MW00983545

A WHOLE NEW WORLD

Luggage! As I wander round the department, looking at Louis Vuitton suitcases and calfskin bags, I'm quite thrown. Why on earth have I never considered luggage before?

I should explain. For years now I've kind of operated under an informal shopping cycle. A bit like a farmer's crop rotation system. Except, instead of wheat-maize-barley-fallow, mine pretty much goes clothes-makeup-shoes-clothes (I don't bother with fallow). Shopping is actually very similar to farming a field. You can't keep buying the same thing—you have to have a bit of variety. Otherwise you get bored and stop enjoying yourself.

And I thought I had all the areas covered. To be honest, I was quite blasé about it. But look what I've been missing out on all this time. Look what I've been denying myself. I feel quite shaky as I realize the opportunities I've just been throwing away over the years. Suitcases, weekend bags, monogrammed hatboxes. . . . With weak legs I wander into a corner and sit down on a carpeted pedestal next to a red leather vanity case.

How can I have just blithely led my life ignoring an entire retail sector?

SOPHIE KINSELLA

confessions of a SHOPAHOLIC

A DELTA TRADE PAPERBACK

A Delta Book
Published by
Dell Publishing
a division of
Random House, Inc.
1540 Broadway
New York, New York 10036

Cover design by Belina Huey
Cover art © 2001 by Diane Bigda

Book design by Susan Yuran

Library of Congress Cataloging-in-Publication Information:
Kinsella, Sophie
Confessions of a shopaholic / Sophie Kinsella.
p. cm.
ISBN 0-385-33548-2
1. Young women—Fiction. 2. London (England)—Fiction.
3. Shopping—Fiction. 4. Debt—Fiction. I. Title.
PR6061.I54 C6 2001
823'.92—dc21 00-060398

Manufactured in the United States of America
First published in 2000 by Transworld, United Kingdom
Published simultaneously in Canada

February 2001

BVG 30 29

confessions of a SHOPAHOLIC

· ENDWICH BANK ·

1 Stallion Square
London W1 3HW

Ms. Rebecca Bloomwood
Flat 4
63 Jarvis Road
Bristol BS1 0DN

6 July 1997

Dear Ms. Bloomwood:

Congratulations! As a recent graduate of Bristol University you are undoubtedly proud of your performance.

We at Endwich are also proud of our performance as a flexible, caring bank with accounts to suit everyone. We pride ourselves particularly in our farsighted approach when it comes to customers of a caliber such as yours.

We are therefore offering you, Ms. Bloomwood—as a graduate—a free extended overdraft facility of £2,000 during the first two years of your career. Should you decide to open an account with Endwich, this facility will be available immediately.* I do hope you decide to take advantage of this unique offer and look forward to receiving your completed form.

Once again, congratulations!

Yours sincerely,

Nigel Fairs
Graduate Marketing Manager

*(*subject to status*)

• ENDWICH -- BECAUSE WE CARE •

· ENDWICH BANK ·

FULHAM BRANCH

3 Fulham Road

London SW6 9JH

Ms. Rebecca Bloomwood
Flat 2
4 Burney Rd.
London SW6 8FD

10 September 1999

Dear Ms. Bloomwood:

Further to my letters of 3 May, 29 July, and 14 August, you will be aware that your free graduate overdraft facility is due to end on 19 September 1999. You will also be aware that you have substantially exceeded the agreed limit of £2,000.

The current balance stands at a debit of £3,794.56.

Perhaps you would be kind enough to telephone my assistant, Erica Parnell, at the above number to arrange a meeting concerning this matter.

Yours sincerely,

Derek Smeath
Manager

• ENDWICH -- BECAUSE WE CARE •

· ENDWICH BANK ·

FULHAM BRANCH
3 Fulham Road
London SW6 9JH

Ms. Rebecca Bloomwood
Flat 2
4 Burney Rd.
London SW6 8FD

22 September 1999

Dear Ms. Bloomwood:

I am sorry to hear that you have broken your leg.

When you have recovered, perhaps you would be kind enough to ring my assistant, Erica Parnell, and arrange a meeting to discuss your ongoing overdraft needs.

Yours sincerely,

Derek Smeath
Manager

• ENDWICH -- BECAUSE WE CARE •

One

OK. DON'T PANIC. Don't *panic*. It's only a VISA bill. It's a piece of paper; a few numbers. I mean, just how scary can a few numbers be?

I stare out of the office window at a bus driving down Oxford Street, willing myself to open the white envelope sitting on my cluttered desk. It's only a piece of paper, I tell myself for the thousandth time. And I'm not stupid, am I? I know exactly how much this VISA bill will be.

Sort of. Roughly.

It'll be about . . . £200. Three hundred, maybe. Yes, maybe £300. Three-fifty, max.

I casually close my eyes and start to tot up. There was that suit in Jigsaw. And there was dinner with Suze at Quaglinos. And there was that gorgeous red and yellow rug. The rug was £200, come to think of it. But it was definitely worth every penny—everyone's admired it. Or, at least, Suze has.

And the Jigsaw suit was on sale—30 percent off. So that was actually *saving* money.

I open my eyes and reach for the bill. As my fingers hit the paper I remember new contact lenses. Ninety-five pounds. Quite a lot. But, I mean, I had to get those, didn't I? What am I supposed to do, walk around in a blur?

And I had to buy some new solutions and a cute case and some hypoallergenic eyeliner. So that takes it up to . . . £400?

At the desk next to mine, Clare Edwards looks up from her post. She's sorting all her letters into neat piles, just like she does every morning. She puts rubber bands round them and puts labels on them saying things like "Answer immediately" and "Not urgent but respond." I loathe Clare Edwards.

"OK, Becky?" she says.

"Fine," I say lightly. "Just reading a letter."

I reach gaily into the envelope, but my fingers don't quite pull out the bill. They remain clutched around it while my mind is seized—as it is every month—by my secret dream.

Do you want to know about my secret dream? It's based on a story I once read in *The Daily World* about a mix-up at a bank. I loved this story so much, I cut it out and stuck it onto my wardrobe door. Two credit card bills were sent to the wrong people, and—get this—each person paid the wrong bill without realizing. They paid off each other's bills *without even checking them.*

And ever since I read that story, my secret fantasy has been that the same thing will happen to me. I mean, I know it sounds unlikely—but if it happened once, it can happen again, can't it? Some dotty old woman in Cornwall will be sent my humongous bill and will pay it without even looking at it. And I'll be sent her bill for three tins of cat food at fifty-nine pence each. Which, naturally, I'll pay without question. Fair's fair, after all.

A smile is plastered over my face as I gaze out of the window. I'm convinced that this month it'll happen—my secret dream is about to come true. But when I eventually pull the bill out of the envelope—goaded by Clare's curious gaze—my smile falters, then disappears. Something hot is blocking my throat. I think it could be panic.

The page is black with type. A series of familiar names rushes past my eyes like a mini shopping mall. I try to take them in, but they're moving too fast. Thorntons, I manage to glimpse. Thorntons Chocolates? What was I doing in Thorntons Chocolates? I'm supposed to be on a diet. This bill *can't* be right. This can't be me. I can't possibly have spent all this money.

Don't panic! I yell internally. The key is not to panic. Just read each entry slowly, one by one. I take a deep breath and force myself to focus calmly, starting at the top.

WHSmith (well, that's OK. Everyone needs stationery.)
Boots (everyone needs shampoo)
Specsavers (essential)
Oddbins (bottle of wine—essential)
Our Price (Our Price? *Oh yes. The new Charlatans album. Well, I had to have that, didn't I?)*
Bella Pasta (supper with Caitlin)
Oddbins (bottle of wine—essential)
Esso (petrol doesn't count)
Quaglinos (expensive—but it was a one-off)
Pret à Manger (that time I ran out of cash)
Oddbins (bottle of wine—essential)
Rugs to Riches (what? Oh yes. Stupid rug.)
La Senza (sexy underwear for date with James)
Agent Provocateur (even sexier underwear for date with James. Like I needed it.)
Body Shop (that skin brusher thing which I must use)
Next (fairly boring white shirt—but it was in the sale)
Millets . . .

I stop in my tracks. Millets? I never go into Millets. What would I be doing in Millets? I stare at the statement in puzzlement, wrinkling my brow and trying to think—and then suddenly, the truth dawns on me. It's obvious. Someone else has been using my card.

Oh my God. I, Rebecca Bloomwood, have been the victim of a crime.

Now it all makes sense. Some criminal's pinched my credit

card and forged my signature. Who knows where else they've used it? No wonder my statement's so black with figures! Someone's gone on a spending spree round London with my card—and they thought they would just get away with it.

But how? I scrabble in my bag for my purse, open it—and there's my VISA card, staring up at me. I take it out and run my fingers over the glossy surface. Someone must have pinched it from my purse, used it—*and then put it back.* It must be someone I know. Oh my God. Who?

I look suspiciously round the office. Whoever it is, isn't very bright. Using my card at Millets! It's almost laughable. As if I'd ever shop there.

"I've never even been into Millets!" I say aloud.

"Yes you have," says Clare.

"What?" I turn to her. "No I haven't."

"You bought Michael's leaving present from Millets, didn't you?"

I feel my smile disappear. Oh, bugger. Of course. The blue anorak for Michael. The blue sodding anorak from Millets.

When Michael, our deputy editor, left three weeks ago, I volunteered to buy his present. I took the brown envelope full of coins and notes into the shop and picked out an anorak (take it from me, he's that kind of guy). And at the last minute, now I remember, I decided to pay on credit and keep all that handy cash for myself.

I can vividly remember fishing out the four £5 notes and carefully putting them in my wallet, sorting out the pound coins and putting them in my coin compartment, and pouring the rest of the change into the bottom of my bag. Oh good, I remember thinking. I won't have to go to the cash machine. I'd thought that sixty quid would last me for weeks.

So what happened to it? I can't have just *spent* sixty quid without realizing it, can I?

"Why are you asking, anyway?" says Clare, and she leans forward. I can see her beady little X-ray eyes gleaming behind her specs. She knows I'm looking at my VISA bill. "No reason," I say, briskly turning to the second page of my statement.

But I've been put off my stride. Instead of doing what I normally do—look at the minimum payment required and ignore the total completely—I find myself staring straight at the bottom figure.

Nine hundred and forty-nine pounds, sixty-three pence. In clear black and white.

For thirty seconds I am completely motionless. Then, without changing expression, I stuff the bill back into the envelope. I honestly feel as though this piece of paper has nothing to do with me. Perhaps, if I carelessly let it drop down on the floor behind my computer, it will disappear. The cleaners will sweep it up and I can claim I never got it. They can't charge me for a bill I never received, can they?

I'm already composing a letter in my head. "Dear Managing Director of VISA. Your letter has confused me. What bill are you talking about, precisely? I never received any bill from your company. I did not care for your tone and should warn you, I am writing to Anne Robinson of *Watchdog*."

Or I could always move abroad.

"Becky?" My head jerks up and I see Clare holding this month's news list. "Have you finished the piece on Lloyds?"

"Nearly," I lie. As she's watching me, I feel forced to summon it up on my computer screen, just to show I'm willing.

"This high-yield, 60-day access account offers tiered rates of interest on investments of over £2,000," I type onto the screen, copying directly from a press release in front of me. "Long-term savers may also be interested in a new stepped-rate bond which requires a minimum of £5,000."

I type a full stop, take a sip of coffee, and turn to the second page of the press release.

This is what I do, by the way. I'm a journalist on a financial magazine. I'm paid to tell other people how to organize their money.

Of course, being a financial journalist is not the career I always wanted. No one who writes about personal finance ever meant to do it. People tell you they "fell into" personal finance. They're lying. What they mean is they couldn't get a job writing about anything more interesting. They mean they applied for jobs at *The Times* and *The Express* and *Marie-Claire* and *Vogue* and *GQ*, and all they got back was "Piss off."

So they started applying to *Metalwork Monthly* and *Cheese-makers Gazette* and *What Investment Plan?* And they were taken on as the crappiest editorial assistant possible on no money whatsoever and were grateful. And they've stayed on writing about metal, or cheese, or savings, ever since—because that's all they know. I myself started on the catchily titled *Personal Investment Periodical*. I learned how to copy out a press release and nod at press conferences and ask questions that sounded as though I knew what I was talking about. After a year and a half—believe it or not—I was head-hunted to *Successful Saving*.

Of course, I still know nothing about finance. People at the bus stop know more about finance than me. Schoolchildren know more than me. I've been doing this job for three years now, and I'm still expecting someone to catch me out.

That afternoon, Philip, the editor, calls my name, and I jump in fright.

"Rebecca?" he says. "A word." And he beckons me over to his desk. His voice seems lower all of a sudden, almost conspiratorial, and he's smiling at me, as though he's about to give me a piece of good news.

Promotion, I think. It must be. He read the piece I wrote on international equity securities last week (in which I likened the hunt for long-term growth to the hunt for the perfect pair of summer mules) and was bowled over by how exciting I made it all sound. He *knows* it's unfair I earn less than Clare, so he's going to promote me to her level. Or even above. And he's telling me discreetly so Clare won't get jealous.

A wide smile plasters itself over my face and I get up and walk the three yards or so to his desk, trying to stay calm but already planning what I'll buy with my raise. I'll get that swirly coat in Whistles. And some black high-heeled boots from Pied à Terre. Maybe I'll go on holiday. And I'll pay off that blasted VISA bill once and for all. I feel buoyant with relief. I *knew* everything would be OK . . .

"Rebecca?" He's thrusting a card at me. "I can't make this press conference," he says. "But it could be quite interesting. Will you go? It's at Brandon Communications."

I can feel the elated expression falling off my face like jelly. He's not promoting me. I'm not getting a raise. I feel betrayed. *Why* did he smile at me like that? He must have known he was lifting my hopes.

"Something wrong?" inquires Philip.

"No," I mutter. But I can't bring myself to smile. In front of me, my new swirly coat and high-heeled boots are disappearing into a puddle, like the Wicked Witch of the West. No promotion. Just a press conference about . . . I turn over the card. About a new unit trust. How could anyone *possibly* describe that as interesting?

Two

There's just one essential purchase I have to make on the way to the press conference—and that's the *Financial Times*. The *FT* is by far the best accessory a girl can have. Its major advantages are:

1. It's a nice color.
2. It only costs eighty-five pence.
3. If you walk into a room with it tucked under your arm, people take you seriously. With an *FT* under your arm, you can talk about the most frivolous things in the world, and instead of thinking you're an airhead, people think you're a heavyweight intellectual who has broader interests, too.

At my interview for *Successful Saving*, I went in holding copies of the *Financial Times* and the *Investor's Chronicle*—and I didn't get asked about finance once. As I remember it, we spent the whole time talking about holiday villas and gossiping about other editors.

So I stop at a newsstand and buy a copy of the *FT*. There's some huge headline about Rutland Bank on the front page, and

I'm thinking maybe I should at least skim it, when I catch my reflection in the window of Denny and George.

I don't look bad, I think. I'm wearing my black skirt from French Connection, and a plain white T-shirt from Knickerbox, and a little angora cardigan which I got from M&S but looks like it might be Agnès b. And my new square-toed shoes from Hobbs. Even better, although no one can see them, I know that underneath I'm wearing my gorgeous new matching knickers and bra with embroidered yellow rosebuds. They're the best bit of my entire outfit. In fact, I almost wish I could be run over so that the world would see them.

It's a habit of mine, itemizing all the clothes I'm wearing, as though for a fashion page. I've been doing it for years—ever since I used to read *Just Seventeen*. Every issue, they'd stop a girl on the street, take a picture of her, and list all her clothes. "T-Shirt: Chelsea Girl, Jeans: Top Shop, Shoes: borrowed from friend." I used to read those lists avidly, and to this day, if I buy something from a shop that's a bit uncool, I cut the label out. So that if I'm ever stopped in the street, I can pretend I don't know where it's from.

So anyway. There I am, with the *FT* tucked under my arm, thinking I look pretty good, and half wishing someone from *Just Seventeen* would pop up with a camera—when suddenly my eyes focus and snap to attention, and my heart stops. In the window of Denny and George is a discreet sign. It's dark green with cream lettering, and it says: SALE.

I stare at it, and my skin's all prickly. It can't be true. Denny and George can't be having a sale. They never have a sale. Their scarves and pashminas are so coveted, they could probably sell them at twice the price. Everyone I know in the entire world aspires to owning a Denny and George scarf. (Except my mum and dad, obviously. My mum thinks if you can't buy it at Bentalls of Kingston, you don't need it.)

I swallow, take a couple of steps forward, then push open the door of the tiny shop. The door pings, and the nice blond girl who works there looks up. I don't know her name but I've always liked her. Unlike some snotty cows in clothes shops, she doesn't mind if you stand for ages staring at clothes you really can't afford to buy. Usually what happens is, I spend half an hour lusting after scarves in Denny and George, then go off to Accessorize and buy something to cheer myself up. I've got a whole drawerful of Denny and George substitutes.

"Hi," I say, trying to stay calm. "You're . . . you're having a sale."

"Yes." The blond girl smiles. "Bit unusual for us."

My eyes sweep the room. I can see rows of scarves, neatly folded, with dark green "50 percent off" signs above them. Printed velvet, beaded silk, embroidered cashmere, all with the distinctive "Denny and George" signature. They're everywhere. I don't know where to start. I think I'm having a panic attack.

"You always liked this one, I think," says the nice blond girl, taking out a shimmering gray-blue scarf from the pile in front of her.

Oh God, yes. I remember this one. It's made of silky velvet, overprinted in a paler blue and dotted with iridescent beads. As I stare at it, I can feel little invisible strings, silently tugging me toward it. I have to touch it. I have to wear it. It's the most beautiful thing I've ever seen. The girl looks at the label. "Reduced from £340 to £120." She comes and drapes the scarf around my neck and I gape at my reflection.

There is no question. I have to have this scarf. I *have* to have it. It makes my eyes look bigger, it makes my haircut look more expensive, it makes me look like a different person. I'll be able to wear it with everything. People will refer to me as the Girl in the Denny and George Scarf.

"I'd snap it up if I were you." The girl smiles at me. "There's only one of these left."

Involuntarily, I clutch at it.

"I'll have it," I gasp. "I'll have it."

As she's laying it out on tissue paper, I take out my purse, open it up, and reach for my VISA card in one seamless, automatic action—but my fingers hit bare leather. I stop in surprise and start to rummage through all the pockets of my purse, wondering if I stuffed my card back in somewhere with a receipt or if it's hidden underneath a business card . . . And then, with a sickening thud, I remember. It's on my desk.

How could I have been so stupid? How could I have left my VISA card on my desk? What was I *thinking*?

The nice blond girl is putting the wrapped scarf into a dark green Denny and George box. My mouth is dry with panic. What am I going to do?

"How would you like to pay?" she says pleasantly.

My face flames red and I swallow hard.

"I've just realized I've left my credit card at the office," I stutter.

"Oh," says the girl, and her hands pause.

"Can you hold it for me?" The girl looks dubious.

"For how long?"

"Until tomorrow?" I say desperately. Oh God. She's pulling a face. Doesn't she understand?

"I'm afraid not," she says. "We're not supposed to reserve sale stock."

"Just until later this afternoon, then," I say quickly. "What time do you close?"

"Six."

Six! I feel a combination of relief and adrenaline sweeping through me. Challenge, Rebecca. I'll go to the press conference, leave as soon as I can, then take a taxi back to the office. I'll grab my VISA card, tell Philip I left my notebook behind, come here, and buy the scarf.

"Can you hold it until then?" I say beseechingly. "Please? *Please?*" The girl relents.

"OK. I'll put it behind the counter."

"Thanks," I gasp. I hurry out of the shop and down the road

toward Brandon Communications. Please let the press conference be short, I pray. Please don't let the questions go on too long. Please God, *please* let me have that scarf.

As I arrive at Brandon Communications, I can feel myself begin to relax. I do have three whole hours, after all. And my scarf is safely behind the counter. No one's going to steal it from me.

There's a sign up in the foyer saying that the Foreland Exotic Opportunities press conference is happening in the Artemis Suite, and a man in uniform is directing everybody down the corridor. This means it must be quite big. Not television-cameras-CNN-world's-press-on-tenterhooks big, obviously. But fairly-good-turnout big. A relatively important event in our dull little world.

As I enter the room, there's already a buzz of people milling around, and waitresses circulating with canapés. The journalists are knocking back the champagne as if they've never seen it before; the PR girls are looking supercilious and sipping water. A waiter offers me a glass of champagne and I take two. One for now, one to put under my chair for the boring bits.

In the far corner of the room I can see Elly Granger from *Investor's Weekly News*. She's been pinned into a corner by two earnest men in suits and is nodding at them, with a glassy look in her eye. Elly's great. She's only been on *Investor's Weekly News* for six months, and already she's applied for forty-three other jobs. What she really wants to be is a beauty editor on a magazine, and I think she'd be really good at it. Every time I see her, she's got a new lipstick on—and she always wears really interesting clothes. Like today, she's wearing an orange chiffony shirt over a pair of white cotton trousers, espadrilles, and a big wooden necklace, the kind I could never wear in a million years.

What *I* really want to be is Fiona Phillips on *GMTV*. I could really see myself, sitting on that sofa, joshing with Eamonn every morning and interviewing lots of soap stars. Sometimes, when we're very drunk, we make pacts that if we're not somewhere more exciting in three months, we'll both leave our jobs. But then the thought of no money—even for a month—is almost more scary than the thought of writing about depository trust companies for the rest of my life.

"Rebecca. Glad you could make it."

I look up, and almost choke on my champagne. It's Luke Brandon, head honcho of Brandon Communications, staring straight at me as if he knows exactly what I'm thinking. Staring straight down at me, I should say. He must be well over six feet tall with dark hair and dark eyes and . . . wow. Isn't that suit nice? An expensive suit like that almost makes you want to be a man. It's inky blue with a faint purple stripe, single-breasted, with proper horn buttons. As I run my eyes over it I find myself wondering if it's by Oswald Boateng, and whether the jacket's got a silk lining in some stunning color. If this were someone else, I might ask—but not Luke Brandon, no way.

I've only met him a few times, and I've always felt slightly uneasy around him. For a start, he's got such a scary reputation. Everyone talks all the time about what a genius he is, even Philip, my boss. He started Brandon Communications from nothing, and now it's the biggest financial PR company in London. A few months ago he was listed in *The Mail* as one of the cleverest entrepreneurs of his generation. It said his IQ was phenomenally high and he had a photographic memory.

But it's not just that. It's that he always seems to have a frown on his face when he's talking to me. It'll probably turn out that the famous Luke Brandon is not only a complete genius but he can read minds, too. He knows that when I'm staring up at some boring graph, nodding intelligently, I'm really thinking about a gorgeous black top I saw in Joseph and whether I can afford the trousers as well.

"You know Alicia, don't you?" Luke is saying, and he gestures to the immaculate blond girl beside him.

I don't know Alicia, as it happens. But I don't need to. They're all the same, the girls at Brandon C, as they call it. They're well dressed, well spoken, are married to bankers, and have zero sense of humor. Alicia falls into the identikit pattern exactly, with her baby-blue suit, silk Hermès scarf, and matching baby-blue shoes, which I've seen in Russell and Bromley, and they cost an absolute fortune. (I *bet* she's got the bag as well.) She's also got a suntan, which must mean she's just come back from Mauritius or somewhere, and suddenly I feel a bit pale and weedy in comparison.

"Rebecca," she says coolly, grasping my hand. "You're on *Successful Saving,* aren't you?"

"That's right," I say, equally coolly.

"It's very good of you to come today," says Alicia. "I know you journalists are terribly busy."

"No problem," I say. "We like to attend as many press conferences as we can. Keep up with industry events." I feel pleased with my response. I'm almost fooling myself.

Alicia nods seriously, as though everything I say is incredibly important to her.

"So, tell me, Rebecca. What do you think about today's news?" She gestures to the *FT* under my arm. "Quite a surprise, didn't you think?"

Oh God. What's she talking about?

"It's certainly interesting," I say, still smiling, playing for time. I glance around the room for a clue, but there's nothing. What's she talking about? Have interest rates gone up or something?

"I have to say, I think it's bad news for the industry," says Alicia earnestly. "But of course, you must have your own views."

She's looking at me, waiting for an answer. I can feel my cheeks flaming bright red. How can I get out of this? After this, I promise myself, I'm going to read the papers every day. I'm never going to be caught out like this again.

"I agree with you," I say eventually. "I think it's very bad news." My voice feels strangled. I take a quick swig of champagne and pray for an earthquake.

"Were you expecting it?" Alicia says. "I know you journalists are always ahead of the game."

"I . . . I certainly saw it coming," I say, and I'm pretty sure I sound convincing.

"And now this rumor about Scottish Prime and Flagstaff Life going the same way!" She looks at me intently. "Do you think that's really on the cards?"

"It's . . . it's difficult to say," I reply, and take a gulp of champagne. What rumor? Why can't she leave me alone?

Then I make the mistake of glancing up at Luke Brandon. He's staring at me, his mouth twitching slightly. Oh shit. He *knows* I don't have a clue, doesn't he?

"Alicia," he says abruptly, "that's Maggie Stevens coming in. Could you—"

"Absolutely," she says, trained like a racehorse, and starts to move smoothly toward the door.

"And Alicia—" adds Luke, and she quickly turns back. "I want to know exactly who fucked up on those figures."

"Yes," gulps Alicia, and walks off.

God he's scary. And now we're on our own. I think I might quickly run away.

"Well," I say brightly. "I must just go and . . ."

But Luke Brandon is leaning toward me.

"SBG announced that they've taken over Rutland Bank this morning," he says quietly.

And of course, now that he says it, I remember that front-page headline.

"I know they did," I reply haughtily. "I read it in the *FT*." And before he can say anything else, I walk off, to talk to Elly.

As the press conference is about to start, Elly and I sidle toward the back and grab two seats together. We're in one of the bigger conference rooms and there must be about a hundred chairs arranged in rows, facing a podium and a large screen. I open my notebook, write "Brandon Communications" at the top of the page, and start doodling swirly flowers down the side. Beside me, Elly's dialing her telephone horoscope on her mobile phone.

I take a sip of champagne, lean back, and prepare to relax. There's no point listening at press conferences. The information's always in the press pack, and you can work out what they were talking about later. In fact, I'm wondering whether anyone would notice if I took out a pot of Hard Candy and did my nails, when suddenly the awful Alicia ducks her head down to mine.

"Rebecca?"

"Yes?" I say lazily.

"Phone call for you. It's your editor."

"Philip?" I say stupidly. As though I've a whole array of editors to choose from.

"Yes." She looks at me as though I'm a moron and gestures to a phone on a table at the back. Elly gives me a questioning look and I shrug back. Philip's never phoned me at a press conference before.

I feel rather excited and important as I walk to the back of the room. Perhaps there's an emergency at the office. Perhaps he's scooped an incredible story and wants me to fly to New York to follow up a lead.

"Hello, Philip?" I say into the receiver—then immediately I wish I'd said something thrusting and impressive, like a simple "Yep."

"Rebecca, listen, sorry to be a bore," says Philip, "but I've got a migraine coming on. I'm going to head off home."

"Oh," I say puzzledly.

"And I wondered if you could run a small errand for me."

An errand? If he wants somebody to buy him Tylenol, he should get a secretary.

"I'm not sure," I say discouragingly. "I'm a bit tied up here."

"When you've finished there. The Social Security Select

Committee is releasing its report at five o'clock. Can you go and pick it up? You can go straight to Westminster from your press conference."

What? I stare at the phone in horror. No, I can't pick up a bloody report. I need to pick up my VISA card! I need to secure my scarf.

"Can't Clare go?" I say. "I was going to come back to the office and finish my research on . . ." What am I supposed to be writing about this month? "On mortgages."

"Clare's got a briefing in the City. And Westminster's on your way home to Trendy Fulham, isn't it?"

Philip *always* has to make a joke about me living in Fulham. Just because he lives in Harpenden and thinks anyone who doesn't live in lovely leafy suburbia is mad.

"You can just hop off the tube," he's saying, "pick it up, and hop back on again."

Oh God. I close my eyes and think quickly. An hour here. Rush back to the office, pick up my VISA card, back to Denny and George, get my scarf, rush to Westminster, pick up the report. I should just about make it.

"Fine," I say. "Leave it to me."

I sit back down, just as the lights dim and the words *Far Eastern Opportunities* appear on the screen in front of us. There is a colorful series of pictures from Hong Kong, Thailand, and other exotic places, which would usually have me thinking wistfully about going on holiday. But today I can't relax, or even feel sorry for the new girl from *Portfolio Week,* who's frantically trying to write everything down and will probably ask five questions because she thinks she should. I'm too concerned about my scarf. What if I don't make it back in time? What if someone puts in a higher offer? The very thought makes me panic.

Then, just as the pictures of Thailand disappear and the boring graphs begin, I have a flash of inspiration. Of course! I'll pay cash for the scarf. No one can argue with cash. I can get £100 out on my cash card, so all I need is another £20, and the scarf is mine.

I tear a piece of paper out of my notebook, write on it "Can you lend me twenty quid?" and pass it to Elly, who's still surreptitiously listening to her mobile phone. I wonder what she's listening to. It can't still be her horoscope, surely? She looks down, shakes her head, and writes, "No can do. Bloody machine swallowed my card. Living off luncheon vouchers at moment."

Damn. I hesitate, then write, "What about credit card? I'll pay you back, honest. And what are you listening to?"

I pass the page to her and suddenly the lights go up. The presentation has ended and I didn't hear a word of it. People shift around on their seats and a PR girl starts handing out glossy brochures. Elly finishes her call and grins at me.

"Love life prediction," she says, tapping in another number. "It's really accurate stuff."

"Load of old bullshit, more like." I shake my head disapprovingly. "I can't believe you go for all that rubbish. Call yourself a financial journalist?"

"No," says Elly. "Do you?" And we both start to giggle, until some old bag from one of the nationals turns round and gives us an angry glare.

"Ladies and gentlemen." A piercing voice interrupts us and I look up. It's Alicia, standing up at the front of the room. She's got very good legs, I note resentfully. "As you can see, the Foreland Exotic Opportunities Savings Plan represents an entirely new approach to investment." She looks around the room, meets my eye, and smiles coldly.

"Exotic Opportunities," I whisper scornfully to Elly and point to the leaflet. "Exotic prices, more like. Have you seen how much they're charging?"

(I always turn to the charges first. Just like I always look at the price tag first.)

Elly rolls her eyes sympathetically, still listening to the phone.

"Foreland Investments are all about adding value," Alicia is saying in her snooty voice. "Foreland Investments offer you more."

"They charge more, you lose more," I say aloud without thinking, and there's a laugh around the room. God, how embarrassing. And now Luke Brandon's lifting his head, too. Quickly I look down and pretend to be writing notes.

Although to be honest, I don't know why I even pretend to write notes. It's not as if we ever put anything in the magazine except the puff that comes on the press release. Foreland Investments takes out a whopping double-page spread advertisement every month, *and* they took Philip on some fantastic research (ha-ha) trip to Thailand last year—so we're never allowed to say anything except how wonderful they are. Like that's really any help to our readers.

As Alicia carries on speaking, I lean toward Elly.

"So, listen," I whisper. "Can I borrow your credit card?"

"All used up," hisses Elly apologetically. "I'm up to my limit. Why do you think I'm living off LVs?"

"But I need money!" I whisper. "I'm desperate! I need twenty quid!"

I've spoken more loudly than I intended and Alicia stops speaking.

"Perhaps you should have invested with Foreland Investments, Rebecca," says Alicia, and another titter goes round the room. A few faces turn round to gawk at me, and I stare back at them lividly. They're fellow journalists, for God's sake. They should be on my side. National Union of Journalists solidarity and all that.

Not that I've ever actually got round to joining the NUJ. But still.

"What do you need twenty quid for?" says Luke Brandon, from the front of the room.

"I . . . my aunt," I say defiantly. "She's in hospital and I wanted to get her a present."

The room is silent. Then, to my disbelief, Luke Brandon reaches into his pocket, takes out a £20 note, and gives it to a guy in the front row of journalists. He hesitates, then passes it back to the row behind. And so it goes on, a twenty-quid note being passed from hand to hand, making its way to me like a fan at a gig being passed over the crowd. As I take hold of it, a round of applause goes round the room and I blush.

"Thanks," I say awkwardly. "I'll pay you back, of course."

"My best wishes to your aunt," says Luke Brandon.

"Thanks," I say again. Then I glance at Alicia, and feel a little dart of triumph. She looks utterly deflated.

Toward the end of the question-and-answer session, people begin slipping out to get back to their offices. This is usually when I slip out to go and buy a cappuccino and browse in a few shops. But today I don't. Today I decide I will stick it out until the last dismal question about tax structures. Then I'll go up to the front and thank Luke Brandon in person for his kind, if embarrassing, gesture. And then I'll go and get my scarf. Yippee!

But to my surprise, after only a few questions, Luke Brandon gets up, whispers something to Alicia, and heads for the door.

"Thanks," I mutter as he passes my chair, but I'm not sure he even hears me.

The tube stops in a tunnel for no apparent reason. Five minutes go by, then ten minutes. I can't believe my bad luck. Normally, of course, I long for the tube to break down—so I've got an excuse to stay out of the office for longer. But today I behave like a stressed businessman with an ulcer. I tap my fingers and sigh, and peer out of the window into the blackness.

Part of my brain knows that I've got plenty of time to get to Denny and George before it closes. Another part knows that even if I don't make it, it's unlikely the blond girl will sell my scarf to someone else. But the possibility is there. So until I've got that scarf in my hands I won't be able to relax.

As the train finally gets going again I sink into my seat with a dramatic sigh and look at the pale, silent man on my left. He's wearing jeans and sneakers, and I notice his shirt is on inside out. Gosh, I think in admiration, did he read the article on deconstructing fashion in last month's *Vogue,* too? I'm about to ask him—then I take another look at his jeans (really nasty fake 501s) and his sneakers (very new, very white)—and something tells me he didn't.

"Thank God!" I say instead. "I was getting desperate there."

"It's frustrating," he agrees quietly.

"They just don't think, do they?" I say. "I mean, some of us have got crucial things we need to be doing. I'm in a terrible hurry!"

"I'm in a bit of a hurry myself," says the man.

"If that train hadn't started moving, I don't know what I would have done." I shake my head. "You feel so . . . impotent!"

"I know exactly what you mean," says the man intensely. "They don't realize that some of us . . ." He gestures toward me. "We aren't just idly traveling. It *matters* whether we arrive or not."

"Absolutely!" I say. "Where are you off to?"

"My wife's in labor," he says. "Our fourth."

"Oh," I say, taken aback. "Well . . . Gosh. Congratulations. I hope you—"

"She took an hour and a half last time," says the man, rubbing his damp forehead. "And I've been on this tube for forty minutes already. Still. At least we're moving now."

He gives a little shrug, then smiles at me.

"How about you? What's your urgent business?"

Oh God.

"I . . . ahm . . . I'm going to . . ."

I stop feebly and clear my throat, feeling rather sheepish. I *can't* tell this man that my urgent business consists of picking up a scarf from Denny and George.

I mean, a scarf. It's not even a suit or a coat, or something worthy like that.

"It's not that important," I mumble.

"I don't believe that," he says nicely.

Oh, now I feel awful. I glance up—and thank goodness, it's my stop.

"Good luck," I say, hastily getting up. "I really hope you get there in time."

As I walk along the pavement I'm feeling a bit shamefaced. I should have got out my 120 quid and given it to that man for his baby, instead of buying a pointless scarf. I mean, when you think about it, what's more important? Clothes—or the miracle of new life?

As I ponder this issue, I feel quite deep and philosophical. In fact, I'm so engrossed, I almost walk past my turning. But I look up just in time and turn the corner—and feel a jolt. There's a girl coming toward me and she's carrying a Denny and George carrier bag. And suddenly everything is swept from my mind.

Oh my God.

What if she's got my scarf?

What if she asked for it specially and that assistant sold it to her, thinking I wasn't going to come back?

My heart starts to beat in panic and I begin to stride along the street toward the shop. As I arrive at the door and push it open, I can barely breathe for fear. What if it's gone? What will I do?

But the blond girl smiles as I enter.

"Hi!" she says. "It's waiting for you."

"Oh, thanks," I say in relief and subside weakly against the counter.

I honestly feel as though I've run an obstacle course to get here. In fact, I think, they should list shopping as a cardiovascular activity. My heart never beats as fast as it does when I see a "reduced by 50 percent" sign.

I count out the money in tens and twenties and wait, almost shivering as she ducks behind the counter and produces the green box. She slides it into a thick glossy bag with dark green cord handles and hands it to me, and I almost want to cry out loud, the moment is so wonderful.

That moment. That instant when your fingers curl round the handles of a shiny, uncreased bag—and all the gorgeous new things inside it become yours. What's it like? It's like going hungry for days, then cramming your mouth full of warm buttered toast. It's like waking up and realizing it's the weekend. It's like the better moments of sex. Everything else is blocked out of your mind. It's pure, selfish pleasure.

I walk slowly out of the shop, still in a haze of delight. I've got a Denny and George scarf. I've got a Denny and George scarf! I've got . . .

"Rebecca." A man's voice interrupts my thoughts. I look up and my stomach gives a lurch of horror. It's Luke Brandon.

Luke Brandon is standing on the street, right in front of me, and he's staring down at my carrier bag. I feel myself growing flustered. What's he doing here on the pavement anyway? Don't people like that have chauffeurs? Shouldn't he be whisking off to some vital financial reception or something?

"Did you get it all right?" he says, frowning slightly.

"What?"

"Your aunt's present."

"Oh yes," I say, and swallow. "Yes, I . . . I got it."

"Is that it?" He gestures to the bag and I feel a guilty blush spread over my cheeks.

"Yes," I say eventually. "I thought a . . . a scarf would be nice."

"Very generous of you. Denny and George." He raises his eyebrows. "Your aunt must be a stylish lady."

"She is," I say, and clear my throat. "She's terribly creative and original."

"I'm sure she is," says Luke, and pauses. "What's her name?"

Oh God. I should have run as soon as I saw him, while I had

a chance. Now I'm paralyzed. I can't think of a single female name.

"Erm . . . Ermintrude," I hear myself saying.

"Aunt Ermintrude," says Luke thoughtfully. "Well, give her my best wishes."

He nods at me, and walks off, and I stand, clutching my bag, trying to work out if he guessed or not.

· ENDWICH BANK ·

FULHAM BRANCH
3 Fulham Road
London SW6 9JH

Ms. Rebecca Bloomwood
Flat 2
4 Burney Rd.
London SW6 8FD

17 November 1999

Dear Ms. Bloomwood:

I am sorry to hear that you have glandular fever.

When you have recovered, perhaps you would be kind enough to ring my assistant, Erica Parnell, and arrange a meeting to discuss your situation.

Yours sincerely,

Derek Smeath
Manager

• ENDWICH -- BECAUSE WE CARE •

Three

I WALK THROUGH THE DOOR of our flat to see Suze, my flatmate, sitting in one of her strange yoga positions, with her eyes closed. Her fair hair is scrunched up in a knot, and she's wearing black leggings together with the ancient T-shirt she always wears for yoga. It's the one her dad was wearing when he rowed Oxford to victory, and she says it gives her good vibes.

For a moment I'm silent. I don't want to disturb her in case yoga is like sleepwalking and you're not meant to wake people when they're doing it. But then Suze opens her eyes and looks up—and the first thing she says is "Denny and George! Becky, you're not serious."

"Yes," I say, grinning from ear to ear. "I bought myself a scarf."

"Show me!" says Suze, unwinding herself from the floor. "Show-me-show-me-show-me!" She comes over and starts tugging at the strings of the carrier, like a kid. "I want to see your new scarf! Show me!"

This is why I love sharing a flat with Suze. Julia, my old flatmate, would have wrinkled her brow and said, "Denny and who?" or, "That's a lot of money for a scarf." But Suze completely and utterly understands. If anything, she's worse than me.

But then, she can afford to be. Although she's twenty-five, like me, her parents still give her pocket money. It's called an "allowance" and apparently comes from some family trust—but as far as I can see, it's pocket money. Her parents also bought her a flat in Fulham as a twenty-first birthday present and she's been living in it ever since, half working and half dossing about.

She was in PR for a (very) short while, and that's when I met her, on a press trip to an offshore bank on Guernsey. As a matter of fact, she was working for Brandon Communications. Without being rude—she admits it herself—she was the worst PR girl I've ever come across. She completely forgot which bank she was supposed to be promoting, and started talking enthusiastically about one of their competitors. The man from the bank looked crosser and crosser, while all the journalists pissed themselves laughing. Suze got in big trouble over that. In fact, that's when she decided PR wasn't the career for her. (The other way of putting it is that Luke Brandon gave her the sack as soon as they got back to London. Another reason not to like him.)

But the two of us had a whale of a time sloshing back wine until the early hours. Actually, Suze had a secret little weep at about two A.M. and said she was hopeless at every job she'd tried and what was she going to do? I said I thought she was *far* too interesting and creative to be one of those snooty Brandon C girls. Which I wasn't just saying to be nice, it's completely true. I gave her a big hug and she cried some more, then we both cheered up and ordered another bottle of wine, and tried on all each other's clothes. I lent Suze my belt with the square silver buckle, which, come to think of it, she's never given back. And we kept in touch ever since.

Then, when Julia suddenly upped and ran off with the professor supervising her Ph.D. (she was a dark horse, that one), Suze suggested I move in with her. I'm sure the rent she charges is too low, but I've never insisted I pay the full market rate, because I couldn't afford it. As market rates go, I'm nearer Elephant and

Castle than Fulham on my salary. How can normal people afford to live in such hideously expensive places?

"Bex, open it up!" Suze is begging. "Let me see!" She's grabbing inside the bag with eager long fingers, and I pull it away quickly before she rips it. This bag is going on the back of my door along with my other prestige carrier bags, to be used in a casual manner when I need to impress. (Thank God they didn't print special "Sale" bags. I *hate* shops that do that. What's the point of having a posh bag with "Sale" splashed all over it?)

Very slowly, I take the dark green box out of the bag, remove the lid, and unfold the tissue paper. Then, almost reverentially, I lift up the scarf. It's beautiful. It's even more beautiful here than it was in the shop. I drape it around my neck and grin stupidly at Suze.

"Oh, Bex," she murmurs. "It's gorgeous!"

For a moment we are both silent. It's as though we're communing with a higher being. The god of shopping.

Then Suze has to go and ruin it all.

"You can wear it to see James this weekend," she says.

"I can't," I say almost crossly, taking it off again. "I'm not seeing him."

"How come?"

"I'm not seeing him anymore." I try to give a nonchalant shrug.

"Really?" Suze's eyes widen. "Why not? You didn't tell me!"

"I know." I look away from her eager gaze. "It's a bit . . . awkward."

"Did you chuck him? You hadn't even shagged him!" Suze's voice is rising in excitement. She's desperate to know. But am I desperate to tell? For a moment I consider being discreet. Then I think, oh, what the hell?

"I know," I say. "That was the problem."

"What do you mean?" Suze leans forward. "Bex, what are you talking about?"

I take a deep breath and turn to face her.

"He didn't want to."

"Didn't fancy you?"

"No. He—" I close my eyes, barely able to believe this myself. "He doesn't believe in sex before marriage."

"You're joking." I open my eyes to see Suze looking at me in horror—as if she's just heard the worst profanity known to mankind. "You are joking, Becky." She's actually pleading with me.

"I'm not." I manage a weak smile. "It was a bit embarrassing, actually. I kind of . . . pounced on him, and he had to fight me off."

The cringingly awful memory which I had successfully suppressed starts to resurface. I'd met James at a party a few weeks back, and this was the crucial third date. We'd been out for a really nice meal, which he'd insisted on paying for, and had gone back to his place, and had ended up kissing on the sofa.

Well, what was I *supposed* to think? There he was, there I was—and make no mistake, if his mind was saying no, his body was certainly saying yes, yes, yes. So, being a modern girl, I reached for his trouser zip and began to pull it down. When he reached down and brushed me aside I thought he was playing games, and carried on, even more enthusiastically.

Thinking back, perhaps it took me longer than it should have to guess that he wasn't playing ball, so to speak. In fact, he actually had to punch me in the face to get me off him—although he was very apologetic about it afterward.

Suze is gazing at me incredulously. Then she breaks into gurgles of laughter.

"He had to fight you off? Bex, you man-eater!"

"Don't!" I protest, half laughing, half embarrassed. "He was really sweet about it. He asked, was I prepared to wait for him?"

"And you said, not bloody likely!"

"Sort of." I look away.

In fact, carried away with the moment, I seem to remember issuing him a bit of a challenge. "Resist me now if you can, James," I recall saying in a husky voice, gazing at him with what I thought were limpid, sexual eyes. "But you'll be knocking at my door within the week."

Well, it's been over a week now, and I haven't heard a peep. Which, if you think about it, is pretty unflattering.

"But that's hideous!" Suze is saying. "What about sexual compatibility?"

"Dunno." I shrug. "I guess he's willing to take that gamble."

Suze gives a sudden giggle. "Did you get a look at his . . ."

"No! He wouldn't let me near it!"

"But could you feel it? Was it tiny?" Suze's eyes gleam wickedly. "I bet it's teeny. He's hoping to kid some poor girl into marrying him and being stuck with a teeny todger all her life. Narrow escape, Bex!" She reaches for her packet of Silk Cut and lights up.

"Stay away!" I say. "I don't want my scarf smelling of smoke!"

"So what *are* you doing this weekend?" she asks, taking a drag. "Will you be OK? Do you want to come down to the country?"

This is how Suze always refers to her family's second home in Hampshire. *The Country.* As though her parents own some small, independent nation that nobody else knows about.

"No, 's'OK," I say, morosely picking up the TV guide. "I'm going to Surrey. Visit my parents."

"Oh well," says Suze. "Give your mum my love."

"I will," I say. "And you give my love to Pepper."

Pepper is Suze's horse. She rides him about three times a year, if that, but whenever her parents suggest selling him she gets all hysterical. Apparently he costs £15,000 a year to run. Fifteen thousand pounds. And what does he do for his money? Just stands in a stable and eats apples. I wouldn't mind being a horse.

"Oh yeah, that reminds me," says Suze. "The council tax bill came in. It's three hundred each."

"Three hundred pounds?" I look at her in dismay. "What, straight away?"

"Yeah. Actually, it's late. Just write me a check or something."

"Fine," I say airily. "Three hundred quid coming up."

I reach for my bag and write a check out straight away. Suze is so generous about the rent, I always pay my share of the bills, and sometimes add a bit extra. But still, I'm feeling cold as I hand it over. Three hundred pounds gone, just like that. And I've still got that bloody VISA bill to think of. Not a great month.

"Oh, and someone called," adds Suze, and squints at a piece of paper. "Erica Parsnip. Is that right?"

"Erica *Parsnip*?" Sometimes I think Suze's mind has been expanded just a little too often.

"Parnell. Erica Parnell from Endwich Bank. Can you call her."

I stare at Suze, frozen in horror.

"She called here? She called this number?"

"Yes. This afternoon."

"Oh shit." My heart starts to thump. "What did you say? Did you say I've got glandular fever?"

"What?" It's Suze's turn to stare. "Of course I didn't say you've got bloody glandular fever!"

"Did she ask about my leg? Anything about my health at all?"

"No! She just said where were you? And I said you were at work—"

"Suze!" I wail in dismay.

"Well, what was I *supposed* to say?"

"You were supposed to say I was in bed with glandular fever and a broken leg!"

"Well, thanks for the warning!" Suze gazes at me, eyes narrowed, and crosses her legs back into the lotus position. Suze has got the longest, thinnest, wiriest legs I've ever known. When she's wearing black leggings she looks just like a spider. "What's the big deal, anyway?" she says. "Are you overdrawn?"

Am I overdrawn?

I smile back as reassuringly as I can. If Suze had any idea

of my real situation, she'd need more than yoga to calm her down.

"Just a tad." I give a careless shrug. "But I'm sure it'll work itself out. No need to worry!"

There's silence, and I look up to see Suze tearing up my check. For a moment I'm completely silenced, then I stutter, "Suze! Don't be stupid!"

"Pay me back when you're in the black," she says firmly.

"Thanks, Suze," I say in a suddenly thickened voice—and as I give her a big hug I can feel tears jumping into my eyes. Suze has got to be the best friend I've ever had.

But there's a tense feeling in my stomach, which stays with me all evening and is still there when I wake up the next morning. A feeling I can't even shift by thinking about my Denny and George scarf. I lie in bed staring up at the ceiling and, for the first time in months, calculate how much I owe to everybody. The bank, VISA, my Harvey Nichols card, my Debenhams card, my Fenwicks card . . . And now Suze, too.

It's about . . . let's think . . . it's about £6,000.

A cold feeling creeps over me as I contemplate this figure. How on earth am I going to find £6,000? I could save £6 a week for a thousand weeks. Or £12 a week for five hundred weeks. Or . . . or £60 a week for a hundred weeks. That's more like it. But how the hell am I going to find £60 a week?

Or I could bone up on lots of general knowledge and go on a game show. Or invent something really clever. Or I could . . . win the lottery. At the thought, a lovely warm glow creeps over me, and I close my eyes and snuggle back down into bed. The lottery is by far the best solution.

I wouldn't aim to win the jackpot of course—that's *completely* unlikely. But one of those minor prizes. There seem to be heaps of those going around. Say, £100,000. That would do. I could pay off all my debts, buy a car, buy a flat . . .

Actually, better make it £200,000. Or a quarter of a million.

Or, even better, one of those shared jackpots. "The five winners will each receive £1.3 million." (I love the way they say that: "One point three." As if that extra £300,000 is a tiny, insignificant amount. As if you wouldn't notice whether it was there or not.)

One point three million should see me straight. And it's not being greedy, is it, to want to share your jackpot? Please, God, I think, let me win the lottery and I promise to share nicely.

And so, on the way down to my parents' house I stop off at a petrol station to buy a couple of lottery tickets. Choosing the numbers takes about half an hour. I know 44 always does well, and 42. But what about the rest? I write out a few series of numbers on a piece of paper and squint at them, trying to imagine them on the telly.

1 6 9 16 23 44

No! Terrible! What am I thinking of? One never comes up, for a start. And 6 and 9 look wrong, too.

3 14 21 25 36 44

That's a bit better. I fill in the numbers on the ticket.

5 11 18 27 28 42

I'm quite impressed by this one. It *looks* like a winner. I can just imagine Moira Stewart reading it out on the news. "One ticket-holder, believed to live in southwest London, has won an estimated jackpot of £10 million."

For a moment, I feel faint. What'll I do with £10 million? Where will I start?

Well, a huge party to begin with. Somewhere smart but cool, with loads of champagne and dancing and a taxi service so no one has to drive. And going-home presents, like really nice bubble bath or something. (Does Calvin Klein do bubble bath?)

Then I'll buy houses for all my family and friends, of course. I lean against the lottery stand and close my eyes to concentrate. Suppose I buy twenty houses at £250,000 each. That'll leave me . . . 5 million. Plus about £50,000 on the party.

So that's £4,950,000. Oh, and I need £6,000 to pay off all my credit cards and overdraft. Plus £300 for Suze. Call it £7,000. So that leaves . . . £4,943,000.

Obviously, I'll do loads for charity. In fact, I'll probably set up a charitable foundation. I'll support all those unfashionable charities that get ignored, like skin diseases and home helps for the elderly. And I'll send a great big check to my old English teacher, Mrs. James, so she can restock the school library. Perhaps they'll even rename it after me. The Bloomwood Library.

Oh, and £300 for that swirly coat in Whistles, which I *must* buy before they're all snapped up. So how much does that leave? Four million, nine hundred and forty-three thousand, minus—

"Excuse me." A voice interrupts me and I look up dazedly. The woman behind is trying to get at the pen.

"Sorry," I say, and politely make way. But the interruption has made me lose track of my calculations. Was it 4 million or 5 million?

Then, as I see the woman looking at my bit of paper covered in scribbled numbers, an awful thought strikes me. What if one of my rejected sets of numbers actually comes up? What if **1 6 9 16 23 44** comes up tonight and I haven't entered it? All my life, I'd never forgive myself.

I quickly fill in tickets for all the combinations of numbers written on my bit of paper. That's nine tickets in all. Nine quid—quite a lot of money, really. I almost feel bad about spending it. But then, that's nine times as many chances of winning, isn't it?

And I now have a very good feeling about **1 6 9 16 23 44**. Why has that particular set of numbers leapt into my mind and stayed there? Maybe someone, somewhere, is trying to tell me something.

Four

WHEN I ARRIVE at my parents' house, they are in the middle of an argument. Dad is halfway up a stepladder in the garden, poking at the gutter on the side of the house, and Mum is sitting at the wrought-iron garden table, leafing through a Past Times catalogue. Neither of them even looks up when I walk through the patio doors.

"All I'm saying is that they should set a good example!" Mum is exclaiming. She's looking good, I think as I sit down. New hair color—pale brown with just a hint of gray—and a very nice red polo-neck jumper. Perhaps I'll borrow that tomorrow.

"And you think exposing themselves to danger is a good example, is it?" replies Dad, looking down from the ladder. He's got quite a few more gray hairs, I notice with a slight shock. Mind you, gray hair looks quite distinguished on him. "You think that would solve the problem?"

"Danger!" says Mum derisively. "Don't be so melodramatic, Graham. Is that the opinion you really have of British society?"

"Hi, Mum," I say. "Hi, Dad."

"Becky agrees with me. Don't you, darling?" says Mum, and points to a page of Past Times, full of 1930s reproduction jewelry and trinket boxes. "Lovely cardigan," she adds *sotto voce*. "Look at that embroidery!" I follow her gaze and see a long, purple coat-like garment covered in colorful Art Deco swirls. I'd save the page and get it for her birthday—if I didn't know she'll probably have bought it herself by next week.

"Of course Becky doesn't agree with you!" retorts my dad. "It's the most ridiculous idea I've ever heard."

"No it's not!" says Mum indignantly. "Becky, you think it would be a good idea for the royal family to travel by public transport, don't you, darling?"

"Well . . ." I say cautiously. "I hadn't really . . ."

"You think the queen should travel to official engagements on the ninety-three bus?" scoffs Dad.

"And why not? Maybe then the ninety-three bus would become more efficient!"

"So," I say, sitting down next to Mum. "How are things?"

"You realize this country is on the verge of gridlock?" says Mum, as if she hasn't heard me. "If more people don't start using public transport, our roads are going to seize up."

My dad shakes his head.

"And you think the queen traveling on the ninety-three bus would solve the problem. Never mind the security problems, never mind the fact that she'd be able to do far fewer engagements . . ."

"I didn't mean the queen, necessarily," retorts Mum. "But some of those others. Princess Michael of Kent, for example. She could travel by tube, every so often, couldn't she? These people need to learn about real life."

The last time my mum traveled on the tube was about 1983.

"Shall I make some coffee?" I say brightly.

"If you ask me, this gridlock business is utter nonsense," says my dad. He jumps down from the stepladder and brushes the dirt off his hands. "It's all propaganda."

"Propaganda?" exclaims my mum in outrage.

"Right," I say hurriedly. "Well, I'll go and put the kettle on."

I walk back into the house, flick the kettle on in the kitchen, and sit down at the table in a nice patch of sunshine. I've already forgotten what my mum and dad are arguing about. They'll just go round and round in circles and agree it's all the fault of Tony Blair. Anyway, I've got more important things to think about. I'm trying to figure out exactly how much I should give to Philip, my boss, after I win the lottery. I can't leave him out, of course—but is cash a bit tacky? Would a present be better? Really nice cufflinks, perhaps. Or one of those picnic hampers with all the plates inside. (Clare Edwards, obviously, will get nothing.)

Sitting alone in the sunny kitchen, I feel as though I have a little glowing secret inside me. I'm going to win the lottery. Tonight, my life is going to change. God, I can't wait. Ten million pounds. Just think, tomorrow I'll be able to buy anything I want. Anything!

The newspaper's open in front of me at the property section and I carelessly pick it up to peruse expensive houses. Where shall I live? Chelsea? Notting Hill? Mayfair? *Belgravia,* I read. *Magnificent seven-bedroom detached house with staff annex and mature garden.* Well, that sounds all right. I could cope with seven bedrooms in Belgravia. My eye flicks complacently down to the price and stops still with shock. Six point five million pounds. That's how much they're asking. Six and a half million.

I feel stunned and slightly angry. Are they serious? I haven't got anything like £6.5 million. I've only got about . . . 4 million left. Or was it 5? I stare at the page, feeling cheated. Lottery winners are supposed to be able to buy anything they want—but already I'm feeling poor and inadequate.

I shove the paper aside and reach for a freebie brochure full of gorgeous white duvet covers at £100 each. That's more like it. When I've won the lottery I'll only ever have crisp white duvet covers, I decide. And I'll have a white cast-iron bed and painted wooden shutters and a fluffy white dressing gown . . .

"So, how's the world of finance?" Mum's voice interrupts me and I look up. She's bustling into the kitchen, still holding her

Past Times catalogue. "Have you made the coffee? Chop chop, darling!"

"I was going to," I say, and make a half move from my chair. But, as always, Mum's there before me. She reaches for a ceramic storage jar I've never seen before and spoons coffee into a new gold cafétière.

Mum's terrible. She's always buying new stuff for the kitchen—and she just gives the old stuff to charity shops. New kettles, new toasters . . . We've already had three new rubbish bins this year—dark green, then chrome, and now yellow translucent plastic. I mean, what a waste of money.

"That's a nice skirt!" she says, looking at me as though for the first time. "Where's that from?"

"DKNY," I mumble back.

"Very pretty," she says. "Was it expensive?"

"Not really," I say. "About fifty quid."

This is not strictly true. It was nearer 150. But there's no point telling Mum how much things really cost, because she'd have a coronary. Or, in fact, she'd tell my dad first—and then they'd both have coronaries, and I'd be an orphan.

So what I do is work in two systems simultaneously. Real prices and Mum prices. It's a bit like when everything in the shop is 20 percent off, and you walk around mentally reducing everything. After a while, you get quite practiced.

The only difference is, I operate a sliding-scale system, a bit like income tax. It starts off at 20 percent (if it really cost £20, I say it cost £16) and rises up to . . . well, to 90 percent if necessary. I once bought a pair of boots that cost £200, and I told Mum they were £20 in the sale. And she believed me.

"So, are you looking for a flat?" she says, glancing over my shoulder at the property pages.

"No," I say sulkily, and flick over a page of my brochure. My parents are always on at me to buy a flat. Do they know how much flats cost?

"Apparently, Thomas has bought a very nice little starter

home in Reigate," she says, nodding toward our next-door neighbors. "He commutes." She says this with an air of satisfaction, as though she's telling me he's won the Nobel Peace Prize.

"Well, I can't afford a flat," I say. "*Or* a starter home."

Not yet, anyway, I think. Not until eight o'clock tonight. Hee hee hee.

"Money troubles?" says Dad, coming into the kitchen. "You know, there are two solutions to money troubles."

His eyes are twinkling, and I just know he's about to give me some clever little aphorism. Dad has a saying for every subject under the sun—as well as a wide selection of limericks and truly terrible jokes. Sometimes I like listening to them. Sometimes I don't.

"C.B.," says Dad, his eyes twinkling. "Or M.M.M."

He pauses for effect and I turn the page of my brochure, pretending I can't hear him.

"Cut Back," says my dad, "or Make More Money. One or the other. Which is it to be, Becky?"

"Oh, both, I expect," I say airily, and turn another page of my brochure. To be honest, I almost feel sorry for Dad. It'll be quite a shock for him when his only daughter becomes a multimillionaire overnight.

After lunch, Mum and I go along to a craft fair in the local primary school. I'm really just going to keep Mum company, and I'm certainly not planning to buy anything—but when we get there, I find a stall full of amazing handmade cards, only £1.50 each! So I buy ten. After all, you always need cards, don't you? There's also a gorgeous blue ceramic plant holder with little elephants going round it—and I've been saying for ages we should have more plants in the flat. So I buy that, too. Only fifteen quid. Craft fairs are such a bargain, aren't they? You go along thinking they'll be complete rubbish—but you can always find *something* you want.

Mum's really happy, too, as she's found a pair of candlesticks for her collection. She's got collections of candlesticks, toast racks, pottery jugs, glass animals, embroidered samplers, and thimbles. (Personally, I don't think the thimbles count as a proper collection, because she got the whole lot, including the cabinet, from an ad at the back of the *Mail on Sunday* magazine. But she never tells anybody that. In fact, I shouldn't have mentioned it.)

So anyway, we're both feeling rather pleased with ourselves, and decide to go for a cup of tea. Then, on the way out, we pass one of those really sad stalls which no one is going near; the kind people glance at once, then quickly walk past. The poor guy behind it looks really sorry for himself, so I pause to have a look. And no wonder no one's stopping. He's selling weird-shaped wooden bowls, and matching wooden cutlery. What on earth is the point of wooden cutlery?

"That's nice!" I say brightly, and pick one of the bowls up.

"Hand-crafted applewood," he says. "Took a week to make."

Well, it was a waste of a week, if you ask me. It's shapeless and the wood's a nasty shade of brown. But as I go to put it back down again, he looks so doleful I feel sorry for him and turn it over to look at the price, thinking if it's a fiver I'll buy it. But it's eighty quid! I show the price to Mum, and she pulls a little face.

"That particular piece was featured in *Elle Decoration* last month," says the man mournfully, and produces a cutout page. And at his words, I freeze. *Elle Decoration*? Is he joking?

He's not joking. There on the page, in full color, is a picture of a room, completely empty except for a suede beanbag, a low table, and a wooden bowl. I stare at it incredulously.

"Was it this exact one?" I ask, trying not to sound too excited. "This exact bowl?" As he nods, my grasp tightens round the bowl. I can't believe it. I'm holding a piece of *Elle Decoration*. How cool is that? Now I feel incredibly stylish and trendy—and wish I were wearing white linen trousers and had my hair slicked back like Yasmin Le Bon to match.

It just shows I've got good taste. Didn't I pick out this bowl—

sorry, this *piece*—all by myself? Didn't I spot its quality? Already I can see our sitting room redesigned entirely around it, all pale and minimalist. Eighty quid. That's nothing for a timeless piece of style like this.

"I'll have it," I say determinedly, and reach inside my bag for my checkbook. The thing is, I remind myself, buying cheap is actually a false economy. It's much better to spend a little more and make a serious purchase that'll last for a lifetime. And this bowl is quite clearly a classic. Suze is going to be *so* impressed.

When we get back home, Mum goes straight inside, but I stay in the driveway, carefully transferring my purchases from her car to mine.

"Becky! What a surprise!"

Oh God. It's Martin Webster from next door, leaning over the fence with a rake in his hand and a huge friendly smile on his face. Martin has this way of always making me feel guilty, I don't know why.

Actually I do know why. It's because I know he was always hoping I would grow up and marry Tom, his son. And I haven't. The history of my relationship with Tom is: he asked me out once when we were both about sixteen and I said no, I was going out with Adam Moore. That was the end of it and thank God for that. To be perfectly honest, I would rather marry Martin himself than marry Tom.

"Hi!" I say overenthusiastically. "How are you?"

"Oh, we're all doing well," says Martin. "You heard Tom's bought a house?"

"Yes," I say. "In Reigate. Fantastic!"

"It's got two bedrooms, shower room, reception room, and open-plan kitchen," he recites. "Limed oak units in the kitchen."

"Gosh," I say. "How fab."

"Tom's thrilled with it," says Martin. "Janice!" he adds in a yell. "Come and see who's here!"

A moment later, Janice appears on the front doorstep, wearing her floral apron.

"Becky!" she says. "What a stranger you've become! How long is it?"

Now I feel guilty for not visiting my parents more often.

"Well," I say, trying to give a nonchalant smile. "You know. I'm quite busy with my job and everything."

"Oh yes," says Janice, giving an awe-stricken nod. "Your *job*."

Somewhere along the line, Janice and Martin have got it into their heads that I'm this high-powered financial whiz kid. I've tried telling them that really, I'm not—but the more I deny it, the more high powered they think I am. It's a catch-22. They now think I'm high powered *and* modest.

Still, who cares? It's actually quite fun, playing a financial genius.

"Yes, actually we've been quite busy lately," I say coolly. "What with the merger of SBG and Rutland."

"Of course," breathes Janice.

"You know, that reminds me," says Martin suddenly. "Becky, wait there. Back in two ticks." He disappears before I can say anything, and I'm left awkwardly with Janice.

"So," I say inanely. "I hear Tom's got limed oak units in his kitchen!"

This is literally the only thing I can think of to say. I smile at Janice, and wait for her to reply. But instead, she's beaming at me delightedly. Her face is all lit up—and suddenly I realize I've made a huge mistake. I shouldn't have mentioned Tom's bloody starter home. I shouldn't have mentioned the limed oak units. She'll think I suddenly fancy Tom, now he's got a starter home to his name.

"It's limed oak and Mediterranean tiles," she says proudly. "It was a choice of Mediterranean or Farmhouse Quarry, and Tom chose Mediterranean."

For an instant I consider saying I would have chosen Farmhouse Quarry. But that seems a bit mean.

"Lovely," I say. "And two bedrooms!"

Why can't I get off the subject of this bloody starter home?

"He wanted two bedrooms," says Janice. "After all, you never know, do you?" She smiles coyly at me, and ridiculously, I feel myself start to blush. Why am I blushing? This is so stupid. Now she thinks I fancy Tom. She's picturing us together in the starter home, making supper together in the limed oak kitchen.

I should say something. I should say, "Janice, I don't fancy Tom. He's too tall and his breath smells." But how on earth can I say that?

"Well, do give him my love," I hear myself saying instead.

"I certainly will," she says, and pauses. "Does he have your London number?"

Aarrgh!

"I think so," I lie, smiling brightly. "And he can always get me here if he wants." Now everything I say sounds like some saucy double entendre. I can just imagine how this conversation will be reported back to Tom. "She was asking *all* about your starter home. And she asked you to call her!"

Life would be a lot easier if conversations were rewindable and erasable, like videos. Or if you could instruct people to disregard what you just said, like in a courtroom. *Please strike from the record all references to starter homes and limed oak kitchens.*

Luckily, at that moment, Martin reappears, clutching a piece of paper.

"Thought you might cast your eye over this," he says. "We've had this with-profits fund with Flagstaff Life for fifteen years. Now we're thinking of transferring to their new unit-linked growth fund. What do you think?"

I don't know. What's he talking about, anyway? Some kind of savings plan? Please don't ask me, I want to say. Please ask someone who knows what they're talking about. But there's no way they'll believe that I'm not a financial genius—so I'll just have to do the best I can.

I run my eye over the piece of paper in what I hope looks like a knowledgeable fashion and nod several times. It's a letter making some kind of special offer if investors switch to this new fund. Sounds reasonable enough.

"The company wrote to us, saying we might want a higher return in our retirement years," says Martin. "There's a guaranteed sum, too."

"And they'll send us a carriage clock," chimes in Janice. "Swiss-made."

"Mmm," I say, studying the letterhead intently. "Well, I should think that's quite a good idea."

Flagstaff Life, I'm thinking. I'm sure I've heard something about them recently. Which ones are Flagstaff Life? Oh yes! They're the ones who threw a champagne party at Soho Soho. That's right. And Elly got incredibly pissed and told David Salisbury from *The Times* that she loved him. It was a bloody good party, come to think of it. One of the best.

Hmm. But wasn't there something else? Something I've heard recently? I wrinkle my nose, trying to remember . . . but it's gone. I've probably got it wrong, anyway.

"D'you rate them as a company?" says Martin.

"Oh yes," I say, looking up. "They're very well regarded among the profession."

"Well then," says Martin, looking pleased. "If Becky thinks it's a good idea . . ."

"Yes, but, I really wouldn't just listen to me!" I say quickly. "I mean, a financial adviser or someone would know far more . . ."

"Listen to her!" says Martin with a little chuckle. "The financial expert herself."

"You know, Tom sometimes buys your magazine," puts in Janice. "Not that he's got much money now, what with the mortgage and everything . . . But he says your articles are very good! Tom says—"

"How nice!" I cut in. "Well, look, I really must go. Lovely to see you. And love to Tom!"

And I turn into the house so quickly, I bump my knee on the

door frame. Then I feel a bit bad, and wish I'd said good-bye nicely. But honestly! If I hear one more word about bloody Tom and his bloody kitchen, I'll go mad.

By the time I sit down in front of the National Lottery, however, I've forgotten all about them. We've had a nice supper—chicken Provençale from Marks and Spencer, and a nice bottle of Pinot Grigio, which I brought. I know the chicken Provençale comes from Marks and Spencer because I've bought it myself, quite a few times. I recognized the sun-dried tomatoes and the olives, and everything. Mum, of course, still acted like she'd made it from scratch, from her own recipe.

I don't know why she bothers. It isn't like anyone would care—especially when it's just me and Dad. And I mean, it's pretty obvious that there are never any raw ingredients in our kitchen. There are lots of empty cardboard boxes and lots of fully prepared meals—and nothing in between. But still Mum never ever admits she's bought a ready-made meal, not even when it's a pie in a foil container. My dad will eat one of those pies, full of plastic mushrooms and gloopy sauce, and then say, with a perfectly straight face, "Delicious, my love." And my mum will smile back, looking all pleased with herself.

But tonight it's not foil pie, it's chicken Provençale. (To be fair, I suppose it almost does look homemade—except no one would ever cut a red pepper up that small for themselves, would they? People have more important things to do.) So anyway, we've eaten it and we've drunk a fair amount of the Pinot Grigio, and there's an apple crumble in the oven—and I've suggested, casually, that we all go and watch telly. Because I know from looking at the clock that the National Lottery program has already started. In a matter of minutes, it's all going to happen. I cannot wait.

Luckily, my parents aren't the sort who want to make conversation about politics or talk about books. We've already caught up with all the family news, and I've told them how my work's going, and they've told me about their holiday in Corsica—so by now, we're grinding to a bit of a halt. We need the telly on, if only as a conversational sounding board.

So we all troop into the sitting room, and my dad lights the gas flame-effect fire and turns on the telly. And there it is! The National Lottery, in glorious Technicolor. The lights are shining, and Dale Winton is joshing with Tiffany from *EastEnders*, and every so often the audience gives an excited whoop. My stomach's getting tighter and tighter, and my heart's going thump-thump-thump. Because in a few minutes those balls are going to fall. In a few minutes I'm going to be a millionaire. I just *know* I am.

I lean calmly back on the sofa and think what I'll do when I win. At the very instant that I win, I mean. Do I scream? Do I keep quiet? Maybe I shouldn't tell anyone for twenty-four hours. Maybe I shouldn't tell anyone *at all*.

This new thought transfixes me. I could be a secret winner! I could have all the money and none of the pressure. If people asked me how I could afford so many designer clothes I'd just tell them I was doing lots of freelance work. Yes! And I could transform all my friends' lives anonymously, like a good angel.

I'm just working out how big a house I could manage to buy without everyone twigging, when a voice on the screen alerts me.

"Question to number three."

What?

"My favorite animal is the flamingo because it's pink, fluffy, and has long legs." The girl sitting on the stool excitedly unwinds a pair of long glossy legs, and the audience goes wild. I stare at her dazedly. What's going on? Why are we watching *Blind Date*?

"Now, this show used to be fun," says Mum. "But it's gone downhill."

"You call this rubbish fun?" retorts my dad incredulously.

"Listen, Dad, actually, could we turn back to—"

"I didn't say it was fun *now*. I said—"

"Dad!" I say, trying not to sound too panicky. "Could we just go back to BBC1 for a moment?"

Blind Date disappears and I sigh with relief. The next moment, an earnest man in a suit fills the screen.

"What the police failed to appreciate," he says in a nasal voice, "is that the witnesses were not sufficiently—"

"Dad!"

"Where's the television guide?" he says impatiently. "There's got to be something better than this."

"There's the lottery!" I almost scream. "I want to watch the lottery!"

I know strictly speaking that whether I watch it or not won't affect my chances of winning—but I don't want to miss the great moment, do I? You might think I'm a bit mad, but I feel that if I watch it, I can kind of communicate with the balls through the screen. I'll stare hard at them as they get tossed around and silently urge on my winning numbers. It's a bit like supporting a team. *Team 1 6 9 16 23 44.*

Except the numbers never come out in order, do they?

Team 44 1 23 6 9 16. Possibly. Or *Team 23 6 1 . . .*

Suddenly there's a round of applause and Martine McCutcheon's finished her song. Oh my God. It's about to happen. My life is about to change.

"The lottery's become terribly commercialized, hasn't it?" says my mum, as Dale Winton leads Martine over to the red button. "It's a shame, really."

"What do you mean, it's *become* commercialized?" retorts my dad.

"People used to play the lottery because they wanted to support the charities."

"No they didn't! Don't be ridiculous! No one gives a fig about the charities. This is all about self, self, self." Dad gestures toward Dale Winton with the remote control and the screen goes dead.

"Dad!" I wail.

"So you think no one cares about the charities?" says my mum into the silence.

"That's not what I said."

"Dad! Put it back on!" I screech. "Put-it-back-on!" I'm about to wrestle him for the remote control when he flicks it back on again.

I stare at the screen in utter disbelief. The first ball has already dropped. And it's 44. My number 44.

". . . last appeared three weeks ago. And here comes the second ball . . . And it's number 1."

I can't move. It's taking place, before my very eyes. I'm actually winning the lottery. I'm winning the bloody lottery!

Now that it's happening, I feel surprisingly calm about it. It's as if I've known, all my life, that this would happen. Sitting here silently on the sofa, I feel as though I'm in a fly-on-the-wall documentary about myself. "Becky Bloomwood always secretly knew she would win the lottery one day. But on the day it happened, even she couldn't have predicted . . ."

"And another low one. Number 3."

What? My mind snaps to and I stare perplexedly at the screen. That can't be right. They mean 23.

"And number 2, last week's bonus ball."

I feel cold all over. What the hell is going on? What *are* these numbers?

"And another low one! Number 4. A popular number—it's had twelve appearances so far this year. And finally . . . number 5! Well, I never! This is a bit of a first! Now, lining them up in order . . ."

No. This can't be serious. This has to be a mistake. The winning lottery numbers cannot possibly be 1, 2, 3, 4, 5, 44. That's not a lottery combination, it's a . . . it's an act of torture.

And I was winning. I was *winning*.

"Look at that!" my mum's saying. "Absolutely incredible! One–two–three–four–five–forty-four."

"And why should that be incredible?" replies Dad. "It's as likely as any other combination."

"It can't be!"

"Jane, do you know *anything* about the laws of probability?"

Quietly I get up and leave the room, as the National Lottery theme tune blares out of the telly. I walk into the kitchen, sit down at the table, and bury my head in my hands. I feel slightly shaky, to tell you the truth. How could I lose? I was living in a big house and going on holiday to Barbados with all my friends, and walking into Agnès b and buying anything I wanted. It felt so real.

And now, instead, I'm sitting in my parents' kitchen, and I can't afford to go on holiday and I've just spent eighty quid on a wooden bowl I don't even like.

Miserably, I turn on the kettle, pick up a copy of *Woman's Journal* lying on the counter, and flick through it—but even that doesn't cheer me up. Everything seems to remind me of money. Maybe my dad's right, I find myself thinking dolefully. Maybe Cut Back is the answer. Suppose . . . suppose I cut back enough to save sixty quid a week. I'd have £6,000 in a hundred weeks.

And suddenly my brain is alert. Six thousand quid. That's not bad, is it? And if you think about it, it can't be *that* hard to save sixty quid a week. It's only the same as a couple of meals out. I mean, you'd hardly notice it.

God, yes. That's what I'll do. Sixty quid a week, every week. Maybe I'll even pay it into a special account. That new Lloyds high-yield sixty-day access account with the tiered interest rates. It'll be fantastic! I'll be completely on top of my finances—and when I've paid off my bills I'll just keep saving. It'll become a habit to be frugal. And at the end of every year I'll splash out on one classic investment like an Armani suit. Or maybe Christian Dior. Something really classy, anyway.

I'll start on Monday, I think excitedly, spooning chocolate Ovaltine into a cup. What I'll do is, I just won't spend *anything*. All my spare money will mount up, and I'll be rich. This is going to be so great.

OCTAGON ▸ *flair...style...vision*

FINANCIAL SERVICES DEPARTMENT
8TH FLOOR TOWER HOUSE
LONDON ROAD WINCHESTER SO 44 3DR

Ms. Rebecca Bloomwood
Flat 2
4 Burney Rd.
London SW6 8FD

Charge Card Number 7854 4567

2 March 2000

Dear Ms. Bloomwood:

Our records suggest that we have not received payment for your latest Octagon Silver Card bill. If you have paid within the last few days, please ignore this letter.

Your outstanding bill is currently £235.76. The minimum payment is £43.00. You may pay by cash, check, or on the enclosed bank giro credit slip. We look forward to receiving your payment.

Yours sincerely,

John Hunter
Customer Accounts Manager

OCTAGON ▸ *flair...style...vision*

FINANCIAL SERVICES DEPARTMENT
8TH FLOOR TOWER HOUSE
LONDON ROAD WINCHESTER S0 44 3DR

Ms. Rebecca Bloomwood
Flat 2
4 Burney Rd.
London SW6 8FD

Charge Card Number 7854 4567

2 March 2000

Dear Ms. Bloomwood:

There's never been a better time to spend!

For a limited time, we are offering EXTRA POINTS on all purchases over £50 made with your Octagon Silver Card*—so take the opportunity now to add more points to your total and take advantage of some of our Pointholders' Gifts.

Some of the fantastic gifts we are offering include:

An Italian leather bag	**1,000 points**
A case of pink champagne	**2,000 points**
Two flights to Paris**	**5,000 points**
(Your current level is:	35 points)

And remember, during this special offer period, you will gain two points for every £5 spent! We look forward to welcoming you soon to take advantage of this unique offer.

Yours sincerely,

Adrian Smith
Customer Services Manager

**excluding purchases at restaurants, pharmacy, newsstand, and hairdresser*
***certain restrictions apply—see enclosed leaflet*

Five

FRUGALITY. SIMPLICITY. These are my new watchwords. A new, uncluttered, Zen-like life, in which I spend nothing. Spend *nothing*. I mean, when you think about it, how much money do we all waste every day? No wonder I'm in a little bit of debt. And really, it's not my fault. I've merely been succumbing to the Western drag of materialism—which you have to have the strength of elephants to resist. At least, that's what it says in my new book.

You see, yesterday, when Mum and I went into Waterstone's to buy her paperback for the week, I sidled off to the self-help section and bought the most wonderful book I've ever read. Quite honestly, it's going to change my life. I've got it now, in my bag. It's called *Controlling Your Cash* by David E. Barton, and it's fantastic. What it says is that we can all fritter away money without realizing it, and that most of us could easily cut our cash consumption by half in just one week.

In one week!

You just have to do things like make your own sandwiches instead of eating in restaurants and ride a bike to work instead of taking the tube. When you start thinking about it, you can save money everywhere. And as David E. Barton says, there are lots of free pleasures which we forget because we're so busy spending money, like parks and museums and the simple joy of a country walk.

Come to think of it, why don't we put information like this in *Successful Saving*? It's so much more useful than knowing about some fancy new unit trust which might make a profit or might not. I mean, with this scheme you start making money straight away!

It's all so easy and straightforward. And the best thing is, you have to start out by going shopping! The book says you should begin by itemizing every single purchase in a single normal spending day and plot it on a graph. It stresses that you should be honest and not suddenly curtail or alter your spending pattern—which is lucky, because it's Suze's birthday on Friday and I've got to get her a present.

So on Monday morning, I stop off at Lucio's on the way into work and buy an extralarge cappuccino and a chocolate muffin, just like I usually do. I have to admit I feel a bit sorrowful as I hand over my money, because this is my last-ever cappuccino and my last-ever chocolate muffin. My new frugality starts tomorrow—and cappuccinos aren't allowed. David E. Barton says if you have a coffee habit you should make it at home and take it into the office in a flask, and if you like eating snacks you should buy cheap cakes from the supermarket. "The coffee merchants are fleecing you for what is little more than hot water and polystyrene," he points out—and I suppose he's right. But I will miss my morning cappuccino. Still, I've promised myself I'll follow the rules of the book—and I will.

As I come out of the coffee shop, clutching my last-ever cup, I realize I don't actually have a flask for coffee. But that's OK, I'll buy one. There are some lovely sleek chrome ones in Habitat. Flasks are actually quite trendy these days. I think Alessi might even do one. Wouldn't that be cool? Drinking coffee out of an Alessi flask. Much cooler than a take-away cappuccino.

So I'm feeling quite happy as I walk along the street. When I get to Smiths I pop in and stock up on a few magazines to keep me going—and I also buy a sweet little silver notebook and pen to write down everything I spend. I'm going to be really rigorous about this, because David E. Barton says the very act of noting down purchases should have a curtailing effect. So when I get into work, I start my list.

Cappuccino	*£1.50*
Muffin	*£1.00*
Notebook	*£3.99*
Pen	*£1.20*
Magazines	*£6.40*

Which makes a grand total so far of . . . £14.09.

Gosh. I suppose that's quite a lot, bearing in mind it's only nine-forty in the morning.

But the notebook and pen don't count, do they? They're like course requirements. I mean, how on earth are you supposed to note down all your purchases without a notebook and pen? So I subtract both of those, and now my total comes to . . . £8.90. Which is much better.

Anyway, I'm at work now. I probably won't spend anything else all day.

But somehow, spending nothing is absolutely impossible. First of all, Guy from Accounts comes round with yet another leaving present to give to. Then I have to go out and get some lunch. I'm very restrained with my sandwich—I choose egg and cress, which is the cheapest one at Boots, and I don't even like egg and cress.

David E. Barton says that when you make a real effort, particularly in the early stages, you should reward yourself—so I pick up some coconut bath oil from the Natural range as a little treat. Then I notice there are double advantage points on the moisturizer I use.

I *love* advantage points. Aren't they a wonderful invention? If you spend enough, you can get really good prizes, like a beauty day at a hotel. Last Christmas I was really canny—I let my points build up until I'd accumulated enough to buy my granny's Christmas present. What happened in fact was, I'd already built up 1,653 points—and I needed 1,800 to buy her a heated roller set. So I bought myself a great big bottle of Samsara perfume, and that gave me 150 extra points on my card—and then I got the heated roller set absolutely free! The only thing is, I don't much like Samsara perfume—but I didn't realize that until I got home. Still, never mind.

The clever way to use advantage points—as with all special offers—is to spot the opportunity and use it, because it may not come your way again. So I grab three pots of moisturizer and buy them. Double advantage points! I mean, it's just free money, isn't it?

Then I have to get Suze's birthday present. I've actually already bought her a set of aromatherapy oils—but the other day I saw this gorgeous pink angora cardigan in Benetton, and I know she'd love it. I can always take the aromatherapy oils back or give them to someone for Christmas.

So I go into Benetton and pick up the pink cardigan. I'm about to pay . . . when I notice they've got it in gray as well. The most perfect, soft, dove-gray angora cardigan, with little pearly buttons.

Oh *God*. You see, the thing is, I've been looking for a nice gray cardigan for ages. Honestly, I have. You can ask Suze, my mum, anybody. And the other thing is, I'm not actually *on* my new frugal regime yet, am I? I'm just monitoring myself.

David E. Barton says I should act as naturally as possible. So really, I *ought* to act on my natural impulses and buy it. It would be false not to. It would ruin the whole point.

It only costs forty-five quid. And I can put it on VISA.

Look at it another way—what's forty-five quid in the grand scheme of things? I mean, it's nothing, is it?

So I buy it. The most perfect little cardigan in the world.

People will call me the Girl in the Gray Cardigan. I'll be able to *live* in it. Really, it's an investment.

After lunch, I have to go and visit Image Store to choose a front-cover picture for the next issue. This is my absolute favorite job—I can't understand why Philip always offloads it onto someone else. It basically means you get to go and sit drinking coffee all afternoon, looking at rows and rows of transparencies.

Because, of course, we don't have the editorial budget to create our own front covers. God, no. When I first started out in journalism, I thought I'd be able to go to shoots, and meet models, and have a really glamorous time. But we don't even have a cameraman. All our sorts of magazines use picture libraries like Image Store, and the same images tend to go round and round. There's a picture of a roaring tiger that's been on at least three personal finance covers in the last year. Still, the readers don't mind, do they? They're not exactly buying the magazines to look at Kate Moss.

The good thing is that Elly's editor doesn't like choosing front covers either—and they use Image Store, too. So we always try to work it that we'll go together and have a good natter over the pics. Even better, Image Store is all the way over in Notting Hill Gate, so you can legitimately take ages getting there and back. Usually I don't bother going back to the office. Really, it's the perfect way to spend a weekday afternoon.

I get there before Elly and mutter, "Becky Bloomwood from *Successful Saving*," to the girl at reception, wishing I could say "Becky Bloomwood from *Vogue*" or "Becky Bloomwood from *Wall Street Journal*." Then I sit on a squashy black leather chair, flicking through a catalogue of pictures of glossy happy families, until one of the trendy young men who works there comes and leads me to my own illuminated table.

"I'm Paul," he says, "and I'll be looking after you today. Do you know what you're looking for?"

"Well . . ." I say, and pull out my notebook. We had a meeting about the cover yesterday and eventually decided on "Portfolio Management: Getting the Right Balance." And before your head falls off with boredom, let me just point out that last month, the cover line was "Deposit Accounts: Put to the Test."

Why can't we just *once* put self-tanning creams to the test instead? Oh well.

"I'm looking for pictures of scales," I say, reading off my list. "Or tightropes, unicycles . . ."

"Balancing images," says Paul. "No problem. Would you like a coffee?"

"Yes, please," I beam, and relax back in my chair. You see what I mean? It's so nice here. And I'm being *paid* to sit in this chair, doing nothing at all.

A few moments later, Elly appears with Paul, and I look at her in surprise. She's looking really smart, in an aubergine-colored suit and high heels.

"So it's swimmers, boats, and European images," says Paul to her.

"That's it," says Elly, and sinks into the chair beside me.

"Let me guess," I say. "Something about floating currencies."

"Very good," says Elly. "Actually, it's 'Europe: Sink or Swim'?" She says it in an incredibly dramatic voice, and Paul and I both start giggling. When he's walked away, I look her up and down.

"So how come you're so smart?"

"I always look smart," she parries. "You know that." Paul's already wheeling trolley-loads of transparencies toward us and she looks over at them. "Are these yours or mine?'

She's avoiding the subject. What's going on?

"Have you got an interview?" I say, in a sudden flash of genius. She looks at me, flushes, then pulls a sheet of transparencies out of the trolley.

"Circus acts," she says. "People juggling. Is that what you wanted?"

"Elly! Have you got an interview? Tell me!"

There's silence for a while. Elly stares down at the sheet, then looks up.

"Yes," she says, and bites her lip. "But—"

"That's fantastic!" I exclaim, and a couple of smooth-looking girls in the corner look up. "Who for?" I say more quietly. "It's not *Cosmo,* is it?"

We're interrupted by Paul, who comes over with a coffee and puts it in front of Elly.

"Swimmers coming up," he says, then grins and walks off.

"Who's it for?" I repeat. Elly applies for so many jobs, I lose track.

"It's Wetherby's," she says, and a pink flush creeps over her face.

"Wetherby's Investments?" She gives a very slight nod, and I frown in bemusement. Why is she applying to Wetherby's Investments? "Have they got an in-house magazine or something?"

"I'm not applying to be a journalist," she says in a low voice. "I'm applying to be a fund manager."

"*What?*" I say, appalled.

I know friends should be supportive of each other's life decisions and all that. But I'm sorry, a *fund manager*?

"I probably won't even get it," she says, and looks away. "It's no big deal."

"But . . ."

I'm speechless. How can Elly even be thinking of becoming a fund manager? Fund managers aren't real people. They're the characters we laugh at on press trips.

"It's just an idea," she says defensively. "Maybe I want to show Carol I can do something else. You know?"

"So it's like . . . a bargaining tool?" I hazard.

"Yes," she says, and gives a little shrug. "That's it. A bargaining tool."

But she doesn't sound exactly convinced—and she's not nearly as chatty as usual during the rest of the afternoon. What's happened to her? I'm still puzzling over it as I make my way home from Image Store. I walk down to High Street Kensington, cross over the road, and hesitate in front of Marks and Spencer.

The tube is to my right. The shops are to my left.

I must *ignore* the shops. I must practice frugality, go straight home, and plot my expenditure graph. If I need entertainment, I can watch some nice free television and perhaps make some inexpensive, nutritious soup.

But there's nothing good on tonight, at least not until *EastEnders*. And I don't want soup. I really feel as if I need something to cheer me up. And besides—my mind's working fast—I'll be giving it all up tomorrow, won't I? It's like the beginning of Lent. This is my Shopping Pancake Day. I need to cram it all in before the fast begins.

With a surge of excitement I hurry toward the Barkers Centre. I won't go mad, I promise myself. Just one little treat to see me through. I've already got my cardigan—so not clothes . . . and I bought some new kitten heels the other day—so not that . . . although there are some nice Prada-type shoes in Hobbs . . . Hmm. I'm not sure.

I arrive at the cosmetics department of Barkers and suddenly I know. Makeup! That's what I need. A new mascara, and maybe a new lipstick. Happily I start to wander around the bright, heady room, dodging sprays of perfume and painting lipsticks onto the back of my hand. I want a really pale lipstick, I decide. Sort of nudey beige/pink, and a lip liner to go with it . . .

At the Clarins counter, my attention is grabbed by a big promotional sign.

BUY TWO SKIN-CARE PRODUCTS, AND RECEIVE FREE BEAUTY BAG, CONTAINING TRIAL-SIZE CLEANSER, TONER, AND MOISTURIZER, AUTUMN BLAZE LIPSTICK, EXTRA STRENGTH MASCARA AND SAMPLE-SIZE EAU DYNAMISANTE. STOCKS LIMITED SO HURRY.

But this is fantastic! Do you know how much Clarins lipstick usually costs? And here they are, giving it away! Excitedly I start rooting through all the skin-care products, trying to decide which two to buy. How about some neck cream? I've never used that before. And some of this Revitalizing Moisturizer. And then I'll get a free lipstick! It's a complete bargain.

"Hi," I say to the woman in the white uniform. "I'd like the Neck Cream and the Revitalizing Moisturizer. And the beauty bag," I add, suddenly petrified that I might be too late; that the limited stocks might have run out.

But they haven't! Thank God. As my VISA card's processing, the woman hands me my shiny red beauty bag (which I have to admit is a bit smaller than I was expecting) and I excitedly open it up. And there, sure enough, is my free lipstick!

It's a kind of browny-red color. A bit weird, actually. But if I mix it up a bit with some of my others and add a bit of lip gloss, it'll look really good.

By the time I get home, I'm exhausted. I open the door to the flat and Suze comes rushing up, like a puppy.

"What did you get?" she cries.

"Don't look!" I cry back. "You're not allowed to look! It's your present."

"My present!" Suze gets overexcited about birthdays. Well, to be honest, so do I.

I hurry into my bedroom and hide the Benetton bag in the wardrobe. Then I unpack all the rest of my shopping and get out my little silver notebook to itemize my purchases. David E. Barton says this should be done *straight away,* before items can be forgotten.

"D'you want a drink?" comes Suze's voice through the door.

"Yes, please!" I shout back, writing in my book, and a moment later she comes in with a glass of wine.

"*EastEnders* in a minute," she says.

"Thanks," I say absently, and keep on writing. I'm following the rules of the book exactly, taking out all my receipts and writing them all down, and I'm feeling really pleased with myself. It just shows, as David E. Barton says, that with a bit of application, anyone can gain control of their finances.

Come to think of it, I've bought quite a lot of moisturizer today, haven't I? To be honest, when I was at the Clarins counter, buying my Revitalizing Moisturizer, I forgot about all those pots I'd bought at Boots. Still, never mind. You always need moisturizer. It's a staple, like bread and milk, and David E. Barton says you should never scrimp on staples. And apart from that, I don't think I've done too badly. Of course I haven't added it all up yet, but . . .

OK. So here is my final and complete list:

Cappuccino	*£1.50*
Muffin	*£1.00*
~~*Notebook*~~	~~*£3.99*~~
~~*Pen*~~	~~*£1.20*~~
Magazines	*£6.40*
Leaving present	*£4.00*
Egg and cress sandwich	*99p*
Coconut bath oil	*£2.55*
Boots Moisturizers	*£20.97*
Two cardigans	*£90.00*
Evening Standard	*35p*
Clarins Neck Cream	*£14.50*
Clarins Moisturizer	*£32.50*
Beauty Bag	*Free!*
Banana smoothie	*£2.00*
Carrot cake	*£1.20*

And that comes to a grand total of . . . £177.96

I stare at this figure in utter shock.

No, I'm sorry, that just can't be right. It *can't* be right. I can't have spent over £170 in one day.

I mean, it isn't even the weekend. I've been at work. I wouldn't have had *time* to spend that much. There has to be something wrong somewhere. Maybe I haven't added it up right. Or maybe I've entered something twice.

My eye runs more carefully down the list and suddenly stops in triumph. "Two cardigans." I knew it! I only bought . . .

Oh yes. I did buy two, didn't I? Blast. Oh, this is too depressing. I'm going to go and watch *EastEnders*.

OCTAGON ▸ *flair...style...vision*

FINANCIAL SERVICES DEPARTMENT
8TH FLOOR TOWER HOUSE
LONDON ROAD WINCHESTER SO 44 3DR

Ms. Rebecca Bloomwood
Flat 2
4 Burney Rd.
London SW6 8FD

Charge Card Number 7854 4567

5 March 2000

Dear Ms. Bloomwood:

Thank you for your check for £43.00, received today.

Unfortunately, the check is unsigned. No doubt just an oversight on your part. I am therefore returning it to you and request that you sign it and return to us.

As you are no doubt aware, this payment is already late by eight days.

I look forward to receiving your signed check.

Yours sincerely,

John Hunter
Customer Accounts Manager

• ENDWICH BANK •
FULHAM BRANCH
3 Fulham Road
London SW6 9JH

Ms. Rebecca Bloomwood
Flat 2
4 Burney Rd.
London SW6 8FD

5 March 2000

Dear Ms. Bloomwood:

Thank you for your answer-machine message of Sunday 4 March.

I am sorry to hear that your dog has died.

Nevertheless, I must insist that you make contact with myself or my assistant, Erica Parnell, within the next few days, in order to discuss your situation.

Yours sincerely,

Derek Smeath
Manager

• ENDWICH -- BECAUSE WE CARE •

Six

OK, I THINK FIRMLY the next day. The thing is not to get freaked out by how much I happened to spend yesterday. It's water under the bridge. The point is, today is the beginning of my new frugal life. From now on, I'm just going to spend absolutely nothing. David E. Barton says you should aim to cut your expenditure by half in the first week, but I reckon I can do much better than that. I mean, not wanting to be rude, but these self-help books are always for people with absolutely zero self-control, aren't they? And I gave up smoking easily enough. (Except socially, but that doesn't count.)

I feel quite exhilarated as I make myself a cheese sandwich and wrap it up in tinfoil. I've already saved a couple of quid, just by doing that! I haven't got a flask (must buy one at the weekend), so I can't take in coffee, but there's a bottle of Peach Herbal Blast in the fridge so I decide I'll take that instead. It'll be healthier, too.

In fact, it makes you wonder why people buy shop-made sandwiches at all. Look how cheap and easy it is to make your own. And it's the same with curries. David E. Barton says instead of forking out for expensive takeaway meals you should learn how to make your own curries and stir-fries, for a fraction of the cost. So that's what I'm going to do this weekend, after I've been to a museum or maybe just walked along the river, enjoying the scenery.

As I walk along to the tube I feel pure and refreshed. Stern, almost. Look at all these people on the street, scurrying around, thinking about nothing but money. Money, money, money. It's an obsession. But once you relinquish money altogether, it ceases to have any relevance. Already I feel I'm in a completely different mindset. Less materialistic, more philosophical. More *spiritual*. As David E. Barton says, we all fail to appreciate each day just how much we already possess. Light, air, freedom, the companionship of friends . . . I mean, these are the things that matter, aren't they?

It's almost frightening, the transformation that's already occurred within me. For example, I walk past the magazine kiosk at the tube station and idly glance over, but I don't feel the slightest desire to buy any of the magazines. Magazines are irrelevant in my new life. (Plus I've already read most of them.)

So I get on the tube feeling serene and impervious, like a Buddhist monk. When I get off the tube at the other end, I walk straight past the discount shoe shop without even looking, and straight past Lucio's, too. No cappuccino today. No muffin. No spending at all—just straight to the office.

It's quite an easy time of the month for *Successful Saving*. We've only just put the latest issue of the magazine to bed, which basically means we can laze around for a few days doing nothing, before getting our acts together for the next issue. Of course, we're meant to be starting on research for next month's article. In fact, I'm supposed to be making phone calls to a list of stockbrokers today, asking for their investment tips for the next six months. But I already know what they're all going to say. Jon Burrins will go on about the problems with e-commerce stocks, George Steadman will enthuse about some tiny biotechnology company, and Steve Fox will tell me how he wants to get out of the stockbroking game and start an organic farm.

Somehow the whole morning goes by and I haven't done anything, just changed the screen saver on my computer to three yellow fish and an octopus, and written out an expense claim form. To be honest, I can't really concentrate on proper work. I suppose I'm too exhilarated by my new pure self. I keep trying to work out how much I'll have saved by the end of the month and what I'll be able to afford in Jigsaw.

At lunchtime I take out my sandwich wrapped in foil—and for the first time that day, I feel a bit depressed. The bread's gone all soggy, and some pickle's leaked out onto the foil, and it really doesn't look very appetizing at all. What I crave at that moment is Pret à Manger walnut bread and a chocolate brownie.

Don't think about it, I instruct myself firmly. Think how much money you're saving. So somehow I force myself to eat my soggy effort, and swig down some Peach Herbal Blast. When I've finished, I throw away my foil, screw the top back on the Peach Herbal Blast bottle, and put it in our tiny office fridge. And that's about . . . five minutes of my lunch break gone.

So what am I supposed to do next? Where am I supposed to go?

I slump miserably at my desk. God, this frugality is hard going. I leaf dispiritedly through a few folders . . . then raise my head and stare out of the window, at all the busy Oxford Street shoppers clutching carrier bags. I want to get out there so desperately, I'm actually leaning forward in my chair, like a plant toward the light. I'm craving the bright lights and warm air, the racks of merchandise, even the bleep of the cash registers. But I can't go. This morning I told myself that I wouldn't go near the shops all day. I *promised* myself—and I can't break my own promise.

Then a brilliant thought occurs to me. I need to get a curry recipe for my homemade takeaway, don't I? David E. Barton says recipe books are a waste of money. He says you should use the recipes printed on the sides of food packets, or take books out of the library. But I've got an even better idea. I'll go into Smith's and *copy out* a curry recipe to make on Saturday night. That way, I can go into a shop, but I don't need to spend any money. Already I'm scrambling to my feet, reaching for my coat. Shops, here I come!

As I walk into Smith's I feel my whole body expand in relief. There's a thrill about walking into a shop—any shop—which you can't beat. It's partly the anticipation, partly the buzzy, welcoming atmosphere, partly just the lovely *newness* of everything. Shiny new magazines, shiny new pencils, shiny new protractors. Not that I've needed a protractor since I was eleven—but don't they look nice, all clean and unscratched in their packets? There's a new range of leopard-print stationery that I haven't seen before, and for a moment I'm almost tempted to linger. But instead I force myself to stride on past, down to the back of the shop where the books are stacked.

There's a whole array of Indian recipe books, and I pick up one at random, flicking over the pages and wondering what sort of recipe I should go for. I hadn't realized quite how complicated this Indian cookery is. Perhaps I should write down a couple, to be on the safe side.

I look around cautiously and take out my notebook and pen. I'm a bit wary, because I know Smith's doesn't like you copying down stuff out of their books. The reason I know this is because Suze once got asked to leave the Smith's in Victoria. She was copying out a page of the street atlas, because she'd forgotten hers—and they told her she had to either buy it or leave. (Which doesn't make any sense, because they let you read the magazines for free, don't they?)

So anyway, when I'm sure no one's looking, I start copying out the recipe for "Tiger Prawn Biriani." I'm halfway through the list of spices when a girl in WHSmith uniform comes round the corner, so I quickly close the book and walk off a little, pretending I'm browsing. When I think I'm safe, I open it again—but before I can write anything down, an old woman in a blue coat says loudly, "Is that any good, dear?"

"What?" I say.

"The book!" She gestures to the recipe book with her umbrella. "I need a present for my daughter-in-law, and she comes from India. So I thought I'd get a nice Indian recipe book. Is that a good one, would you say?"

"I'm afraid I don't know," I say. "I haven't read it yet."

"Oh," she says, and starts to wander off. And I ought to keep my mouth shut and mind my own business—but I just can't leave it there, I have to clear my throat and say, "Excuse me—but doesn't she have lots of Indian recipes already?"

"Who, dear?" says the woman, turning round.

"Your daughter-in-law!" Already I'm regretting this. "If she's Indian, doesn't she already know how to cook Indian food?"

"Oh," says the old woman. She seems completely flummoxed. "Well, what should I get, then?"

Oh God.

"I don't know," I say. "Maybe a book on . . . on something else?"

"That's a good idea!" she says brightly, and comes toward me. "You show me, dear."

"Well," I say, looking helplessly around the racks of books. "What's she interested in? Does she . . . have any particular hobby?"

"She likes the fresh air," says the woman thoughtfully. "Walking in the countryside."

"Perfect!" I say in relief. "Why not try the travel section for a walking book?"

I point the woman in the right direction, then hurry off to do my copying. I reach the CD and video section, which is always quite empty, and hide behind a rack of Teletubbies videos. I glance around and check no one's about, then open the book again. Okay, turn to page 214, "Tiger Prawn Biriani" . . . I start copying again, and I've just got to the end of the list of spices, when a stern voice says in my ear, "Excuse me?"

I'm so startled, my pen jerks off my notebook and, to my

horror, makes a blue line, straight across a photograph of perfectly cooked basmati rice. Quickly I shift my hand, almost covering up the mark, and turn round innocently. A man in a white shirt and a name badge is looking at me disapprovingly.

"This isn't a public library, you know," he says.

"I'm just browsing," I say hurriedly, and make to close the book. But the man's finger comes out of nowhere and lands on the page before I can get it shut. Slowly he opens the book out again and we both stare at my blue Biro line.

"Browsing is one thing," says the man sternly. "Defacing shop stock is another."

"It was an accident!" I say. "You startled me!"

"Hmm," says the man, and gives me a hard stare. "Were you actually intending to buy this book? Or any book?"

There's a pause—then, rather shamefacedly, I say, "No."

"I see," says the man, tightening his lips. "Well, I'm afraid this matter will have to go to the manager. Obviously, we can't sell this book now, so it's our loss. If you could come with me and explain to her exactly what you were doing when the defacement occurred . . ."

Is he serious? Isn't he just going to tell me kindly that it doesn't matter and would I like a loyalty card? My heart starts to thud in panic. What am I going to do? Obviously, I can't buy the book, under my new frugal regime. But I don't want to go and see the manager, either.

"Lynn?" the man's calling to an assistant at the pen counter. "Could you page Glenys for me, please?"

He really *is* serious. He's looking all pleased with himself, as though he's caught a shoplifter. Can they prosecute you for making Biro marks in books? Maybe it counts as vandalism. I'll have a criminal record. I won't ever be able to go to America.

"Look, I'll buy it, okay?" I say breathlessly. "I'll buy the bloody book." I wrench it from the man's grasp and hurry off to the checkout before he can say anything else.

Standing at the next checkout is the old woman in the blue coat, and she calls triumphantly, "I took your advice! I've got her one of those traveling books. I think she'll really like it!"

"Oh good," I reply, handing my recipe book over to be scanned.

"It's called *The Rough Guide to India,*" says the old woman, showing me the fat blue paperback. "Have you heard of it?"

"Oh," I say. "Well, yes, but—"

"That's £24.99, please," says the girl at my till.

What? I look at the girl in dismay. Twenty-five quid, just for recipes? Why couldn't I have picked up some cheap paperback? Damn. *Damn.* Very reluctantly, I take out my credit card and hand it over. Shopping is one thing, being forced into purchases against your will is something else. I mean, I could have bought some nice underwear with that twenty-five quid.

On the other hand, I think as I walk away, that's quite a lot of new points on my Club Card. The equivalent to . . . fifty pence! And now I'll be able to make loads of delicious, exotic curries and save all that wasted takeaway money. Really, I've got to think of this book as an investment.

I don't want to boast, but apart from that one purchase, I do incredibly well over the next couple of days. The only things I buy are a really nice chrome flask to take coffee into the office. (And some coffee beans and an electric grinder.) And some flowers and champagne for Suze's birthday.

But I'm allowed to get those, because, as David E. Barton says, you must treasure your friends. He says the simple act of breaking bread with friends is one of the oldest, most essential parts of human life. "Do not stop giving your friends gifts," he says. "They need not be extravagant—use your creativity and try making them yourself."

So I've bought Suze a half bottle of champagne instead of a whole one—and instead of buying expensive croissants from the patisserie, I'm going to make them out of that special dough you get in tubes.

In the evening we're going out to Terrazza for supper with Suze's cousins Fenella and Tarquin—and, to be honest, it might be quite an expensive evening. But that's OK, because it counts as breaking bread with friends. (Except the bread at Terrazza is sun-dried tomato focaccia and costs £4.50 a basket.)

Fenella and Tarquin arrive at six o'clock, and as soon as she sees them, Suze starts squealing with excitement. I stay in my bedroom and finish my makeup, putting off the moment of having to go out and say hello. I'm not that keen on Fenella and Tarquin. In fact, to be honest with you, I think they're a bit weird. For a start, they look weird. They're both very skinny, but in a pale, bony way, and have the same slightly protruding teeth. Fenella does make a bit of an effort with clothes and makeup, and doesn't look *too* bad. But Tarquin, frankly, looks just like a stoat. Or a weasel. Some bony little creature, anyway. They do strange things, too. They ride around on a tandem and wear matching jumpers knitted by their old nanny and have this family language which no one else can understand. Like they call sandwiches "witchies." And a drink is a "titchy" (except if it's water, which is "Ho"). Take it from me, it gets irritating after a while.

But Suze loves them. She spent all her childhood summers with them in Scotland and she just can't see that they're a bit strange. The worst thing is, *she* starts talking about witchies and titchies when she's with them.

Still, there's nothing I can do about it—they're here now. I finish brushing on my mascara and stand up, looking at my reflection. I'm pretty pleased with what I see. I'm wearing a really simple black top and black trousers—and, tied loosely round my neck, my gorgeous, *gorgeous* Denny and George scarf. God, that was a good buy. It looks fantastic.

I linger a bit, then resignedly open my bedroom door.

"Hi, Bex!" says Suze, looking up with bright eyes. She's sitting cross-legged on the floor of the corridor, ripping open a present, while Fenella and Tarquin stand nearby, looking on. They're not wearing matching jumpers today, thank God, but Fenella's wearing a very odd red skirt made out of hairy tweed, and Tarquin's double-breasted suit looks as if it were tailored during the First World War.

"Hi!" I say, and kiss each of them politely.

"Oh, wow!" cries Suze, as she pulls out a picture in an old gilt frame. "I don't believe it! I don't *believe* it!" She's looking from Tarquin to Fenella with shining eyes, and I look at the picture interestedly over her shoulder. But to be honest, I can't say I'm impressed. For a start it's really dingy—all sludgy greens and browns—and for another start, it just shows a horse standing still in a field. I mean, couldn't it have been jumping over a fence or rearing up or something? Or maybe trotting along in Hyde Park, ridden by a girl in one of those lovely *Pride and Prejudice* dresses.

"Happy Bad Day!" Tarquin and Fenella chime in unison. (That's another thing. They call birthdays bad days, ever since . . . Oh God. It really is too boring to explain.)

"It's absolutely gorgeous!" I say enthusiastically. "Absolutely beautiful!"

"It is, isn't it?" says Tarquin earnestly. "Just look at those colors."

"Mmm, lovely," I say, nodding.

"And the brushwork. It's exquisite. We were thrilled when we came across it."

"It's a really wonderful picture," I say. "Makes you want to just . . . gallop off over the downs!"

What *is* this drivel I'm coming out with? Why can't I just be honest and say I don't like it?

"Do you ride?" says Tarquin, looking up at me in slight surprise.

I've ridden once. On my cousin's horse. And I fell off and vowed never to do it again. But I'm not going to admit that to Mr. Horse of the Year.

"I used to," I say, and give a modest little smile. "Not very well."

"I'm sure you'd get back into it," says Tarquin, gazing at me. "Have you ever hunted?"

Hunted? Little furry foxes? Is he joking?

"Hey," says Suze, fondly propping the picture against the wall. "Shall we have a titchy before we go?"

"Absolutely!" I say, turning quickly away from Tarquin. "Good idea."

"Oooh, yes," says Fenella. "Have you got any champagne?"

"Should have," says Suze, and goes into the kitchen. At that moment the phone rings and I go to answer it.

"Hello?"

"Hello, may I speak to Rebecca Bloomwood?" says a strange woman's voice.

"Yes," I say idly. I'm listening to Suze opening and shutting cupboard doors in the kitchen and wondering if we have actually got any champagne, apart from the dregs of the half bottle we drank for breakfast . . . "Speaking."

"Ms. Bloomwood, this is Erica Parnell from Endwich Bank," says the voice, and I freeze.

Shit. It's the bank. Oh God, they sent me that letter, didn't they, and I never did anything about it.

What am I going to say? Quick, what am I going to say?

"Ms. Bloomwood?" says Erica Parnell.

OK, what I'll say is, I'm fully aware that my overdraft is slightly larger than it should be, and I'm planning to take remedial action within the next few days. Yes, that sounds good. "Remedial action" sounds very good. OK—go.

Firmly I tell myself not to panic—these people are human—and take a big breath. And then, in one seamless, unplanned movement, my hand puts down the receiver.

I stare at the silent phone for a few seconds, not quite able to believe what I've just done. *What* did I do that for? Erica Parnell knew it was me, didn't she? Any minute, she'll ring back. She's probably pressing redial now, and she'll be really angry . . .

Quickly I take the phone off the hook and hide it under a cushion. Now she can't get me. I'm safe.

"Who was that?" says Suze, coming into the room.

"No one," I say, and force a bright smile. I don't want to spoil Suze's birthday with my stupid problems. "Just a wrong . . . Listen, let's not have drinks here. Let's go out!"

"Oh," says Suze. "OK!"

"Much more fun," I gabble, trying to head her away from the phone. "We can go to some really nice bar and have cocktails, and then go on to Terrazza."

What I'll do in future, I'm thinking, is screen all my calls. Or answer in a foreign accent. Or, even better, change the number. Go ex-directory.

"What's going on?" says Fenella, appearing at the door.

"Nothing!" I hear myself say. "We're going out for a titchy and then on to sups."

Oh, I don't believe it. I'm turning into one of them.

As we arrive at Terrazza, I'm feeling a lot calmer. Of course, Erica Parnell will have thought we were cut off by a fault on the line or something. She'll never have thought I put the phone down on her. I mean, we're two civilized adults, aren't we? Adults just don't *do* things like that.

And if I ever meet her, which I hope to God I never do, I'll just keep very cool and say, "It was odd what happened, that time you phoned me, wasn't it?" Or even better, I'll accuse *her* of putting the phone down on *me*. (In a jokey way, of course.)

Terrazza is full, buzzing with people and cigarette smoke and chatter, and as we sit down with our huge silver menus I feel myself relax even more. I love eating out. And I reckon I deserve a real treat, after being so frugal over the last few days. It hasn't been easy, keeping to such a tight regime, but somehow I've managed it. I'm keeping to it so well! On Saturday I'm going to monitor my spending pattern again, and I'm sure it'll have gone down by at least 70 percent.

"What shall we have to drink?" says Suze. "Tarquin, you choose."

"Oh, look!" shrieks Fenella. "There's Eddie Lazenby! I must just say hello." She leaps to her feet and makes for a balding guy in a blazer, ten tables away. How she spotted him in this throng, I've no idea.

"Suze!" cries another voice, and we all look up. A blond girl in a tiny pastel-pink suit is heading toward our table, arms stretched out for a hug. "And Tarkie!"

"Hello, Tory," says Tarquin, getting to his feet. "How's Mungo?"

"He's over there!" says Tory. "You must come and say hello!"

How is it that Fenella and Tarquin spend most of their time in the middle of Perthshire, but the minute they set foot in London, they're besieged by long-lost friends?

"Eddie says hi," announces Fenella, returning to the table. "Tory! How are you? How's Mungo?"

"Oh, he's fine," says Tory. "But listen, have you heard? Caspar's back in town!"

"No!" everyone exclaims, and I'm almost tempted to join in. No one has bothered to introduce me to Tory, but that's the way it goes. You join the gang by osmosis. One minute you're a complete stranger, the next you're shrieking away with the rest of them, going "Did you *hear* about Venetia and Sebastian?"

"Look, we *must* order," says Suze. "We'll come and say hello in a minute, Tory."

"Okay, ciao," says Tory, and she sashays off.

"Suze!" cries another voice, and a girl in a little black dress comes rushing up. "And Fenny!"

"Milla!" they both cry. "How are you? How's Benjy?"

Oh God, it just doesn't stop. Here I am, staring at the menu, pretending to be really interested in the starters but really feeling like some utter loser that no one wants to talk to. It's not fair.

I want to table-hop, too. *I* want to bump into old friends I've known since babyhood. (Although to be honest, the only person I've known that long is Tom from next door, and he'll be in his limed oak kitchen in Reigate.)

But just in case, I lower my menu and gaze hopefully around the restaurant. Please, God, just once, let there be someone I recognize. It doesn't have to be anyone I like, or even know that well—just someone I can rush up to and go mwah mwah and shriek, "We must do lunch!" *Anyone*'ll do. Anyone at all . . .

And then, with a disbelieving thrill, I spot a familiar face, a few tables away! It's Luke Brandon, sitting at a table with a smartly dressed older man and woman.

Well, he's not exactly an old friend—but I know him, don't I? And I *so* want to table-hop like the others.

"Oh look, there's Luke!" I shriek (quietly, so he doesn't hear). "I simply *must* go and say hello!"

As the others look at me in surprise, I toss my hair back, leap to my feet, and hurry off, full of a sudden exhilaration. I can do it, too! I'm table-hopping at Terrazza. I'm an It-girl!

It's only when I get within a few feet of his table that I slow down and wonder what I'm actually going to say to him.

Well . . . I'll just be polite. Say hello and—ah, genius! I can thank him again for his kind loan of twenty quid.

Shit, I did pay him back, didn't I?

Yes. Yes, I sent him that nice recycled card with poppies on it and a check. That's right. Now don't panic, just be cool and It.

"Hi!" I say as soon as I get within earshot of his table, but the hubbub around us is so loud, he doesn't hear me. No wonder all Fenella's friends have got such screechy voices. You need about sixty-five decibels, just to be heard. "Hi!" I try again, louder, but still no response. Luke is talking earnestly to the older man, and the woman's listening intently. None of them even glances up.

This is getting a bit embarrassing. I'm standing, marooned, being utterly ignored by the person I want to table-hop with. Nobody else ever seems to have this problem. Why isn't he leaping up, shrieking "Have you *heard* about Foreland Investments?" It's not fair. What shall I do? Shall I just creep away? Shall I pretend I was heading toward the Ladies'?

A waiter barges past me with a tray, and I'm pushed helplessly forward, toward Luke's table—and at that moment, he looks up. He stares at me blankly as though he doesn't even know who I am, and I feel my stomach give a little flip of dismay. But I've got to go through with it now.

"Hi, Luke!" I say brightly. "I just thought I'd say . . . hello!"

"Well, hello," Luke says eventually. "Mum, Dad, this is Rebecca Bloomwood. Rebecca—my parents."

Oh God. What have I done? I've table-hopped an intimate family gathering. Leave, quick.

"Hello," I say, and give a feeble smile. "Well, I won't keep you from . . ."

"So how do you know Luke?" inquires Mrs. Brandon.

"Rebecca is a leading financial journalist," says Luke, taking a sip of wine. (Is that really what he thinks? Gosh, I must drop that into a conversation with Clare Edwards. And Philip, come to that.)

I grin confidently at Mr. Brandon, feeling like a mover and a shaker. I'm a leading financial journalist hobnobbing with a leading entrepreneur at a leading London restaurant. How cool is that?

"Financial journalist, eh?" grunts Mr. Brandon, and lowers his reading glasses to have a better look at me. "So what do *you* think of the chancellor's announcement?"

I'm never going to table-hop again. Never.

"Well," I begin confidently, wondering if I could suddenly pretend to spot an old friend across the room.

"Dad, I'm sure Rebecca doesn't want to talk shop," says Luke, his lips twitching slightly.

"Quite right!" says Mrs. Brandon, and smiles at me. "That's a lovely scarf, Rebecca. Is it Denny and George?"

"Yes, it is!" I say brightly, full of relief. "I was so pleased, I got it last week in the sale!"

Out of the corner of my eye, I can see that Luke Brandon is staring at me with an odd expression. Why? Why is he looking so . . .

Oh fuck. How can I be so *stupid*?

"In the sale . . . for my aunt," I continue, trying to think as quickly as I can. "I bought it for my aunt, as a present. But she . . . died."

There's a shocked silence and I look down. I can't quite believe what I've just said.

"Oh dear," says Mr. Brandon gruffly.

"Aunt Ermintrude died?" says Luke in a strange voice.

"Yes," I reply, forcing myself to look up. "It was terribly sad."

"How awful!" says Mrs. Brandon sympathetically.

"She was in hospital, wasn't she?" says Luke, pouring himself a glass of water. "What was wrong with her?"

For an instant I'm silenced.

"It was . . . her leg," I hear myself say.

"Her leg?" Mrs. Brandon's staring at me anxiously. "What was wrong with her leg?"

"It . . . swelled up and got septic," I say after a pause. "And they had to amputate it and then she died."

"Christ," says Mr. Brandon, shaking his head. "Bloody doctors." He gives me a suddenly fierce look. "Did she go private?"

"Umm . . . I'm not sure," I say, starting to back away. Why didn't I just say she *gave* me the bloody scarf? "Anyway, lovely to see you, Luke. Must dash, my friends will be missing me!"

I give a nonchalant kind of wave without quite looking Luke in the eye and then quickly turn round and walk back to Suze, my legs trembling and my fingers twisted tightly by my sides. God, what a fiasco.

I've managed to recompose myself by the time our food arrives. The food! I've ordered grilled scallops and as I take my first bite, I nearly swoon. After so many torturous days of cheap, functional food, this is like going to heaven. I feel almost tearful—like a prisoner returning to the real world, or children after the war, when rationing stopped. After my scallops I have steak béarnaise and chips—and when all the others say no thanks to the pudding menu, I order chocolate mousse. Because who knows when I'm next going to be in a restaurant like this? There could be months ahead of cheese sandwiches and homemade coffee in a flask, with nothing to relieve the monotony.

While I'm waiting for my chocolate mousse, Suze and Fenella decide they simply must go and talk to Benjy, on the other side of the room. So they leap up, both lighting cigarettes as they do so, and Tarquin stays behind to keep me company. He doesn't seem quite as into table-hopping as the others. In fact, he's been pretty quiet all evening. I've also noticed that he's drunk more than any of us. Any moment I'm expecting his head to land on the table.

For a while there's silence between us. To be honest, Tarquin is so weird, I don't know how to talk to him. Then, suddenly, he says, "Do you like Wagner?"

"Oh yes," I say at once. I'm not sure I've ever heard any Wagner, but I don't want to sound uncultured. And I have been to the opera before, though I think that was Mozart.

" 'The Liebestod' from *Tristan,*" he says, and shakes his head. " 'The Liebestod.' "

"Mmm," I say, and nod in what I hope is an intelligent manner. I pour myself some wine, fill his glass up, too, and look around to see where Suze has got to. Typical of her just to disappear off and leave me with her drunken cousin.

"Dah-dah-*dah*-dah, daaaah dah dah . . ."

Oh my God, now he's singing. Not loudly, but really intensely. And he's staring into my eyes as though he expects me to join in.

"Dah-dah-*dah*-dah . . ."

Now he's closed his eyes and is swaying. This is getting embarrassing.

"Da diddle-idy da-a-da-a daaaah dah . . ."

"Lovely," I say brightly. "You can't beat Wagner, can you?"

"Tristan," he says. *"Und Isolde."* He opens his eyes. "You'd make a beautiful Isolde."

I'd make a *what*? While I'm still staring at him, he lifts my hand to his lips and starts kissing it. For a few seconds I'm too shocked to move.

"Tarquin," I say as firmly as I can, trying to pull my hand away. "Tarquin, please—" I look up and desperately scan the room for Suze—and, as I do so, meet the eye of Luke Brandon, making his way out of the restaurant. He frowns slightly, lifts his hand in farewell, then disappears out of the door.

"Your skin smells like roses," murmurs Tarquin against my skin.

"Oh, shut up!" I say crossly, and yank my hand out of his grasp so hard I get a row of teeth marks on my skin. "Just leave me alone!"

I would slap him, but he'd probably take it as a come-on.

Just then, Suze and Fenella arrive back at the table, full of news about Binky and Minky—and Tarquin reverts into silence. And for the rest of the evening, even when we say good-bye, he barely looks at me. Thank God. He must have got the message.

Seven

It doesn't seem he has, though, because on Saturday, I receive a card of a pre-Raphaelite girl looking coyly over her shoulder. Inside, Tarquin has written:

Many apologies for my uncouth behavior. I hope to make it up to you. Tickets to Bayreuth—or, failing that, dinner?

Tarquin.

Dinner with Tarquin. Can you imagine? And what's he going on about, anyway? I've never heard of Bayreuth. Is it a new show or something? Or does he mean Beirut? Why would we want to go to Beirut, for God's sake?

Anyway, I've got more important things to think about today. This is my sixth day of Cutting Back—and, crucially, my first weekend. David E. Barton says this is often when one's frugal regime cracks, as the office routine is no longer there as a distraction and the day stretches empty, waiting to be filled with the familiar comfort of shopping.

But I'm too strong-willed to crack. I've got my day completely sussed—and I'm not going *near* any shops. This morning I'm going to visit a museum and then tonight, instead of wasting lots of money on an expensive takeaway, I'm cooking a homemade curry for me and Suze. I'm actually quite excited about it.

My entire budget for today is as follows:

Travel to museum:	*free (I already have a travelcard)*
Museum:	*free*
Curry:	*£2.50 (David E. Barton says you can make a wonderful curry for four people for less than £5.00—and there are only two of us.)*
Total daily expenditure:	*£2.50*

That's more like it. Plus I get to experience culture instead of mindless materialism. I have chosen the Victoria & Albert Museum because I have never been to it before. In fact, I'm not even sure what they have in it. Statues of Queen Victoria and Prince Albert, or something?

Anyway, whatever they have, it will be very interesting and stimulating, I'm sure. And above all, free!

As I come out of South Kensington tube, the sun's shining brightly and I stride along, feeling pleased with myself. Normally I waste my Saturday mornings watching *Live and Kicking* and getting ready to go to the shops. But look at this! I suddenly feel very grown-up and metropolitan, like someone in a Woody Allen film. I just need a long woolly scarf and some sunglasses and I'll look like Diane Keaton.

And on Monday, when people ask me how my weekend was, I'll be able to say, "Actually, I went to the V&A." No, what I'll say is "I caught an exhibition." That sounds much cooler. (Why *do* people say they "caught" an exhibition, by the way? It's not as though all the paintings were thundering past like bulls at Pamplona.)

Then they'll say, "Really? I didn't know you were into art, Rebecca." And I'll say, "Oh yes. I spend most of my free time at museums." And they'll give me an impressed look and say . . .

Come to think of it, I've walked straight past the entrance. Silly me. Too busy thinking about the conversation between me and . . . actually, the person I realize I've pictured in this little scene is Luke Brandon. How weird. Why should that be? Because I table-hopped with him, I suppose. Anyway. Concentrate. Museum.

Quickly I retrace my steps and walk nonchalantly into the entrance hall, trying to look as though I come here all the time. Not like that bunch of Japanese tourists clustering round their guide. Ha! I think proudly, I'm no tourist. This is my heritage. *My* culture. I pick up a map carelessly as though I don't really need it, and look at a list of talks on things like *Ceramics of the Yuan and Early Ming Dynasties*. Then, casually, I begin to walk through to the first gallery.

"Excuse me?" A woman at a desk is calling to me. "Have you paid?"

Have I *what*? You don't have to pay to get into museums! Oh, of course—she's just joking with me. I give a friendly little laugh, and carry on.

"Excuse me!" she says, in a sharper voice, and a bloke in security uniform appears out of nowhere. "Have you paid for admission?"

"It's free!" I say in surprise.

"I'm afraid not," she says, and points to a sign behind me. I turn to read it, and nearly keel over in astonishment.

Admission £5.00.

I feel quite faint with shock. What's happened to the world? They're *charging* for admission to a museum. This is outrageous. Everyone knows museums are supposed to be free. If you start charging for museums, no one will ever go! Our cultural heritage will be lost to a whole generation, excluded by a punitive financial barrier. The nation will be dumbed down still further, and civilized society will face the very brink of collapse. Is that what you want, Tony Blair?

Plus, I don't have £5. I deliberately came out with no cash except £2.50 for my curry ingredients. Oh God, this is annoying. I mean, here I am, all ready for some culture. I *want* to go in and look at . . . well, whatever's in there—and I can't!

Now all the Japanese tourists are staring at me, as if I'm some sort of criminal. Go away! I think crossly. Go and look at some art.

"We take credit cards," says the woman. "VISA, Switch, American Express."

"Oh," I say. "Well . . . OK."

"The season ticket is £15," she says, as I reach for my purse, "but it gives you unlimited access for a year."

Unlimited access for a year! Now wait just a minute. David E. Barton says what you're supposed to do, when you make any purchase, is estimate the "cost per use," which you get by dividing the price by the number of times you use it. Let's suppose that from now on I come to the V&A once a month. (I should think that's quite realistic.) If I buy a season ticket, that's only . . . £1.25 a visit.

Well, that's a bargain, isn't it? It's actually a very good investment, when you come to think of it.

"OK, I'll have the season ticket," I say, and hand over my VISA card. Hah! Culture here I come.

I start off really well. I look at my little map, and peer at each exhibit, and carefully read all the little cards.

Chalice made from silver, Dutch, 16th century

Plaque depicting Holy Trinity, Italian mid–15th century

Blue and white earthenware bowl, early 17th century

That bowl's really nice, I find myself thinking in sudden interest, and wonder how much it is. It looks quite expensive . . . I'm just peering to see if there's a price tag when I remember where I am. Of course. There aren't any prices here.

Which is a bit of a mistake, I think. Because it kind of takes the fun out of it, doesn't it? You wander round, just looking at things, and it all gets a bit boring after a while. Whereas if they put price tags on, you'd be far more interested. In fact, I think all museums should put prices on their exhibits. You'd look at a silver chalice or a marble statue or the *Mona Lisa* or whatever, and admire it for its beauty and historical importance and everything—and then you'd reach for the price tag and gasp, "Hey, look how much this one is!" It would really liven things up.

I might write to the Victoria & Albert and suggest this to them. I am a season-ticket holder, after all. They should listen to my opinion.

In the meantime, let's move on to the next glass case.

Carved goblet, English, mid–15th century

God, I could die for a cup of coffee. How long have I been here? It must be . . .

Oh. Only fifteen minutes.

When I get to the gallery showing a history of fashion, I become quite rigorous and scholarly. In fact, I spend longer there than anywhere else. But then the dresses and shoes come to an end and it's back to more statues and little fiddly things in cases. I keep looking at my watch, and my feet hurt . . . and in the end I sink down onto a sofa.

Don't get me wrong, I like museums. I do. And I'm really interested in Korean art. It's just that the floors are really hard, and I'm wearing quite tight boots, and it's hot so I've taken off my jacket but now it keeps slithering around in my arms. And it's weird, but I keep thinking I can hear the sound of a cash till. It must be in my imagination.

I'm sitting blankly, wondering if I can summon the energy to stand up again, when the group of Japanese tourists comes into the gallery, and I feel compelled to get to my feet and pretend I'm looking at something. I peer vaguely at a piece of tapestry, then stride off down a corridor lined with exhibits of old Indian tiles. I'm just thinking that maybe we should get the Fired Earth catalogue and retile the bathroom, when I glimpse something through a metal grille and stop dead with shock.

Am I dreaming? Is it a mirage? I can see a cash register, and a queue of people, and a display cabinet with price tags . . .

Oh my God, I was right! It's a shop! There's a *shop,* right there in front of me!

Suddenly my steps have more spring in them; my energy has miraculously returned. Following the bleeping sound of the cash register, I hurry round the corner to the shop entrance and pause on the threshold, telling myself not to raise my hopes, not to be disappointed if it's just bookmarks and tea towels.

But it's not. It's bloody fantastic! Why isn't this place better known? There's a whole range of gorgeous jewelry, and loads of really interesting books on art, and there's all this amazing pottery, and greeting cards, and . . .

Oh. But I'm not supposed to be buying anything today, am I? Damn.

This is awful. What's the point of discovering a new shop and then not being able to buy anything in it? It's not fair. Everyone else is buying stuff, everyone else is having fun. For a while I hover disconsolately beside a display of mugs, watching as an Australian woman buys a pile of books on sculpture. She's chatting away to the sales assistant, and suddenly I hear her say something about Christmas. And then I have a flash of pure genius.

Christmas shopping! I can do all my Christmas shopping here! I know March is a bit early, but why not be organized? And then when Christmas arrives I won't have to go near the horrible Christmas crowds. I can't believe I haven't thought of doing this before. And it's not breaking the rules, because I'd have to buy

Christmas presents *sometime*, wouldn't I? All I'm doing is shifting the buying process forward a bit. It makes perfect sense.

And so, about an hour later, I emerge happily with two carrier bags. I've bought a photograph album covered in William Morris print, an old-fashioned wooden jigsaw puzzle, a book of fashion photographs, and a fantastic ceramic teapot. God, I *love* Christmas shopping. I'm not sure what I'll give to who—but the point is, these are all timeless and unique items that would enhance any home. (Or at least the ceramic teapot is, because that's what it said on the little leaflet.) So I reckon I've done really well.

In fact, this morning has been a great success. As I emerge from the museum, I feel incredibly content and uplifted. It just shows the effect that a morning of pure culture has on the soul. From now on, I decide, I'm going to spend every Saturday morning at a museum.

When I get back home, the second post is on the doormat and there's a square envelope addressed to me in writing I don't recognize. I rip it open as I lug my carrier bags to my room—and then stop in surprise. It's a card from Luke Brandon. How did he get my home address?

> *Dear Rebecca,* it says, *It was good to bump into you the other night, and I do hope you had an enjoyable evening. I now realize that I never thanked you for the prompt repayment of my loan. Much appreciated.*
>
> *With all best wishes—and, of course, deepest sympathy on the loss of your Aunt Ermintrude. (If it's any consolation, I can't imagine that scarf could suit anyone better than you.)*
>
> *Luke.*

For a while I stare at it silently. I'm quite taken aback. Gosh, I think cautiously. It's nice of him to write, isn't it? A nice handwritten card like this, just to thank me for *my* card. I mean, he's not just being polite, is he? You don't have to send a thank-you card to someone just because they repaid your twenty quid.

Or do you? Maybe, these days, you do. Everyone seems to send cards for everything. I haven't got a clue what's done and what's not anymore. (I *knew* I should have read that etiquette book I got in my stocking.) Is this card just a polite thank-you? Or is it something else? And if so . . . what?

Is he taking the piss?

Oh God, that's it. He knows Aunt Ermintrude doesn't exist. He's just pulling my leg to embarrass me.

But then . . . would he go to all the trouble of buying a card, writing in it, and sending it, just to pull my leg?

Oh, I don't know. Who cares? I don't even like him, anyway.

Having been so cultured all morning, I deserve a bit of a treat in the afternoon, so I buy myself *Vogue* and a bag of Minstrels, and lie on the sofa for a bit. God, I've missed little treats like this. I haven't read a magazine for . . . well, it must be a week, except Suze's copy of *Cosmo* yesterday. And I can't *remember* the last time I tasted chocolate.

I can't spend too long enjoying myself, though, because I've got to go out and buy the stuff for our homemade curry. So after I've read my horoscope, I close *Vogue* and get out my new Indian recipe book. I'm quite excited, actually. I've never made curry before.

I've gone off the tiger prawn recipe because it turns out tiger prawns are very expensive. So what I'm going to make instead is chicken and mushroom Balti. It all looks very cheap and easy, and I just need to write out my shopping list.

When I've finished I'm a bit taken aback. The list is quite a lot longer than I'd thought it would be. I hadn't realized you needed so many spices just to make one curry. I've just looked in the kitchen, and we don't have a Balti pan, or a grinder for grinding spices, or a blender for making the aromatic paste. Or a wooden spoon or any scales that work.

Still, never mind. What I'll do is quickly go to Peter Jones and buy all the equipment we need for the kitchen, and then I'll get the food and come back and start cooking. The thing to remember is, we only have to buy all this stuff once—and then we're fully equipped to make delicious curries every night. I'll just have to think of it as an investment.

By the time Suze arrives back from Camden Market that evening, I am dressed in my new stripy apron, grinding up roasted spices in our new grinder.

"Phew!" she says, coming into the kitchen. "What a stink!"

"It's aromatic spices," I say a bit crossly, and take a swig of wine. To be honest, this is all a bit more difficult than I'd thought. I'm trying to make something called Balti masala mix, which we will be able to keep in a jar and use for months, but all the spices seem to be disappearing into the grinder and refusing to come back out. Where are they going?

"I'm absolutely starving," says Suze, pouring herself a glass of wine. "Will it be ready soon?"

"I don't know," I say, peering into the grinder. "If I can just get these bloody spices out . . ."

"Oh well," says Suze. "I might just make some toast." She pops a couple of pieces of bread in the toaster and then starts picking up all my little bags and pots of spices and looking at them.

"What's allspice?" she says, holding up a pot curiously. "Is it all the spices, mixed together?"

"I don't know," I say, banging the grinder on the counter. A tiny dusting of powder falls out and I stare at it angrily. What happened to a whole jarful that I could keep for months? Now I'll have to roast some more of the bloody things.

"Because if it is, couldn't you just use that and forget all the others?"

"No!" I say. "I'm making a fresh and distinct Balti blend."

"OK," says Suze, shrugging. "You're the expert."

Right, I think, taking another swig of wine. Start again. Coriander seeds, fennel seeds, cumin seeds, peppercorns . . . By this time, I've given up measuring, I'm just throwing everything in. They say cooking should be instinctive, anyway.

"What's this?" says Suze, looking at Luke Brandon's card on the kitchen table. "Luke Brandon? How come he sent you a card?"

"Oh, you know," I say, shrugging casually. "He was just being polite."

"Polite?" Suze wrinkles her brow, turning the card over in her hands. "No way. You don't have to send a card to someone just because they returned your twenty quid."

"Really?" My voice is slightly higher than usual, but that must be because of the roasting aromatic spices. "I thought maybe that's what people did these days."

"Oh no," says Suze assuredly. "What happens is, the money's lent, it's returned with a thank-you letter, and that's the end of the matter. This card"— she waves it at me —"this is something extra."

This is why I love sharing a flat with Suze. She knows stuff like this, because she mixes in the right social circles. You know she once had dinner with the duchess of Kent? Not that I'm boasting, or anything.

"So what do you think it means?" I say, trying not to sound too tense.

"I reckon he's being friendly," she says, and puts the card back on the table.

Friendly. Of course, that's it. He's being friendly. Which is a good thing, of course. So why do I feel ever so slightly disappointed? I stare at the card, which has a face by Picasso on the front. What does that mean?

"Are those spices supposed to be going black, by the way?" says Suze, spreading peanut butter on her toast.

"Oh God!" I whip the Balti pan off the stove and look at the blackened coriander seeds. This is driving me crazy. Okay, tip them away and start again. Coriander seeds, fennel seeds, cumin seeds, peppercorns, bay leaves. That's the last of the bay leaves. This one had better not go wrong.

Somehow, miraculously, it doesn't. Forty minutes later, I actually have a curry bubbling away in my Balti pan! This is fantastic! It smells wonderful, and it looks just like it does in the book—and I didn't even follow the recipe very carefully. It just shows, I have a natural affinity with Indian cookery. And the more I practice, the more accomplished I'll become. Like David E. Barton says, I'll be able to knock up a quick, delicious curry in the time it takes to call the delivery firm. And look how much money I've saved!

Triumphantly I drain my basmati rice, take my ready-made nans out of the oven, and serve everything out onto plates. Then I sprinkle chopped fresh coriander over everything—and honestly, it looks like something out of *Marie-Claire*. I carry the plates through and put one in front of Suze.

"Wow!" she says. "This looks fantastic!"

"I know," I say proudly, sitting down opposite her. "Isn't it great?"

I watch as she takes her first forkful—then put a forkful into my mouth.

"Mmm! Delicious!" says Suze, chewing with relish. "Quite hot," she adds after a while.

"It's got chili powder in," I say. "And fresh chilies. But it's nice, though, isn't it?"

"It's wonderful!" says Suze. "Bex, you're so clever! I could never make this in a million years!"

But as she's chewing, a slightly strange expression is coming over her face. To be honest, I'm feeling a bit breathless, too. This curry is quite hot. In fact, it's bloody hot.

Suze has put down her plate and is taking a large slug of wine. She looks up, and I see her cheeks are red.

"OK?" I say, forcing myself to smile through the pain in my mouth.

"Yeah, great!" she says, and takes a huge bite of nan. I look down at my plate and resolutely take another forkful of curry. Immediately, my nose starts to run. Suze is sniffing, too, I notice, but as I meet her eye she smiles brightly.

Oh God, this is hot. My mouth can't stand it. My cheeks are burning, and my eyes are starting to water. How much chili powder did I put in this bloody thing? Only about one teaspoonful . . . or maybe it was two. I just kind of trusted my instincts and chucked in what looked about right. Well, so much for my instincts.

Tears start running down my face, and I give an enormous sniff.

"Are you OK?" says Suze in alarm.

"I'm fine!" I say, putting down my fork. "Just . . . you know. A bit hot."

But actually, I'm not OK. And it's not just the heat that's making tears run down my face. Suddenly I feel like a complete failure. I can't even get a quick and easy curry right. And look how much money I spent on it, with the Balti pan and the apron and all the spices . . . Oh, it's all gone wrong, hasn't it? I haven't Cut Back at all. This week's been a complete disaster.

I give a huge sob and put my plate on the floor.

"It's horrible!" I say miserably, and tears begin to stream down my face. "Don't eat it, Suze. It'll poison you."

"Bex! Don't be silly!" says Suze. "It's fantastic!" She looks at me, then puts her own plate on the floor. "Oh, Bex." She shuffles across the floor, reaches up, and gives me a hug. "Don't worry. It's just a bit hot. But otherwise, it's brilliant! And the nan is delicious! Honestly. Don't get upset."

I open my mouth to reply, and instead hear myself giving another huge sob.

"Bex, don't!" wails Suze, practically crying herself. "It's delicious! It's the most delicious curry I've ever tasted."

"It's not just the curry!" I sob, wiping my eyes. "The point was, I was supposed to be Cutting Back. This curry was only supposed to cost £2.50."

"But . . . why?" asks Suze perplexedly. "Was it a bet, or something!"

"No!" I wail. "It was because I'm in debt! And my dad said I should Cut Back or Make More Money. So I've been trying to Cut Back. But it hasn't worked . . ." I break off, shuddering with sobs. "I'm just a complete failure."

"Of course you're not a failure!" says Suze at once. "Bex, you're the opposite of a failure. It's just . . ." She hesitates. "It's just that maybe . . ."

"What?"

There's silence, then Suze says seriously, "I think you might have chosen the wrong option, Becky. I don't think you're a Cut Back kind of person."

"Really?" I sniff, and wipe my eyes. "Do you think?"

"I think you should go for Make More Money instead." Suze pauses thoughtfully. "In fact, to be honest, I don't know why anyone would choose Cut Back. I think Make More Money is a *much* better option. If I ever had to choose, that's definitely the one I'd go for."

"Yes," I say slowly. "Yes, maybe you're right. Maybe that's what I should do." I reach down with a shaky hand and take a bite of warm nan—and Suze is right. Without the curry, it's delicious. "But how shall I do it?" I say eventually. "How shall I make more money?"

There's silence for a while, with both of us thoughtfully chewing on nan. Then Suze brightens.

"I know. Look at this!" She reaches for a magazine and flips to the classified ads at the back. "Look what it says here. 'Need extra money? Join the Fine Frames family. Make thousands, working from home in your spare time. Full kit supplied.' You see? It's easy."

Wow. I'm quite impressed. Thousands. That's not bad.

"Yes," I say shakily, "maybe I'll do that."

"Or you could invent something," says Suze.

"Like what?"

"Oh, anything," she says confidently. "You're really clever. Remember when the coffee filter broke, and you made a new one out of a knee-high?"

"Yes," I say, and a tiny glow of pride spreads over me. "Yes, I did, didn't I?"

"You could easily be an inventor. Or . . . I know! Set up an Internet company. They're worth millions!"

You know, she's right. There's loads of things I could do to Make More Money. Loads of things! It's just a question of lateral thinking. Suddenly I feel a lot better. Suze is *such* a good friend. I reach forward and give her a hug.

"Thanks, Suze," I say. "You're a star."

"No problem," she says, and hugs me back. "So, you cut out this ad and start making your thousands . . ." She pauses. "And I'll go and phone up for a takeaway curry, shall I?"

"Yes please," I say in a small voice. "A takeaway would be lovely."

REBECCA BLOOMWOOD'S CUT-BACK PROJECT

HOMEMADE CURRY, SATURDAY 24TH MARCH

Proposed Budget:	**£2.50**
Actual Expenditure:	
Balti pan	£15.00
Electric grinder	£14.99
Blender	£18.99
Wooden spoon	35p
Apron	£9.99
Two chicken breasts	£1.98
300g mushrooms	79p
Onion	29p
Coriander seeds	£1.29
Fennel seeds	£1.29
Allspice	£1.29
Cumin seeds	£1.29
Cloves	£1.39
Ground ginger	£1.95
Bay leaves	£1.40
Chili powder	

OH GOD, FORGET IT.

PGNI FIRST BANK VISA

7 CAMEL SQUARE

LIVERPOOL L1 5NP

Ms. Rebecca Bloomwood
Flat 2
4 Burney Rd.
London SW6 8FD

6 March 2000

Dear Ms. Bloomwood:

PGNI First Bank VISA Card No. 1475839204847586

Thank you for your letter of 2 March.

I can assure you that our computers are regularly checked, and that the possibility of a "glitch," as you put it, is remote. Nor have we been affected by the millennium bug. All accounts are entirely accurate.

You may write to Anne Robinson at *Watchdog* if you wish, but I am sure she will agree that you have no grounds for complaint.

Our records inform us that payment on your VISA account is now overdue. As you will see from your most recent VISA card statement, the minimum payment required is £105.40. I look forward to receiving your payment, as soon as possible.

Yours sincerely,

Peter Johnson
Customer Accounts Executive

eight

OK, SO PERHAPS the Cutting Back didn't go that well. But it doesn't matter, because that's all in the past. That was negative thinking—now I'm seriously into positive thinking. Onward and upward. Growth and prosperity. M.M.M. It's the obvious solution, when you think about it. And you know what? Suze is absolutely right. Making More Money suits my personality far better than Cutting Back did. I'm already feeling much happier. Just the fact that I don't have to make any more grotty cheese sandwiches, or go to any more museums, has lifted a huge weight off my soul. And I'm allowed to buy all the cappuccinos I like, and start looking in shop windows again. Oh, the relief! I've even chucked *Controlling Your Cash* in the bin. I never did think it was any good.

The only small thing—tiny niggle—is I'm not quite sure how I'm going to do it. Make More Money, I mean. But now I've decided to go ahead with it, something will turn up. I'm sure of it.

When I get into work on Monday, Clare Edwards is already at her desk—surprise—and on the phone.

"Yes," she's saying softly. "Well, it's certainly been a wonderful first year."

When she sees me, to my surprise, she blushes a faint pink and turns away slightly. "Yes, I understand," she whispers, scribbling in her notepad. "But what about the future?"

God knows why she's being so secretive. As if I'm interested in her tedious life. I sit down at my desk, briskly flip on my computer, and open my diary. Oh goody, I've got a press conference in the City. Even if it is some boring old pensions launch, at least it means a trip out of the office and, with any luck, a nice glass of champagne. Work can be quite fun, sometimes. And Philip isn't in yet, which means we can sit and gossip for a while.

"So, Clare," I say, as she puts the phone down, "how was your weekend?"

I look over, expecting to hear the usual thrilling account of what shelf she put up where with her boyfriend—but Clare doesn't even seem to have heard what I said.

"Clare?" I say puzzledly. She's staring at me with pink cheeks, as though I've caught her stealing pens from the stationery cupboard.

"Listen," she says in a rush. "That conversation you heard me having just now . . . could you not mention it to Philip?"

I stare at her in bemusement. What's she talking about? Oh wow—is she having an affair? But then, why should Philip care? He's her editor, not her—

Oh my God. She's not having an affair with *Philip,* is she?

"Clare, what's going on!" I say excitedly.

There's a long pause, as Clare blushes deep red. I can't believe this. A piece of office scandal at last! And involving Clare Edwards, of all people!

"Oh, come on, Clare," I whisper. "You can tell me. I won't tell anyone." I lean forward sympathetically. "I might even be able to help."

"Yes," says Clare, rubbing her face. "Yes, that's true. I could do with a bit of advice. The pressure's starting to get to me."

"Start from the beginning," I say calmly, just like Dear Abby. "When did it all begin?"

"OK, I'll tell you," whispers Clare, and looks nervously about. "It was about . . . six months ago."

"And what happened?"

"It all began on that Scottish press trip," she says slowly. "I was away from home . . . I said yes without even thinking. I suppose I was flattered, more than anything else."

"It's the old story," I say wisely. God, I'm enjoying this.

"If Philip knew what I was doing, he'd go crazy," she says despairingly. "But it's just so easy. I use a different name—and no one knows!"

"You use a different name?" I say, impressed in spite of myself.

"Several," she says, and gives a bitter little laugh. "You've probably seen some of them around." She exhales sharply. "I know I'm taking a risk—but I can't stop. To be honest, you get used to the money."

Money? Is she a *prostitute*?

"Clare, what exactly are you—"

"At first it was just a little piece on mortgages in *The Mail*," she says, as though she hasn't heard me. "I thought I could handle it. But then I was asked to do a full-length feature on life insurance in *The Sunday Times*. Then *Pension* and *Portfolio* got in on the act. And now it's about three articles every week. I have to do it all in secret, try to act normally . . ." She breaks off and shakes her head. "Sometimes it gets me down. But I just can't say no anymore. I'm hooked."

I do not believe it. She's talking about work. Work! There I was, thinking she was having a steamy affair, ready to hear all the exciting details—and all the time it was just boring old . . .

Then something she's just said tweaks at my mind.

"Did you say the money was good?" I say casually.

"Oh yes," she says. "About three hundred quid a piece. That's how we could afford our flat."

Three hundred quid!

Nine hundred quid a week! Bloody hell!

This is the answer. It's easy. I'll become a high-flying freelance journalist, just like Clare, and earn nine hundred quid a week. What I have to do is start networking and making contacts at events instead of always sitting at the back with Elly. I must shake hands firmly with all the finance editors of the nationals and wear my name badge prominently instead of putting it straight in my bag, and then phone them up with ideas when I get back to the office. And then I'll have £900 a week. Hah!

So when I arrive at the press conference, I pin my name badge on firmly, take a cup of coffee (no champagne—blast), and head toward Moira Channing of the *Daily Herald*.

"Hello," I say, nodding in what I hope is a serious manner. "Becky Bloomwood, *Successful Saving*."

"Hello," she says without interest, and turns back to the other woman in the group. "So we had the second lot of builders back, and *really* read them the riot act."

"Oh, Moira, you poor thing," says the other woman. I squint at her badge and see that she's Lavinia Bellimore, freelance. Well, there's no point impressing her—she's the competition.

Anyway, she doesn't give me a second glance. The two chat away about extensions and school fees, completely ignoring me—and after a bit I mutter, "Good to meet you," and creep away. God, I'd forgotten how unfriendly they are. Still, never mind. I'll just have to find someone else.

So after a bit I sidle up to a very tall guy on his own, and smile at him.

"Becky Bloomwood, *Successful Saving*," I say.

"Geoffrey Norris, freelance," he says, and flashes his badge at me. Oh for God's sake. The place is crawling with freelancers!

"Who do you write for?" I ask politely, thinking at least I might pick up some tips.

"It depends," he says shiftily. His eyes keep darting backward and forward, and he's refusing to meet my eye. "I used to be on *Monetary Matters*. But they sacked me."

"Oh dear," I say.

"They're bastards over there," he says, and drains his coffee. "Bastards! Don't go near them. That's my advice."

"OK, I'll remember that!" I say brightly, edging away. "Actually, I just have to . . ." And I turn, and walk quickly away. Why do I always find myself talking to weirdos?

Just then, a buzzer goes off, and people start to find their seats. Deliberately, I head for the second row, pick up the glossy brochure that's waiting for me on my seat, and take out my notebook. I wish I wore glasses, then I'd look even more serious. I'm just writing down Sacrum Asset Management Pension Fund Launch in capitals at the top of the page, when a middle-aged man I've never seen before plonks himself down next to me. He's got disheveled brown hair and smells of cigarettes, and is wearing an old-looking jacket over a dark red shirt with no tie. Plus, I suddenly notice, sneakers on his feet. *Sneakers* to a press conference? He sits down, leans back comfortably, and looks around with twinkling brown eyes.

"It's a joke, isn't it?" he murmurs, then meets my eye. "All this gloss. All this show." He gestures around. "You don't fall for it, do you?"

Oh God. *Another* weirdo.

"Absolutely not," I say politely, and look for his name badge, but I can't see one.

"Glad to hear it," says the man, and shakes his head. "Bloody fat cats." He gestures to the front, where three men in expensive suits are sitting down behind the table. "You won't find *them* surviving on fifty quid a week, will you?"

"Well . . . no," I say. "More like fifty quid a minute." The man gives an appreciative laugh.

"That's a good line. I might use that." He extends his hand. "Eric Foreman, *Daily World*."

"Daily World?" I say, impressed in spite of myself. Gosh, *The Daily World.* I have to confess a little secret here—I really like *The Daily World.* I know it's only a tabloid, but it's so easy to read, especially if you're on a train. (My arms must be very weak or something, because holding *The Times* makes them ache after a while. And then all the pages get messed up. It's a nightmare.) And some of the articles in the "Female World" section are actually rather interesting.

But hang on—surely I've met *The Daily World*'s personal finance editor. Surely it's that drippy woman called Marjorie? So who's this guy?

"I haven't seen you around before," I say casually. "Are you new?"

Eric Foreman gives a chuckle. "I've been on the paper for ten years. But this finance stuff isn't usually my scene." He lowers his voice. "I'm here to stir up a bit of trouble, as it goes. The editor's brought me on board for a new campaign we're running, 'Can We Trust the Money Men?' "

He even *talks* in a tabloid voice.

"That sounds great," I say.

"Could be, could be. As long as I can get past all this technical stuff." He pulls a face. "Never been good at figures."

"I wouldn't worry," I say kindly. "You don't actually need to know very much. You'll soon pick up what's important. Basically, these guys are launching a new pension plan . . ." I glance at the brochure ". . . and the gimmick is, there's a discount for investors under the age of twenty-five. Which makes sense, of course, because the sooner you start retirement planning, the better."

"Oh absolutely," echoes Eric Foreman, a tiny smile at his mouth. "May I ask, do you have a pension?"

"Well . . . no," I admit. "I don't at the moment . . . but I'm absolutely intending to, as soon as I decide which one."

Which is true. As *soon* as I clear all my debts, I'm going to start a pension plan, and also invest in a long-term equity-based investment fund. I may even put some spare money into emerging markets. I mean, it makes sense, doesn't it?

"Glad to hear it," says Eric Foreman, grinning. "Very wise of you." He peers at my name badge. "And you are . . ."

"Rebecca Bloomwood, *Successful Saving,*" I say, in my best networking manner.

"Glad to meet you, Rebecca," he says, and fishes in his pocket for a business card.

"Oh, thanks," I say, hastily reaching into my bag for my own business cards. Yes! I think triumphantly as I hand it over. I'm networking with the national newspapers! I'm swapping business cards!

Just then the microphones all come on with a screech of feedback, and a dark-haired girl at the podium clears her throat. Behind her is a lit-up screen, with the words *Sacrum Asset Management* against a sunset.

I remember this girl now. She was really snotty to me at a press briefing last year. But Philip likes her, because she sends him a bottle of champagne every Christmas, so I'll have to give this new pension plan a nice write-up.

"Ladies and gentlemen," she says. "My name is Maria Freeman, and I'm delighted to welcome you all to the launch of the Sacrum Asset Management Pension Series. This is an innovative range of products designed to combine flexibility and security with the powerful performance associated with Sacrum."

A graph appears on the screen before us, with a wiggly red line rising and falling above a thinner black one.

"As Graph 1 shows," says Maria Freeman confidently, pointing to the wiggly red line, "our UK Enterprise Fund has consistently outperformed the rest of its particular sector."

"Hmm," murmurs Eric Foreman to me, frowning at his brochure. "So, what's going on here, then? I heard a rumor that Sacrum Asset Management wasn't doing too well." He jabs at the graph. "But look at this. Outperforming the sector."

"Yeah, right," I murmur back. "And what sector would that be? The Crap Investments Sector? The Lose All Your Money Sector?"

Eric Foreman looks at me and his mouth twists slightly.

"You think they've fiddled their figures?" he whispers.

"It's not exactly fiddling," I explain. "They just compare themselves to whoever's worse than themselves, and then call themselves the winners." I point to the graph in the brochure. "Look. They haven't actually specified what this so-called sector is."

"Well, blow me," says Eric Foreman, and looks up at the Sacrum team sitting on the platform. "They're canny bastards, aren't they?"

Really, this guy has no idea. I feel almost sorry for him.

Maria Freeman is droning on again, and I stifle a yawn. The trouble with sitting near the front is you have to pretend to look interested and be writing notes. "Pensions," I write, and draw a swirly line underneath. Then I make the line into the stem of a vine and start drawing little bunches of grapes and leaves all the way along.

"In a moment I'll be introducing Mike Dillon, who heads up the investment team, and he'll be telling you a little about their methods. In the meantime, if there are any questions . . ."

"Yes," says Eric Foreman. "I've got a question." I look up from my grapevine, slightly surprised.

"Oh yes?" Maria Freeman smiles sweetly at him. "And you are . . ."

"Eric Foreman, *Daily World*. I'd like to know, how much do you all get paid?" He gestures with his hand along the table.

"What?" Maria Freeman turns pink, then regains her composure. "Oh, you mean charges. Well, we'll be dealing with those . . ."

"I don't mean charges," says Eric Foreman. "I mean, how-much-do-you-get-paid? You, Mike Dillon." He jabs at him with his finger. "What are you on? Six figures, is it? And bearing in mind what a *disaster* the performance of Sacrum Asset Management was last year—shouldn't you be out on the streets?"

I'm absolutely stunned. I've never seen anything like this at a press conference. Never!

There's a kerfuffle at the table, and then Mike Dillon leans forward toward his microphone.

"If we could get on with the presentation," he says, "and . . . and leave other questions for later." He's looking decidedly uncomfortable.

"Just one more thing," says Eric Foreman. "What would you say to one of our readers who invested in your Safe Prospects plan and lost ten grand?" He glances briefly at me and winks. "Show them a nice reassuring graph like that one, would you? Tell them you were 'top of the sector'?"

Oh, this is fantastic! All the Sacrum people look like they want to die.

"A press release on the subject of Safe Prospects was issued at the time," says Maria and smiles icily at Eric. "However, this press conference is restricted to the subject of the new Pension Series. If you could just wait until the presentation is over . . ."

"Don't worry," says Eric Foreman comfortably. "I won't be staying to hear the bullshit. I reckon I've got everything I need already." He stands up and grins at me. "Good to meet you, Rebecca," he says quietly. "And thanks for your expertise." He extends his hand and I shake it, without quite knowing what I'm doing. And then, as everyone is turning in their seats and whispering, he makes his way along the row and out of the room.

"Ladies and gentlemen," says Maria Freeman, two bright spots burning on her cheeks. "Due to this . . . disturbance, we will have a short break before we resume. Please help yourself to tea and coffee. Thank you." She turns off the microphone, climbs down from the podium, and hurries over to the huddle of Sacrum Asset Management personnel.

"You should *never* have let him in!" I hear one of them saying.

"I didn't know who he was!" replies Maria defensively. "He said he was a stringer for *The Wall Street Journal*!"

Well, this is more like it! I haven't seen so much excitement since Alan Derring from the *Daily Investor* stood up at a Provident Assurance press conference and told everyone he was becoming a woman and wanted us all to call him Andrea.

I head toward the back to get another cup of coffee, and find Elly standing by the coffee table. Excellent. I haven't seen Elly for ages.

"Hi," she grins. "I like your new friend. Very entertaining."

"I know!" I say delightedly. "Isn't he cool?" I reach for a posh chocolate biscuit wrapped in gold foil, and give my cup to the waitress to be refilled. Then I take another couple of biscuits and pop them in my bag. (No point wasting them.)

Around us there is an excited buzz of conversation; the Sacrum people are still clustered at the front. This is great. We'll be able to natter for hours.

"So listen," I say to Elly. "Have you applied for any jobs recently?" I take a sip of coffee. "Because I saw one for *New Woman* the other day in the *Media Guardian,* and I meant to ring you. It said it was essential to have experience on a consumer title, but I thought you could say—"

"Becky," interrupts Elly in an odd voice, "you know which job I've been going for."

"What?" I stare at her. "Not that fund manager job. But that wasn't serious. That was just a bargaining tool."

"I took it," she says, and I gaze at her in shock.

Suddenly a voice comes from the podium, and we both look up.

"Ladies and gentlemen," Maria is saying. "If you would like to resume your seats . . ."

I'm sorry, but I can't go and sit back down there. I *have* to hear about this.

"Come on," I say quickly to Elly. "We don't need to stay. We've got our press packs. Let's go and have lunch."

There's a pause—and for an awful moment I think she's going to say no, she *wants* to stay and hear about personal pensions. But then she grins and takes my arm—and to the obvious dismay of the girl at the door, we waltz out of the room.

There's a Café Rouge around the corner, and we go straight in and order a bottle of white wine. I'm still in slight shock, to tell you the truth. Elly Granger is going to become a Wetherby's fund manager. She's deserting me. I won't have anyone to play with anymore.

And how *can* she? She wanted to be beauty editor on *Marie-Claire*, for God's sake!

"So, what decided you?" I say cautiously as our wine arrives.

"Oh, I don't know," she says, and sighs. "I just kept thinking, where am I going? You know, I keep applying for all these glam jobs in journalism and never even getting an interview . . ."

"You would have got one eventually," I say robustly. "I know you would."

"Maybe," she says. "Or maybe not. And in the meantime, I'm writing about all this boring financial stuff—and I suddenly thought, why not just sod it and *do* boring financial stuff? At least I'll have a proper career."

"You were in a proper career!"

"No I wasn't, I was hopeless! I was paddling around with no aim, no game plan, no prospects . . ." Elly breaks off as she sees my face. "I mean, I was quite different from you," she adds hurriedly. "You're much more sorted out than I was."

Sorted out? Is she joking?

"So when do you start?" I say, to change the subject—because to be honest, I feel a bit thrown by all this. I don't have a game plan, I don't have prospects. Maybe I'm hopeless, too. Maybe I should rethink my career. Oh God, this is depressing.

"Next week," says Elly, and takes a swig of wine. "I'm going to be based at the Silk Street office."

"Oh right," I say miserably.

"And I've had to buy loads of new clothes," she adds, and pulls a little face. "They're all really smart at Wetherby's."

New clothes? *New clothes?* Right, now I really am jealous.

"I went into Karen Millen and practically bought it out," she says, eating a marinated olive. "Spent about a thousand quid."

"Blimey," I say, feeling slightly awe-stricken. "A thousand quid, all at once?"

"Well, I had to," she says apologetically. "And anyway, I'll be earning more now."

"Really?"

"Oh yes," she says, and gives a little laugh. "Lots more."

"Like . . . how much?" I ask, feeling tweaks of curiosity.

"I'm starting off on forty grand," she says, and gives a careless shrug. "After that, who knows? What they said is . . ."

And she starts talking about career structures and ladders and bonuses. But I can't hear a word, I'm too shell-shocked.

Forty grand?

Forty grand? But I only earn—

Actually, should I be telling you how much I earn? Isn't it one of those things like religion, you're not supposed to mention in polite company? Or maybe we're all allowed to talk about money these days. Suze would know.

Oh well, sod it. You know everything else, don't you? The truth is, I earn £21,000. And I thought that was a lot! I remember really well, when I moved jobs, I jumped from £18,000 to £21,000, and I thought I'd made the big time. I was so excited about it, I used to write endless lists of what I would buy with all that extra money.

But now it sounds like nothing. I should be earning forty grand, like Elly, and buying all my clothes at Karen Millen. Oh, it's not fair. My life's a complete disaster.

As I'm walking back to the office, I feel pretty morose. Maybe I should give up journalism and become a fund manager, too. Or a merchant banker. They earn a pretty good whack, don't they? Maybe I could join Goldman Sachs or somewhere. They earn about a million a year, don't they? God, that would be good. I wonder how you get a job like that.

But on the other hand . . . do I really want to be a banker? I wouldn't mind the clothes-from-Karen-Millen part of it. In fact, I think I'd do that really well. But I'm not so sure about the rest. The getting-up-early-and-working-hideously-hard part. Not that I'm lazy or anything—but I quite like the fact that I can go and spend the afternoon at Image Store, or flick through the papers pretending to be doing research, and no one gives me a hard time. It doesn't sound as if Elly will be doing much of that in her new job. In fact, there doesn't seem to be anything remotely fun or creative about it. And aren't bankers rather humorless? Their press conferences certainly are—so imagine *working* with them. It all sounds quite scary.

Hmm. If only there were some way that I could get all the nice clothes—but not have to do the dreary work. One but not the other. If only there were a way . . . My eyes are automatically flicking into all the shop windows as I pass, checking out the displays—and suddenly I stop in my tracks.

This is a sign from God. It has to be.

I'm standing outside Ally Smith—which has some gorgeous full-length coats in the window—and there's a handwritten sign in the glass pane of the door. "Wanted. Saturday sales assistants. Inquire within."

I almost feel faint as I stare at the sign. It's as though lightning has struck, or something. Why on *earth* haven't I thought of this before? It's pure genius. I'll get a Saturday job! I'll work in a clothes shop! That way, I'll make loads of extra money *and* I'll get a discount on all the clothes! And let's face it, working in a shop has got to be more fun than becoming a fund manager, hasn't it? I can choose all my own clothes as I help the customers. I'll actually be getting *paid* to go shopping!

This is bloody fantastic, I think, striding into the shop with a friendly smile on my face. I *knew* something good was going to happen today. I just had a feeling about it.

Half an hour later, I come out with an even bigger smile on my face. I've got a job! I've got a Saturday job! I'm going to work from eight-thirty to five-thirty every Saturday, and get £4.80 an hour, and 10 percent off all the clothes! And after three months, it goes up to 20 percent! All my money troubles are over.

Thank God it was a quiet afternoon. They let me fill in the application form on the spot, and Danielle, the manager, gave me an interview straight away. At first, she looked a bit dubious—especially when I said I had a full-time job as a financial journalist and was doing this to get extra money and clothes. "It'll be hard work," she kept saying. "You do realize that? It'll be very hard work." But I think what changed her mind was when we started talking about the stock. I love Ally Smith—so of course I knew the price of every single item in the shop and whether they have anything similar in Jigsaw or French Connection. Eventually Danielle gave me a funny look and said, "Well, you obviously like clothes." And then she gave me the job! I can't wait. I start this Saturday. Isn't it great?

As I arrive back at the office I feel exhilarated with my success. I look around—and suddenly this mundane office life seems far too boring and limited for a creative spirit like mine. I don't belong here, among fusty piles of press releases and grimly tapping computers. I belong out there, among the bright spotlights and cashmere cardigans of Ally Smith. Maybe I'll go into retail full time, I think, as I sit back down at my desk. Maybe I'll start my own chain of designer stores! I'll be one of those people featured in articles about incredibly successful entrepreneurs. "Becky Bloomwood was working as a financial journalist when she devised the innovative concept of Bloomwood Stores. Now a successful chain around the country, the idea came to her one day as she . . ."

The phone rings and I pick it up.

"Yes?" I say absently. "Rebecca Bloomwood here." I nearly add, "of Bloomwood Stores," but maybe that's a tad premature.

"Ms. Bloomwood, this is Derek Smeath from Endwich Bank."

What? I'm so shocked, I drop the phone onto my desk with a clatter and have to scrabble around to pick it up. All the while, my heart's thumping like a rabbit. How does Derek Smeath know where I work? How did he get my number?

"Are you OK?" says Clare Edwards curiously.

"Yes," I gulp. "Yes, fine."

And now she's looking at me. Now I can't just put the phone down and pretend it was a wrong number. I've got to talk to him. OK, what I'll do is be really brisk and cheerful and try and get rid of him as quickly as possible.

"Hi!" I say into the phone. "Sorry about that! The thing is, I was just a bit busy with something else. You know how it is!"

"Ms. Bloomwood, I've written you several letters," says Derek Smeath. "And to none of them have I had a satisfactory response."

Oh, he sounds really cross. This is horrible. Why did he have to come along and spoil my day?

"I've been very busy, I'm afraid," I say. "My . . . my aunt was very ill. I had to go and be with her."

"I see," he says. "Nevertheless—"

"And then she died," I add.

"I'm sorry to hear that," says Derek Smeath. He doesn't *sound* sorry. "But that doesn't alter the fact that your current account stands at a balance of—"

Has this man got no heart? As he starts talking about balances and overdrafts and agreements, I deliberately tune out so I don't hear anything that will upset me. I'm staring at the fake woodgrain on my desk, wondering if I could pretend to drop the receiver accidentally back down onto the phone. This is awful. What am I going to do? *What am I going to do?*

"And if the situation is not resolved," he's saying sternly, "I'm afraid I will be forced to—"

"It's OK," I hear myself interrupting. "It's OK, because . . . I'm coming into some money soon." Even as I say the words, I feel my cheeks flame guiltily. But I mean, what else am I supposed to do?

"Oh yes?"

"Yes," I say, and swallow. "The thing is, my . . . my aunt left me some money in her will."

Which is kind of almost true. I mean, obviously Aunt Ermintrude would have left me some money. After all, I was her favorite niece, wasn't I? Did anyone else buy her Denny and George scarves? "I'll get it in a couple of weeks," I add for good measure. "A thousand pounds."

Then I realize I should have made it ten thousand—that would have really impressed him. Oh well, too late now.

"You're saying that in two weeks' time you'll be paying a check for a thousand pounds into your account," says Derek Smeath.

"Erm . . . yes," I say after a pause. "I suppose I am."

"I'm glad to hear it," he says. "I've made a note of our conversation, Ms. Bloomwood, and I'll be expecting the arrival of a thousand pounds into your account on Monday 26 March."

"Good," I say boldly. "Is that it?"

"For the moment. Good-bye, Ms. Bloomwood."

"Good-bye," I say, and put the phone down.

Got rid of him. Thank God.

OCTAGON ▸ *flair...style...vision*

FINANCIAL SERVICES DEPARTMENT
8TH FLOOR TOWER HOUSE
LONDON ROAD WINCHESTER S0 44 3DR

Ms. Rebecca Bloomwood
Flat 2
4 Burney Rd.
London SW6 8FD

Charge Card Number 7854 4567

9 March 2000

Dear Ms. Bloomwood:

Thank you for your prompt return of a signed check for £43.

Unfortunately, although this check is signed, it appears to be dated 14 February 2200. No doubt just an oversight on your part.

Octagon Shops cannot accept postdated checks as payment, and I am therefore returning it to you with the request that you return to us a signed check, dated with the date of signature.

Alternatively you can pay by cash or on the enclosed bank giro credit slip. A leaflet is enclosed for your information.

I look forward to receiving your payment.

Yours sincerely,

John Hunter
Customer Accounts Manager

Nine

WHEN I GET HOME that night, there's a pile of post in the hall for me—but I ignore it because my package from Fine Frames has arrived! It cost me £100 to buy, which is quite expensive, but apparently it will give you a return of £300 in only a few hours. Inside the package there's a leaflet full of photographs of people who make fortunes from doing Fine Frames—some of them make a hundred thousand a year! It makes me wonder what I'm doing, being a journalist.

So after supper, I sit down in front of *Changing Rooms* and open the kit. Suze is out tonight, so it's nice and easy to concentrate.

"Welcome to the best-kept secret in Britain . . ." says the leaflet. "The Fine Frames home-working family! Join other members and earn £££ in the comfort of your own home. Our easy-to-follow instructions will aid you as you embark on the biggest money-making enterprise of your life. Perhaps you will use your earnings to buy a car, or a boat—or to treat someone special. And remember—the amount you earn is completely up to you!"

I'm utterly gripped. Why on earth haven't I done this before? This is a *fantastic* scheme! I'll work incredibly hard for two weeks, then pay off all my debts, go on holiday, and buy loads of new clothes.

I start ripping at the packaging, and suddenly a pile of fabric strips falls onto the floor. Some are plain, and some are a flowered pattern. It's a pretty hideous pattern actually—but then, who cares? My job is just to make the frames and collect the money. I reach for the instructions and find them under a load of cardboard pieces. And sure enough, they're incredibly simple. What you have to do is glue wadding onto the cardboard frame, put the fabric over the top for that luxury upholstered effect, then glue braid along the back to hide the join. And that's it! It's completely simple and you get £2 a frame. There are 150 in the package—so if I do thirty a night for a week I'll have made three hundred quid just like that in my spare time!

OK, let's get started. Frame, wadding, glue, fabric, braid.

Oh God. Oh *God*. Who designed these bloody things? There just isn't enough fabric to fit over the frame and the wadding. Or at least you have to stretch it really hard—and it's such flimsy fabric, it rips. I've got glue on the carpet, and I've bent two of the cardboard frames from pulling them, and the only frame I've actually completed looks really wonky. And I've been doing it for . . .

I yawn, look at the time, and feel a jolt of shock. It's eleven-thirty, which means I've been working for three hours. In that time I've made one dodgy-looking frame which I'm not sure they'll accept, and ruined two. And I was supposed to be making thirty!

At that moment the door opens and Suze is back.

"Hi!" she says, coming into the sitting room. "Nice evening?"

"Not really," I begin disgruntledly. "I've been making these things . . ."

"Well, never mind," she says dramatically. "Because guess what? You've got a secret admirer."

"What?" I say, startled.

"Someone really likes you," she says, taking off her coat. "I heard it tonight. You'll never guess who!"

Luke Brandon pops into my mind before I can stop it. How ridiculous. And how would Suze have found that out, anyway? Stupid idea. Very stupid. Impossible.

She could have bumped into him at the cinema, whispers my brain. She does know him, after all, doesn't she? And he could have said . . .

"It's my cousin!" she says triumphantly. "Tarquin. He *really* likes you."

Oh for God's sake.

"He's got this secret little crush on you," she continues happily. "In fact, he's had one ever since he met you!"

"Really?" I say. "Well, I had sort of . . . guessed." Suze's eyes light up.

"So you already know about it?"

"Well," I say, and shrug awkwardly. What can I say? I can't tell her that her beloved cousin gives me the creeps. So instead I start to pick at the fabric on the photo frame in front of me, and a delighted smile spreads over Suze's face.

"He's really keen on you!" she says. "I said he should just ring you and ask you out. You wouldn't mind, would you?"

"Of course not," I say feebly.

"Wouldn't that be great?" said Suze. "If you two got married. I could be bridesmaid!"

"Yes," I say, and force myself to smile brightly. "Lovely."

What I'll do, I think, is agree to a date just to be polite—and then cancel at the last moment. And hopefully Tarquin'll have to go back to Scotland or something, and we can forget all about it.

But to be honest, I could really do without it. Now I've got two reasons to dread the phone ringing.

However, to my relief, Saturday arrives and I haven't heard a word from Tarquin. *Or* Derek Smeath. Everyone's finally leaving me alone to get on with my life!

On the slightly more negative side, I was planning to make 150 frames this week—but so far I've only made three, and none of them looks like the one in the picture. One doesn't have enough wadding in it, one doesn't quite meet at the corner, and the third has got a smear of glue on the front, which hasn't come off. I just can't understand why I'm finding it so difficult. Some people make hundreds of these things every week, without any effort. Mrs. S. of Ruislip even takes her family on a cruise every year on her earnings. How come they can do it and I can't? It's really depressing. I mean, I'm supposed to be bright, aren't I? I've got a degree, for God's sake.

Still, never mind, I tell myself. It's my new job at Ally Smith today—so at least I'll be earning some extra money there.

And I'm quite excited about it. Here starts a whole new career in fashion! I spend a long time choosing a cool outfit to wear on my first day—and eventually settle on black trousers from Jigsaw, a little cashmere (well, half cashmere) T-shirt, and a pink wrap-around top, which actually came from Ally Smith.

I'm quite pleased with the way I look, and am expecting Danielle to make some appreciative comment when I arrive at the shop—but she doesn't even seem to notice. She just says, "Hi. The trousers and T-shirts are in the stock room. Pick out your size and change in the cubicle."

Oh, right. Now I come to think of it, all the assistants at Ally Smith do wear the same outfits. Almost like a . . . well, a uniform, I suppose. Reluctantly I get changed and look at myself—and, to tell you the truth, I'm disappointed. These gray trousers don't really flatter me—and the T-shirt's just plain boring. I'm almost tempted to ask Danielle if I can pick out another outfit to wear—

but she seems a bit busy, so I don't. Maybe next week I'll have a little word.

But even though I don't like the outfit, I still feel a frisson of excitement as I come out onto the shop floor. The spotlights are shining brightly; the floor's all shiny and polished; music's playing and there's a sense of anticipation in the air. It's almost like being a performer. I glance at myself in a mirror and murmur, "How can I help you?" Or maybe it should be "*Can* I help you?" I'm going to be the most charming shop assistant ever, I decide. People will come here just to be assisted by me, and I'll have a fantastic rapport with all the customers. And then I'll appear in the *Evening Standard* in some quirky column about favorite shops.

No one's told me what to do yet, so—using my initiative, very good—I walk up to a woman with blond hair, who's tapping away at the till, and say, "Shall I have a quick go?"

"What?" she says, not looking up.

"I'd better learn how to work the till, hadn't I? Before all the customers arrive?"

Then the woman does look up and, to my surprise, bursts into laughter.

"On the till? You think you're going to go straight onto the till?"

"Oh," I say, blushing a little. "Well, I thought . . ."

"You're a beginner, darling," she says. "You're not going near the till. Go with Kelly. She'll show you what you'll be doing today."

Folding jumpers. Folding bloody jumpers. That's what I'm here to do. Rush round after customers who have picked up cardigans and left them all crumpled—and fold them back up again. By eleven o'clock I'm absolutely exhausted—and, to be honest, not enjoying myself very much at all. Do you know how depressing it is to fold a cardigan in exactly the right Ally Smith way and put it back on the shelf, all neatly lined up—just to see someone casually pull it down again, look at it, pull a face, and discard it? You want to scream at them, LEAVE IT ALONE IF YOU'RE

NOT GOING TO BUY IT! I watched one girl even pick up a cardigan *identical* to the one she already had on!

And I'm not getting to chat to the customers, either. It's as if they see through you when you're a shop assistant. No one's asked me a single interesting question, like "Does this shirt go with these shoes?" or, "Where can I find a really nice black skirt under £60?" I'd *love* to answer stuff like that. I could really help people! But the only questions I've been asked are "Is there a loo?" and, "Where's the nearest Midland cashpoint?" I haven't built up a single rapport with anyone.

Oh, it's depressing. The only thing that keeps me going is an end-of-stock reduced rack at the back of the shop. I keep sidling toward it and looking at a pair of zebra-print jeans, reduced from £180 to £90. I remember those jeans. I've even tried them on. And here they are, out of the blue—reduced. I just can't keep my eyes off them. They're even in my size.

I mean, I know I'm not really supposed to be spending money—but this is a complete one-off. They're the coolest jeans you've ever seen. And £90 is *nothing* for a pair of really good jeans. If you were in Gucci, you'd be paying at least £500. Oh God, I want them. I *want* them.

I'm just loitering at the back, eyeing them up for the hundredth time, when Danielle comes striding up and I jump guiltily. But all she says is "Can you go onto fitting room duty now? Sarah'll show you the ropes."

No more folding jumpers! Thank God!

To my relief, this fitting room lark is a lot more fun. Ally Smith has really nice fitting rooms, with lots of space and individual cubicles, and my job is to stand at the entrance and check how many items people are taking in with them. It's really interesting to see what people are trying on. One girl's buying *loads* of stuff, and keeps saying how her boyfriend told her to go mad for her birthday, and he would pay.

Huh. Well, it's all right for some. Still, never mind, at least I'm earning money. It's eleven-thirty, which means I've earned . . .

£14.40 so far. Well, that's not bad, is it? I could get some nice makeup for that.

Except that I'm not going to waste this money on makeup. Of course not—I mean, that's not why I'm here, is it? I'm going to be really sensible. What I'm going to do is buy the zebra-print jeans—just because they're a one-off and it would be a crime not to—and then put all the rest toward my bank balance. I just can't *wait* to put them on. I get a break at two-thirty, so what I'll do is nip to the reduced rack and take them to the staff room, just to make sure they fit, and . . .

Suddenly my face freezes. Hang on.

Hang on a moment. What's that girl holding over her arm? She's holding my zebra-print jeans! She's coming toward the fitting rooms. Oh my God. She wants to try them on. But they're mine! I saw them first!

I'm almost giddy with panic. I mean, a normal pair of jeans, I wouldn't bother about. But these are unique. They're *meant* for me. I've mentally reorganized my entire wardrobe around them, and have already planned to wear them at least three times next week. I can't lose them. Not now.

"Hi!" she says brightly as she approaches.

"Hi," I gulp, trying to stay calm. "Ahm . . . how many items have you got?"

"Four," she says, showing me the hangers. Behind me are tokens hanging on the wall, marked One, Two, Three, and Four. The girl's waiting for me to give her a token marked Four and let her in. But I can't.

I physically cannot let her go in there with my jeans.

"Actually," I hear myself saying, "you're only allowed three items."

"Really?" she says in surprise. "But . . ." She gestures to the tokens.

"I know," I say. "But they've just changed the rules. Sorry about that." And I flash her a quick smile.

"Oh, OK," says the girl. "Well, I'll leave out—"

"These," I say, and grab the zebra-print jeans.

"No," she says. "Actually, I think I'll—"

"We have to take the top item," I explain hurriedly. "Sorry about that."

Thank *God* for bossy shop assistants and stupid pointless rules. People are so used to them that this girl doesn't even question me. She just rolls her eyes, grabs the Three token, and pushes her way past into the fitting room, leaving me holding the precious jeans.

OK, now what? From inside the girl's cubicle, I can hear zips being undone and hangers being clattered. She won't take long to try on those three things. And then she'll be out, wanting the zebra-print jeans. Oh God. What can I do? For a few moments I'm frozen with indecision. Then the sound of a cubicle curtain being rattled back jolts me into action. It's not her—but it could have been. Quickly I stuff the zebra-print jeans out of sight behind the curtain and stand up again, a bright smile on my face.

Please let the girl find something else she likes, I pray feverishly. Please let her forget all about the jeans. Maybe she's not even that keen on them. Maybe she picked them up on impulse. She didn't really look like a jeans person to me.

A moment later, Danielle comes striding up, a clipboard in her hands.

"All right?" she says. "Coping, are you?"

"I'm doing fine," I say. "Really enjoying it."

"I'm just rostering in breaks," she says. "If you could manage to last until three, you can have an hour then."

"Fine," I say in my positive, employee-of-the-month voice, even though I'm thinking *Three? I'll be starving!*

"Good," she says, and moves off into the corner to write on her piece of paper, just as a voice says,

"Hi. Can I have those jeans now?"

It's the girl, back again. How can she have tried on all those other things so quickly? Is she Houdini?

"Hi!" I say, ignoring the last bit of what she said. "Any good? That black skirt's really nice. I think it would really suit you. The way the splits go at the—"

"Not really," she says, interrupting me, and shoves the lot back at me, all mussed up and off their hangers. "It was really the jeans I wanted. Can I have them?"

I stare at her desperately. I *can't* relinquish my treasured jeans. I just know this girl wouldn't love them like I would. She'd probably wear them once and chuck them out—or never wear them at all! And *I saw them first*.

"What jeans were they?" I say, wrinkling my brow sympathetically. "Blue ones? You can get them over there, next to the—"

"No!" says the girl impatiently. "The zebra-print jeans I had a minute ago."

"Oh," I say vaguely. "Oh yes. I'm not sure where they went. Maybe someone else took them."

"Oh for God's sake!" she says, looking at me as if I'm an imbecile. "This is ridiculous! I gave them to you about thirty seconds ago! How can you have lost them?"

Shit. She's really angry. Her voice is getting quite loud, and people are starting to look. Oh, *why* couldn't she have liked the black skirt instead?

"Is there a problem?" chimes in a syrupy voice, and I look up in horror. Danielle's coming over toward us, a sweet-but-menacing look on her face. OK, keep calm, I tell myself firmly. No one can prove anything either way.

"I gave this assistant a pair of jeans to look after because I had four items, which is apparently too many," the girl begins explaining.

"Four items?" says Danielle. "But you're allowed four items in the fitting room." And she turns to look at me with an expression which isn't very friendly.

"*Are* you?" I say innocently. "Oh God, I'm sorry. I thought it was three. I'm new," I add apologetically.

"I *thought* it was four!" says the girl. "I mean, you've got tokens with bloody 'Four' written on them!" She gives an impatient sigh. "So anyway, I gave her the jeans, and tried on the other things—and then I came out for the jeans, and they've gone."

"Gone?" says Danielle sharply. "Gone where?"

"I'm not sure," I say, trying to look as baffled as the next person. "Maybe another customer took them."

"But you were holding them!" says the girl. "So what—did someone just come up to you and whip them out of your fingers?"

I flinch at the tone of her voice. I would never speak to a shop assistant like that, even if I was cross. Anyway, how can she be so obsessed with a pair of *jeans*?

"Maybe you could get another pair from the rack," I say, trying to sound helpful. "Or some capri pants? I bet you'd look really nice in—"

"There *isn't* another pair," she says icily. "They were from the reduced rack. And I don't like capri pants."

"Rebecca, think!" says Danielle. "Did you put the jeans down somewhere?"

"I must have done," I say, twisting my fingers into a knot. "It's been so busy in here, I must have put them on the rail, and . . . and I suppose another customer must have walked off with them." I give an apologetic little shrug as though to say "Customers, eh?"

"Wait a minute!" says the girl sharply. "What's that?"

I follow her gaze and freeze. The zebra-print jeans have rolled out from under the curtain. For a moment we all stare at them.

"Gosh!" I manage at last. "There they are!"

"And what exactly are they doing down there?" asks Danielle.

"I don't know!" I say. "Maybe they . . ." I swallow, trying to think as quickly as I can. "Maybe . . ."

"You *took* them!" says the girl incredulously. "You bloody took them! You wouldn't let me try them on, and then you hid them!"

"That's ridiculous!" I say, trying to sound convincing—but I can feel my cheeks flushing a guilty red.

"You little . . ." The girl breaks off and turns to Danielle. "I want to make an official complaint."

"Rebecca," says Danielle. "Into my office, please."

I jump in fright at her voice and follow her slowly to her office. Around the shop, I can see all the other staff looking at me and nudging each other. How utterly mortifying. Still, it'll be OK. I'll just say I'm really sorry and promise not to do it again, and maybe offer to work overtime. Just as long as I don't get . . .

I don't believe it. She's fired me. I haven't even worked there for a day, and I've been kicked out. I was so shocked when she told me, I almost became tearful. I mean, apart from the incident with the zebra-print jeans, I thought I was doing really well. But apparently hiding stuff from customers is one of those automatic-firing things. (Which is really unfair, because she never told me that at the interview.)

As I get changed out of my gray trousers and T-shirt, there's a heavy feeling in my heart. My retail career is over before it's even begun. I was only given twenty quid for the hours I've done today—and Danielle said that was being generous. And when I asked if I could quickly buy some clothes using my staff discount, she looked at me as if she wanted to hit me.

It's all gone wrong. No job, no money, no discount, just twenty bloody quid. Miserably I start to walk along the street, shoving my hands in my pockets. Twenty bloody quid. What am I supposed to do with—

"Rebecca!" My head jerks up and I find myself looking dazedly at a face which I know I recognize. But who is it? It's . . . it's . . . it's . . .

"Tom!" I exclaim in the nick of time. "Hi there! What a surprise!"

Well, blow me down. Tom Webster, up in London. He's just as tall and gangly as ever—but somehow looking slightly cooler with it than usual. He's wearing a thin blue sweater over a T-shirt and . . . are those really Armani jeans? This doesn't make sense. What's he doing here anyway? Shouldn't he be in Reigate, grouting his Mediterranean tiles or something?

"This is Lucy," he says proudly, and pulls forward a slim girl with big blue eyes, holding about sixty-five carrier bags. And I don't believe it. It's the girl who was buying all that stuff in Ally Smith. The girl whose boyfriend was paying. *Surely* she didn't mean . . .

"You're going out together?" I say stupidly. "You and her?"

"Yes," says Tom, and grins at me. "Have been for some time now."

But this doesn't make any sense. Why haven't Janice and Martin mentioned Tom's girlfriend? They've mentioned every other bloody thing in his life.

And fancy Tom having a girlfriend!

"Hi," says Lucy.

"Hi there," I say. "I'm Rebecca. Next-door neighbor. Childhood friend. All that."

"Oh, *you're* Rebecca," she says, and gives a swift glance at Tom.

What does that mean? Have they been talking about me? God, does Tom still fancy me? How embarrassing.

"That's me!" I say brightly, and give a little laugh.

"You know, I'm sure I've seen you somewhere before," says Lucy thoughtfully—and then her eyes crinkle in recognition. "You work at Ally Smith, don't you?"

"No!" I say, a little too sharply.

"Oh," she says. "I thought I saw you—"

God, I can't have it going back to my parents that I work in a shop. They'll think I've been lying about my entire life in London and that secretly I'm broke and living in squalor.

"Research," I say quickly. "I'm a journalist, actually."

"Rebecca's a financial journalist," says Tom. "Really knows her stuff."

"Oh, right," says Lucy, and I give her a supercilious smile.

"Mum and Dad always listen to Rebecca," says Tom. "Dad

was talking about it just the other day. Said you'd been very helpful on some financial matter. Switching funds or something."

I nod vaguely, and give him a special, old-friends smile. Not that I'm jealous, or anything—but I do feel a little twinge seeing Tom smiling down at this Lucy character who, frankly, has very boring hair, even if her clothes are quite nice. Come to think of it, Tom's wearing quite nice clothes himself. Oh, what's going on? This is all wrong. Tom belongs in his starter home in Reigate, not prancing around expensive shops looking halfway decent.

"Anyway," he says. "We must get going."

"Train to catch?" I say patronizingly. "It must be hard, living so far out."

"It's not so bad," says Lucy. "I commute to Wetherby's every morning and it only takes forty minutes."

"You work for Wetherby's?" I say, aghast. Why am I *surrounded* by City high-flyers?

"Yes," she says. "I'm one of their political advisers."

What? What does that mean? Is she really brainy, or something? Oh God, this gets worse and worse.

"And we're not catching our train just yet," says Tom, smiling down at Lucy. "We're off to Tiffany first. Choose a little something for Lucy's birthday next week." He lifts a hand and starts twisting a lock of her hair round his finger.

I can't cope with this anymore. It's not fair. Why haven't *I* got a boyfriend to buy me stuff in Tiffany's?

"Well, lovely to see you," I gabble. "Give my love to your mum and dad. Funny they didn't mention Lucy," I can't resist adding. "I saw them the other day, and they didn't mention her once."

I shoot an innocent glance at Lucy. But she and Tom are exchanging looks again.

"They probably didn't want to—" begins Tom, and stops abruptly.

"What?" I say.

There's a long, awkward silence. Then Lucy says, "Tom, I'll

just look in this shop window for a second," and walks off, leaving the two of us alone.

God, what drama! I'm obviously the third person in their relationship.

"Tom, what's going on?" I say, and give a little laugh.

But it's obvious, isn't it? He's still hankering after me. And Lucy knows it.

"Oh God," says Tom, and rubs his face. "Look, Rebecca, this isn't easy for me. But the thing is, Mum and Dad are aware of your . . . feelings for me. They didn't want to mention Lucy to you, because they thought you'd be . . ." He exhales sharply. "Disappointed."

What? Is this some kind of *joke*? I have never been more dumbfounded in all my life. For a few seconds I can't even move for astonishment.

"My feelings for *you*?" I stutter at last. "Are you joking?"

"Look, it's pretty obvious," he says, shrugging. "Mum and Dad told me how the other day, you kept on asking how I was, and all about my new house . . ." There's a slightly pitying look in his eye. Oh my God, I can't stand this. How can he think . . . "I really like you, Becky," he adds. "I just don't . . ."

"I was being *polite*!" I roar. "I don't *fancy* you!"

"Look," he says. "Let's just leave it, shall we?"

"But I *don't*!" I cry furiously. "I never did fancy you! That's why I didn't go out with you when you asked me! When we were both sixteen, remember?"

I break off and look at him triumphantly—to see that his face hasn't moved a bit. He isn't listening. Or if he is, he's thinking that the fact I've dragged in our teenage past means I'm obsessed by him. And the more I try to argue the point, the more obsessed he'll think I am. Oh God, this is horrendous.

"OK," I say, trying to gather together the remaining shreds of my dignity. "OK, we're obviously not communicating here, so I'll just leave you to it." I glance over at Lucy, who's looking in a shop window and obviously pretending not to be listening.

"Honestly, I'm not after your boyfriend," I call. "And I never was. Bye."

And I stride off down the street, a nonchalant smile plastered stiffly across my face.

As I round the corner, however, the smile gradually slips, and I sit heavily down on a bench. I feel humiliated. Of course, the whole thing's laughable. That Tom Webster should think I'm in love with *him*. Just serves me right for being too polite to his parents and feigning interest in his bloody limed oak units. Next time I'll yawn loudly, or walk away. Or produce a boyfriend of my own.

I know all this. I know I shouldn't care two hoots what Tom Webster or his girlfriend think. But even so . . . I have to admit, I feel a bit low. Why haven't I got a boyfriend? There isn't even anyone I fancy at the moment. The last serious boyfriend I had was Robert Hayman, who sells advertising for *Portfolio News,* and we split up three months ago. And I didn't even much like him. He used to call me "Love" and jokingly put his hands over my eyes during the rude bits in films. Even when I told him not to, he still kept doing it. It used to drive me *mad*. Just remembering it now makes me feel all tense and scratchy.

But still, he was a boyfriend, wasn't he? He was someone to phone up during work, and go to parties with and use as ammunition against creeps. Maybe I shouldn't have chucked him. Maybe he was all right.

I give a gusty sigh, stand up, and start walking along the street again. All in all, it hasn't been a great day. I've lost a job and been patronized by Tom Webster. And now I haven't got anything to do tonight. I thought I'd be too knackered after working all day, so I didn't bother to organize anything.

Still, at least I've got twenty quid.

Twenty quid. I'll buy myself a nice cappuccino and a chocolate brownie. And a couple of magazines.

And maybe something from Accessorize. Or some boots. In fact I really *need* some new boots—and I've seen some really nice ones in Hobbs with square toes and quite a low heel. I'll go there after my coffee, and look at the dresses, too. God, I deserve a treat, after today. And I need some new tights for work, and a nail file. And maybe a book to read on the tube . . .

By the time I join the queue at Starbucks, I feel happier already.

PGNI FIRST BANK VISA

7 CAMEL SQUARE

LIVERPOOL L1 5NP

Ms. Rebecca Bloomwood
Flat 2
4 Burney Rd.
London SW6 8FD

10 March 2000

Dear Ms. Bloomwood:

PGNI First Bank VISA Card No. 1475839204847586

Thank you for your letter of 6 March.

Your offer of a free subscription to *Successful Saving* magazine is most kind, as is your invitation to dinner at The Ivy. Unfortunately, employees of PGNI First Bank are prohibited from accepting such gifts.

I look forward to receiving your outstanding payment of £105.40, as soon as possible.

Yours sincerely,

Peter Johnson
Customer Accounts Executive

Ten

ON MONDAY MORNING I wake early, feeling rather hollow inside. My gaze flits to the pile of unopened carrier bags in the corner of my room and then quickly flits away again. I know I spent too much money on Saturday. I know I shouldn't have bought two pairs of boots. I know I shouldn't have bought that purple dress. In all, I spent . . . Actually, I don't want to think about how much I spent. Think about something else, quick, I instruct myself. Something else. Anything'll do.

I'm well aware that at the back of my mind, thumping quietly like a drumbeat, are the twin horrors of Guilt and Panic.

Guilt Guilt Guilt Guilt.

Panic Panic Panic Panic.

If I let them, they'd swoop in and take over. I'd feel completely paralyzed with misery and fear. So the trick I've learned is simply not to listen. My mind is very well trained like that.

My other trick is to distract myself with different thoughts and activities. So I get up, switch the radio on, take a shower, and get dressed. The thumping's still there at the back of my head, but gradually, gradually, it's fading away. As I go into the kitchen and make a cup of coffee, I can barely hear it anymore. A cautious relief floods over me, like that feeling you get when a painkiller finally gets rid of your headache. I can relax. I'm going to be all right.

On the way out I pause in the hall to check my appearance in the mirror (Top: River Island, Skirt: French Connection, Tights: Pretty Polly Velvets, Shoes: Ravel) and reach for my coat (Coat: House of Fraser sale). Just then the post plops through the door, and I go to pick it up. There's a handwritten letter for Suze and a postcard from the Maldives. And for me, there are two ominous-looking window envelopes. One from VISA, one from Endwich Bank.

For a moment, my heart stands still. Why another letter from the bank? And VISA. What do they want? Can't they just leave me alone?

Carefully I place Suze's post on the ledge in the hall and shove my own two letters in my pocket, telling myself I'll read them on the way to work. Once I get on the tube, I'll open them both and I'll read them, however unpleasant they may be.

Honestly. As I'm walking along the pavement, I promise my intention is to read the letters.

But then I turn into the next street—and there's a skip outside someone's house. A huge great yellow skip, already half full of stuff. Builders are coming in and out of the house, tossing old bits of wood and upholstery into the skip. Loads of rubbish, all jumbled up together.

And a little thought creeps into my mind.

My steps slow down as I approach the skip and I pause, staring intently at it as though I'm interested in the words printed on the side. I stand there, trying to appear casual, until the builders have gone back into the house and no one's looking. Then, in one motion, I reach for the two letters, pull them out of my pocket, and drop them over the side, into the skip.

Gone.

As I'm standing there, a builder pushes past me with two

sacks of broken plaster, and heaves them into the skip. And now they really are gone. Buried beneath a layer of plaster, unread. No one will ever find them.

Gone for good.

Quickly I turn away from the skip and begin to walk on again. Already my step's lighter and I'm feeling buoyant.

Before long, I'm feeling completely purged of guilt. I mean, it's not my fault if I never read the letters, is it? It's not my fault if I never got them, is it? As I bound along toward the tube station I honestly feel as though neither of those letters ever existed.

When I arrive at work, I switch on my computer, click efficiently to a new document, and start typing my piece on pensions. Perhaps if I work really hard, it's occurred to me, Philip will give me a raise. I'll stay late every night and impress him with my dedication to the job, and he'll realize that I'm considerably undervalued. Perhaps he'll even make me associate editor, or something.

"These days," I type briskly, "none of us can rely on the government to take care of us in our old age. Therefore pension planning should be done as early as possible, ideally as soon as you are earning an income."

"Morning, Clare," says Philip, coming into the office in his overcoat. "Morning, Rebecca."

Hah! Now is the time to impress him.

"Morning, Philip," I say, in a friendly-yet-professional manner. Then, instead of leaning back in my chair and asking him how his weekend was, I turn back to my computer and start typing again. In fact, I'm typing so fast that the screen is filled with lots of splodgy typos. It has to be said, I'm not the best typist in the world. But who cares? I look very businesslike, that's the point.

"The bwst ootion is oftwn yoor compaamy occupatinoa lscheme, bt if tehis is not posibsle, a wide vareiety of peronanlas penion lans is on ther markte, ranign from . . ." I break off, reach for a pension brochure, and flip quickly through it, as though scanning for some crucial piece of information.

"Good weekend, Rebecca?" says Philip.

"Fine, thanks," I say, glancing up from the brochure as though surprised to be interrupted while I'm at work.

"I was round your neck of the woods on Saturday," he says. "The Fulham Road. Trendy Fulham."

"Right," I say absently.

"It's the place to be, these days, isn't it? My wife was reading an article about it. Full of It-girls, all living on trust funds."

"I suppose so," I say vaguely.

"That's what we'll have to call you," he says, and gives a little guffaw. "The office It-girl."

"Right," I say, and smile at him. After all, he's the boss. He can call me whatever he—

Hang on a minute. Philip hasn't got the idea that I'm rich, has he? He doesn't think I've got a trust fund or something ridiculous, does he?

"Rebecca," says Clare, looking up from her telephone. "I've got a call for you. Someone called Tarquin."

Philip gives a little grin, as though to say "What else?" and ambles off to his desk. I stare after him in frustration. This is all wrong. If Philip thinks I've got some kind of private income, he'll never give me a raise.

But what on earth could have given him that idea?

"Becky," says Clare meaningfully, gesturing to my ringing phone.

"Oh," I say. "Yes, OK." I pick up the receiver, and say, "Hi. Rebecca Bloomwood here."

"Becky" comes Tarquin's unmistakable, reedy voice. He sounds rather nervous, as if he's been gearing up to this phone call for ages. Perhaps he has. "It's so nice to hear your voice. You know, I've been thinking about you a lot."

"Really?" I say, trying not to sound too encouraging. I mean, he is Suze's cousin and I don't want to hurt the poor bloke.

"I'd . . . I'd very much like to spend some more time in your company," he says. "May I take you out to dinner?"

Oh God. What am I supposed to say to that? It's such an innocuous request. I mean, it's not as if he's said, Can I sleep with you? or even Can I kiss you? If I say no to dinner, it's like saying "You're so unbearable, I can't even stand sharing a table with you for two hours."

And Suze has been so sweet to me recently, and if I turn her darling Tarkie down flat, she'll be really upset.

"I suppose so," I say, aware that I don't sound too thrilled—and also aware that maybe I should just come clean and say "I don't fancy you." But somehow I can't face it. To be honest, it would be a lot easier just to go out to dinner with him. I mean, how bad can it be?

And anyway, I don't have to actually *go*. I'll call at the last moment and cancel. Easy.

"I'm in London until Sunday," says Tarquin.

"Let's make it Saturday night, then!" I say brightly. "Just before you leave."

"Seven o'clock?"

"How about eight?" I suggest.

"OK," he says. "Eight o'clock." And he rings off, without mentioning a venue. But since I'm not actually going to meet him, this doesn't really matter. I put the phone down, give an impatient sigh, and start typing again.

"Although solid investment performance is important, flexibility is equally vital when choosing a pension plan, particularly for the younger investor. New on the market this year is the . . ." I break off and reach for a brochure. "Sun Assurance 'Later Years' Retirement Plan, which . . ."

"So, was that guy asking you out?" says Clare Edwards.

"Yes, he was, actually," I say, looking up carelessly. And in spite of myself, I feel a little flip of pleasure. Because Clare doesn't know what Tarquin's like, does she? For all she knows, he's incredibly good-looking and witty. "We're going out on Saturday night." I give her a nonchalant smile and start typing again.

"Oh right," she says, and snaps an elastic band round a pile of letters. "You know, Luke Brandon was asking me if you had a boyfriend the other day."

For an instant I can't move. Luke Brandon wants to know if I've got a boyfriend?

"Really?" I say, trying to sound normal. "When . . . when was this?"

"Oh, just the other day," she says. "I was at a briefing at Brandon Communications, and he asked me. Just casually. You know."

"And what did you say?"

"I said no," said Clare, and gives me a little grin. "You don't fancy him, do you?"

"Of course not," I say, and roll my eyes.

But I have to admit, I feel quite cheerful as I turn back to my computer and start typing again. Luke Brandon. I mean, not that I like him or anything—but still. "This plan," I type, "offers full death benefits and an optional lump sum on retirement. For example, assuming 7 percent growth, a typical woman aged 30 who invested £100 a month would receive . . ."

You know what? I suddenly think, stopping midsentence. This is boring. I'm better than this.

I'm better than sitting here in this crappy office, typing out the details from a brochure, trying to turn them into some kind of credible journalism. I deserve to do something more interesting than this. Or more well paid. Or both.

I stop typing and rest my chin on my hands. It's time for a new start. Why don't I do what Elly's doing? I'm not afraid of a bit of hard work, am I? Why don't I get my life in order, go to a City head-hunter, and land myself a new job? I'll have a huge income and a company car and wear Karen Millen suits every day. And I'll never have to worry about money again.

I feel exhilarated. This is it! This is the answer to everything. I'll be a . . .

"Clare?" I say casually. "Who earns the most in the City?"

"I don't know," says Clare, frowning thoughtfully. "Maybe futures brokers?"

That's it, then. I'll be a futures broker. Easy.

And it is easy. So easy that ten o'clock the next morning sees me walking nervously up to the front doors of William Green, top City head-hunters. As I push the door open I glimpse my own reflection and feel a little thrill go through my stomach. Am I *really* doing this?

You bet I am. I'm wearing my smartest black suit, and tights and high heels, with an *FT* under my arm, obviously. And I'm carrying the briefcase with the combination lock, which my mum gave me one Christmas and which I've never used. This is partly because it's really heavy and bumpy—and partly because I've forgotten the combination, so I can't actually open it. But it looks the part. And that's what counts.

Jill Foxton, the woman I'm meeting, was really nice on the phone when I told her about wanting to change careers, and sounded pretty impressed by all my experience. I quickly typed up a curriculum vitae and e-mailed it to her—and, OK, I padded it a bit, but that's what they expect, isn't it? It's all about selling yourself. And it worked, because she phoned back only about ten minutes after receiving it, and asked if I'd come in and see her, as she thought she had some interesting opportunities for me.

I was so excited, I could barely keep still. I went straight into Philip and told him I wanted to take tomorrow off to take my nephew to the zoo—and he didn't suspect a thing. He's going to be gobsmacked when he finds out I've turned overnight into a high-flying futures broker.

"Hi," I say confidently to the woman at reception. "I'm here to see Jill Foxton. It's Rebecca Bloomwood."

"Of . . ."

I can't say *Successful Saving*. It might get back to Philip that I've been looking for a new job.

"Of . . . just of nowhere, really," I say and give a relaxed little laugh. "Just Rebecca Bloomwood. I have a ten o'clock appointment."

"Fine," she says, and smiles. "Take a seat."

I pick up my briefcase and walk over to the black leather chairs, trying not to give away how nervous I feel. I sit down, run my eye hopefully over the magazines on the coffee table (but there's nothing interesting, just things like *The Economist*), then lean back and look around. This foyer is pretty impressive, I have to admit. There's a fountain in the middle, and glass stairs rising in a curve—and, what seems like several miles away, I can see lots of state-of-the-art lifts. Not just one lift, or two—but about ten. Blimey. This place must be huge.

"Rebecca?" A blond girl in a pale trouser suit is suddenly in front of me. Nice suit, I think. Very nice suit.

"Hi!" I say. "Jill!"

"No, I'm Amy," she smiles. "Jill's assistant."

Wow. That's pretty cool. Sending your assistant to pick up your visitors, as if you're too grand and busy to do it yourself. Maybe that's what I'll get my assistant to do when I'm an important futures broker and Elly comes over for lunch. Or maybe I'll have a *male* assistant—and we'll fall in love! God, it would be just like a movie. The high-flying woman and the cute but sensitive . . .

"Rebecca?" I come to and see Amy staring at me curiously. "Are you ready?"

"Of course!" I say gaily, and pick up my briefcase. As we stride off over the glossy floor, I surreptitiously run my gaze over Amy's trouser suit again—and find my eye landing on an Emporio Armani label. I can't quite believe it. The *assistants* wear Emporio Armani! So what's Jill herself going to be in? Couture Dior? God, I love this place already.

We go up to the sixth floor and begin to walk along endless carpeted corridors.

"So you want to be a futures broker," says Amy after a while.

"Yes," I say. "That's the idea."

"And you already know a bit about it."

"Well, you know." I give a modest smile. "I've written extensively on most areas of finance, so I do feel quite well equipped."

"That's good," says Amy, and gives me a smile. "Some people turn up with no idea. Then Jill asks them a few standard questions, and . . ." She makes a gesture with her hand. I don't know what it means, but it doesn't look good.

"Right!" I say, forcing myself to speak in an easy tone. "So—what sort of questions?"

"Oh, nothing to worry about!" says Amy. "She'll probably ask you . . . oh, I don't know. Something like 'How do you trade a butterfly?' or, 'What's the difference between open outlay and OR?' Or, 'How would you calculate the expiry date of a futures instrument?' Really basic stuff."

"Right," I say, and swallow. "Great."

Something in me is telling me to turn and run—but we've already arrived at a pale blond-wood door.

"Here we are," says Amy, and smiles at me. "Would you like tea or coffee?"

"Coffee, please," I say, wishing I could say "A stiff gin, please." Amy knocks on the door, opens it and ushers me in, and says, "Rebecca Bloomwood."

"Rebecca!" says a dark-haired woman behind the desk, and gets up to shake my hand.

To my slight surprise, Jill is not nearly as well dressed as Amy. She's wearing a blue, rather mumsy-looking suit, and boring court shoes. But still, never mind, she's the boss. And her office is pretty amazing.

"It's very good to meet you," she says, gesturing to a chair in front of her desk. "And let me say straight away, I was extremely impressed by your CV."

"Really?" I say, feeling relief creep over me. That can't be bad, can it? *Extremely impressed*. Maybe it won't matter I don't know the answers to those questions.

"Particularly by your languages," adds Jill. "*Very* good. You do seem to be one of those rare breeds, an all-rounder."

"Well, my French is really only conversational," I say modestly. "*Voici la plume de ma tante*, and all that!"

Jill gives an appreciative laugh, and I beam back at her.

"But Finnish!" she says, reaching for the cup of coffee on her desk. "That's quite unusual."

I keep smiling and hope we move off the subject of languages. To be honest, "fluent in Finnish" went in because I thought "conversational French" looked a bit bare on its own. And after all, who speaks Finnish, for God's sake? No one.

"And your financial knowledge," she says, pulling my CV toward her. "You seemed to have covered a lot of different areas during your years in financial journalism." She looks up. "What attracts you to derivatives in particular?"

What? What's she talking about? Oh yes. Derivatives. They're futures, aren't they? And they have something to do with the price of a security. Or a commodity. Something like that.

"Well," I begin confidently—and am interrupted as Amy comes in with a cup of coffee.

"Thanks," I say, and look up, hoping we've moved onto something else. But she's still waiting for an answer. "I think the excitement of futures is the . . . um, their speculative nature, combined with the ability to control risk with hedge positions," I hear myself saying.

Wow. How on earth did I come out with that?

"They're an extremely challenging area," I add quickly, "and I think . . ." What do I think? Should I throw in a quick reference to butterflies or expiry dates or something? Or Barings Bank? Probably better not. "I think I'd be well suited to that particular field," I finish at last.

"I see," says Jill Foxton, and leans back in her chair. "The reason

I ask is, there's a position we have in banking, which I think might also suit you. I don't know what you would feel about that."

A position in banking? Has she actually found me a job? I don't believe it!

"Well, that would be fine by me," I say, trying not to sound too joyful. "I mean, I'd miss the futures—but then, banking's good, too, isn't it?"

Jill laughs. I think she thinks I'm joking or something.

"The client is a triple-A-rated foreign bank, looking for a new recruit in the London arm of their debt financing division."

"Right," I say intelligently.

"I don't know whether you're familiar with the principles of European back-to-back arbitrage?"

"Absolutely," I say confidently. "I wrote an article on that very subject last year."

Which isn't *quite* true, but I can always read a book about it, can't I?

"Obviously I'm not trying to rush you into any decision," she says, "but if you do want a change of career, I'd say this would be perfect for you. There'd be an interview, but I can't see any problems there." She smiles at me. "And we'll be able to negotiate you a very attractive package."

"Really?" Suddenly, I can't quite breathe. She's going to negotiate an attractive package. For me!

"Oh yes," says Jill. "Well, you must realize you're a bit of a one-off." She gives me a confidential smile. "You know, when your CV came through yesterday, I actually whooped! I mean, the *coincidence*!"

"Absolutely," I say, beaming at her. God, this is fantastic. This is a bloody dream come true. I'm going to be a banker! And not just any old banker—a triple-A-rated banker!

"So," says Jill casually. "Shall we go and meet your new employer?"

"What?" I say in astonishment, and a little smile spreads over her face.

"I didn't want to tell you until I'd met you—but the recruitment director of Bank of Helsinki is over here for a meeting with our managing director. I just *know* he's going to love you. We can have the whole thing wrapped up by this afternoon!"

"Excellent!" I say, and get to my feet. Ha-ha-ha! I'm going to be a banker!

It's only as we're halfway down the corridor that her words begin to impinge on my mind. Bank of Helsinki.

Bank of Helsinki. That doesn't mean . . . Surely she doesn't think . . .

"I can't wait to hear the two of you talking away in Finnish," says Jill pleasantly, as we begin to climb a flight of stairs. "It's not a language I know at all."

Oh my God. *Oh my God. No.*

"But then, my languages have always been hopeless," she adds comfortably. "I'm not talented in that department, not like you!"

I flash her a little smile and keep walking, without missing a step. But I can hardly breathe. Shit. What am I going to do? *What the fuck am I going to do?*

We turn a corner and begin to walk calmly down another corridor. And I'm doing pretty well. As long as we just keep walking, I'm OK.

"Was Finnish a hard language to learn?" asks Jill.

"Not that hard," I hear myself saying in a scratchy voice. "My . . . my father's half Finnish."

"Yes, I thought it must be something like that," says Jill. "I mean, it's not the sort of thing you learn at school, is it?" And she gives a jolly little laugh.

It's all right for her, I think desperately. She's not the one being led to her death. Oh God, this is terrible. People keep passing us and glancing at me and smiling, as if to say "So that's the Finnish-speaker!"

Why did I put I was fluent in Finnish? *Why?*

"All right?" says Jill. "Not nervous?"

"Oh no!" I say at once, and force a grin onto my face. "Of course I'm not nervous!"

Maybe I'll be able to busk it, I think suddenly. I mean, the guy won't conduct the whole bloody interview in Finnish, will he? He'll just say "Haållø," or whatever it is, and I'll say "Haållø" back, and then before he can say anything else, I'll quickly say, "You know, my technical Finnish is a bit rusty these days. Would you mind if we spoke in English?" And he'll say . . .

"Nearly there," says Jill, and smiles at me.

"Good," I say brightly, and clasp my sweaty hand more tightly round my briefcase handle. Oh God. Please save me from this. Please . . .

"Here we are!" she says, and stops at a door marked "Conference Room." She knocks twice, then pushes it open. There's a roomful of people sitting round a table, and they all turn to look at me.

"Jan Virtanen," she says. "I'd like you to meet Rebecca Bloomwood."

A bearded man rises from his chair, give me a huge smile, and extends his hand.

"Neiti Bloomwood," he says cheerfully. "Nautin erittain paljon tapaamisestamme. Onko oiken, etta teilla on jonkinlainen yhteys Suomeen?"

I stare speechlessly at him. My face is glowing, as though I'm consumed with happiness. Everyone in the room is waiting for me to answer, I've got to say something.

"I . . . erm . . . erm . . . Haållø!" I lift my hand in a friendly little wave and smile around the room.

But nobody smiles back.

"Erm . . . I've just got to . . ." I start backing away. "Just got to . . ."

I turn. And I run.

Eleven

I ARRIVE BACK DOWN in the foyer, panting slightly. Which is not surprising, since I've just run about a half marathon along endless corridors, trying to get out of this place. I descend the final flight of stairs (couldn't risk waiting for the elevators in case the Finnish brigade suddenly turned up), then pause to catch my breath. I straighten my skirt, transfer my briefcase from one sweaty hand to the other, and begin to walk calmly across the foyer toward the door, as though I've come out of an utterly ordinary, utterly unspectacular meeting. I don't look right and I don't look left. I don't think about the fact that I've just completely shredded any chances I had of becoming a top City banker. All I can think about is getting to that glass door and getting outside before anyone can . . .

"Rebecca!" comes a voice behind my voice, and I freeze. Shit. They've got me.

"Haållø!" I gulp, turning round. "Haåll . . . Oh. Hell . . . Hello."

It's Luke Brandon.

It's Luke Brandon, standing right in front of me, looking down at me with that amused smile he always seems to have.

"This isn't the sort of place I would have expected to find you," he says. "You're not after a City job, are you?"

And why shouldn't I be? Doesn't he think I'm clever enough?

"Actually," I say haughtily, "I'm thinking of a change of career. Maybe into foreign banking. Or futures broking."

"Really?" he says. "That's a shame."

A shame? What does that mean? Why is it a shame? As I look up at him, his dark eyes meet mine, and I feel a little flicker, deep inside me. Out of nowhere, Clare's words pop into my head. *Luke Brandon was asking me if you had a boyfriend.*

"What . . ." I clear my throat. "What are *you* doing here, anyway?"

"Oh, I recruit from here quite often," he says. "They're very efficient. Soulless, but efficient." He shrugs, then looks at my shiny briefcase. "Have they fixed you up with anything yet?"

"I've . . . I've got a number of options open to me," I say. "I'm just considering my next move."

Which, to be honest, is straight out the door.

"I see," he says, and pauses. "Did you take the day off to come here?"

"Yes," I say. "Of course I did."

What does he think? That I just sloped off for a couple of hours and said I was at a press conference?

Actually, that's not a bad idea. I might try that next time.

"So—what are you up to now?" he asks.

Don't say "nothing." *Never* say "nothing."

"Well, I've got some bits and pieces to do," I say. "Calls to make, people to see. That kind of thing."

"Ah," he says, nodding. "Yes. Well. Don't let me keep you." He looks around the foyer. "And I hope it all works out for you, job-wise."

"Thanks," I say, giving him a businesslike smile.

And then he's gone, walking off toward the doors, and I'm left holding my clunky briefcase, feeling just a bit disappointed. I wait until he's disappeared, then wander slowly over to the doors myself and go out onto the street. And then I stop. To tell you the truth, I'm not quite sure what to do next. I'd kind of planned to spend the day ringing everyone up and telling them about my fab new job as a futures broker. Instead of which . . . Well, anyway. Let's not think about that.

But I can't stand still on the pavement outside William Green all day. People will start thinking I'm a piece of installation art or something. So eventually I begin walking along the street, figuring I'll arrive at a tube soon enough and then I can decide what to do. I come to a corner and I'm just waiting for the traffic to stop, when a taxi pulls up beside me.

"I know you're a very busy woman, with a lot to do," comes Luke Brandon's voice, and my head jerks up in shock. There he is, leaning out of the taxi window, his dark eyes crinkled up in a little smile. "But if you had the odd half-hour to spare—you wouldn't be interested in doing a little shopping, would you?"

This day is unreal. Completely and utterly unreal.

I get into the taxi, put my clunky briefcase on the floor, and shoot a nervous look at Luke as I sit down. I'm already slightly regretting this. What if he asks me a question about interest rates? What if he wants to talk about the Bundesbank or American growth prospects? But all he says is "Harrods, please," to the driver.

As we zoom off, I can't stop a smile coming to my face. I thought I was going to have to go home and be all miserable on my own—and instead, I'm on my way to Harrods, and someone else is paying. I mean, you can't get more perfect than that.

As we drive along, I look out of the window at the crowded streets. Although it's March, there are still a few SALE signs in the shop windows left over from January, and I find myself peering at the displays, wondering if there are any bargains I might have missed. We pause outside a branch of Lloyds Bank. I look idly at the window, and at the queue of people inside, and hear myself saying "You know what? Banks should run January sales. Everyone else does."

There's silence and I look up, to see a look of amusement on Luke Brandon's face.

"Banks?" he says.

"Why not?" I say defensively. "They could reduce their charges for a month or something. And so could building societies. Big posters in the windows, 'Prices Slashed' . . ." I think for a moment. "Or maybe they should have April sales, after the end of the tax year. Investment houses could do it, too. 'Fifty percent off a selected range of funds.' "

"A unit trust sale," says Luke Brandon slowly. "Reductions on all upfront charges."

"Exactly," I say. "Everyone's a sucker for a sale. Even rich people."

The taxi moves on again, and I gaze out at a woman in a gorgeous white coat, wondering where she got it. Maybe at Harrods. Maybe I should buy a white coat, too. I'll wear nothing but white all winter. A snowy white coat and a white fur hat. People will start calling me the Girl in the White Coat.

When I look back again, Luke's writing something down in a little notebook. He looks up and meets my eye for a moment, then says, "Rebecca, are you serious about leaving journalism?"

"Oh," I say vaguely. To be honest, I'd forgotten all about leaving journalism. "I don't know. Maybe."

"And you really think banking would suit you better?"

"Who knows?" I say, feeling a bit rattled at his tone. It's all right for him. He doesn't have to worry about his career—he's got his own multimillion-pound company. I've only got my own multimillion-pound overdraft. "Elly Granger is leaving *Investor's Weekly News,*" I add. "She's joining Wetherby's as a fund manager."

"I heard," he says. "Doesn't surprise me. But you're nothing like Elly Granger."

Really? This comment intrigues me. If I'm not like Elly, who am I like, then? Someone really cool like Kristin Scott Thomas, maybe.

"You have imagination," adds Luke. "She doesn't."

Wow! Now I really am gobsmacked. Luke Brandon thinks I have imagination? Gosh. That's good, isn't it. That's quite flattering, really. *You have imagination.* Mmm, yes, I like that. Unless . . .

Hang on. It's not some polite way of saying he thinks I'm stupid, is it? Or a liar? Like "creative accounting." Perhaps he's trying to say that none of my articles is accurate.

Oh God, now I don't know whether to look pleased or not.

To cover up my embarrassment, I look out of the window. We've stopped at a traffic light, and a very large lady in a pink velour jogging suit is trying to cross the road. She's holding several bags of shopping and a pug dog, and she keeps losing grasp of one or other of them and having to put something down. I almost want to leap out and help her. Then, suddenly, she loses her grasp of one of the bags, and drops it on the ground. It falls open—and three huge tubs of ice cream come out of it and start rolling down the road.

Don't laugh, I instruct myself. Be mature. Don't laugh. I clamp my lips together, but I can't stop a little giggle escaping.

I glance at Luke, and his lips are clamped together, too.

Then the woman starts chasing her ice cream down the road, pug dog in tow, and that's it. I can't stop myself giggling. And when the pug dog reaches the ice cream before the lady, and starts trying to get the lid off with its teeth, I think I'm going to die laughing. I look over at Luke, and I can't believe it. He's laughing helplessly, too, wiping the tears from his eyes. I didn't think Luke Brandon *ever* laughed.

"Oh God," I manage at last. "I know you shouldn't laugh at people. But I mean . . ."

"That dog!" Luke starts laughing again. "That bloody dog!"

"That outfit!" I give a little shudder as we start to move off again, past the pink woman. She's bending over the ice cream, her huge pink bottom thrust up in the air . . . "I'm sorry, but pink velour jogging suits should be banned from this planet."

"I couldn't agree more," says Luke, nodding seriously. "Pink velour jogging suits are hereby banned. Along with cravats."

"And men's briefs," I say without thinking—then blush pink. How could I mention men's briefs in front of Luke Brandon? "And toffee-flavored popcorn," I quickly add.

"Right," says Luke. "So we're banning pink velour jogging suits, cravats, men's briefs, toffee-flavored popcorn . . ."

"And punters with no change," comes the taxi driver's voice from the front.

"Fair enough," says Luke, giving a little shrug. "Punters with no change."

"And punters who vomit. They're the worst."

"OK . . ."

"And punters who don't know where the fuck they're going."

Luke and I exchange glances and I begin to giggle again.

"And punters who don't speak the bloody language. Drive you crazy."

"Right," says Luke. "So . . . most punters, in fact."

"Don't get me wrong," says the taxi driver. "I've got nothing against foreigners . . ." He pulls up outside Harrods. "Here we are. Going shopping, are you?"

"That's right," says Luke, getting out his wallet.

"So—what're you after?"

I look at Luke expectantly. He hasn't told me what we're here to buy. Clothes? A new aftershave? Will I have to keep smelling his cheek? (I wouldn't mind that, actually.) Furniture? Something dull like a new desk?

"Luggage," he says, and hands a tenner to the driver. "Keep the change."

Luggage! Suitcases and holdalls and stuff like that. As I wander round the department, looking at Louis Vuitton suitcases and calfskin bags, I'm quite thrown. Quite shocked by myself. Luggage. Why on earth have I never considered luggage before?

I should explain—for years now, I've kind of operated under an informal shopping cycle. A bit like a farmer's crop rotation system. Except, instead of wheat-maize-barley-fallow, mine pretty much goes clothes-makeup-shoes-clothes. (I don't usually bother with fallow.) Shopping is actually very similar to farming a field. You can't keep buying the same thing—you have to have a bit of variety.

But look what I've been missing out on all this time. Look what I've been denying myself. I feel quite shaky as I realize the opportunities I've just been throwing away over the years. Suitcases, weekend bags, monogrammed hatboxes . . . With weak legs I wander into a corner and sit down on a carpeted pedestal next to a red leather vanity case.

How can I have overlooked luggage for so long? How can I have just blithely led my life *ignoring an entire retail sector*?

"So—what do you think?" says Luke, coming up to me. "Anything worth buying?"

And now, of course, I feel like a fraud. Why couldn't he have wanted to buy a really good white shirt, or a cashmere scarf? Or even hand cream? I would have been able to advise him authoritatively and even quote prices. But luggage. I'm a beginner at luggage.

"Well," I say, playing for time. "It depends. They all look great."

"They do, don't they?" He follows my gaze around the department. "But which one would you choose? If you had to buy one of these suitcases, which one would it be?"

It's no good. I can't bluff.

"To be honest," I say, "this isn't really my field."

"What isn't?" he says, sounding incredulous. "Shopping?"

"Luggage," I explain. "It's not an area I've put a lot of time into. I should have done, I know, but . . ."

"Well . . . never mind," says Luke, his mouth twisting into a smile. "As a nonexpert, which one would you choose?"

Well, that's different.

"Hmm," I say, and get to my feet in a businesslike manner. "Well, let's have a closer look."

God, we have fun. We line up eight suitcases in a row, and give them marks for looks, heaviness, quality of lining, number of interior pockets, and efficiency of wheels. (I test this by striding the length of the department, pulling the case behind me. By this time, the assistant has just given up and left us to it.) Then we look to see if they have a matching holdall and give that marks, too.

The prices don't seem to matter to Luke. Which is a bloody good thing, because they're astronomical—and at first sight, so scary, they make me want to run away. But it's amazing how quickly £1,000 can start to seem like a very reasonable sum for a suitcase—especially since the Louis Vuitton monogrammed trunk costs about ten times as much. In fact, after a while I find myself thinking quite seriously that I too should really invest in a quality suitcase, instead of my battered old canvas bag.

But today is Luke's shopping trip, not mine. And, strangely enough, it's almost more fun choosing for someone else than for yourself. In the end, we narrow it down to a dark green leather case, which has wonderful trundly wheels, or the palest beige calfskin case, which is a bit heavier, but has a stunning silk lining and is so soft, I can't stop running my fingers over it. And it has a matching holdall and vanity case—and they're just as beautiful. God, if it were me, I'd . . .

But then, it's not up to me, is it? It's Luke who's buying the case. He's the one who's got to choose. We sit down on the floor, side by side, and look at them.

"The green one would be more practical," says Luke eventually.

"Mmm," I say noncommittally. "I suppose it would."

"It's lighter—and the wheels are better."

"Mmm."

"And that pale calfskin would probably scuff in a matter of minutes. Green's a more sensible color."

"Mmm," I say, trying to sound as though I agree with him.

He gives me a quizzical look and says, "Right, well, I think we've made our choice, don't you?" And, still sitting on the floor, he calls over the assistant.

"Yes, sir?" says the assistant, and Luke nods at him.

"I'd like to buy one of these pale beige suitcases, please."

"Oh!" I say, and I can't stop a smile of delight spreading over my face. "You're getting the one I liked best!"

"Rule of life," says Luke, getting to his feet and brushing down his trousers. "If you bother to ask someone's advice, then bother to listen to it."

"But I didn't say which one . . ."

"You didn't have to," says Luke, reaching out a hand to pull me to my feet. "Your mmms gave it all away."

His hand is surprisingly strong round mine, and as he pulls me up, I feel a slight swooping in my stomach. He smells nice, too. Some expensive aftershave, which I don't recognize. For a moment, neither of us says anything.

"Right," says Luke at last. "Well, I'd better pay for it, I suppose."

"Yes," I say, suddenly feeling ridiculously nervous. "Yes, I suppose you had."

He walks off to the checkout and starts talking to the assistant, and I perch next to a display of leather suit-carriers, suddenly feeling a bit awkward. I mean, what happens next?

Well, we'll just say good-bye politely, won't we? Luke'll probably have to get back to the office. He can't hang around shopping all day. And if he asks me what I'm doing next, I tell myself, I really will say I'm busy. I'll pretend I've got some important meeting arranged or something.

"All sorted out," he says, coming back. "Rebecca, I'm incredibly grateful to you for your help."

"Great!" I say brightly. "Well, I must be on my—"

"So I was wondering," says Luke, before I can continue. "Would you like some lunch?"

This is turning into my perfect day. Shopping at Harrods, and lunch at Harvey Nichols. I mean, what could be better than that? We go straight up to the Fifth Floor restaurant, and Luke orders a bottle of chilled white wine and raises his glass in a toast.

"To luggage," he says, and smiles.

"Luggage," I reply happily, and take a sip. It's just about the most delicious wine I've ever tasted. Luke picks up his menu and starts to read it, and I pick mine up, too—but to be honest, I'm not reading a word. I'm just sitting in a happy glow. I'm looking around with relish at all the smart women coming in to have lunch here, and making notes of their outfits and wondering where that girl over there got her pink boots from. And now, for some reason, I'm thinking about that nice card Luke sent me. And I'm wondering whether it was just being friendly—or . . . or whether it was something else.

At this thought, my stomach flips so hard I almost feel sick, and very quickly I take another sip of wine. Well, a gulp, really. Then I put down my glass, count to five, and say casually, "Thanks for your card, by the way."

"What?" he says, looking up. "Oh, you're welcome." He reaches for his glass and takes a sip of wine. "It was nice to bump into you that night."

"It's a great place," I say. "Great for table-hopping."

As soon as I've said this, I feel myself blush. But Luke just smiles and says, "Indeed." Then he puts down his glass and says, "Do you know what you want?"

"Ahm . . ." I say, glancing hurriedly at the menu. "I think I'll just have . . . erm . . . fish cakes. And rocket salad."

Damn, I've just spotted squid. I should have had that. Oh well, too late now.

"Good choice," says Luke, smiling at me. "And thanks again for coming along today. It's always good to have a second opinion."

"No problem," I say lightly, and take a sip of wine. "Hope you enjoy the case."

"Oh, it's not for me," he says after a pause. "It's for Sacha."

"Oh, right," I say pleasantly. "Who's Sacha? Your sister?"

"My girlfriend," says Luke, and turns away to beckon to a waiter.

And I stare at him, unable to move.

His girlfriend. I've been helping him choose a suitcase for his girlfriend.

Suddenly I don't feel hungry anymore. I don't want fish cakes and rocket salad. I don't even want to be here. My happy glow is fading away, and underneath I feel chilly and rather stupid. Luke Brandon's got a girlfriend. Of course he has. Some beautiful smart girl called Sacha, who has manicured nails and travels everywhere with expensive cases. I'm a fool, aren't I? I should have known there'd be a Sacha somewhere on the scene. I mean, it's obvious.

Except . . . Except it's not that obvious. In fact, it's not obvious at all. Luke hasn't mentioned his girlfriend all morning. Why hasn't he? Why didn't he just *say* the suitcase was for her in the first place? Why did he let me sit on the floor beside him in Harrods and laugh as I marched up and down, testing the wheels? I wouldn't have behaved anything like that if I'd known we were buying a case for his girlfriend. And he must have known that. He must have known.

A cold feeling begins to creep over me. This is all wrong.

"All right?" says Luke, turning back to me.

"No," I hear myself saying. "No, it's not. You didn't tell me that case was for your girlfriend. You didn't even tell me you *had* a girlfriend."

Oh God. I've done it now. I've been completely uncool. But somehow I don't care.

"I see," says Luke after a pause. He picks up a piece of bread and begins to break it up with his fingers, then looks up. "Sacha and I have been together awhile now," he says kindly. "I'm sorry if I gave . . . any other impression."

He's patronizing me. I can't bear it.

"That's not the point," I say, feeling my cheeks flushing beet red. "It's just . . . it's all wrong."

"Wrong?" he says, looking amused.

"You should have told me we were choosing a case for your girlfriend," I say doggedly, staring down at the table. "It would have made things . . . different."

There's silence and I raise my eyes, to see Luke looking at me as though I'm crazy.

"Rebecca," he says, "you're getting this all out of proportion. I wanted your opinion on suitcases. End of story."

"And are you going to tell your girlfriend you asked my advice?"

"Of course I am!" says Luke, and gives a little laugh. "I expect she'll be rather amused."

I stare at him in silence, feeling mortification creep over me. My throat's tight, and there's a pain growing in my chest. *Amused.* Sacha will be amused when she hears about me.

Well, of course she will. Who wouldn't be amused by hearing about the girl who spent her entire morning testing out suitcases for another woman? The girl who got completely the wrong end of the stick. The girl who was so stupid, she thought Luke Brandon might actually like her.

I swallow hard, feeling sick with humiliation. For the first time, I'm realizing how Luke Brandon sees me. How they all see me. I'm just the comedy turn, aren't I? I'm the scatty girl who gets things wrong and makes people laugh. The girl who didn't know SBG and Rutland Bank had merged. The girl no one would ever think of taking seriously. Luke didn't bother telling me we were choosing a suitcase for his girlfriend because I don't matter. He's only buying me lunch because he hasn't got anything else to do—and probably because he thinks I might do something entertaining like drop my fork, which he can laugh about when he gets back to the office.

"I'm sorry," I say in a wobbly voice, and stand up. "I haven't got time for lunch after all."

"Rebecca, don't be silly!" says Luke. "Look, I'm sorry you didn't know about my girlfriend." He raises his eyebrows quizzically, and I almost want to hit him. "But we can still be friends, can't we?"

"No," I say stiffly, aware that my voice is thick and my eyes smarting. "No, we can't. Friends treat each other with respect. But you don't respect me, do you, Luke? You just think I'm a joke. A nothing. Well . . ." I swallow hard. "Well, I'm not."

And before he can say anything else I turn and quickly make my way out of the restaurant, half blinded by disappointed tears.

PGNI FIRST BANK VISA

7 CAMEL SQUARE
LIVERPOOL L1 5NP

Ms. Rebecca Bloomwood
Flat 2
4 Burney Rd.
London SW6 8FD

15 March 2000

Dear Ms. Bloomwood:

PGNI First Bank VISA Card No. 1475839204847586

Thank you for your payment of £10.00, received on 13 March.

As I have pointed out several times, the minimum payment required was in fact £105.40.

The balance currently overdue is therefore £95.40. I look forward to receiving your payment as soon as possible.

If satisfactory payment is not received within seven days, further action will have to be taken.

Yours sincerely,

Peter Johnson
Customer Accounts Executive

BANK OF LONDON
LONDON HOUSE MILL STREET EC3R 4DW

Ms. Rebecca Boomwood
Flat 2
4 Burney Rd.
London SW6 8FD

18 March 2000

Dear Ms. Boomwood:

Just think . . .

What kind of difference would a personal loan make to your life?

A new car, perhaps. Improvements to the home. A boat for those weekend breaks. Or maybe just the peace of mind, knowing that all those bills can easily be taken care of.

Bank of London will offer loans for almost any purpose—so don't wait any longer! Turn your life into the lifestyle you deserve.

With a Bank of London Easifone Loan, you don't even have to fill in any forms. Simply call one of our friendly 24-hour operators on **0100 45 46 47 48** and let us do the rest.

Just think . . .

We look forward to hearing from you.

Yours sincerely,

Sue Skepper
Marketing Executive

P.S. Why delay? Pick up the phone now and dial 0100 45 46 47 48. It couldn't be easier!

Twelve

I ARRIVE HOME that afternoon, feeling weary and miserable. Suddenly, triple-A-rated jobs in banking and Harrods with Luke Brandon seem miles away. Real life isn't swanning round Knightsbridge in a taxi, choosing £1,000 suitcases, is it? This is real life. Home to a tiny flat which still smells of curry, and a pile of nasty letters from the bank, and no idea what to do about them.

I put my key in the lock, and as I open the door, I hear Suze cry, "Bex? Is that you?"

"Yes!" I say, trying to sound cheerful. "Where are you?"

"Here," she says, appearing at the door of my bedroom. Her face is all pink, and there's a shine in her eyes. "Guess what! I've got a surprise for you!"

"What is it?" I say, putting down my briefcase. To be honest, I'm not in the mood for one of Suze's surprises. She'll just have moved my bed to a different place, or something. And all I want is to sit down and have a cup of tea and something to eat. I never did get any lunch.

"Come and see. No, no, shut your eyes, first. I'll lead you."

"OK," I say reluctantly. I close my eyes and allow her to take my hand. We start to walk along the corridor—and of course, as we near my bedroom door, I start feeling a little tingle of anticipation in spite of myself. I always fall for things like this.

"Da-daaa! You can look now!"

I open my eyes and look dazedly around my room, wondering what mad thing Suze has done. At least she hasn't painted the walls or touched the curtains, and my computer's safely switched off. So what on earth can she have . . .

And then I see them. On my bed. Piles and piles of upholstered frames. All made up perfectly, with no wonky corners, and the braid glued neatly in place. I can't quite believe my eyes. There must be at least . . .

"I've done a hundred," says Suze behind me. "And I'm going to do the rest tomorrow! Aren't they fab?"

I turn and stare incredulously at her. "You . . . you did all these?"

"Yes!" she says proudly. "It was easy, once I got into a rhythm. I did it in front of *Morning Coffee*. Oh, I wish you'd seen it. They had *such* a good phone-in, about men who dress up in women's clothes! Emma was being all sympathetic, but Rory looked like he wanted to—"

"Wait," I say, trying to get my head round this. "Wait. Suze, I don't understand. This must have taken you *ages*." My eye runs disbelievingly over the pile of frames again. "Why . . . why on earth did you—"

"Well, you weren't getting very far with them, were you?" says Suze. "I just thought I'd give you a helping hand."

"A helping hand?" I echo weakly.

"I'll do the rest tomorrow, and then I'll ring up the delivery people," says Suze. "You know, it's a very good system. You don't have to post them, or anything. They just come and pick them up! And then they'll send you a check. It should come to about £284. Pretty good, huh?"

"Hang on." I turn round. "What do you mean, they'll send me a check?" Suze looks at me as though I'm stupid.

"Well, Bex, they are *your* frames."

"But you made them! Suze, you should get the money!"

"But I did them for you!" says Suze, and stares at me. "I did them so you could make your three hundred quid!"

I stare at her silently, feeling a sudden thickness in my throat. Suze made all these frames for me. Slowly I sit down on the bed, pick up one of the frames, and run my finger along the fabric. It's absolutely perfect. You could sell it in Liberty's.

"Suze, it's your money. Not mine," I say eventually. "It's your project now."

"Well, that's where you're wrong," says Suze, and a triumphant look spreads over her face. "I've got my own project."

She comes over to the bed, reaches behind the pile of made-up frames, and pulls something out. It's a photo frame, but it's nothing like a Fine Frame. It's upholstered in silver furry fabric, and the word ANGEL is appliquéd in pink across the top, and there are little silver pom-poms at the corners. It's the coolest, kitschest frame I've ever seen.

"Do you like it?" she says, a bit nervously.

"I love it!" I say, grabbing it from her hands and looking more closely at it. "Where did you get it?"

"I didn't get it anywhere," she says. "I made it."

"What?" I stare at her. "You . . . made this?"

"Yes. During *Neighbours*. It was awful, actually. Beth found out about Joey and Skye."

I'm completely astounded. How come Suze suddenly turns out to be so talented?

"So what do you reckon?" she says, taking the frame back and turning it over in her fingers. "Could I sell these?"

Could she sell these?

"Suze," I say quite seriously. "You're going to be a millionaire."

And we spend the rest of the evening getting very pissed and eating ice cream, as we always do when something good or bad happens to either one of us. We map out Suze's career as a high-flying businesswoman, and get quite hysterical trying to decide if she should wear Chanel or Prada when she goes to meet the queen. Somehow the discussion ends with us trying on each other's smartest outfits (Suze looks really good in my new Hobbs dress, much better than me), and by the time I get into bed, I've forgotten all about Luke Brandon, and Bank of Helsinki, and the rest of my disastrous day.

The next morning, it all comes rushing back to me like a horror movie. I wake up feeling pale and shaky, and desperately wishing I could take a sickie. I don't want to go to work. I want to stay at home under the duvet, watching daytime telly and being a millionairess entrepreneur with Suze.

But it's the busiest week of the month, and Philip'll never believe I'm ill.

So, somehow, I haul myself out of bed and into some clothes and onto the tube. At Lucio's I buy myself an extralarge cappuccino, and a muffin, *and* a chocolate brownie. I don't care if I get fat. I just need sugar and caffeine and chocolate, and as much as possible.

Luckily it's so busy, no one's talking very much, so I don't have to bother telling everyone at the office what I did on my day off. Clare's tapping away at something and there's a pile of pages on my desk, ready for me to proofread. So after checking my e-mails—none—I scrunch miserably up in my chair, pick up the first one, and start to scan it.

"Market efficiencies dictate that greater risks must accompany greater reward. Fund managers understand the balance sheets and market momentum driving volatile stocks."

Oh God, this is boring.

"These experts therefore minimize risk in a way that the average investor cannot. For the small-time investor . . ."

"Rebecca?" I look up, to see Philip approaching my desk, holding a piece of paper. He doesn't look very happy, and for one terrible moment, I think he's spoken to Jill Foxton at William Green, has discovered everything, and is about to fire me. But as he gets nearer, I see it's only some dull-looking press release.

"I want you to go to this instead of me," he says. "It's on Friday. I'd go myself, but I'm going to be tied up here with Marketing."

"Oh," I say without enthusiasm, and take the piece of paper. "OK. What is it?"

"Personal Finance Fair at Olympia," he says. "We always cover it."

Yawn. Yawn yawn yawn . . .

"Barclays are giving a champagne lunchtime reception," he adds.

"Oh right!" I say, with more interest. "Well, OK. It sounds quite good. What exactly is it—"

I glance down at the paper, and my heart stops as I see the Brandon Communications logo at the top of the page.

"It's basically just a big fair," says Philip. "All sectors of personal finance. Talks, stands, events. Just cover whatever sounds interesting. I leave it up to you."

"OK," I say after a pause. "Fine."

I mean, what do I care if Luke Brandon might be there? I'll just ignore him. I'll show him about as much respect as he showed me. And if he tries to talk to me, I'll just lift my chin firmly in the air, and turn on my heel, and . . .

"How are the pages going?" says Philip.

"Oh, great," I say, and pick the top one up again. "Should be finished soon." He gives a little nod and walks away, and I begin to read again.

". . . for the small-time investor, the risks attached to such stocks may outweigh the potential for reward."

Oh God, this is boring. I can't even bring myself to focus on what the words mean.

"More and more investors are therefore demanding the combination of stock-market performance with a high level of security.

One option is to invest in a Tracker fund, which automatically 'tracks' the top one hundred companies at any time . . ."

Hmm. Actually, that gives me a thought. I reach for my Filofax, flip it open, and dial Elly's new direct number at Wetherby's.

"Eleanor Granger," comes her voice, sounding a bit far-off and echoey. Must be a dodgy line.

"Hi, Elly, it's Becky," I say. "Listen, whatever happened to Tracker bars? They're really yummy, aren't they? And I haven't eaten one for . . ."

There's a scuffly sort of sound on the line, and I gape at the receiver in surprise. In the distance, I can hear Elly, saying "I'm sorry. I'll just be a . . ."

"Becky!" she hisses down the phone. "I was on speaker-phone! Our head of department was in my office."

"Oh God!" I say, aghast. "Sorry! Is he still there?"

"No," says Elly, and sighs. "God knows what he thinks of me now."

"Oh well," I say reassuringly. "He's got a sense of humor, hasn't he?"

Elly doesn't reply.

"Oh well," I say again, less certainly. "Anyway, are you free for a drink at lunchtime?"

"Not really," she says. "Sorry, Becky, I've really got to go." And she puts the phone down.

No one likes me anymore. Suddenly I feel a bit small and sad, and I scrunch up even more in my chair. Oh God, I hate today. I hate everything. I want to go hooome.

By the time Friday arrives, I have to say I feel a lot more cheerful. This is primarily because:

1. It's Friday.
2. I'm spending all day out of the office.
3. Elly phoned yesterday and said sorry she was so

abrupt, but someone else came into the office just as we were talking. *And* she's going to be at the Personal Finance Fair.

Plus:

4. I have completely put the Luke Brandon incident from my mind. Who cares about him, anyway?

So as I get ready to go, I feel quite bouncy and positive. I put on my new gray cardigan over a short black shirt, and my new Hobbs boots—dark gray suede—and I have to say, I look bloody good in them. God, I love new clothes. If everyone could just wear new clothes every day, I reckon depression wouldn't exist anymore.

As I'm about to leave, a pile of letters comes through the letterbox for me. Several of them look like bills, and one is yet another letter from Endwich Bank. But I have a clever new solution to all these nasty letters: I just put them in my dressing table drawer and close it. It's the only way to stop getting stressed out about it. And it really does work. As I thrust the drawer shut and head out of the front door, I've already forgotten all about them.

The conference is buzzing by the time I get there. I give my name to the press officer at reception and I'm given a big, shiny courtesy carrier bag with the logo of HSBC on the side. Inside this, I find an enormous press pack complete with a photo of all the conference organizers lifting glasses of champagne to each other, a voucher for two drinks at the Sun Alliance Pimm's Stand, a raffle ticket to win £1,000 (invested in the unit trust of my choice), a big lollipop advertising Eastgate Insurance, and my name badge with PRESS stamped across the top. There's also a white envelope with the ticket to the Barclays Champagne Reception inside, and I put that carefully in my bag. Then I fasten my name badge prominently on my lapel and start to walk around the arena.

Normally, of course, the rule is to throw away your name badge. But the great thing about being PRESS at one of these events is that people fall over themselves to ply you with free stuff. A lot of it's just boring old leaflets about savings plans, but some of them are giving out free gifts and snacks, too. So after an hour, I've accumulated two pens, a paper knife, a mini box of Ferrero Rocher chocolates, a helium balloon with Save & Prosper on the side, and a T-shirt with a cartoon on the front, sponsored by some mobile phone company. I've had two free cappuccinos, a *pain au chocolat,* some apple cider (from Somerset Savings), a mini pack of Smarties, and my Pimm's from Sun Alliance. (I haven't written a single note in my notebook, or asked a single question—but never mind.)

I've seen that some people are carrying quite neat little silver desk clocks, and I wouldn't mind one of those, so I'm just wandering along, trying to work out what direction they're coming from, when a voice says, "Becky!"

I look up—and it's Elly! She's standing at the Wetherby's display with a couple of guys in suits, waving at me to come over.

"Hi!" I say delightedly. "How *are* you?"

"Fine!" she says, beaming. "Really getting along well." And she does look the part, I have to say. She's wearing a bright red suit (Karen Millen, no doubt), and some really nice square-toed shoes, and her hair's tied back. The only thing I don't go for is the earrings. Why is she suddenly wearing pearl earrings? Maybe it's just to blend in with the others.

"God, I can't believe you're actually one of them!" I say, lowering my voice slightly. "I'll be interviewing you next!" I tilt my head earnestly, like Martin Bashir on *Panorama*. " 'Ms. Granger, could you tell me the aims and principles of Wetherby's Investments?' "

Elly gives a little laugh, then reaches into a box beside her.

"I'll give you this," she says, and hands me a brochure.

"Oh thanks," I say ironically, and stuff it into my bag. I suppose she has to look good in front of her colleagues.

"It's actually quite an exciting time at Wetherby's," continues Elly. "You know we're launching a whole new range of funds next month? There are five altogether. UK Growth, UK Prospects, European Growth, European Prospects, and . . ."

Why is she telling me this, exactly?

"Elly . . ."

"And US Growth!" she finishes triumphantly. There isn't a flicker of humor in her eyes. Suddenly I find myself remembering Luke saying he wasn't surprised by Elly joining Wetherby's.

"Right," I say after a pause. "Well, that sounds . . . fab!"

"I could arrange for our PR people to give you a call, if you like," she says. "Fill you in a bit more."

What?

"No," I say hurriedly. "No, it's OK. So, erm . . . what are you doing afterward? Do you want to go for a drink?"

"No can do," she says apologetically. "I'm going to look at a flat."

"Are you moving?" I say in surprise. Elly lives in the coolest flat in Camden, with two guys who are in a band and get her into loads of free gigs and stuff. I can't think why she'd want to move.

"Actually, I'm buying," she says. "I'm looking around Streatham, Tooting . . . I just want to get on the first rung of that property ladder."

"Right," I say feebly. "Good idea."

"You should do it yourself, you know, Becky," she says. "You can't hang around in a student flat forever. Real life has to begin sometime!" She glances at one of her men in suits, and he gives a little laugh.

It's not a student flat, I think indignantly. And anyway, who defines "real life"? Who says "real life" is property ladders and hideous pearl earrings? "Shit-boring tedious life," more like.

"Are you going to the Barclays Champagne Reception?" I say as a last gasp, thinking maybe we can go and have some fun together. But she pulls a little face and shakes her head.

"I might pop in," she says, "but I'll be quite tied up here."

"OK," I say. "Well, I'll . . . I'll see you later."

I move away from the stand and slowly start walking toward the corner where the Champagne Reception's being held, feeling slightly dispirited. In spite of myself, a part of me starts wondering if maybe Elly's right and I'm wrong. Maybe I should be talking about property ladders and growth funds, too. Oh God, I'm missing the gene which makes you grow up and buy a flat in Streatham and start visiting Homebase every weekend. Everyone's moving on without me, into a world I don't understand.

But as I get near the entrance to the Champagne Reception, I feel my spirits rising. Whose spirits *don't* rise at the thought of free champagne? It's all being held in a huge tent, and there's a huge banner, and a band playing music, and a girl in a sash at the entrance, handing out Barclays key rings. When she sees my badge, she gives me a wide smile, hands me a white glossy press pack, and says, "Bear with me a moment." Then she walks off to a little group of people, murmurs in the ear of a man in a suit, and comes back. "Someone will be with you soon," she says. "In the meantime, let me get you a glass of champagne."

You see what I mean about being PRESS? Everywhere you go, you get special treatment. I accept a glass of champagne, stuff the press pack into my carrier bag, and take a sip. Oh, it's delicious. Icy cold and sharp and bubbly. Maybe I'll stay here for a couple of hours, I think, just drinking champagne until there's none left. They won't dare chuck me out, I'm PRESS. In fact, maybe I'll . . .

"Rebecca. Glad you could make it."

I look up and feel myself freeze. The man in the suit was Luke Brandon. Luke Brandon's standing in front of me, with an expression I can't quite read. And suddenly I feel sick. All that stuff I planned about playing it cool and icy isn't going to work—

because just seeing his face, I feel hot with humiliation, all over again.

"Hi," I mutter, looking down. Why am I even saying hi to him?

"I was hoping you'd come," he says in a low, serious voice. "I very much wanted to—"

"Yes," I interrupt. "Well, I . . . I can't talk, I've got to mingle. I'm here to work, you know."

I'm trying to sound dignified, but there's a wobble in my voice, and I can feel my cheeks flush as he keeps gazing at me. So I turn away before he can say anything else, and march off toward the other side of the tent. I don't quite know where I'm heading, but I've just got to keep walking until I find someone to talk to.

The trouble is, I can't see anyone I recognize. It's all just groups of bank-type people laughing loudly together and talking about golf. They all seem really tall and broad-shouldered, and I can't even catch anyone's eye. God, this is embarrassing. I feel like a six-year-old at a grown-up's party. In the corner I spot Moira Channing from the *Daily Herald,* and she gives me a half flicker of recognition—but I'm certainly not going to talk to her. OK, just keep walking, I tell myself. Pretend you're on your way somewhere. Don't panic.

Then I see Luke Brandon on the other side of the tent. His head jerks up as he sees me, and and he starts heading toward me. Oh God, quick. Quick. I've *got* to find somebody to talk to.

Right, how about this couple standing together? The guy's middle-aged, the woman's quite a lot younger, and they don't look as if they know too many people, either. Thank God. Whoever they are, I'll just ask them how they're enjoying the Personal Finance Fair and whether they're finding it useful, and pretend I'm making notes for my article. And when Luke Brandon arrives, I'll be too engrossed in conversation even to notice him. OK, go.

I take a gulp of champagne, approach the man, and smile brightly.

"Hi there," I say. "Rebecca Bloomwood, *Successful Saving*."

"Hello," he says, turning toward me and extending his hand. "Derek Smeath from Endwich Bank. And this is my assistant, Erica."

Oh my God.

I can't speak. I can't shake his hand. I can't run. My whole body's paralyzed.

"Hi!" says Erica, giving me a friendly smile. "I'm Erica Parnell."

"Yes," I say, after a huge pause. "Yes, hi."

Please don't recognize my name. Please don't recognize my voice.

"Are you a journalist, then?" she says, looking at my name badge and frowning. "Your name seems quite familiar."

"Yes," I manage. "Yes, you . . . you might have read some of my articles."

"I expect I have," she says, and takes an unconcerned sip of champagne. "We get all the financial mags in the office. Quite good, some of them."

Slowly the circulation is returning to my body. It's going to be OK, I tell myself. They don't have a clue.

"You journalists have to be expert on everything, I suppose," says Derek, who has given up trying to shake my hand and is swigging his champagne instead.

"Yes, we do really," I reply, and risk a smile. "We get to know all areas of personal finance—from banking to unit trusts to life insurance."

"And how do you acquire all this knowledge?"

"Oh, we just pick it up along the way," I say smoothly.

You know what? This is quite fun, actually, now that I've relaxed. And Derek Smeath isn't at all scary in the flesh. In fact, he's rather cozy and friendly, like some nice sitcom uncle.

"I've often thought," says Erica Parnell, "that they should do a fly-on-the-wall documentary about a bank." She gives me an expectant look and I nod vigorously.

"Good idea!" I say. "I think that would be fascinating."

"You should *see* some of the characters we get in! People who have absolutely no idea about their finances. Don't we, Derek?"

"You'd be amazed," says Derek. "Utterly amazed. The lengths people go to, just to avoid paying off their overdrafts! Or even talking to us!"

"Really?" I say, as though astonished.

"You wouldn't believe it!" says Erica. "I sometimes wonder—"

"Rebecca!" A voice booms behind me and I turn round in shock to see Philip, clutching a glass of champagne and grinning at me. What's *he* doing here?

"Hi," he says. "Marketing canceled the meeting, so I thought I'd pop along after all. How's it all going?"

"Oh, great!" I say, and take a gulp of champagne. "This is Derek, and Erica . . . this is my editor, Philip Page."

"Endwich Bank, eh?" says Philip, looking at Derek Smeath's name badge. "You must know Martin Gollinger, then."

"We're not head office, I'm afraid," says Derek, giving a little laugh. "I'm the manager of our Fulham branch."

"Fulham!" says Philip. "Trendy Fulham."

And suddenly a warning bell goes off in my head. Dong-dong-dong! I've got to do something. I've got to say something; change the subject. But it's too late. I'm the spectator on the mountain, watching the trains collide in the valley below.

"Rebecca lives in Fulham," Philip's saying. "Who do you bank with, Rebecca? You're probably one of Derek's customers!" He laughs loudly at his own joke, and Derek laughs politely, too.

But I can't laugh. I'm frozen to the spot, watching Erica Parnell's face as it changes. As realization slowly dawns. She meets my eye, and I feel something icy drip down my spine.

"Rebecca Bloomwood," she says, in quite a different voice. "I *thought* I knew that name. Do you live in Burney Road, Rebecca?"

"That's clever!" says Philip. "How did you know that?" And he takes another swig of champagne.

Shut up, Philip, I think frantically. Shut *up*.

"So you do?" Her voice is sweet but sharp. Oh God, now Philip's looking at me, waiting for me to answer.

"Yes," I say in a strangled voice. I'm gripping my champagne glass so hard, I think I might break it.

"Derek, have you realized who this is?" says Erica pleasantly. "This is Rebecca Bloomwood, one of our customers. I think you spoke to her the other day. Remember?" Her voice hardens. "The one with the dead dog?"

There's silence. I don't dare look at Derek Smeath's face. I don't dare look at anything except the floor.

"Well, there's a coincidence!" says Philip. "More champagne, anyone?"

"Rebecca Bloomwood," says Derek Smeath. He sounds quite faint. "I don't believe it."

"Yes!" I say, desperately slugging back the last of my champagne. "Ha-ha-ha! It's a small world. Well, I must be off and interview some more . . ."

"Wait!" says Erica, her voice like a dagger. "We were hoping to have a little meeting with you, Rebecca. Weren't we, Derek?"

"Indeed we were," says Derek Smeath. I feel a sudden trickle of fear. This man isn't like a cozy sitcom uncle anymore. He's like a scary exam monitor, who's just caught you cheating. "That is," he adds pointedly, "assuming your legs are both intact and you aren't suffering from any dreaded lurgey?"

"What's this?" says Philip cheerfully.

"How *is* the leg, by the way?" says Erica sweetly.

"Fine," I mumble. "Fine, thanks."

"Good," says Derek Smeath. "So we'll say Monday at nine-thirty, shall we?" He looks at Philip. "You don't mind if Rebecca joins us for a quick meeting on Monday morning, do you?"

"Of course not!" says Philip.

"And if she doesn't turn up," says Derek Smeath, "we'll know where to find her, won't we?" He gives me a sharp look, and I feel my stomach contract in fright.

"Rebecca'll turn up!" says Philip. He gives me a jokey grin, lifts his glass, and wanders off. Oh God, I think in panic. Don't leave me alone with them.

"Well, I'll look forward to seeing you," says Derek Smeath. He pauses, and gives me a beady look. "And if I remember rightly from our telephone conversation the other day, you'll be coming into some funds by then."

Oh shit. I thought he'd have forgotten about that.

"That's right," I say after a pause. "Absolutely. My aunt's money. Well remembered! My aunt left me some money recently," I explain to Erica Parnell.

Erica Parnell doesn't look impressed.

"Good," says Derek Smeath. "Then I'll expect you on Monday."

"Fine," I say, and smile even more confidently at him. "Looking forward to it already!"

OCTAGON ▸ *flair...style...vision*

FINANCIAL SERVICES DEPARTMENT
8TH FLOOR TOWER HOUSE
LONDON ROAD WINCHESTER S0 44 3DR

Ms. Rebecca Bloomwood
Flat 2
4 Burney Rd.
London SW6 8FD

Charge Card Number 7854 4567

15 March 2000

Dear Ms. Bloomwood:

FINAL REMINDER

Further to my letter of 9 March, there is still an outstanding balance of £235.76 on your Octagon Silver Card. Should payment not arrive within the next seven days, your account will be frozen and further action will be taken.

I was glad to hear that you have found the Lord and accepted Jesus Christ as your savior; unfortunately this has no bearing on the matter.

I look forward to receiving your payment shortly.

Yours sincerely,

Grant Ellesmore
Customer Finance Manager

Thirteen

THIS IS BAD. I mean, I'm not just being paranoid, am I? This is really bad.

As I sit on the tube on my way home, I stare at my reflection—outwardly calm and relaxed. But inside, my mind's scurrying around like a spider, trying to find a way out. Round and round and round, legs flailing, no escape . . . OK, stop. Stop! Calm down and let's go through the options one more time.

Option One: Go to meeting and tell the truth.

I just can't. I *can't* go along on Monday morning and admit that there isn't £1,000 from my aunt and there never will be. What will they do to me? They'll get all serious, won't they? They'll sit me down and start going through all my expenditures and . . . Oh God, I feel sick at the thought of it. I can't do it. I can't go. End of story.

Option Two: Go to meeting and lie.

So, what, tell them the £1,000 is absolutely on its way, and that further funds will be coming through soon. Hmm. Possible. The trouble is, I don't think they'll believe me. So they'll still get all serious, sit me down, give me a lecture. No way.

Option Three: Don't go to meeting.

But if I don't, Derek Smeath will phone Philip and they'll start talking. Maybe the whole story will come out, and he'll find out I didn't actually break my leg. Or have glandular fever. And after that I won't ever be able to go back into the office. I'll be unemployed. My life will be over at the age of twenty-five.

Option Four: Go to meeting with check for £1,000.

Perfect. Waltz in, hand over the check, say "Will there be anything else?" and waltz out again.

But how do I get £1,000 before Monday morning? *How?*

Option Five: Run away.

Which would be very childish and immature. Not worth considering.

I wonder where I could go? Maybe abroad somewhere. Las Vegas. Yes, and I could win a fortune at the casinos. A million pounds or something. Even more, perhaps. And then, yes, then I'd fax Derek Smeath, saying I'm closing my bank account due to his lack of faith in me.

God yes! Wouldn't that be great? "Dear Mr. Smeath, I was a little surprised at your recent implication that I have insufficient funds to cover my overdraft. As this check for £1.2 million shows, I have ample funds at my disposal, which I will shortly be moving to one of your competitors. Perhaps they will treat me with more respect. P.S., I am copying this letter to your superiors."

I love this idea so much, I lean back and wallow in it for a while, amending the letter over and over in my head. "Dear Mr. Smeath, as I tried to inform you discreetly at our last encounter, I am in fact a millionairess. If only you had trusted me, things might have been different."

God, he'll be sorry, won't he? He'll probably phone up and apologize. Try and keep my business and say he hadn't meant to offend me. But it'll be too late. Hah! Ha-ha-ha-ha . . .

Oh blast. Missed my stop.

When I get home, Suze is sitting on the floor, surrounded by magazines.

"Hi!" she says brightly. "Guess what? I'm going to be in *Vogue*!"

"What?" I say disbelievingly. "Were you spotted on the streets or something?" Suze has got an excellent figure. She could easily be a model. But still . . . *Vogue*!

"Not me, silly!" she says. "My frames."

"Your *frames* are going to be in *Vogue*?" Now I really am disbelieving.

"In the June issue! I'm going to be in a piece called 'Just Relax: Designers Who Are Bringing the Fun Back into Interiors.' It's cool, isn't it? The only thing is, I've only made two frames so far, so I need to make a few more in case people want to buy them."

"Right," I say, trying to grasp all this. "So—how come *Vogue* is doing a piece about you? Did they . . . hear about you?" I mean, she only started making frames four days ago!

"No, silly!" she says, and laughs. "I phoned up Lally. Have you met Lally?" I shake my head. "Well, she's fashion editor of *Vogue* now, and she spoke to Perdy, who's the interiors editor, and Perdy phoned me back—and when I told her what my frames were like, she just went wild."

"Gosh," I say. "Well done."

"She told me what to say in my interview, too," Suze adds, and clears her throat importantly. "I want to create spaces for people to enjoy, not admire. There's a bit of the child in all of us. Life's too short for minimalism."

"Oh right," I say. "Great!"

"No, wait, there was something else, too." Suze frowns thoughtfully. "Oh yes, my designs are inspired by the imaginative spirit of Gaudi. I'm going to phone up Charlie now," she adds happily. "I'm *sure* he's something at *Tatler*."

"Great," I say again.

And it is great.

I'm really glad for Suze. Of course I am. If Suze gets in *Vogue,* I'll be the proudest person in the world.

But at the same time there's a part of me that's thinking, How come everything happens so easily for her? I bet Suze has never had to face a nasty bank manager in her life. And I bet she never will have to, either.

Immediately I feel a huge spasm of guilt. Why can't I just be glad for Suze and nothing else? Dispiritedly I sink down onto the floor and begin to flip through a magazine.

"By the way," says Suze, looking up from the phone. "Tarquin rang about an hour ago, to arrange your date." She grins wickedly. "Are you looking forward to it?"

"Oh," I say dully. "Of course I am."

I'd forgotten all about it, to be honest. But it's OK—I'll just wait until tomorrow afternoon and say I've got period pain. Easy. No one ever questions that, especially men.

"Oh yes," says Suze, gesturing to a *Harper's and Queen* open on the floor. "And look who I came across just now in the Hundred Richest Bachelors list! Oh hi, Charlie," she says into the phone. "It's Suze! Listen—"

I look down at the open *Harper's and Queen* and freeze. Luke Brandon is staring out of the page at me, an easy smile on his face.

Number 31, reads the caption. *Age 32. Estimated wealth: £10 million. Scarily intelligent entrepreneur. Lives in Chelsea; currently dating Sacha de Bonneville, daughter of the French billionaire.*

I don't want to know this. Why would I be interested in who Luke Brandon is dating? Not remotely interested.

Sacha. Sacha, with her million-pound suitcase and perfect figure and whole wardrobe full of Prada. She'll have immaculate nails, won't she? Of course she will. And hair that never goes wrong. And some really sexy French accent, and incredibly long legs . . .

Anyway, I'm not interested. Savagely I flip the page backward and start reading about Number 17, who sounds much nicer.

Dave Kington. Age 28. Estimated wealth: £20 million. Former striker for Manchester United, now management guru and sportswear entrepreneur. Lives in Hertfordshire, recently split from girlfriend, model Cherisse.

And anyway, Luke Brandon's boring. Everyone says so. All he does is work. Obsessed with money, probably.

Number 16, Ernest Flight. Age 52. Estimated wealth: £22 million. Chairman and major shareholder of the Flight Foods Corporation. Lives in Nottinghamshire, recently divorced from third wife Susan.

I don't even think he's that good-looking. Too tall. And he probably doesn't go to the gym or anything. Too busy. He's probably hideous underneath his clothes.

Number 15, Tarquin Cleath-Stuart. Age 26. Estimated wealth: £25 million. Landowner since inheriting family estate at age 19. V. publicity-shy. Lives in Perthshire and London with old nanny; currently single.

Anyway, what kind of man buys luggage as a present? I mean, a *suitcase*, for God's sake, when he had the whole of Harrods to choose from. He could have bought his girlfriend a necklace, or some clothes. Or he could have . . . He could have . . .

Hang on a moment, what was that?

What was that?

No. That can't be— Surely that's not—

And suddenly, I can't breathe. I can't move. My entire frame is concentrated on the blurry picture in front of me. Tarquin Cleath-Stuart? Tarquin Suze's-Cousin? *Tarquin?*

Tarquin . . . has . . . twenty-five . . . million . . . pounds?

I think I'm going to pass out, if I can ever ungrip my hand from this page. I'm staring at the fifteenth richest bachelor in Britain—and I know him.

Not only do I know him, I'm having dinner with him tomorrow night.

OH. MY. GOD.

I'm going to be a millionairess. A multimillionairess. I knew it. Didn't I know it? I *knew* it. Tarquin's going to fall in love with me and ask me to marry him and we'll get married in a gorgeous Scottish castle just like in *Four Weddings* (except with nobody dying on us).

Of course, I'll love him, too. By then.

I know I haven't exactly been attracted to him in the past . . . but it's all a matter of willpower, isn't it? I bet that's what most long-term successful couples would say counts in a relationship. Willpower and a desire to make it work. Both of which I absolutely have. You know what? I actually fancy him more already. Well, not exactly *fancy* . . . but just the thought of him makes me feel all excited, which must mean something, mustn't it?

It's going to happen. I'm going to be Mrs. Tarquin Cleath-Stuart and have £25 million.

And what will Derek Smeath say *then*? Hah!

Hah!

"D'you want a cup of tea?" says Suze, putting down the phone. "Charlie's such a poppet. He's going to feature me in Britain's Up-and-Coming-Talent."

"Excellent," I say vaguely, and clear my throat. "Just . . . just looking at Tarquin here."

I have to check. I have to check there isn't some other Tarquin Cleath-Stuart. Please God, *please* let me be going out with the rich one.

"Oh yes," says Suze casually. "He's always in those things." She runs her eyes down the text and shakes her head. "God, they always exaggerate everything. Twenty-five million pounds!"

My heart stops.

"Hasn't he got £25 million, then?" I says carelessly.

"Oh, no!" She laughs as though the idea's ridiculous. "The estate's worth about . . . Oh, I don't know, £18 million."

Eighteen million pounds. Well, that'll do. That'll do nicely.

"These magazines!" I say, and roll my eyes sympathetically.

"Earl Grey?" says Suze, getting up. "Or normal?"

"Earl Grey," I say, even though I actually prefer Typhoo. Because I'd better start acting posh, hadn't I, if I'm going to be the girlfriend of someone called Tarquin Cleath-Stuart.

Rebecca Cleath-Stuart.

Becky Cleath-Stuart.

Hi, it's Rebecca Cleath-Stuart here. Yes, Tarquin's wife. We met at . . . Yes, I was wearing Chanel. How clever of you!

"By the way," I add, "did Tarquin say where I should meet him?"

"Oh, he's going to come and pick you up," says Suze.

But of course he is. The fifteenth richest bachelor in Britain doesn't just meet you at a tube station, does he? He doesn't just say "See you under the big clock at Waterloo." He comes and picks you up.

Oh, this is it. This is it! Forget Luke Brandon, forget suitcases. My new life has finally begun.

I have never spent so long on getting ready for a date in my life. Never. The process starts at eight on Saturday morning when I look at my open wardrobe and realize that I don't have a *single* thing to wear—and only ends at seven-thirty that evening when I give my lashes another layer of mascara, spray myself in Coco Chanel, and walk into the sitting room for Suze's verdict.

"Wow!" she says, looking up from a frame she is upholstering in distressed denim. "You look . . . bloody amazing!"

And I have to say, I agree. I'm wearing all black—but expensive black. The kind of deep, soft black you fall into. A simple sleeveless dress from Whistles, the highest of Jimmy Choos, a pair of stunning uncut amethyst earrings. And please don't ask how much it all cost, because that's irrelevant. This is investment shopping. The biggest investment of my life.

I haven't eaten anything all day so I'm nice and thin, and for once my hair has fallen perfectly into shape. I look . . . well, I've never looked better in my life.

But of course, looks are only part of the package, aren't they? Which is why I cannily stopped off at Waterstones on the way home and bought a book on Wagner. I've been reading it all afternoon, while I waited for my nails to dry, and have even memorized a few little passages to throw into the conversation.

I'm not sure what else Tarquin is into, apart from Wagner. Still, that should be enough to keep us going. And anyway, I expect he's planning to take me somewhere really glamorous with a jazz band, so we'll be too busy dancing cheek to cheek to make conversation.

The doorbell rings and I give a little start. I have to admit, my heart is pounding with nerves. But at the same time I feel strangely cool. This is it. Here begins my new multimillion-pound existence. Luke Brandon, eat your heart out.

"I'll get it," says Suze, grinning at me, and disappears out into the hall. A moment later I hear her saying "Tarkie!"

"Suze!"

I glance at myself in the mirror, take a deep breath, and turn to face the door, just as Tarquin appears. His head is as bony as ever, and he's wearing another of his odd-looking suits. But somehow none of that seems to matter anymore. In fact, I'm not really taking in the way he looks. I'm just staring at him. Staring and staring at him, unable to speak; unable to frame any thought at all except: twenty-five million pounds.

Twenty-five million pounds.

The sort of thought that makes you feel dizzy and elated, like a fairground ride. I suddenly want to run around the room, yelling "Twenty-five million! Twenty-five million!" throwing bank notes up in the air as if I were in some Hollywood comedy caper.

But I don't. Of course I don't. I say, "Hi, Tarquin," and give him a dazzling smile.

"Hi, Becky," he says. "You look wonderful."

"Thanks," I say, and look bashfully down at my dress.

"D'you want to stay for a titchy?" says Suze, who is looking on fondly, as if she's my mother and this is senior prom night and I'm dating the most popular boy in school.

"Ermm . . . no, I think we'll just get going," says Tarquin, meeting my eye. "What do you think, Becky?"

"Absolutely," I say. "Let's go."

Fourteen

A TAXI IS CHUGGING OUTSIDE in the road, and Tarquin ushers me inside. To be honest, I'm a bit disappointed it isn't a chauffeur-driven limousine—but still. This is pretty good, too. Being whisked off in a taxi by one of Britain's most eligible bachelors to . . . who knows where? The Savoy? Claridges? Dancing at Annabel's? Tarquin hasn't told me yet where we're going.

Oh God, maybe it'll be one of those mad places where everything is served under a silver dome and there's a million knives and forks and snooty waiters looking on, just waiting to catch you out.

"I thought we'd just have a nice quiet supper," says Tarquin, looking over at me.

"Lovely," I say. "Nice quiet supper. Perfect."

Thank God. That probably means we're not heading for silver domes. We're going to some tiny tucked-away place that hardly anyone knows about. Some little private club where you have to knock on an anonymous-looking door in a back street, and you get inside and it's packed with celebrities sitting on sofas, behaving like normal people. Yes! And maybe Tarquin knows them all!

But of course he knows them all. He's a multimillionaire, isn't he?

I look out of the window and see that we're driving past Harrods. And for just a moment, my stomach tightens painfully as I remember the last time I was here. Bloody suitcases. Bloody Luke Brandon. Huh. In fact, I wish he was walking along the road right now, so I could give him a careless, I'm-with-the-fifteenth-richest-single-man-in-Britain wave.

"OK," says Tarquin suddenly to the taxi driver. "You can drop us here." He grins at me. "Practically on the doorstep."

"Great," I say, and reach for the door.

Practically on the doorstep of where? As I get out I look around, wondering where on earth we're going. We're at Hyde Park Corner. What's at Hyde Park Corner? I turn round slowly, and glimpse a sign—and suddenly I realize what's going on. We're going to the Lanesborough!

Wow. How classy is that? Dinner at the Lanesborough. But naturally. Where else would one go on a first date?

"So," says Tarquin, appearing at my side. "I just thought we could get a bite to eat and then . . . see."

"Sounds good," I say, as we start walking.

Excellent! Dinner at the Lanesborough and then on to some glam nightclub. This is all shaping up wonderfully.

We walk straight past the entrance to the Lanesborough, but I'm not fazed by that. Everyone knows VIPs always go in through the back to avoid the paparazzi. Not that I can actually see any paparazzi, but it probably becomes a habit. We'll duck into some back alley, and walk through the kitchens while the chefs pretend they can't see us, and then emerge in the foyer. This is so cool.

"I'm sure you've been here before," says Tarquin apologetically. "Not the most original choice."

"Don't be silly!" I say, as we stop and head toward a pair of glass doors. "I simply adore . . ."

Hang on, where are we? This isn't the back entrance to anywhere. This is . . .

Pizza on the Park.

Tarquin's taking me to Pizza Express. I don't believe it. The fifteenth richest man in the country is taking me to bloody Pizza Express.

". . . pizza," I finish weakly. "Love the stuff."

"Oh good!" says Tarquin. "I thought we probably didn't want anywhere too flashy."

"Oh no." I pull what I think is a very convincing face. "I hate flashy places. Much better to have a nice quiet pizza together."

"That's what I thought," says Tarquin, turning to look at me. "But now I feel rather bad. You've dressed up so nicely . . ." He pauses doubtfully, gazing at my outfit. (As well he might. I didn't go and spend a fortune in Whistles for Pizza Express.) "I mean, if you wanted to, we could go somewhere a bit smarter. The Lanesborough's just around the corner . . ."

He raises his eyes questioningly, and I'm about to say "Oh, yes, please!" when suddenly, in a blinding flash, I realize what's going on. This is a test, isn't it? It's like choosing out of three caskets in a fairy tale. Everyone knows the rules. You *never* choose the gold shiny one. Or even the quite impressive silver one. What you're supposed to do is choose the dull little lead one, and then there's a flash of light and it turns into a mountain of jewels. So this is it. Tarquin's testing me, to see whether I like him for himself.

Which, frankly, I find rather insulting. I mean, who does he think I am?

"No, let's stay here," I say, and touch his arm briefly. "Much more relaxed. Much more . . . fun."

Which is actually quite true. And I do like pizza. And that yummy garlic bread. Mmm. You know, now I come to think about it, this is quite a good choice.

As the waiter hands us our menus, I give a cursory flash down the list, but I already know what I want. It's what I always have when I go to Pizza Express—Fiorentina. The one with spinach and an egg. I know, it sounds weird, but honestly, it's delicious.

"Would you like an aperitif?" says the waiter, and I'm about to say what I usually do, which is Oh, let's just have a bottle of wine, when I think, Sod it, I'm having dinner with a multi-millionaire here. I'm bloody well going to have a gin and tonic.

"A gin and tonic," I say firmly, and look at Tarquin, daring him to look taken aback. But he grins at me and says, "Unless you wanted champagne?"

"Oh," I say, completely thrown.

"I always think champagne and pizza is a good combination," he says, and looks at the waiter. "A bottle of Moet, please."

Well, this is more like it. This is a lot more like it. Champagne and pizza. And Tarquin is actually being quite normal.

The champagne arrives and we toast each other and take a few sips. I'm really starting to enjoy myself. Then I spot Tarquin's bony hand edging slowly toward mine on the table. And in a reflex action—completely without meaning to—I whip my fingers away, pretending I have to scratch my ear. A flicker of disappointment passes over his face and I find myself giving a really fake, embarrassed cough and looking intently at a picture on the wall to my left.

I can do this, I tell myself firmly. I *can* be attracted to him. It's just a matter of self-control and possibly also getting very drunk. So I lift my glass and take several huge gulps. I can feel the bubbles surging into my head, singing happily "I'm going to be a millionaire's wife! I'm going to be a millionaire's wife!" And when I look back at Tarquin, he already seems a bit more attractive (in a stoaty kind of way). Alcohol is obviously going to be the key to our marital happiness.

My head is filled with a happy vision of our wedding day. Me in some wonderful designer dress; my mum and dad looking on proudly. No more money troubles ever. *Ever.* The fifteenth richest man in the country. A house in Belgravia. Mrs. Tarquin Cleath-Stuart. Just imagining it, I feel almost faint with longing.

I smile as warmly as I can at Tarquin, who hesitates—then smiles back. Phew. I haven't wrecked things. It's all still on. Now we just need to discover that we're utter soul mates with loads of things in common.

"I love the—" I say.

"Do you—"

We both speak at once.

"Sorry," I say. "Do carry on."

"No, *you* carry on," says Tarquin.

"Oh," I say. "Well . . . I was just going to say again how much I love the picture you gave Suze." No harm in complimenting his taste again. "I *love* horses," I add for good measure.

"Then we should go riding together," says Tarquin. "I know a very good livery near Hyde Park. Not quite the same as in the country, of course . . ."

"What a wonderful idea!" I say. "That would be such fun!"

There's no way anyone's getting me on a horse. Not even in Hyde Park. But that's OK, I'll just go along with the plan and then, on the day, say I've twisted my ankle or something.

"Do you like dogs?" asks Tarquin.

"I love dogs," I say confidently.

Which is sort of true. I wouldn't actually like to *have* a dog—too much hard work and hairs everywhere. But I like seeing Labradors running across the park. And cute little puppies. That kind of thing.

We lapse into silence, and I take a few sips of champagne.

"Do you like *EastEnders*?" I ask eventually. "Or are you a . . . a *Coronation Street* person?"

"I've never watched either, I'm afraid," says Tarquin apologetically. "I'm sure they're very good."

"Well . . . they're OK," I say. "Sometimes they're really good, and other times . . ." I tail off a bit feebly, and smile at him. "You know."

"Absolutely," exclaims Tarquin, as though I've said something really interesting.

There's another awkward silence. This is getting a bit sticky.

"Are there good shops, where you live in Scotland?" I say at last. Tarquin pulls a little face.

"I wouldn't know. Never go near shops if I can help it."

"Oh right," I say, and take a deep gulp of champagne. "No, I . . . I hate shops, too. Can't *stand* shopping."

"Really?" says Tarquin in surprise. "I thought all girls loved shopping."

"Not me!" I say. "I'd far rather be . . . out on the moors, riding along. With a couple of dogs running behind."

"Sounds perfect," says Tarquin, smiling at me. "We'll have to do it sometime."

This is more like it! Common interests. Shared pursuits.

And OK, maybe I haven't been completely honest, maybe they aren't exactly my interests at the moment. But they could be. They *can* be. I can easily get to like dogs and horses, if I have to.

"Or . . . or listening to Wagner, of course," I say casually.

"Do you really like Wagner?" says Tarquin. "Not everyone does."

"I *adore* Wagner," I insist. "He's my favorite composer." OK, quick—what did that book say? "I love the . . . er . . . sonorous melodic strands which interweave in the Prelude."

"The Prelude to what?" says Tarquin interestedly.

Oh shit. Is there more than one Prelude? I take a gulp of champagne, playing for time, desperately trying to recall something else from the book. But the only other bit I can remember is "Richard Wagner was born in Leipzig."

"All the Preludes," I say at last. "I think they're all . . . fab."

"Right," says Tarquin, looking a bit surprised.

Oh God. That wasn't the right thing to say, was it? Change the subject. Change the subject.

Luckily, at that moment, a waiter arrives with our garlic bread, and we can get off the subject of Wagner. And Tarquin orders some more champagne. Somehow, I think we're going to need it.

Which means that by the time I'm halfway through my Fiorentina, I've drunk almost an entire bottle of champagne and I'm . . . Well, frankly, I'm completely pissed. My face is tingling and my eyes are sparkling, and my arm gestures are a lot more erratic than usual. But this doesn't matter. In fact, being pissed is a *good* thing—because it means I'm also delightfully witty and lively and am more-or-less carrying the conversation single-handedly. Tarquin is also pissed, but not as much as me. He's got quieter and quieter, and kind of thoughtful. And he keeps gazing at me.

As I finish my last scraps of pizza and lean back pleasurably, he stares at me silently for a moment, then reaches into his pocket and produces a little box.

"Here," he says. "This is for you."

I have to admit, for one heart-stopping moment I think, This is it! He's proposing!

But of course, he's not proposing, is he? He's just giving me a little present.

I knew that.

So I open it, and find a leather box, and inside is a little gold brooch in the shape of a horse. Lots of fine detail; beautifully crafted. A little green stone (emerald?) for the eye.

Really not my kind of thing.

"It's gorgeous," I breathe in awe. "Absolutely . . . stunning."

"It's rather jolly, isn't it?" says Tarquin. "Thought you'd like it."

"I *adore* it." I turn it over in my fingers then look up at him and blink a couple of times with misty eyes. God, I'm drunk. I think I'm actually *seeing* through champagne. "This is so thoughtful of you," I murmur.

Plus, I don't really wear brooches. I mean, where are you supposed to put them? Slap bang in the middle of a really nice top? I mean, come on. And they always leave great brooch-holes everywhere.

"It'll look lovely on you," says Tarquin after a pause—and suddenly I realize he's expecting me to put it on.

Aaargh! It'll ruin my lovely Whistles dress! And who wants a horse galloping across their tits, anyway!

"I *must* put it on," I say, and open the clasp. Gingerly, I thread it through the fabric of my dress and clasp it shut, already feeling it pull the dress out of shape.

"It looks wonderful," says Tarquin, meeting my gaze. "But then . . . you always look wonderful."

I feel a dart of apprehension as I see him leaning forward. He's going to try and hold my hand again, isn't he? And probably kiss me. I glance at Tarquin's lips—parted and slightly moist—and give an involuntary shudder. Oh God. I'm not quite ready for this. I mean, obviously I *do* want to kiss Tarquin, of course I do. In fact, I find him incredibly attractive. It's just . . . I think I need some more champagne first.

"That scarf you were wearing the other night," says Tarquin. "It was simply stunning. I looked at you in that, and I thought . . ."

Now I can see his hand edging toward mine.

"My Denny and George scarf!" I cut in brightly, before he can say anything else. "Yes, that's lovely, isn't it? It was my aunt's, but she died. It was really sad, actually."

Just keep talking, I think. Keep talking brightly and gesture a lot.

"But anyway, she left me her scarf," I continue hurriedly. "So I'll always remember her through that. Poor Aunt Ermintrude."

"I'm really sorry," says Tarquin, looking taken aback. "I had no idea."

"No. Well . . . her memory lives on through her good works," I say, and give him a little smile. "She was a very charitable woman. Very . . . giving."

"Is there some sort of foundation in her name?" says Tarquin. "When my uncle died—"

"Yes!" I say gratefully. "Exactly that. The . . . the Ermintrude Bloomwood Foundation for . . . violinists," I improvise, catching sight of a poster for a musical evening. "Violinists in Mozambique. That was her cause."

"Violinists in Mozambique?" echoes Tarquin.

"Oh, absolutely!" I hear myself babbling. "There's a desperate shortage of classical musicians out there. And culture is so enriching, whatever one's material circumstances."

I can't *believe* I'm coming out with all this rubbish. I glance apprehensively up at Tarquin—and to my complete disbelief, he looks really interested.

"So, what exactly is the foundation aiming to do?" he asks.

What am I getting myself into here?

"To . . . to fund six violin teachers a year," I say after a pause. "Of course, they need specialist training, and special violins to take out there. But the results will be very worthwhile. They're going to teach people how to make violins, too, so they'll be self-sufficient and not dependent on the West."

"Really?" Tarquin's brow is furrowed. Have I said something that doesn't make sense?

"Anyway," I give a little laugh. "That's enough about me and my family. Have you seen any good films recently?"

This is good. We can talk about films, and then the bill will come, and then . . .

"Wait a moment," says Tarquin. "Tell me—how's the project going so far?"

"Oh," I say. "Ahm . . . quite well. Considering. I haven't really kept up with its progress recently. You know, these things are always—"

"I'd really like to contribute something," he says, interrupting me.

What?

He'd like to *what*?

"Do you know who I should make the check payable to?" he says, reaching into his jacket pocket. "Is it the Bloomwood Foundation?"

And as I watch, paralyzed in astonishment, he brings out a Coutts checkbook.

A pale gray Coutts checkbook.

The fifteenth richest man in the country.

"I'm . . . I'm not sure," I hear myself say, as though from a great distance. "I'm not sure of the *exact* wording."

"Well, I'll make it payable to you, then, shall I?" he says. "And you can pass it on." Briskly he starts to write.

Pay Rebecca Bloomwood.

The sum of.

Five . . .

Five hundred pounds. It must be. He wouldn't just give five miserable . . .

Thousand pounds.

T. A. J. Cleath-Stuart.

I can't believe my eyes. Five thousand pounds, on a check, addressed to me.

Five thousand pounds, which belongs to Aunt Ermintrude and the violin teachers of Mozambique.

If they existed.

"Here you are," says Tarquin, and hands me the check—and as though in a dream, I find myself reaching out toward it.

Pay Rebecca Bloomwood the sum of five thousand pounds.

I read the words again slowly—and feel a wave of relief so strong, it makes me want to burst into tears. The sum of five thousand pounds. More than my overdraft and my VISA bill put together. This check would solve all my problems, wouldn't it? It would solve all my problems in one go. And, OK, I'm not exactly violinists in Mozambique—but Tarquin would never know the difference, would he?

And anyway, what's £5,000 to a multimillionaire like Tarquin? He probably wouldn't even notice whether I paid it in or not. A pathetic £5,000, when he's got £25 million! If you work it out as a fraction of his wealth it's . . . well, it's laughable, isn't it? It's the equivalent of about fifty pence to normal people. Why am I even hesitating?

"Rebecca?"

Tarquin is staring at me—and I realize my hand is still inches away from the check. *Come on, take it,* I instruct myself firmly. *It's yours. Take the check and put it in your bag.* With a heroic effort, I stretch out my hand further, willing myself to close my fingers around the check. I'm getting closer . . . closer . . . almost there . . . my fingers are trembling with the effort . . .

It's no good, I can't. I just can't do it. I can't take his money.

"I can't take it," I say in a rush. I pull my hand away and feel myself flushing. "I mean . . . I'm not actually sure the foundation is accepting money yet."

"Oh right," says Tarquin, looking slightly taken aback.

"I'll tell you who to make a check payable to when I've got more details," I say, and take a deep gulp of champagne. "You'd better tear that up."

He slowly rips the paper, but I can't look. I stare into my champagne glass, feeling like crying. Five thousand pounds. It would have changed my life. It would have solved everything. I would have written out checks immediately to Suze, to VISA, to Octagon . . . to all of them. Then I would have taken this check and presented it to Derek Smeath on Monday morning. Perhaps I wouldn't have cleared every single penny of overdraft, but I would have made a start. A bloody good start.

Tarquin reaches for the box of matches on the table, sets the scraps of paper alight in the ashtray, and we both watch as they briefly flame. Then he puts down the matches, smiles at me, and says, "Do excuse me a minute."

He gets up from the table and heads off toward the back of the restaurant, and I take another gulp of champagne. Then I lean my head in my hands and give a little sigh. Oh well, I think, trying to be philosophical. Maybe I'll win £5,000 in a raffle or something. Maybe Derek Smeath's computer will go haywire and he'll be forced to cancel all my debts and start again. Maybe some utter stranger really *will* pay off my VISA bill for me by mistake.

Maybe Tarquin will come back from the loo and ask me to marry him.

I raise my eyes, and they fall with an idle curiosity on the Coutts checkbook, which Tarquin has left on the table. That's the checkbook of the fifteenth richest unmarried man in the country. Wow. I wonder what it's like inside? He probably writes enormous checks all the time, doesn't he? He probably spends more money in a day than I spend in a year.

On impulse, I pull the checkbook toward me and open it. I don't know quite what I'm looking for—really, I'm just hoping to find some excitingly huge amount. But the first stub is only for £30. Pathetic! I flip on a bit, and find £520. Payable to Arundel & Son, whoever they are. Then, a bit later on, there's one for £7,515 to American Express. Well, that's more like it. But I mean, really, it's not the most exciting read in the world. This could be anybody's checkbook. This could practically be mine.

I close it and push it back toward his place, and glance up. As I do so, my heart freezes. Tarquin is staring straight at me.

He's standing by the bar, being directed to the other side of the restaurant by a waiter. But he isn't looking at the waiter. He's looking at me. As our eyes meet, my stomach lurches. Oh, damn.

Damn. What exactly did he see?

Quickly I pull my hand back from his checkbook and take a sip of champagne. Then I look up and pretend to spot him for the first time. I give a bright little smile, and after a pause he smiles back. Then he disappears off again and I sink back into my chair, trying to look relaxed.

OK, don't panic, I instruct myself. Just behave naturally. He probably didn't see you. And even if he did—it's not the hugest crime in the world, is it, looking at his checkbook? If he asks me what I was doing, I'll say I was . . . checking he'd filled in his stub correctly. Yes. That's what I'll say I was doing if he mentions it.

But he doesn't. He comes back to the table, silently pockets his checkbook, and says politely, "Have you finished?"

"Yes," I say. "Yes, I have, thanks."

I'm trying to sound as natural as possible—but I'm aware my voice sounds guilty, and my cheeks are hot.

"Right," he says. "Well, I've paid the bill . . . so shall we go?"

And that's it. That's the end of the date. With impeccable courtesy, Tarquin ushers me to the door of Pizza on the Park, hails a taxi, and pays the driver the fare back to Fulham. I don't dare ask him if he'd like to come back or go for a drink somewhere else. There's a coldness about my spine which stops me uttering the words. So we kiss each other on the cheek and he tells me he had a delightful evening, and I thank him again for a lovely time.

And I sit in the taxi all the way back to Fulham with a jumpy stomach, wondering what exactly he saw.

I say good-night to the taxi driver and reach for my keys. I'm thinking that I'll go and run a hot bath and sit in it, and calmly try to work out exactly what happened back there. Did Tarquin really see me looking through his checkbook? Maybe he just saw me pushing it back toward his place in a helpful manner. Maybe he saw nothing at all.

But then why did he suddenly become all stiff and polite? He must have seen something; suspected something. And then he'll have noticed the way I flushed and couldn't meet his eye. Oh God, why do I always have to look so guilty? I wasn't even *doing* anything. I was just curious.

Perhaps I should have quickly said something—made some joke about it. Turned it into a lighthearted, amusing incident. But what kind of joke can you make about leafing through someone's private checkbook? Oh God, I'm so *stupid*. Why did I ever touch the bloody thing? I should have just sat, quietly sipping my drink.

But in my defense . . . he left it on the table, didn't he? He can't be that secretive about it. And I don't *know* that he saw me looking through it, do I? Maybe I'm just paranoid.

As I put my key into the lock, I'm actually feeling quite positive. OK, so Tarquin wasn't that friendly just now—but he might have been feeling ill or something. Or maybe he just didn't want to rush me. What I'll do is, tomorrow I'll send a nice chatty note to him, saying thanks again, and suggesting we go and see some Wagner together. Excellent idea. And I'll mug up a bit about the Preludes, so that if he asks me which one again, I'll know exactly what to say. Yes! This is all going to be fine. I need never have worried.

I swing the door open, taking off my coat—and then my heart gives a flip. Suze is waiting for me in the hall. She's sitting on the stairs, waiting for me—and there's a reproachful expression on her face.

"Oh, Bex," she says, and shakes her head. "I've just been speaking to Tarquin."

"Oh right," I say, trying to sound natural—but aware that my voice is a frightened squeak. I turn away, take my coat, and slowly unwind my scarf, playing for time. What exactly has he said to her?

"I don't suppose there's any point asking you *why*?" she says after a pause.

"Well," I falter, feeling sick. God, I could do with a cigarette.

"I'm not *blaming* you, or anything. I just think you should have . . ." She shakes her head and sighs. "Couldn't you have let him down more gently? He sounded quite upset. The poor thing was really keen on you, you know."

This isn't quite making sense. Let him down more gently?

"What exactly—" I lick my dry lips. "What exactly did he say?"

"Well, he was only really phoning to tell me you'd left your umbrella behind," says Suze. "Apparently one of the waiters came rushing out with it. But of course I asked him how the date had gone . . ."

"And . . . and what did he say?"

"Well," says Suze, and gives a little shrug. "He said you'd had a really nice time—but you'd pretty much made it clear you didn't want to see him again."

"Oh."

I sink down onto the floor, feeling rather weak. So that's it. Tarquin did see me leafing through his checkbook. I've ruined my chances with him completely.

But he didn't tell Suze what I'd done. He protected me. Pretended it was my decision not to carry things on. He was a gentleman.

In fact—he was a gentleman all evening, wasn't he? He was kind to me, and charming, and polite. And all I did, all throughout the date, was tell him lies.

Suddenly I want to cry.

"I just think it's such a shame," says Suze. "I mean, I know it's up to you and everything—but he's such a sweet guy. And he's had a crush on you for ages! You two would go perfectly together." She gives me a wheedling look. "Isn't there *any* chance you might go out with him again?"

"I . . . I honestly don't think so," I say in a scratchy voice. "Suze . . . I'm a bit tired. I think I'll go to bed."

And without meeting her eye, I get up and slowly walk down the corridor to my room.

BANK OF LONDON

LONDON HOUSE MILL STREET EC3R 4DW

Ms. Rebecca Boomwood
Flat 2
4 Burney Rd.
London SW6 8FD

23 March 2000

Dear Ms. Boomwood:

Thank you very much for your application for a Bank of London Easifone Loan.

Unfortunately, "buying clothes and makeup" was not deemed a suitable purpose for such a substantial unsecured loan, and your application has been turned down by our credit team.

Thank you very much for considering Bank of London.

Yours sincerely,

Margaret Hopkins
Loans Adviser

· ENDWICH BANK ·

FULHAM BRANCH
3 Fulham Road
London SW6 9JH

Ms. Rebecca Bloomwood
Flat 2
4 Burney Rd.
London SW6 8FD

23 March 2000

Dear Ms. Bloomwood:

I am writing to confirm our meeting at 9:30 A.M. on Monday 26 March, here at our Fulham office. Please ask for me at reception.

I look forward to seeing you then.

Yours sincerely,

Derek Smeath
Manager

· ENDWICH -- BECAUSE WE CARE ·

Fifteen

I HAVE NEVER IN MY LIFE felt as terrible as I do when I wake up the next morning. Never.

The first thing I feel is pain. Exploding sparks of pain as I try to move my head; as I try to open my eyes; as I try to work out a few basics like: Who am I? What day is it? Where should I be right now?

For a while I lie quite still, panting with the exertion of just being alive. In fact, my face is growing scarlet and I'm almost starting to hyperventilate, so I force myself to slow down and breathe regularly. *In . . . out, in . . . out.* And then surely everything will come back to me and I will feel better. *In . . . out, in . . . out.*

OK . . . Rebecca. That's right. I'm Rebecca Bloomwood, aren't I? *In . . . out, in . . . out.*

What else? Dinner. I had dinner somewhere last night. *In . . . out, in . . . out.*

Pizza. I had pizza. And who was I with, again? *In . . . out, in . . .*

Tarquin.

Out.

Oh God. Tarquin.

Leafing through checkbook. Everything ruined. All my own fault.

A familiar wave of despair floods over me and I close my eyes, trying to calm my throbbing head. At the same time, I remember that last night, when I went back to my room, I found the half bottle of malt whisky which Scottish Prudential once gave me, still sitting on my dressing table. I opened it up—even though I don't like whisky—and drank . . . well, certainly a few cupfuls. Which might possibly explain why I'm feeling so ill now.

Slowly I struggle to a sitting position and listen for sounds of Suze, but I can't hear anything. The flat's empty. It's just me.

Me and my thoughts.

Which, to be honest, I can't endure. My head's pounding and I feel pale and shaky—but I've got to get moving; distract myself. I'll go out, have a cup of coffee somewhere quiet and try to get myself together.

I manage to get out of bed, stagger to my chest of drawers, and stare at myself in the mirror. I don't like what I see. My skin's green, my mouth is dry, and my hair's sticking to my skin in clumps. But worst of all is the expression in my eyes: a blank, miserable self-loathing. Last night I was given a chance—a fantastic opportunity on a silver platter. I threw it in the bin—and hurt a really sweet, decent chap, to boot. God, I'm a disaster. I don't deserve to live.

I head to King's Road, to lose myself in the anonymous bustle. The air's crisp and fresh, and as I stride along it's almost possible to forget about last night. Almost, but not quite.

I go into Aroma, order a large cappuccino, and try to drink it normally. As if everything's fine and I'm just another girl out on a Sunday for some shopping. But I can't do it. I can't escape my thoughts. They're churning round in my head, like a record that won't stop, over and over and over.

If only I hadn't picked up his checkbook. If only I hadn't

been so *stupid*. It was all going so well. He really liked me. We were holding hands. He was planning to ask me out again. If only I could go back; if only I could play the evening again . . .

Don't think about it. Don't think about what could have been. It's too unbearable. If I'd played it right, I'd probably be sitting here drinking coffee with Tarquin, wouldn't I? I'd probably be well on my way to becoming the fifteenth richest woman in the country.

Instead of which, I have unpaid bills stacked up in my dressing table drawer. I have a meeting with my bank manager on Monday morning. I have no idea what I'm going to do. No idea at all.

Miserably I take a sip of coffee and unwrap my little chocolate. I'm not in the mood for chocolate, but I stuff it into my mouth anyway.

The worst thing—the very worst thing of all—is that I was actually starting to quite like Tarquin. Maybe he isn't God's gift in the looks department, but he's very kind, and quite funny, in his own way. And that brooch—it's really quite sweet.

And the way he didn't tell Suze what he'd seen me doing. And the way he *believed* me when I told him I liked dogs and Wagner and bloody violinists in Mozambique. The way he was so completely, utterly unsuspicious.

Now I really am going to start crying.

Roughly I brush at my eyes, drain my cup, and stand up. Out on the street I hesitate, then begin walking briskly again. Maybe the breeze will blow these unbearable thoughts out of my head.

But I stride and stride, and I still feel no better. My head's aching and my eyes are red and I could really do with a drink or something. Just a little something, to make me feel a bit better. A drink, or a cigarette, or . . .

I look up, and I'm in front of Octagon. My favorite shop in the whole world. Three floors of clothes, accessories, furnishings, gifts, coffee shops, juice bars, and a florist which makes you want to buy enough bouquets to fill your house.

I've got my purse with me.

Just something small, to cheer me up. A T-shirt or something. Or even some bubble bath. I *need* to buy myself something. I won't spend much. I'll just go in, and . . .

I'm already pushing my way through the doors. Oh God, the relief. The warmth, the light. This is where I belong. This is my natural habitat.

Except that even as I'm heading toward the T-shirts, I'm not quite as happy as I should be. I look through the racks, trying to summon the excitement I usually feel at buying myself a little treat—but somehow today I feel a bit empty. Still, I choose a cropped top with a silver star in the middle and put it over my arm, telling myself I feel better already. Then I spot a rack of dressing gowns. I could do with a new dressing gown, as a matter of fact.

As I finger a lovely white waffle robe, I can hear a little voice at the back of my head, like a radio turned down low. *Don't do it. You're in debt. Don't do it. You're in debt.*

But quite frankly, what does it matter now? It's too late to make any difference. I'm already in debt; I might as well be more in debt. Almost savagely, I pull the dressing gown down from the rack and put it over my arm. Then I reach for the matching waffle slippers. No point buying one without the other.

The checkout point is directly to my left, but I ignore it. I'm not done yet. I head for the escalators and go up to the home-furnishing floor. Time for a new duvet set. White, to match my new dressing gown. And a pair of bolster cushions.

Every time I add something to my pile, I feel a little whoosh of pleasure, like a firework going off. And for a moment, everything's all right. But then, gradually, the light and sparkles disappear, and I'm left with cold dark blackness again. So I look feverishly around for something else. A huge scented candle. A bottle of Jo Malone shower gel. A bag of handmade potpourri. As I add each one, I feel a whoosh—and then blackness. But the whooshes are getting shorter and shorter each time. Why won't the pleasure stay? Why don't I feel happier?

"Can I help you?" says a voice, interrupting my thoughts. A young assistant, dressed in the Octagon outfit of white shirt and linen trousers, has come up and is looking at my pile of stuff on the floor. "Would you like me to hold some of these while you continue shopping?"

"Oh," I say blankly, and look down at the stuff I've accumulated. It's actually quite a lot by now. "No, don't worry. I'll just . . . I'll just pay for this lot."

Somehow, between us, we manage to lug all my shopping across the beechwood floor to the stylish granite checkout point in the middle, and the assistant begins to scan everything through. The bolster cushions have been reduced, which I hadn't realized, and while she's checking the exact price, a queue begins to form behind me.

"That'll be £370.56," she says eventually, and smiles at me. "How would you like to pay?"

"Erm . . . debit card," I say, and reach for my purse. As she's swiping it, I eye up my carrier bags and wonder how I'm going to get all this stuff home.

But immediately my thoughts bounce away. I don't want to think about home. I don't want to think about Suze, or Tarquin, or last night. Or any of it.

"I'm sorry," says the girl apologetically, "but there's something wrong with your card. It won't authorize the purchase." She hands it back to me. "Do you have anything else?"

"Oh," I say, slightly flustered. "Well . . . here's my VISA card."

How embarrassing. And anyway, what's wrong with my card? It looks all right to me. I must call the bank about this.

The bank. Meeting tomorrow, with Derek Smeath. Oh God. Quick, think about something else. Look at the floor. Glance about the shop. There's quite a big line of people now, and I can hear coughing and clearing of throats. Everyone's waiting for me. As I meet the eye of the woman behind me, I smile awkwardly.

"No," says the girl. "This one's no good either."

"What?" I whip round in shock. How can my VISA card be no good? It's my *VISA* card, for God's sake. Accepted all over the world. What's going on? It doesn't make any sense. It doesn't make any . . .

My words stop midstream, and a nasty chill feeling begins to creep over me. All those letters. Those letters I've been putting in my dressing table drawer. Surely they can't have . . .

No. They can't have done.

My heart starts to thump in panic. I know I haven't been that great at paying my bills—but I need my VISA card. I *need* it. They can't just cancel it, just like that.

"There are other people waiting," says the girl, gesturing to the queue. "So if you aren't able to pay . . ."

"Of course I'm able to pay," I say stiffly. With trembling hands I scrabble in my purse and eventually produce my silver Octagon charge card. It was buried under all the others, so I can't have used it for a while. "Here," I say. "I'll put it all on this."

"Fine," says the girl curtly, and swipes the card.

It's only as we're waiting silently for the authorization that I begin to wonder whether I've actually paid off my Octagon account. They sent me a nasty letter a while ago, didn't they? Something about an outstanding balance. But I'm sure I paid it off, ages ago. Or at least some of it. Didn't I? I'm sure I . . .

"I'm just going to have to make a quick call," says the assistant, staring at her machine. She reaches for the phone next to the till.

"Hi," she says. "Yes, if I can give you an account number . . ."

Behind me, somebody sighs loudly. I can feel my face growing hotter and hotter. I don't dare look round. I don't dare move.

"I see," says the assistant eventually, and puts down the phone. She looks up—and at the sight of her face, my stomach gives a lurch. Her expression isn't apologetic or polite anymore. It's plain unfriendly.

"Our financial services department would like you to contact them urgently," she says curtly. "I'll give you the number."

"Right," I say, trying to sound relaxed. As though this is a fairly normal request. "OK. Well, I'll do that. Thanks." I hold my hand out for my charge card. I'm not interested in my shopping anymore. All I want to do is get out of here as quickly as possible.

"I'm sorry, I'm afraid your account's been frozen," says the assistant without lowering her voice. "I'm going to have to retain your card."

I stare at her in disbelief, feeling my face prickling with shock. Behind me there's an interested rustle as everybody hears this and starts nudging each other.

"So, unless you have another means of paying . . ." she adds, looking at my heap of stuff on the counter. My waffle robe. My new duvet set. My scented candle. A huge, conspicuous pile of stuff. Stuff I don't need. Stuff I can't pay for. Suddenly the sight of it all makes me feel sick.

Numbly I shake my head. I feel as if I've been caught stealing.

"Elsa," calls the assistant. "Will you deal with this, please? The customer isn't going to make the purchase after all." She gestures to the pile of stuff, and the other assistant moves it along the counter, out of the way, her face deliberately blank.

"Next, please."

The woman behind me steps forward, avoiding my eye in embarrassment, and slowly I turn away. I have never felt so humiliated in all my life. The whole floor seems to be looking at me—all the customers, all the sales assistants, all whispering and nudging. *Did you see? Did you see what happened?*

With wobbling legs I walk away, not looking right or left. This is a nightmare. I just have to get out, as quickly as possible. I have to get out of the shop and onto the street and go . . .

Go where? Home, I suppose.

But I can't go back and face Suze. She's been so kind to me

and how have I behaved? She has no idea what a horrible person I am. If I go home, I'll have to hear her telling me again how sweet Tarquin is. Or even worse, risk bumping into him. Oh God. The very thought makes me feel sick.

What am I going to do? Where am I going to go?

Shakily I begin to walk along the pavement, looking away from the mocking window displays. What can I do? Where can I go? I feel empty, almost light-headed with panic.

I pause at a corner, waiting for a traffic light to change, and look blankly at a display of cashmere jumpers to my left. And suddenly, at the sight of a scarlet Pringle golfing jumper, I feel tears of relief springing to my eyes. There's one place I can go. One place I can always go.

Sixteen

When I turn up at my parents' house that afternoon without warning, saying I want to stay for a few days, I can't say they seem shocked.

In fact, so unsurprised do they seem that I begin to wonder if they've been expecting this eventuality all along, ever since I moved to London. Have they been waiting every week for me to arrive on the doorsteps with no luggage and red eyes? They're certainly behaving as calmly as a hospital casualty team operating an emergency procedure.

Except that surely the casualty team wouldn't keep arguing about the best way to resuscitate the patient? After a few minutes, I feel like going outside, letting them decide on their plan of action, and ringing the bell again.

"You go upstairs and have a nice hot bath," says Mum, as soon as I've put down my handbag. "I expect you're exhausted!"

"She doesn't have to have a bath if she doesn't want to!" retorts Dad. "She might want a drink! D'you want a drink, darling?"

"Is that *wise*?" says Mum, shooting him a meaningful what-if-she's-an-alkie? look, which presumably I'm not supposed to notice.

"I don't want a drink, thanks," I say. "But I'd love a cup of tea."

"Of course you would!" says Mum. "Graham, go and put the kettle on." And she gives him another meaningful look. As soon as he's disappeared into the kitchen, she comes close to me and says, in a lowered voice, "Are you feeling all right, darling? Is anything . . . wrong?"

Oh God, there's nothing like your mother's sympathetic voice to make you want to burst into tears.

"Well," I say, in a slightly uncertain voice. "Things have been better. I'm just . . . in a bit of a difficult situation at the moment. But it'll be all right in the end." I give a small shrug and look away.

"Because . . ." She lowers her voice even more. "Your father isn't as old-fashioned as he seems. And I know that if it were a case of us looking after a . . . a little one, while you pursued your career . . ."

What?

"Mum, don't worry!" I exclaim sharply. "I'm not pregnant!"

"I never said you were," she says, and flushes a little. "I just wanted to offer you our support."

My parents watch too many soap operas, that's their trouble. In fact, they were probably *hoping* I was pregnant. By my wicked married lover whom they could then murder and bury under the patio.

And what's this "offer you our support" business, anyway? My mum would never have said that before she started watching Ricki Lake.

"Well, come on," she says. "Let's sit you down with a nice cup of tea."

And so I follow her into the kitchen, and we all sit down with a cup of tea. And I have to say, it is very nice. Hot strong tea and a chocolate bourbon biscuit. Perfect. I close my eyes and take a few sips, and then open them again, to see both my parents gazing at me with naked curiosity all over their faces. Immediately my mother changes her expression to a smile, and my father gives a little cough—but I can tell, they are *gagging* to know what's wrong.

"So," I say cautiously, and both their heads jerk up. "You're both well, are you?"

"Oh yes," says my mother. "Yes, *we're* fine."

There's another silence.

"Becky?" says my father gravely, and both Mum and I swivel to face him. "Are you in some kind of trouble we should know about? Only tell us if you want to," he adds hastily. "And I want you to know—we're there for you."

That's another bloody Ricki Lake–ism, too. My parents should really get out more.

"Are you all right, darling?" says Mum gently—and she sounds so kind and understanding that, in spite of myself, I find myself putting down my cup with a bit of a clatter and saying "To tell you the truth, I am in a spot of bother. I didn't want to worry you, so I haven't said anything before now . . ." I can feel tears gathering in my eyes.

"What is it?" says Mum in a panicky voice. "You're on drugs, aren't you?"

"No, I'm not on drugs!" I exclaim. "I'm just . . . It's just that I . . . I'm . . ." I take a deep gulp of tea. This is even harder than I thought it would be. Come on, Rebecca, just *say* it.

I close my eyes and clench my hand tightly around my mug.

"The truth is . . ." I say slowly.

"Yes?" says Mum.

"The truth is . . ." I open my eyes. "I'm being stalked. By a man called . . . called Derek Smeath."

There's silence apart from a long hiss as my father sucks in breath.

"I knew it!" says my mother in a sharp, brittle voice. "I knew it! I knew there was something wrong!"

"We all knew there was something wrong!" says my father, and rests his elbows heavily on the table. "How long has this been going on, Becky?"

"Oh, ahm . . . months now," I say, staring into my tea. "It's just . . . pestering, really. It's not serious or anything. But I just couldn't deal with it anymore."

"And who is this Derek Smeath?" says Dad. "Do we know him?"

"I don't think so. I came across him . . . I came across him through work."

"Of course you did!" says Mum. "A young, pretty girl like you, with a high-profile career . . . I knew this was going to happen!"

"Is he another journalist?" says Dad, and I shake my head.

"He works for Endwich Bank. He does things like . . . like phone up and pretend he's in charge of my bank account. He's really convincing."

There's silence while my parents digest this and I eat another chocolate bourbon.

"Well," says Mum at last. "I think we'll have to phone the police."

"No!" I exclaim, spluttering crumbs all over the table. "I don't want the police! He's never threatened me or anything. In fact, he's not really a stalker at all. He's just a pain. I thought if I disappeared for a while . . ."

"I see," says Dad, and glances at Mum. "Well, that makes sense."

"So what I suggest," I say, meshing my hands tightly in my lap, "is that if he rings, you say I've gone abroad and you don't have a number for me. And . . . if anyone else rings, say the same thing. Even Suze. I've left her a message saying I'm OK—but I don't want anyone to know where I am."

"Are you sure?" says Mum, wrinkling her brow. "Wouldn't it be better to go to the police?"

"No!" I say quickly. "That would only make him feel important. I just want to vanish for a bit."

"Fine," says Dad. "As far as we're concerned, you're not here."

He reaches across the table and clasps my hand. And as I see the worry on his face, I hate myself for what I'm doing.

But I simply can't tell my kind, loving parents that their so-called successful daughter with her so-called top job is in fact a disorganized, deceitful mess, up to her eyeballs in debt.

And so we have supper (Waitrose Cumberland Pie) and watch an Agatha Christie adaption together, and then I go upstairs to my old bedroom, put on an old nightie, and go to bed. And when I wake up the next morning, I feel more happy and rested than I have for weeks.

Above all, staring at my old bedroom ceiling, I feel safe. Cocooned from the world; wrapped up in cotton wool. No one can get me here. No one even *knows* I'm here. I won't get any nasty letters and I won't get any nasty phone calls and I won't get any nasty visitors. It's like a sanctuary. I feel as if I'm fifteen again, with nothing to worry about but my homework. (And I haven't even got any of that.)

It's at least nine o'clock before I rouse myself and get out of bed, and as I do so, it occurs to me that miles away in London, Derek Smeath is expecting me to arrive for a meeting in half an hour. A slight twinge passes through my stomach and for a moment I consider phoning up the bank and giving some excuse. But even as I'm considering it, I know I'm not going to do it. I don't even want to acknowledge the bank's existence. I want to forget all about it.

None of it exists anymore. Not the bank, not VISA, not Octagon. All eliminated from my life, just like that.

The only call I make is to the office, because I don't want them sacking me in my absence. I phone at nine-twenty—before Philip gets in—and get Mavis on reception.

"Hello, Mavis?" I croak. "It's Rebecca Bloomwood here. Can you tell Philip I'm ill?"

"You poor thing!" says Mavis. "Is it bronchitis?"

"I'm not sure," I croak. "I've got a doctor's appointment later. I must go. Bye."

And that's it. One phone call, and I'm free. No one suspects anything—why should they? I feel light with relief. It's so easy to escape. I should have done this long ago.

At the back of my mind, like a nasty little gremlin, is the knowledge that I won't be able to stay here forever. That sooner or later things will start to catch up with me. But the point is—not yet. And in the meantime, I'm not even going to think about it. I'm just going to have a nice cup of tea and watch *Morning Coffee* and blank my mind out completely.

As I go into the kitchen, Dad's sitting at the table, reading the paper. There's the smell of toast in the air, and Radio Four in the background. Just like when I was younger and lived at home. Life was simple then. No bills, no demands, no threatening letters. An enormous wave of nostalgia overcomes me, and I turn away to fill the kettle, blinking slightly.

"Interesting news," says Dad, jabbing at *The Daily Telegraph*.

"Oh yes?" I say, putting a tea bag in a mug. "What's that?"

"Scottish Prime has taken over Flagstaff Life."

"Oh right," I say vaguely. "Right. Yes, I think I'd heard that was going to happen."

"All the Flagstaff Life investors are going to receive huge windfall payments. The biggest ever, apparently."

"Gosh," I say, trying to sound interested. I reach for a copy of *Good Housekeeping*, flick it open, and begin to read my horoscope.

But something's niggling at my mind. Flagstaff Life. Why does that sound familiar? Who was I talking to about . . .

"Martin and Janice next door!" I exclaim suddenly. "They're with Flagstaff Life! Have been for fifteen years."

"Then they'll do very well," says Dad. "The longer you've been with them, the more you get, apparently."

He turns the page with a rustle, and I sit down at the table with my cup of tea and a *Good Housekeeping* article on making

Easter cakes. It's not fair, I find myself thinking resentfully. Why can't I get a windfall payment? Why doesn't Endwich Bank get taken over? Then they could pay me a windfall big enough to wipe out my overdraft.

"Any plans for the day?" says Dad, looking up.

"Not really," I say, and take a sip of tea.

Any plans for the rest of my life? Not really.

In the end, I spend a pleasant, unchallenging morning helping Mum sort out a pile of clothes for a jumble sale, and at twelve-thirty we go into the kitchen to make a sandwich. As I look at the clock, the fact that I was supposed to be at Endwich Bank three hours ago flickers through my mind—but very far off, like a distant clock chiming. My whole London life seems remote and unreal now. *This* is where I belong. Away from the madding crowd; at home with Mum and Dad, having a nice relaxed uncomplicated time.

After lunch I wander out into the garden with one of Mum's mail-order catalogues, and go and sit on the bench by the apple tree. A moment later, I hear a voice from over the garden fence, and look up. It's Martin from next door. Hmm. I'm not feeling very well disposed toward Martin at the moment.

"Hello, Becky," he says softly. "Are you all right?"

"I'm fine, thanks," I say shortly. *And I don't fancy your son,* I feel like adding.

"Becky," says Janice, appearing beside Martin, holding a garden trowel. She gives me an awestricken look. "We heard about your . . . *stalker,*" she whispers.

"It's criminal," says Martin fiercely. "These people should be locked up."

"If there's anything we can do," says Janice. "Anything at all. You just let us know."

"I'm fine, really," I say, softening. "I just want to stay here for a while. Get away from it all."

"Of course you do," says Martin. "Wise girl."

"I was saying to Martin this morning," says Janice, "you should hire a bodyguard."

"Can't be too careful," says Martin. "Not these days."

"The price of fame," says Janice, sorrowfully shaking her head. "The price of fame."

"Well, anyway," I say, trying to get off the subject of my stalker. "How are you?"

"Oh, we're both well," says Martin. "I suppose." To my surprise there's a forced cheerfulness to his voice. He glances at Janice, who frowns and shakes her head slightly.

"Anyway, you must be pleased with the news," I say brightly. "About Flagstaff Life."

There's silence.

"Well," says Martin. "We would have been."

"No one could have known," says Janice, giving a little shrug. "It's just one of those things. Just the luck of the draw."

"What is?" I say, puzzled. "I thought you were getting some huge great windfall."

"It appears . . ." Martin rubs his face. "It appears not in our case."

"But . . . but why?"

"Martin phoned them up this morning," says Janice. "To see how much we would be getting. They were saying in the papers that long-term investors would be getting *thousands*. But—" She glances at Martin.

"But what?" I say, feeling a twinge of alarm.

"Apparently we're no longer eligible," says Martin awkwardly. "Since we switched our investment. Our old fund would have qualified, but . . ." He coughs. "I mean, we will get *something*—but it'll only be about £100."

I stare at him blankly.

"But you only switched—"

"Two weeks ago," he says. "That's the irony. If we'd just held on a little bit longer . . . Still, what's done is done. No point whining about it." He gives a resigned shrug and smiles at Janice, who smiles back.

And I look away and bite my lip.

A nasty cold feeling is creeping over me. They took the decision to switch their money based on my advice, didn't they? They asked me if they should switch funds, and I said go ahead. But now I come to think of it . . . hadn't I already heard a rumor about this takeover? Oh God. Could I have stopped this?

"We could never have known these windfalls would happen," says Janice, and puts her hand comfortingly on his arm. "They keep these things secret right up until the last minute, don't they, Becky?"

My throat's too tight to answer. I can remember exactly now. It was Alicia who first mentioned the takeover. The day before I came down here. And then Philip said something about it in the office. Something about with-profits holders doing well. Except . . . I wasn't really listening. I think I was doing my nails at the time.

"Twenty thousand pounds, they reckon we would have got if we'd stayed," says Martin gloomily. "Makes you sick to think about it. Still, Janice is right. We couldn't have known. Nobody knew."

Oh God. This is all my fault. It's all my fault. If I'd just used my brain and *thought* for once . . .

"Oh, Becky, don't look so upset!" says Janice. "This isn't your fault! You didn't know! Nobody knew! None of us could have—"

"I knew," I hear myself saying miserably.

There's a flabbergasted silence.

"What?" says Janice faintly.

"I didn't *know,* exactly," I say, staring at the ground. "But I heard a sort of rumor about it a while ago. I should have said something when you asked me. I should have warned you to wait. But I just . . . didn't think. I didn't remember." I force myself to look up and meet Martin's astonished gaze. "I . . . I'm really sorry. It's all my fault."

There's silence, during which Janice and Martin glance at each other and I hunch my shoulders, loathing myself. Inside, I can hear the phone ringing, and footsteps as someone goes to answer it.

"I see," says Martin eventually. "Well . . . not to worry. These things happen."

"Don't blame yourself, Becky," says Janice kindly. "It was our decision to switch funds, not yours."

"And remember, you've been under a lot of pressure yourself recently," adds Martin, putting a sympathetic hand on my arm. "What with this dreadful stalking business."

Now I really feel like dirt. I don't deserve these people's kindness. I've just lost them £20,000, through being too bloody lazy to keep up with events I'm supposed to know about. I'm a financial journalist, for God's sake.

And suddenly, standing there in my parents' garden on a Monday afternoon, I'm plunged to the lowest ebb of my life. What have I got going for me? Nothing. Not one thing. I can't control my money, I can't do my job, and I haven't got a boyfriend. I've hurt my best friend, I've lied to my parents—and now I've ruined my neighbors.

"Becky?"

My father's voice interrupts us all, and I look up in surprise. He's striding across the lawn toward us, a perturbed look on his face.

"Becky, don't be alarmed," he says, "but I've just had that Derek Smeath chap on the phone."

"What?" I say, feeling my face drain in horror.

"The stalker?" exclaims Janice, and Dad gives a sober nod.

"Quite an unpleasant fellow, I would say. He was really quite aggressive toward me."

"But how does he know Becky's here?" says Janice.

"Obviously just taking potluck," says Dad. "I was very civil, simply told him you weren't here and that I had no idea where you were."

"And . . . and what did he say?" I say in a strangled voice.

"Came out with some nonsense about a meeting you'd set up with him." Dad shakes his head. "The chap's obviously deluded."

"You should change your number," advises Martin. "Go ex-directory."

"But where was he phoning from?" says Janice, her voice rising in alarm. "He could be anywhere!" She starts looking agitatedly around the garden as though expecting him to jump out from behind a bush.

"Exactly," says Dad. "So, Becky, I think maybe you should come inside now. You never know with these characters."

"OK," I say numbly. I can't quite believe this is happening. I look at Dad's kind, concerned face and suddenly I can barely meet his eye. Oh, *why* didn't I tell him and Mum the truth? Why did I let myself get into this situation?

"You look quite shaken up, dear," says Janice, and pats me on the shoulder. "You go and have a nice sit down."

"Yes," I say. "Yes, I think I will."

And Dad leads me off gently toward the house, as though I were some kind of invalid.

This is all getting out of hand. Now not only do I feel like an utter failure, I don't feel safe anymore, either. I feel exposed and edgy. I sit on the sofa next to Mum, drinking tea and watching *Countdown,* and every time there's a sound outside, I jump.

What if Derek Smeath's on his way here? How long would it take him to drive here from London? An hour and a half? Two, if the traffic's bad?

He wouldn't do that. He's a busy man.

But he *might.*

Or send the bailiffs round. Oh God. Threatening men in leather jackets. My stomach is squeezed tight with fear. In fact, I'm beginning to feel as though I genuinely am being stalked.

As the commercial break begins, Mum reaches for a catalogue

full of gardening things. "Look at this lovely birdbath," she says. "I'm going to get one for the garden."

"Great," I mutter, unable to concentrate.

"They've got some super window boxes, too," she says. "You could do with some nice window boxes in your flat."

"Yes," I say. "Maybe."

"Shall I put you down for a couple? They're not expensive."

"No, it's OK."

"You can pay by check, or VISA . . ." she says, flipping over the page.

"No, really, Mum," I say, my voice sharpening slightly.

"You could just phone up with your VISA card, and have them delivered—"

"Mum, stop it!" I cry. "I don't want them, OK?"

Mum gives me a surprised, slightly reproving look and turns to the next page of her catalogue. And I gaze back at her, full of a choking panic. My VISA card doesn't work. My debit card doesn't work. Nothing works. And she has no idea.

Don't think about it. Don't think about it. I grab for an ancient copy of the *Radio Times* on the coffee table and begin to leaf through it blindly.

"It's a shame about poor Martin and Janice, isn't it?" says Mum, looking up. "Fancy switching funds two weeks before the takeover! Such bad luck!"

"I know," I mumble, staring down at a page of listings. I don't want to be reminded about Martin and Janice.

"It seems a terrible coincidence," says Mum, shaking her head. "That the company should launch this new fund just before the takeover. You know, there must be a lot of people who did exactly what Martin and Janice did, who have lost out. Dreadful, really." She looks at the television. "Oh look, it's starting again."

The cheery *Countdown* music begins to play, and a round of applause rattles noisily from the television. But I'm not listening to it, or even paying any attention to the vowels and consonants. I'm thinking about what Mum has just said. A terrible coincidence—but it wasn't exactly a coincidence, was it? The bank actually wrote to Janice and Martin, suggesting that they switch funds. They even offered an incentive, didn't they? A carriage clock.

Suddenly I feel alert. I want to see the letter from Flagstaff Life—and find out exactly how long before the takeover they sent it.

" 'ENDING,' " says Mum, staring at the screen. "That's six. Ooh, there's an S. Can you have 'ENDINGS'?"

"I'm just . . . popping next door," I say, getting to my feet. "I won't be a minute."

As Martin opens the front door, I see that he and Janice have also been sitting in front of the telly, watching *Countdown*.

"Hi," I say sheepishly. "I was just wondering—could I have a quick chat?"

"Of course!" says Martin. "Come on in! Would you like a sherry?"

"Oh," I say, a little taken aback. I mean, not that I'm against drinking, obviously—but it isn't even five o'clock yet. "Well—OK then."

"Never too early for a sherry!" says Martin.

"I'll have another one, thanks, Martin," comes Janice's voice from the sitting room.

Blow me down. They're a pair of alcoholics!

Oh God, perhaps this is my fault too. Perhaps their financial mishap has driven them to seek solace in alcohol and daytime television.

"I was just wondering," I say nervously as Martin pours dark brown sherry into a schooner. "Just out of interest, could I have a look at that letter you got from Flagstaff Life, asking you to switch funds? I was wondering when they sent it."

"It arrived the very day we saw you," says Martin. "Why do you want to see it?" He raises his glass. "Your good health."

"Cheers," I say, and take a sip. "I'm just wondering—"

"Come into the living room," he interrupts, and ushers me through from the hall. "Here you are, my love," he adds, and gives Janice her sherry. "Bottoms up!"

"Sssh," she replies. "It's the numbers game! I need to concentrate."

"I thought I might do a little investigation into this," I whisper to Martin as the *Countdown* clock ticks round. "I feel so bad about it."

"Fifty times 4 is 200," says Janice suddenly. "Six minus 3 is 3, times 7 is 21 and add it on."

"Well done, love!" says Martin, and roots about in a carved oak sideboard. "Here's the letter," he says. "So—do you want to write an article or something?"

"Possibly," I say. "You wouldn't mind, would you?"

"Mind?" He gives a little shrug. "No, I wouldn't think so."

"Sssh!" says Janice. "It's the Countdown Conundrum."

"Right," I whisper. "Well, I'll just . . . I'll just take this, shall I?"

"Explicate!" yells Janice. "No, exploited!"

"And . . . thanks for the sherry." I take a huge gulp, shuddering slightly at its sticky sweetness, then put my glass down and tiptoe out of the room.

Half an hour later, sitting in my bedroom, I've read the letter from Flagstaff Life six times and I'm sure there's something fishy about it. How many investors must have switched funds after receiving this crappy carriage clock offer—and missed out on their windfall? More to the point, how much money must Flagstaff Life have saved? Suddenly I really want to know. There's a growing indignation in me; a growing determination to find out exactly what's been going on and, if it's what I suspect, to expose it. To print the truth and warn others. For the first time in my life, I'm actually *interested* in a financial story.

And I don't just want to write it up for *Successful Saving,* either.

This deserves the widest audience possible. Eric Foreman's card is still in my purse, with his direct telephone number printed at the top, and I take it out. I go to the phone and quickly punch in the number before I can change my mind.

"Eric Foreman, *Daily World,*" comes his voice, booming down the line.

Am I really doing this?

"Hi," I say nervously. "I don't know if you remember me. Rebecca Bloomwood from *Successful Saving*. We met at the Sacrum Asset Management press conference."

"That's right, so we did," he says cheerfully. "How are you, my love?"

"I'm fine," I say, and clench my hand tightly around the receiver. "Absolutely fine. Ahm . . . I was just wondering, are you still running your series on 'Can We Trust the Money Men?' "

"We are, as it goes," says Eric Foreman. "Why?"

"It's just . . ." I swallow. "I think I've got a story that might interest you."

Seventeen

I HAVE NEVER before worked so hard on an article. Never.

Mind you, I've never before been asked to write one so quickly. At *Successful Saving,* we get a whole month to write our articles—and we complain about that. When Eric Foreman said, "Can you do it by tomorrow?" I thought he was joking at first. I jauntily replied, "Of course!" and nearly added, "In fact, I'll have it with you in five minutes' time!" Then, *just* in time, I realized he was serious. Crikey.

So I'm round at Martin and Janice's first thing the next morning with a Dictaphone, writing down exactly all the information on their investment and trying to get in lots of heart-wrenching details as advised by Eric.

"We need human interest," he told me over the phone. "None of your dull financial reporting here. Make us feel sorry for them. Make us weep. A hardworking, ordinary couple, who thought they could rely on a few savings to see them through their old age. Ripped off by the fat cats. What kind of house do these people live in?"

"Ahmm . . . a four-bedroom detached house in Surrey."

"Well, for Christ's sake don't put that in!" he boomed. "I want honest, poor, and proud. Never demanded a penny off the state, saved to provide for themselves. Trusted a respectable financial institution. And all it did was kick them in the face." He paused, and it sounded as if he might be picking his teeth. "That kind of thing. Think you can manage it?"

"I . . . ahm . . . yes! Of course!" I stuttered.

Oh God, I thought as I put down the phone. What have I got myself into?

But it's too late to change my mind now. So the next thing is to persuade Janice and Martin that they don't mind appearing in *The Daily World*. The trouble is, it's not exactly *The Financial Times*, is it? Or even the normal *Times*. (Still, it could be a lot worse. It could be *The Sun*—and they'd end up sandwiched between a topless model and a blurred paparazzi shot of Posh Spice.)

Luckily, however, they're so bowled over that I'm making all this effort on their behalf, they don't seem to care which newspaper I'm writing for. And when they hear that a photographer's coming over at midday to take their picture, you'd think the queen was coming to visit.

"My hair!" says Janice in dismay, staring into the mirror. "Have I time to get Maureen in to give me a blow-dry?"

"Not really. And it looks lovely," I say reassuringly. "Anyway, they want you as natural as possible. Just . . . honest, ordinary people." I glance around the living room, trying to pick up poignant details to put into my article.

An anniversary card from their son stands proudly on the well-polished mantelpiece. But there will be no celebration this year for Martin and Janice Webster.

"I must phone Phyllis!" says Janice. "She won't believe it!"

"You weren't ever a soldier, or anything?" I say thoughtfully to Martin. "Or a . . . a fireman? Anything like that. Before you became a travel agent."

"Not really, love," says Martin, wrinkling his brow. "Just the Cadets at school."

"Oh, right," I say, brightening. "That might do."

Martin Webster fingers the Cadet badge he was so proud to wear as a youth. His life has been one of hard work and service for others. Now, in his retirement years, he should be enjoying the rewards he deserves.

But the fat cats have conned him out of his nest egg.* The Daily World *asks . . .

"I've photocopied all the documents for you," says Martin. "All the paperwork. I don't know if it'll be any use . . ."

"Oh thanks," I say, taking the pile of pages from him. "I'll have a good read through these."

When honest Martin Webster received a letter from Flagstaff Life, inviting him to switch investment funds, he trusted the money men to know what was best for him.

Two weeks later he discovered they had tricked him out of a £20,000 windfall.

"My wife is ill as a result of all this," he said. "I'm so worried."

Hmm.

"Janice?" I say, looking up casually. "Do you feel all right? Not . . . unwell, or anything?"

"A bit nervous, to be honest, dear," she says, looking round from the mirror. "I'm never very good at having my picture taken."

"My nerves are shot to pieces," said Mrs. Webster in a ragged voice. "I've never felt so betrayed in all my life."

"Well, I think I've got enough now," I say, getting up and switching off my Dictaphone. "I might have to *slightly* digress from what's on the tape—just to make the story work. You don't mind, do you?"

"Of course not!" says Janice. "You write what you like, Becky! We trust you."

I look at her soft, friendly face and feel a sudden shot of determination. This time I'll get it right.

"So what happens now?" says Martin.

"I'll have to go and talk to Flagstaff Life," I say. "Get them to give their defense."

"What defense?" says Martin. "There is no defense for what they did to us!"

I grin at him. "Exactly."

I'm full of happy adrenaline. All I need to do is get a quote from Flagstaff Life, and I can start writing the piece. I haven't got long: it needs to be finished by two o'clock if it's going to make tomorrow's edition. Why has work never seemed so exciting before?

Briskly I reach for the phone and dial Flagstaff's number—only to be told by the switchboard operator that all press inquiries are dealt with out of house. She gives me a number, which seems rather familiar, and I frown at it for a moment, then punch it in.

"Hello," says a smooth voice. "Brandon Communications."

Of course. Suddenly I feel a bit shaky. The word *Brandon* has hit me right in the stomach like a punch. I'd forgotten all about Luke Brandon. To be honest, I'd forgotten all about the rest of my life. And frankly, I don't want to be reminded of it.

But it's OK—I don't have to speak to him personally, do I?

"Hi!" I say. "It's Rebecca Bloomwood here. Ermm . . . I just wanted to talk to somebody about Flagstaff Life."

"Let me check . . ." says the voice. "Yes, that's Luke Brandon's client. I'll just put you through to his assistant . . ." And the voice disappears before I can say anything.

Oh God.

I can't do this. I can't speak to Luke Brandon. My questions are jotted down on a piece of paper in front of me, but as I stare at them, I'm not reading them. I'm remembering the humiliation I felt that day in Harvey Nichols. That horrible plunge in my stomach, as I heard the patronizing note in his voice and suddenly realized what he thought of me. A nothing. A joke.

OK, I *can* do this, I tell myself firmly. I'll just be very stern and businesslike and ask my questions, and . . .

"Rebecca!" comes a voice in my ear. "How are you! It's Alicia here."

"Oh," I say in surprise. "I thought I was going to speak to Luke. It's about Flagstaff Life."

"Yes, well," says Alicia. "Luke Brandon is a very busy man. I'm sure I can answer any questions you have."

"Oh, right," I say, and pause. "But they're not your client, are they?"

"I'm sure that won't matter in this case," she says, and gives a little laugh. "What did you want to know?"

"Right," I say, and look at my list. "Was it a deliberate strategy for Flagstaff Life to invite their investors to move out of with-profits just before they announced windfalls? Some people lost out a lot, you know."

"Right . . ." she says. "Thanks, Camilla, I'll have smoked salmon and lettuce."

"What?" I say.

"Sorry, yes, I am with you," she says. "Just jotting it down . . . I'll have to get back to you on that, I'm afraid."

"Well, I need a response soon!" I say, giving her my number. "My deadline's in a few hours."

"Got that," says Alicia. Suddenly her voice goes muffled. "No, smoked salmon. OK then, Chinese chicken. Yes." The muffle disappears. "So, Rebecca, any other questions? Tell you what, shall I send you our latest press pack? That's bound to answer any other queries. Or you could fax in your questions."

"Fine," I say curtly. "Fine, I'll do that." And I put the phone down.

For a while I stare straight ahead in brooding silence. Stupid patronizing cow. Can't even be bothered to take my questions seriously.

Then gradually it comes to me that this is the way I always get treated when I ring up press offices. No one's ever in any hurry to answer my questions, are they? People are always putting me on hold, saying they'll ring me back and not bothering. I've never minded before—I've rather enjoyed hanging on to a phone, listening to "Greensleeves." I've never cared before whether people took me seriously or not.

But today I do care. Today what I'm doing *does* seem important, and I *do* want to be taken seriously. This article isn't just about a press release and a bunch of numbers. Martin and Janice aren't hypothetical examples dreamed up by some marketing department. They're real people with real lives. That money would have made a huge difference to them.

I'll show Alicia, I think fiercely. I'll show them all, Luke Brandon included. Show them that I, Rebecca Bloomwood, am not a joke.

With a sudden determination I reach for my dad's typewriter. I feed in some paper, switch on my Dictaphone, take a deep breath, and begin to type.

Two hours later, I fax my 950-word article to Eric Foreman.

Eighteen

THE NEXT MORNING, I wake at six o'clock. It's pathetic, I know, but I'm as excited as a little kid on Christmas Day (or as me on Christmas Day, to be perfectly honest).

I lie in bed, telling myself to be grown-up and laid-back and not think about it—but I just can't resist it. My mind swims with images of the piles of newspapers in newsstands all over the country. Of the copies of *The Daily World* being dropped on people's doormats this morning; all the people who are going to be opening their papers, yawning, wondering what's in the news.

And what are they going to see?

They're going to see my name! Rebecca Bloomwood in print in *The Daily World*! My first national byline: "By Rebecca Bloomwood." Doesn't that sound cool? "By Rebecca Bloomwood."

I know the piece has gone in, because Eric Foreman phoned me up yesterday afternoon and told me the editor was really pleased with it. And they've got it on a color page—so the picture of Janice and Martin will be in full color. Really high profile. I can't quite believe it. *The Daily World!*

Even as I'm lying here, it occurs to me, there's already a whole pile of *Daily Worlds* at the newsstand in the parade of shops round the corner. A whole pile of pristine, unopened copies. And the newsstand opens at . . . what time? Six, I seem to remember. And now it's five past six. So in *theory,* I could go and buy one right now if I wanted to. I could just get up, slip on some clothes, go down to the newsstand, and buy one.

Not that I would, of course. I'm not quite so sad and desperate that I'm going to rush down as soon as the shop's opened, just to see my name. I mean, what do you take me for? No, what I'll do is just saunter down casually later on—perhaps at eleven or midday—pick up the paper and flip through it in mild interest and then saunter home again. I probably won't even bother to buy a copy. I mean—I've seen my name in print before. It's hardly a big deal. No need to make a song and dance about it.

I'm going to turn over now and go back to sleep. I can't think why I'm awake so early. Must be the birds or something. Hmm . . . close my eyes, plump up my pillow, think about something else . . . I wonder what I'll have for breakfast when I get up?

But I've never seen my name in *The Daily World,* says a little voice in my head. I've never seen it in a national newspaper.

This is killing me. I can't wait any longer, I've *got* to see it.

Abruptly I get out of bed, throw on my clothes, and tiptoe down the stairs. As I close the door, I feel just like the girl in that Beatles song about leaving home. Outside the air has a sweet, new-day smell, and the road is completely quiet. Gosh, it's nice being up early. Why on earth don't I get up at six more often? I should do this every day. A power walk before breakfast, like people do in New York. Burn off loads of calories and then return home to an energizing breakfast of oats and freshly squeezed orange juice. Perfect. This will be my new regime.

But as I reach the little parade of shops I feel a stab of nerves, and without quite meaning to, I slow my walk to a funereal pace. Maybe I'll just buy myself a Mars Bar and go home again. Or a Mint Aero, if they've got them.

Cautiously, I push at the door and wince at the ping! as it opens. I really don't want to draw attention to myself this morning. What if the guy behind the counter has read my article and thinks it's rubbish? This is nerve-racking. I should never have become a journalist. I should have become a beautician, like I always wanted to. Maybe it's not too late. I'll retrain, open my own boutique . . .

"Hello, Becky!"

I look up and feel my face jerk in surprise. Martin Webster's standing at the counter, holding a copy of *The Daily World*. "I just happened to be awake," he explains sheepishly. "Thought I'd just come down, have a little look . . ."

"Oh," I say. "Erm . . . me too." I give a nonchalant shrug. "Since I was awake anyway . . ."

My eye falls on the newspaper and I feel my stomach flip over. I'm going to expire with nerves. Please, just kill me quickly.

"So—what . . . what's it like?" I say in a strangled voice.

"Well," says Martin, gazing at the page as though perplexed. "It's certainly big." He turns the paper round to face me, and I nearly keel over. There, in full color, is a picture of Martin and Janice staring miserably up at the camera, below the headline COUPLE CHEATED BY FAT CATS AT FLAGSTAFF LIFE.

Shaking slightly, I take the paper from Martin. My eye skips across the page to the first column of text . . . and there it is! "By Rebecca Bloomwood." That's my name! That's me!

There's a ping at the door of the shop, and we both look round. And there, to my utter astonishment, is Dad.

"Oh," he says, and gives an embarrassed little cough. "Your mother wanted me to buy a copy. And since I was awake anyway . . ."

"So was I," says Martin quickly.

"Me too," I say.

"Well," says Dad. "So—is it in?"

"Oh yes," I say, "it's in." I turn the paper round so he can see it.

"Gosh," he says. "It's big, isn't it?"

"The photo's good, don't you think?" says Martin enthusiastically. "Brings out the flowers in our curtains beautifully."

"Yes, the photo's great," I agree.

I'm not going to demean myself by asking what he thought of the article itself. If he wants to compliment my writing, he will. If he doesn't—then it really doesn't matter. The point is, *I'm* proud of it.

"And Janice looks very nice, I thought," says Martin, still gazing at the photograph.

"Very nice," agrees Dad. "If a little mournful."

"You see, these professionals, they know how to light a shot," says Martin. "The way the sunlight falls just here, on her—"

"What about my article?" I wail piteously. "Did you like that?"

"Oh, it's very good!" says Martin. "Sorry, Becky, I should have said! I haven't read it all yet, but it seems to capture the situation exactly. Makes me out to be quite a hero!" He frowns. "Although I never did fight in the Falklands, you know."

"Oh well," I say hurriedly. "That's neither here nor there, really."

"So you wrote all this yesterday?" says Dad. "On my typewriter?" He seems astounded.

"Yes," I say smugly. "It looks good, doesn't it? Have you seen my byline? 'By Rebecca Bloomwood.' "

"Janice'll be thrilled," says Martin. "I'm going to buy two copies."

"I'm going to buy three," says Dad. "Your granny will love to see this."

"And I'll buy one," I say. "Or two, perhaps." I carelessly reach for a handful and plonk them on the counter.

"Six copies?" says the cashier. "Are you sure?"

"I need them for my records," I say, and blush slightly.

When we get home, Mum and Janice are both waiting at our front door, desperate to see a copy.

"My hair!" wails Janice as soon as she sees the picture. "It looks terrible! What have they done to it?"

"No, it doesn't, love!" protests Martin. "You look very nice."

"Your curtains look lovely, Janice," says Mum, looking over her shoulder.

"They do, don't they?" says Martin eagerly. "That's just what I said."

I give up. What kind of family have I got, that are more interested in curtains than top financial journalism? Anyway, I don't care. I'm mesmerized by my byline. "By Rebecca Bloomwood." "By Rebecca Bloomwood."

After everyone's peered at the paper, Mum invites Janice and Martin round to our house for breakfast, and Dad goes and puts on some coffee. There's a rather festive air to the proceedings, and everyone keeps laughing a lot. I don't think any of us can quite believe that Janice and Martin are in *The Daily World*. (And me, of course. "By Rebecca Bloomwood.")

At ten o'clock, I slope off and ring up Eric Foreman. Just casually, you know. To let him know I've seen it.

"Looks good, doesn't it?" he says cheerfully. "The editor's really going for this series, so if you come up with any more stories like this just give me a shout. I like your style. Just right for *The Daily World*."

"Excellent," I say, feeling a glow of pleasure.

"Oh, and while I'm at it," he adds, "you'd better give me your bank details."

My stomach gives a nasty lurch. Why does Eric Foreman want my bank details? Shit, is he going to check that my own finances are in order or something? Is he going to run a credit check on me?

"Everything's done by transfer these days," he's saying. "Four hundred quid. That all right?"

What? What's he—

Oh my God, he's going to *pay* me. But of course he is. Of course he is!

"That's fine," I hear myself say. "No problem. I'll just, ahm . . . give you my account number, shall I?"

Four hundred quid! I think dazedly as I scrabble for my checkbook. Just like that! I can't quite believe it.

"Excellent," says Eric Foreman, writing the details down. "I'll sort that out for you with Accounts." Then he pauses. "Tell me, would you be in the market for writing general features? Human interest stories, that kind of thing?"

Would I be in the market? Is he kidding?

"Sure," I say, trying not to sound too thrilled. "In fact . . . I'd probably prefer it to finance."

"Oh right," he says. "Well, I'll keep an eye out for bits that might suit you. As I say, I think you've got the right style for us."

"Great," I say. "Thanks."

As I put the phone down, there's a huge smile on my face. I've got the right style for *The Daily World*! Hah!

The phone rings again, and I pick it up, wondering if it's Eric Foreman offering me some more work already.

"Hello, Rebecca Bloomwood," I say in a businesslike voice.

"Rebecca," says Luke Brandon's curt voice—and my heart freezes. "Could you please tell me what the fuck is going on?"

Shit.

He sounds really angry. For an instant I'm paralyzed. My throat feels dry; my hand is sweaty round the receiver. Oh God. What am I going to say? What am I going to say to him?

But hang on a minute. *I* haven't done anything wrong.

"I don't know what you mean," I say, playing for time. Keep calm, I tell myself. Calm and cool.

"Your tawdry effort in *The Daily World*," he says scathingly. "Your one-sided, unbalanced, probably libelous little story."

For a second I'm so shocked I can't speak. Tawdry? Libelous?

"It's not tawdry!" I splutter at last. "It's a good piece. And it's certainly not libelous. I can prove everything I said."

"And I suppose getting the other side of the story would have been inconvenient," he snaps. "I suppose you were too busy writing your purple prose to approach Flagstaff Life and ask for their version of events. You'd rather have a good story than spoil it by trying to give a balanced picture."

"I *tried* to get the other side of the story!" I exclaim furiously. "I phoned your PR company yesterday and told them I was writing the piece!"

There's silence.

"Who did you speak to?" says Luke.

"Alicia," I reply. "I asked her a very clear question about Flagstaff's policy on switching funds, and she told me she'd get back to me. I *told* her I had an urgent deadline."

Luke gives an impatient sigh. "What the fuck were you doing, speaking to Alicia? Flagstaff's my client, not hers."

"I know! I said that to her! But she said you were a very busy man and she could deal with me."

"Did you tell her you were writing for *The Daily World*?"

"No," I say, and feel myself flush slightly red. "I didn't specify who I was writing for. But I would have told her if she'd asked me. She just didn't bother. She just assumed I couldn't possibly be doing anything important." In spite of myself, my voice is rising in emotion. "Well, she was wrong, wasn't she? You were all wrong. And maybe now you'll start treating everybody with respect. Not just the people you *think* are important."

I break off, panting slightly, and there's a bemused silence.

"Rebecca," says Luke at last, "if this is about what happened between us that day—if this is some kind of petty revenge—"

I'm really going to explode now.

"Don't you bloody insult me!" I yell. "Don't you bloody try and make this personal! This is about two innocent people being hoodwinked by one of your big-shot clients, nothing else. I told the truth, and if you didn't have a chance to respond, it's your own company's incompetence that's to blame. I was completely professional, I gave you every opportunity to put out your side of the story. *Every* opportunity. And if you blew it, that's not my fault."

And without giving him the chance to reply, I slam the phone down.

I'm feeling quite shaken as I go back into the kitchen. To think I ever liked Luke Brandon. To think I table-hopped with him. To think I let him lend me twenty quid. He's just an arrogant, self-centered, chauvinistic—

"Telephone!" says Mum. "Shall I get it?"

It'll be him again, won't it? Ringing back to apologize. Well, he needn't think I'm that easily won round. I stand by every word I said. And I'll tell him so. In fact, I'll add that—

"It's for you, Becky," says Mum.

"Fine," I say coolly, and make my way to the telephone. I don't hurry; I don't panic. I feel completely in control.

"Hello?" I say.

"Rebecca? Eric Foreman here."

"Oh!" I say in surprise. "Hi!"

"Bit of news about your piece."

"Oh yes?" I say, trying to sound calm. But my stomach's churning. What if Luke Brandon's spoken to him? Oh shit, I did check all the facts, didn't I?

"I've just had *Morning Coffee* on the phone," he says. "You know, the TV program? Rory and Emma. They're interested in your story."

"What?" I say stupidly.

"There's a new series they're doing on finance, 'Managing Your Money.' They get some financial expert in every week, tell the viewers how to keep tabs on their dosh." Eric Foreman lowers his voice. "Frankly, they're running out of stuff to talk about. They've done mortgages, store cards, pensions, all the usual cobblers . . ."

"Right," I say, trying to sound focused. But as his words slowly sink in, I'm a bit dazed. Rory and Emma read my article? Rory and Emma themselves? I have a sudden vision of them holding the paper together, jostling for a good view.

But of course, that's silly, isn't it? They'd have a copy each.

"So, anyway, they want to have you on the show tomorrow morning," Eric Foreman's saying. "Talk about this windfall story, warn their viewers to take care. You interested in that kind of thing? If not, I can easily tell them you're too busy."

"No!" I say quickly. "No. Tell them I'm . . ." I swallow. "I'm interested."

As I put down the phone, I feel faint. I'm going to be on television.

BANK OF HELSINKI

Helsinki House
124 Lombard St.
London EC2D 9YF

Rebecca Bloomwood
c/o William Green Recruitment
39 Farringdon Square
London EC4 7TD

27 March 2000

Dere Rebecca Bloomwood:

Finnish Finnish Finnish Finnish Finnish Finnish Finnish Finnish Finnish Finnish Finnish Finnish "*Daily World*" Finnish

More Finnish More Finnish

Finnish good-bye,

Jan Virtanen

Nineteen

THE CAR TO TAKE ME to the television studios arrives promptly at seven-thirty the next morning. When the doorbell rings, Mum, Dad, and I all jump, even though we've been waiting in a tense silence for ten minutes.

"Well," says Dad gruffly, glancing at his watch. "They're here, anyway."

Ever since I told him about the arrangements, Dad's been predicting that the car won't turn up and that he'll have to drive me to the studios himself. He even worked out a route last night, and phoned up Uncle Malcolm as a standby. (To be honest, I think he was quite looking forward to it.)

"Oh, Becky," says Mum in a trembling voice. "Good luck, darling." She looks at me, then shakes her head. "Our little Becky, on television. I can't believe it."

I start to get up, but Dad puts out a restraining arm.

"Now, before you answer the door, Becky," he says. "You are sure, aren't you? About the risk you're taking." He glances at Mum, who bites her lip.

"I'll be fine!" I say, trying to sound as soothing as possible. "Honestly, Dad, we've been over it all."

Last night, it suddenly occurred to Dad that if I went on the telly, my stalker would know where I was. At first he was adamant I'd have to call the whole thing off—and it took an awful lot of persuasion to convince him and Mum I'd be perfectly safe in the TV studios. They were even talking about hiring a bodyguard, can you believe it? I mean, what on earth would I look like, turning up with a bodyguard?

Actually, I'd look pretty cool and mysterious, wouldn't I? That might have been quite a good idea.

The doorbell rings again and I leap to my feet.

"Well," says Dad. "You just be careful."

"I will, don't worry!" I say, picking up my bag. I walk to the door calmly, trying not to give away how excited I feel. Inside I feel as light as a bubble.

I just can't believe how well everything's going. Not only am I going to be on the telly, but everyone's being so nice to me! Yesterday I had several phone conversations with an assistant producer of *Morning Coffee*, who's a really sweet girl called Zelda. We went over exactly what I was going to say on the program, then she arranged for a car to come and pick me up—and when I told her I was at my parents' house with none of my clothes handy, she thought for a bit—then said I could choose something to wear from the wardrobe. I mean, how cool is that? Choosing any outfit I like from the wardrobe! Maybe they'll let me keep it afterward, too.

As I open the front door, my stomach gives an excited leap. There, waiting in the drive, is a portly, middle-aged man in a blue blazer and cap, standing next to a shiny black car. My own private chauffeur! This just gets better and better.

"Miss Bloomwood?" says the driver.

"Yes," I say, unable to stop myself from grinning in delight. I'm about to reach for the door handle—but he gets there before me, opens the car door with a flourish, and stands to attention, waiting for me to get in. God, this is like being a film star or something!

I glance back toward the house and see Mum and Dad standing on the front step, both looking utterly gobsmacked.

"Well—bye then!" I say, trying to sound casual, as though I always ride around in a chauffeur-driven car. "See you later!"

"Becky, is that you?" comes a voice from next door, and Janice appears on the other side of the hedge in her dressing gown. Her eyes grow large as they take in the car and she glances at Mum, who raises her shoulders, as though to say "I know, isn't it unbelievable?"

"Morning, Janice," says Dad.

"Morning, Graham," says Janice dazedly. "Oh, Becky! I've never seen anything like it. In all the years . . . If Tom could only see you . . ." She breaks off and looks at Mum. "Have you taken any photographs?"

"We haven't!" says Mum in dismay. "It didn't even occur to us. Graham, quick—go and get the camera."

"No, wait, I'll get our camcorder!" says Janice. "It won't take me two ticks. We could have the car arriving in the drive, and Becky walking out of the front door . . . and maybe we could use *The Four Seasons* as the soundtrack, and then cut straight to . . ."

"No!" I say hastily, seeing a flicker of amusement pass across the face of the driver. And I was doing so well at looking nonchalant and professional. "We haven't got time for any pictures. I have to get to the studios!"

"Yes," says Janice, suddenly looking anxious. "Yes, you don't want to be late." She glances fearfully at her watch, as though afraid the program might already have started. "It's on at eleven, isn't it?"

"Eleven o'clock the program starts," says Dad. "Set the video for five to, that's what I've been telling people."

"That's what we'll do," says Janice. "Just in case." She gives a little sigh. "I shan't dare to go to the loo all morning, just in case I miss it!"

There's an awed silence as I get into the car. The driver closes the door smartly, then walks around to the driver's door. I press the button to lower my window and grin out at Mum and Dad.

"Becky, darling, what will you do afterward?" says Mum. "Come back here or go back to the flat?"

Immediately I feel my smile falter, and look down, pretending to fiddle with the window controls. I don't want to think about afterward.

In fact, I can't even visualize afterward. I'm going to be on the telly . . . and that's as far as it goes. The rest of my life is shut securely away in a box at the back of my head and I don't even want to remember it's there.

"I . . . I'm not sure," I say. "I'll see what happens."

"They'll probably take you out to lunch afterward," says Dad knowledgeably. "These showbiz types are always having lunch with each other."

"Liquid lunches," puts in Janice, and gives a little laugh.

"At The Ivy," says Mum. "That's where all the actors meet up, isn't it?"

"The Ivy's old hat!" retorts Dad. "They'll take her to the Groucho Club."

"The Groucho Club!" says Janice, clasping her hands. "Isn't that where Kate Moss goes?"

This is getting ridiculous.

"We'd better go," I say, and the driver nods.

"Good luck, sweetheart," calls Dad. I close the window and lean back, and the car purrs out of the drive.

For a while, we drive in silence. I keep casually glancing out of the window to see if anyone's looking at me in my chauffeur-driven car and wondering who I am (that new girl on *EastEnders*, perhaps). Although we're whizzing along the highway so fast, I probably look like a blur.

"So," says the driver after a while. "You're appearing on *Morning Coffee*, are you?"

"Yes, I am," I say, and immediately feel a joyful smile plaster itself over my face. God, I must *stop* this. I bet Jeremy Paxman doesn't start grinning inanely every time someone asks him if he's appearing on *University Challenge*.

"So what're you on for?" says the driver, interrupting my thoughts.

I'm about to reply "To be famous and maybe get some free clothes," when I realize what he means.

"A financial story," I say coolly. "I wrote a piece in *The Daily World*, and the producers read it and wanted me on the show."

"Been on television before?"

"No," I admit reluctantly. "No, I haven't."

We pull up at some lights and the driver turns round in his seat to survey me.

"You'll be fine," he says. "Just don't let the nerves get to you."

"Nerves?" I say, and give a little laugh. "I'm not nervous! I'm just . . . looking forward to it."

"Glad to hear it," says the driver, turning back. "You'll be OK, then. Some people, they get onto that sofa, thinking they're fine, relaxed, happy as a clam . . . then they see that red light, and it hits them that 2.5 million people around the country are all watching them. Makes some people start to panic."

"Oh," I say after a slight pause. "Well . . . I'm nothing like them! I'll be fine!"

"Good," says the driver.

"Good," I echo, a little less certainly, and look out of the window.

I'll be fine. Of course I will. I've never been nervous in my life before, and I'm certainly not going to start . . .

Two point five million people.

Gosh. When you think about it—that is quite a lot, isn't it? Two point five million people, all sitting at home, staring at the screen. Staring at my face. Waiting for what I'm going to say next.

OK, don't think about it. The important thing is just to keep remembering how well prepared I am. I rehearsed for ages in front of the mirror last night and I know what I'm going to say practically by heart.

It all has to be very basic and simple, Zelda said—because apparently 76 percent of the *Morning Coffee* audience are housewives looking after toddlers, who have very short attention spans. She kept apologizing for what she called the "dumbing-down effect" and saying a financial expert like myself must feel really frustrated by it—and of course, I agreed with her.

But to be honest, I'm quite relieved. In fact, the more dumbed down the better, as far as I'm concerned. I mean, writing a *Daily World* article with all my notes to hand was one thing, but answering tricky questions on live TV is quite another.

So anyway, I'm going to start off by saying "If you were offered a choice between a carriage clock and £20,000, which would you choose?" Rory or Emma will reply, "Twenty thousand pounds, of course!" and I'll say, "Exactly. Twenty thousand pounds." I'll pause briefly, to let that figure sink into the audience's mind, and then I'll say, "Unfortunately, when Flagstaff Life offered their customers a carriage clock to transfer their savings, they didn't tell them that if they did so, they would *lose* a £20,000 windfall!"

That sounds quite good, don't you think? Rory and Emma will ask a few very easy questions like "What can people do to protect themselves?" and I'll give nice simple answers. And right at the end, just to keep it light, we're going to talk about all the different things you could buy with £20,000.

Actually, that's the bit I'm looking forward to most of all. I've already thought of loads of things. Did you know, with £20,000 you could buy forty Gucci watches, *and* have enough left over for a bag?

The *Morning Coffee* studios are in Maida Vale, and as we draw near to the gates, familiar from the opening credits of the show, I feel a dart of excitement. I'm actually going to be on television!

The doorman waves us through the barrier, we pull up outside a pair of huge double doors, and the driver opens the door for me. As I get out, my legs are shaking slightly, but I force myself to walk confidently up the steps, into the reception hall, and up to the desk.

"I'm here for *Morning Coffee,*" I say, and give a little laugh as I realize what I've just said. "I mean . . ."

"I know what you mean," says the receptionist, kindly but wearily. She looks up my name on a list, jabs a number into her phone, and says, "Jane? Rebecca Bloomwood's here." Then she gestures to a row of squashy chairs and says, "Someone will be with you shortly."

I walk over to the seating area and sit down opposite a middle-aged woman with lots of wild dark hair and a big amber necklace round her neck. She's lighting up a cigarette, and even though I don't really smoke anymore, I suddenly feel as though I could do with one myself.

Not that I'm nervous or anything. I just fancy a cigarette.

"Excuse me," calls the receptionist. "This is a no-smoking area."

"Damn," says the woman in a raspy voice. She takes a long drag, then stubs the cigarette out on a saucer and smiles at me conspiratorially. "Are you a guest on the show?" she says.

"Yes," I say. "Are you?"

The woman nods. "Promoting my new novel, *Blood Red Sunset*." She lowers her voice to a thrilling throb. "A searing tale of love, greed, and murder, set in the ruthless world of South American money launderers."

"Gosh," I say. "That sounds really—"

"Let me give you a copy," interrupts the woman. She reaches into a Mulberry holdall by her side and pulls out a vividly colored hardback book. "Remind me of your name?"

Remind her?

"It's Rebecca," I say. "Rebecca Bloomwood."

"To Becca," the woman says aloud, as she scrawls inside the front page. "With love and great affection." She signs with a flourish and hands the book to me.

"Thanks very much . . ." Quickly I look at the cover. "Elisabeth."

Elisabeth Plover. To be honest, I've never heard of her.

"I expect you're wondering how I came to know such a lot about such a violent, dangerous world," says Elisabeth. She leans forward and gazes at me with huge green eyes. "The truth is, I lived with a money launderer for three long months. I loved him; I learned from him . . . and then I betrayed him." Her voice dies to a trembling whisper. "I still remember the look he gave me as the police dragged him away. He knew what I'd done. He knew I was his Judas Iscariot. And yet, in a strange kind of way, I think he loved me for it."

"Wow," I say, impressed in spite of myself. "Did all this happen in South America?"

"Brighton," she says after a slight pause. "But money launderers are the same the world over."

"Rebecca?" says a voice, before I can think of a reply to this, and we both look up to see a girl with smooth dark hair, in jeans and a black polo neck, walking swiftly toward us. "I'm Zelda. We spoke yesterday?"

"Zelda!" exclaims Elisabeth, getting to her feet. "How have you been, my darling?" She holds out her arms, and Zelda stares at her.

"I'm sorry," she says, "have we—" She stops as her gaze falls on my copy of *Blood Red Sunset*. "Oh yes, that's right. Elisabeth Plover. One of the researchers will be down for you in a minute. Meanwhile, do help yourself to coffee." She flashes her a smile, then turns to me. "Rebecca, are you ready?"

"Yes!" I say eagerly, leaping up from my chair. (I have to admit, I feel quite flattered that Zelda's come down to get me herself. I mean, she obviously doesn't come down for everyone.)

"Great to meet you," says Zelda, shaking my hand. "Great to have you on the show. Now, as usual, we're completely frantic—so if it's OK by you, I thought we'd just head straight off to hair and makeup and we can talk on the way."

"Absolutely," I say, trying not to sound too excited. "Good idea."

Hair and makeup! This is so cool!

"There's been a slight change of plan which I need to fill you in on," says Zelda. "Nothing to worry about . . . Any word from Bella yet?" she adds to the receptionist.

The receptionist shakes her head, and Zelda mutters something which sounds like "Stupid cow."

"OK, let's go," she says, heading off toward a pair of swing doors. "I'm afraid it's even more crazy than usual today. One of our regulars has let us down, so we're searching for a replacement, and there's been an accident in the kitchen . . ." She pushes through the swing doors and now we're striding along a green-carpeted corridor buzzing with people. "Plus, we've got Heaven Sent 7 in today," she adds over her shoulder. "Which means the switchboard gets jammed with fans calling in, and we have to find dressing room space for seven enormous egos."

"Right," I say nonchalantly. But underneath I'm jumping with excitement. Heaven Sent 7? But I mean . . . they're really famous! And I'm appearing on the same show as them! I mean—I'll get to meet them and everything, won't I? Maybe we'll all go out for a drink afterward and become really good friends. They're all a bit younger than me, but that won't matter. I'll be like their older sister.

Or maybe I'll *go out* with one of them! God, yes. That nice one with the dark hair. Nathan. (Or is it Ethan? Whatever he's called.) He'll catch my eye after the show and quietly ask me out to dinner without the others. We'll go to some tiny little restaurant, and at first it'll be all quiet and discreet, but then the press will find out and we'll become one of those really famous couples who go to premieres all the time. And I'll wear . . .

"OK, here we are," says Zelda, and I look up dazedly.

We're standing in the doorway of a room lined with mirrors and spotlights. Three people are sitting in chairs in front of the mirrors, wearing capes and having makeup applied by trendy-looking girls in jeans; another is having her hair blow-dried. Music is playing in the background, there's a friendly level of chatter, and in the air are the mingled scents of hair spray, face powder, and coffee.

It's basically my idea of heaven.

"So," says Zelda, leading me toward a girl with red hair. "Chloe will do your makeup, and then we'll pop you along to wardrobe. OK?"

"Fine," I say, my eyes widening as I take in Chloe's collection of makeup. There's about a zillion brushes, pots, and tubes littered over the counter in front of us, all really good brands like Chanel and MAC.

"Now, about your slot," continues Zelda as I sit down on a swivel chair. "As I say, we've gone for a rather different format from the one we talked about previously . . ."

"Zelda!" comes a man's voice from outside. "Bella's on the line for you!"

"Oh shit," says Zelda. "Look, Rebecca, I've got to go and take this call, but I'll come back as soon as I can. OK?"

"Fine!" I say happily, as Chloe drapes a cape round me and pulls my hair back into a wide towel band. In the background, the radio's playing my favorite song by Lenny Kravitz.

"I'll just cleanse and tone, and then give you a base," says Chloe. "If you could shut your eyes . . ."

I close my eyes and, after a few seconds, feel a cool, creamy liquid being massaged into my face. It's the most delicious sensation in the world. I could sit here all day.

"So," says Chloe after a while. "What are you on the show for?"

"Errm . . . finance," I say vaguely. "A piece on finance."

To be honest, I'm feeling so relaxed, I can hardly remember what I'm doing here.

"Oh, yeah," says Chloe, efficiently smoothing foundation over my face. "They were talking earlier about some financial thing." She reaches for a palette of eyeshadows, blends a couple of colors together, then picks up a brush. "So, are you a financial expert, then?"

"Well," I say, a little awkwardly. "You know."

"Wow," says Chloe, starting to apply eyeshadow to my eyelids. "I don't understand the first thing about money."

"Me neither!" chimes in a dark-haired girl from across the room. "My accountant's given up trying to explain it all to me. As soon he says the word 'tax-year,' my mind glazes over."

I'm about to reply sympathetically "Me too!" and launch into a nice girly chat—but then I stop myself. The memory of Janice and Martin is a bit too raw for me to be flippant.

"You probably know quite a lot more about your finances than you realize," I say instead. "If you *really* don't know . . . then you should take advice from someone who does."

"You mean a financial expert like you?" says the girl.

I smile back, trying to look confident—but all this talk of my being a "financial expert" is unnerving me. I feel as though any minute now, someone's going to walk in, ask me an impossible question about South African bond yields, and then denounce me as a fraud. Thank goodness I know exactly what I'm going to say on air.

"Sorry, Rebecca," says Chloe, "I'm going to have to interrupt. Now, I was thinking a raspberry red for the lips. Is that OK by you?"

What with all this chatting, I haven't really been paying attention to what she's been doing to my face. But as I look at my reflection properly, I can't quite believe it. My eyes are huge; I've suddenly got amazing cheekbones . . . honestly, I look like a different person. Why on earth don't I wear makeup like this every day?

"Wow!" I breathe.

"It's easier because you're so calm," observes Chloe, reaching into a black vanity case. "We get some people in here, really trembling with nerves. Even celebrities. We can hardly do their makeup."

"Really?" I say, and lean forward, ready to hear some insider gossip. But Zelda's voice interrupts us.

"Sorry about that, Rebecca!" she exclaims. "Right, how are we doing? Makeup looks good. What about hair?"

"It's nicely cut," says Chloe, picking up a few strands of my hair and dropping them back down again, just like Nicky Clarke on a makeover. "I'll just give it a blow-dry for sheen."

"Fine," says Zelda. "And then we'll get her along to wardrobe." She glances at something on her clipboard, then sits down on a swivel chair next to me. "OK, so, Rebecca, we need to talk about your item."

"Excellent," I say, matching her businesslike tone. "Well, I've prepared it all just as you wanted. Really simple and straightforward."

"Yup," says Zelda. "Well, that's the thing. We had a talk at the meeting yesterday, and you'll be glad to hear, we don't need it too basic, after all." She smiles. "You'll be able to get as technical as you like!"

"Oh, right," I say, taken aback. "Well . . . good! That's great! Although I might still keep it fairly low—"

"We want to avoid talking down to the audience. I mean, they're not morons!" Zelda lowers her voice slightly. "Plus we had some new audience research in yesterday, and apparently 80 percent of our viewers feel patronized by some or all of the show's content. Basically, we need to redress that balance. So we've had a complete change of plan for your item!" She beams at me. "What we thought is, instead of a simple interview, we'd have more of a high-powered debate."

"A high-powered debate?" I echo, trying not to sound as alarmed as I feel.

"Absolutely!" says Zelda. "What we want is a really heated discussion! Opinions flying, voices raised. That kind of thing."

Opinions?

"So is that OK?" says Zelda, frowning at me. "You look a bit—"

"I'm fine!" I force myself to smile brightly. "Just . . . looking forward to it! A nice high-powered debate. Great!" I clear my throat. "And . . . and who will I be debating with?"

"A representative from Flagstaff Life," says Zelda triumphantly. "Head-to-head with the enemy. It'll make great television!"

"Zelda!" comes a voice from outside the room. "Bella again!"

"Oh, for Christ's sake!" says Zelda, leaping up. "Rebecca, I'll be back in a sec."

"Fine," I manage. "See you in a minute."

"OK," says Chloe cheerfully. "While she's gone, let me put on that lipstick."

She reaches for a long brush and begins to paint in my lips, and I stare at my reflection, trying to keep calm, trying not to panic. But my throat's so tight, I can't swallow. I've never felt so frightened in all my life.

I can't talk in a high-powered debate!

Why did I ever want to be on television?

"Rebecca, could you try to keep your lips still?" says Chloe with a puzzled frown. "They're really shaking."

"Sorry," I whisper, staring at my reflection like a frozen rabbit. She's right, I'm trembling all over. Oh God, this is no good. I've got to calm down. Think happy thoughts. Think Zen.

In an effort to distract myself, I focus on the reflection in the mirror. In the background I can see Zelda standing in the corridor, talking into a phone with a furious expression on her face.

"Yup," I can hear her saying curtly. "Yup. But the point is, Bella, we pay you a retainer to *be* available. What the fuck am I supposed to do now?" She looks up, sees someone, and lifts a hand in greeting. "OK, Bella, I do see that . . ."

A blond woman and two men appear in the corridor, and

Zelda nods to them apologetically. I can't see their faces, but they're all wearing smart overcoats and holding briefcases, and one of the men is holding a folder bulging with papers. The blond woman's coat is actually rather nice, I find myself thinking. And she's got a *gorgeous* Louis Vuitton bag. I wonder who she is.

"Yup," Zelda's saying. "Yup. Well, if *you* can suggest an alternative phone-in subject . . ."

She raises her eyebrows at the blond woman, who shrugs and turns away to look at a poster on the wall. And as she does so, my heart nearly stops dead.

Because I recognize her. It's Alicia. Alicia from Brandon Communications is standing five yards away from me.

I almost want to laugh at the incongruity of it. What's she doing here? What's Alicia Bitch Long-legs doing here, for God's sake?

One of the men turns round to say something to her—and as I see his face, I think I recognize him, too. He's another one of the Brandon C lot, isn't he? One of those young, eager, baby-faced types.

But what on earth are they all doing here? What's going on? Surely it can't be—

They can't all be here because of—

No. Oh no. Suddenly I feel rather cold.

"Luke!" comes Zelda's voice from the corridor, and I feel a swoop of dismay. "*So* glad you could make it. We always love having you on the show. You know, I had no idea you represented Flagstaff Life, until Sandy said . . ."

This isn't happening. Please tell me this isn't happening.

"The journalist who wrote the piece is already here," Zelda's saying, "and I've primed her on what's happening. I think it's going to make really great television, the two of you arguing away!"

She starts moving down the corridor, and in the mirror I see Alicia and the eager young man begin to follow her. Then the third overcoated man starts to come into view. And although my stomach's churning painfully, I can't stop myself. I slowly turn my head as he passes the door.

I meet Luke Brandon's grave, dark eyes and he meets mine, and for a few still seconds, we just stare at each other. Then abruptly he looks away and strides off down the corridor. And I'm left, gazing helplessly at my painted reflection, feeling sick with panic.

POINTS FOR TELEVISION INTERVIEW

SIMPLE AND BASIC FINANCIAL ADVICE

1. Prefer clock/twenty grand? Obvious.
2. Flagstaff Life ripped off innocent customers. Beware.

Ermm . . .

3. Always be very careful with your money.
4. Don't put it all in one investment but diversify.
5. Don't lose it by mistake
6. Don't

THINGS YOU CAN BUY WITH £20,000

1. Nice car; e.g., small BMW
2. Pearl and diamond necklace from Aspreys plus big diamond ring
3. 3 couture evening dresses; e.g., from John Galliano
4. Steinway grand piano
5. 5 gorgeous leather sofas from the Conran shop
6. 40 Gucci watches, plus bag
7. Flowers delivered every month for 42 years
8. 55 pedigree Labrador puppies
9. 80 cashmere jumpers
10. 666 Wonderbras
11. 454 pots Helena Rubinstein moisturizer
12. 800 bottles of champagne
13. 2,860 Fiorentina pizzas
14. 15,384 tubes of Pringles
15. 90,909 packets of Polo mints
16.

Twenty

By ELEVEN TWENTY-FIVE, I'm sitting on a brown upholstered chair in the green room. I'm dressed in a midnight-blue Jasper Conran suit, sheer tights, and a pair of suede high heels. What with my makeup and blown-dry hair, I've never looked smarter in my life. But I can't enjoy any of it. All I can think of is the fact that in fifteen minutes, I've got to sit on a sofa and discuss high-powered finance with Luke Brandon on live television.

The very thought of it makes me feel like whimpering. Or laughing wildly. I mean, it's like some kind of sick joke. Luke Brandon against me. Luke Brandon, with his genius IQ and bloody photographic memory—against me. He'll walk all over me. He'll *massacre* me.

"Darling, have a croissant," says Elisabeth Plover, who's sitting opposite me, munching a *pain au chocolat*. "They're simply sublime. Every bite like a ray of golden Provençal sun."

"No thanks," I say. "I . . . I'm not really hungry."

I don't understand how she can eat. I honestly feel as though I'm about to throw up at any moment. How on earth do people appear on television every day? How does Fiona Phillips do it? No wonder they're all so thin.

"Coming up!" comes Rory's voice from the television monitor in the corner of the room, and both our heads automatically swivel round to see the screen filled with a picture of the beach at sunset. "What is it like, to live with a gangster and then, risking everything, betray him? Our next guest has written an explosive novel based on her dark and dangerous background . . ."

". . . And we introduce a new series of in-depth discussions," chimes in Emma. The picture changes to one of pound coins raining onto the floor, and my stomach gives a nasty flip. "*Morning Coffee* turns the spotlight on the issue of financial scandal, with two leading industry experts coming head-to-head in debate."

Is that me? Oh God, I don't want to be a leading industry expert. I want to go home and watch reruns of *The Simpsons*.

"But first!" says Rory cheerily. "Scott Robertson's getting all fired up in the kitchen."

The picture switches abruptly to a man in a chef's hat grinning and brandishing a blowtorch. I stare at him for a few moments, then look down again, clenching my hands tightly in my lap. I can't quite believe that in fifteen minutes it'll be me up on that screen. Sitting on the sofa. Trying to think of something to say.

To distract myself, I unscrew my crappy piece of paper for the thousandth time and read through my paltry notes. Maybe it won't be so bad, I find myself thinking hopefully, as my eyes circle the same few sentences again and again. Maybe I'm worrying about nothing. We'll probably keep the whole thing at the level of a casual chat. Keep it simple and friendly. After all . . .

"Good morning, Rebecca," comes a voice from the door. Slowly I look up—and as I do so, my heart sinks. Luke Brandon is standing in the doorway. He's wearing an immaculate dark suit, his hair is shining, and his face is bronze with makeup. There isn't an ounce of friendliness in his face. His jaw is tight; his eyes are hard and businesslike. As they meet mine, they don't even flicker.

For a few moments we gaze at each other without speaking. I can hear my pulse beating loudly in my ears; my face feels hot beneath all the makeup. Then, summoning all my inner resources, I force myself to say calmly, "Hello, Luke."

There's an interested silence as he walks into the room. Even Elisabeth Plover seems intrigued by him.

"I know that face," she says, leaning forward. "I know it. You're an actor, aren't you? Shakespearean, of course. I believe I saw you in *Lear* three years ago."

"I don't think so," says Luke curtly.

"You're right!" says Elisabeth, slapping the table. "It was *Hamlet*. I remember it well. The desperate pain, the guilt, the final tragedy . . ." She shakes her head solemnly. "I'll never forget that voice of yours. Every word was like a stab wound."

"I'm sorry to hear it," says Luke, and looks at me. "Rebecca—"

"Luke, here are the final figures," interrupts Alicia, hurrying into the room and handing him a piece of paper. "Hello, Rebecca," she adds, giving me a snide look. "All prepared?"

"Yes, I am, actually," I say, crumpling my paper into a ball in my lap. "Very well prepared."

"Glad to hear it," says Alicia, raising her eyebrows. "It should be an interesting debate."

"Yes," I say defiantly. "Very."

God, she's a cow.

"I've just had John from Flagstaff on the phone," adds Alicia to Luke in a lowered voice. "He was very keen that you should mention the new Foresight Savings Series. Obviously, I told him—"

"This is a damage limitation exercise," says Luke curtly. "Not a bloody plug-fest. He'll be bloody lucky if he . . ." He glances at me and I look away as though I'm not remotely interested in what he's talking about. Casually I glance at my watch and feel a leap of fright as I see the time. Ten minutes. Ten minutes to go.

"OK," says Zelda, coming into the room. "Elisabeth, we're ready for you."

"Marvelous," says Elisabeth, taking a last mouthful of *pain au chocolat.* "Now, I do *look* all right, don't I?" She stands up and a shower of crumbs falls off her skirt.

"You've got a piece of croissant in your hair," says Zelda, reaching up and removing it. "Other than that—what can I say?" She catches my eye and I have a hysterical desire to giggle.

"Luke!" says the baby-faced guy, rushing in with a mobile phone. "John Bateson on the line for you. And a couple of packages have arrived . . ."

"Thanks, Tim," says Alicia, taking the packages and ripping them open. She pulls out a bunch of papers and begins scanning them quickly, marking things every so often in pencil. Meanwhile, Tim sits down, opens a laptop computer, and starts typing.

"Yes, John, I do see your bloody point," Luke's saying in a low, tight voice. "But if you had just kept me better informed—"

"Tim," says Alicia, looking up. "Can you quickly check the return on the Flagstaff Premium Pension over the last three, five, and ten?"

"Absolutely," says Tim, and starts tapping at his computer.

"Tim," says Luke, looking up from the phone. "Can you print out the Flagstaff Foresight press release draft for me ASAP? Thanks."

I can't quite believe what I'm seeing. They've practically set up an office, here in the *Morning Coffee* green room. An entire office of Brandon Communications staff complete with computers and modems and phones . . . pitted against me and my crumpled piece of notebook paper.

As I watch Tim's laptop efficiently spewing out pages, and Alicia handing sheets of paper to Luke, a resigned feeling starts to creep over me. I mean, let's face it. I'll never beat this lot, will I? I haven't got a chance. I should just give up now. Tell them I'm ill or something. Run home and hide under my duvet.

"OK, everyone?" says Zelda, poking her head round the door. "On in seven minutes."

"Fine," says Luke.

"Fine," I echo in a wobbly voice.

"Oh, and Rebecca, there's a package for you," says Zelda. She comes into the room and hands me a large, square box. "I'll be back in a minute."

"Thanks, Zelda," I say in surprise, and, with a sudden lift of spirits, begin to rip the box open. I've no idea what it is or who it's from—but it's got to be something helpful, hasn't it? Special last-minute information from Eric Foreman, maybe. A graph, or a series of figures that I can produce at the crucial moment. Or some secret document that Luke doesn't know about.

Out of the corner of my eye I can see that all the Brandonites have stopped what they're doing and are watching, too. Well, that'll show them. They're not the only ones to get packages delivered to the green room. They're not the only ones to have resources. Finally I get the sticky tape undone and open the flaps of the box.

And as everyone watches, a big red helium balloon, with "GOOD LUCK" emblazoned across it, floats up to the ceiling. There's a card attached to the string, and, without looking anyone in the eye, I rip it open.

Immediately I wish I hadn't.

"Good luck to you, good luck to you, whatever you're about to do," sings a tinny electronic voice.

I slam the card shut and feel a surge of embarrassment. From the other side of the room I can hear little sniggers going on, and I look up to see Alicia smirking. She whispers something into Luke's ear, and an amused expression spreads across his face.

He's laughing at me. They're all laughing at Rebecca Bloomwood and her singing balloon. For a few moments I can't move for mortification. My chest is rising and falling swiftly; I've never felt less like a leading industry expert in my life.

Then, on the other side of the room, I hear Alicia murmur some malicious little comment and give a snort of laughter. Deep inside me, something snaps. Sod them, I think suddenly. Sod them all. They're probably only jealous, anyway. They wish they had balloons, too.

Defiantly I open the card again to read the message.

"No matter if it's rain or shine, we all know that you'll be fine," sings the card's tinny voice at once. *"Hold your head up, keep it high—all that matters is you try."*

To Becky, I read. *With love and thanks for all your wonderful help. We're so proud to know you. From your friends Janice and Martin.*

I stare down at the card, reading the words over and over, and feel my eyes grow hot with tears. Janice and Martin *have* been good friends over the years. They've always been kind to me, even when I gave them such disastrous advice. I owe this to them. And I'm bloody well not going to let them down.

I blink a few times, take a deep breath, and look up to see Luke Brandon gazing at me, his eyes dark and expressionless.

"Friends," I say coolly. "Sending me their good wishes."

Carefully I place the card on the coffee table, making sure it stays open so it'll keep singing, then pull my balloon down from the ceiling and tie it to the back of my chair.

"OK," comes Zelda's voice from the door. "Luke and Rebecca. Are you ready?"

"Couldn't be readier," I say calmly, and walk past Luke to the door.

Twenty-one

As we stride along the corridors to the set, neither Luke nor I says a word. I dart a glance at him as we turn a corner—and his face is even steelier than it was before.

Well, that's fine. I can do hard and businesslike, too. Firmly I lift my chin and begin to take longer strides, pretending to be Alexis Carrington in *Dynasty*.

"So, do you two already know each other?" says Zelda, who's walking along between us.

"We do, as it happens," says Luke shortly.

"In a business context," I say, equally shortly. "Luke's always trying to promote some financial product or other. And I'm always trying to avoid his calls."

Zelda gives an appreciative laugh and I see Luke's eyes flash angrily. But I really don't care. I don't care how angry he gets. In fact, the angrier he gets, the better I feel.

"So—Luke, you must have been quite pissed off at Rebecca's article in *The Daily World*," says Zelda.

"I wasn't pleased," says Luke. "By any of it," he adds in a lower voice.

What does that mean? I turn my head, and to my astonishment, he's looking at me with a sober expression. Almost apologetic. Hmm. This must be an old PR trick. Soften up your opponent and then go in for the kill. But *I'm* not going to fall for it.

"He phoned me up to complain," I say airily to Zelda. "Can't cope with the truth, eh, Luke? Can't cope with seeing what's under the PR gloss?"

There's silence and I dart another look at him. Now he looks so furious, I think for a terrifying moment that he's going to hit me. Then his face changes and, in an icily calm voice, he says, "Let's just get on the fucking set and get this over with, shall we?"

Zelda raises her eyebrows at me and I grin back. This is more like it.

"OK," says Zelda as we approach a set of double swing doors. "Here we are. Keep your voices down when we go in."

She pushes open the doors and ushers us in, and for a moment my cool act falters. I feel all shaky and awed, like Laura Dern in *Jurassic Park* when she sees the dinosaurs for the first time. Because there it is, in real life. The real live *Morning Coffee* set. With the sofa and all the plants and everything, all lit up by the brightest, most dazzling lights I've ever seen in my life.

This is just unreal. How many zillion times have I sat at home, watching this on the telly? And now I'm actually going to be part of it.

"We've got a couple of minutes till the commercial break," says Zelda, leading us across the floor, across a load of trailing cables. "Rory and Emma are still with Elisabeth in the library set."

She gestures to us to sit down on opposite sides of the coffee table, and, gingerly, I do so. The sofa's harder than I was expecting, and kind of . . . different. Everything's different. The plants seem bigger than they do on the screen, and the coffee table is smaller. God, this is weird. The lights are so bright on my face, I can hardly see anything, and I'm not quite sure how to sit. A girl comes and threads a microphone cable under my shirt and clips it to my lapel. Awkwardly, I lift my hand to push my hair back, and immediately Zelda comes hurrying over.

"Try not to move too much, OK, Rebecca?" she says. "We don't want to hear a load of rustling."

"Right," I say. "Sorry."

Suddenly my voice doesn't seem to be working properly. I feel as though a wad of cotton's been stuffed into my throat. I glance up at a nearby camera and, to my horror, see it zooming toward me.

"OK, Rebecca," says Zelda, hurrying over again, "one more golden rule—don't look at the camera, all right? Just behave naturally!"

"Fine," I say huskily.

Behave naturally. Easy-peasy.

"Thirty seconds till the news bulletin," she says, looking at her watch. "Everything OK, Luke?"

"Fine," says Luke calmly. He's sitting on his sofa as though he's been there all his life. Typical.

I shift on my seat, tug nervously at my skirt, and smooth my jacket down. They always say that television puts ten pounds on you, which means my legs will look really fat. Maybe I should cross them the other way. Or not cross them at all? But then maybe they'll look even fatter.

"Hello!" comes a high-pitched voice from across the set before I can make up my mind. My head jerks up, and I feel an excited twinge in my stomach. It's Emma March in the flesh! She's wearing a pink suit and hurrying toward the sofa, closely followed by Rory, who looks even more square-jawed than usual. God, it's weird seeing celebrities up close. They don't look quite real, somehow.

"Hello!" Emma says cheerfully, and sits down on the sofa. "So you're the finance people, are you? Gosh, I'm dying for a wee." She frowns into the lights. "How long is this slot, Zelda?"

"Hi there!" says Rory, and shakes my hand. "Roberta."

"It's Rebecca!" says Emma, and rolls her eyes at me sympathetically. "Honestly, he's hopeless." She wriggles on the sofa. "Gosh, I really need to go."

"Too late now," says Rory.

"But isn't it really unhealthy not to go when you need to?" Emma wrinkles her brow anxiously. "Didn't we have a phone-in on it once? That weird girl phoned up who only went once a day. And Dr. James said . . . what did he say?"

"Search me," says Rory cheerfully. "These phone-ins always go over my head. Now I'm warning you, Rebecca," he adds, turning to me, "I can never follow any of this finance stuff. Far too brainy for me." He gives me a wide grin and I smile weakly back.

"Ten seconds," calls Zelda from the side of the set, and my stomach gives a tweak of fear. Over the loudspeakers I can hear the *Morning Coffee* theme music, signaling the end of a commercial break.

"Who starts?" says Emma, squinting at the TelePrompTer. "Oh, me."

So this is it. I feel almost light-headed with fear. I don't know where I'm supposed to be looking; I don't know when I'm supposed to speak. My legs are trembling and my hands are clenched tightly in my lap. The lights are dazzling my eyes; a camera's zooming in on my left, but I've got to try to ignore it.

"Welcome back!" says Emma suddenly to the camera. "Now, which would you rather have? A carriage clock or £20,000?"

What? I think in shock. But that's *my* line. That's what I was going to say.

"The answer's obvious, isn't it?" continues Emma blithely. "We'd all prefer the £20,000."

"Absolutely!" interjects Rory with a cheerful smile.

"But when some Flagstaff Life investors received a letter inviting them to move their savings recently," says Emma, suddenly putting on a sober face, "they didn't realize that if they did so, they would lose out on a £20,000 windfall. Rebecca Bloomwood is the journalist who uncovered this story—Rebecca, do you think this kind of deception is commonplace?"

And suddenly everyone's looking at me, waiting for me to reply. The camera's trained on my face; the studio's silent.

Two point five million people, all watching at home.

I can't breathe.

"Do you think investors need to be cautious?" prompts Emma.

"Yes," I manage in a strange, woolly voice. "Yes, I think they should."

"Luke Brandon, you represent Flagstaff Life," says Emma, turning away. "Do you think—"

Shit, I think miserably. That was pathetic. Pathetic! What's happened to my voice, for God's sake? What's happened to all my prepared answers?

And now I'm not even listening to Luke's reply. Come on, Rebecca. Concentrate.

"What you must remember," Luke's saying smoothly, "is that nobody's *entitled* to a windfall. This isn't a case of deception!" He smiles at Emma. "This is simply a case of a few investors being a little too greedy for their own good. They believe they've missed out—so they're deliberately stirring up bad publicity for the company. Meanwhile, there are thousands of people who *have* benefited from Flagstaff Life."

What? What's he saying?

"I see," says Emma, nodding her head. "So, Luke, would you agree that—"

"Wait a minute!" I hear myself interrupting. "Just . . . just wait a minute. Mr. Brandon, did you just call the *investors* greedy?"

"Not all," says Luke. "But some, yes."

I stare at him in disbelief, my skin prickling with outrage. An image of Janice and Martin comes into my mind—the sweetest, least greedy people in the world—and for a few moments I'm so angry, I can't speak.

"The truth is, the majority of investors with Flagstaff Life have seen record returns over the last five years," Luke's continuing to Emma, who's nodding intelligently. "And that's what they should be concerned with. Good-quality investment. Not flash-in-the-pan windfalls. After all, Flagstaff Life was originally set up to provide—"

"Correct me if I'm wrong, Luke," I cut in, forcing myself to speak calmly. "Correct me if I'm wrong—but I believe Flagstaff Life was originally set up as a mutual company? For the *mutual benefit* of all its members. Not to benefit some at the expense of others."

"Absolutely," replies Luke without flickering. "But that doesn't entitle every investor to a £20,000 windfall, does it?"

"Maybe not," I say, my voice rising slightly. "But surely it entitles them to believe they won't be misled by a company they've put their money with for fifteen years? Janice and Martin Webster trusted Flagstaff Life. They trusted the advice they were given. And look where that trust got them!"

"Investment is a game of luck," says Luke blandly. "Sometimes you win—"

"It wasn't luck!" I hear myself crying furiously. "Of course it wasn't luck! Are you telling me it was compete coincidence that they were advised to switch their funds two weeks before the windfall announcements?"

"My clients were simply making available an offer that they believed would add value to their customers' portfolios," says Luke, giving me a tight smile. "They have assured me that they were simply wishing to benefit their customers. They have assured me that—"

"So you're saying your clients are incompetent, then?" I retort. "You're saying they had all the best intentions—but cocked it up?"

Luke's eyes flash in anger and I feel a thrill of exhilaration.

"I fail to see—"

"Well, we could go on debating all day!" says Emma, shifting slightly on her seat. "But moving onto a slightly more—"

"Come on, Luke," I say, cutting her off. "Come *on*. You can't have it both ways." I lean forward, ticking points off on my hand. "Either Flagstaff Life were incompetent, or they were deliberately trying to save money. Whichever it is, they're in the wrong. The Websters were loyal customers and they should have gotten that money. In my opinion, Flagstaff Life deliberately encouraged them out of the with-profits fund to stop them receiving the windfall. I mean, it's obvious, isn't it?"

I look around for support and see Rory gazing blankly at me.

"It all sounds a bit technical for me," he says with a little laugh. "Bit complicated."

"OK, let's put it another way," I say quickly. "Let's . . ." I close my eyes, searching for inspiration. "Let's . . . suppose I'm in a clothes shop!" I open my eyes again. "I'm in a clothes shop, and I've chosen a wonderful cashmere Nicole Farhi coat. OK?"

"OK," says Rory cautiously.

"I love Nicole Farhi!" says Emma, perking up. "Beautiful knitwear."

"Exactly," I say. "OK, so imagine I'm standing in the checkout queue, minding my own business, when a sales assistant comes up to me and says, 'Why not buy this other coat instead? It's better quality—and I'll throw in a free bottle of perfume.' I've got no reason to distrust the sales assistant, so I think, Wonderful, and I buy the other coat."

"Right," says Rory, nodding. "With you so far."

"But when I get outside," I say carefully, "I discover that this other coat isn't Nicole Farhi and isn't real cashmere. I go back in—and the shop won't give me a refund."

"You were ripped off!" exclaims Rory, as though he's just discovered gravity.

"Exactly," I say. "I was ripped off. And the point is, so were thousands of Flagstaff Life customers. They were persuaded out of their original choice of investment, into a fund which left them £20,000 worse off." I pause, marshaling my thoughts. "Perhaps Flagstaff Life didn't break the law. Perhaps they didn't contravene any regulations. But there's a natural justice in this world, and they didn't just break that, they shattered it. Those customers deserved that windfall. They were loyal, long-standing customers, and they deserved it. And if you're honest, Luke Brandon, you *know* they deserved it."

I finish my speech breathlessly and look at Luke. He's staring at me with an unreadable expression on his face—and in spite of myself, I feel my stomach clench with nerves. I swallow, and try to shift my vision away from his—but somehow I can't move my head. It's as though our eyes are glued together.

"Luke?" says Emma. "Do you have a response to Rebecca's point?"

Luke doesn't respond. He's staring at me, and I'm staring back, feeling my heart thump like a rabbit.

"Luke?" repeats Emma slightly impatiently. "Do you have—"

"Yes," says Luke. "Yes I do. Rebecca—" He shakes his head, almost smiling to himself, then looks up again at me. "Rebecca, you're right."

There's a sudden still silence around the studio.

I open my mouth, but I can't make a sound.

Out of the corner of my eye, I see Rory and Emma glancing at each other puzzledly.

"Sorry, Luke," says Emma. "Do you mean—"

"She's right," says Luke, and gives a shrug. "Rebecca's absolutely right." He reaches for his glass of water, leans back on his sofa, and takes a sip. "If you want my honest opinion, those customers deserved that windfall. I very much wish they *had* received it."

He looks up at me, and he's wearing that same apologetic expression he had in the corridor. This can't be happening. Luke's agreeing with me. How can he be agreeing with me?

"I see," says Emma, sounding a bit affronted. "So, you've changed your position, then?"

There's a pause, while Luke stares thoughtfully into his glass of water. Then he looks up and says, "My company is employed by Flagstaff Life to maintain their public profile. But that doesn't mean that personally I agree with everything they do—or even that I know about it." He pauses. "To tell you the truth, I had no idea any of this was going on until I read about it in Rebecca's article in *The Daily World*. Which, by the way, was a fine piece of investigative journalism," he adds, nodding to me. "Congratulations."

I stare back helplessly, unable even to mutter "Thank you." I've never felt so wrong-footed in all my life. I want to stop and bury my head in my hands and think all of this through slowly and carefully—but I can't, I'm on live television. I'm being watched by 2.5 million people, all around the country.

I hope my legs look OK.

"If I were a Flagstaff customer and this had happened to me, I'd be very angry," Luke continues. "There *is* such a thing as customer loyalty; there *is* such a thing as playing straight. And I would hope that any client of mine, whom I represent in public, would abide by both of those principles."

"I see," says Emma, and turns to the camera. "Well, this is quite a turnaround! Luke Brandon, here to represent Flagstaff Life, now says that what they did was wrong. Any further comment, Luke?"

"To be honest," says Luke, with a wry smile, "I'm not sure I'll be representing Flagstaff Life any more after this."

"Ah," says Rory, leaning forward intelligently. "And can you tell us why that is?"

"Oh, honestly, Rory!" says Emma impatiently. She rolls her eyes and Luke gives a little snort of laughter.

And suddenly everyone's laughing, and I join in too, slightly hysterically. I catch Luke's eye and feel something flash in my chest, then quickly look away again.

"Right, well, anyway," says Emma abruptly, pulling herself together and smiling at the camera. "That's it from the finance experts—but, coming up after the break, the return of hot pants to the catwalk . . ."

". . . and cellulite creams—do they really work?" adds Rory.

"Plus our special guests—Heaven Sent 7—singing live in the studio."

The theme music blares out of the loudspeakers and both Emma and Rory leap to their feet.

"Wonderful debate," says Emma, hurrying off. "Sorry, I'm *dying* for a wee."

"Excellent stuff," adds Rory earnestly. "Didn't understand a word—but great television." He slaps Luke on the back, raises his hand to me, and then hurries off the set.

And all at once it's over. It's just me and Luke, sitting opposite each other on the sofas, with bright lights still shining in our eyes and microphones still clipped to our lapels. I feel slightly shell-shocked.

Did all that really just happen?

"So," I say eventually, and clear my throat.

"So," echoes Luke with a tiny smile. "Well done."

"Thanks," I say, and bite my lip awkwardly in the silence.

I'm wondering if he's in big trouble now. If attacking one of your clients on live TV is the PR equivalent of hiding clothes from the customers.

If he really changed his mind because of my article. Because of me.

But I can't ask that. Can I?

The silence is growing louder and louder and at last I take a deep breath.

"Did you—"

"I was—"

We both speak at once.

"No," I say, flushing red. "You go. Mine wasn't . . . You go."

"OK," says Luke, and gives a little shrug. "I was just going to ask if you'd like to have dinner tonight."

What does he mean, have dinner? Does he mean—

"To discuss a bit of business," he continues. "I very much

liked your idea for a unit trust promotion along the lines of the January sales."

My what?

What idea? What's he . . .

Oh God, *that*. Is he serious? That was just one of my stupid, speak-aloud, brain-not-engaged moments.

"I think it could be a good promotion for a particular client of ours," he's saying, "and I was wondering whether you'd like to consult on the project. On a freelance basis, of course."

Consult. Freelance. Project.

He's serious.

"Oh," I say, and swallow, inexplicably disappointed. "Oh, I see. Well, I . . . I suppose I might be free tonight."

"Good," says Luke. "Shall we say the Ritz?"

"If you like," I say offhandedly, as though I go there all the time.

"Good," says Luke again, and his eyes crinkle into a smile. "I look forward to it."

And then—oh God. To my utter horror, before I can stop myself, I hear myself saying bitchily, "What about Sacha? Doesn't she have plans for you tonight?"

Even as the words hit the air, I feel myself redden. Oh shit. Shit! What did I say that for?

There's a long silence during which I want to slink off somewhere and die.

"Sacha left two weeks ago," says Luke finally, and my head pops up.

"Oh," I say feebly. "Oh dear."

"No warning—she packed up her calfskin suitcase and went." Luke looks up. "Still, it could be worse." He gives a deadpan shrug. "At least I didn't buy the holdall as well."

Oh God, now I'm going to giggle. I mustn't giggle. I *mustn't*.

"I'm really sorry," I manage at last.

"I'm not," says Luke, gazing at me seriously, and the laughter inside me dies away. I stare back at him nervously and feel a tingle spread across my face.

"Rebecca! Luke!"

Our heads jerk round to see Zelda approaching the set, clipboard in hand.

"Fantastic!" she exclaims. "Just what we wanted. Luke, you were great. And Rebecca . . ." She comes and sits next to me on the sofa and pats my shoulder. "You were so wonderful, we were thinking—how would you like to stand in as our phone-in expert later in the show?"

"What?" I stare at her. "But . . . but I can't! I'm not an expert on anything."

"Ha-ha-ha, very good!" Zelda gives an appreciative laugh. "The great thing about you, Rebecca, is you've got the common touch. We see you as finance guru meets girl next door. Informative but approachable. Knowledgeable but down-to-earth. The financial expert people really want to talk to. What do you think, Luke?"

"I think Rebecca will do the job perfectly," says Luke. "I can't think of anyone better qualified. I also think I'd better get out of your way." He stands up and smiles at me. "See you later, Rebecca. Bye, Zelda."

I watch in a daze as he picks his way across the cable-strewn floor toward the exit, half wishing he would look back.

"Right," says Zelda, and squeezes my hand. "Let's get you sorted."

Twenty-two

I WAS MADE TO GO ON TELEVISION. That's the truth. I was absolutely *made* to go on television.

We're sitting on the sofas again, Rory and Emma and me, and Anne from Leeds is admitting over the line that she's never given retirement planning a thought.

I glance at Emma and smile, and she twinkles back. I've never felt so warm and happy in all my life.

What's really strange is that when it was me being interviewed, I felt all tongue-tied and nervous—but on the other side of the sofa, I've been in my element right from the start. God, I could do this all day. I don't even mind the bright lights anymore. They feel normal. And I've practiced the most flattering way to sit in front of the mirror (knees together, feet crossed at the ankle), and I'm sticking to it.

"My mum used to tell me to take out a pension," says Anne, "and I used to laugh at her. But now I've started to panic I've left it too late."

"Rebecca?" says Emma. "Should Anne be concerned?"

Pensions, I think quickly. Come on, what do I know about pensions?

"Well," I say. "Of course, the earlier you start saving, the more you'll accumulate. But that's no reason to panic, Anne. The good thing is, you're thinking about it *now*."

"How old are you exactly, Anne?" says Emma.

"I'm thirty," says Anne. "Thirty last month."

Yes! Thank you, God!

"Ah, well," I say knowledgeably. "A typical woman of thirty, who invested £100 a month, would receive an income of £9,000 on retirement at sixty. That's assuming 7 percent growth."

Bingo. Rory and Emma look *so* impressed. OK, quick, what else?

"But you should also look for flexibility, Anne," I continue. "Choose a scheme which allows you to take a 'holiday' from payments, because you never know when you might need it."

"That's true," says Anne thoughtfully. "I'd like to take a year off sometime and travel a bit."

"Well, there you are!" I say triumphantly. "If you do that, you'll want to be able to pause your pension payments. In fact, what I would do is—"

"Thanks, Rebecca," chimes in Emma. "Wise advice there! Now we're going to go briefly to Davina for news and weather . . ."

I'm rather disappointed at being interrupted. There were so many more things I could have said to Anne. All the points I made in my pensions article are popping up in my head—and now that there's a real person involved, they all suddenly seem a lot more interesting. In fact, the whole subject seems more interesting today. It's as though all this stuff has suddenly got a point.

Believe it or not, I'm really enjoying the questions on this phone-in. I know about mortgages and I know about life insurance and I know about unit trusts. I know so much more than I ever realized! A few minutes ago, Kenneth from St. Austell asked what the annual contribution limit for an ISA is—and the figure £5,000 just jumped right into my head. It's as if some bit of my mind has been storing every single bit of information I've ever written—and now, when I need it, it's all there.

"And after the break," Emma's saying, "since so many of you are ringing in, we'll be coming back to this phone-in: 'Managing Your Money.' "

"Lots of people with money problems out there," chimes in Rory.

"Absolutely," says Emma. "And we want to help. So whatever your query, however big or small, please call in for Rebecca Bloomwood's advice, on 0333 4567." She freezes for a moment, smiling at the camera, then relaxes back in her chair as the light goes off. "Well, this is going very well!" she says brightly, as a makeup girl hurries up and touches up her face with powder. "Isn't it, Zelda?"

"Fantastic!" says Zelda, appearing out of nowhere. "The lines haven't been this busy since we did 'I'd Like to Meet a Spice Girl.' " She looks curiously at me. "Have you ever done a course in television presenting, Rebecca?"

"No," I say honestly. "I haven't. But . . . I've watched a lot of telly."

Zelda roars with laughter. "Good answer! OK, folks, we're back in thirty."

Emma smiles at me and consults a piece of paper in front of her, and Rory leans back and examines his nails.

I've never felt so completely and utterly happy. Never. Not even that time I found a Vivienne Westwood bustier for £60 in the Harvey Nichols sale. (I wonder where that is, actually. I must get round to wearing it sometime.) This beats everything. Life is perfect.

I lean back, full of contentment, and am idly looking around the studio when an oddly familiar figure catches my eye. I peer harder, and my skin starts to prickle in horror. There's a man standing in the gloom of the studio—and honestly, I must be hallucinating or something, because he looks exactly like—

"And . . . welcome back," says Rory, and my attention snaps back to the set. "This morning's phone-in is on financial problems, big and small. Our guest expert is Rebecca Bloomwood and our next caller is Fran from Shrewsbury. Fran?"

"Yes," says Fran. "Hi. Hi, Rebecca."

"Hi there, Fran," I say, smiling warmly. "And what seems to be the trouble?"

"I'm in a mess," says Fran. "I . . . I don't know what to do."

"Are you in debt, Fran?" says Emma gently.

"Yes," says Fran, and gives a shaky sigh. "I'm overdrawn, I owe money on all my credit cards, I've borrowed money off my sister . . . and I just can't stop spending. I just . . . love buying things."

"What sort of things?" says Rory interestedly.

"I don't know, really," says Fran after a pause. "Clothes for me, clothes for the kids, things for the house, just rubbish, really. Then the bills arrive . . . and I throw them away."

Emma gives me a significant look, and I raise my eyebrows back. But my cool act is starting to falter a little at Fran's story.

"It's like a vicious circle," Fran's saying. "The more in debt I am, the worse I feel, so I go out and spend more."

Outstanding bills. Credit card debts. Overdrafts. All the things I've been desperate not to think about are being thrust back into my mind. Desperately I thrust them back out again.

"Rebecca?" she says. "Fran's obviously in a bit of a spot. What should she be doing?"

For an instant I feel like crying *Why ask me?* But I can't crumble, I have to do this. I have to be Rebecca Bloomwood, top financial expert. Summoning all my strength, I force myself to smile sympathetically at the camera.

"Well, Fran," I say. "The first thing you've got to do is . . . is be brave and confront the issue. Contact the bank and tell them you're having trouble managing." I swallow hard, trying to keep my voice steady. "I know myself how hard it can be to tackle this kind of problem—but I can honestly tell you, running away doesn't solve anything. The longer you leave it, the worse it'll get."

"Rebecca," says Emma earnestly. "Would you say this is a common problem?"

"I'm afraid it is," I reply. "It's all too easy to forget those unpaid bills, to put them in a dressing table drawer, or . . . or throw them in a skip . . ."

"A skip?" says Rory, looking puzzled.

"Whatever," I say hurriedly. "Everybody's different."

"I put mine in the dog basket," interjects Fran. "Then he chews them and I can't read them."

"I can understand that," I say, nodding. "But you know what, Fran? Once you take those letters out of the dog basket and actually read them, you'll find they're not nearly as bad as you think."

"You really think so?" says Fran tremulously.

"Open each envelope," I suggest, "and write down all the outstanding amounts. Then make a plan to pay them off, even if it's only £5 a week. You can do it."

There's a long pause.

"Fran?" says Emma. "Are you still there?"

"Yes!" says Fran. "Yes, I'm still here—and I'm going to do it! You've convinced me. Thanks, Becky! I really appreciate your help!"

I beam back at the camera, my confidence restored.

"It's a pleasure," I say. "And you know, Fran, as soon as you turn that corner and wake up to the real world, your life will be transformed."

I make a confident sweeping gesture with my arm, and as I do so, my gaze takes in the whole studio. And . . . oh my God, it's him.

I'm not hallucinating.

It's really him. Standing at the corner of the set, wearing a security badge and sipping something in a polystyrene cup as though he belongs here. Derek Smeath is standing here in the *Morning Coffee* studios, ten yards away from me.

Derek Smeath of Endwich Bank. It doesn't make any sense. What's he doing here?

Oh God, and now he's staring straight at me.

My heart begins to pound, and I swallow hard, trying to keep control of myself.

"Rebecca?" Emma says puzzledly, and I force myself to turn my attention back to the show. But all my confident words are withering on my lips. "So you really think, if she tries, Fran will be able to get her life in order?"

"I . . . that's right," I say, and force a smile. "It's just a question of facing up to it."

I'm trying desperately to stay cool and professional—but all the bits of my life I'd so carefully buried are starting to worm their way out again. Here they come, wriggling into my mind, one piece of dreadful reality after another.

"Well," says Rory. "Let's all hope Fran takes Rebecca's very good advice."

My bank account. Thousands of pounds of debt.

"We're out of time, I'm afraid," says Emma, "but before we go, do you have any last words of advice, Rebecca?"

My VISA card, canceled. My Octagon card, confiscated in front of that whole crowd. God, that was humiliating.

OK, stop it. Concentrate. Concentrate.

"Yes," I say, forcing a confident tone. "I would just say . . . in the same way you might have a medical checkup once a year, do the same with your finances. Don't ignore them until they become a problem!"

My whole terrible, disorganized life. It's all there, isn't it? Waiting for me, like a great big spider. Just waiting to pounce, as soon as this phone-in ends.

"Wise words from our financial expert," says Emma. "Many thanks to Rebecca Bloomwood, and I'm sure we'll all be heeding her advice. Coming up after the break, the results of our makeover in Newcastle and Heaven Sent 7, live in the studio."

There's a frozen pause, then everyone relaxes.

"Right," says Emma, consulting her piece of paper. "Where are we next?"

"Good work, Rebecca," says Rory cheerfully. "Excellent stuff."

"Oh, Zelda!" says Emma, leaping up. "Could I have a quick word? That was fab, Rebecca," she adds. "Really fab."

And suddenly they're both gone. And I'm left alone on the set, exposed and vulnerable. Rebecca Bloomwood, top financial expert, has vanished. All that's left is me, Becky. Shrinking on my seat and frantically trying to avoid Derek Smeath's eye.

I don't have anything to give him. The money from *The Daily World* has got to go straight to Suze. I'm in as much trouble as I ever was. What am I going to do?

Maybe I could slip out at the back.

Maybe I could stick it out here on the sofa. Just sit here until he gets bored and leaves. I mean, he won't dare to come onto the actual set, will he? Or maybe I could *pretend to be someone else*. God yes. I mean, with all this makeup on, I practically look like someone else, anyway. I could just walk quickly past, and if he talks to me, answer in a foreign accent. Or else . . .

And then suddenly I stop, midtrack. It's as though I'm hearing my own thoughts for the first time in my life. And what I hear makes me ashamed of myself.

Who do I think I'm kidding? What exactly will I achieve by dodging Derek Smeath one more time? It's time to grow up, Becky, I tell myself. It's time to stop running away. If Fran from Shrewsbury can do it, then so can Rebecca from London.

I stand up, take a deep breath, and walk slowly across the set to Derek Smeath.

"Hello, Mr. Smeath," I say in polite, calm tones. "What a coincidence to see you here." I hold out my hand for a symbolic, peacemaking handshake, but Derek Smeath doesn't even seem to see it. He's staring at me as though he's seen a goldfish begin to talk.

"Coincidence?" he echoes at last, and a technician gestures to us to keep our voices down. Derek Smeath firmly ushers me out of the studio into a foyer area and turns to face me, and I feel a twinge of fear at his expression.

"Miss Bloomwood," he says. "Miss Bloomwood—" He rubs

his face with his hand, then looks up. "Do you know quite how long I have been writing letters to you? Do you know how long I've been trying to get you into the bank for a meeting?"

"Ahm . . . I'm not quite—"

"Six months," says Derek Smeath, and pauses. "Six long months of excuses and prevarication. Now, I'd just like you to think about what that means for me. It means endless letters. Numerous phone calls. Hours of time and effort on my part and that of my assistant, Erica. Resources which, quite frankly, could be better spent elsewhere." He gestures sharply with his polystyrene cup and some coffee slops onto the floor. "Then finally I pin you down to a cast-iron appointment. Finally I think you're taking your situation seriously . . . And you don't turn up. You disappear completely. I telephone your home to find out where you are, and get accused most unpleasantly of being some kind of stalker!"

"Oh yes," I say, and pull an apologetic face. "Sorry about that. It's just my dad, you know. He's a bit weird."

"I'd all but given up on you," says Derek Smeath, his voice rising. "I'd all but given up. And then I'm passing a television shop this morning, and what should I see, on six different screens, but the missing, vanished Rebecca Bloomwood, advising the nation. And what are you advising them on?" He begins to shake with laughter. (At least, I think it's laughter.) "Finance! *You* are advising the British public . . . on finance!"

I stare at him, taken aback. It's not *that* funny.

"Look, I'm very sorry I couldn't make the last meeting," I say, trying to sound businesslike. "Things were a bit difficult for me at that time. But if we could reschedule . . ."

"Reschedule!" cries Derek Smeath, as though I've just cracked a hysterical joke. "Reschedule!"

I gaze at him indignantly. He's not taking me seriously at all, is he? He hasn't shaken my hand, and he's not even listening to what I'm saying. I'm telling him I want to come in for a meeting—I actually *want* to—and he's just treating me like a joke.

And no wonder, interrupts a tiny voice inside me. *Look at the way you've behaved. Look at the way you've treated him. Frankly, it's a wonder he's being civil to you at all.*

I look up at his face, still crinkled in laughter . . . and suddenly feel very chastened.

Because the truth is, he could have been a lot nastier to me than he has been. He could have taken my card away a long time ago. Or sent the bailiffs round. Or had me blacklisted. He's actually been very nice to me, one way or another, and all I've done is lie and wriggle and run away.

"Listen," I say quickly. "Please. Give me another chance. I really want to sort my finances out. I want to repay my overdraft. But I need you to help me. I'm . . ." I swallow. "I'm asking you to help me, Mr. Smeath."

There's a long pause. Derek Smeath looks around for a place to put his coffee cup, takes a white handkerchief out of his pocket, and rubs his brow with it. Then he puts it away and gives me a long look.

"You're serious," he says at last.

"Yes."

"You'll really make an effort?"

"Yes. And—" I bite my lip. "And I'm very grateful for all the allowances you've made for me. I really am."

Suddenly I feel almost tearful. I want to be good. I want to get my life in order. I want him to tell me what to do to make things right.

"All right," says Derek Smeath at last. "Let's see what we can sort out. You come into the office tomorrow, nine-thirty sharp, and we'll have a little chat."

"Thanks," I say, my whole body subsiding in relief. "Thank you so much. I'll be there. I promise."

"You'd better be," he says. "No more excuses." Then a faint smile passes over his features. "By the way," he adds, gesturing to the set. "I thought you did very well up there, with all your advice."

"Oh," I say in surprise. "Well . . . thanks. That's really . . ." I clear my throat. "How did you get into the studio, anyway? I thought they had quite tight security."

"They do," replies Derek Smeath. "But my daughter works in television." He smiles fondly. "She used to work on this very show."

"Really?" I say incredulously.

God, how amazing. Derek Smeath has a daughter. He's probably got a whole family, come to that. A wife, and everything. Who would have thought it?

"I'd better go," he says, and drains his polystyrene cup. "This was a bit of an unscheduled detour." He gives me a severe look. "And I'll see you tomorrow."

"I'll be there," I say quickly, as he walks off toward the exit. "And . . . and thanks. Thanks a lot."

As he disappears, I sink down onto a nearby chair. I can't quite believe I've just had a pleasant, civilized conversation with Derek Smeath. With Derek Smeath! And actually, he seems quite a sweetheart. He's been so nice and kind to me, and his daughter works in television . . . I mean, who knows, maybe I'll get to know her, too. Maybe I'll become friends with the whole family. Wouldn't that be great? I'll start going to dinner at their house, and his wife will give me a warm hug when I arrive, and I'll help her with the salad and stuff . . .

"Rebecca!" comes a voice from behind me, and I turn round to see Zelda approaching, still clutching her clipboard.

"Hi," I say happily. "How's it going?"

"Great," she says, and pulls up a chair. "Now, I want to have a little talk."

"Oh," I say, suddenly nervous. "OK. What about?"

"We thought you did tremendously well today," says Zelda, crossing one jeaned leg over the other. "*Tremendously* well. I've spoken to Emma and Rory and our senior producer"—she pauses for effect—"and they'd all like to see you back on the show."

I stare at her in disbelief. "You mean—"

"Not every week," says Zelda. "But fairly regularly. We thought maybe three times a month. Do you think your work would allow you to do that?"

"I . . . I don't know," I say dazedly. "I expect it would."

"Excellent!" says Zelda. "We could probably plug your magazine as well, keep them happy." She scribbles something on a piece of paper and looks up. "Now, you don't have an agent, do you? So I'll have to talk money directly with you." She pauses, and looks down at her clipboard. "What we're offering, per slot, is—"

Twenty-three

I PUT MY KEY IN THE LOCK and slowly open the door of the flat. It seems like about a million years since I was here last, and I feel like a completely different person. I've grown up. Or changed. Or something.

"Hi," I say cautiously into the silence, and drop my bag onto the floor. "Is anyone—"

"Bex!" gasps Suze, appearing at the door of the sitting room. She's wearing tight black leggings and holding a half-made denim photograph frame in one hand. "Oh my God! Where've you *been*? What have you been doing? I saw you on *Morning Coffee* and I couldn't believe my eyes! I tried to phone in and speak to you, but they said I had to have a financial problem. So I said, OK, how should I invest half a million? but they said that wasn't really . . ." She breaks off. "Bex, what happened?"

I don't reply straight away. My attention has been grabbed by the pile of letters addressed to me on the table. White, official-looking envelopes, brown window envelopes, envelopes marked menacingly "Final Reminder." The scariest pile of letters you've ever seen.

Except somehow . . . they don't seem quite so scary anymore.

"I was at my parents' house," I say, looking up. "And then I was on television."

"But I phoned your parents! They said they didn't know where you were!"

"I know," I say, flushing slightly. "They were . . . protecting me from a stalker." I look up, to see Suze staring at me in utter incomprehension. Which I suppose is fair enough. "Anyway," I add defensively, "I left you a message on the machine, saying not to worry, I was fine."

"I know," wails Suze, "but that's what they always do in films. And it means the baddies have got you and you've got a gun jammed against your head. Honestly, I thought you were dead! I thought you were, like, cut up into a million pieces somewhere."

I look at her face again. She isn't kidding, she really was worried. I feel awful. I should never have vanished like that. It was completely thoughtless and irresponsible and selfish.

"Oh, Suze." On impulse, I hurry forward and hug her tightly. "I'm really sorry. I never meant to worry you."

"It's OK," says Suze, hugging me back. "I was worried for a bit—but then I knew you must be all right when I saw you on the telly. You were fantastic, by the way."

"Really?" I say, a tiny smile flickering round the corners of my mouth. "Did you really think so?"

"Oh yes!" says Suze. "Much better than whatshisface. Luke Brandon. God, he's arrogant."

"Yes," I say after a tiny pause. "Yes, I suppose he is. But he was actually quite nice to me afterward."

"Really?" says Suze indifferently. "Well, you were brilliant, anyway. Do you want some coffee?"

"Love some," I say, and she disappears into the kitchen.

I pick up my letters and bills and begin slowly to leaf through them. Once upon a time, this lot would have sent me into a blind panic. In fact, they would have gone straight into the bin, unread. But you know what? Today I don't feel a flicker of fear. Honestly, how could I have been so silly about my financial affairs? How could I have been so cowardly? This time I'm just going to face up to them properly. I'm going to sit down with my checkbook and my latest bank statements, and sort methodically through the whole mess.

Staring at the clutch of envelopes in my hand, I feel suddenly very grown-up and responsible. Farsighted and sensible. I'm going to sort my life out and keep my finances in order from now on. I've completely and utterly changed my attitude toward money.

Plus . . .

OK, I wasn't actually going to tell you this. But *Morning Coffee* is paying me absolute loads. *Loads.* You won't believe it, but for every single phone-in I do, I'm going to get—

Oh, I'm all embarrassed now. Let's just say it's . . . it's quite a lot!

I just can't stop smiling about it. I've been floating along ever since they told me. So the point is, I'll easily be able to pay all these bills off now. My VISA bill, and my Octagon bill, and the money I owe Suze—and everything! Finally, *finally* my life is going to be sorted.

"So, why did you just disappear like that?" asks Suze, coming back out of the kitchen and making me jump. "What was wrong?"

"I don't really know," I say with a sigh, putting the letters back down on the hall table. "I just had to get away and think. I was all confused."

"Because of Tarquin?" says Suze at once, and I feel myself stiffen apprehensively.

"Partly," I say after a pause, and swallow. "Why? Has he—"

"I know you're not that keen on Tarkie," says Suze wistfully, "but I think he still really likes you. He came round a couple of nights ago and left you this letter."

She gestures to a cream envelope stuck in the mirror. With slightly trembling hands I take it. Oh God, what's he going to say? I hesitate, then rip it open, and a ticket falls onto the floor.

"The opera!" says Suze, picking it up. "Day after tomorrow." She looks up. "God, it's lucky you came back, Bex."

> *My dear Rebecca,* I'm reading incredulously. *Forgive my reticence in contacting you before. But the more I think about it, the more I realize how much I enjoyed our evening together and how much I would like to repeat it.*
>
> *I enclose a ticket for* Die Meistersinger *at the Opera House. I shall be attending in any case and if you were able to join me, I would be delighted.*
>
> *Yours very sincerely,*
>
> *Tarquin Cleath-Stuart.*

"Oh, Bex, you must go!" says Suze, reading over my shoulder. "You've got to go. He'll be devastated if you don't. I really think he likes you."

I look at the ticket, for two nights' time. "Gala Performance," it says, and I feel a sudden excitement. I've never been to an opera gala! I could wear that divine Ghost dress which I've never had a chance to wear, and I could put my hair up, and meet lots of amazing people . . .

And then, abruptly, I stop. However much fun it would be—it wouldn't be fair or honest to go. I've hurt Tarquin enough.

"I can't go, Suze," I say, thrusting the letter down. "I've . . . I've got plans that night."

"But what about poor Tarkie?" says Suze, crestfallen. "He's so keen on you . . ."

"I know," I say, and take a deep breath. "But I'm not keen on him. I'm really sorry, Suze . . . but that's the truth. If I could change the way I felt . . ."

There's a short silence.

"Oh well," says Suze at last. "Never mind. You can't help it." She disappears into the kitchen and emerges a minute later with two mugs of coffee. "So," she says, handing me one, "what are you up to tonight? Shall we go out together?"

"Sorry, I can't," I say, and clear my throat. "I've got a business meeting."

"Really?" Suze pulls a face. "What a bummer!" She sips at her coffee and leans against the door frame. "Who on earth has business meetings in the evening, anyway?"

"It's . . . it's with Luke Brandon," I say, trying to sound unconcerned. But it's no good, I can feel myself starting to blush.

"Luke Brandon?" says Suze puzzledly. "But what—" She stares at me, and her expression slowly changes. "Oh no. Bex! Don't tell me . . ."

"It's just a business meeting," I say, avoiding her eye. "That's all. Two businesspeople meeting up and talking about business. In a . . . in a business situation. That's all."

And I hurry off to my room.

Business meeting. Clothes for a business meeting. OK, let's have a look.

I pull all my outfits out of the wardrobe and lay them on the bed. Blue suit, black suit, pink suit. Hopeless. Pinstriped suit? Hmm. Maybe overdoing it. Cream suit . . . too weddingy. Green suit . . . isn't that bad luck or something?

"So what are you going to wear?" says Suze, looking in through my open bedroom door. "Are you going to buy something new?" Her face lights up. "Hey, shall we go shopping?"

"Shopping?" I say distractedly. "Ahm . . . maybe."

Somehow today . . . Oh, I don't know. I almost feel too tense to go shopping. Too keyed up. I don't think I'd be able to give it my full attention.

"Bex, did you hear me?" says Suze in surprise. "I said, shall we go shopping?"

"Yes, I know." I glance up at her, then reach for a black top and look at it critically. "Actually, I think I'll take a rain check."

"You mean . . ." Suze pauses. "You mean you *don't* want to go shopping?"

"Exactly."

There's silence, and I look up, to see Suze staring at me.

"I don't understand," she says, and she sounds quite upset. "Why are you being all weird?"

"I'm not being weird!" I give a little shrug. "I just don't feel like shopping."

"Oh God, there's something wrong, isn't there?" wails Suze. "I knew it. Maybe you're really ill." She hurries into the room and reaches for my head. "Have you got a temperature? Does anything hurt?"

"No!" I say, laughing. "Of course not!"

"Have you had a bump on the head?" She wiggles her hand in front of my face. "How many fingers?"

"Suze, I'm fine," I say, thrusting her hand aside. "Honestly. I'm just . . . not in a shopping mood." I hold a gray suit up against myself. "What do you think of this?"

"Honestly, Bex, I'm worried about you," says Suze, shaking her head. "I think you should get yourself checked out. You're so . . . different. It's frightening."

"Yes, well." I reach for a white shirt and smile at her. "Maybe I've changed."

It takes me all afternoon to decide on an outfit. There's a lot of trying on, and mixing and matching, and suddenly remembering things at the back of my wardrobe. (I *must* wear those purple jeans sometime.) But eventually I go for simple and straightforward. My nicest black suit (Jigsaw sale, two years ago), a white T-shirt (M&S), and knee-high black suede boots (Dolce & Gabbana, but I told Mum they were from BHS. Which was a mistake, because then she wanted to get some for herself, and I had to pretend they'd all sold out). I put it all on, screw my hair up into a knot, and stare at myself in the mirror.

"Very nice," says Suze admiringly from the door. "Very sexy."

"Sexy?" I feel a pang of dismay. "I'm not going for sexy! I'm going for businesslike."

"Can't you be both at once?" suggests Suze. "Businesslike *and* sexy?"

"I . . . no," I say after a pause, and look away. "No, I don't want to."

I don't want Luke Brandon to think I've dressed up for him, is what I really mean. I don't want to give him the slightest chance to think I've misconstrued what this meeting is about. Not like last time.

With no warning, a surge of fresh humiliation goes through my body as I remember that awful moment in Harvey Nichols. I shake my head hard, trying to clear it; trying to calm myself. Why the hell did I agree to this bloody dinner, anyway?

"I just want to look as serious and businesslike as possible," I say, and frown sternly at my reflection.

"I know, then," says Suze. "You need some accessories. Some businesswoman-type accessories."

"Like what? A Filofax?"

"Like . . ." Suze pauses thoughtfully. "OK. Wait there—"

I arrive at the Ritz that evening five minutes after our agreed time of seventy-thirty, and as I reach the entrance to the restaurant, I see Luke there already, sitting back looking relaxed and sipping something that looks like a gin and tonic. He's wearing a different suit from the one he was wearing this morning, I can't help noticing, and he's put on a fresh, dark green shirt. He actually looks . . . Well. Quite nice. Quite good-looking.

Not that businessy, in fact.

And, come to think of it, this restaurant isn't very businessy, either. It's all chandeliers and gold garlands and soft pink chairs, and the most beautiful painted ceiling, all clouds and flowers. The whole place is sparkling with light, and it looks . . .

Well, actually, the word that springs to mind is *romantic*.

Oh God. My heart starts thumping with nerves, and I glance

quickly at my reflection in a gilded mirror. I'm wearing the black Jigsaw suit and white T-shirt and black suede boots as originally planned. But now I also have a crisp copy of the *Financial Times* under one arm, a pair of tortoiseshell glasses (with clear glass) perched on my head, my clunky executive briefcase in one hand and—Suze's pièce de résistance—an AppleMac laptop in the other.

Maybe I overdid it.

I'm about to back away and see if I can quickly deposit the briefcase in the cloakroom (or, to be honest, just put it down on a chair and walk away), when Luke looks up, sees me, and smiles. Damn. So I'm forced to go forward over the plushy carpet, trying to look as relaxed as possible, even though one arm is clamped tightly to my side, to stop the *FT* from falling on the floor.

"Hello," says Luke as I arrive at the table. He stands up to greet me, and I realize that I can't shake his hand, because I'm holding the laptop. Flustered, I plunk my briefcase on the floor, transfer the laptop to the other side—nearly dropping the *FT* as I do so—and, with as much poise as possible, hold out my hand.

A flicker of amusement passes over Luke's face and he solemnly shakes it. He gestures to a chair, and watches politely as I put the laptop on the tablecloth, all ready for use.

"That's an impressive machine," he says. "Very . . . high tech."

"Yes," I reply, and give him a brief, cool smile. "I often use it to take notes at business meetings."

"Ah," says Luke, nodding. "Very organized of you."

He's obviously waiting for me to switch it on, so experimentally I press the return key. This, according to Suze, should make the screen spring to life. But nothing happens.

Casually I press the key again—and still nothing. I jab at it, pretending my finger slipped by accident—and *still* nothing. Shit, this is embarrassing. Why do I ever listen to Suze?

"Is there a problem?" says Luke.

"No!" I say at once, and snap the lid shut. "No, I've just— On second thought, I won't use it today." I reach into my bag for a notebook. "I'll jot my notes down in here."

"Good idea," says Luke mildly. "Would you like some champagne?"

"Oh," I say, slightly thrown. "Well . . . OK."

"Excellent," says Luke. "I hoped you would."

He glances up, and a beaming waiter scurries forward with a bottle. Gosh, Krug.

But I'm not going to smile, or look pleased or anything. I'm going to stay thoroughly cool and professional. In fact, I'm only going to have one glass, before moving on to still water. I need to keep a clear head, after all.

While the waiter fills my champagne flute, I write down "Meeting between Rebecca Bloomwood and Luke Brandon" in my notebook. I look at it appraisingly, then underline it twice. There. That looks very efficient.

"So," I say, looking up, and raise my glass. "To business."

"To business," echoes Luke, and gives a wry smile. "Assuming I'm still *in* business, that is . . ."

"Really?" I say anxiously. "You mean—after what you said on *Morning Coffee*? Has it gotten you into trouble?"

He nods and I feel a pang of sympathy for him.

I mean, Suze is right—Luke is pretty arrogant. But I actually thought it was really good of him to stick out his neck like that and say publicly what he really thought about Flagstaff Life. And now, if he's going to be ruined as a result . . . well, it just seems all wrong.

"Have you lost . . . everything?" I say quietly, and Luke laughs.

"I wouldn't go that far. But we've had to do an awful lot of explaining to our other clients this afternoon." He grimaces. "It has to be said, insulting one of your major clients on live television isn't exactly normal PR practice."

"Well, I think they should respect you!" I retort. "For actually saying what you think! I mean, so few people do that these days. It could be like . . . your company motto: 'We tell the truth.' "

I take a gulp of champagne and look up into silence. Luke's gazing at me, a quizzical expression on his face.

"Rebecca, you have the uncanniest knack of hitting the nail right on the head," he says at last. "That's exactly what some of our clients have said. It's as though we've given ourselves a seal of integrity."

"Oh," I say, feeling rather pleased with myself. "Well, that's good. So you're not ruined."

"I'm not ruined," agrees Luke, and gives a little smile. "Just slightly dented."

A waiter appears from nowhere and replenishes my glass, and I take a sip. When I look up, Luke's staring at me again.

"You know, Rebecca, you're an extremely perceptive person," he says. "You see what other people don't."

"Oh well." I wave my champagne glass airily. "Didn't you hear Zelda? I'm 'finance guru meets girl next door.' " I meet his eye and we both start to laugh.

"You're informative meets approachable."

"Knowledgeable meets down-to-earth."

"You're intelligent meets charming, meets bright, meets . . ." Luke tails off, staring down into his drink, then looks up.

"Rebecca, I want to apologize," he says. "I've been wanting to apologize for a while. That lunch in Harvey Nichols . . . you were right. I didn't treat you with the respect you deserved. The respect you deserve."

He breaks off into silence and I stare down at the tablecloth, feeling hot with indignation. It's all very well for him to say this *now,* I'm thinking furiously. It's all very well for him to book a table at the Ritz and order champagne and expect me to smile and say "Oh, that's OK." But underneath all the bright banter, I still feel wounded by that whole episode.

"My piece in *The Daily World* had nothing to do with that

lunch," I say without looking up. "Nothing. And for you to insinuate that it did . . ."

"I know," says Luke, and sighs. "I should never have said that. It was a . . . a defensive, angry remark on a day when, frankly, you had us all on the hop."

"Really?" I can't help a pleased little smile coming to my lips. "I had you all on the hop?"

"Are you joking?" says Luke. "A whole page in *The Daily World* on one of our clients, completely out of the blue?"

Ha. I quite like that idea, actually. The whole of Brandon C thrown into disarray by Janice and Martin Webster.

"Was Alicia on the hop?" I can't resist asking.

"She was hopping as fast as her Pradas would let her," says Luke drily. "Even faster when I discovered she'd actually spoken to you the day before."

Ha!

"Good," I hear myself saying childishly—then wish I hadn't. Top businesswomen don't gloat over their enemies being told off. I should have simply nodded, or said "Ah" meaningfully.

"So, did I have you on the hop, too?" I say, giving a careless little shrug.

There's silence, and after a while I look up. Luke's gazing at me with an unsmiling expression, which makes me feel suddenly light-headed and breathless.

"You've had me on the hop for quite a while, Rebecca," he says quietly. He holds my eyes for a few seconds while I stare back, unable to move—then looks down at his menu. "Shall we order?"

The meal seems to go on all night. We talk and talk and eat, and talk, and eat some more. The food is so delicious I can't say no to anything, and the wine is so delicious I abandon my plan of drinking a businesslike single glass. By the time I'm toying listlessly with chocolate feulliantine, lavender honey ice cream, and caramelized pears, it's about midnight, and my head is starting to droop.

"How's the chocolate thing?" says Luke, finishing a mouthful of cheesecake.

"Nice," I say, and push it toward him. "Not as good as the lemon mousse, though."

That's the other thing—I'm absolutely stuffed to the brim. I couldn't decide between all the scrummy-sounding desserts, so Luke said we should order all the ones we liked the sound of. Which was most of them. So now my stomach feels as though it's the size of a Christmas pudding, and just as heavy.

I honestly feel as if I'll never ever be able to get out of this chair. It's so comfortable, and I'm so warm and cozy, and it's all so pretty, and my head's spinning just enough to make me not want to stand up. Plus . . . I don't want it all to stop. I don't want the evening to end. I've had *such* a good time. The amazing thing is how much Luke makes me laugh. You'd think he'd be all serious and boring and intellectual, but really, he's not. In fact, come to think of it, we haven't talked about that unit trust thingy once.

A waiter comes and clears away all our pudding dishes, and brings us each a cup of coffee. I lean back in my chair, close my eyes, and take a few delicious sips. Oh God, I could stay here forever. I'm actually feeling really sleepy by now—partly because I was so nervous last night about *Morning Coffee,* I hardly slept at all.

"I should go," I say eventually, and force myself to open my eyes. "I should go back to . . ." Where do I live, again? "Fulham. To Fulham."

"Right," says Luke after a pause, and takes a sip of coffee. He puts his cup down and reaches for the milk. And as he does so, his hand brushes against mine—and stops still. At once I feel my whole body stiffen. I can't even blink, in case I break the spell.

OK, I'll admit it—I kind of put my hand in his way.

Just to see what would happen. I mean, he could easily move

his hand back if he wanted to, couldn't he? Pour his milk, make a joke, say good-night.

But he doesn't. Very slowly, he closes his hand over mine.

And now I really can't move. His thumb starts to trace patterns on my wrist, and I can feel how warm and dry his skin is. I look up and meet his gaze, and feel a little jolt inside me. I can't tear my eyes away from his. I can't move my hand. I'm completely transfixed.

"That chap I saw you with in Terrazza," he says after a while, his thumb still drawing leisurely pictures on my skin. "Was he anything—"

"Just . . . you know." I try to give a careless laugh, but I'm feeling so nervous it comes out as a squeak. "Some multimillionaire or other."

Luke stares intently at me for a second, then looks away.

"Right," he says, as though closing the subject. "Well. Perhaps we should get you a taxi." I feel a thud of disappointment, and try not to let it show. "Or maybe . . ." He stops.

There's an endless pause. I can't quite breathe. Maybe what? What?

"I know them pretty well here," says Luke at last. "If we wanted to . . ." He meets my eyes. "I expect we could stay."

I feel an electric shock go through my body.

"Would you like to?"

Unable to speak, I nod my head.

"OK, wait here," says Luke. "I'll go and see if I can get rooms." He gets up and I stare after him in a daze, my hand all cold and bereft.

Rooms. Rooms, plural. So he didn't mean—

He doesn't want to—

Oh God. What's *wrong* with me?

We travel up in the lift in silence with a smart porter. I glance a couple of times at Luke's face, but he's staring impassively ahead. In fact, he's barely said a word since he went off to ask about staying. I feel a bit chilly inside—in fact, to be honest, I'm half wishing they hadn't had any spare rooms for us after all. But it turns out there was a big cancellation tonight—and it also turns out that Luke is some big-shot client of the Ritz. When I commented on how nice they were being to us, he shrugged and said he often puts up business contacts here.

Business contacts. So is that what I am? Oh, it doesn't make any sense. I wish I'd gone home after all.

We walk along an opulent corridor in complete silence—then the porter swings open a door and ushers us into a spectacularly beautiful room, furnished with a big double bed and plushy chairs. He places my briefcase and AppleMac on the luggage rail, then Luke gives him a bill and he disappears.

There's an awkward pause.

"Well," says Luke. "Here you are."

"Yes," I say in a voice which doesn't sound like mine. "Thanks . . . thank you. And for dinner." I clear my throat. "It was delicious."

We seem to have turned into complete strangers.

"Well," says Luke again, and glances at his watch. "It's late. You'll probably be wanting to . . ." He stops, and there's a sharp, waiting silence.

My hands are twisted in a nervous knot. I don't dare look at him.

"I'll be off, then," says Luke at last. "I hope you have a—"

"Don't go," I hear myself say, and blush furiously. "Don't go yet. We could just . . ." I swallow. "Talk, or something."

I look up and meet his eyes, and something fearful starts to pound within me. Slowly he walks toward me, until he's standing just in front of me. I can just smell the scent of his aftershave and hear the crisp cotton rustle of his shirt as he moves. My whole body's prickling with anticipation. Oh God, I want to touch him. But I daren't. I daren't move anything.

"We could just talk, or something," he echoes, and slowly lifts his hands until they cup my face.

And then he kisses me.

His mouth is on mine, gently parting my lips, and I feel a white-hot dart of excitement. His hands are running down my back and cupping my bottom, fingering under the hem of my skirt. And then he pulls me tightly toward him, and suddenly I'm finding it hard to breathe.

It's pretty obvious we're not going to do much talking at all.

Twenty-four

MMM.

Bliss.

Lying in the most comfortable bed in the world, feeling all dreamy and smiley and happy, letting the morning sunlight play on my closed eyelids. Stretching my arms above my head, then collapsing contentedly onto an enormous mound of pillows. Oh, I feel good. I feel . . . sated. Last night was absolutely . . .

Well, let's just say it was . . .

Oh, come on. You don't need to know *that*. Anyway, can't you use your imagination? Of course you can.

I open my eyes, sit up, and reach for my cup of room-service coffee. Luke's in the shower, so it's just me alone with my thoughts. And I don't want to sound all pretentious here—but I do feel this is a pretty significant day in my life.

It's not just Luke—although the whole thing was . . . well, amazing, actually. God, he really knows how to . . .

Anyway. Not the point. The point is, it's not just Luke, and it's not just my new job with *Morning Coffee* (even though every time I remember it, I feel a leap of disbelieving joy).

No, it's more than that. It's that I feel like a completely new person. I feel as though I'm moving on to a new stage in life—with a different outlook, and different priorities. When I look back at the frivolous way I used to think—well, it makes me want to laugh, really. The new Rebecca is so much more levelheaded. So much more responsible. It's as though the tinted glasses have fallen off—and suddenly I can see what's really important in the world and what's not.

I've even been thinking this morning that I might go into politics or something. Luke and I discussed politics a bit last night, and I have to say, I came up with lots of interesting views. I could be a young, intellectual member of parliament, and be interviewed about lots of important issues on television. I'd probably specialize in health, or education, or something like that. Maybe foreign affairs.

Casually I reach for the remote control and switch on the television, thinking I might watch the news. I flick a few times, trying to find BBC1, but the TV seems stuck on rubbish cable channels. Eventually I give up, leave it on something called QVT or something, and lean back down on my pillows.

The truth, I think, taking a sip of coffee, is that I'm quite a serious-minded person. That's probably why Luke and I get on so well.

Mmm, Luke. Mmm, that's a nice thought. I wonder where he is.

I sit up in bed, and am just considering going into the bathroom to surprise him, when a woman's voice from the television attracts my attention.

". . . offering genuine NK Malone sunglasses, in tortoiseshell, black, and white, with that distinctive NKM logo in brushed chrome."

That's interesting, I think idly. NK Malone sunglasses. I've always quite wanted a pair of those.

"Buy all three pairs . . ." the woman pauses ". . . and pay not £400. Not £300. But £200! A saving of at least 40 percent off the recommended retail price."

I stare at the screen, riveted.

But this is incredible. *Incredible.* Do you know how much NK Malone sunglasses usually cost? At least 140 quid. Each! Which means you're saving . . .

"Send no money now," the woman is saying. "Simply call this number . . ."

Excitedly I scrabble for the notebook on my bedside table and scribble down the number. This is an absolute dream come true. NK Malone sunglasses. I can't quite believe it. And three pairs! I'll never have to buy sunglasses again. People will call me the Girl in the NK Malone Shades. (And those Armani ones I bought last year are all wrong now. Completely out of date.) Oh, this is *such* an investment. With shaking hands I reach for the phone and dial the number.

And then I stop.

Wait just a moment. The new Rebecca has more self-control than this. The new Rebecca isn't even *interested* in fashion.

Slowly I put the phone down. I reach for the remote and zap the TV to a different channel. A nature program. Yes, that's more like it. There's a close-up of a tiny green frog and a sober voice-over talking about the effect of drought on the ecosystem. I turn up the volume and settle back, pleased with myself. This is much more me. I'm not going to give those sunglasses a second thought. I'm going to learn about this tiny frog and the eco-system, and global warming. Maybe Luke and I will talk about all these important issues, over breakfast.

NK Malone.

Stop it. *Stop* it. Watch the frog, and that tiny red beetle thing . . .

I've wanted NK Malone sunglasses for so long. And £200 is amazing value for three pairs.

I could always give one pair away as a present.

And I deserve a little treat, don't I? After everything I've been though? Just one little final luxury and that's the end. I *promise.*

Grabbing the phone, I redial the number. I give my name and

address, thank the woman very much indeed, then put down the receiver, a content smile on my face. This day is turning out perfect. And it's only nine o'clock!

I turn off the nature program, snuggle back down under the covers, and close my eyes. Maybe Luke and I will spend all day here, in this lovely room. Maybe we'll have oysters and champagne sent up. (I hope not, actually, because I hate oysters.) Maybe we'll . . .

Nine o'clock, interrupts a little voice in my mind. I frown for a second, shake my head, then turn over to get rid of it. But it's still there, prodding annoyingly at my thoughts.

Nine o'clock. Nine . . .

And suddenly I sit bolt upright in bed, my eyes wide in dismay. Oh my God.

Nine-thirty.

Derek Smeath.

I promised to be there. I *promised.* And here I am, with half an hour to go, all the way over at the Ritz. Oh God. What am I going to do?

I switch off the TV, bury my head in my hands, and try to think calmly and rationally. OK, if I got going straight away, I might make it. If I got dressed as quickly as possible, and ran downstairs and jumped in a taxi—I might just make it. Fulham's not that far away. And I could be a quarter of an hour late, couldn't I? We could still have the meeting. It could still happen.

In theory, it could still happen.

"Hi," says Luke, putting his head round the bathroom door. He's got a white towel wrapped round his body, and a few drops of water are glistening on his shoulders. I never even noticed his shoulders last night, I think, staring at them. God, they're bloody sexy. In fact, all in all, he's pretty damn . . .

"Rebecca? Is everything OK?"

"Oh," I say, starting slightly. "Yes, everything's great. Lovely! Oh, and guess what? I just bought the most wonderful . . ."

And then for some reason I stop myself midstream.

I'm not exactly sure why.

"Just . . . having breakfast," I say instead, and gesture to the room-service tray. "Delicious."

A faintly puzzled look passes over Luke's face, and he disappears back into the bathroom. OK, quick, I tell myself. What am I doing to do? Am I going to get dressed and go? Am I going to make the meeting?

But my hand's already reaching for my bag as though it's got a will of its own; I'm pulling out a business card and punching a number into the phone.

Because, I mean, we don't actually *need* to have a meeting, do we? I'm going to send him a nice big check.

And I'd probably never make it in time, anyway.

And he probably won't even mind. He's probably got loads of other stuff he'd prefer to be doing instead.

"Hello?" I say into the phone, and feel a tingle of pleasure as Luke comes up behind me and begins to nuzzle my ear. "Hello, yes. I'd . . . I'd like to leave a message for Mr. Smeath."

FINE FRAMES LTD.

The happy home working family

230A BURNSIDE ROAD LEEDS L6 4ST

Ms. Rebecca Bloomwood
Flat 2
4 Burney Rd.
London SW6 8FD

7 April 2000

Dear Rebecca:

I write to acknowledge receipt of 136 completed Fine Frames ("Sherborne" style—blue). Thank you very much for your fine work. A check for £272 is enclosed, together with an application form for your next frame-making pack.

Our quality control manager, Mrs. Sandra Rowbotham, has asked me to inform you that she was extremely impressed with the quality of your first batch. Novices rarely come up to the exacting standards of the Fine Frames Quality Promise—it is clear you have a natural gift for frame-making.

I would therefore like to invite you to come and demonstrate your technique at our next Framemakers' Convention, to be held in Wilmslow on June 21. This is an occasion when all the members of the Fine Frames homeworking family gather under one roof, with a chance to exchange frame-making tips and anecdotes. It's a lot of fun, believe me!

We very much look forward to hearing from you.

Happy frame-making!

Malcolm Headley
Managing Director

P.S. Are you the same Rebecca Bloomwood who gives advice on *Morning Coffee?*

· ENDWICH BANK ·

FULHAM BRANCH
3 Fulham Road
London SW6 9JH

Ms. Rebecca Bloomwood
Flat 2
4 Burney Rd.
London SW6 8FD

10 April 2000

Dear Ms. Bloomwood:

Thank you for your recent deposit of £1,000.

Bearing in mind the relatively healthy state of your current account at the present time, I suggest that we might postpone our meeting for the moment.

However, be assured that I shall be keeping a close eye on the situation and will be in touch, should matters change in any way.

With best wishes.

Yours sincerely,

Derek Smeath
Manager

P.S. I look forward to your next performance on *Morning Coffee*.

· ENDWICH -- BECAUSE WE CARE ·

ACKNOWLEDGMENTS

Warmest thanks to Susan Kamil and Zoë Rice for all their guidance, inspiration, and enthusiasm. Also to Kim Witherspoon and David Forrer, Celia Hayley, Mark Lucas and all at LAW, all at Transworld, Valerie Hoskins and Rebecca Watson and Brian Siberell at CAA.

Special thanks to Samantha Wickham, Sarah Manser, Paul Watts, Chantal Rutherford-Brown, my wonderful family, and especially Gemma, who taught me how to shop.

This book is dedicated to my friend and agent, Araminta Whitley.

The Dress . . .

I stare at my reflection and feel a little glow of pleasure. It's a simple dress—but I look fantastic in it. It makes me look really thin! It makes my skin look radiant and . . . God, maybe this is the one!

There's silence in the shop.

"Do you feel it here?" says Cynthia, the owner of the boutique, clutching her stomach.

"I . . . don't know! I think so!" I give an excited little laugh. "I think I might!"

"I knew it. You see? When you find the right dress, it hits you. You can't plan for it. You just know when it's right."

"I've found my wedding dress!" I beam at Suze. "I've found it!"

"At last!" There's a ring of relief to Cynthia's voice. "Let's all have a glass of champagne to celebrate!"

An assistant is carrying past another dress, and I catch sight of an embroidered silk corset bodice, tied up with ribbons.

"Hey, that looks nice," I say. "What's that?"

"Never mind what it is!" says Cynthia, handing me a glass of champagne. "You've found your dress!" She lifts her glass, but I'm still looking at the ribboned bodice.

"Maybe I should just try that one on. Just quickly."

"You don't need to look any further." Cynthia's voice is slightly shrill. "This is the one!"

"Mmm . . ." I pull a tiny face. "You know, I'm not so sure it is."

For an awful moment I think Cynthia's going to throw the champagne at me.

"I thought this was the dress of your dreams!"

"It's the dress of *some* of my dreams," I explain. "I have a lot of dreams. Could we put it down as another possible?"

Also by Sophie Kinsella

CONFESSIONS OF A SHOPAHOLIC

SHOPAHOLIC TAKES MANHATTAN

SOPHIE KINSELLA

SHOPAHOLIC *ties* THE KNOT

DELTA TRADE PAPERBACKS

SHOPAHOLIC TIES THE KNOT
A Delta Book/March 2003

Published by
Bantam Dell
A division of Random House, Inc.
New York, New York

Cover design by Belina Huey

Book design by Karin Batten

Library of Congress Cataloging-in-Publication Data

Kinsella, Sophie.
Shopaholic ties the knot / Sophie Kinsella.
p. cm.
ISBN 0-385-33617-9
1. Bloomwood, Becky (Fictitious character)—Fiction.
2. British—New York (State)—Fiction. 3. Manhattan (New York, N.Y.)—
Fiction. 4. Young women—Fiction. 5. Shopping—Fiction.
6. Weddings—Fiction. I. Title.

PR6061.I54 S57 2003
823'.92—dc21 2002073789

Manufactured in the United States of America
Published simultaneously in Canada
First published in 2002 by Transworld, United Kingdom

BVG 10 9 8

For Abigail,
who would have found
the brilliant solution in a flash

SHOPAHOLIC

ties

THE KNOT

SECOND UNION BANK
53 WALL STREET
NEW YORK, NY 10005

November 7, 2001

Miss Rebecca Bloomwood
Apt. B
251 W. 11th Street
New York, NY 10014

Dear Miss Bloomwood:

New Joint Account No.: 5039 2566 2319

We are pleased to confirm your new joint bank account with Mr. Luke J. Brandon, and enclose explanatory documentation. A debit card will be sent to you under separate cover.

We at Second Union Bank continually pride ourselves on our highly individual approach to clients. Please contact me personally at any time if you have a query, and I will help in any way I can. No matter is too small for my attention.

With kind regards.

Yours sincerely,

Walt Pitman
Director of Customer Relations

SECOND UNION BANK
53 WALL STREET
NEW YORK, NY 10005

December 12, 2001

Miss Rebecca Bloomwood
Apt. B
251 W. 11th Street
New York, NY 10014

Dear Miss Bloomwood:

Thank you for your letter of December 9 regarding your joint account with Mr. Luke J. Brandon. I agree the relationship between bank and client should be one of friendship and cooperation, and in answer to your question, my favorite color is red.

I regret, however, I am unable to reword entries on your forthcoming statement as you request. The particular debit item you refer to will appear on your next statement as "Prada, New York." It cannot be changed to "Gas bill."

Yours sincerely,

Walt Pitman
Director of Customer Relations

SECOND UNION BANK
53 WALL STREET
NEW YORK, NY 10005

January 7, 2002

Miss Rebecca Bloomwood
Apt. B
251 W. 11th Street
New York, NY 10014

Dear Miss Bloomwood:

Thank you for your letter of January 4 regarding your joint account with Mr. Luke J. Brandon, and for the chocolates, which I must return. I agree it is difficult to keep tabs on every tiny purchase, and was sorry to hear that "the odd little misunderstanding" had arisen between you.

Unfortunately, it is impossible to split the statement into half as you suggest, sending half to yourself and half to Mr. Brandon and "keeping it our little secret." All income and outgoings are itemized jointly.

That is why it is called a joint account.

Yours sincerely,

Walt Pitman
Director of Customer Relations

One

OK. DON'T PANIC. The answer will come to me any minute. I just have to think hard about what marriage is all about. It's about love, obviously. And companionship, and mutual support. And . . . soup?

My eye rests on a huge antique silver tureen, complete with ladle. Now, that would make a perfect wedding gift. I can just see it: Suze and Tarquin sitting by the fire, ladling soup into each other's bowls. It'll be all lovely and domestic and heartwarming, and every time they drink soup they'll think of me.

Perhaps I could even have it engraved. "To my best friends Suze and Tarquin on their wedding day with love and affection from Becky." And a little poem, maybe.

Mind you, engraving is quite expensive. I'd better check how much it would all come to.

"Excuse me, how much is this soup tureen?" I say, turning to Arthur Graham, who is the owner of Graham's Antiques. This shop has to be one of my favorites in the West Village. It's small and intimate like someone's home, and everywhere you turn, there's something you might want. Like that fantastic carved chair, and a hand-painted velvet throw, and that amazing grandfather clock over in the corner . . .

"The tureen?" Arthur comes over, dapper in his jacket and tie.

"This is very special. Eighteenth-century silver. Exquisite craftsmanship. You see this detail on the rim?"

"Beautiful!" I look obediently.

"And it's priced at . . ." He consults a little book. "Four thousand dollars."

"Oh, right." My smile falters, and I carefully put the ladle back. "Thanks. I'll . . . keep looking."

So maybe marriage isn't about soup. Maybe it's about . . . chess? I run my hand over a beautiful old chess set, all set up as though a game's in progress. But I'm not sure Suze knows how to play chess.

A clock? No.

A . . . an antique barometer?

Oh God, I'm really clutching at straws here. I can't believe it's Suze's wedding in two days and I still haven't got her and Tarquin a present. Or at least, not one I can actually give them. Months ago I bought them this gorgeous picnic hamper, filled with picnicware, a champagne cooler, really cool knives and forks, and even a rug. It took me ages to choose all the stuff, and I was so pleased with it. But Suze phoned last night to check what time we'd be arriving, and told me her aunt had just given her a fantastic present—a picnic hamper filled with Conran tableware!

Well, no way am I giving Suze the same present as someone else. So here I am in the only place I can think of where I'll find something unique. Except . . . what? She hasn't registered for gifts, because she says she hates the idea of asking people for things. And anyway, I'd never just get her some boring set of plates off a list. Suze is my best friend, and I'm going to be her bridesmaid, and my present has to be something really special.

I can feel myself starting to get anxious. OK, just think laterally. What do Suze and Tarquin enjoy doing?

"Do you have any horse saddles?" I ask in sudden inspiration. "Or . . . bridles?"

"Not at the moment."

Oh well. Anyway, I'd have to get two, wouldn't I? And they probably wouldn't even fit the horses properly . . .

A carved music stand? Except how would I get it home on the plane? And anyway, neither of them plays an instrument. A marble bust of Abraham Lincoln? A picture of . . .

Hang on a minute. I push the bust of Lincoln aside and look

carefully at the old trunk he's been resting on. Now that's rather nice. In fact it's very nice. I undo the straps and gently lift the lid, inhaling the smell of old leather.

Wow. This is stunning. All pale silk and leather straps, and a mirror, and little compartments to put your cuff links in. Suze will adore this, I know she will. She can use it to keep jumpers in and when she and Tarquin go on a cruise a porter can wheel it up the ramp for her and she'll look all glamorous and film-star-like.

And the point is, even if someone else gives them a suitcase or something, one of my great maxims of life is: you can never have too much luggage.

"How much is this trunk?" I ask Arthur Graham a little nervously. Please don't let it be $10,000—

"We've had that awhile." He frowns at it. "I could let you have it for . . . three hundred."

"Perfect." I breathe a sigh of relief. "I'll take it."

Mission accomplished! I've got Suze's wedding present! Thank goodness for that. Now all I need is my bridesmaid's dress, and I'm there.

"It's Miss Bloomwood, isn't it?" says Arthur, opening a large leather-bound notebook. "I'm sure we have your address . . . And yes. Here it is." He smiles at me. "Is that all for today?"

I don't need anything else. I don't even need to look around the rest of the shop.

"Um . . . Well." Idly I glance around again. It's always a good idea to have your eyes open when you're in antique shops, because there are some really good bargains out there. And it's all a good investment. I mean, this is how some people make their money.

Through the door to the back room I see the corner of a lace shawl, and feel a tug of desire. Antique shawls are *so* in at the moment. And since I'm buying the trunk, it occurs to me, Arthur might give it to me for half price. Or maybe even for free!

Oh, come on. I'll just have a quick look. But only at very small things, because I've promised Luke no more furniture.

"I'll have a bit of a browse." I smile back at Arthur. "Thanks."

I head happily into the back room and reach for the lace shawl, but close up it looks a bit ragged. I put it down again and pick up a cocktail shaker. This is nice. Maybe I should get it for Suze as well.

"This is cool!" I beam at Arthur, who has followed me in.

"It's fun, isn't it?" he agrees. "It goes with the 1930s cocktail cabinet."

"Cocktail cabinet?" I echo, feeling prickles of interest. "I didn't see a—"

"Here." He walks over to what I thought was a cupboard, unhooks the front flap, and displays the mirrored Art Deco fittings inside. "You see, here's where your bottles go . . . here are your highballs . . ."

I gaze at it, completely smitten. A real, genuine, 1930s cocktail cabinet. I've *always* wanted a cocktail cabinet.

Just think, if we had one of these in the apartment it would change our lives. Every night Luke and I would mix martinis, and dance to old-fashioned songs, and watch the sun go down. It'd be so atmospheric! We'd have to buy one of those old-fashioned record players with the big horns, and start collecting 78s, and I'd start wearing gorgeous vintage tea dresses.

We have to have this. We *have* to. This isn't some boring chair, or set of shelves. This is different. Luke will understand.

"How much is that?" I say, trying to sound nonchalant. I'm rather good at getting good prices in this shop. The trick is to sound as though you don't care whether you buy it or not.

"This?" Arthur looks at it thoughtfully, and I hold my breath. "This really should be seven hundred dollars. But since you're taking the trunk as well . . . I could let you have the pair for . . . eight hundred?"

Eight hundred dollars. For a wedding present *and* a unique cocktail cabinet that we'll treasure all our lives. I mean, this isn't like buying some pair of shoes that you'll forget about. This is a genuine investment for the future.

"I'll take them!" I beam at Arthur Graham.

"Excellent!" He smiles back. "You have a very good eye."

Luke and I've been living together in New York now for a year, and our apartment is on West 11th Street, in the really nice leafy, atmospheric bit. There are ornate little balconies on all the houses, and stone steps up to all the front doors, and trees all along the pavement. Right opposite us lives someone who plays jazz piano, and on summer evenings we stroll up to the roof terrace that we share with our neighbors, and sit on cushions and drink wine and listen. (At least, we did that one time and I'm sure we will again.)

As I let myself into the house, there's a pile of post for us in the hall, and I quickly flick through it.

Boring . . .

Boring . . .

British *Vogue*!

Boring . . .

Oh. My Saks Fifth Avenue store card bill.

I look at the envelope for moment, then remove it and put it in my bag. Not because I'm hiding it. Simply because there's no particular point in Luke seeing it. I read this really good magazine article recently, entitled "Too Much Information?" in which it said you should filter out the day's events rather than tell your partner every single tiny thing and overload his or her weary mind. It said your home should be a sanctuary, and that no one needs to know *everything*. Which, when you think about it, makes a lot of sense.

I put the rest of the post under my arm and start to walk up the stairs. There aren't any letters from England, but then, I wouldn't expect there to be today, because tonight we're flying home for the wedding! I just can't wait.

Suze is my first friend to take the plunge and get married. She's marrying Tarquin, who's a really sweet guy she's known all her life. (In fact, he's her cousin. But it's legal. They checked.) The wedding's going to be at her parents' house in Hampshire, and there's going to be loads of champagne, and a horse and carriage . . . and best of all, I'm going to be her bridesmaid!

At the thought, I feel a pang of yearning. I'm *so* looking forward to it. Not just being bridesmaid—but seeing Suze, my parents, and my home. It occurred to me yesterday I haven't been back to Britain for over six months, which suddenly seems like a really long time. I completely missed Dad getting elected captain of the golf club, which was his life ambition. And I missed the scandal when Siobhan at the church stole the roof money and used it to go to Cyprus. And worst of all, I missed Suze getting engaged—although she came out to New York two weeks later to show me her ring.

It's not that I mind exactly, because I'm having such a great time out here. My job at Barneys is perfect, and living in the West Village is even more perfect. I love walking through the tiny tucked-away streets, and buying cupcakes at the Magnolia Bakery on Saturday mornings and walking back through the market. Basically, I love everything I have here in New York. Except possibly Luke's mother.

But still. Your home's your home.

As I reach the second floor, I hear music coming from our apartment, and I feel a little fizz of anticipation inside. That'll be Danny, working away. He'll probably have finished by now! My dress will be ready!

Danny Kovitz lives upstairs from us, in his brother's apartment, and he's become one of my best friends since I've been in New York. He's a fabulous designer, really talented—but he's not that successful yet. Five years after leaving fashion school, he's still waiting for his big break to come along. But like he always says, making it as a designer is even harder than making it as an actor. If you don't know the right people or have an ex-Beatle as a father, you might as well forget it. I feel so sorry for him, because he does deserve to succeed. So as soon as Suze asked me to be her bridesmaid, I asked him to make my dress. The great thing is, Suze's wedding is going to be stuffed full of rich, important guests. So hopefully loads of people will ask me who designed my dress, and then a whole word-of-mouth buzz will start, and Danny will be made!

I just can't wait to see what he's done. All the sketches he's shown me have been amazing—and of course, a handmade dress will have far more workmanship and detail than you'd get off the peg. Like, the bodice is going to be a boned, hand-embroidered corset—and Danny suggested putting in a tiny beaded love-knot using the birthstones of all the bridal party, which is just so original.

My only slight worry—tiny niggle—is that the wedding's in two days' time, and I haven't actually tried the dress on yet. Or even seen it. This morning I rang Danny's doorbell to remind him I was leaving for England today, and after he'd eventually staggered to the door, he promised me he'd have it by lunchtime. He told me he always lets his ideas ferment until the véry last minute—then he gets a surge of adrenaline and inspiration. It's just the way he works, he assured me, and he's never missed a deadline yet.

I open the door and call "Hello!" cheerfully. There's no response, so I push open the door to our all-purpose living room. The radio is blaring Madonna, the television is playing MTV, and Danny's novelty robot dog is trying to walk up the side of the sofa.

And Danny is slumped over his sewing machine in a cloud of gold silk, fast asleep.

"Danny?" I say in dismay. "Hey, wake up!"

With a start, Danny sits up and rubs his thin face. His curly hair is rumpled, and his pale blue eyes are even more bloodshot than they were when he answered the door this morning. His skinny frame is clad in an old gray T-shirt and a bony knee is poking out of his ripped jeans, complete with a scab that he got Rollerblading this past weekend. He looks like a ten-year-old with stubble.

"Becky!" he says blearily. "Hi! What are you doing here?"

"This is my apartment. Remember? You were working down here because your electricity fused."

"Oh. Yeah." He looks around dazedly. "Right."

"Are you OK?" I peer at him anxiously. "I got some coffee."

I hand him a cup and he takes a couple of deep gulps. Then his eyes land on the pile of mail in my hand and for the first time, he seems to wake up.

"Hey, is that British *Vogue*?"

"Er . . . yes," I say, putting it down where he can't reach it. "So—how's the dress doing?"

"It's going great! Totally under control."

"Can I try it on yet?"

There's a pause. Danny looks at the mound of gold silk in front of him as though he's never seen it before in his life.

"Not yet, no," he says at last.

"But it will be ready in time?"

"Of course! Absolutely." He puts his foot down and the sewing machine starts whirring busily. "You know what?" he says over the noise. "I could really do with a glass of water."

"Coming up!"

I hurry into the kitchen, turn on the tap, and wait for the cold to come through. The plumbing in this building is a little bit eccentric, and we're always on at Mrs. Watts, the owner, to fix it. But she lives miles away in Florida, and doesn't really seem interested. And other than that, the place is completely wonderful. Our apartment is huge by New York standards, with wooden floors and a fireplace, and enormous floor-to-ceiling windows.

(Of course, Mum and Dad weren't at all impressed when they came over. First they couldn't understand why we didn't live in a house. Then they couldn't understand why the kitchen was so small. Then they started saying wasn't it a shame we didn't have a garden, and did I know that Tom next door had moved into a house with a quarter of an acre? Honestly. If you had a quarter of an acre in New York, someone would just build ten office buildings on it.)

"OK! So how's it—" I walk back into the living room and break off. The sewing machine has stopped, and Danny's reading my copy of *Vogue*.

"Danny!" I wail. "What about my dress!"

"Did you see this?" says Danny, jabbing at the page. "'Hamish Fargle's collection demonstrated his customary flair and wit,'" he reads aloud. "Give me a break! He has zero talent. Zero. You know, he was at school with me. Totally ripped off one of my ideas—" He looks up at me, eyes narrowed. "Is he stocked at Barneys?"

"Erm . . . I don't know," I lie.

Danny is completely obsessed with being stocked at Barneys. It's the only thing he wants in the world. And just because I work there as a personal shopper, he seems to think I should be able to arrange meetings with the head buyer.

In fact, I have arranged meetings with the head buyer for him. The first time, he arrived a week late for the appointment and she'd gone to Milan. The second time, he was showing her a jacket and as she tried it on, all the buttons fell off.

Oh God. What was I thinking, asking him to make my dress?

"Danny, just tell me. Is my dress going to be ready?"

There's a long pause.

"Does it actually have to be ready for today?" says Danny at last. "Like literally *today*?"

"I'm catching a plane in six hours!" My voice rises to a squeak. "I've got to walk down the aisle in less than . . ." I break off and shake my head. "Look, don't worry. I'll wear something else."

"Something else?" Danny puts down *Vogue* and stares at me blankly. "What do you mean, something else?"

"Well . . ."

"Are you *firing* me?" He looks as though I've told him our ten-year marriage is over. "Just because I've run a tad over schedule?"

"I'm not firing you! But I mean, I can't be a bridesmaid without a dress, can I?"

"But what else would you wear?"

"Well . . ." I twist my fingers awkwardly. "I do have this one little reserve dress in my wardrobe . . ."

I can't tell him I've actually got three. And two on hold at Barneys.

"By whom?"

"Er . . . Donna Karan," I say guiltily.

"Donna Karan?" His voice cracks with betrayal. "You prefer Donna Karan to me?"

"Of course not! But I mean, the seams are actually sewn . . ."

"Wear my dress."

"Danny—"

"Wear my dress! Please!" He throws himself down on the floor and walks toward me on his knees. "It'll be ready. I'll work all day and all night."

"We haven't *got* all day and all night! We've got about . . . three hours!"

"Then I'll work all three hours. I'll do it!"

"You can really make a boned embroidered corset from scratch in three hours?" I say incredulously.

Danny looks abashed. "So . . . um . . . we may have to rethink the design very slightly . . ."

"In what way?"

He drums his fingers for a few moments, then looks up. "Do you have a plain white T-shirt?"

"A *T-shirt*?" I can't hide my dismay.

"It'll be great. I promise!" From outside comes the chugging sound of a van pulling up and Danny glances out of the window. "Hey, did you buy another antique?"

An hour later I stare at myself in the mirror. I'm wearing a full sweeping skirt made of gold silk—topped by my white T-shirt, which is now completely unrecognizable. Danny's ripped off the sleeves, sewn on sequins, gathered hems, created lines where there were none—and basically turned it into the most fantastic top I've ever seen.

"I love it." I beam at Danny. "I love it! I'll be the coolest bridesmaid in the world!"

"It's pretty good, isn't it?" Danny gives a casual shrug, but I can see he's pleased with himself.

I take another gulp of my cocktail, draining the glass. "Delicious. Shall we have another one?"

"What was in that?"

"Erm . . ." I squint vaguely at the bottles lined up in the cocktail cabinet. "I'm not sure."

It took a while to get the cocktail cabinet up the stairs and into our apartment. To be honest, it's a bit bigger than I remembered, and I'm not sure it'll fit into that little alcove behind the sofa where I'd planned to put it. But still, it looks fantastic! It's standing proudly in the middle of the room, and we've already put it to good use. As soon as it arrived, Danny went upstairs and raided his brother Randall's drinks cupboard, and I got all the booze I could find in the kitchen. We've had a margarita each and a gimlet, and my invention called the Bloomwood, which consists of vodka, orange, and M&M's, which you scoop out with a spoon.

"Give me the top again. I want to pull in that shoulder tighter."

I peel off the top, hand it to him, and reach for my jumper, not bothering to be modest. I mean, this is Danny. He threads a needle and starts expertly gathering along the hem of the T-shirt. "So, these weird cousin-marrying friends of yours," he says. "What's that about?"

"They're not weird!" I hesitate for a moment. "Well, OK, Tarquin is a tiny bit weird. But Suze isn't weird at all. She's my best friend! You've met her!"

Danny raises an eyebrow. "So—couldn't they find anyone else to marry except their own family? Was it like, 'OK, Mom's taken . . . my sister, too fat . . . the dog . . . mmm, don't like the hair.' "

"Stop it!" I can't help giggling. "They just suddenly realized they were meant for each other."

"Like *Harry Met Sally*." He puts on a film-trailer voice. "They were friends. They came from the same gene pool."

"Danny . . ."

"OK." He relents, and snips off the thread. "So, what about you and Luke?"

"What about us?"

"D'you think you'll get married?"

"I . . . I have no idea!" I say, feeling a slight color coming to my cheeks. "I can't say it's ever crossed my mind."

Which is completely true.

Well, OK. It's not *completely* true. Maybe it has crossed my mind on the very odd occasion. Maybe just occasionally I've doodled "Becky Brandon" on my notepad to see what it looked like. And I might possibly have flicked through *Martha Stewart Weddings* once or twice. Just out of idle curiosity.

Perhaps, also, it's occurred to me that Suze is getting married and she's been going out with Tarquin for less time than me and Luke.

But you know. It's not a big deal. I'm really not into weddings. In fact, if Luke asked me, I'd probably say no.

Well . . . OK. I'd probably say yes.

But the point is, it's not going to happen. Luke doesn't want to get married "for a very long time, if at all." He said that in an interview in the *Telegraph* three years ago, which I found in his file of clippings. (I wasn't poking about. I was looking for an elastic band.) The piece was mainly about his business, but they asked him about personal stuff too—and then they captioned his picture *Brandon: marriage at the bottom of agenda.*

Which is absolutely fine by me. It's at the bottom of my agenda, too.

While Danny's finishing off the dress, I do a little housework. Which is to say I tip the dirty breakfast dishes into the sink where they can soak, dab at a spot on the counter—and then spend some time rearranging the spice jars in the spice rack, according to color. That's such a satisfying job. Almost as good as organizing my felt-tip pens used to be.

"So do you guys find it hard living together?" says Danny, coming to the door and watching me.

"No." I look at him in surprise. "Why?"

"My friend Kirsty just tried living with her boyfriend. Disaster.

All they did was fight. She said she doesn't know how anyone does it."

I slot the cumin jar next to fenugreek (what *is* fenugreek?), feeling rather smug. The truth is, Luke and I have had hardly any problems since living together. Except maybe the incident when I repainted the bathroom and got gold glitter paint on his new suit. But that doesn't count, because, as Luke admitted afterward, he completely overreacted, and anybody with sense would have seen that the paint was wet.

Now that I think about it, perhaps we've had the odd teeny little dispute about how many clothes I buy. Perhaps Luke has on occasion opened the wardrobe door and said in exasperation, "Are you *ever* going to wear any of these?"

Perhaps we've also had the odd argu-frank discussion about how many hours Luke works. He runs his own very successful financial PR company, Brandon Communications, which has branches in London and New York and is expanding all the time. He loves his work, and maybe once or twice I've accused him of loving work more than me.

But the point is, we're a mature, flexible couple who are able to talk things through. We went out to lunch not long ago and had a long talk, during which I sincerely promised I would try to shop a bit less and Luke sincerely promised he would try to work a bit less. And I reckon we're both making a pretty good effort.

"Living together has to be worked at," I say wisely. "You have to be flexible. You have to give as well as take."

"Really?"

"Oh yes. Luke and I share our finances, we share the chores . . . it's all a matter of teamwork. The point is, you can't expect everything to stay as it was before. You have to *accommodate*."

"Really?" Danny looks interested. "So who do you think accommodates more? You or Luke?"

I'm thoughtful for a moment.

"It's difficult to say, really," I say at last. "I expect it's about equal on both sides."

"So, like . . . all this stuff." Danny gestures around the cluttered apartment. "Is it mostly yours or mostly his?"

"Erm . . ." I look around, taking in all my aromatherapy candles, vintage lace cushions, and stacks of magazines. For an instant, my mind flicks back to the immaculate, minimalist apartment Luke had in London.

"You know . . ." I say at last. "A bit of both . . ."

Which is kind of true. I mean, Luke's got his laptop in the bedroom.

"The point is, there's no friction between us," I continue. "We think as one. We're like one unit."

"That's great," says Danny, reaching for an apple from the fruit bowl. "You're lucky."

"I know we are." I look at him confidingly. "You know, Luke and I are so in tune, sometimes there's almost a . . . sixth sense between us."

"Really?" Danny stares at me. "Are you serious?"

"Oh yes. I'll know what he's about to say, or I'll kind of *feel* when he's around . . ."

"Like The Force?"

"I suppose." I give a nonchalant shrug. "It's like a gift. I don't question it too closely—"

"Greetings, Obi-Wan Kenobi," says a deep voice behind us, and Danny and I both jump out of our skins. I swivel round—and there's Luke, standing at the door with an amused grin. His face is flushed from the cold and there are snowflakes in his dark hair, and he's so tall, the room suddenly seems a little smaller.

"Luke!" I exclaim. "You scared us!"

"Sorry," he says. "I assumed you would feel my presence."

"Yes. Well, I did kind of feel something . . ." I say, a little defiantly.

"Of course you did." He gives me a kiss. "Hi, Danny."

"Hi," says Danny, watching as Luke takes off his navy cashmere coat, then loosens his cuffs while simultaneously unknotting his tie, with the same assured, deft movements he always makes.

Once, after a few too many cocktails, Danny asked me, "Does Luke make love the same way he opens a champagne bottle?" And although I shrieked and hit him, and said it was none of his business, I could kind of see what he meant. Luke never fumbles or hesitates or looks confused. He always seems to know exactly what he wants, and he pretty much gets it, whether it's a champagne bottle opening smoothly or a new client for his company, or, in bed, for us to . . .

Well. Anyway. Let's just say, since we've been living together, my horizons have been broadened.

Now he picks up the post and starts to leaf briskly through it. "So how are you, Danny?"

"Good, thanks," says Danny, taking a bite of apple. "How's the world of high finance? Did you see my brother today?" Danny's brother Randall works in a financing company, and Luke's had lunch with him a couple of times.

"Not today, no," says Luke.

"OK, well, when you do," says Danny, "ask him if he's put on weight. Really casually. Just say, 'Why, Randall, you're looking well-covered.' And then maybe comment on his choice of entree. He is so paranoid that he's getting fat. It's hilarious."

"Brotherly love," says Luke. "Beautiful, isn't it?" He comes to the end of the post and looks at me with a slight frown.

"Becky, has our joint account statement come yet?"

"Er . . . no. Not yet." I give him a reassuring smile. "I expect it'll come tomorrow!"

Our bank statement actually came yesterday, but I put it straight in my underwear drawer. I'm slightly concerned about some of the entries, so I'm just going to see if there's anything I can do to rectify the situation. The truth is, despite what I said to Danny, I've been finding this whole joint account thing a bit tricky.

Don't get me wrong, I'm all for sharing money. In fact, hand on heart, I *love* sharing Luke's money. It gives me a real buzz! I just don't love it when he suddenly asks, "What was this seventy dollars in Bloomingdale's for?" and I can't remember. So I've worked out a whole new tactical response—which is so simple, it's brilliant.

It's to spill something on the statement, so he can't read it.

"I'm going to take a shower," says Luke, gathering up the post. And he's almost out of the room—when he stops. Very slowly he turns back and looks at the cocktail cabinet as though seeing it for the first time.

"What is that?" he says slowly.

"It's a cocktail cabinet!" I say brightly.

"Where has it come from?"

"It . . . umm . . . actually, I bought it today."

"Becky . . ." Luke closes his eyes. "I thought we said no more crap."

"It's not crap! It's genuine 1930s! We can make amazing cocktails every night!" I'm feeling a bit nervous at his expression, so I start to gabble. "Look, I know we said no more furniture. But this is different. I mean, when you see a one-off like this, you have to grab it!"

I trail away and bite my lip. Luke silently walks toward the cabinet. He runs a hand along the top, then picks up a cocktail shaker, his mouth tight.

"Luke, I just thought it would be fun! I thought you'd like it. The guy in the shop said I've got a really good eye . . ."

"A really good eye," echoes Luke as though in disbelief.

I gasp and scream as he throws the cocktail shaker in the air, and I'm wincing, waiting for it to land with a crash on the wooden floor—when Luke neatly catches it. Danny and I gape as he throws it again, twirls round, and rolls it down his arm.

I don't believe it. I'm living with Tom Cruise.

"I worked as a barman for a summer," says Luke, his face breaking into a smile.

I never knew that! Luke is so driven and businesslike and you think he doesn't care about anything except work . . . and then all of a sudden, he surprises you.

"Teach me how to do it!" I cry excitedly. "I want to be able to do that!"

"And me!" says Danny. He picks up the other cocktail shaker, gives it an inexpert twirl, then tosses it at me. I make a grab, but it lands on the sofa.

"Butterfingers!" mocks Danny. "Come on, Becky. You need to get in practice for catching the bouquet at this wedding."

"No, I don't!"

"Sure you do. You wanna be next, don't you?"

"Danny . . ." I try to give a lighthearted laugh.

"You two should definitely get married," Danny continues, ignoring me. He picks up the cocktail shaker and begins tossing it from hand to hand. "It's perfect. Look at you. You live together, you don't want to kill each other, you're not already related . . . I could make you a *fabulous* dress . . ." He puts down the shaker with a suddenly intent expression. "Hey, listen, Becky. Promise me, if you get married, I can make your dress."

This is appalling. If he carries on like this, Luke will think I'm trying to pressure him. He might even think I told Danny to bring up the subject deliberately.

I've got to redress the balance somehow. Quickly.

"Actually, I don't want to get married," I hear myself saying. "Not for at least ten years."

"Really?" Danny looks taken aback. "You don't?"

"Is that so?" Luke looks up with an unreadable expression. "I wasn't aware of that."

"Weren't you?" I reply, trying to sound nonchalant. "Well . . . now you know!"

"Why don't you want to get married for ten years?" says Danny.

"I . . . erm . . ." I clear my throat. "As it happens, I have a lot of things I want to do first. I want to concentrate on my career, and I want to . . . explore my full potential . . . and . . . get to know the real me first . . . and . . . be a whole . . . umm . . . rounded person."

I tail off and meet Luke's quizzical gaze slightly defiantly.

"I see," he says, nodding. "Well, that sounds very sensible." He looks at the cocktail shaker in his hand, then puts it down. "I'd better go and pack."

He wasn't supposed to *agree* with me.

Two

We arrive at Heathrow at seven the next morning and pick up our rental car. As we drive along to Suze's parents' house in Hampshire, I peer blearily out of the window at the snowy countryside, the hedgerows and fields and little villages, as though I've never seen them before. After Manhattan, everything looks so tiny and pretty. For the first time I realize why Americans go around calling everything in England "quaint."

"Which way now?" says Luke, as we arrive at yet another little crossroads.

"Erm, you definitely turn left here. I mean . . . right. No, I mean left."

As the car swings round, I fish in my bag for the invitation, just to check the exact address.

Sir Gilbert and Lady Cleath-Stuart
request the pleasure of your company . . .

I stare, slightly mesmerized, at the grand swirly writing. God, I still can't quite believe Suze and Tarquin are getting married.

I mean, of course I *believe* it. After all, they've been going out for well over a year now, and Tarquin's basically moved into the flat I used to share with Suze—although they seem to be spending more and more time in Scotland. They're both really sweet and laid back, and everyone's agreed that they make a brilliant couple.

But just occasionally, when I'm not concentrating, my mind will suddenly yell, "Whaat? Suze and Tarquin?"

I mean, Tarquin used to be Suze's weird geeky cousin. For years he was just that awkward guy in the corner with the ancient jacket and a tendency to hum Wagner in public places. He was the guy who rarely ventured beyond the safe haven of his Scottish castle—and when he did, it was to take me on the worst date of my life (although we don't talk about that anymore).

But now he's . . . well, he's Suze's boyfriend. Still slightly awkward, and still prone to wearing woolly jumpers knitted by his old nanny. Still a bit tatty round the edges. But Suze loves him, and that's what counts.

Oh God, I can't start crying yet. I have to pace myself.

"Harborough Hall," reads Luke, pausing at a pair of crumbling stone pillars. "Is this it?"

"Erm . . ." I sniff, and try to look businesslike. "Yes, this is it. Just drive in."

I've been to Suze's house plenty of times before, but I always forget quite how impressive it is. We sweep down a great big long avenue lined with trees and into a circular gravel drive. The house is large and gray and ancient-looking, with pillars at the front and ivy growing over it.

"Nice house," says Luke as we head toward the huge front door. "How old is it?"

"Dunno," I say vaguely. "It's been in their family for years." I tug at the bell pull to see if by any remote chance it's been mended—but it obviously hadn't. I knock a couple of times with the heavy door knocker—and when there's no answer to that either, I push my way into the huge flagstoned hall, where an old Labrador is asleep by a crackling fire.

"Hello?" I call. "Suze?"

Suddenly I notice that Suze's father is also asleep by the fireplace, in a large winged armchair. I'm a bit scared of Suze's father, actually. I certainly don't want to wake him up.

"Suze?" I say, more quietly.

"Bex! I thought I heard something!"

I look up—and there's Suze standing on the staircase, in a tartan dressing gown with her blond hair streaming down her back and a huge excited smile.

"Suze!"

I bound up the stairs and give her a huge hug. As I pull away we're both a bit pink about the eyes, and I give a shaky laugh. God, I've missed Suze, even more than I'd realized.

"Come up to my room!" says Suze, tugging my hand. "Come and see my dress!"

"Is it really lovely?" I say excitedly. "In the picture it looked amazing."

"It's just perfect! Plus you *have* to see, I've got the coolest corsety thing from Rigby and Peller . . . and these really gorgeous knickers . . ."

Luke clears his throat and we both look round.

"Oh!" says Suze. "Sorry, Luke. There's coffee and newspapers and stuff in the kitchen, through there." She points down a corridor. "You can have bacon and eggs if you like! Mrs. Gearing will make them for you."

"Mrs. Gearing sounds like my kind of woman," says Luke with a smile. "I'll see you later."

Suze's room is light and airy and overlooks the garden. I say *garden.* It's about twelve thousand acres, with lawns running down from the back of the house to a clump of cedar trees and a lake, which Suze nearly drowned in once when she was three. There's also a walled rose garden to the left, all flower beds and gravel paths and hedges, which is where Tarquin proposed to Suze. (Apparently he got down on one knee and when he stood up, gravel was clinging to his trousers. That is *so* Tarquin.) On the right there's an old tennis court and then rough grass, extending all the way to a hedge, beyond which is the village church graveyard. As I look out of the window now, I can see a huge marquee billowing to the rear of the house, and a tented walkway being put up, which will snake past the tennis court and over the grass, all the way to the churchyard gate.

"You're not going to walk to the church?" I say, suddenly fearful for Suze's Emma Hope shoes.

"No, silly! I'm going in the carriage. But all the guests can walk back to the house, and there'll be people handing out hot whiskeys as they go."

"God, it's going to be spectacular!" I say, watching as a man in jeans begins to hammer a stake into the ground. And in spite of myself, I can't help feeling a twinge of envy. I've always dreamed of having some huge, amazing wedding, with horses and carriages and lots of hoopla, ever since . . .

Well, since . . .

To be completely, perfectly honest, ever since Princess Diana's wedding. I was six years old when we all watched it round at our neighbor Janice's house, and I can still remember goggling at her as she got out of the carriage in that dress. It was like Cinderella come to life. It was *better* than Cinderella. I wanted to be her so much, it hurt. Mum had bought me a commemorative book of photographs called *Diana's Big Day*—and the next day I spent ages making my own version called *Becky's Big Day*, with lots of drawings of me in a big frilly dress, wearing a crown. (And, in some versions, carrying a magic wand.)

Maybe I've moved on a little since then. I don't dream about wearing a crumpled cream-colored lampshade for a wedding dress. I've even given up on marrying a member of the royal family. But still, whenever I see a wedding, part of me turns back into that starry-eyed six-year-old.

"I know! Isn't it going to be great?" Suze beams happily. "Now, I must just brush my teeth . . ."

She disappears into the bathroom and I wander over to her dressing table, where the announcement of the engagement is stuck in the mirror. The Hon. Susan Cleath-Stuart and The Hon. Tarquin Cleath-Stuart. Blimey. I always forget Suze is so grand.

"I want a title," I say, as Suze comes back into the room with a hairbrush in her hair. "I feel all left out. How do I get one?"

"Ooh, no you don't," says Suze, wrinkling her nose. "They're crap. People send you letters saying Dear Ms. Hon."

"Still. It'd be so cool. What could I be?"

"Erm . . ." Suze tugs at a tangle in her hair. "Dame Becky Bloomwood?"

"That makes me sound about ninety-three," I say doubtfully.

"What about . . . Becky Bloomwood MBE. Those MBE things are quite easy to get, aren't they?"

"Easy-peasy," says Suze confidently. "You could get one for services to industry or something. I'll nominate you, if you like. Now come on, I want to see your dress!"

"OK!" I heave my case onto the bed, click it open, and carefully draw out Danny's creation. "What do you think?" I proudly hold it up against myself and swoosh the gold silk around. "It's pretty cool, isn't it?"

"It's fantastic!" says Suze, staring at it with wide eyes. "I've never seen anything like it!" She fingers the sequins on the shoulder. "Where did you get it? Is this the one from Barneys?"

"No, this is the one from Danny. Remember, I told you he was making me a dress?"

"That's right." She screws up her face. "Which one's Danny, again?"

"My upstairs neighbor," I remind her. "The designer. The one we bumped into on the stairs that time?"

"Oh yes," says Suze, nodding. "I remember."

But the way she says it, I can tell she doesn't really.

I can't blame her—she only met Danny for about two minutes. He was on his way to visit his parents in Connecticut and she was pretty jet-lagged at the time and they barely spoke. Still. It's weird to think that Suze doesn't really know Danny, and he doesn't know her, when they're both so important to me. It's like I've got two completely separate lives, and the longer I'm in New York, the farther they split apart.

"OK, here's mine," says Suze excitedly.

She opens a wardrobe door and unzips a calico cover—and there's a simply stunning dress, all drifting white silk and velvet with long sleeves and a traditional long train.

"Oh God, Suze," I breathe, my throat tight. "You're going to be so completely beautiful. I still can't believe you're getting married! 'Mrs. Cleath-Stuart.' "

"Ooh, don't call me that!" says Suze, wrinkling her nose. "It sounds like my mother. But actually it *is* quite handy marrying someone in the family," she adds, closing the wardrobe, "because I can keep my name and take his, all at the same time. So I can keep being S C-S for my frames." She reaches into a cardboard box and pulls out a beautiful glass frame, all spirals and whorls. "Look, this is the new range—"

Suze's career is designing photograph frames, which sell all over the country, and last year she diversified into photograph albums, wrapping paper, and gift boxes too.

"The whole theme is shell shapes," she says proudly. "D'you like it?"

"It's beautiful!" I say, running my finger round the spirals. "How did you come up with it?"

"I got the idea from Tarkie, actually! We were out walking one day and he was saying how he used to collect shells when he was a child and about all the different amazing shapes in nature . . . and then it hit me!"

I look at her face, all lit up, and have a sudden image of her and Tarquin walking hand in hand on the blustery moors, in Aran sweaters by The Scotch House.

"Suze, you're going to be so happy with Tarquin," I say heartfeltly.

"D'you think?" She flushes with pleasure. "Really?"

"Definitely. I mean, look at you! You're simply glowing!"

Which is true. I hadn't really noticed it before, but she looks completely different from the old Suze. She's still got the same delicate nose and high cheekbones, but her face is rounder, and kind of softer. And she's still slim, but there's a kind of a fullness . . . almost a . . .

My gaze runs down her body and stops.

Hang on a minute.

No. Surely . . .

No.

"Suze?"

"Yes?"

"Suze, are you . . ." I swallow. "You're not . . . pregnant?"

"No!" she replies indignantly. "Of course not! Honestly, whatever can have given you—" She meets my eye, breaks off, and shrugs. "Oh, all right then, yes I am. How did you guess?"

"How did I guess? From you . . . I mean, you *look* pregnant."

"No, I don't! No one else has guessed!"

"They must have. It's completely obvious!"

"No, it isn't!" She sucks in her stomach and looks at herself in the mirror. "You see? And once I've got my Rigby and Peller on . . ."

I can't get my head round this. Suze is pregnant!

"So—is it a secret? Don't your parents know?"

"Oh no! Nobody knows. Not even Tarkie." She pulls a face. "It's a bit tacksville, being pregnant on your wedding day, don't you think? I thought I'd pretend it's a honeymoon baby."

"But you must be at least three months gone."

"Four months. It's due at the beginning of June."

I stare at her. "So how on earth are you going to pretend it's a honeymoon baby?"

"Um . . ." She thinks for a moment. "It could be a bit premature."

"Four whole *months*?"

"Well, OK then. I'll think of something else," says Suze airily. "It's ages away. Anyway, the important thing is, don't tell anyone."

"OK. I won't." Gingerly I reach out and touch her stomach. Suze is having a baby. She's going to be a mother. And Tarquin's going to be a father. God, it's like we're all suddenly growing up or something.

Suze is right on one point at least. Once she's squeezed into her corset, you can't see the bulge at all. In fact, as we both sit in front of her dressing table on the morning of the wedding, grinning excitedly at each other, she actually looks *thinner* than me, which is a tad unfair.

We've had such a great couple of days, chilling out, watching old videos and eating endless KitKats. (Suze is eating for two, and I need energy after my transatlantic flight.) Luke brought some paperwork with him and has spent most of the time in the library—but for once I don't mind. It's just been so nice to be able to spend some time with Suze. I've heard all about the flat she and Tarquin are buying in London and I've seen pictures of the gorgeous hotel on Antigua where she and Tarquin are going for their honeymoon, and I've tried on most of the new clothes in her wardrobe.

There's been loads going on all over the house, with florists and caterers and relations arriving every minute. What's a bit weird is, none of the family seems particularly bothered by it. Suze's mother has been out hunting both the days that I've been here, and her father has been in his study. Mrs. Gearing, their housekeeper, is the one who's been organizing the marquee and flowers and everything—and even she seems pretty relaxed. When I asked Suze about it she just shrugged and said, "I suppose we're used to throwing big parties."

Last night there was a grand drinks party for Suze and Tarquin's relations who have all come down from Scotland, and I was expecting everyone to be talking about the wedding then, at least. But every time I tried to get anyone excited about the flowers, or how romantic it all was, I got blank looks. It was only when Suze mentioned that Tarquin was going to buy her a horse as a wedding present that they all suddenly got animated, and started talking about breeders they knew, and horses they'd bought, and how their great chum had a very nice young chestnut mare Suze might be interested in.

I mean, honestly. No one even *asked* me what my dress was like.

Anyway. I don't care, because it looks wonderful. We both look wonderful. We've both been made up by a fantastic makeup artist, and our hair is up in sleek chignons. The photographer has taken so-called "candid" pictures of me buttoning Suze into her dress (he made us do it three times, in fact my arms were aching by the end). Now Suze is umming and aahing over about six family tiaras while I take sips of champagne. Just to keep me from getting nervous.

"What about your mother?" says the hairdresser to Suze, as she pulls wispy blond tendrils round her face. "Does she want a blow-dry?"

"I doubt it," says Suze, pulling a face. "She's not really into that kind of stuff."

"What's she wearing?" I ask.

"God knows," says Suze. "The first thing that comes to hand, probably." She meets my eye, and I pull a tiny sympathetic face. Last night Suze's mother came downstairs for drinks in a dirndl skirt and patterned woolly jumper, with a large diamond brooch on the front. Mind you, Tarquin's mother looked even worse. I really don't know where Suze has managed to get her sense of style.

"Bex, could you just go and make sure she doesn't put on some hideous old gardening dress?" says Suze. "She'll listen to you, I know she will."

"Well . . . OK," I say doubtfully. "I'll try."

As I let myself out of the room, I see Luke coming along the corridor in his morning dress.

"You look very beautiful," he says with a smile.

"Do I?" I do a little twirl. "It's a lovely dress, isn't it? And it fits so well—"

"I wasn't looking at the dress," says Luke. His eyes meet mine with a wicked glint and I feel a flicker of pleasure. "Is Suze decent?" he adds. "I just wanted to wish her well."

"Oh yes," I say. "Go on in. Hey, Luke, you'll never guess!"

I've been absolutely dying to tell Luke about Suze's baby for the last two days, and now the words slip out before I can stop them.

"What?"

"She's . . ." I can't tell him, I just can't. Suze would kill me. "She's . . . got a really nice wedding dress," I finish lamely.

"Good!" says Luke, giving me a curious look. "There's a surprise. Well, I'll just pop in and have a quick word. See you later."

I cautiously make my way to Suze's mother's bedroom and give a gentle knock.

"Hellooo?" thunders a voice in return, and the door is flung open by Suze's mother, Caroline. She's about six feet tall with long rangy legs, gray hair in a knot, and a weatherbeaten face that creases into a smile when she sees me.

"Rebecca!" she booms, and looks at her watch. "Not time yet, is it?"

"Not quite!" I smile gingerly and run my eyes over her outfit of ancient navy blue sweatshirt, jodhpurs, and riding boots. She's got an amazing figure for a woman her age. No wonder Suze is so skinny. I glance around the room, but I can't see any telltale suit-carriers or hatboxes.

"So, um, Caroline . . . I was just wondering what you were planning to wear today. As mother of the bride!"

"Mother of the bride?" She stares at me. "Good God, I suppose I am. Hadn't thought of it like that."

"Right! So, you . . . haven't got a special outfit ready?"

"Bit early to be dressing up, isn't it?" says Caroline. "I'll just fling something on before we go."

"Well, why don't I help you choose?" I say firmly, and head toward the wardrobe. I throw open the doors, preparing myself for a shock—and gape in astonishment.

This has got to be the most extraordinary collection of clothes I've ever seen. Riding habits, ball dresses, and thirties suits are jostling for space with Indian saris, Mexican ponchos . . . and an extraordinary array of tribal jewelry.

"These clothes!" I breathe.

"I know." Caroline looks at them dismissively. "A load of old rubbish, really."

"Old *rubbish*? My God, if you found any of these in a vintage shop in New York . . ." I pull out a pale blue satin coat edged with ribbon. "This is fantastic."

"D'you like it?" says Caroline in surprise. "Have it."

"I couldn't!"

"Dear girl, I don't want it."

"But surely the sentimental value . . . I mean, your memories—"

"My memories are in here." She taps her head. "Not in there." She surveys the melee of clothes, then picks up a small piece of bone on a leather cord. "Now, *this* I'm rather fond of."

"That?" I say, trying to summon some enthusiasm. "Well, it's—"

"It was given to me by a Masai chief, many years ago now. We were driving at dawn to find a pride of elephants, when a chieftain flagged us down. A tribeswoman was in a fever after giving birth. We helped bring down her temperature and the tribe honored us with gifts. Have you been to the Masai Mara, Rebecca?"

"Er . . . no. I've never actually been to—"

"And this little lovely." She picks up an embroidered purse. "I bought this at a street market in Konya. Bartered for it with my last packet of cigarettes before we trekked up the Nemrut Dagi. Have you been to Turkey?"

"No, not there, either," I say, feeling rather inadequate. God, I feel undertraveled. I scrabble around in my mind, trying to think of somewhere I've been that will impress her—but it's a pretty paltry lineup, now that I think about it. France a few times, Spain, Crete . . . and that's about it. Why haven't I been anywhere exciting? Why haven't I been trekking round Mongolia?

I was going to go to Thailand once, come to think of it. But then I decided to go to France instead and spend the money I saved on a Lulu Guinness handbag.

"I haven't really traveled much at all," I admit reluctantly.

"Well, you must, dear girl!" booms Caroline. "You must broaden your horizons. Learn about life from real people. One of the dearest friends I have in the world is a Bolivian peasant woman. We ground maize together on the plains of the Llanos."

"Wow."

A little clock on the mantelpiece chimes the half hour, and I suddenly realize we're not getting anywhere.

"So anyway . . . did you have any ideas for a wedding outfit?"

"Something warm and colorful," says Caroline, reaching for a thick red and yellow poncho.

"Erm . . . I'm not so sure that would be entirely appropriate . . ." I push between the jackets and dresses, and suddenly see a flash of apricot silk. "Ooh! This is nice." I haul it out—and I don't believe it. It's Balenciaga.

"My going-away outfit," says Caroline reminiscently. "We traveled on the Orient Express to Venice, then explored the caves of Postojna. Do you know that region?"

"You have to wear this!" I say, my voice rising to a squeak of excitement. "You'll look spectacular. And it's so romantic, wearing your own going-away outfit!"

"I suppose it might be rather fun." She holds it up against herself with red, weatherbeaten hands that make me wince every time I look at them. "That should still fit, shouldn't it? Now, there must be a hat around here somewhere . . ." She puts down the suit and starts rooting around on a shelf.

"So—you must be really happy for Suze," I say, picking up an enameled hand mirror and examining it.

"Tarquin's a dear boy." She turns round and taps her beaky nose confidentially. "Very well endowed."

This is true. Tarquin is the fifteenth richest person in the country, or something. But I'm a bit surprised at Suze's mother bringing it up.

"Well, yes . . ." I say. "Although I don't suppose Suze really needs the money . . ."

"I'm not talking about money!" She gives me a knowing smile and suddenly I realize what she means.

"Oh!" I feel myself blushing furiously. "Right! I see!"

"All the Cleath-Stuart men are the same. They're famous for it. Never a divorce in the family," she adds, plonking a green felt hat on top of her head.

Gosh. I'm going to look at Tarquin a bit differently now.

It takes me a while to persuade Caroline out of the green felt hat and into a chic black cloche. As I'm walking back along the corridor toward Suze's room, I hear some familiar voices in the hall downstairs.

"It's common knowledge. Foot-and-mouth was caused by carrier pigeons."

"Pigeons? You're telling me that this huge epidemic, which has wiped out stocks of cattle across Europe, was caused by a few harmless pigeons?"

"Harmless? Graham, they're vermin!"

Mum and Dad! I hurry to the banisters—and there they are, standing by the fireplace. Dad's in morning dress with a top hat under his arm, and Mum's dressed in a navy jacket, floral skirt, and bright red shoes, which don't quite match her red hat.

"Mum?"

"Becky!"

"Mum! Dad!" I hurry down the stairs and envelop them both in a hug, breathing in the familiar scent of Yardley's talc and Tweed.

This trip is getting more emotional by the minute. I haven't seen my parents since they came out to visit me in New York four months ago. And even then, they only stayed for three days before going off to Florida to see the Everglades.

"Mum, you look amazing! Have you done something to your hair?"

"Maureen put some highlights in," she says, looking pleased. "And I popped next door to Janice this morning, so she could do my face. You know, she's taken a course in professional makeup. She's a real expert!"

"I can . . . see!" I say feebly, looking at the lurid stripes of blusher and highlighter painted on Mum's cheeks. Maybe I can manage to wipe them off accidentally on purpose.

"So, is Luke here?" says Mum, looking around with bright eyes, like a squirrel searching for a nut.

"Somewhere around," I say—and Mum and Dad exchange glances.

"He is here, though?" Mum gives a tense little laugh. "You did fly on the same plane, didn't you?"

"Mum, don't worry. He's here. Really."

Mum still doesn't look convinced—and I can't honestly blame her. The truth is, there was this tiny incident at the last wedding we all attended. Luke didn't turn up, and I was completely desperate, and I resorted to . . . um . . .

Well. It was only a tiny white lie. I mean, he *could* have been there, mingling somewhere. If they hadn't had that stupid group photograph, no one would ever have known.

"Jane! Graham! Hello!"

There's Luke, striding through the front door. Thank God for that.

"Luke!" Mum gives a relieved trill of laughter. "You're here! Graham, he's here!"

"Of course he's here!" says my father, rolling his eyes. "Where did you think he was? On the moon?"

"How are you, Jane?" says Luke with a smile, and kisses her on the cheek.

Mum's face is pink with happiness, and she's clutching onto Luke's arm as though he might vanish in a puff of smoke. He gives me a little smile, and I beam happily back. I've been looking forward to this day for so long, and now it's actually here. It's like Christmas. In fact, it's better than Christmas. Through the open front door I can see wedding guests walking past on the snowy gravel in morning dress and smart hats. In the distance, the church bells are pealing, and there's a kind of excited, expectant atmosphere.

"And where's the blushing bride?" says Dad.

"I'm here," comes Suze's voice. We all look up—and there she is, floating down the stairs, clutching a stunning bouquet of roses and ivy.

"Oh, Suzie," says Mum, and claps a hand to her mouth. "Oh, that dress! Oh . . . Becky! You're going to look—" She turns to me with softened eyes and for the first time seems to take in my dress. "Becky . . . is that what you're wearing? You'll freeze!"

"No, I won't. The church is going to be heated."

"It's lovely, isn't it?" says Suze. "So unusual."

"But it's only a T-shirt!" She gives a dissatisfied tug at the sleeve. "And what's this frayed bit? It isn't even finished properly!"

"It's customized," I explain. "It's completely unique."

"Unique? Don't you have to match the others?"

"There aren't any others," explains Suze. "The only other person I would have asked is Tarquin's sister, Fenny. But she said if she was a bridesmaid again she'd jinx her chances of marriage. You know what they say, 'Three times a bridesmaid.' Well, she's been one about ninety-three times! And she's got her eye on this chap who works in the City, so she doesn't want to take any chances."

There's a short silence. I can see Mum's brain working hard. Oh God, *please* don't—

"Becky love, how many times have you been a bridesmaid?" she says, a little too casually. "There was Uncle Malcolm and Aunt Sylvia's wedding . . . but I think that's it, isn't it?"

"And Ruthie and Paul's," I remind her.

"You weren't a bridesmaid at that," says Mum at once. "You were a . . . flower girl. So it's twice, including today. Yes, twice."

"Did you get that, Luke?" says Dad with a grin. "Twice."

Honestly, what are my parents *like*?

"Well, anyway!" I say, trying quickly to think of another subject. "So . . . er . . ."

"Of course, Becky has a good ten years before she needs to worry about anything like that . . ." says Luke conversationally.

"What?" Mum stiffens, and her eyes dart from Luke to me and back again. "What did you say?"

"Becky wants to wait at least ten years before she gets married," says Luke. "Isn't that right, Becky?"

There's a stunned silence. I can feel my face growing hot.

"Um . . ." I clear my throat and try to give a nonchalant smile. "That's . . . that's right."

"Really?" says Suze, staring at me, wide-eyed. "I never knew that! Why?"

"So I can . . . um . . . explore my full potential," I mumble, not daring to look at Mum. "And . . . get to know the real me."

"Get to know the real you?" Mum's voice is slightly shrill. "Why do you need ten years to do that? I could show it to you in ten minutes!"

"But Bex, how old will you be in ten years' time?" says Suze, wrinkling her brow.

"I won't necessarily need ten whole years exactly," I say, feeling a little rattled. "You know, maybe . . . eight will be long enough."

"Eight?" Mum looks as though she wants to burst into tears.

"Luke," says Suze, looking perturbed. "Did you know about this?"

"We discussed it the other day," says Luke with an easy smile.

"But I don't understand," she persists. "What about the—"

"The time?" Luke cuts her off neatly. "You're right. I think we should all get going. You know, it's five to two."

"Five minutes?" Suze suddenly looks petrified. "Really? But I'm not ready! Bex, where are your flowers?"

"Er . . . in your room, I think. I put them down somewhere . . ."

"Well, get them! And where's Daddy got to? Oh shit, I want a cigarette—"

"Suze, you can't *smoke*!" I say in horror. "It's bad for the—" I stop myself just in time.

"For the dress?" suggests Luke helpfully.

"Yes. She might . . . drop ash on it."

By the time I've found my flowers in Suze's bathroom, redone my lipstick, and come downstairs again, only Luke is left in the hall.

"Your parents have gone over," he says. "Suze says we should go over too, and she'll come with her father in the carriage. And I've found a coat for you," he adds, proffering a sheepskin jacket. "Your mother's right, you can't walk over like that."

"OK," I agree reluctantly. "But I'm taking it off in the church."

"Did you know your dress is unraveling at the back, by the way?" he says as he puts it on.

"Really?" I look at him in dismay. "Does it look awful?"

"It looks very nice." His mouth twitches into a smile. "But you might want to find a safety pin after the service."

"Bloody Danny!" I shake my head. "I knew I should have gone for Donna Karan."

As Luke and I make our way over the gravel to the tented walkway, the air is still and silent and a watery sun is coming out. The pealing bells have diminished to a single chiming, and there's no one about except a sole scurrying waiter. Everyone else must already be inside.

"Sorry if I brought up a sensitive subject just then," says Luke as we begin to walk toward the church.

"Sensitive?" I raised my eyebrows. "Oh, what, *that*. That's not a sensitive subject at all!"

"Your mother seemed a bit upset . . ."

"Mum? Honestly, she's not bothered either way. In fact . . . she was joking!"

"Joking?"

"Yes!" I say, a little defiantly. "Joking."

"I see." Luke takes my arm as I stumble slightly on the matting. "So you're still determined to wait eight years before you get married."

"Absolutely." I nod. "At least eight years."

In the distance I can hear hooves on gravel, which must be Suze's carriage setting off.

"Or you know, maybe six," I add casually. "Or . . . five, possibly. It all depends."

There's a long silence, broken only by the soft, rhythmic sound of our footsteps on the walkway. The atmosphere is growing very strange between us, and I don't quite dare look at Luke. I clear my throat and rub my nose, and try to think of a comment about the weather.

We reach the church gate, and Luke turns to look at me—and suddenly his face is stripped of its usual quizzical expression.

"Seriously, Becky," he says. "Do you really want to wait five years?"

"I . . . I don't know," I say, confused. "Do you?"

There's a moment of stillness between us, and my heart starts to thump.

Oh my God. Oh my God. Maybe he's going to . . . Maybe he's about to—

"Ah! The bridesmaid!" The vicar bustles out of the porch and Luke and I both jump. "All set to walk up the aisle?"

"I, er . . . think so," I say, aware of Luke's gaze. "Yes."

"Good! You'd better get inside!" adds the vicar to Luke. "You don't want to miss the moment!"

"No," he says, after a pause. "No, I don't."

He drops a kiss on my shoulder and walks inside without saying anything else, and I stare after him, still completely confused.

Did we just talk about . . . Was Luke really saying . . .

Then there's the sound of hooves, and I'm jolted out of my reverie. I turn to see Suze's carriage coming down the road like something out of a fairy tale. Her veil is blowing in the wind and she's smiling radiantly at some people who have stopped to watch, and I've never seen her look more beautiful.

I honestly wasn't planning to cry. In fact, I'd already planned a way to stop myself doing so, which is to recite the alphabet backward in a French accent. But even as I'm helping Suze straighten her train I'm feeling damp around the eyes. And as the organ music swells and we start to process slowly forward into the packed church, I'm having to sniff hard every two beats, along with the organ. Suze is holding tightly to her father's arm and her train is gliding along the old stone floor. I'm walking behind, trying not to tap my heels on the floor, and hoping no one will notice my dress unraveling.

We reach the front—and there's Tarquin waiting, with his best man. He's as tall and bony as ever, and his face still reminds me of a stoat, but I have to admit he's looking pretty striking in his sporran and kilt. He's gazing at Suze with such transparent love and admiration that I can feel my nose starting to prickle again. He turns briefly, meets my eye, and grins nervously—and I give an embarrassed little smile back. To be honest, I'll never be able to look at him again without thinking about what Caroline said.

The vicar begins his "Dearly beloved" speech, and I feel myself relax with pleasure. I'm going to relish every single, familiar word. This is like watching the start of a favorite movie, with my two best friends playing the main parts.

"Susan, wilt thou take this man to be thy wedded husband?" The vicar's got huge bushy eyebrows, which he raises at every question, as though he's afraid the answer might be no. "Wilt thou love him, comfort him, honor, and keep him in sickness and in health; and, forsaking all others, keep thee only unto him, so long as ye both shall live?"

There's a pause—then Suze says, "I will," in a voice as clear as a bell.

I wish bridesmaids got to say something. It wouldn't have to be anything very much, just a quick "Yes" or "I do."

When we come to the bit where Suze and Tarquin have to hold hands, Suze gives me her bouquet, and I take the opportunity to turn round and have a quick peek at the congregation. The place is crammed to the gills, in fact there isn't even room for everyone to sit down. There are lots of strapping men in kilts and women in velvet suits, and there's Fenny and a whole crowd of her London friends, all wearing Philip Treacy hats, it looks like. And there's Mum, squashed right up against Dad, with a tissue pressed to her eyes. She looks up and sees me and I give a little smile—but all she does is sob again.

I turn back and Suze and Tarquin are kneeling down, and the vicar is intoning severely, "Those whom God has joined together, let no man put asunder."

I look at Suze as she beams radiantly at Tarquin. She's completely lost in him. She belongs to him now. And to my surprise, I suddenly feel slightly hollow inside. Suze is married. It's all changed.

It's a year since I went off to live in New York, and I've loved every minute of it. Of course I have. But subconsciously, I realize, I've always had it in the back of my mind that if everything went wrong, I could come back to Fulham and have my old life with Suze.

Suze doesn't need me anymore. She's got someone else, who will always come first in her life. I watch as the vicar places his hands on Suze's and Tarquin's heads to bless them—and my throat feels a little tight as I remember all the times we've had together. The time I cooked a horrible curry to save money and she kept saying how delicious it was even while her mouth was burning. The time she tried to seduce my bank manager so he would extend my overdraft. Every time I've got myself into trouble, she's been there for me.

And now it's all over.

Suddenly I feel in need of a little reassurance. I turn round and quickly scan the rows of guests, looking for Luke's face. For a few moments I can't spot him, and although I keep wearing my confident smile, I feel a ridiculous panic rising inside me, like a child realizing she's been left behind at school; that everyone else has been collected but her.

Until suddenly I see him. Standing behind a pillar toward the back, tall and dark and solid, his eyes fixed on mine. Looking at me and no one else. And as I gaze back at him, I feel restored. I've been collected too; it's OK.

We emerge into the churchyard, the sound of bells behind us, and a crowd of people who have gathered outside on the road start to cheer.

"Congratulations!" I cry, giving Suze a huge hug. "And to you, Tarquin!"

I've always been a teeny bit awkward around Tarquin. But now I see him with Suze—married to Suze—the awkwardness seems to melt away.

"I know you'll be really happy," I say warmly, and give him a kiss on the cheek, and we both laugh as someone throws confetti at us. Guests are already piling out of the church like sweets out of a jar, talking and laughing and calling to each other in loud confident voices. They swarm around Suze and Tarquin, kissing and hugging and shaking hands, and I move away a little, wondering where Luke is.

The whole churchyard is filling up with people, and I can't help staring at some of Suze's relations. Her granny is coming out of the church very slowly and regally, holding a stick, and is being followed by a dutiful-looking young man in morning dress. A thin, pale girl with huge eyes is wearing an enormous black hat, holding a pug and chain-smoking. There's a whole army of almost identical brothers in kilts standing by the church gate, and I remember Suze telling me about her aunt who had six boys before finally getting twin girls.

"Here. Put this on." Luke's voice is suddenly in my ear, and I turn round, to see him holding out the sheepskin jacket. "You must be freezing."

"Don't worry. I'm fine!"

"Becky, there's snow on the ground," says Luke firmly, and drapes the coat round my shoulders. "Very good wedding," he adds.

"Yes." I look up at him carefully, wondering if by any chance we can work the conversation back to what we were talking about before the service. But now Luke's looking at Suze and Tarquin, who are being photographed under the oak tree. Suze looks absolutely radiant, but Tarquin looks as though he's facing gunfire.

"He's a very nice chap," he says, nodding toward Tarquin. "Bit odd, but nice."

"Yes. He is. Luke—"

"Would you like a glass of hot whiskey?" interrupts a waiter, coming up with a tray. "Or champagne?"

"Hot whiskey," I say gratefully. "Thanks." I take a few sips and close my eyes as the warmth spreads through my body. If only it could get down to my feet, which, to be honest, are completely freezing.

"Bridesmaid!" cries Suze suddenly. "Where's Bex? We need you for a photograph!"

My eyes open.

"Here," I shout, slipping the sheepskin coat off my shoulders. "Luke, hold my drink—"

I hurry through the melee and join Suze and Tarquin. And it's funny, but now that all these people are looking at me, I don't feel cold anymore. I smile my most radiant smile, and hold my flowers nicely, and link arms with Suze when the photographer tells me to, and, in between shots, wave at Mum and Dad, who have pushed their way to the front of the crowd.

"We'll head back to the house soon," says Mrs. Gearing, coming up to kiss Suze. "People are getting chilly. You can finish the pictures there."

"OK," says Suze. "But let's just take some of me and Bex together."

"Good idea!" says Tarquin at once, and heads off in obvious relief to talk to his father, who looks exactly like Tarquin but forty years older. The photographer takes a few shots of me and Suze beaming at each other, then pauses to reload his camera. Suze accepts a glass of whiskey from a waiter and I reach surreptitiously behind me to see how much of my dress has unraveled.

"Bex, listen," comes a voice in my ear. I look round, and Suze is gazing at me earnestly. She's so close I can see each individual speck of glitter in her eyeshadow. "I need to ask you something. You don't really want to wait ten years before you get married, do you?"

"Well . . . no," I admit. "Not really."

"And you do think Luke's the one? Just . . . honestly. Between ourselves."

There's a long pause. Behind me I can hear someone saying, "Of course, our house is fairly modern. I think it was built in 1853—"

"Yes," I say eventually, feeling a deep pink rising through my cheeks. "Yes. I think he is."

Suze looks at me searchingly for a few moments longer—then abruptly seems to come to a decision. "Right!" she says, putting down her whiskey. "I'm going to throw my bouquet."

"What?" I stare at her in bewilderment. "Suze, don't be stupid. You can't throw your bouquet yet!"

"Yes I can! I can throw it when I like."

"You ought to throw it when you leave for your honeymoon!"

"I don't care," says Suze obstinately. "I can't wait any longer. I'm going to throw it now."

"But you're supposed to do it at the *end*!"

"Who's the bride? You or me? If I wait till the end it won't be any fun! Now, stand over there." She points with an imperious hand to a small mound of snowy grass. "And put your flowers down. You'll never catch it if you're holding things! Tarkie?" She raises her voice. "I'm going to throw my bouquet now, OK?"

"OK!" Tarquin calls back cheerfully. "Good idea."

"Go on, Bex!"

"Honestly! I don't even want to catch it!" I say, slightly grumpily.

But I suppose I am the only bridesmaid—so I put my flowers down on the grass, and go and stand on the mound as instructed.

"I want a picture of this," Suze is saying to the photographer. "And where's Luke?"

The slightly weird thing is, no one else is coming with me. Everyone else has melted away. Suddenly I notice that Tarquin and his best man are going around murmuring in people's ears, and gradually all the guests are turning to me with bright, expectant faces.

"Ready, Bex?" calls Suze.

"Wait!" I cry. "You haven't got enough people! There should be lots of us, all standing together . . ."

I feel so stupid, up here on my own. Honestly, Suze is doing this all wrong. Hasn't she *been* to any weddings?

"Wait, Suze!" I cry again, but it's too late.

"Catch, Bex!" she yells. "Caaatch!"

The bouquet comes looping high through the air, and I have to jump slightly to catch it. It's bigger and heavier than I expected, and for a moment I just stare dazedly at it, half secretly delighted and half completely furious with Suze.

And then my eyes focus. And I see the little envelope. *To Becky.*

An envelope addressed to me in Suze's bouquet?

I look up bewilderedly at Suze, and with a shining face she nods toward the envelope.

With trembling fingers, I open the card. There's something lumpy inside. It's . . .

It's a ring, all wrapped up in cotton wool. I take it out, feeling dizzy. There's a message in the card, written in Luke's handwriting. And it says . . .

It says *Will You* . . .

I stare at it in disbelief, trying to keep control of myself, but the world is shimmering, and blood is pounding through my head.

I look up dazedly, and there's Luke, coming forward through the people, his face serious but his eyes warm.

"Becky—" he begins, and there's a tiny intake of breath around the churchyard. "Will you—"

"Yes! Yeee-esssss!" I hear the joyful sound ripping through the churchyard before I even realize I've opened my mouth. I'm so charged up with emotion, my voice doesn't even *sound* like mine. In fact, it sounds more like . . .

Mum.

I don't believe it.

As I whip round, she claps a hand over her mouth in horror. "Sorry!" she whispers, and a ripple of laughter runs round the crowd.

"Mrs. Bloomwood, I'd be honored," says Luke, his eyes crinkling into a smile. "But I believe you're already taken."

Then he looks at me again.

"Becky, if I had to wait five years, then I would. Or eight—or even ten." He pauses, and there's complete silence except for a tiny gust of wind, blowing confetti about the churchyard. "But I hope that one day—preferably rather sooner than that—you'll do me the honor of marrying me?"

My throat's so tight, I can't speak. I give a tiny nod, and Luke takes my hand. He unfolds my fingers and takes out the ring. My heart is hammering. Luke wants to marry me. He must have been planning this all along. Without saying a thing.

I look at the ring, and feel my eyes start to blur. It's an antique diamond ring, set in gold, with tiny curved claws. I've never seen another quite like it. It's perfect.

"May I?"

"Yes," I whisper, and watch as he slides it onto my finger. He looks at me again, his eyes more tender than I've ever seen them, and kisses me, and the cheering starts.

I don't believe it. I'm engaged.

Three

OK. Now, I may be engaged, but I'm not going to get carried away.

No way.

I know some girls go mad, planning the biggest wedding in the universe and thinking about nothing else . . . but that's not going to be me. I'm not going to let this take over my life. I mean, let's get our priorities right here. The most important thing is not the dress, or the shoes, or what kind of flowers we have, is it? It's making the promise of lifelong commitment. It's pledging our troth to one another.

I pause, halfway through putting on my moisturizer, and gaze at the reflection in my old bedroom mirror. "I, Becky," I murmur solemnly. "I, Rebecca. Take thee, Luke."

Those ancient words just send a shiver up your spine, don't they?

"To be thine . . . mine . . . husband. For better, for richer . . ."

I break off with a puzzled frown. That doesn't sound quite right. Still, I can learn it properly nearer the time. The point is, the vows are what matters, nothing else. We don't have to go over the top. Just a simple, elegant ceremony. No fuss, no hoopla. I mean, Romeo and Juliet didn't need a big wedding with sugared almonds and vol-au-vents, did they?

In fact, maybe we should even get married in secret, like they did! Suddenly I'm gripped by a vision of Luke and me kneeling before an Italian priest in the dead of night, in some tiny stone chapel. God, that would be romantic. And then somehow Luke would think I was dead, and he'd commit suicide, and so would I, and it would be incredibly tragic, and everyone would say we did it for love and the whole world should learn from our example . . .

"Karaoke?" Luke's voice outside the bedroom door brings me back to reality. "Well, it's certainly a possibility . . ."

The door opens and he holds out a cup of coffee to me. He and I have been staying here at my parents' house since Suze's wedding, and when I left the breakfast table, he was refereeing my parents as they argued over whether or not the moon landings actually happened.

"Your mother's already found a possible date for the wedding," he says. "What do you think about the—"

"Luke!" I put up a hand to stop him. "Luke. Let's just take this one step at a time, shall we?" I give him a kind smile. "I mean, we've only just got engaged. Let's just get our heads round that first. There's no need to dash into setting dates."

I glance at myself in the mirror, feeling quite grown-up and proud of myself. For once in my life I'm not getting overexcited.

"You're right," says Luke after a pause. "No, you are right. And the date your mother suggested would be a terrible hurry."

"Really?" I take a thoughtful sip of coffee. "So . . . just out of interest . . . when was it?"

"June 22nd. This year." He shakes his head. "Crazy, really. It's only a few months away."

"Madness!" I say, rolling my eyes. "I mean, there's no hurry, is there?"

June 22nd. Honestly! What is Mum thinking?

Although . . . I suppose a summer wedding would be nice in theory.

There's nothing actually *stopping* us getting married this year.

And if we did make it June, I could start looking at wedding dresses straight away. I could start trying on tiaras. I could start reading *Brides*! Yes!

"On the other hand," I add casually, "there's no *real* reason to delay, is there? I mean, now we've decided, in one sense, we might as well just . . . do it. Why hang around?"

"Are you sure? Becky, I don't want you to feel pressured—"

"It's OK. I'm quite sure. Let's get married in June!" I give him an exhilarated beam. "Shall we go and register today?"

Oops. That just kind of slipped out.

"Today?" says Luke, looking taken aback. "You're not serious."

"Of course not!" I give a lighthearted laugh. "I'm joking! Although, you know, we *could* go and start looking at a few things, purely for information . . ."

"Becky, I'm busy today, remember?" He glances at his watch. "In fact, I must get going."

"Oh yes," I say, trying to muster some enthusiasm. "Yes, you don't want to be late, do you?"

Luke's spending the day with his mother, Elinor, who is over in London on her way to Switzerland. The official version is that she's going there to stay with some old friends and "enjoy the mountain air." Of course everyone knows she's really going to have her face lifted for the zillionth time.

Then this afternoon, Mum, Dad, and I are going up to meet them for tea at Claridges. Everyone has been exclaiming about what a lucky coincidence it is that Elinor's over here, so the two families will be able to meet. But every time I think about it, my stomach turns over. I wouldn't mind if it was Luke's real parents—his dad and stepmum, who are really lovely and live in Devon. But they've just gone out to Australia, where Luke's sister has moved, and they probably won't be back until just before the wedding. So all we're left with to represent Luke is Elinor.

Elinor Sherman. My future mother-in-law.

OK . . . let's not think about that.

"Luke . . ." I pause, trying to find the right words. "How do you think it'll be? Our parents meeting for the first time? You know—your mother . . . and my mother . . . I mean, they're not exactly similar, are they?"

"It'll be fine! They'll get on wonderfully, I'm sure."

He honestly hasn't a clue what I'm talking about.

I know it's a good thing that Luke adores his mother. I know sons should love their mothers. And I know he hardly ever saw her when he was tiny, and he's trying to make up for lost time . . . but still. *How* can he be so devoted to Elinor?

As I arrive downstairs in the kitchen, Mum's tidying up the breakfast things with one hand and holding the portable phone in the other.

"Yes," she's saying. "That's right. Bloomwood, B-l-o-o-m-w-o-o-d. Of Oxshott, Surrey. And you'll fax that over? Thank you.

"Good." She puts away the phone and beams at me. "That's the announcement gone in the Surrey *Post.*"

"*Another* announcement? Mum, how many have you done?"

"Just the standard number!" she says defensively. "The *Times,* the *Telegraph,* the Oxshott *Herald,* and the Esher *Gazette.*"

"And the Surrey *Post.*"

"Yes. So only . . . five."

"Five!"

"Becky, you only get married once!" says Mum.

"I know. But honestly . . ."

"Now, listen." Mum is rather pink in the face. "You're our only daughter, Becky, and we're not going to spare any expense. We want you to have the wedding of your dreams. Whether it's the announcements, or the flowers, or a horse and carriage like Suzie had . . . we want you to have it."

"Mum, I wanted to talk to you about that," I say awkwardly. "Luke and I will contribute to the cost—"

"Nonsense!" says Mum briskly. "We wouldn't hear of it."

"But—"

"We've always hoped we'd be paying for a wedding one day. We've been putting money aside especially, for a few years now."

"Really?" I stare at her, feeling a sudden swell of emotion. Mum and Dad have been saving all this time, and they never said a word. "I . . . I had no idea."

"Yes, well. We weren't going to tell you, were we? Now!" Mum snaps back into businesslike mode. "Did Luke tell you we've found a date? You know, it wasn't easy! Everywhere's booked up. But I've spoken to Peter at the church, he's had a cancellation, and he can fit us in at three on that Saturday. Otherwise it would be a question of waiting until November."

"November?" I pull a face. "That's not very weddingy."

"Exactly. So I told him to pencil it in. I've put it on the calendar, look."

I glance over at the fridge calendar, which has a different recipe using Nescafé for each month. And sure enough, there in June is a big felt-tipped "BECKY'S WEDDING."

I stare at it, feeling slightly weird. I am going to get married. It's something I've secretly thought about for so long—and now it really is happening.

"I've been having a few ideas about the marquee," adds Mum. "I saw a beautiful striped one in a magazine somewhere, and I thought, 'I must show that to Becky . . .' "

She reaches behind her and hauls out a stack of glossy magazines. *Brides. Modern Bride. Wedding and Home.* All shiny and succulent and inviting, like a plate of sticky doughnuts.

"Gosh!" I say, forcing myself not to reach greedily for one. "I haven't read any of those bridal things yet. I don't even know what they're like!"

"Neither have I," says Mum at once, as she flicks expertly through an issue of *Wedding and Home.* "Not properly. I've just glanced through for the odd idea. I mean, they're really just adverts mainly . . ."

I hesitate, my fingers running over the cover of *You and Your Wedding.* I can hardly believe I'm actually allowed to read these now. Openly! I don't have to sidle up to the rack and take tiny, guilty peeks, like stuffing a biscuit into my mouth and all the time wondering if someone will see me.

The habit's so ingrained I almost can't break it, even though I've got an engagement ring on my finger now.

"I suppose it makes sense to have a very brief look," I say casually. "You know, just for basic information . . . just to be aware what's available . . ."

Oh, sod it. Mum's not even listening, anyway, so I might as well give up pretending I'm not going to read every single one of these magazines avidly from cover to cover. Happily I sink into a chair and reach for *Brides,* and for the next ten minutes we're both completely silent, gorging on pictures.

"There!" says Mum suddenly. She turns her magazine round so I can see a picture of a billowing white and silver striped marquee. "Isn't that nice?"

"Very pretty." I run my gaze down interestedly to the picture of the bridesmaids' dresses, and the bride's bouquet . . . and then my eye comes to rest on the dateline.

"Mum!" I exclaim. "This is from last year! How come you were looking at wedding magazines last year!"

"I've no idea!" says Mum shiftly. "I must have . . . picked it up in a doctor's waiting room or something. Anyway. Are you getting any ideas?"

"Well . . . I don't know," I say vaguely. "I suppose I just want something simple."

A vision of myself in a big white dress and sparkly tiara suddenly pops into my head. Getting out of a carriage at St. Paul's Cathedral . . . my handsome prince waiting for me . . . cheering crowds . . .

OK, stop. I'm *not* going to go over the top. I've already decided that.

"I agree," Mum is saying. "You want something elegant and tasteful. Oh, look, grapes covered with gold leaf. We could do that!" She turns a page. "Look, identical twin bridesmaids! Don't they look pretty? Do you know anyone with twins, love?"

"No," I say regretfully. "I don't think so. Ooh, you can buy a special wedding countdown alarm clock! And a wedding organizer with matching bridal diary for those special memories. Do you think I should get one of those?"

"Definitely," says Mum. "If you don't, you'll only wish you had." She puts down her magazine. "You know, Becky, one thing I will say to you is, don't do this by half-measures. Remember, you only do it once—"

"Hellooo?" We both look up as there's a tap on the back door. "It's only me!" Janice's bright eyes look through the glass, and she gives a little wave. Janice is our next-door neighbor and I've known her forever. She's wearing a floral shirtwaister in a virulent shade of turquoise, and eye shadow to match, and there's a folder under her arm.

"Janice!" cries Mum. "Come on in and have a coffee."

"I'd love one," says Janice. "I've brought my Canderel." She comes in and gives me a hug. "And here's the special girl! Becky love, congratulations!"

"Thanks," I say, with a bashful grin.

"Just look at that ring!"

"Two carats," says Mum at once. "Antique. It's a family heirloom."

"A family heirloom!" echoes Janice breathlessly. "Oh, Becky!" She picks up a copy of *Modern Bride* and gives a wistful little sigh. "But how are you going to organize the wedding, living in New York?"

"Becky doesn't have to worry about a thing," says Mum firmly. "I can do it all. It's traditional, anyway."

"Well, you know where I am if you want any help," says Janice. "Have you set a date yet?"

"June 22nd," says Mum over the shriek of the coffee grinder. "Three o'clock at St. Mary's."

"Three o'clock!" says Janice. "Lovely." She puts down the magazine and gives me a suddenly earnest look. "Now, Becky, there's something I want to say. To both of you."

"Oh yes?" I say, slightly apprehensively, and Mum puts down the coffeepot.

Janice takes a deep breath. "It would give me great pleasure to do your wedding makeup. You and the whole bridal party."

"Janice!" exclaims my mother in delight. "What a kind thought! Think of that, Becky. Professional makeup!"

"Er . . . fantastic!"

"I've learned such a lot on my course, all the tricks of the trade. I've got a whole book full of photographs you can browse through, to choose your style. In fact I've brought it with me, look!" Janice opens the folder and begins to flip over laminated cards of women who look as though they had their makeup applied during the seventies. "This look is called Prom Princess, for the younger face," she says breathlessly. "Now, here we have Radiant Spring Bride, with extra-waterproof mascara . . . Or Cleopatra, if you wanted something more dramatic?"

"Great!" I say feebly. "Perhaps I'll have a look nearer the time."

There is no way in a million years I'm letting Janice near my face.

"And you'll be getting Wendy to do the cake, will you?" asks Janice as Mum puts a cup of coffee in front of her.

"Oh, no question," says Mum. "Wendy Prince, who lives on Maybury Avenue," she adds to me. "You remember, she did Dad's retirement cake with the lawnmower on it? The things that woman can do with a nozzle!"

I remember that cake. The icing was virulent green and the lawnmower was made out of a painted matchbox. You could still see "Swan" through the green.

"You know, there are some really amazing wedding cakes in here," I say, tentatively holding out an issue of *Brides*. "From this special place in London. Maybe we could go and have a look."

"Oh, but love, we have to ask Wendy!" says Mum in surprise. "She'd be devastated if we didn't. You know her husband's just had a stroke? Those sugar roses are what's keeping her going."

"Oh, right," I say, putting down the magazine guiltily. "I didn't know. Well . . . OK then. I'm sure it'll be lovely."

"We were very pleased with Tom and Lucy's wedding cake." Janice sighs. "We've saved the top tier for the first christening. You know, they're with us at the moment. They'll be round to offer their congratulations, I'm sure. Can you believe they've been married a year and a half already!"

"Have they?" Mum takes a sip of coffee and gives a brief smile.

Tom and Lucy's wedding is still a very slightly sore point in our family. I mean, we love Janice and Martin to bits so we never say anything, but to be honest, we're none of us very keen on Lucy.

"Are there any signs of them . . ." Mum makes a vague, euphemistic gesture. "Starting a family," she adds in a whisper.

"Not yet." Janice's smile flickers briefly. "Martin and I think they probably want to *enjoy* each other first. They're such a happy young couple. They just dote on each other! And of course, Lucy's got her career—"

"I suppose so," says Mum consideringly. "Although it doesn't do to wait *too* long . . ."

"Well, I know," agrees Janice. They both turn to look at me—and suddenly I realize what they're driving at.

For God's sake, I've only been engaged a day! Give me a chance!

I escape to the garden and wander round for a bit, sipping my coffee. The snow is starting to melt outside, and you can just see patches of green lawn and bits of rosebush. As I pick my way down the gravel path, I find myself thinking how nice it is to be in an

English garden again, even if it is a bit cold. Manhattan doesn't have any gardens like this. There's Central Park, and there's the odd little flowery square. But it doesn't have any proper English gardens, with lawns and trees and flower beds.

I've reached the rose arbor and am looking back at the house, imagining what a marquee will look like on the lawn, when suddenly there's a rumble of conversation from the garden next door. I wonder if it's Martin, and I'm about to pop my head over the fence and say "Hello!" when a girl's voice comes clearly over the snow, saying: "Define *frigid*! Because if you ask me—"

It's Lucy. And she sounds furious! There's a mumbled reply, which can only be Tom.

"And you're such a bloody expert, are you?"

Mumble mumble.

"Oh, give me a break."

I edge surreptitiously toward the fence, wishing desperately I could hear both sides.

"Yeah, well, maybe if we had more of a life, maybe if you actually organized something once in a blue moon, maybe if we weren't stuck in such a bloody rut . . ."

Lucy's voice is so hectoring. And now Tom's voice is raised defensively in return.

"We went out to . . . all you could do was complain . . . made a real bloody effort . . ."

Crack!

Shit. *Shit.* I've stepped on a twig.

For an instant I consider running. But it's too late, their heads have already appeared over the garden fence, Tom's all pink and distressed, and Lucy's tight with anger.

"Oh, hi!" I say, trying to look relaxed. "How are *you*? I'm just . . . um . . . having a little stroll . . . and I dropped my . . . hanky."

"Your hanky?" Lucy looks suspiciously at the ground. "I can't see any hanky."

"Well . . . erm . . . So . . . how's married life?"

"Fine," says Lucy shortly. "Congratulations, by the way."

"Thanks."

There's an awkward pause, and I find myself running my eyes over Lucy's outfit, taking in her top (black polo-neck, probably

M&S), trousers (Earl Jeans, quite cool, actually), and boots (high-heeled with laces, Russell & Bromley).

This is something I've always done, checking out people's clothes and listing them in my mind like on a fashion page. I thought I was the only one who did it. But then I moved to New York—and there, everyone does it. Seriously, everybody. The first time you meet anyone, whether it's a rich society lady or a doorman, they give you a swift, three-second top-to-toe sweep. You can see them costing your entire outfit to the nearest dollar before they even say hello. I call it the Manhattan Onceover.

"So how's New York?"

"It's great! Really exciting . . . I love my job . . . it's such a great place to live!"

"I've never been," says Tom wistfully. "I wanted to go there for our honeymoon."

"Tom, don't start that again," says Lucy sharply. "OK?"

"Maybe I could come and visit," says Tom. "I could come for the weekend."

"Er . . . yes! Maybe! You could both come . . ." I tail off lamely as Lucy rolls her eyes and stomps toward the house. "Anyway, lovely to see you and I'm glad married life is treating you . . . er . . . treating you, anyway."

I hurry back into the kitchen, dying to tell Mum what I just heard, but it's empty.

"Hey, Mum!" I call. "I just saw Tom and Lucy!"

I hurry up the stairs, and Mum is halfway down the loft ladder, pulling down a big white squashy bundle all wrapped up in plastic.

"What's that?" I ask, helping her to get it down.

"Don't say anything," she says, with suppressed excitement. "Just . . ." Her hands are trembling as she unzips the plastic cover. "Just . . . look!"

"It's your wedding dress!" I say in astonishment as she pulls out the white frothy lace. "I didn't know you still had that!"

"Of course I've still got it!" She brushes away some sheets of tissue paper. "Thirty years old, but still as good as new. Now, Becky, it's only a thought . . ."

"What's a thought?" I say, helping her to shake out the train.

"It might not even fit you . . ."

Slowly I look up at her. She's serious.

"Actually, I don't think it will," I say, trying to sound casual. "I'm sure you were much thinner than me! And . . . shorter."

"But we're the same height!" says Mum in puzzlement. "Oh, go on, try it, Becky!"

Five minutes later I stare at myself in the mirror in Mum's bedroom. I look like a sausage roll in layered frills. The bodice is tight and lacy, with ruffled sleeves and a ruffled neckline. It's tight down to my hips where there are more ruffles, and then it fans out into a tiered train.

I have never worn anything less flattering in my life.

"Oh, Becky!" I look up—and to my horror, Mum's in tears. "I'm so silly!" she says, laughing and brushing at her eyes. "It's just . . . my little girl, in the dress I wore . . ."

"Oh, Mum . . ." Impulsively I give her a hug. "It's a . . . a really lovely dress . . ."

How exactly do I add, But I'm not wearing it?

"And it fits you perfectly," gulps Mum, and rummages for a tissue. "But it's your decision." She blows her nose. "If you don't think it suits you . . . just say so. I won't mind."

"I . . . well . . ."

Oh God.

"I'll . . . think about it," I manage at last, and give Mum a lame smile.

We put the wedding dress back in its bag, and have some sandwiches for lunch, and watch an old episode of *Changing Rooms* on the new cable telly Mum and Dad have had installed. And then, although it's a bit early, I go upstairs and start getting ready to see Elinor. Luke's mother is one of those Manhattan women who always look completely and utterly immaculate, and today of all days I want to match her in the smartness stakes.

I put on the DKNY suit I bought myself for Christmas, brand-new tights, and my new Prada sample sale shoes. Then I survey my appearance carefully, looking all over for specks or creases. I'm not going to be caught out this time. I'm not going to have a single stray thread or crumpled bit which her beady X-ray eyes can zoom in on.

I've just about decided that I look OK, when Mum comes busting into my bedroom. She's dressed smartly in a purple Windsmoor suit and her face is glowing with anticipation.

"How do I look?" she says with a little laugh. "Smart enough for Claridges?"

"You look lovely, Mum! That color really suits you. Let me just . . ."

I reach for a tissue, dampen it under the tap, and wipe at her cheeks where she's copied Janice's badger-look approach to blusher.

"There. Perfect."

"Thank you, darling!" Mum peers at herself in the wardrobe mirror. "Well, this will be nice. Meeting Luke's mother at last."

"Mmm," I say noncommittally.

"I expect we'll get to be quite good friends! What with getting together over the wedding preparations . . . You know, Margot across the road is such good friends with her son-in-law's mother, they take holidays together. She says she hasn't lost a daughter, she's gained a friend!"

Mum sounds really excited. How can I prepare her for the truth?

"And Elinor certainly sounds lovely! The way Luke describes her. He seems so fond of her!"

"Yes, he is," I admit grudgingly. "Incredibly fond."

"He was telling us this morning about all the wonderful charity work she does. She must have a heart of gold!"

As Mum prattles on, I tune out and remember a conversation I had with Luke's stepmum, Annabel, when she and his dad came out to visit us.

I completely adore Annabel. She's very different from Elinor, much softer and quieter, but with a lovely smile that lights up her whole face. She and Luke's father live in a sleepy area of Devon near the beach, and I really wish we could spend more time with them. But Luke left home at eighteen, and he hardly ever goes back. In fact, I get the feeling he thinks his father slightly wasted his life by settling down as a provincial lawyer, instead of conquering the world.

When they came to New York, Annabel and I ended up having an afternoon alone together. We walked around Central Park talking about loads of different things, and it seemed as though no subject was off-limits. So at last I took a deep breath and asked her what I've always wanted to know—which is how she can stand Luke being so dazzled by Elinor. I mean, Elinor may be his biological mother, but Annabel has been there for him all his life. She was the one who looked after him when he was ill and helped him with his homework and cooked his supper every night. And now she's been pushed aside.

For an instant I could see the pain in Annabel's face. But then she kind of smiled and said she completely understood it. That Luke had been desperate to know his real mother since he was a tiny child, and now that he was getting the chance to spend time with her, he should be allowed to enjoy it.

"Imagine your fairy godmother came along," she said. "Wouldn't you be dazzled? Wouldn't you forget about everyone else for a while? He needs this time with her."

"She's not his fairy godmother!" I retorted. "She's the wicked old witch!"

"Becky, she's his natural mother," Annabel said, with a gentle reproof. Then she changed the subject. She wouldn't bitch about Elinor, or anything.

Annabel is a saint.

"It's such a shame they didn't get to see each other while Luke was growing up!" Mum is saying. "What a tragic story." She lowers her voice, even though Luke's left the house. "Luke was telling me only this morning how his mother was desperate to take him with her to America. But her new American husband wouldn't allow it! Poor woman. She must have been in misery. Leaving her child behind!"

"Well, yes, maybe," I say, feeling a slight rebellion. "Except . . . she didn't *have* to leave, did she? If she was in so much misery, why didn't she tell the new husband where to go?"

Mum looks at me in surprise. "That's very harsh, Becky."

"Oh . . . I suppose so." I give a little shrug and reach for my lip liner.

I don't want to stir things up before we even begin. So I won't say what I really think, which is that Elinor never showed any interest in Luke until his PR company started doing so well in New York. Luke has always been desperate to impress her—in fact, that's the real reason he expanded to New York in the first place, though he won't admit it. But she completely ignored him, like the cow she is, until he started winning a few really big contracts and being mentioned in the papers and she suddenly realized he could be useful to her. Just before Christmas, she started her own charity—the Elinor Sherman Foundation—and made Luke a director. Then she had a great big gala concert to launch it—and guess who spent about twenty-five hours a day helping her out with it until he was so exhausted, Christmas was a complete washout?

But I can't say anything to him about it. When I once brought up the subject, Luke got all defensive and said I'd always had a problem with his mother (which is kind of true) and she was sacrificing loads of her time to help the needy and what more did I want, blood?

To which I couldn't really find a reply.

"She's probably a very lonely woman," Mum is musing. "Poor thing, all on her own. Living in her little flat. Does she have a cat to keep her company?"

"Mum . . ." I put a hand to my head. "Elinor doesn't live in a 'little flat.' It's a duplex on Park Avenue."

"A duplex? What—like a maisonette?" Mum pulls a sympathetic little face. "Oh, but it's not the same as a nice house, is it?"

Oh, I give up. There's no point.

As we walk into the foyer at Claridges, it's full of smart people having tea. Waiters in gray jackets are striding around with green and white striped teapots, and everyone's chattering brightly and I can't see Luke or Elinor anywhere. As I peer around, I'm seized by sudden hope. Maybe they're not here. Maybe Elinor couldn't make it! We can just go and have a nice cup of tea on our own! Thank God for—

"Becky?"

I swivel round—and my heart sinks. There they are, on a sofa in the corner. Luke's wearing that radiant expression he gets whenever he sees his mother, and Elinor's sitting on the edge of her seat in a houndstooth suit trimmed with fur. Her hair is a stiff lacquered helmet and her legs, encased in pale stockings, seem to have got even thinner. She looks up, apparently expressionless—but I can see from the flicker of her eyelids that she's giving both Mum and Dad the Manhattan Onceover.

"Is that her?" whispers Mum in astonishment, as we give our coats in. "Goodness! She's very . . . young!"

"No, she's not," I mutter. "She's had a lot of help."

Mum gazes at me incomprehendingly for a moment before the penny drops. "You mean . . . she's had a *face-lift*?"

"Not just one. So keep off the subject, OK?"

We both stand waiting as Dad hands in his coat, and I can see Mum's mind working, digesting this new piece of information, trying to fit it in somewhere.

"Poor woman," she says suddenly. "It must be terrible, to feel so insecure. That's living in America for you, I'm sure."

As we approach the sofa, Elinor looks up and her mouth extends by three millimeters, which is her equivalent to a smile.

"Good afternoon, Rebecca. And felicitations on your engagement. Most unexpected."

What's that supposed to mean?

"Thanks very much!" I say, forcing a smile. "Elinor, I'd like to introduce my parents, Jane and Graham Bloomwood."

"How do you do?" says Dad with a friendly smile, and holds out his hand. He looks so distinguished in his dark gray suit, I feel a twinge of pride. He's actually very handsome, my dad, even though his hair is going a bit gray.

"Graham, don't stand on ceremony!" exclaims Mum. "We're going to be family now!" Before I can stop her she's enveloping a startled Elinor in a hug. "We're so pleased to meet you, Elinor! Luke's told us all about you!" As she stands up again I see she's rumpled Elinor's collar, and can't help giving a tiny giggle.

"Isn't this nice?" Mum continues as she sits down. "Very grand!" She looks around, her eyes bright. "Now, what are we going to have? A nice cup of tea, or something stronger to celebrate?"

"Tea, I think," says Elinor. "Luke . . ."

"I'll go and sort it out," says Luke, leaping to his feet.

I hate the way he behaves around his mother. Normally he's so strong and assured. But with Elinor it's as though she's the president of some huge multinational and he's some junior minion. He hasn't even said hello to me yet.

"Now, Elinor," says Mum. "I've brought you a little something. I saw them yesterday and I couldn't resist!"

She pulls out a package wrapped in gold paper and hands it to Elinor. A little stiffly, Elinor takes off the paper—and pulls out a blue padded notebook, with the words "His Mum" emblazoned on the front in swirly silver writing. She stares at it as though Mum's presented her with a dead rat.

"I've got a matching one!" says Mum triumphantly. She reaches in her bag and brings out an equivalent "Her Mum" notebook, in pink. "They're called the Mums' Planning Kit! There's a space for us to write in our menus, guest lists . . . color schemes . . . and here's a plastic pocket for swatches, look . . . This way we can keep coordinated! And this is the ideas page . . . I've already jotted down a few thoughts, so if you want to contribute anything . . . or if there's any particular food you like . . . The point is, we want you to be involved as much as possible." She pats Elinor's hand. "In fact, if you'd like to come and stay for a while, so we could really get to know each other . . ."

"My schedule is rather full, I'm afraid," says Elinor with a wintry smile as Luke reappears, holding his mobile.

"The tea's on its way. And . . . I've just had rather a nice phone call." He looks around with a suppressed smile. "We've just landed NorthWest Bank as a client. We're going to manage the launch of an entire new retail division. It's going to be huge."

"Luke!" I exclaim. "That's wonderful!"

Luke's been wooing NorthWest for absolutely ages, and last week he admitted he'd thought he'd lost them to another agency. So this is really fantastic.

"Well done, Luke," says Dad.

"That's brilliant, love!" chimes in Mum.

The only one who hasn't said anything is Elinor. She's not even paying attention, but looking in her Hermès bag.

"What do you think, Elinor?" I say deliberately. "It's good news, isn't it?"

"I hope this won't interfere with your work for the foundation," she says, and snaps her bag shut.

"It shouldn't," says Luke easily.

"Of course, Luke's work for your foundation is voluntary," I point out sweetly. "Whereas this is his business."

"Indeed." Elinor gives me a stony look. "Well, Luke, if you don't have time—"

"Of course I've got time," says Luke, shooting me a glance of annoyance. "It won't be a problem."

Great. Now they're both pissed off with me.

Mum has been watching this exchange in slight bewilderment, and as the tea arrives her face clears in relief.

"Just what the doctor ordered!" she exclaims as a waiter places a teapot and silver cake stand on our table. "Elinor, shall I pour for you?"

"Have a scone," says Dad heartily to Elinor. "And some clotted cream?"

"I don't think so." Elinor shrinks slightly as though cream particles might be floating through the air and invading her body. She takes a sip of tea, then looks at her watch. "I must go, I'm afraid."

"What?" Mum looks up in surprise. "Already?"

"Luke, could you fetch the car?"

"Absolutely," says Luke, draining his cup.

"What?" Now it's my turn to stare. "Luke, what's going on?"

"I'm going to drive my mother to the airport," says Luke.

"Why? Why can't she take a taxi?"

As the words come out of my mouth I realize I sound a bit rude—but honestly. This was supposed to be a nice family meeting. We've only been here about three seconds.

"There are some things I need to discuss with Luke," says Elinor, picking up her handbag. "We can do so in the car." She stands up and brushes an imaginary crumb off her lap. "So nice to meet you," she says to Mum.

"You too!" exclaims Mum, leaping up in a last-ditch attempt at friendliness. "Lovely to meet you, Elinor! I'll get your number from Becky and we can have some nice chats about what we're going to wear! We don't want to clash with each other, do we?"

"Indeed," says Elinor, glancing at Mum's shoes. "Good-bye, Rebecca." Elinor nods at Dad. "Graham."

"Good-bye, Elinor," says Dad in an outwardly polite voice—but as I glance at him I can tell he's not at all impressed. "See you later,

Luke." As they disappear through the doors, he looks at his watch. "Twelve minutes."

"What do you mean?" says Mum.

"That's how long she gave us."

"Graham! I'm sure she didn't mean . . ." Mum breaks off as she notices the blue "His Mum" book, still lying on the table amid the wrapping paper. "Elinor's left her wedding planner behind!" she cries, grabbing it. "Becky, run after her."

"Mum . . ." I take a deep breath. "I wouldn't bother. I'm not sure she's that interested."

"I wouldn't count on her for any help," says Dad. He reaches for the clotted cream and piles a huge amount onto his scone.

"Oh." Mum looks from my face to Dad's—then slowly subsides into her seat, clutching the book. "Oh, I see."

She takes a sip of tea, and I can see her struggling hard to think of something nice to say.

"Well . . . she probably just doesn't want to interfere!" she says at last. "It's completely understandable."

But even she doesn't look that convinced. God, I hate Elinor.

"Mum, let's finish our tea," I say. "And then why don't we go to the sales?"

"Yes," says Mum after a pause. "Yes, let's do that! Now you mention it, I could do with some new gloves." She takes a sip of tea and looks more cheerful. "And perhaps a nice bag."

"We'll have a lovely time," I say, and squeeze her arm. "Just us."

FRANTON, BINTON AND OGLEBY
ATTORNEYS AT LAW
739 THIRD AVENUE
SUITE 503
NEW YORK, NY 10017

Miss Rebecca Bloomwood
251 W. 11th Street, Apt. B
New York, NY 10014

February 11, 2002

Dear Miss Bloomwood:

May we be the very first to congratulate you on your engagement to Mr. Luke Brandon, the report of which we saw in *The New York Observer*. This must be a very happy time for you, and we send you our wholehearted good wishes.

We are sure that at this time, you will be inundated with many unwanted, even tasteless offers. However, we offer a unique and personal service to which we would like to draw your attention.

As divorce lawyers with over 30 years' experience between us, we know the difference a good attorney can make. Let us all hope and pray that you and Mr. Brandon never reach that painful moment. But if you do, we are specialists in the following areas:

- **Contesting** prenuptial agreements
- **Negotiating** alimony
- **Obtaining** court injunctions
- **Uncovering** information (with the help of our in-house private detective)

We do not ask that you contact us now. Simply place this letter with your other wedding memorabilia—and should the need arise you will know where we are.

Many congratulations again!

Ernest P. Franton
Associate Partner

ANGELS OF ETERNAL PEACE CEMETERY

WESTCHESTER HILLS, WESTCHESTER COUNTY, NEW YORK

Miss Rebecca Bloomwood
251 W. 11th Street, Apt. B
New York, NY 10014

February 13, 2002

Dear Miss Bloomwood:

May we be the very first to congratulate you on your engagement to Mr. Luke Brandon, the report of which we saw in *The New York Observer*. This must be a very happy time for you, and we send you our wholehearted good wishes.

We are sure that at this time, you will be inundated with many unwanted, even tasteless offers. However, we offer a unique and personal service to which we would like to draw your attention.

A wedding gift with a difference.

What better way for your guests to show their appreciation of the love you have for each other, than by giving you adjoining cemetery plots? In the peace and tranquility of our meticulously tended gardens, you and your husband will rest together as you have lived together, for all eternity.*

A pair of plots in the prestigious Garden of Redemption is currently available at the special offer price of $6,500. Why not add it to your wedding list—and let your loved ones give you the gift that will truly last forever?**

Again, many congratulations, and may you have a long and blissful married life together.

Hank Hamburg
Director of Sales

* In case of divorce, plots can be moved to opposite sides of cemetery.

** Hamburg Family Mortuaries, Inc., reserves the right to reallocate grave space, giving 30 days' notice in the event of redevelopment of the land (see attached terms and conditions).

Four

WHO CARES ABOUT bloody Elinor, anyway?

We'll have a lovely wedding, with or without her help. As Mum said, it's her loss, and she'll regret it on the day, when she doesn't feel part of the celebrations. We cheered up quite a lot after we left Claridges, actually. We went to the Selfridges sale and Mum found a nice new bag and I got some volumizing mascara, while Dad went and had a pint of beer, like he always does. Then we all went out for supper, and by the time we got home we were all a lot more cheerful and finding the whole situation quite funny.

The next day, when Janice came round for coffee, we told her all about tea with Elinor and she was really indignant on our behalf, and said if Elinor thought she was getting her makeup done for free, she had another think coming! Then Dad joined in and did a good imitation of Elinor looking at the clotted cream as if it was about to mug her and we all started giggling hysterically—until Luke came downstairs and asked what was funny, and we had to pretend we were laughing at a joke on the radio.

I really don't know what to do about Luke and his mother. Part of me thinks I should be honest. I should tell him how upset she made us all, and how Mum was really hurt. But the trouble is, I've tried to be honest with him in the past about Elinor and it's always led to a huge row. And I *really* don't want to have any rows now, while we're just engaged, and all blissful and happy. So I didn't say anything.

The following day we left to come back to New York, and when we said good-bye, Mum gave Luke a huge affectionate hug, as though to make up for the way she feels about Elinor. After all, he can't help his mother, can he? Then she hugged me, and wrote down my fax number for the zillionth time and promised she'd be in touch as soon as she'd talked to some caterers.

Apart from the small issue of Elinor, everything is going perfectly. Just to prove it, on the plane back to New York, I did this quiz in *Wedding and Home* on "Are You Ready for Marriage?" And we got the top marks! It said, "Congratulations! You are a committed and loving couple, able to work through your problems. The lines of communication are open between you and you see eye to eye on most issues."

OK, maybe I did cheat a tiny bit. Like for the question "Which part of your wedding are you most looking forward to?" I was going to put (a) "Choosing my shoes" until I saw that (c) "Making a lifelong commitment" got ten points whereas (a) only got two.

But then, I'm sure everyone else has a little peek at the answers too. They probably factor it in somehow.

At least I didn't put (d) "Dessert" (no points).

"Becky?"

"Yes?"

We arrived back at the apartment an hour ago and Luke is going through the post. "You haven't seen that joint account statement, have you? I'll have to give them a ring."

"Oh, it came. Sorry, I forgot to tell you."

I hurry into the bedroom and take the statement from its hiding place, feeling a slight beat of apprehension.

Come to think of it, there was a question about financial matters in that quiz. I think I ticked (b) "We have similar patterns of expenditure and money is never an issue between us."

"Here you are," I say lightly, handing him the sheet of paper.

"I just don't see why we keep going overdrawn on this account," Luke's saying. "Our household expenses can't increase every month . . ." He peers at the page, which is covered in thick white blobs. "Becky . . . why has this statement got Wite-Out all over it?"

"I know!" I say apologetically. "I'm sorry about that. The bottle was there, and I was moving some books, and it just . . . tipped over."

"But it's almost impossible to read!"

"Is it?" I say innocently. "That's a shame. Still, never mind. These things happen . . ." And I'm about to pluck it from his fingers when suddenly his eyes narrow.

"Does that say . . ." He starts scraping at the statement with his fingernail, and suddenly a big blob of Wite-Out falls off.

Damn. I should have used tomato ketchup, like last month.

"Miù Miù. I *thought* so. Becky, what's Miù Miù doing in here?" He scrapes again, and Wite-Out starts to shower off the page like snow.

Oh God. Please don't see—

"Sephora . . . and Joseph . . . No wonder we're overdrawn!" He gives me an exasperated look. "Becky, this account is supposed to be for household expenses. Not skirts from Miù Miù!"

OK. Fight or flight.

I cross my arms defiantly and lift my chin. "So . . . a skirt isn't a household expense. Is that what you're saying?"

Luke stares at me. "Of course that's what I'm saying!"

"Well, you know, maybe that's the problem. Maybe the two of us just need to clarify our definitions a little."

"I see," says Luke after a pause, and I can see his mouth twitching slightly. "So you're telling me that you would classify a Miù Miù skirt as a household expense."

"I . . . might! It's 'in the household,' isn't it? And anyway," I continue quickly. "Anyway. At the end of the day, what does it matter? What does *any* of it matter? We have our health, we have each other, we have the . . . the beauty of life. Those are the things that matter. Not money. Not bank accounts. Not the mundane, soul-destroying details." I make a sweeping gesture with my hand, feeling as though I'm making an Oscar-winning speech. "We're on this planet for all too short a time, Luke. All too short a time. And when we come to the end, which will count for more? A number on a piece of paper—or the love between two people? Knowing that a few meaningless figures balanced—or knowing that you were the person you wanted to be?"

As I reach the end, I'm choked by my own brilliance. I look up in a daze, half expecting Luke to be near tears and whispering, "You had me at 'And.' "

"Very stirring," says Luke crisply. "Just for the record, in my book 'household expenses' means joint expenses pertaining to the running of this apartment and our lives. Food, fuel, cleaning products, and so on."

"Fine!" I shrug. "If that's the narrow . . . frankly *limited* definition you want to use—then fine."

The doorbell rings and I open it to see Danny standing in the hallway.

"Danny, is a Miù Miù skirt a household expense?" I say.

"Absolutely," says Danny, coming into the living area.

"You see?" I raise my eyebrows at Luke. "But fine, we'll go with your definition . . ."

"So did you hear?" says Danny morosely.

"Hear what?"

"Mrs. Watts is selling."

"What?" I stare at him. "Are you serious?"

"As soon as the lease is up, we're out."

"She can't do that!"

"She's the owner. She can do what she likes."

"But . . ." I stare at Danny in dismay, then turn to Luke, who is putting some papers into his briefcase. "Luke, did you hear that? Mrs. Watts is selling!"

"I know."

"You *knew*? Why didn't you tell me?"

"Sorry. I meant to." Luke looks unconcerned.

"What will we do?"

"Move."

"But I don't want to move. I like it here!"

I look around the room with a pang. This is the place where Luke and I have been happy for the last year. I don't want to be uprooted from it.

"So you want to hear where this leaves me?" says Danny. "Randall's getting an apartment with his girlfriend."

I look at him in alarm. "He's throwing you out?"

"Practically. He says I have to start contributing, otherwise I can start looking for a new place. Like, how am I supposed to do that?" Danny raises his hands. "Until I have my new collection ready, it just won't be possible. He might as well just . . . order me a cardboard box."

"So, er . . . how is the new collection coming on?" I ask cautiously.

"You know, being a designer isn't as easy as it looks," says Danny defensively. "You can't just be creative to order. It's all a matter of inspiration."

"Maybe you could get a job," says Luke, reaching for his coat.

"A job?"

"They must need designers at, I don't know, Gap?"

"Gap?" Danny stares at him. "You think I should spend my life designing *polo shirts*? So how about, ooh, two sleeves right here, three buttons on the placket, some ribbing . . . How can I contain my excitement?"

"What will we do?" I say plaintively to Luke.

"About Danny?"

"About our apartment!"

"We'll find somewhere," says Luke reassuringly. "Which reminds me. My mother wants to have lunch with you today."

"She's back?" I say in dismay. "I mean . . . she's back!"

"They had to postpone her surgery." Luke pulls a little face. "The clinic was placed under investigation by the Swiss medical authorities while she was there and all the procedures were put on hold. So . . . one o'clock, La Goulue?"

"Fine." I shrug unenthusiastically.

Then, as the door closes behind Luke, I feel a bit bad. Maybe Elinor's had a change of heart. Maybe she wants to bury the hatchet and get involved with the wedding. You never know.

I'd planned to be really cool and only tell people I was engaged if they asked me "How was your trip?"

But when the time comes I find myself running into the personal shopping department at Barneys where I work, thrusting out my hand, and yelling "Look!"

Erin, who works there with me, looks up startled, peers at my hand, then claps her hands over her mouth. "Oh my God! Oh my God!"

"I know!"

"You're engaged? To Luke?"

"Yes, of course to Luke! We're getting married in June!"

"What are you going to wear?" she gabbles. "I'm so jealous! Let me see the ring! Where did you get it? When I get engaged I'm going straight to Harry Winstons. And forget a month's salary, we're talking at least three years' . . ." She tails off as she examines my ring. "Wow."

"It's Luke's family's," I say. "His grandmother's."

"Oh right. So . . . it isn't new?" Her face falls slightly. "Oh well . . ."

"It's . . . vintage," I say carefully—and her entire expression lifts again.

"Vintage! A vintage ring! That's such a cool idea!"

"Congratulations, Becky," says Christina, my boss, and gives me a warm smile. "I know you and Luke will be very happy together."

"Can I try it on?" says Erin. "No! I'm sorry. Forget I mentioned it. I just . . . A vintage ring!"

She's still gazing at it as my first client, Laurel Johnson, comes into the department. Laurel is president of a company that leases private jets and is one of my favorite clients, even though she tells me all the time how she thinks everything in the store is overpriced and she'd buy all her clothes from Kmart if it weren't for her job.

"What's this I see?" she says, taking off her coat and shaking out her dark curly hair.

"I'm engaged!" I say, beaming.

"Engaged!" She comes over and scrutinizes the ring with dark, intelligent eyes. "Well, I hope you'll be very happy. I'm sure you will be. I'm sure your husband will have sense enough to keep his dick out of the little blonde who came to work as his intern and told him she'd never met a man who filled her with awe before. *Awe.* I ask you. Did you ever hear such a—" She stops midtrack, claps her hand to her mouth, and gives me a rueful look. "Damn."

"Never mind," I say comfortingly. "You were provoked."

Laurel has made a New Year's resolution not to talk about her ex-husband or his mistress anymore, because her therapist, Hans, has told her it isn't healthy for her. Unfortunately she's finding this resolution quite hard to keep. Not that I blame her. He sounds like a complete pig.

"You know what Hans told me last week?" she says as I open the door of my fitting room. "He told me to write down a list of everything I wanted to say about that woman—and then tear it up. He said I'd feel a sense of freedom."

"Oh right," I say interestedly. "So what happened?"

"I wrote it all down," says Laurel. "And then I mailed it to her."

"Laurel!"

"I know. I know. Not helpful."

"Well, come on in," I say, trying not to laugh, "and tell me what you've been up to. I'm a little behind this morning . . ."

One of the best things about working as a personal shopper is you get really close to your clients. In fact, some of them feel like friends. When I first met Laurel, she'd just split up with her husband. She was really low, and had zero self-confidence. Now, I'm not trying to boast, but when I found her the perfect Armani dress to wear to this huge ballet gala that he was going to be at—when I watched her staring at herself in the mirror, raising her chin and smiling and feeling like an attractive woman again—I honestly felt I'd made a difference to her life.

This morning Laurel is looking for a couple of suits for work. I know her so well now it's easy to pick out what will sit well on her tall frame. We have a nice easy chat, and talk about the new Brad Pitt movie, and Laurel tells me all about her new, very sexy golf coach.

"My entire game has fallen to pieces," she says, pulling a face. "I'm no longer aiming to hit the ball in the hole. I'm just aiming to look thin and attractive and the ball can go where the hell it likes."

As she gets changed back into her own daywear I come out of the fitting room, holding a pile of clothes.

"I can't possibly wear that," comes a muffled voice from Erin's room.

"If you just try it—" I can hear Erin saying.

"You know I never wear that color!" The voice rises, and I freeze.

That's a British accent.

"I'm not wasting my time anymore! If you bring me things I can't wear—"

Tiny spiders are crawling up and down my back. I don't believe it. It can't be—

"But you asked for a new look!" says Erin helplessly.

"Call me when you've got what I asked for."

And before I can move, here she is, walking out of Erin's fitting room, as tall and blonde and immaculate as ever, her lips already curving into a supercilious smile. Her hair is sleek and her blue eyes are sparkling and she looks on top of the world.

Alicia Billington.

Alicia Bitch Longlegs.

I meet her eyes—and it's like an electric shock all over my body. Inside my tailored gray trousers, I can feel my legs starting to tremble. I haven't laid eyes on Alicia Billington for well over a year. I should be able to deal with this. But it's as though that time has concertinaed into nothing. The memories of all our encounters are as strong and sore as ever. What she did to me. What she tried to do to Luke.

She's looking at me with the same patronizing air she used to use when she was a PR girl and I was a brand-new financial reporter. And although I tell myself firmly that I've grown up a lot since then, that I'm a strong woman with a successful career and nothing to prove . . . I can still feel myself shrinking inside. Turning back into the girl who always felt a bit of a flake, who never knew quite what to say.

"Rebecca!" she says, looking a me as though highly amused. "Well, I never!"

"Hi, Alicia," I say, and somehow force myself to smile courteously. "How are you?"

"I had heard you were working in a shop, but I thought that must be a joke." She gives a little laugh. "Yet . . . here you are. Makes sense, really."

I don't just "work in a shop"! I want to yell furiously. I'm a personal shopper! It's a skilled profession! I help people!

"And you're still with Luke, are you?" She gives me mock concerned look. "Is his company finally back on track? I know he went through a rough time."

I cannot believe this girl. It was she who tried to sabotage Luke's company. It was she who set up a rival PR company that went bust. It was she who lost all her boyfriend's money—and apparently had to be bailed out by her dad.

And now she's behaving as though she won.

I swallow several times, trying to find the right response. I know I'm worth more than Alicia. I should be able to come up with the perfect, polite, yet witty retort. But somehow it doesn't come.

"I'm living in New York myself," she says airily. "So I expect we'll see each other again. Maybe you'll sell me a pair of shoes." She gives me a final patronizing smile, hoists her Chanel bag on her shoulder, and walks out of the department.

When she's left, there's silence all around.

"Who was *that*?" says Laurel at last, who has come out of the fitting room only half dressed, without me noticing.

"That was . . . Alicia Bitch Longlegs," I say, half dazed.

"Alicia Bitch Fatass more like," says Laurel. "I always say, there's no bitch like an English bitch." She gives me a hug. "Don't worry about it. Whoever she is, she's just jealous."

"Thanks," I say, and rub my head, trying to clear my thoughts. But I'm still a bit shell-shocked, to be honest. I never thought I'd have to set eyes on Alicia again.

"Becky, I'm so sorry!" says Erin, as Laurel goes back into the fitting room. "I had no idea you and Alicia knew each other!"

"I had no idea she was a client of yours!"

"She doesn't show up very often." Erin pulls a face. "I never met anyone so fussy. So what's the story between you two?"

Oh, nothing! I want to say. She just trashed me to the tabloids and nearly ruined Luke's career, and has been a complete bitch to me from the very first moment I met her. Nothing to speak of.

"We just have a bit of a history," I say at last.

"You know she's engaged too? To Peter Blake. Very old money."

"I don't understand." My brow wrinkles. "I thought she got married last year. To a British guy. Ed . . . somebody?"

"She did! Except she didn't. Oh my God, didn't you hear the story?" A pair of customers are wandering past the personal shopping area, and Erin lowers her voice. "They had the wedding and they were at the reception—when in walks Peter Blake as someone's date. Alicia hadn't known he was coming, but apparently the minute she found out who he was, she totally zeroed in on him. So they started chatting and were really getting on—like, *really* getting on . . . but what can Alicia do, she's married!" Erin's face is shiny with glee. “So she went up to the priest and said she wanted an annulment.”

“She did *what*?”

“She asked for an annulment! At her own wedding reception! She said they hadn’t consummated it so it didn’t count.” Erin gives a little gurgle of laughter. “Can you believe it?”

I can’t help giving a halfhearted laugh in response. “I can believe anything of Alicia.”

“She said she always gets what she wants. Apparently the wedding is going to be to *die* for. But she’s a complete bridezilla. Like, she’s practically forced one of the ushers to have a nose job, and she’s sacked every florist in New York . . . the wedding planner’s going nuts! Who’s your wedding planner?”

“My mum,” I reply, and Erin’s eyes widen.

“Your mom’s a wedding planner? I never knew that!”

“No, you moron!” I giggle, starting to cheer up. “My mum’s organizing the wedding. She’s got it all under control already.”

“Oh right.” Erin nods. “Well—that probably makes things easier. So you can keep your distance.”

“Yes. It should be really simple. Cross fingers!” I add, and we both laugh.

Five

I ARRIVE AT LA Goulue at one o'clock on the dot, but Elinor isn't there yet. I'm shown to a table and sip my mineral water while I wait for her. The place is busy, as it always is at this time, mostly with smartly dressed women. All around me is chatter and the gleam of expensive teeth and jewels, and I take the opportunity to eavesdrop shamelessly. At the table next to mine, a woman wearing heavy eyeliner and an enormous brooch is saying emphatically, "You simply cannot furnish an apartment these days under one hundred thousand dollars."

"So I said to Edgar, 'I am a human being,' " says a red-haired girl on my other side.

Her friend chews on a celery stick and looks at her with bright, avid eyes. "So what did he say?"

"One room, you're talking thirty thousand."

"He said, 'Hilary—' "

"Rebecca?"

I look up, a bit annoyed to miss what Edgar said, to see Elinor approaching the table, wearing a cream jacket with large black buttons and carrying a matching clutch bag. To my surprise she's not alone. A woman with a shiny chestnut bob, wearing a navy blue suit and holding a large Coach bag, is with her.

"Rebecca, may I present Robyn de Bendern," says Elinor. "One of New York's finest wedding planners."

"Oh," I say, taken aback. "Well . . . Hello!"

"Rebecca," says Robyn, taking both my hands and gazing intently into my eyes. "We meet at last. I'm so delighted to meet you. *So* delighted!"

"Me too!" I say, trying to match her vivacity while simultaneously racking my brain. Did Elinor mention meeting a wedding planner? Am I supposed to know about this?

"Such a pretty face!" says Robyn, without letting go of my hands. She's taking in every inch of me, and I find myself reciprocating. She looks in her forties, immaculately made up with bright hazel eyes, sharp cheekbones, and a wide smile exposing a row of immaculate teeth. Her air of enthusiasm is infectious, but her eyes are appraising as she takes a step back and sweeps over the rest of me.

"Such a young, fresh look. My dear, you'll make a stunning bride. Do you know yet what you'll be wearing on the day?"

"Er . . . a wedding dress?" I say stupidly, and Robyn bursts into peals of laughter.

"That humor!" she cries. "You British girls! You were quite right," she adds to Elinor, who gives a gracious nod.

Elinor was right? What about?

Have they been talking about me?

"Thanks!" I say, trying to take an unobtrusive step backward. "Shall we . . ." I nod toward the table.

"Let's," says Robyn, as though I've made the most genius suggestion she's ever heard. "Let's do that." As she sits down I notice she's wearing a brooch of two intertwined wedding rings, encrusted with diamonds.

"You like this?" says Robyn. "The Gilbrooks gave it to me after I planned their daughter's wedding. Now *that* was a drama! Poor Bitty Gilbrook's nail broke at the last minute and we had to fly her manicurist in by helicopter . . ." She pauses as though lost in memories, then snaps to. "So, Rebecca." She beams at me and I can't help beaming back. "Lucky, lucky girl. Tell me, are you enjoying every moment?"

"Well—"

"What I always say is, the first week after you're engaged is the most precious time of all. You have to *savor* it."

"Actually, it's been a couple of weeks now—"

"Savor it," says Robyn, lifting a finger. "Wallow in it. What I always say is, no one else can have those memories for you."

"Well, OK!" I say with a grin. "I'll . . . wallow in it!"

"Before we start," says Elinor, "I must give you one of these." She reaches into her bag and puts an invitation down on the table. What's this?

Mrs. Elinor Sherman requests the pleasure of your company . . .

Wow. Elinor's holding an engagement party! For us!

"Gosh!" I look up. "Well . . . thanks. I didn't know we were having an engagement party!"

"I discussed the matter with Luke."

"Really? He never mentioned it to me."

"It must have slipped his mind." Elinor gives me a cold, gracious smile. "I will have a stack of these delivered to your apartment and you can invite some friends of your own. Say . . . ten."

"Well . . . er . . . thanks."

"Now, shall we have some champagne, to celebrate?"

"What a lovely idea!" says Robyn. "What I always say is, if you can't celebrate a wedding, what can you celebrate?" She gives me a twinkling smile and I smile back. I'm warming to this woman. But I still don't know what she's doing here.

"Erm . . . I was just wondering, Robyn," I say hesitantly. "Are you here in a . . . professional capacity?"

"Oh no. No, no, nooooo." Robyn shakes her head. "It's not a profession. It's a *calling*. The hours I put in . . . the sheer love I put into my job . . ."

"Right." I glance uncertainly at Elinor. "Well, the thing is—I'm not sure I'm going to need any help. Although it's very kind of you—"

"No help?" Robyn throws back her head and peals with laughter. "You're not going to need any help? Please! Do you know how much organization a wedding takes?"

"Well—"

"Have you ever done it before?"

"No, but—"

"A lot of girls think your way," says Robyn, nodding. "Do you know who those girls are?"

"Um—"

"They're the girls who end up *weeping* into their wedding cake, because they're too stressed out to enjoy the fun! Do you want to be those girls?"

"No!" I say in alarm.

"Right! Of course you don't!" She sits back, looking like a teacher whose class has finally cracked two plus two. "Rebecca, I will take that strain off you. I will take on the headaches, the hard work, the sheer *stress* of the situation . . . Ah, here's the champagne!"

Maybe she has got a point, I think as a waiter pours champagne into three flutes. Maybe it would be a good idea to get a little extra help. Although how exactly she'll coordinate with Mum . . .

"I will become your best friend, Becky," Robyn's saying, beaming at me. "By the time of your wedding, I'll know you *better* than your best friend does. People call my methods unorthodox; they say I get too close. But when they see the results . . ."

"Robyn is unparalleled in this city," says Elinor, taking a sip of champagne, and Robyn gives a modest smile.

"So let's start with the basics," she says, and takes out a large, leather-bound notebook. "The wedding's on June 22nd . . ."

"Yes."

"Rebecca and Luke . . ."

"Yes."

"At the Plaza Hotel . . ."

"What?" I stare at her. "No, that's not—"

"I'm taking it that both the ceremony and reception will take place there?" She looks up at Elinor.

"I think so," says Elinor, nodding. "Much easier that way."

"Excuse me—"

"So—the ceremony in the Terrace Room?" She scribbles for a moment. "And then the reception in the Ballroom. Lovely. And how many?"

"Wait a minute!" I say, planting a hand on her notebook. "What are you talking about?"

"Your wedding," says Elinor. "To my son."

"At the Plaza Hotel," says Robyn with a beam. "I don't need to tell you how lucky you are, getting the date you wanted! Luckily it was a client of mine who made the cancellation, so I was able to snap it right up for you then and there . . ."

"I'm not getting married at the Plaza Hotel!"

Robyn looks sharply at Elinor, concern creasing her brow. "I thought you'd spoken to John Ferguson?"

"I have," replies Elinor crisply. "I spoke with him yesterday."

"Good! Because as you know, we're on a very tight schedule. A Plaza wedding in less than five months? There are some wedding planners who would simply say, impossible! I am not that wedding planner. I did a wedding once in three days. Three days! Of course, that was on a beach, so it was a little different—"

"What do you mean, the Plaza's booked?" I turn in my chair. "Elinor, we're getting married in Oxshott. You know we are."

"Oxshott?" Robyn wrinkles her brow. "I don't know it. Is it upstate?"

"Some provisional arrangements have been made," says Elinor dismissively. "They can easily be cancelled."

"They're not provisional!" I stare at Elinor in fury. "And they can't be cancelled!"

"You know, I sense some tension here," says Robyn brightly. "So I'll just go make a few calls . . ." She picks up her mobile and moves off to the side of the restaurant, and Elinor and I are left glaring at each other.

I take a deep breath, trying to stay calm. "Elinor, I'm not getting married in New York. I'm getting married at home. Mum's already started organizing it. You know she has!"

"You are not getting married in some unknown backyard in England," says Elinor crisply. "Do you know who Luke is? Do you know who *I* am?"

"What's that got to do with anything?"

"For someone with a modicum of intelligence, you're very naive." Elinor takes a sip of champagne. "This is the most important social event in all our lives. It must be done properly. Lavishly. The Plaza is unsurpassed for weddings. You must be aware of that."

"But Mum's already started planning!"

"Then she can stop planning. Rebecca, your mother will be grateful to have the wedding taken off her hands. It goes without saying, I will fund the entire event. She can attend as a guest."

"She won't want to attend as some guest! It's her daughter's wedding! She wants to be the hostess! She wants to organize it!"

"So!" A cheerful voice interrupts us. "Are we resolved?" Robyn appears back at the table, putting her mobile away.

"I've booked an appointment for us to see the Terrace Room after lunch," says Elinor frostily. "I would be glad if you would at least be courteous enough to come and view it with us."

I stare at her mutinously, tempted to throw down my napkin and say no way. I can't believe Luke knows anything about this. In fact, I feel like ringing him up right now and telling him exactly what I think.

But then I remember he's at a board lunch . . . and I also remember him asking me to give his mother a chance. Well, fine. I'll give her a chance. I'll go along and see the room, and walk around and nod politely and say nothing. And then tonight I'll tell her equally politely that I'm still getting married in Oxshott.

"All right," I say at last.

"Good." Elinor's mouth moves a few millimeters. "Shall we order?"

Throughout lunch, Elinor and Robyn talk about all the New York weddings they've ever been to, and I eat my food silently, resisting their attempts to draw me into the conversation. Outwardly I'm calm, but inside I can't stop seething. How dare Elinor try and take over? How dare she just hire a wedding planner without even consulting me? How dare she call Mum's garden an "unknown backyard"?

She's just an interfering cow, and if she thinks I'm going to get married in some huge anonymous New York hotel instead of at home with all my friends and family, she can just think again.

We finish lunch and decline coffee, and head outside. It's a brisk, breezy day with clouds scudding along the blue sky.

As we walk toward the Plaza, Robyn smiles at me. "I can understand if you're a little tense. It can be very stressful, planning a New York wedding. Some of my clients get very . . . wound up, shall we say."

I'm not planning a New York wedding! I want to yell. I'm planning an Oxshott wedding! But instead I just smile and say, "I suppose."

"I have one client in particular who's really quite demanding . . ." Robyn exhales sharply. "But as I say, it is a stressful business . . . Ah. Here we are! Isn't it an impressive sight?"

As I look up at the opulent facade of the Plaza I grudgingly have to admit it looks pretty good. It stretches up above Plaza Square like a wedding cake, with flags flying above a grand porticoed entrance.

"Have you been to a wedding here before?" asks Robyn.

"No. I've never been inside at all."

"Ah! Well . . . In we go . . ." says Robyn, ushering Elinor and me up the steps, past uniformed porters, through a revolving door, and into an enormous reception hall with a high, ornate ceiling, a marble floor, and huge gilded pillars. Directly in front of us is a light, bright area filled with palms and trellises where people are drinking coffee and a harp is playing and waiters in gray uniforms are hurrying around with silver coffeepots.

I suppose, if I'm honest, this is quite impressive too.

"Along here," says Robyn, taking my arm and leading us to a cordoned-off staircase. She unclasps a heavy rope cordon and we head up a grand staircase, and through another vast marble hall. Everywhere I look are ornate carvings, antiques, wall hangings, the hugest chandeliers I've ever seen . . .

"This is Mr. Ferguson, the executive director of catering."

Out of nowhere, a dapper man in a jacket has appeared. He shakes my hand and beams at me.

"Welcome to the Plaza, Rebecca! And may I say, you've made a very wise choice. There's nothing in the world like a Plaza wedding."

"Right!" I say politely. "Well, it seems a very nice hotel . . ."

"Whatever your fantasy, whatever your cherished dream, we'll do everything we can to create it for you. Isn't that right, Robyn?"

"That's right!" says Robyn fondly. "You simply couldn't be in better hands."

"Shall we go and look at the Terrace Room first?" Mr. Ferguson's eyes twinkle. "This is the room where the ceremony will take place. I think you'll like it."

We sweep back through the vast marble hall and he opens a pair of double doors, and we walk into an enormous room, surrounded by a white balustraded terrace. At one end is a marble fountain, at the other steps up to a raised area. Everywhere I look, people are scurrying around, arranging flowers and draping chiffon and placing gilt chairs in angled rows on the richly patterned carpet.

Wow.

This is actually . . . quite nice.

Oh, sod it. It's amazing.

"You're in luck!" says Mr. Ferguson with a beam. "We have a wedding on Saturday, so you can see the room 'in action,' as it were."

"Nice flowers," says Robyn politely, then leans toward me and whispers, "We'll have something far more special than these."

More special than these? They're the hugest, most spectacular flower arrangements I've ever seen in my life! Cascading roses, and tulips, and lilies . . . and are those orchids?

"So, you'll come in through these double doors," says Robyn, leading me along the terrace, "and then the bugles will play . . . or trumpets . . . whatever you wish . . . You'll pause in front of the grotto, arrange your train, have some photographs. And then the string orchestra will begin . . ."

"String orchestra?" I echo dazedly.

"I've spoken to the New York Phil," she adds to Elinor. "They're checking their tour schedule, so, fingers crossed . . ."

The *New York Phil*?

"The bride on Saturday is having seven harpists," says Mr. Ferguson. "And a soprano soloist from the Met."

Robyn and Elinor look at each other.

"Now *that's* an idea," says Robyn, and reaches for her notebook. "I'll get onto it."

"Shall we go and look at the Baroque Room now?" suggests Mr. Ferguson, and leads us to a large, old-fashioned elevator.

"The night before the wedding, you'll probably want to take a suite upstairs and enjoy the spa facilities," he says pleasantly as we travel upward. "Then on the day, you can bring in your own professional hair and makeup people." He smiles. "But I expect you've already thought of that."

"I . . . er . . ." My mind flicks madly back to Janice and Radiant Spring Bride. "Kind of . . ."

"The guests will be served cocktails as they pass along the corridor," explains Robyn as we leave the elevator. "Then this is the Baroque Room, where hors d'oeuvres will be served before we go into the Grand Ballroom. I expect you haven't even given hors d'oeuvres a thought yet!"

"Well . . . um . . . you know . . ." I'm about to say that everyone likes minisausages.

"But for example," she continues, "you could consider a caviar bar, an oyster bar, a Mediterranean meze table, sushi, perhaps . . ."

"Right," I gulp. "That . . . sounds good."

"And of course, the space itself can be themed however you like." She gestures around the room. "We can transform it into a Venetian carnival, a Japanese garden, a medieval banqueting hall . . . wherever your imagination takes you!"

"And then into the Grand Ballroom for the main reception!" says Mr. Ferguson cheerfully. He throws open a pair of double doors and . . . oh my God. This room is the most spectacular of all. It's all white and gold, with a high ceiling and theatrical boxes, and tables set around the vast, polished dance floor.

"That's where you and Luke will lead the dancing," says Robyn with a happy sigh. "I always say, that's the moment of a wedding I love the most. The first dance."

I gaze at the shining floor, and have a sudden vision of Luke and me whirling round among the candlelight and everyone looking on.

And seven harps.

And the New York Phil.

And caviar . . . and oysters . . . and cocktails . . .

"Rebecca, are you all right?" says Mr. Ferguson, suddenly seeing my expression.

"I think she's a little overwhelmed," says Robyn with a little laugh. "It's a lot to take in, isn't it?"

"Well . . . yes. I suppose so."

I take a deep breath and turn away for a moment. OK, let's not get carried away. This may all be very glitzy, but I am *not* going to be swayed by any of it. I've decided I'm going to get married in England—and that's what I'm going to do. End of story.

Except . . . just look at it all.

"Come and sit down," says Robyn, patting a gilt chair beside her. "Now, I know from your point of view it still seems far off. But we're on a pretty tight schedule . . . so I just wanted to talk to you about your overall view of the wedding. What's your fantasy? What, for you, is the image of pure romance? A lot of my clients say Scarlett and Rhett, or Fred and Ginger . . ." She looks at me with sparkling eyes, her pen poised expectantly over the page.

This has gone far enough. I have to tell this woman that none of this is actually going to happen. Come on, Becky. Get back to reality.

"I . . ."

"Yes?"

"I've always loved the end of *Sleeping Beauty,* when they dance together," I hear myself saying.

"The ballet," says Elinor approvingly.

"No, actually, I meant . . . the Disney film."

"Oh!" Robyn looks momentarily puzzled. "I'll have to catch that again! Well . . . I'm sure that will be inspirational too . . ."

She starts writing in her book and I bite my inner lip.

I have to call a halt to all this. Come on. Say something!

For some reason my mouth stays closed. I look around, taking in the molded ceiling; the gilding; the twinkling chandeliers.

Robyn follows my gaze and smiles at me. "Becky, you know, you're a very lucky girl." She squeezes my arm affectionately. "We're going to have so much fun!"

HOUSE OF LORDS

APPPOINTMENTS COMMISSION

NOMINATION FORM

Please summarize here why you are suitable for recommendation as a nonparty political peer and how you, personally, would make an effective contribution to the work of the House of Lords. Please support this with a CV clearly showing your major achievements and highlighting relevant skills and experience.

APPLICATION TO BE A LIFE PEER

Name: Rebecca Bloomwood

Address: Apt. B
251 W. 11th Street
New York, NY 10014

Preferred title: Baroness Rebecca Bloomwood of Harvey Nichols

Major achievements:

Patriotism
I have served Great Britain for many years, bolstering the economy through the medium of retail.

Trade Relations
Since living in New York I have promoted international trade between Britain and America, e.g., I always buy imported Twinings tea and Marmite.

Public Speaking
I have appeared on television chairing debates on current affairs (in the world of fashion).

Cultural Expertise
I am a collector of antiques and fine art, most notably 1930s cocktail cabinets and barware.

Personal contribution if appointed:
As a new member of the House of Lords, I would personally be very willing to take on the role of fashion consultant, an area hitherto neglected—yet vital to the very lifeblood of democracy.

SECOND UNION BANK
53 WALL STREET
NEW YORK, NY 10005

February 21, 2002

Miss Rebecca Bloomwood
Apt. B
251 W. 11th Street
New York, NY 10014

Dear Miss Bloomwood:

Thank you for your letter of February 20.

I am afraid I could not comment on whether or not a Miù Miù skirt is a household expense.

Yours sincerely,

Walt Pitman
Director of Customer Relations

Six

I'M NOT GOING to get married in New York. Of course I'm not. It's unthinkable. I'm going to get married at home, just like I planned, with a nice marquee in the garden. There's absolutely no reason to change my plans. None at all.

Except . . . it would be amazing. Walking down that aisle in front of four hundred people, to the sound of a string orchestra, with amazing flower arrangements everywhere. Having the huge, dreamy, Lady Di wedding I always fantasized about but thought was beyond my grasp. I mean, it'd be *Becky's Big Day* come to life.

Then we'd all sit down to some incredible dinner . . . Robyn gave me some sample dinner menus, and the food! Rosace of Maine Lobster . . . Fowl Consommé with Quenelles of Pheasant . . . Wild Rice with Pignoli Nuts . . .

I know Oxshott and Ashtead Quality Caterers are good—but I'm not sure they even know what a pignoli nut is. (To be honest, I don't either. But that's not the point.)

And maybe Elinor's right, Mum would be *grateful* if we took the whole thing off her hands. Yes. Maybe she's finding the organization more of a strain than she's letting on. Maybe she's already wishing she hadn't volunteered to do the whole thing. Whereas if we get married at the Plaza, she won't have to do anything, just turn up. Plus Mum and Dad wouldn't have to pay for a thing . . . I mean, it would be doing them a favor!

So as I'm walking back to Barneys, I take out my mobile and dial the number for home. As Mum answers I can hear the closing music of *Crimewatch* in the background, and I suddenly feel a wave of nostalgia for home. I can just imagine Mum and Dad sitting there, with the curtains drawn and the gas-effect fire flickering cozily.

"Hi, Mum?"

"Becky!" exclaims Mum. "I'm so glad you've phoned! I've been trying to fax you through some menus from the catering company, but your machine won't work. Dad says, have you checked your paper recently?"

"Um . . . I don't know. Listen, Mum—"

"And listen to this! Janice's sister-in-law knows someone who works at a balloon printing company! She says if we order two hundred or more balloons we can have the helium for free!"

"Great! Look, I was just thinking about the wedding, actually . . ."

Why do I suddenly feel nervous?

"Oh yes? Graham, turn the television down."

"It was just occurring to me . . . just as a possibility"—I give a shrill laugh—"that Luke and I could get married in America!"

"America?" There's a long pause. "What do you mean, America?"

"It was just a thought! You know, since Luke and I live here already . . ."

"You've lived there for one year, Becky!" Mum sounds quite shocked. "This is your home!"

"Well, yes . . . but I was just thinking . . ." I say feebly.

Somehow I was hoping that Mum would say "What a fantastic idea!" and make it really easy.

"How would we organize a wedding in America?"

"I don't know!" I swallow. "Maybe we could have it at a . . . a big hotel."

"A *hotel*?" Mum sounds as though I've gone mad.

"And maybe Elinor would help . . ." I plow on. "I'm sure she'd contribute . . . you know, if it was more expensive . . ."

There's a sharp intake of breath at the other end of the phone and I wince. Damn. I should never have mentioned Elinor.

"Yes, well. We don't want her contributions, thank you. We can manage very well by ourselves. Is this Elinor's idea, then, a hotel? Does she think we can't put on a nice wedding?"

"No!" I say hastily. "It's just . . . it's nothing! I was just . . ."

"Dad says, if she's so keen on hotels, she can stay at one instead of with us."

Oh God. I'm just making everything worse.

"Look . . . forget it. It was a silly idea." I rub my face. "So—how are the plans going?"

We chat for a few more minutes, and I hear all about the nice man from the marquee company and how his quote was very reasonable, and how his son was at school with cousin Alex, isn't it a small world? By the end of our conversation Mum sounds completely mollified and all talk of American hotels has been forgotten.

I say good-bye, turn off the phone, and exhale sharply. Right. Well, that's decided. I might as well call Elinor and tell her. No point in hanging around.

I turn on my mobile again, dial two digits, and then stop.

On the other hand—is there any point in rushing straight into a decision?

I mean, you never know. Maybe Mum and Dad will talk it over this evening and change their minds. Maybe they'll come out to have a look. Maybe if they actually *saw* the Plaza . . . if they saw how magical it was all going to be . . . how luxurious . . . how glamorous . . . I can't quite bear to give it up. Not quite yet.

When I get home, Luke is sitting at the table, frowning over some papers.

"You came home early!" I say, pleased.

"I had some papers to go over," says Luke. "Thought I'd get some peace and quiet here."

"Oh, right."

As I get near I see that they're all headed "The Elinor Sherman Foundation." I open my mouth to say something—then close it again.

"So," he says, looking up with a little smile, "what did you think of the Plaza?"

"You *knew* about it?" I stare at him.

"Yes. Of course I did. I would have come along too if I hadn't had a lunch appointment."

"But, Luke . . ." I take a deep breath, trying not to overreact. "You know my mother's planning a wedding in England."

"It's early days, surely?"

"You shouldn't have just fixed up a meeting like that!"

"My mother thought it would be a good way to surprise you. So did I."

"Spring it on me, you mean!" I retort crossly, and Luke looks at me, puzzled.

"Didn't you like the Plaza? I thought you'd be overwhelmed!"

"Of course I *liked* it. That's not the point."

"I know how much you've always wanted a big, magnificent wedding. When my mother offered to host a wedding at the Plaza, it seemed like a gift. In fact, it was my idea to surprise you. I thought you'd be thrilled."

He looks a bit deflated and immediately guilt pours over me. It hadn't occurred to me that Luke might have been in on the whole thing.

"Luke, I am thrilled! It's just . . . I don't think Mum would be very happy, us getting married in America."

"Can't you talk her round?"

"It's not that easy. Your mother's been pretty high-handed, you know—"

"High-handed? She's only trying to give us a wonderful wedding."

"If she really wanted to, she could give us a wonderful wedding in England," I point out. "Or she could help Mum and Dad—and they could *all* give us a wonderful wedding! But instead, she talks about their garden as an 'unknown backyard'!" Resentment flares up inside me again as I remember Elinor's dismissive voice.

"I'm sure she didn't mean—"

"Just because it isn't in the middle of New York! I mean, she doesn't know anything about it!"

"OK, fine," says Luke shortly. "You've made your point. You don't want the wedding. But if you ask me, my mother's being incredibly generous. Offering to pay for a wedding at the Plaza, plus she's arranged us a pretty lavish engagement party . . ."

"Who said I want a lavish engagement party?" I retort before I can stop myself.

"That's a bit churlish, isn't it?"

"Maybe I don't care about all the glitz and the glamour and the . . . the material things! Maybe my family is more important to me! And tradition . . . and . . . and honor. You know, Luke, we're only on this planet for a short time . . ."

"Enough!" says Luke in exasperation. "You win! If it's really going to be a problem, forget it! You don't have to come to the engagement party if you don't want to—and we'll get married in Oxshott. Happy now?"

"I . . ." I break off, and rub my nose. Of course, it is a fairly amazing offer. And if I *could* somehow persuade Mum and Dad, maybe we'd all have the most fantastic time of our lives.

"It's not necessarily a question of getting married in Oxshott," I say at last. "It's a question of . . . of . . . coming to the right decision. Look, you were the one saying we didn't have to rush into anything . . ."

Luke's expression softens, and he gets up.

"I know." He sighs. "Look, Becky, I'm sorry."

"I'm sorry too," I mumble.

"Oh, this is ridiculous." He puts his arms around me and kisses my forehead. "All I wanted to do was give you the wedding you've always dreamed of. If you really don't want to get married at the Plaza, then of course we won't."

"What about your mother?"

"We'll just explain to her how you feel." Luke gazes at me for a few moments. "Becky, it doesn't matter to me where we get married. It doesn't matter to me whether we have pink flowers or blue flowers. What matters to me is we're going to become a couple—and the whole world is going to know it."

He sounds so sure and steady, I feel a sudden lump in my throat.

"That's what matters to me too," I say, and swallow hard. "That's the most important thing."

"OK. So let's agree. You can make the decision. Just tell me where to turn up—and I'll turn up."

"OK." I smile back at him. "I promise to give you at least forty-eight hours' notice."

"Twenty-four will do." He kisses me again, then points to the sideboard. "That arrived, by the way. An engagement present."

I look over and gape. It's a robin's-egg-blue box, tied up with white ribbon. A present from Tiffany!

"Shall I open it?"

"Go ahead."

Excitedly I untie the ribbon and open the box to find a blue glass bowl nestling in tissue paper, and a card reading "With best wishes from Marty and Alison Gerber."

"Wow! This is nice! Who are the Gerbers?"

"I don't know. Friends of my mother's."

"So . . . will everyone who comes to the party bring us a present?"

"I expect so."

"Oh . . . right."

Gosh. When Tom and Lucy had their engagement party, only about three people brought presents. And they certainly weren't from Tiffany. I stare at the bowl thoughtfully, running my finger over its gleaming surface.

You know, maybe Luke does have a point. Maybe it would be churlish to throw Elinor's generosity back in her face.

OK, what I'll do is, I'll wait until the engagement party's over. And *then* I'll decide.

The engagement party is at six o'clock the following Friday. I mean to get there early, but we have a frantic day at work, with three big emergencies—one of which involves our most demanding celebrity client, who clearly has *not* got over her recent breakup, whatever she may say in *People* magazine. Anyway, so I don't arrive until ten past six, feeling a little flustered. On the plus side, I'm wearing a completely fabulous black strapless dress, which fits me perfectly. (Actually, it was earmarked for Regan Hartman, one of my clients. But I'll just tell her I don't think it would suit her after all.)

Elinor's duplex is in a grand building on Park Avenue, with the most enormous marble-floored foyer and walnut-lined elevators that always smell of expensive scent. As I step out at the sixth floor I can hear the hubbub and tinkle of piano music. There's a queue of people waiting at the door, and I wait politely behind an elderly couple in matching fur coats. I can just see through to the apartment, which is dimly lit and already seems to be full of people.

To be honest, I've never really liked Elinor's apartment. It's all done in pale blue, with silk sofas and heavy curtains and the dullest pictures in the world hanging on the walls. I can't believe she really likes any of them. In fact, I can't believe she ever *looks* at any of them.

"Good evening." A voice interrupts my thoughts and I realize I've reached the head of the queue. A woman in a black trouser suit, holding a clipboard, is giving me a professional smile.

"May I have your name?"

"Rebecca Bloomwood," I say modestly, expecting her to gasp, or at least light up with recognition.

"Bloomwood . . . Bloomwood . . ." The woman looks down the list, turns a page, and runs her finger to the bottom before looking up. "I don't see it."

"Really?" I stare at her. "It must be there somewhere!"

"I'll look again . . ." The woman goes up to the top and runs her eyes down more slowly. "No," she says at last. "I'm afraid not. Sorry." She turns to a blond woman who has just arrived. "Good evening! May I take your name?"

"But . . . but . . . the party's for me!"

"Vanessa Dillon."

"Ah yes," says the door woman, and crosses off her name with a smile. "Please go in. Serge will take your coat. Could you please step aside, miss?" she adds coldly to me. "You're blocking the doorway."

"You have to let me in! I must be on the list!" I peer inside the door, hoping to see Luke, or even Elinor—but it's just a load of people I don't recognize. "Please! Honestly, I'm supposed to be here!"

The woman in black sighs. "Do you have your invitation with you?"

"No! I don't have one. I'm the . . . the engagee!"

"The what?" She stares at me blankly.

"The party's for *me*! And Luke . . . oh God . . ." I peer again into the party and suddenly spot Robyn, dressed in a silver beaded top and floaty skirt.

"Robyn!" I call, as discreetly as I can. "Robyn! They won't let me in!"

"Becky!" Robyn's face lights up. "At last!" She beckons gaily with her champagne glass with one hand, while with the other she moves a pair of men in dinner jackets out of my path. "Come on, belle of the ball!"

"You see?" I say desperately. "I'm not gate-crashing! The party's being given *for me*!"

The blond woman stares at me for a long time—then shrugs. "OK. You can go in. Serge will take your coat. Do you have a gift?"

A gift? Has she listened to anything I've been saying?

"No, I don't."

The woman rolls her eyes as though to say, "That figures"—then turns to the next person in the queue, and I hurry in before she changes her mind.

"I can't stay long," says Robyn as I join her. "I have three rehearsal dinners to go to. But I particularly wanted to see you tonight, because I have exciting news. A *very* talented event designer is going to be working on your wedding! Sheldon Lloyd, no less!"

"Wow!" I say, trying to match her tone even though I have no idea who Sheldon Lloyd is. "Gosh."

"You're bowled over, aren't you? What I always say is, if you want to make things happen, make them happen now! So I've been speaking with Sheldon and we've been tossing around some ideas. He thought your Sleeping Beauty concept was *fabulous,* by the way. Really original." She looks around and lowers her voice. "His idea is . . . we turn the Terrace Room into an enchanted forest."

"Really?"

"Yes! I'm so thrilled, I just have to show you!"

She opens her bag and pulls out a sketch, and I stare at it in disbelief.

"We'll have birch trees imported from Switzerland, and garlands of fairy lights. You'll walk down an avenue of trees, with their branches hanging over you. Pine needles will give off a wonderful scent as you walk, flowers will magically blossom as you pass, and trained songbirds will sing overhead. . . . What do you think about an animatronic squirrel?"

"Erm . . ." I pull a little face.

"No, I wasn't sure about that, either. OK . . . we'll forget the woodland creatures." She takes out a pen and scores out an entry. "But otherwise . . . it's going to be fabulous. Don't you think?"

"I . . . Well . . ."

Should I tell her I'm still not quite decided about whether to get married in New York?

Oh, but I can't. She'll stop all the preparations on the spot. She'll go and tell Elinor, and there'll be a terrible fuss.

And the thing is, I'm sure we will end up going for the Plaza in the end. Once I've worked out exactly how to win Mum round. I mean, we'd be mad not to.

"You know, Sheldon has worked for many Hollywood stars," says Robyn, lowering her voice still further. "When we meet him you can look at his portfolio. I'm telling you, it's quite something."

"Really?" I feel a sparkle of excitement. "It all sounds . . . fantastic!"

"Good!" She looks at her watch. "Now, I have to run. But I'll be in touch." She squeezes my hand, downs her champagne, and hurries toward the door—and I stare after her, still a little dazzled.

Hollywood stars! I mean, if Mum knew about that, wouldn't she see the whole thing differently? Wouldn't she realize what an amazing opportunity this is?

The trouble is, I can't quite pluck up courage to bring up the subject again. I didn't even dare tell her about this party. She'd only get all upset and say, "Doesn't Elinor think we can throw a nice engagement party?" or something. And then I'd feel even more guilty than I already do. Oh God. I just need a way to introduce the idea into her head once more, without her immediately getting upset. Maybe if I spoke to Janice . . . if I told her about the Hollywood stars . . .

A burst of laughter nearby brings me out of my thoughts, and I realize I'm standing all alone. I take a sip of champagne and look for someone to join. The slightly weird thing is, this is supposed to be an engagement party for me and Luke. But there must be at least a hundred people here, and I don't know any of them. At least, I dimly recognize the odd face here and there—but not really well enough to bound up and say hello. I try smiling at a woman coming in, but she eyes me suspiciously and pushes her way toward a group standing by the window. You know, whoever said Americans were friendlier than the British can't ever have been to New York.

Danny should be here somewhere, I think, peering through the throng. I invited Erin and Christina too—but they were both still hard at it when I left Barneys. I expect they'll be along later.

Oh come on, I've got to talk to someone. I should at least let Elinor know I'm here. I'm just elbowing my way past a group of women in matching black Armani when I hear someone saying "Do you know the bride?"

I freeze behind a pillar, trying to pretend I'm not eavesdropping.

"No. Does anybody?"

"Where do they live?"

"The West Village somewhere. But apparently they're moving to this building."

I stare at the pillar in bemusement. What's that?

"Oh really? I thought it was impossible to get in here."

"Not if you're related to Elinor Sherman!" The women laugh gaily and move off into the melee, and I stare blankly at a molded curlicue.

They must have got that wrong. There's no way we're moving here. No way.

I wander aimlessly around for another few minutes, find myself a glass of champagne, and try to keep a cheerful smile on my face. But try as I might, it keeps slipping. This isn't exactly how I pictured my engagement party would be. First of all the door-people try to stop me going in. Then I don't know anybody. Then the only things to eat are low-fat, high-protein cubes of fish—and even then, the wait staff look taken aback when you actually eat them.

I can't help thinking back slightly wistfully to Tom and Lucy's engagement party. It wasn't nearly as grand as this, of course. Janice made a big bowl of punch and there was a barbecue, and Martin sang "Are You Lonesome Tonight?" on the karaoke machine. But still. At least it was fun. At last I knew people. I knew more people at that party than I do at this one—

"Becky! Why are you hiding?" I look up and feel a swoosh of relief. There's Luke.

"Luke! At last!" I say, moving forward—then gasp in joy as I see a familiar, balding, middle-aged man standing beside him, grinning cheerfully at me. "Michael!" I throw my arms around him and give him a big hug.

Michael Ellis has to be one of my favorite people in the world. He's based in Washington, where he heads up an incredibly successful advertising agency. He's also Luke's partner in the American arm of Brandon Communications, and has been like a mentor figure to him. And to me, for that matter. If it weren't for some advice Michael gave me a while ago, I'd never have moved to New York in the first place.

"Luke said you might be coming!" I say, beaming at him.

"You think I'd miss this?" Michael twinkles at me. "Congratulations!" He raises his glass toward me. "You know, Becky, I'll bet you're regretting not taking up my offer of a job now. You could have had real prospects in Washington. Whereas instead . . ." He shakes his head. "Look at the way things have turned out for you. Great job, got your man, a wedding at the Plaza . . ."

"Who told you about the Plaza?" I say in surprise.

"Oh, just about everybody I've spoken to. Sounds like it's going to be some event."

"Well . . ." I give a bashful shrug.

"Is your mom excited about it?"

"I . . . er . . . well . . ." I take a sip of champagne to avoid having to answer.

"She's not here tonight, I take it?"

"No. Well, it is quite a long way!" My laugh is a little shrill, and I take another sip, draining my glass.

"Let me get you another," says Luke, taking my glass. "And I'll find my mother. She was asking where you were . . . I've just asked Michael to be best man," he adds as he walks off. "Luckily he said yes."

"Really?" I say, and beam at Michael in delight. "Fantastic! I can't think of a better choice."

"I'm very honored to be asked," says Michael. "Unless you want me to marry you, of course. I'm a bit rusty, but I could probably remember the words . . ."

"Really?" I say in surprise. "Are you secretly a minister, as well as everything else?"

"No." He throws back his head and laughs. "But a few years back, some friends wanted me to marry them. I pulled some strings and got registered as an officiant."

"Well, I think you'd make a great minister! Father Michael. People would flock to your church."

"An atheist minister." Michael raises his eyebrows. "I guess I wouldn't be the first." He takes a sip of champagne. "So how's the shopping business?"

"It's great, thanks." I beam at him.

"You know, I recommend you to everyone I meet. 'You need clothes, go to Becky Bloomwood at Barneys.' I tell busboys, businessmen, random people I meet on the street . . ."

"I wondered why I kept getting all these strange people through." I smile at him.

"Seriously, I wanted to ask a small favor." Michael lowers his voice slightly. "I'd be grateful if you could help out my daughter, Lucy. She just broke up with a guy and I think she's going through a patch of lacking self-confidence. I told her I knew who could fix her up."

"Absolutely," I say, feeling touched. "I'd be glad to help."

"You won't bankrupt her, though. Because she's only on a lawyer's salary."

"I'll try not to," I say, laughing. "How about you?"

"You think I need help?"

"To be honest, you look pretty good already." I gesture to his immaculate dark gray suit, which I'm certain didn't give him much change out of $3,000.

"I always dress up when I know I'm going to be seeing the beautiful people," says Michael. He looks around the party with an amused expression, and I follow his gaze. A nearby group of six middle-aged women are talking at each other animatedly, seemingly without taking breath. "Are these your friends?"

"Not really," I admit. "I don't know many people here."

"I guessed as much." He gives me a quizzical smile and takes a sip of champagne. "So . . . how are you getting along with your future mother-in-law?" His expression is so innocent, I want to laugh.

"Oh, like a house on fire," I say, grinning. "Can't you tell?"

"What are you talking about?" says Luke, suddenly appearing at my shoulder. He hands me a full glass of champagne and I shoot a glance at Michael.

"We were just talking about wedding plans," says Michael easily. "Have you decided on a honeymoon location yet?"

"We haven't really talked about it." I look at Luke. "But I've had some ideas. We need to go somewhere really nice and hot. And glamorous. And somewhere I've never been before."

"You know, I'm not sure I'll be able to fit in much of a honeymoon," says Luke with a small frown. "We've just taken on NorthWest and that means we may be looking at expanding again. So we might have to make do with a long weekend."

"A long weekend?" I stare at him in dismay. "That's not a honeymoon!"

"Luke," says Michael reprovingly. "That won't do. You have to take your wife on a nice honeymoon. As best man, I insist. Where have you never been, Becky? Venice? Rome? India? Africa?"

"I haven't been to any of them!"

"I see." Michael raises his eyebrows. "This could turn out to be some honeymoon."

"Everyone has seen the world except me. I never even had a gap year. I never did Australia, or Thailand . . ."

"Neither did I," says Luke, shrugging.

"I haven't *done* anything! You know, Suze's mother's best friend in the whole world is a Bolivian peasant." I look at Luke impressively. "They ground maize together on the plains of the Llanos!"

"Looks like it's Bolivia," says Michael to Luke.

"You want to grind maize on our honeymoon?"

"I just think maybe we should broaden our horizons a bit. Like . . . go backpacking, maybe."

"Becky, are you aware of the concept of backpacking?" says Luke mildly. "All your possessions in one rucksack. Which you have to *carry*. Not FedEx."

"I could do that!" I say indignantly. "Easily! And we'd meet loads of really interesting people—"

"I know interesting people already."

"You know bankers and PR people! Do you know any Bolivian peasants? Do you know any homeless people?"

"I can't say I do," says Luke. "Do you?"

"Well . . . no," I admit after a pause. "But that's not the point. We should!"

"OK, Becky," says Luke lifting a hand. "I have a solution. You organize the honeymoon. Anywhere you want, as long as it doesn't take more than two weeks."

"Really?" I gape at him. "Are you serious?"

"I'm serious. You're right, we can't get married and not have a proper honeymoon." He smiles at me. "Surprise me."

"Well, OK. I will!"

I take a sip of champagne, feeling all bubbly with excitement. How cool is this? I get to choose the honeymoon! Maybe we should go to an amazing spa in Thailand, or something. Or some spectacular safari . . .

"Speaking of homeless," says Luke to Michael, "we'll be out on the streets in September."

"Really?" says Michael. "What happened?"

"The lease on our apartment is up—and the owner's selling. Everyone out."

"Oh!" I say, suddenly diverted from pleasant visions of me and Luke standing on top of one of the pyramids. "That reminds me. Luke, I heard this really odd conversation just now. Some people were saying that we were going to move to this building. Where did they get that from?"

"It's a possibility," says Luke.

"What?" I stare at him blankly. "What do you mean, it's a possibility? Have you gone mad?"

"Why not?"

I lower my voice a little. "Do you really think I want to live in this stuffy building full of horrible old women who look at you as though you smell?"

"Becky—" interrupts Michael, jerking his head meaningfully.

"It's true!" I turn to him. "Not one of the people who lives in this building is nice! I've met them, and they're all absolutely—"

Abruptly I halt, as I realize what Michael's trying to tell me.

"Except . . . for . . . Luke's mother," I add, trying to sound as natural as possible. "Of course."

"Good evening, Rebecca," comes a chilly voice behind me, and I stand up, cheeks flaming.

There she is, standing behind me, wearing a long white Grecian-style dress that falls in pleats to the ground. She's so thin and pale, she looks just like one of her own pillars.

"Hello, Elinor," I say politely. "You look lovely. I'm sorry I was a little late."

"Rebecca," she replies, and offers me a cheek. "I hope you've been circulating? Not just sitting here with Luke?"

"Er . . . kind of . . ."

"This is a good opportunity for you to meet some important people," she says. "The president of this building, for example."

"Right." I nod. "Well, er . . . maybe."

This is probably not the moment to tell her that there's no way in a million years I'm moving to this building.

"I'll introduce you to her later. But now I'm about to make the toast," she says. "If you would both come over to the podium."

"Excellent!" I say, trying to sound enthusiastic, and take a gulp of champagne.

"Mother, you've met Michael," says Luke.

"Indeed," says Elinor with a gracious smile. "How do you do?"

"Very well, thank you," says Michael pleasantly. "I intended to come to the launch of your foundation but unfortunately couldn't make it up from Washington. I hear it went very well, though?"

"It did. Thank you."

"And now another happy occasion." He gestures around the room. "I was just saying to Luke, how lucky he was to have landed such a beautiful, talented, accomplished girl as Becky."

"Indeed." Elinor's smile freezes slightly.

"But you must feel the same way."

There's silence.

"Of course," says Elinor at last. She extends her hand and, after a tiny hesitation, places it on my shoulder.

Oh God. Her fingers are all cold. It's like being touched by the ice queen. I glance at Luke, and he's glowing with pleasure.

"So! The toast!" I say brightly. "Lead the way!"

"See you later, Michael," says Luke.

"Have a good one," replies Michael, and gives me the tiniest of winks. "Luke," he adds more quietly as she moves away, "on the subject of your mother's charity, I'd like to have a word later."

"Right," says Luke after a pause. "Fine."

Is it my imagination or does he look slightly defensive?

"But do the toast first," says Michael pleasantly. "We're not here to talk business."

As I walk through the room with Luke and Elinor, I can see people starting to turn and murmur. A little podium has been set up at one end of the room, and as we step up onto it I start to feel a little nervous for the first time. Silence has fallen around the room and the entire assembled gathering is looking at us.

Two hundred eyes, all giving me the Manhattan Onceover.

Trying to stay unself-conscious, I search among the crowd for faces I recognize. But apart from Michael at the back, there isn't a single one.

I keep smiling, but inside I feel a bit low. Where are my friends? I know Christina and Erin are on their way—but where's Danny? He promised he was going to come.

"Ladies and gentlemen," says Elinor graciously, "welcome. It gives me enormous pleasure to welcome you here tonight on this happy occasion. Particularly Marcia Fox, president of this building, and Guinevere von . . ."

"I don't care about your stupid list!" comes a high-pitched voice from the door, and a couple of heads at the back turn to look.

". . . von Landlenburg, associate of the Elinor Sherman Foundation . . ." says Elinor, her jaw growing more rigid.

"Let me in, you stupid cow!"

There's a scuffling sound and a small scream, and the whole room turns to see what's going on.

"Get your hands off me. I'm pregnant, OK? If anything happens I'll sue!"

"I don't believe it!" I shriek in delight, and jump down off the podium. "Suze!"

"Bex!" Suze appears through the door, looking tanned and healthy, with beads in her hair and a sizable bump showing through her dress. "Surprise!"

Seven

"WE THOUGHT WE'D surprise you!" says Suze after the fuss has died down and Elinor has made her toast—in which she mentions me and Luke once, and the Elinor Sherman Foundation six times. "Like a last bit of our honeymoon! So we turned up at your flat . . ."

"And I was, as ever, running perfectly on time . . ." puts in Danny, giving me an apologetic grin.

"So Danny said why didn't we come along to the party and give you a bit of a shock?"

"It's so great to see you." I give her an affectionate hug. "And Tarquin." We all glance toward Tarquin, who has been surrounded by a group of avidly interested New York ladies.

"Do you live in a castle?" I can hear one of them saying.

"Well . . . um, yes. Actually, I do."

"Do you know Prince Charles?" says another, goggling.

"We've played polo once or twice . . ." Tarquin looks around, desperate to escape.

"You *have* to meet my daughter," says one of the ladies, putting a clamplike arm round his shoulders. "She loves England. She visited Hampton Court *six times*."

"He is spectacular," says a low voice in my ear, and I look round to see Danny gazing over my shoulder at Tarquin. "Utterly spectacular. Is he a model?"

"Is he a *what*?"

"I mean, this story about him being a farmer." Danny drags on his cigarette. "It's bullshit, right?"

"You think Tarquin should be a *model*?" I can't help a snort of laughter erupting through me.

"What?" says Danny defensively. "He has a fantastic look. I could design a whole collection around him. Prince Charles meets . . . Rupert Everett . . . meets—"

"Danny, you do know he's straight?"

"Of course I know he's straight! What do you take me for?" Danny gives a thoughtful pause. "But he went to English boarding school, right?"

"Danny!" I give him a shove and look up. "Hi, Tarquin! You managed to get away!"

"Hello!" says Tarquin, looking a bit harassed. "Suze, darling, have you given Becky the stuff from her mother?"

"Oh, it's back at the hotel," says Suze, and turns to me. "Bex, we dropped in on your mum and dad on the way to the airport. They are so obsessed!" She giggles. "They can't talk about anything but the wedding."

"I'm not surprised," says Danny. "It sounds like it's going to be fairly amazing. Catherine Zeta-Jones, eat your heart out."

"Catherine Zeta-Jones?" says Suze interestedly. "What do you mean?"

I feel my body stiffen all over. Shit. Think.

"Danny," I say casually. "I think the editor of *Women's Wear Daily* is over there."

"Really? Where?" Danny's head swivels round. "I'll be back in a second." He disappears off into the party and I subside in relief.

"When we were there, they were having this huge argument about how big the marquee should be," says Suze with another giggle. "They made us sit on the lawn, pretending to be guests."

I don't want to hear about this. I take a gulp of champagne and try to think of another topic.

"Have you told Becky the other thing that happened?" says Tarquin, looking suddenly grave.

"Er . . . no, not yet," says Suze guiltily, and Tarquin gives a deep, solemn sigh.

"Becky, Suze has something she needs to confess."

"That's right." Suze bites her lip and looks abashed. "We were at your parents' house, and I asked to look at your mum's wedding dress. So we were all admiring it, and I was holding a cup of coffee . . ." She hangs her head. "And then—I don't know how it happened, but . . . I spilled my coffee on the dress."

I stare at her incredulously. "On the dress? Are you serious?"

"We offered to clean it, of course," says Tarquin. "But I'm not sure it will be wearable. We're so incredibly sorry, Becky. And we'll pay for another dress, of course." He looks at his empty glass. "Can I get anyone another drink?"

"So the dress is . . . ruined?" I say, just to be sure.

"Yes, and it wasn't easy, I can tell you!" says Suze as soon as Tarquin is out of earshot. "The first time I tried, your mum whisked it away just in time. Then she started getting all worried and saying she'd better put it away. I had to practically *throw* my coffee cup at it, just as she was packing it up—and even then it only just caught the train. Of course, your mum hates me now," she adds gloomily. "I shouldn't think I'll get invited to the wedding."

"Oh, Suze. She doesn't really. And thank you *so* much. You're a complete star. I honestly didn't think you'd manage it."

"Well, I couldn't let you look like a lamb cutlet, could I?" Suze grins. "The weird thing is, in her wedding pictures, your mum looks really lovely in it. But in real life . . ." She pulls a little face.

"Exactly. Oh, Suze, I'm so glad you're here." Impulsively I give her a hug. "I thought you'd be all . . . married. What's being married like, anyway?"

"Kind of the same," says Suze after a pause. "Except we have more plates—"

I feel a tapping on my shoulder and look up to see a red-haired woman wearing a pale silk trouser suit.

"Laura Redburn Seymour," she says, extending her hand. "My husband and I have to go, but I just wanted to say I just heard about your wedding plans. I got married in exactly the same place, fifteen years ago. And let me tell you, when you walk down that aisle, there's no feeling like it." She clasps her hands and smiles at her husband, who looks exactly like Clark Kent.

"Gosh," I say. "Well . . . thank you!"

"Were you brought up in Oxshott, then?" asks Suze cheerfully. "That's a coincidence!"

Oh, fuck.

"I'm sorry?" says Laura Redburn Seymour.

"Oxshott!" says Suze. "You know!"

"Ox? What ox?" Laura Redburn Seymour looks confusedly at her husband.

"We don't believe in hunting," says Clark Kent a little coldly. "Good evening. And congratulations again," he adds to me.

As the two walk off, Suze stares at me in puzzlement. "Bex. Did that make any sense?"

"I . . . erm . . ." I rub my nose, playing for time.

I really don't know why, but I have a strong feeling that I don't want to tell Suze about the Plaza.

OK. I do know why. It's because I know exactly what she'll say.

"Yes!" I say at last. "I think it did, kind of."

"No, it didn't! She didn't get married in Oxshott. Why did she think you would be walking up the same aisle as her?"

"Well . . . you know . . . they're American. Nothing they say makes sense . . . So, er . . . wedding dress shopping! Shall we go tomorrow?"

"Ooh, definitely!" says Suze, her brow immediately unfurling. "Where shall we go? Does Barneys have a bridal department?"

Thank God Suze is so sweet and unsuspicious.

"Yes, it does," I say. "I've had a quick look, but I haven't tried anything on yet. The only thing is, I haven't got an appointment, and it's a Saturday tomorrow." I wrinkle my brow. "We could try Vera Wang but that'll probably be all booked up . . ."

"I want to go baby shopping as well. I've got a list."

"I've bought a couple of things," I say, looking fondly at her bump. "You know. Just little presents."

"I want a really nice mobile . . ."

"Don't worry, I've got you one of those. And some really cute little outfits!"

"Bex! You shouldn't have!"

"There was a sale on at Baby Gap!" I say defensively.

"Excuse me?" interrupts a voice, and we both look up to see a lady in black and pearls approaching. "I couldn't help overhearing your conversation just now. My name is Cynthia Harrison. I'm a great friend of Elinor's and also of Robyn, your wedding planner. You're in very good hands there!"

"Oh, right!" I say politely. "That's nice to hear!"

"If you're looking for a wedding dress, may I invite you both along to my new bridal boutique, Dream Dress?" Cynthia Harrison beams at me. "I've been selling wedding dresses for twenty years, and this very week I've opened a store on Madison Avenue. We have a huge selection of designer gowns, shoes, and accessories. Personal service in a luxurious environment. All your bridal needs catered to, however great or small."

She stops rather abruptly, as though she's been reading off a card.

"Well . . . OK! We'll come tomorrow!"

"Shall we say eleven o'clock?" suggests Cynthia, and I glance at Suze, who nods.

"Eleven it is. Thank you very much!"

As Cynthia Harrison departs, I grin at Suze excitedly. But she's peering over at the other side of the room.

"What's up with Luke?" she says.

"What do you mean?" I turn round and stare. Luke and Michael are in the corner of the room, away from everyone else, and it looks as though they're arguing.

As I watch, Luke raises his voice defensively, and I catch the words "the bigger picture, for God's sake!"

"What are they talking about?" says Suze.

"I've got no idea!"

I strain as hard as I can, but I can only hear the odd phrase.

". . . simply don't feel . . . appropriate . . ." Michael is saying.

". . . short term . . . feel it's entirely appropriate . . ."

Luke looks really rattled.

". . . wrong impression . . . abusing your position . . ."

". . . had enough of this!"

I watch in dismay as Luke stalks off, out of the room. Michael looks completely taken aback by his reaction. For a moment he's stock still—then he reaches for his glass and takes a slug of whiskey.

I can't believe it. I've never known Luke and Michael to have a cross word before. I mean, Luke adores Michael. He practically sees him as a father figure. What on earth can be going on?

"I'll be back in a minute," I murmur to Suze, and hurry, as discreetly as possible, over to where Michael is still standing, staring into space.

"What was all that about?" I demand as soon as I reach him. "Why were you and Luke fighting?"

Michael looks up, startled—then quickly composes his features into a smile.

"Just a little business disagreement," he says. "Nothing to worry about. So, have you decided on a honeymoon location yet?"

"Michael, come on. It's me! Tell me what's going on." I lower my voice. "What did you mean, Luke's abusing his position? What's happened?"

There's a long pause and I can see Michael weighing up whether or not to tell me.

"Did you know," he says at last, "that at least one member of staff from Brandon Communications has been redeployed to work for the Elinor Sherman Foundation?"

"What?" I stare at him in shock. "Are you serious?"

"I've recently discovered that a new assistant at the company has been assigned to work for Luke's mother. Brandon Communications is still paying her salary—but essentially she's Elinor's full-time lackey. Naturally she's unhappy about the situation." Michael sighs. "All I wanted to do was raise the point, but Luke's very defensive."

"He hasn't said anything about this to me!" I say incredulously.

"He hasn't said anything about it to anybody. I only found out because it so happens that this assistant knows my daughter, and felt she could call me up." Michael lowers his voice. "The real danger is that she might complain to the investors. Then Luke would be in trouble."

"It's his mother," I say at last. "You know what a hold she's got over him. He'll do anything to impress her."

"I know," says Michael. "And I can understand that. Everyone has their own hang-ups." He looks at his watch. "I have to go, I'm afraid."

"You can't leave! Not without talking to him again!"

"I'm not sure that would do any good right now." Michael looks at me kindly. "Becky, don't let this spoil your evening. And don't go and give Luke a hard time. It's obviously a very sensitive topic." He squeezes my arm. "I'm sure it'll all work out."

"I won't. I promise!" I force myself to smile brightly. "And thanks for coming, Michael. It meant a lot to us. Both of us."

I give him a warm hug and watch as he walks away. Then, when he's gone, I head out of the room. I have to talk to Luke, as quickly as possible.

Obviously, Michael's right. It's a very sensitive subject, so I won't go charging in. I'll just ask a few probing, tactful questions, and gently steer him in the right direction. Just like a future wife should.

Eventually I find him upstairs, sitting in a chair in his mother's bedroom, staring into space.

"Luke, I just spoke to Michael!" I exclaim. "He told me you were sending the Brandon Communications staff over to work for your mother's charity!"

Oops. That didn't quite come out right.

"One assistant," says Luke without turning his head. "OK?"

"Can't she hire her own assistant? Luke, what if your investors find out?"

"Becky, I'm not completely stupid. This whole charity thing will be good for the company too." At last he turns his head to look at me. "This business is all about image. When I'm photographed handing over some enormous check to a deserving charity, the positive effect will be enormous. These days, people want to be associated with companies that give something back. I've already planned a photo opportunity in the *New York Post* in a couple of weeks' time, plus a couple of carefully placed features. The effect on our profile will be huge!"

"So why didn't Michael see it like that?"

"He wasn't listening. All he could talk about was how I was 'setting the wrong precedent.' "

"Well, maybe he has a point! I mean, surely you hire staff in order to work for you, not to send off to other companies—"

"This is a one-off example," says Luke impatiently. "And in my opinion, the benefits to the company will far outweigh any costs."

"Michael's your partner! You should listen to him. You should trust him."

"And he should trust me!" retorts Luke angrily. "There won't be a problem with the investors. Believe me, when they see the publicity we're going to generate, they'll be more than happy. If Michael could just *understand* that, instead of quibbling over stupid details . . . Where is he, anyway?"

"Michael had to go," I say—and see Luke's face tighten in shock.

"He left? Oh, well. Great."

"It wasn't like that. He had to." I sit down on the bed and take hold of Luke's hand. "Luke, don't fight with Michael. He's been such a good friend. Come on, remember everything he's done for you? Remember the speech he made on your birthday?"

I'm trying to lighten the atmosphere, but Luke doesn't seem to notice. His face is taut and defensive and his shoulders are hunched up. He's not going to listen to a word I say. I give an inward sigh and take a sip of champagne. I'll just have to wait until a better time.

There's silence for a few minutes—and after a while we both relax. It's as though we've called a truce.

"I'd better go," I say at last. "Suze doesn't know anybody down there."

"How long is she in New York for?" asks Luke, looking up.

"Just a few days."

I look idly around the room. I've never been in Elinor's bedroom before. It's immaculate, like the rest of the place, with pale walls and lots of expensive-looking custom-made furniture.

"Hey, guess what," I say, suddenly remembering. "Suze and I are going to choose a wedding dress tomorrow!"

Luke looks at me in surprise. "I thought you were going to wear your mother's wedding dress."

"Yes. Well." I frown. "The thing is, there was this awful accident . . ."

And all I can say is thank God. Thank God for Suze and her well-aimed cup of coffee.

As we approach the window of Dream Dress on Madison Avenue the next morning, I suddenly realize what Mum was asking me to do. *How* could she want me to dress up in white frills, instead of one of these gorgeous, amazing, Oscar-winner creations? We open the door and silently look around the hushed showroom, with its champagne-colored carpet and painted trompe l'oeil clouds on the ceiling—and, hanging in gleaming, glittery, sheeny rows on two sides of the room, wedding dresses.

I can feel overexcitement rising through me like a fountain. Any minute I might giggle out loud.

"Rebecca!" Cynthia has spotted us and is coming forward with a beam. "I'm so glad you came. Welcome to Dream Dress, where our motto is—"

"Ooh, I bet I know!" interrupts Suze. "Is it 'Live out your dream at Dream Dress'?"

"No. It's not." Cynthia smiles.

"Is it 'Dreams come true at Dream Dress'?"

"No." Cynthia's smile tightens slightly. "It's 'We'll find your Dream Dress.'"

"Oh, lovely!" Suze nods politely.

Cynthia ushers us into the hushed room and seats us on a cream sofa. "I'll be with you in a moment," she says pleasantly. "Have a browse through some magazines meanwhile." Suze and I grin excitedly at each other—then she reaches for *Contemporary Bride,* and I pick up *Martha Stewart Weddings*.

I adore *Martha Stewart Weddings*.

Secretly, I want to *be Martha Stewart Weddings*. I just want to crawl inside the pages with all those beautiful people getting married in Nantucket and South Carolina and riding to the chapel on horses and making their own place-card holders out of frosted russet apples.

I stare at a picture of a wholesome-looking couple standing in a poppy field against a staggeringly beautiful backdrop of mountains. You know, maybe we should get married in a poppy field too, and I could have barley twined round my hair and Luke could make us a loving seat with his own bare hands because his family has worked in wood crafting for six generations. Then we'd ride back to the house in an old country wagon—

"What's 'French white-glove service'?" says Suze, peering puzzledly at an ad.

"I dunno." I look up dazedly. "Hey, Suze, look at this. Shall I make my own bouquet?"

"Do what?"

"Look!" I point to the page. "You can make your own flowers out of crepe paper for an imaginative and individual bouquet."

"You? Make paper flowers?"

"I could!" I say, slightly nettled by her tone. "I'm a very creative person, you know."

"And what if it rains?"

"It won't rain—" I stop myself abruptly.

I was about to say, "It won't rain in the Plaza."

"I just . . . know it won't rain," I say instead, and quickly turn a page. "Ooh, look at those shoes!"

"Ladies! Let's begin." We both look up to see Cynthia coming back, a clipboard in her hand. She sits down on a small gilt chair and we both look at her attentively.

"Nothing in your life," she says, "can prepare you for the experience of buying your wedding dress. You may think you know about buying clothes." Cynthia gives a little smile and shakes her head. "Buying a wedding dress is different. We at Dream Dresses like to say, you don't choose your dress . . ."

"Your dress chooses you?" suggests Suze.

"No," says Cynthia with a flash of annoyance. "You don't *choose* your dress," she repeats, turning to me, "you *meet* your dress. You've met your man . . . now it's time to meet your dress. And let me assure you, there is a dress waiting for you. It might be the first dress you try on." Cynthia gestures to a halter-top sheath hanging up nearby. "It might be the twentieth. But when you put on the right dress . . . it'll hit you here." She clasps her solar plexus. "It's like falling in love. You'll know."

"Really?" I look around, feeling tentacles of excitement. "How will I know?"

"Let's just say . . . you'll know." She gives me a wise smile. "Have you had any ideas at all yet?"

"Well, obviously I've had a few thoughts . . ."

"Good! It's always helpful if we can narrow the search down a little. So before we start, let me ask you a few basic questions." She unscrews her pen. "Were you after something simple?"

"Absolutely," I say, nodding my head. "Really simple and elegant. Or else quite elaborate," I add, my eye catching sight of an amazing dress with roses cascading down the back.

"Right. So . . . simple or elaborate . . ." She scribbles on her notebook. "Did you want beading or embroidery?"

"Maybe."

"OK . . . now. Sleeves or strapless?"

"Possibly strapless," I say thoughtfully. "Or else sleeves."

"Did you want a train?"

"Ooh, yes!"

"But you wouldn't mind if you didn't have a train, would you?" puts in Suze, who is leafing through *Wedding Hair.* "I mean, you could always have one of those really long veils for the procession."

"That's true. But I do like the idea of a train . . ." I stare at her, gripped by a sudden thought. "Hey, Suze, if I waited a couple of years to get married, your baby would be two—and it could hold my train up!"

"Oh!" Suze claps her hand over her mouth. "That would be so sweet! Except, what if it fell over? Or screamed?"

"I wouldn't mind! And we could get it a really gorgeous little outfit . . ."

"If we could just get back to the subject . . ." Cynthia smiles at us and surveys her clipboard. "So we're after something either simple or elaborate, with sleeves or strapless, possibly with beading and/or embroidery and either with a train or without."

"Exactly!" My eye follows hers around the shop. "But you know, I'm quite flexible."

"Right." Cynthia stares at her notes silently for a few moments. "Right," she says again. "Well, the only way you can know is by trying a few dresses on . . . so let's get started!"

Why have I never done this before? Trying on wedding dresses is simply the most fun I've had ever, in my whole life. Cynthia shows me into a large fitting room with gold and white cherub wallpaper and a big mirror and gives me a lacy basque and high satin shoes to put on—and then her assistant brings in dresses in lots of five. I try on silk chiffon sheaths with low backs, ballerina dresses with tight bodices and layers of tulle, dresses made from duchesse satin and lace, starkly plain dresses with dramatic trains, simple dresses, glittery dresses . . .

"When you see the right one, you'll know," Cynthia keeps saying as the assistant heaves the hangers up onto the hooks. "Just . . . keep trying."

"I will!" I say happily, as I step into a strapless dress with beaded lace and a swooshy skirt. I come outside and parade around in front of Suze.

"That's fantastic!" she says. "Even better than the one with the little straps."

"I know! But I still quite like that one with the lace sleeves off the shoulder . . ." I stare critically at myself. "How many have I tried on now?"

"That takes us up to . . . thirty-five," says Cynthia, looking at her list.

"And how many have I marked so far as possibles?"

"Thirty-two."

"Really?" I look up in surprise. "Which ones didn't I like?"

"The two pink dresses and the coatdress."

"Oh no, I still quite like the coatdress. Put it down as a possible." I parade a bit more, then look around the shop, trying to see if there's anything I haven't looked at yet. I stop in front of a rail of baby flower-girls' dresses and sigh, slightly more heavily than I meant to. "God, it's tricky, isn't it? I mean . . . one dress. *One.*"

"I don't think Becky's ever bought one thing before," says Suze to Cynthia. "It's a bit of a culture shock."

"I don't see why you can't wear more than one. I mean, it's supposed to be the happiest day of your life, isn't it? You should be allowed *five* dresses."

"That would be cool!" says Suze. "You could have a really sweet romantic one for walking in, then a more elegant one to walk out . . . then one for cocktails . . ."

"And a really sexy one for dancing . . . and another one for . . ."

"For Luke to rip off you," says Suze, her eyes gleaming.

"Ladies," says Cynthia, giving a little laugh. "Rebecca. I know it's hard . . . but you are going to have to choose sometime! For a June wedding, you're already leaving it very late."

"How can I be leaving it late?" I say in astonishment. "I've only just got engaged!"

Cynthia shakes her head. "In wedding dress terms, that's late.

What we recommend is that if brides think they may have a short engagement, they begin to look for a dress *before* they get engaged."

"Oh God." I give a gusty sigh. "I had no idea it was all going to be so difficult."

"Try on that one at the end," suggests Suze. "The one with the chiffon trumpet sleeves. You haven't tried that, have you?"

"Oh," I say, looking at it in surprise. "No, I haven't."

I carry the dress back to the fitting room, clamber out of the swooshy skirt, and step into it.

It skims sleekly over my hips, hugs my waist, and falls to the floor in a tiny, rippling train. The neckline flatters my face, and the color is just right against my skin. It feels good. It looks good.

"Hey," says Suze, sitting up as I come out. "Now, that's nice."

"It's nice, isn't it?" I say, stepping up onto the podium.

I stare at my reflection and a feel a little glow of pleasure. It's a simple dress—but I look fantastic in it. It makes me look really thin! It makes my skin look radiant and . . . God, maybe this is the one!

There's silence in the shop.

"Do you feel it here?" says Cynthia, clutching her stomach.

"I . . . don't know! I think so!" I give an excited little laugh. "I think I might!"

"I knew it. You see? When you find the right dress, it just hits you. You can't plan for it, you can't work it out on paper. You just know when it's right."

"I've found my wedding dress!" I beam at Suze. "I've found it!"

"At last!" There's a ring of relief to Cynthia's voice. "Let's all have a glass of champagne to celebrate!"

As she disappears I admire myself again. It just shows, you can't tell. Who would have thought I'd go for trumpet sleeves?

An assistant is carrying past another dress and I catch sight of an embroidered silk corset bodice, tied up with ribbons.

"Hey, that looks nice," I say. "What's that?"

"Never mind what that is!" says Cynthia, handing me a glass of champagne. "You've found your dress!" She lifts her glass, but I'm still looking at the ribboned bodice.

"Maybe I should just try that one on. Just quickly."

"You know what I was thinking?" says Suze, looking up from *Brides*. "Maybe you should have a dress that *isn't* a wedding dress. Like a color!"

"Wow!" I stare at Suze, my imagination gripped. "Like red or something."

"Or a trouser suit!" suggests Suze, showing me a magazine picture. "Don't those look cool?"

"But you've found your dress!" chips in Cynthia, her voice slightly shrill. "You don't need to look any further! This is The One!"

"Mmm . . ." I pull a tiny face. "You know . . . I'm not so sure it is."

For an awful moment I think Cynthia's going to throw the champagne at me.

"I thought this was the dress of your dreams!"

"It's the dress of *some* of my dreams," I explain. "I have a lot of dreams. Could we put it down as another possible?"

"Right," she says at last. "Another possible. I'll just write that down."

As she walks off, Suze leans back on the sofa and beams at me. "Oh, Bex, it's going to be so romantic! Tarkie and I went to look at the church you're getting married in. It's beautiful!"

"It is nice," I agree, quelling an automatic wave of guilt.

Although nothing's been decided yet. I haven't definitely chosen the Plaza. We still might get married in Oxshott.

Maybe.

"Your mum's planning to put this gorgeous arch of roses over the gate, and bunches of roses on all the pews . . . and then everyone will get a rose buttonhole. She thought maybe yellow, but it depends on the other colors . . ."

"Oh, right. Well, I'm not really sure yet . . ." I tail off as I see the shop door opening behind me.

Robyn is coming into the shop, dressed in a mauve suit and clutching her Mulberry bag. She catches my eye in the mirror and gives a little wave.

What's Robyn doing here?

"And then on the tables, maybe some sweet little posies . . ."

Robyn's heading toward us. I'm not sure I like this.

"Hey, Suze!" I turn with what I hope is a natural smile. "Why don't you go and look at those . . . um . . . ring cushions over there?"

"What?" Suze stares at me as though I've gone mad. "You're not having a ring cushion, are you? *Please* don't tell me you've turned into an American."

"Well, then . . . the tiaras. I might have one of those!"

"Bex, what's wrong?"

"Nothing!" I say brightly. "I just thought you might want to . . . oh, hi, Robyn!" As she approaches, I force myself to give her a friendly smile.

"Becky!" says Robyn, clasping her hands. "Isn't that gown beautiful? Don't you look adorable? Is that the one, do you think?"

"I'm not sure yet." My smile is so fixed, it's hurting. "So, Robyn, how on earth did you know I'd be here? You must be telepathic!"

"Cynthia told me you'd be coming in. She's an old friend." Robyn turns to Suze. "And is this your chum from England?"

"Oh . . . yes. Suze, Robyn, Robyn, Suze."

"Suze? The maid of honor herself? Oh, it's a pleasure to meet you, Suze! You'll look simply wonderful in—" She stops abruptly as her gaze takes in Suze's stomach. "Dear, are you *expecting*?"

"I'll have had the baby by then," Suze assures her.

"Good!" Robyn's face relaxes. "As I say, you'll look wonderful in violet!"

"Violet?" Suze looks puzzled. "I thought I was wearing blue."

"No, definitely violet!"

"Bex, I'm sure your mum said—"

"Well, anyway!" I interrupt hurriedly. "Robyn, I'm a bit tied up here—"

"I know, and I don't want to get in your way. But since I'm here, there's just a couple of things . . . Two seconds, I promise!" She reaches into her bag and pulls out her notebook. "First of all, the New York Philharmonic will unfortunately be on tour at the time of the wedding, but I'm working on an alternative. Now, what else . . ." She consults her notebook.

"Great!" I dart a quick glance at Suze, who's staring at Robyn with a puzzled frown on her face. "You know, maybe you should just give me a call sometime, and we can talk about all this . . ."

"It won't take long! So the other thing was . . . we've scheduled in a tasting at the Plaza on the 23rd in the chef's dining room. I passed on your views on monkfish, so they're having a rethink on that . . ." Robyn flips a page. "Oh, and I still really need that guest list from you!" She looks up and wags her finger in mock reproof. "We'll be needing to think about invitations before we know it! Especially for the overseas guests!"

"OK. I'll . . . I'll get into it," I mumble.

I don't dare look at Suze.

"Great! And I'm meeting you at Antoine's on Monday, ten o'clock. Those cakes . . . you are going to swoon. Now I have to run." She closes her notebook and smiles at Suze. "Nice to meet you, Suze. See you at the wedding!"

"See you there!" says Suze in a too-cheerful voice. "Absolutely."

The door closes behind Robyn and I swallow hard, my face tingling.

"So, ahm . . . I might as well get changed."

I head to the fitting room without meeting Suze's eye. A moment later, she's in there with me.

"Who was that?" she says lightly as I unzip the dress.

"That was . . . Robyn! She's nice, isn't she?"

"And what was she talking about?"

"Just . . . wedding chitchat . . . you know . . . Can you help me out of this corset?"

"Why does she think you're getting married at the Plaza?"

"I . . . um . . . I don't know!"

"Yes you do! And that woman at the party!" Suddenly Suze's voice is as severe as she can manage. "Bex, what's going on?"

"Nothing!"

Suze grabs my shoulder. "Bex, stop it! You're not getting married at the Plaza. Are you?"

I stare at her, feeling my face grow hotter and hotter.

"It's . . . an option," I say at last.

"What do you mean, it's an option?" Suze stares at me, her grip on me loosening. "How can it be an option?"

I adjust the dress on the hanger, playing for time, trying to stifle the guilt rising inside me. If I behave as though this is a completely normal situation, then maybe it will be.

"It's just that . . . well, Elinor's offered to throw this really spectacular wedding for me and Luke. And I haven't quite decided whether or not to take her up." I see Suze's expression. "What?"

"What do you mean 'what?' " expostulates Suze. "What about

(a) your mum's already *organizing* your wedding? What about (b) Elinor is a complete cow? What about (c) you've gone off your head? Why on *earth* would you want to get married at the Plaza?"

"Because . . . because . . ." I close my eyes briefly. "Suze, you have to see it. We're going to have a great big string orchestra, and caviar, and an oyster bar . . . and Tiffany frames for everyone on the tables . . . and Cristal champagne . . . and the whole place will be this magical enchanted forest, and we're going to have real birch trees and songbirds . . ."

"Real birch trees?" Suze pulls a face. "What do you want those for?"

"It's going to be like *Sleeping Beauty*! And I'm going to be the princess, and Luke's going to be the . . ." I tail off feebly to see Suze staring at me reproachfully.

"What about your mum?"

There's silence, and I pretend to be preoccupied unhooking my basque. I don't want to have to think about Mum right at the moment.

"Bex! What about your mum?"

"I'll just have to . . . talk her round," I say at last.

"Talk her *round*?"

"She said herself I shouldn't do the wedding by halves!" I say defensively. "If she came and saw the Plaza, and saw all the plans—"

"But she's done such a lot of preparation already! When we were there she could talk about nothing else. Her and—what's your neighbor called?"

"Janice."

"That's right. They're calling your kitchen the control center. There's about six pin boards up, and lists, and bits of material everywhere . . . And they're so happy doing it." Suze stares at me earnestly. "Becky, you can't just tell them it's all off. You can't."

"Elinor would fly them over!" There's a guilty edge to my voice, which I pretend I can't hear. "I mean, they'd have a fantastic time! It would be a once-in-a-lifetime experience for them too! They could stay in the Plaza, and dance all night, and see New York . . . They'd have the most fabulous holiday ever!"

I'm trying desperately to paint a picture that, deep down, I know isn't true. As I meet Suze's eyes I can feel shame pouring over me, and I quickly look away.

"Have you said this to your mum?"

"No. I . . . I haven't told her anything about it. Not yet. Not until I'm 100 percent sure." There's a pause while Suze's eyes narrow.

"Bex, you are going to do something about this, aren't you?" she says suddenly. "Promise me you're not just going to bury your head in the sand and pretend it isn't happening."

"Honestly! I wouldn't do that!" I say indignantly.

"This is me, remember!" retorts Suze. "I know what you're like! You used to throw all your bank statements into the trash and hope a complete stranger would pay off your bills!"

This is what happens. You tell your friends your most personal secrets, and they use them against you.

"I've grown up a lot since then," I say, trying to sound dignified. "And I will sort it out. I just need to . . . to think it through."

There's a long silence. Outside, I can hear Cynthia saying "Here at Dream Dress, our motto is, you don't *choose* your dress . . ."

"Look, Bex," says Suze at last. "I can't make this decision for you. No one can. All I can say is, if you're going to pull out of your mum's wedding, you're going to have to do it quickly."

THE PINES
43 Elton Road
Oxshott
Surrey

FAX MESSAGE

TO BECKY BLOOMWOOD

FROM MUM

20 March 2002

Becky, darling! Wonderful news!

You might have heard that Suzie spilt her coffee all over the wedding dress. She was devastated, poor thing.

But I took the dress to the cleaners . . . and they worked miracles! It's as white as snow again and you'll be able to wear it after all!

Much love and talk soon,

Mum xxxxxxxxx

Eight

OK. SUZE IS right. I can't dither anymore. I have to decide.

The day after she's left to go home I sit down in my fitting room at lunchtime with a piece of paper and a pen. I'm just going to have to do this logically. Work out the pros and cons, weigh them all up—and make a rational decision. Right. Let's go.

For Oxshott

1. Mum will be happy
2. Dad will be happy
3. It'll be a lovely wedding

I stare at the list for a few seconds—then make a new heading.

For New York

1. I get to have the most amazing wedding in the world

I bury my head in my hands. It isn't any easier on paper.

In fact it's harder, because it's thrusting the dilemma right in my face, instead of where I want it—which is in a little box at the back of my mind where I don't have to look at it.

"Becky?"

"Yes?" I look up, automatically covering up the sheet of paper with my hand. Standing at the door of my fitting room is Elise, one of my clients. She's a thirty-five-year-old corporate lawyer who's just been assigned to Hong Kong for a year. I'll quite miss her actually. She's always nice to chat to, even though she doesn't really have a sense of humor. I think she'd *like* to have one—it's just that she doesn't quite understand what jokes are for.

"Hi, Elise!" I say in surprise. "Do we have an appointment? I thought you were leaving today."

"Tomorrow. But I wanted to buy you a wedding gift before I go."

"Oh! You don't have to do that!" I exclaim, secretly pleased.

"I just need to find out where you're registered."

"Well, actually, we haven't registered yet," I say, feeling a flicker of frustration. It's not *my* fault we haven't registered yet. It's Luke's! He keeps saying he's too busy to spend a day in the shops, which frankly just doesn't make sense.

"You haven't?" Elise frowns. "So how can I buy you a gift?"

"Well . . . um . . . you could just . . . buy something. Maybe."

"Without a list?" Elise stares at me blankly. "But what would I get?"

"I don't know! Anything you felt like!" I give a little laugh. "Maybe a . . . toaster?"

"A toaster. OK." Elise roots around in her bag for a piece of paper. "What model?"

"I've no idea! It was just off the top of my head! Look, Elise, just . . . I don't know, get me something in Hong Kong."

"Are you registering there too?" Elise looks alert. "Which store?"

"No! I just meant . . ." I sigh. "OK, look. When we register, I'll let you know the details. You can probably do it online."

"Well. OK." Elise puts her piece of paper away, giving me a reproving look. "But you really should register. People will be wanting to buy you gifts."

"Sorry," I say. "But anyway, have a fabulous time in Hong Kong."

"Thanks." Elise hesitates, then awkwardly comes forward and pecks me on the cheek. "Bye, Becky. Thanks for all your help."

When she's gone, I sit down again and look at my piece of paper, trying to concentrate.

But I can't stop thinking about what Elise said.

What if she's right? What if there are loads of people out there, all trying to get us presents and unable to?

Suddenly I feel a fresh stab of fear. What if they abandon the attempt in frustration? Or what if they all buy us nasty green glass decanters, like the one Auntie Jean bought for Mum and Dad that *still* gets brought out every Christmas?

This is serious. I pick up my phone and speed-dial Luke's number.

As it rings, I suddenly remember promising the other day to stop phoning him at work with what he called "wedding trivia." I'd made him stay on the line for half an hour while I described three different table settings, and apparently he missed a really important call from Japan.

But surely this is an exception?

"Listen!" I say urgently as he picks up. "We need to register! We can't put it off any longer!"

"Becky, I'm in a meeting. Can this wait?"

"No! It's important!"

There's silence—then I hear Luke saying, "If you could excuse me for a moment—"

"OK," he says, returning to the phone. "Start again. What's the problem?"

"The problem is, people are trying to buy us presents! We need a list! If there's nothing for them to buy, who knows what they might get us!"

"Well, let's register, then."

"I've been wanting to!" I squeak in frustration. "You know I have! I've been waiting and *waiting* for you to have a spare day, or even an evening—"

"I've been tied up with things," he says, a defensive edge to his voice. "That's just the way it is."

I know why he's so defensive. It's because he's been working every night on some stupid promotion for Elinor's charity. And he knows what I think about that.

"Well, we need to get started," I say. "We need to decide what we want."

"Look, Becky. Do I really need to be there?"

"Of course you need to be there! Don't you care what plates we have?"

"Frankly, no."

"No?" I take a deep breath, about to launch into a tirade along the lines of, "If you don't care about our plates, then maybe you don't care about our relationship!"

Then, just in time I realize, this way I get to choose everything exactly as I want it.

"Well, OK," I say. "I'll do it."

"Great. And I agreed we'd have a drink with my mother tonight, at her apartment. Six thirty."

"Oh," I say, pulling a face. "All right. See you then. Shall I call you after I've been to Tiffany to let you know what I registered?"

"Becky," says Luke, deadpan. "If you call me again with any more wedding talk during office hours, it's entirely possible we may not be *having* a wedding."

"Fine!" I say. "Fine! If you're not interested, I'll just organize it all and see you at the altar, shall I? Would that suit you?"

There's a pause, and I can tell Luke's laughing.

"Do you want an honest answer or the *Cosmo* 'Does Your Man Really Love You?' full marks answer?"

"Give me the full marks answer," I say after a moment's thought.

"I want to be involved in every tiny detail of our wedding," says Luke earnestly. "I understand that if I show any lack of interest at any stage it is a sign that I am not committed to you as a woman and beautiful, caring, all-round special person, and, frankly, don't deserve you."

"That was pretty good, I suppose," I say, a little grudgingly. "Now give me the honest answer."

"See you at the altar."

"Ha-di-ha. Well, all I can say is, you'll be sorry when I put you in a pink tuxedo."

"You're right," says Luke. "I will. Now I have to go. Really. I'll see you later."

"Bye."

I put down the phone, reach for my coat, and pick up my bag. As I'm zipping it up, I glance at my piece of paper again and bite my lip. Maybe I should stay here and think a bit more, and try to come to a decision.

But then . . . whether we get married in England or America, we'll need a wedding present list, won't we? So in a way it's *more* sensible to go and register first—and decide about which country to get married in later.

Exactly.

OK, so perhaps I should have realized that lots of brides might want to register at Tiffany. And this is a very busy time of day, and they only have so many members of staff available at one time. I told them it was an emergency, and I have to say, they were very sympathetic, but even so, they couldn't fit me in right at that moment. They asked if I could possibly come back at two o'clock, or tomorrow.

But I'm *working* at two o'clock. And tomorrow I'll be so busy, I already know I won't get a proper lunch hour. God, how are you supposed to plan a wedding and have a job at the same time? As I walk back to Barneys, I'm fizzing with frustration. Now that I've decided to register, I can't wait a minute longer. I want to do it *now,* while I'm all excited, and before anyone goes and buys us a green decanter. I'm just wondering whether I should quickly call all our relations to let them know there *will* be a list . . . when my eye is caught by an ad for Crate and Barrel. "Walk right in and register," it says, above a picture of a big shiny tea kettle.

I stop still in the middle of the street. There's a huge Crate and Barrel about two minutes away. I mean, it's not Tiffany—but it's presents, isn't it? It's all cool pans and stuff . . . Oh, I'm going. I start to walk again, quicker and quicker, until I'm almost running down the sidewalk.

It's only as I'm pushing my way into the store, out of breath, that I realize I don't know anything about registering. In fact, I don't know much about wedding lists at all. For Tom and Lucy's wedding I chipped in with Mum and Dad, and Mum organized it all—and the only other person I know who's got married is Suze, and she and Tarquin didn't have a list.

I look randomly around the shop, wondering where to start. It's bright and light, with colorful tables here and there laid out as though for dinner, and lots of displays full of gleaming glasses, racks of knives, and stainless-steel cookware.

As I wander toward a pyramid of shiny saucepans, I notice a girl in a high swingy ponytail who is going around marking things on a form. I edge nearer, trying to see what she's doing, and spot the words "Crate and Barrel Registry" on the paper. She's registering! OK, I can watch what she does.

"Hey," she says, looking up. "You know anything about cookware? You know what this thing is?"

She holds up a pan, and I can't help hiding a smile. Honestly. These Manhattanites don't know anything. She's probably never cooked a meal in her life!

"It's a frying pan," I say kindly. "You use it to fry things with."

"OK. What about this?"

She holds up another pan with a ridged surface and two looped handles. Blimey. What on earth's that for?

"I . . . um . . . I think it's an . . . omelette . . . griddle . . . skillet . . . pan."

"Oh, right." She looks at it puzzledly and I back quickly away. I pass a display of pottery cereal bowls and find myself at a computer terminal marked "Registry." Maybe this is where you get the forms.

"Welcome to Crate and Barrel," says a cheerful message on the screen. "Please enter the choice you require."

Distractedly I punch a few times at the screen. I'm half listening to a couple behind me arguing about plates.

"I just don't want to *be* taupe stoneware," the girl is saying almost tearfully.

"Well, what do you want to be?" retorts the man.

"I don't know!"

"Are you saying *I'm* taupe stoneware, Marie?"

Oh God, I must stop eavesdropping. I look down at the screen again, and stop in surprise. I've arrived at the place where you look up people's lists so you can buy them a gift. I'm about to press "Clear" and walk away, when I pause.

It would be quite cool to see what other people put down, wouldn't it?

Cautiously I enter the name "R. Smith" and press "Enter."

To my astonishment the screen starts filling up with a whole series of couples' names.

Rachel Smith and David Forsyth, Oak Springs, Miss.

Annie M. Winters and Rod Smith, Raleigh, N.C.

Richard Smith and Fay Bullock, Wheaton, Ill.

Leroy Elms and Rachelle F. Smith . . .

This is so cool! OK, let's see what Rachel and David chose. I press "Enter" and a moment later the machine starts spewing out pieces of paper.

Glass Caviar/Shrimp Server	4
Footed Cake Platter with Dome	1
Water Lily Bowl	2
Classic Decanter 28 oz.	

Wow, that all sounds really nice. I definitely want a water lily bowl. And a shrimp server.

OK, now let's see what Annie and Rod chose. I press "Enter" again, and another list starts appearing in front of me.

Gosh, Annie and Rod are keen on barware! I wonder why they want three ice buckets.

This is completely addictive! Let's see what Richard and Fay are getting. And then Leroy and Rachelle . . . I print them both out, and am just wondering whether to try another name, like Brown, when a voice says, "Can I help you, miss?" My head jerks up and I see a salesman wearing a name badge reading "Bud" smiling at me. "Are you having some trouble locating the list you want?"

I feel myself prickle with embarrassment.

I *can't* admit I'm just snooping.

"I . . . actually . . . I've just found it." I grab randomly for Richard and Fay's list. "They're friends of mine. Richard and Fay." I clear my throat. "I want to buy them a wedding present. That's why I'm here. Also, I want to register myself."

"Well, let's deal with the purchase first. What would you like to buy?"

"Umm . . . well . . ." I look down at the list. "Um . . ."

Come on. I'm not really going to buy a present for a pair of complete strangers. Just admit the truth. I was nosy.

"Actually . . . I think I'll leave it for another day," I say. "But I would like to register a list myself."

"No problem!" says Bud cheerily. "Here's the form for you to fill in as you go around . . . you'll see that most of our merchandise breaks down into sections . . ."

"Oh, right. What sort of—"

"Kitchenware, flatware, hollowware, barware, stemware, glassware . . ." He pauses for breath. "And miscellaneous."

"Right . . ."

"It can be a little overwhelming, deciding what you're going to want in your new home." He smiles at me. "So what I suggest is, you start with the basics. Think about your everyday needs—and work up from there. If you need me, just give me a shout!"

"Great! Thanks very much!"

Bud moves away and I look around the store with a fizz of anticipation. I haven't been so excited since I used to write out lists for Father Christmas. And even then, Mum would stand over my shoulder, saying things like "I'm not sure Father Christmas can give you the *real* ruby slippers, darling. Why not ask for a nice coloring book instead?"

Now, no one's telling me what I can or can't have. I can write down anything I like! I can ask for those plates over there . . . and that jug . . . and that chair . . . I mean, if I wanted to, I could ask for everything! The whole shop!

You know. In theory.

But I'm not going to get carried away. I'll start with everyday needs, just as Bud suggested. Feeling pleasantly grown-up, I wander toward a display of kitchen equipment and start perusing the shelves.

Ooh. Lobster crackers! Let's get some of those. And those cute little corn holders. And those sweet little plastic daisies. I don't know what they're for, but they look so gorgeous!

I note the numbers carefully down on my list. OK. What else? As I look around again, my attention is caught by a gleaming array of chrome.

Wow. We just have to have a frozen yogurt maker. And a waffle maker. And a bread cooker, and a juicer, and a Pro Chef Premium Toaster Oven. I write down all the numbers and look around with a sigh of satisfaction. Why on earth have I never registered before? Shopping without spending any money!

You know, I should have got married a long time ago.

"Excuse me?" The girl with the ponytail is over in the knife section. "Do you know what poultry shears are?" She holds up a piece of equipment I've never seen before in my life.

"They're . . . shears for poultry . . . I guess . . ."

For a moment we stare at each other blankly, then the girl shrugs, says "OK," and writes it down on her list.

Maybe I'll get some poultry shears too. And one of those cool herb-chopper things. And a professional blowtorch for making crème brûlée.

Not that I've ever made crème brûlée—but you know. When I'm married, I'm bound to. I have a sudden vision of myself in an apron, nonchalantly brûléeing with one hand and drizzling a homemade fruit coulis with the other, while Luke and an assortment of witty guests look on admiringly.

"So where else are you registering?" says the girl, picking up an egg whisk and peering at it.

I look at her in surprise. "What do you mean? Are you allowed more than one list?"

"Of course! I'm having three. Here, Williams-Sonoma, and Bloomies. It's really cool there, you scan everything on this gun—"

"Three lists!" I can't keep the elation out of my voice.

And actually, when you think about it, why stop at three?

So by the time I arrive at Elinor's apartment that evening I've made appointments to register at Tiffany, Bergdorf, Bloomingdale's, and Barneys, ordered the Williams-Sonoma catalogue, and started an online wedding list.

I haven't managed to think any more about where we're going to get married—but then, first things first.

As Elinor opens the door, music is playing and the apartment smells pleasantly of flowers. Elinor's wearing a wrap dress and her hair looks slightly softer than usual—and as she kisses me she gives my hand a little squeeze.

"Luke's already here," she says as we walk along the corridor. "That's a pretty pair of shoes. Are they new?"

"Er, actually, they are. They're Dolce and Gabbana! Thanks!" I can't help gaping at her in astonishment. I've never known Elinor to compliment me before. Not once.

"You look like you've lost a little weight," she adds. "It suits you."

I'm so gobsmacked I stop, right in the middle of the doorway—then have to hurry to catch up. Is Elinor Sherman finally, after all this time, going to start making an effort to be nice to me? I can't quite believe it.

But then . . . come to think of it, she was quite nice at the end of the engagement party too. She said it had been a mistake about me not being on the door list and that she was really sorry.

Actually no, she didn't exactly say she was sorry—she said she would sue the party planners. But still. That shows concern, doesn't it?

God, maybe Elinor has a hidden nice side, I find myself thinking. Maybe there's a whole different persona under that icy exterior. Yes! She's all vulnerable and insecure but she's put up a protective shell around herself. And I'm the only one who can see beneath it, and when I coax the true Elinor into the world, all New York society will marvel, and Luke will love me even more, and people will call me The Girl Who Changed Elinor Sherman, and—

"Becky?" Luke's voice penetrates my thoughts. "Are you all right?"

"Yes," I say, realizing with a start that I'm blundering into the coffee table. "Yes, I'm fine!"

I sit down next to him on the sofa, Elinor hands me a glass of icy-cold wine, and I sip it, gazing out the window over the glittering Manhattan lights stretching into the distance. Elinor and Luke are in the middle of some discussion about the foundation, and I nibble a salted almond and tune out. Somehow I've arrived in the middle of a dreamlike picture in which Elinor is saying to a crowded room, "Becky Bloomwood is not only a model daughter-in-law, but a valued friend," and I'm smiling modestly as people start applauding, when there's a snapping sound, and I come to, slightly spilling my drink.

Elinor has closed the crocodile notebook she's been writing in. She puts it away, turns down the music slightly, and looks directly at me.

"Rebecca," she says.

"Yes?"

"I asked you here tonight because there's something I'd like to discuss with you." She refreshes my drink and I smile at her.

"Oh yes?"

"As you know, Luke is a very wealthy young man."

"Oh. Right," I say, a little embarrassed. "Well . . . yes, I suppose so."

"I've been speaking with my lawyers . . . and with Luke's lawyers . . . and we are all agreed. So if I could just give you this . . ." She gives me a glittering smile and hands over a thick white envelope—then hands another to Luke.

As I take it I feel a tingle of anticipation. You see? Elinor's already becoming friendlier. This is just like *Dallas.* She's probably making me an associate of some family company or something, to welcome me into the dynasty. God, yes! And I'll get to go to board meetings and everything and we'll mount some amazing takeover together and I'll wear big earrings . . .

Excitedly, I open the envelope and pull out a thick, typed document. But as I read the words I can feel my excitement ebb away.

Memorandum of Agreement
Between Luke James Brandon (hereinafter called "The Groom")
and Rebecca Jane Bloomwood (hereinafter called "The Bride") of—

I don't get it. Memorandum of what agreement? Is this—

Surely this isn't a—

I look bewilderedly at Luke, but he's flipping over the pages, looking as taken aback as me.

"Mother, what's this?" he says.

"It's simply a precaution," says Elinor with a distant smile. "A form of insurance."

Oh my God. It is. It's a prenuptial contract.

Feeling slightly sick, I flip through the contract. It's about ten pages long, with headings like "Property Settlement in the Case of Divorce."

"Insurance against what, exactly?" Luke's voice is unreadable.

"Let's not pretend we're living in a fairy-tale world," says Elinor crisply. "We all know what might happen."

"What's that, exactly?"

"Don't be obstructive, Luke. You know perfectly well what I mean. And bearing in mind Rebecca's . . . shall we say, history of spending?" She glances meaningfully at my shoes—and with a start of humiliation I realize why she asked me about them.

She wasn't trying to be nice. She was gathering ammunition to attack me.

Oh, how could I be so *stupid*? There is no soft center to Elinor. It just doesn't exist.

"Let me get this straight," I say, breathing hard. "You think I'm just after Luke for his money."

"Becky, of course she doesn't," exclaims Luke.

"Yes, she does!"

"A prenuptial contract is simply a sensible premarital step."

"Well, it's a step I really don't think we need to take," says Luke with a little laugh.

"I would beg to differ," says Elinor. "I'm only trying to protect you. Both of you," she adds unconvincingly.

"What do you think, I'm going to . . . divorce Luke and get all his money?"

Just like you did with your husbands, I'm about to add, but stop myself just in time. "You think that's why I want to marry him?"

"Becky—"

"You may, of course, look the contract over in your own time—"

"I don't need to look it over."

"Do I take it you're refusing to sign?" Elinor gives me a triumphant look as though I've confirmed every suspicion she had.

"No!" I say in a trembling voice. "I'm not refusing to sign! I'll sign whatever you like! I'm not going to have you think I want Luke's money!" I grab the pen off the table and furiously start scrawling my signature on the first page, so hard I rip the paper.

"Becky, don't be stupid!" exclaims Luke. "Mother—"

"It's fine! I'll sign every single . . . bloody . . ."

My face is hot and my eyes a little blurry as I turn the pages, signing again and again without even looking at the text above. *Rebecca Bloomwood. Rebecca Bloomwood.*

"Well, I'm not signing it," says Luke. "I never wanted a prenup! And I'm certainly not going to sign something I've never seen before in my life."

"There. Done." I put down my pen and pick up my bag. "I think I'll go now. Bye, Elinor."

"Becky—" says Luke. "Mother, what on *earth* possessed you to do this?"

As I head out of Elinor's apartment my head is still pounding. I wait for the lift for a few seconds—but when it doesn't come, head for the stairs instead. I feel shaky with fury, with mortification. She thinks I'm a gold digger.

Is that what everyone thinks?

"Becky!" Luke is coming down the stairs after me, three at a time. "Becky, wait. I'm so sorry. I had no idea . . ." As we reach the ground floor he envelops me in his arms and I stand there rigidly.

"Believe me. That was as much of a shock for me as it was for you."

"Well . . . you know . . . I think you should sign it," I say, staring at the floor. "You should protect yourself. It's only sensible."

"Becky. This is me. This is *us*." Gently he lifts my chin until I haven't got anywhere to look except into his dark eyes. "I know you're angry. Of course you are. But you have to excuse my mother. She's lived in America a long time. Prenups are standard issue here. She didn't mean—"

"She did," I say, feeling a fresh surge of humiliation. "That's exactly what she meant. She thinks I've got some plan to . . . to take all your money and spend the whole lot on shoes!"

"That's not your plan?" Luke feigns shock. "You're telling me this now? Well, if you're going to change the ground rules, perhaps we *should* have a prenup—"

I give a half-smile—but I'm still raw inside.

"I know loads of people have prenups here," I say. "I know that. But she shouldn't just . . . draw one up without consulting either of us! Do you know how she made me feel?"

"I know." Luke strokes my back soothingly. "I'm furious with her."

"You're not."

"Of course I am."

"No, you're not! You're never furious with her! That's the trouble." I break away from his arms, trying to keep calm.

"Becky?" Luke stares at me. "Is something else wrong?"

"It's not just this. It's . . . everything! The way she's taken over the wedding. The way she was so supercilious and horrible with my parents . . ."

"She's naturally a very formal person," says Luke defensively. "It doesn't mean she's trying to be supercilious. If your parents really got to know her—"

"And the way she uses you!" I know I'm on dangerous ground—but now I've started, I can't stop everything pouring out. "You've given her hours and hours of your time. You've provided staff for her charity. You've even fallen out with Michael because of her. I just don't understand it! You *know* Michael cares about you. You *know* he's only got your best interests at heart. But because of your mother, you're not even talking to him."

Luke's face flinches, and I can see I've touched a nerve.

"And now she wants us to move to this building. Don't you see? She just wants to get her claws into you! She'll have you running errands for her all day long, and she'll never leave us alone . . . Luke, you're already giving her so much!"

"What's wrong with that?" Luke's expression is gradually becoming tighter. "She's my mother."

"I know she is! But come on. She was never even interested in you before you became a success over here. Remember our first trip to New York? You were so desperate to impress her—and she didn't even make the effort to see you! But now that you've made it here, you've got a name, you've got contacts in the media, you've got resources—and all of a sudden she wants to get all the credit and just *use* you . . ."

"That's not true."

"It is true! You just can't see it! You're too dazzled by her!"

"Look, Becky, it's easy for you to criticize," says Luke hotly. "You have a fantastic relationship with your mother. I barely saw mine when I was growing up—"

"Exactly!" I cry, before I can stop myself. "That proves my point! She didn't give a shit about you then either!"

Oh, bugger. I shouldn't have said that. A flash of pain passes through Luke's eyes and suddenly he looks about ten years old.

"You know that's not true," he says. "My mother wanted me. It wasn't her fault."

"I know. I'm sorry—" I move toward him, but he jerks away.

"Put yourself in her shoes for a change, Becky. Think about what she's gone through. Having to leave behind her child; having to put on a brave face. She's been used to hiding her feelings for so long, no wonder her manner can be a little awkward."

Listening to him, I almost want to cry. He's got it all worked out. He's still like the boy who made every excuse in the world for why his mother never came to see him.

"But now we're having a chance to forge our relationship once again," Luke is saying. "Maybe she is a bit tactless now and then. But she's doing her best."

Yeah, right, I want to say. She's really trying hard with me.

Instead I give a tiny shrug and mumble, "I suppose so."

Luke walks over and takes hold of my hand. "Come back upstairs. We'll have another drink. Forget this ever happened."

"No." I exhale sharply. "I think I'll . . . go home. You go. I'll see you later."

As I make my way home it starts to rain, big splashy drops that puddle in the gutters and drip off canopies. They spatter on my hot cheeks and wet my hair and make marks on my new suede-trimmed shoes. But I barely notice them. I'm still too wound up by the evening; by Elinor's gimlet gaze; by my own humiliation; by my frustration with Luke.

The moment I get inside the apartment there's a crack of thunder outside. I switch all the lights on and the television, and pick up the post. There's an envelope from Mum and I open it first. A swatch of fabric falls out and a long letter smelling faintly of her perfume.

> Darling Becky,
>
> Hope all's well in the Big Apple!
>
> Here's the color we were thinking of for the table napkins. Janice says we should have pink but I think this pale plum is very pretty, especially with the colors we were thinking of for the flowers. But let me know what you think, you're the bride, darling!
>
> The photographer that Dennis recommended came round yesterday and we were all very impressed. Dad has heard good things about him at the golf club, which is always a good sign. He can do color and black-and-white, and includes a photograph album in the price, which seems a very good deal. Also, he can turn the picture you like best into one hundred mini jigsaw puzzles to send to all the guests as a little thank-you!
>
> The most important thing of all, I told him, is that we have

lots of pictures of you by the flowering cherry tree. We planted that when you were born, and it's always been my secret dream that our little baby Rebecca would grow up and one day stand beside it on her wedding day. You are our only child and this day is so important to us.

Yours with lots of love,
Mum

By the end, I'm crying. I don't know why I ever thought I wanted to get married in New York. I don't know why I let Elinor even show me the stupid Plaza. Home is where I want to get married. With Mum and Dad, and the cherry tree, and my friends, and everything that really matters to me.

That's it, I've made my choice.

"Becky?"

I give a startled jump and turn round. There's Luke, standing at the door, out of breath and drenched from head to foot. His hair is plastered to his head and raindrops are still running down his face. "Becky . . ." he says urgently. "I'm sorry. I'm so sorry. I shouldn't have let you go like that. I saw the rain . . . I don't know what I was thinking—" He breaks off as he sees my tear-stained face. "Are you all right?"

"I'm fine." I wipe my eyes. "And Luke . . . I'm sorry too."

Luke gazes at me for a long time, his face trembling, his eyes burning.

"Becky Bloomwood," he says at last. "You're the most generous-spirited . . . giving . . . loving . . . I don't deserve . . ."

He breaks off and comes toward me, his face almost fierce with intent. As he kisses me, raindrops spatter from his hair onto my mouth and mingle with the warm salty taste of him. I close my eyes and let my body gradually unwind, the pleasure gradually begin. I can already feel him hard and determined, gripping my hips and wanting me right now, right this minute, to say sorry, to say he loves me, to say he'll do anything for me . . .

God, I love make-up sex.

Nine

I WAKE UP THE next morning all snug and contented and happy with myself. As I lie in bed, curled up against Luke, I'm full of a strong inner resolve. I've sorted out my priorities. Nothing will change my mind now.

"Luke?" I say, as he makes a move to get out of bed.

"Mmm?" He turns and kisses me, and he's all warm and delicious and lovely.

"Don't go. Stay here. All day."

"All day?"

"We could pretend we were ill." I stretch luxuriously out on the pillows. "Actually, I do feel rather ill."

"Oh, really? Which bit?"

"My . . . tummy."

"Looks fine to me," says Luke, peeking under the duvet. "Feels fine . . . Sorry. You don't get a note."

"Spoilsport."

I watch as he gets out of bed, puts on a robe, and heads for the bathroom.

"Luke?" I say again as he reaches the door.

"What?"

I open my mouth to tell him I made a big decision last night. That I want to get married in Oxshott, just like we originally planned. That I'm going to cancel the Plaza. That if Elinor is furious, then so be it.

Then I close it again.

"What is it?" says Luke.

"Just . . . don't use up all my shampoo," I say at last.

I can't face bringing up the subject of the wedding. Not now, when everything's so lovely and happy between us. And anyway, Luke doesn't care where we get married. He said so himself.

I've taken the morning off work for the cake-tasting meeting with Robyn, but our appointment's not until ten. So after Luke's gone I slowly pad around the apartment, making myself some breakfast and thinking about what I'm going to say to Elinor.

The thing is to be direct. Firm and direct but pleasant. Grown-up and professional, like businesspeople who have to fire other businesspeople. Stay calm and use phrases like "We chose to go another way."

"Hello, Elinor," I say to my reflection. "I have something I need to say to you. I have chosen to go another way."

No. She'll think I'm becoming a lesbian.

"Hello, Elinor," I try again. "I've been bouncing around your wedding-scenario proposal. And while it has many merits . . ."

OK, come on. Just do it.

Ignoring my butterflies, I pick up the phone and dial Elinor's number.

"Elinor Sherman is unable to take your call . . ."

She's out.

I can't just leave her a message saying the wedding's off. Can I?

Could I?

No.

I put the phone down hurriedly, before the bleep sounds. OK. What shall I do now?

Well, it's obvious. I'll call Robyn. The important thing is that I tell *someone,* before anything else gets done.

I gather my thoughts for a moment, then dial Robyn's number.

"Hello! Do I hear wedding bells? I hope so, because this is Robyn de Bendern, the answer to your wedding planning prayers. I'm afraid I'm unavailable at present, but your call is so important to me . . ."

Robyn's probably already on her way to meet me at the cake-maker's studio, it occurs to me. I could call her there. Or I could leave a message.

But as I hear her bright, chirruping voice, I feel a pang of guilt.

Robyn's already put so much into this. In fact, I've already become quite fond of her. I just can't tell her it's all off over the phone. Feeling suddenly firm, I put down the phone and reach for my bag.

I'll be a grown-up, go along to the cake studio, and break the news to her face-to-face.

And I'll deal with Elinor later.

To be honest, I don't really like wedding cake. I always take a piece because it's bad luck or something if you don't, but actually all that fruitcake and marzipan and icing like blocks of chalk makes me feel a bit sick. And I'm so nervous at the thought of telling Robyn it's all off that I can't imagine eating anything.

Even so, my mouth can't help watering as I arrive at the cake studio. It's big and light, with huge windows and the sweetest, most delicious sugary-buttery smell wafting through the air. There are huge mounted cakes on display, and rows of flower decorations in transparent boxes, and people at marble tables, carefully making roses out of icing and painting strands of sugar ivy.

As I hover at the entrance, a skinny girl in jeans and strappy high heels is being led out by her mother, and they're in the middle of a row.

"You only had to taste it," the mother is saying furiously. "How many calories could that be?"

"I don't care," retorts the girl tearfully. "I'm going to be a size two on my wedding day if it kills me."

Size two!

Anxiously I glance at my thighs. Should I be aiming for size two as well? Is that the size brides are supposed to be?

"Becky!" I look up to see Robyn, who seems a little flustered. "Hello! You made it."

"Robyn." As I see her, I feel my stomach clench with apprehension. "Listen. I need to talk to you. I tried calling Elinor, but she was . . . Anyway. There's something I need to . . . tell you."

"Absolutely," says Robyn distractedly. "Antoine and I will be with you in a moment, but we have a slight crisis on our hands." She lowers her voice. "There was an accident with one of the cakes. Very unfortunate."

"Miss Bloomwood?" I look up to see a man with gray hair and

twinkling eyes in a white chef's outfit. "I am Antoine Montignac. The cake maker of cake makers. Perhaps you have seen me in my television show?"

"Antoine, I don't think we've quite resolved the problem with the . . . other client . . ." says Robyn anxiously.

"I come in a moment." He dismisses her with his hand. "Miss Bloomwood. Sit down."

"Actually, I'm not sure I really want to . . ." I begin. But before I know what I'm doing, I've been seated on a plushy chair at a polished table, and Antoine is spreading glossy portfolios in front of me.

"I can create for you the cake that will surpass all your dreams," he announces modestly. "No image is beyond my powers of creativity."

"Really?" I look at a photograph of a spectacular six-tier cake decorated with sugar tulips, then turn the page to see one in the shape of five different butterflies. These are the hugest cakes I've ever seen in my life. And the decorations!

"So, are these all fruitcakes inside?"

"Fruitcake? *Non, non, non!*" Antoine laughs. "This is very English notion, the fruitcake at the wedding. This particular cake . . ." He points to the butterfly cake. "It was a light angel sponge, each tier layered with three different fillings: burnt orange caramel, passion-fruit-mango, and hazelnut soufflé."

Gosh.

"If you like chocolate, we can construct a cake purely from different varieties of chocolate." He turns to another page. "This was a dark chocolate sponge layered with chocolate fondant, white chocolate cream, and a Grand Marnier truffle filling."

I had no idea wedding cakes could be anything like this. I flip through dazedly, looking at cake after spectacular cake.

"If you do not want the traditional tiers, I can make for you a cake to represent something you love. A favorite painting . . . or a sculpture . . ." He looks at me again. "A Louis Vuitton trunk, perhaps . . ."

A Louis Vuitton trunk wedding cake! How cool would that be?

"Antoine? If you could just come here a moment?" Robyn pokes her head out of a small meeting room to the right—and although she's smiling, she sounds pretty harassed.

"Excuse me, Miss Bloomwood," says Antoine apologetically. "Davina. Some cake for Miss Bloomwood to taste."

A smiling assistant disappears through a pair of double doors—

then returns with a glass of champagne and a china plate holding two slices of cake and a sugar lily. She hands me a fork and says, "This one is passion-fruit-mango, strawberry, and tangerine mousseline, and this is caramel creme with pistachio and mocha truffle. Enjoy!"

Wow. Each slice is a light sponge, with three different pastel-colored fillings. I don't know where to start!

OK . . . let's go for mocha truffle.

I put a piece in my mouth and nearly swoon. Now *this* is what wedding cakes should all be like. Why don't we have these in England?

I take a few sips of champagne and nibble the sugar lily, which is all yummy and lemony—then take a second piece and munch blissfully, watching a girl nearby as she painstakingly makes a spray of lilies of the valley.

You know, maybe I should get Suze a nice cake for her baby's christening. I mean, I'll get a present as well—but I could always buy a cake as a little extra.

"Do you know how much these cakes are?" I ask the girl as I polish off the second slice.

"Well . . . it really varies," she says, looking up. "But I guess they start at about a thousand dollars."

I nearly choke on my champagne. A thousand dollars? They *start* at $1,000?

For a *cake*?

I mean, how much have I eaten, just now? That must have been at least $50 worth of cake on my plate!

"Would you like another slice?" says the girl, and glances at the meeting room. "It looks like Antoine is still held up."

"Ooh, well . . . Why not! And could I try one of those sugar tulips? You know. Just for research purposes."

"Sure," says the girl pleasantly. "Whatever you like."

She gives me a tulip and a spray of tiny white flowers, and I crunch through them happily, washing them down with champagne.

Then I look idly around and spy a huge, elaborate flower, yellow and white with tiny drops of dew. Wow. That looks yummy. I reach over a display of sugar hearts, pick it up, and it's almost in my mouth when I hear a yell.

"Stooooop!" A guy in whites is pounding across the studio toward me. "Don't eat the jonquil!"

"Oops!" I say, stopping just in time. "Sorry. I didn't realize. Is it very special?"

"It took me three hours to make," he says, taking it gently from my hand. "No harm done, though." He smiles at me, but I notice there's sweat on his forehead.

Hmm. Maybe I should just stick to the champagne from now on. I take another sip, and am looking around for the bottle, when raised voices start coming from the side room where Robyn and Antoine are closeted.

"I deed not do this deliberately! Mademoiselle, I do not have a vendetta."

"You do! You bloody hate me, don't you?" comes a muffled voice.

I can hear Robyn's voice, saying something soothing, which I can't make out.

"It's just one thing after another!" The girl's voice is raised now—and as I hear it clearly, I freeze, glass halfway to my mouth.

I don't believe it.

It can't be.

"This bloody wedding is jinxed!" she's exclaiming. "Right from the word *go,* everything's gone wrong."

The door swings open and now I can hear her properly.

It is. It's Alicia.

I feel my whole body stiffen.

"First the Plaza couldn't fit us in! Now this fiasco with the cake! And do you know what I just heard?"

"What?" says Robyn fearfully.

"My maid of honor dyed her hair red! She won't match the others! Of all the bloody inconsiderate, selfish . . ."

The door is flung open and out stalks Alicia, her stilettos echoing like gunfire on the wooden floor. When she sees me, she stops dead and I look at her, my heart thumping hard.

"Hi, Alicia," I say, forcing myself to sound relaxed. "Sorry to hear about your cake. That was delicious, by the way, Antoine."

"What?" says Alicia blankly. Her eyes flash to my engagement ring, to my face, back to my ring, to my shoes, to my bag—taking in my skirt on the way—and finally back to my ring. It's like the Manhattan Onceover in a hall of mirrors.

"You're getting married?" she says at last. "To Luke?"

"Yes." I glance nonchalantly at the diamond on my left hand, then smile innocently up at her.

I'm starting to relax now. I'm starting to enjoy this.

(Also, I just gave Alicia the Manhattan Oncecover myself. And my ring is a teeny bit bigger than hers. Not that I'm comparing or anything.)

"How come you didn't say?"

You didn't ask, I want to reply, but instead I just give a little shrug.

"So where are you getting married?" Alicia's old supercilious expression is returning and I can see her getting ready to pounce.

"Well . . . as it happens . . ." I clear my throat.

OK, this is the moment. This is the time to make the big announcement. To tell Robyn I've changed my mind. I'm going to get married in Oxshott.

"Actually . . ."

I take a deep breath. Come on. It's like a Band-Aid. The quicker I do it, the quicker it'll be over. Just say it.

And I really am on the brink of it—when I make the fatal mistake of looking up. Alicia's looking as patronizing and smug as she ever did. I feel years of feeling stupid and small welling up in me like a volcano—and I just can't help it, I hear my voice saying, "Actually, we're getting married at the Plaza."

Alicia's face snaps in shock, like an elastic band. "The Plaza? Really?"

"It should be rather lovely," I add casually. "Such a beautiful venue, the Plaza. Is that where you're getting married?"

"No," says Alicia, her chin rather tight. "They couldn't fit us in at such short notice. When did you book?"

"Oh . . . a week or two ago," I say, and give a vague shrug.

Yes! Yes! Her expression!

"It's going to be wonderful," puts in Robyn enthusiastically. "I spoke to the designer this morning, by the way. He's ordered two hundred birch trees, and they're going to send over some samples of pine needles . . ."

I can see Alicia's brain working hard.

"*You're* the one having the enchanted forest in the Plaza," she says at last. "I've heard about that. Sheldon Lloyd's designing it. Is that true?"

"That's the one," I say, and smile at Robyn, who beams back as though I'm an old ally.

"Mees Bloomwood." Antoine appears from nowhere and presses my hand to his lips. "I am now completely at your service. I apologize for the delay. One of these irritating little matters . . ."

Alicia's face goes rigid.

"Well," she says. "I'll be off then."

"Au revoir," says Antoine, without even looking up.

"Bye, Alicia," I say innocently. "Have a lovely wedding."

As she stalks out, I subside back in my seat, heart still pumping wth exhilaration. That was one of the best moments of my life. Finally getting the better of Alicia Bitch Longlegs. Finally! I mean, how often has she been horrible to me? Answer: approximately one thousand times. And how often have I had the perfect put-down at my lips? Answer: never.

Until today!

I can see Robyn and Antoine exchanging looks, and I'm dying to ask them what they think of Alicia. But . . . it wouldn't be becoming in a bride-to-be.

Plus if they bitch about her, they might bitch about me too.

"Now!" says Robyn. "On to something more pleasant. You've seen the details of Becky's wedding, Antoine."

"Indeed," says Antoine, beaming at me. "Eet will be a most beautiful event."

"I know," I hear myself saying happily. "I'm so looking forward to it!"

"So . . . we discuss the cake . . . I must fetch some pictures for you . . . meanwhile, can I offer you some more champagne, perhaps?"

"Yes, please," I say, and hold out my glass. "That would be lovely!"

The champagne fizzes, pale and delicious, into my glass. Then Antoine disappears off again and I take a sip, smiling to hide the fact that inside, I'm feeling a slight unease.

Now that Alicia's gone, there's no need to pretend anymore. What I should do is put my glass down, take Robyn aside, apologize for having wasted her time—and inform her that the wedding is off and I'm getting married in Oxshott. Quite simple and straightforward.

That's what I should do.

But . . . something very strange has happened since this morning. I can't quite explain it—but somehow, sitting here, drinking champagne and eating thousand-dollar cake, I just don't *feel* like someone who's going to get married in a garden in Oxshott.

If I'm really honest, hand on heart—I feel exactly like someone who's going to have a huge, luxurious wedding at the Plaza.

More than that, I *want* to be someone who's going to have a huge, luxurious wedding at the Plaza. I *want* to be that girl who swans around expensive cake shops and has people running after her and gets treated like a princess. If I call off the wedding, then it'll all stop. Everyone will stop making a fuss. I'll stop being that special, glossy person.

Oh God, what's happened to me? I was so resolved this morning.

Determinedly I close my eyes and force myself to think back to Mum and her flowering cherry tree. But even that doesn't work. Perhaps it's the champagne—but instead of being overcome with emotion, and thinking: I *must* get married at home, I find myself thinking: Maybe we can incorporate the cherry tree into the enchanted forest.

"All right, Becky?" says Robyn, beaming at me. "Penny for them!"

"Oh!" I say, my head jerking up guiltily. "I was just thinking that . . . the um . . . wedding will be fantastic."

What am I going to do? Am I going to say something?

Am I *not* going to say anything?

Come *on*, Becky. Decide.

"So—you want to see what I have in my bag?" says Robyn brightly.

"Er . . . yes, please."

"Ta-daah!" She pulls out a thick, embossed card, covered in swirly writing, and hands it to me.

Mrs. Elinor Sherman
requests the honour of your presence
at the marriage of
Rebecca Bloomwood
to her son
Luke Brandon

I stare at it, my heart thumping hard.

This is real. This is really real. Here it is, in black and white.

Or at least, bronze and taupe.

I take the stiff card from her and turn it over and over in my fingers.

"What do you think?" Robyn beams. "It's exquisite, isn't it? The card is 80 percent linen."

"It's . . . lovely." I swallow. "It seems very soon to be sending out invitations, though."

"We aren't sending them out yet! But I always like to get the invitations done early. What I always say is, you can't proofread too many times. We don't want to be asking our guests to wear 'evening press,' like one bride I could mention . . ." She trills with laughter.

"Right." I stare down at the words again.

Saturday June 22nd at seven o'clock
at the Plaza Hotel
New York City

This is serious. If I'm going to say anything, I have to say it now. If I'm going to call this wedding off, I have to do it now. Right this minute.

My mouth remains closed.

Does this really mean I'm choosing the Plaza after all? That I'm selling out? That I'm choosing the gloss and glitter? That I'm going with Elinor instead of Mum and Dad?

"I thought you'd like to send one to your mother!" says Robyn.

My head jerks up sharply—but Robyn's face is blithely innocent. "Such a shame she isn't here to get involved with the preparations. But she'll love to see this, won't she?"

"Yes," I say after a long pause. "Yes, she'll . . . love it."

I put the invitation into my bag and snap the clasp shut, feeling slightly sick.

So this is it. New York it is.

Mum will understand. When I tell her all about it properly, she'll come round. She has to.

Antoine's new mandarin and lychee cake is fabulous. But somehow as I nibble at it, my appetite's gone.

After I've tried several more flavors and am no nearer a decision, Antoine and Robyn exchange looks and suggest I probably need time to think. So with one last sugar rose for my purse, I say good-bye and head to Barneys, where I deal with all my clients perfectly pleasantly, as though nothing's on my mind.

But all the time I'm thinking about the call I've got to make. About how I'm going to break the news to Mum. About how I'm going to *explain* to Mum.

I won't say anything as strong as I definitely want to get married in the Plaza. Not initially. I'll just tell her that it's there as a possibility, if we both want it. That's the key phrase. *If we both want it.*

The truth is, I didn't present it properly to her before. She'll probably leap at the chance once I explain it all to her fully. Once I tell her about the enchanted forest and the string orchestra, and the dance band and the thousand-dollar cake. A lovely luxury wedding, all expenses paid! I mean, who wouldn't leap at it?

But my heart's thumping as I climb the stairs to our apartment. I know I'm not being honest with myself. I know what Mum really wants.

I also know that if I make enough fuss, she'll do anything I ask her.

I close the door behind me and take a deep breath. Two seconds later, the doorbell rings behind me and I jump with fright. God, I'm on edge at the moment.

"Hi," I say, opening it. "Oh, Danny, it's you. Listen, I need to make quite an important phone call. So if you wouldn't mind—"

"OK, I have to ask you a favor," he says, coming into the apartment and completely ignoring me.

"What is it?"

"Randall's been pressuring me. He's like, where exactly do you sell your clothes? Who exactly are your customers? Do you have a business plan? So I'm like, of course I have a business plan, Randall. I'm planning to buy up Coca-Cola next year, what do you think?"

"Danny?"

"So then he starts saying if I don't have any genuine client base I should give up and he's not going to subsidize me anymore. He used the word *subsidize*! Can you believe it?"

"Well," I say distractedly. "He does pay your rent. And he bought you all those rolls of pink suede you wanted . . ."

"OK," says Danny after a pause. "OK. So the pink suede was a mistake. But Jesus! He just wouldn't leave it alone. I told him about your dress—but he was like, Daniel, you can't base a commercial enterprise on one customer who lives downstairs." Danny chews the skin on his thumb nervously. "So I told him I just had a big order from a department store."

"Really? Which one?"

"Barneys."

I look at him, my attention finally caught.

"*Barneys?* Danny, why did you say Barneys?"

"So you can back me up! If he asks you, you stock me, OK? And all your clients are falling over themselves to buy my stuff, you've never known anything like it in the history of the store."

"You're mad. He'll never fall for it. And what will you say when he wants some money?"

"I'll have money by then!"

"What if he checks up? What if he goes to Barneys to look?"

"He won't check up," says Danny scornfully. "He only has time to talk to me once a month, let alone make unscheduled visits to Barneys. But if he meets you on the stairs, go along with my story. That's all I'm asking."

"Well . . . all right," I say at last.

Honestly. As if I haven't got enough to worry about already.

"Danny, I really must make this call . . ." I say helplessly.

"So did you find somewhere else to live yet?" he says, flopping down into an armchair.

"We haven't had time."

"You haven't even thought about it?"

"Elinor wants us to move to her building and I've said no. That's as far as we've got."

"Really?" Danny stares at me. "But don't you want to stay in the Village?"

"Of course I do! There's no way I'm moving there."

"So what are you going to do?"

"I . . . don't know! I've just got too many other things to think about at the moment. Speaking of which—"

"Pre-wedding stress," says Danny knowingly. "The solution is a double martini." He opens up the cocktail cabinet and a sheaf of wedding list brochures falls out onto the floor.

"Hey!" he says reproachfully, picking them up. "Did you register without me? I cannot believe that! I have been dying to register my entire life! Did you ask for a cappuccino maker?"

"Er . . . yes. I think so—"

"Big mistake. You'll use it three times, then you'll be back at Starbucks. Listen, if you ever want me to take delivery of any presents, you know I'm right upstairs . . ."

"Yeah, right." I give him a look. "After Christmas."

Christmas is still a slightly sore point with me. I thought I'd be really clever and order a load of presents off the Internet. But they never arrived, so I spent Christmas Eve rushing round the shops buying replacements. Then on Christmas morning we went upstairs to have a drink with Danny and Randall—to find Danny sitting in the silk robe I'd bought for Elinor, eating the chocolates that were meant for Samantha at work.

"Hey, what was I supposed to think?" he says defensively. "It was Christmas, they were gift-wrapped . . . it was like, Yes, Daniel, there *is* a Santa Claus—" He reaches for the Martini bottle and sloshes it into the cocktail shaker. "Strong? Extra strong?"

"Danny, I *really* have to make this phone call. I'll be back in a minute."

I unplug the phone and take it into the bedroom, then close the door and try to focus my thoughts again.

Right. I can do this. Calm and collected. I dial our home number and wait with slight dread as the ringing tone sounds.

"Hello?" comes a tinny-sounding voice.

"Hello?" I reply puzzledly. Even allowing for long distance, that's not Mum's voice.

"Becky! It's Janice! How are you, love?"

This is bizarre. Did I dial next-door's number by mistake?

"I'm . . . fine."

"Oh, good! Now, while you're on the phone, which do you prefer, Evian or Vittel?"

"Vittel," I say automatically. "Janice—"

"Lovely. And for sparkling water? It's only that a lot of people drink water these days, you know, what with being healthy . . . What do you think of Perrier?"

"I . . . I don't know. Janice—" I take a deep breath. "Is Mum there?"

"Didn't you know, love? Your parents have gone away! To the Lake District."

I feel a plunge of frustration. How can I have forgotten about their trip to the Lake District?

"I've just popped in to see to the plants. If it's an emergency I can look up the number they left—"

"No, it's . . . it's OK."

My frustration has started to subside. Instead I'm feeing a tiny secret relief. This kind of lets me off the hook for the moment. I mean, it's not my fault if they're away, is it?

"Are you sure?" says Janice. "If it's important, I can easily get the number . . ."

"No, honestly, it's fine! Nothing important," I hear myself saying. "Well, lovely to speak to you . . . bye then!" I thrust down the receiver, trembling slightly.

It's only for a few more days. It won't make any difference either way.

I walk back into the living room to find Danny reclining on the sofa, flipping channels.

"All OK?" he says, lifting his head.

"Fine," I say. "Let's have that drink."

"In the shaker," he says, nodding his head toward the cabinet, just as the front door opens.

"Hi!" I call. "Luke, is that you? You're just in time for a—"

I stop abruptly as Luke enters the room and stare at him in dismay. His face is pale and hollow, his eyes even darker than usual. I've never seen him look like this before.

Danny and I glance at each other and I feel my heart plunge in dread.

"Luke!" I gulp. "Are you OK?"

"I've been trying to call for an hour," he says. "You weren't at work, the line here was busy . . ."

"I was probably on my way home. And then I had to make a call." Anxiously I take a step toward him. "What's happened, Luke? Is it work?"

"It's Michael," says Luke. "I've just heard. He's had a heart attack."

Ten

MICHAEL'S ROOM IS on the fourth floor of the George Washington University Hospital. We walk along the corridors in silence, both staring straight ahead. We arrived in Washington last night. Our hotel bed was very big and comfortable, but even so, neither of us slept very well. In fact, I'm not sure Luke slept at all. He hasn't said much, but I know he's feeling eaten up with guilt.

"He could have died," he said last night, as we were both lying awake in the darkness.

"But he didn't," I replied, and reached for his hand.

"But he could have."

And when you think about it, it's true. He could have. Every time I think about it I feel a horrible lurch in my tummy. I've never before known anyone close to me to be ill. I mean, there was my great-aunt Muriel, who had something wrong with her kidneys—but I only met her about twice. And all my grandparents are still alive except Grandpa Bloomwood, who died when I was two, so I never even knew him.

In fact, I've hardly ever been into a hospital before, unless you count *ER* and *Terms of Endearment.* As we walk along, past scary signs like "Oncology" and "Renal Unit," I realize yet again how sheltered my life has been.

We arrive at room 465 and Luke stops.

"This is it," he says. "Ready?" He knocks gently and, after a moment, pushes the door open.

Michael is lying asleep in a big clanky metal bed, with about six huge flower arrangements on the table next to him and more around the room. There's a drip attached to his hand and another tube going from his chest to some machine with little lights. His face is pale and drawn and he looks . . . vulnerable.

I don't like this. I've never seen Michael in anything other than an expensive suit, holding an expensive drink. Big and reassuring and indestructible. Not lying in a bed in a hospital gown.

I glance at Luke and he's staring at Michael, pale-faced. He looks like he wants to cry.

Oh God. Now *I* want to cry.

Then Michael opens his eyes, and I feel a swoosh of relief. His eyes, at least, are exactly the same. The same warmth. The same flash of humor.

"Now, you didn't have to come all this way," he says. His voice sounds dry and even more gravelly than usual.

"Michael," says Luke, taking an eager step forward. "How are you feeling?"

"Better. Better than I was feeling." Michael's eyes run quizzically over Luke. "How are *you* feeling? You look terrible."

"I feel terrible," says Luke. "I feel absolutely . . ." He breaks off and swallows.

"Really?" says Michael. "Maybe you should have some tests run. It's a very reassuring process. I now know that I have angina. On the other hand, my lymph is fine and I'm not allergic to peanuts." His eyes rest on the fruit basket in Luke's hand. "Is that for me?"

"Yes!" says Luke, seeming to come to. "Just a little . . . Shall I put it here?"

He clears a space among the exotic flower arrangements, and as he does so I notice one of the attached cards has a White House heading. Gosh.

"Fruit," says Michael, nodding. "Very thoughtful. You've been talking to my doctor. They're extremely strict here. Visitors who bring candy are marched to a little room and forced to jog for ten minutes."

"Michael . . ." Luke takes a deep breath, and I can see his hands gripping the handle of the fruit basket. "Michael, I just wanted to say . . . I'm sorry. About our argument."

"It's forgotten. Really."

"It's not. Not by me."

"Luke." Michael gives Luke a kind look. "It's not a big deal."

"But I just feel—"

"We had a disagreement, that's all. Since then I've been thinking about what you said. You do have a point. If Brandon Communications is publicly associated with a worthy cause, it can only do the company profile good."

"I should never have acted without consulting you," mutters Luke.

"Well. As you said, it's your company. You have executive control. I respect that."

"And I respect your advice," says Luke at once. "I always will."

"So. Shall we agree to bury the hatchet?" Michael extends his hand, all bruised from where the drip needle goes into it—and after a moment, Luke gently takes it.

Now I'm completely choked.

"I'll just get some . . . water . . ." I mumble, and back out of the room, breathing hard.

I *can't* burst into tears in front of Michael. He'll think I'm completely pathetic.

Or else he'll think I'm crying because I know something he doesn't. He'll think we've seen his medical charts and it wasn't angina at all. It was a brain clot that is inoperable except by a specialist from Chicago who's turned down Michael's case because of an old feud between the hospitals . . .

OK, look, I *must* stop confusing this with *ER*.

I walk to a nearby reception area, taking deep breaths to calm myself down, and sit down next to a middle-aged woman. There are people sitting on upholstered seats and a couple of patients in wheelchairs with drips, and I see a frail old woman greeting what must be her grandchildren. As she sees them, her whole face lights up and suddenly she looks ten years younger—and to my horror I find myself sniffing again.

"Are you all right?" I look up and see the middle-aged woman offering me a tissue. She smiles—but her eyes are red-rimmed. "It gets to you, doesn't it?" she says as I blow my nose. "Is a relation of yours in here?"

"Just a friend. How about you?"

"My husband, Ken," says the woman. "He's had bypass surgery. He's doing fine, though." She gives a half-smile. "He hates to see me upset."

"God. I'm . . . really sorry."

I feel a shiver go down my back as I try to imagine how I'd be feeling if it were Luke in that hospital bed.

"He should be be OK, if he starts looking after himself. These men. They take it all for granted." She shakes her head. "But coming in here . . . it teaches you what's important, doesn't it?"

"Absolutely," I say fervently.

We sit quietly for a while, and I think anxiously about Luke. Maybe I'll get him to start going to the gym a bit more. And eating that low-fat spread stuff that lowers your cholesterol. Just to be on the safe side.

"I should go back," says the woman, looking at her watch. She smiles at me. "Good to meet you."

"You too." I watch as she walks off down the corridor, then stand up and head back to Michael's room, shaking back my hair and putting on a cheerful expression. No more dissolving into tears.

"Hi!" says Luke as I enter. He's sitting on a chair by Michael's bed, and the atmosphere is a lot more relaxed, thank goodness.

"I was just telling Luke," says Michael as I sit down. "My daughter's on at me to retire. Or at least downscale. Move to New York."

"Really? Ooh, yes, do! We'd love that."

"It's a good idea," says Luke. "Bearing in mind you currently do about six full-time jobs."

"I really like your daughter," I say enthusiastically. "We had such fun when she came into Barneys. How's her new job going?"

Michael's daughter is an attorney who specializes in patent law, and just exudes extreme cleverness. On the other hand, she hadn't spotted that she was choosing colors that did nothing for her skin tone until I pointed it out to her.

"Very well indeed, thanks. She just moved to Finerman Wallstein," Michael adds to Luke. "Very swanky offices."

"I know them," says Luke. "I use them for personal matters. In fact, last time I went in there was a few weeks ago. Just about my will. Next time, I'll call in on her."

"Do that," says Michael. "She'd like it."

"Have you made a will, Luke?" I say with interest.

"Of course I've made a will." Luke stares at me. "Haven't you?"

"No," I say—then look from Luke to Michael. "What? What is it?"

"Everyone should make a will," says Michael gravely.

"It never even *occurred* to me you might not have made one," says Luke, shaking his head.

"It never even occurred to me to make one!" I say defensively. "I mean, I'm only twenty-seven."

"I'll make an appointment with my lawyer," says Luke. "We need to sort this out."

"Well. OK. But honestly . . ." I give a little shrug. Then a thought occurs to me. "So, who have you left everything to?"

"You," says Luke. "Minus the odd little bequest."

"Me?" I gape at him. "Really? Me?"

"It is customary for husbands to leave their property to their wives," he says with a small smile. "Or do you object?"

"No! Of course not! I just . . . kind of . . . didn't expect it."

I feel a strange glow of pleasure inside me. Luke's leaving everything to me!

I don't know why that should be a surprise. I mean, we live together. We're getting married. It's obvious. But still, I can't help feeling a bit proud.

"Do I take it you're not planning to leave anything to me?" inquires Luke mildly.

"Of course!" I exclaim. "I mean—of course I will!"

"No pressure," says Luke, grinning at Michael.

"I will!" I say, growing flustered. "I just hadn't really thought about it!"

To cover my confusion I reach for a pear and start munching it. Come to think of it, why *have* I never made a will?

I suppose because I've never really thought I'll die. But I could easily, couldn't I? I mean, our train could crash on the way back to New York. Or an ax murderer could break into our apartment . . .

And who would get all my stuff?

Luke's right. This is an emergency.

"Becky? Are you OK?" I look up to see Luke putting on his coat. "We must go."

"Thanks for coming," says Michael, and squeezes my hand as I bend to kiss him. "I really appreciate it."

"And I'll be in touch about the wedding," says Luke, and smiles at Michael. "No skiving your best-man duties."

"Absolutely not!" says Michael. "But that reminds me, I got a little confused at the engagement party, talking to different people. Are you two getting married in New York or England?"

"New York," says Luke, frowning in slight puzzlement. "That has been finally decided, hasn't it, Becky? I never even asked how your mother took the news."

"I . . . um . . ." I play for time, wrapping my scarf around my neck.

I can't admit the truth. I can't admit that Mum still doesn't know about the Plaza.

Not here. Not now.

"Yes!" I say, feeling my cheeks flame. "Yes, she was fine. New York it is!"

As we get onto the train, Luke looks pale and drained. I think it upset him more than he's letting on, seeing Michael looking so helpless. He sits staring out of the darkening window, and I try to think of something that will cheer him up.

"Look!" I say at last. I reach into my bag and take out a book I bought just the other day called *The Promise of Your Life.* "We need to talk about composing our wedding vows."

"Composing them?" Luke frowns. "Aren't they always the same?"

"No! That's old hat. Everyone writes their own these days. Listen to this. 'Your wedding vows are the chance for you to show the world what you mean to each other. Together with the proclamation by the officiant that you are now married, they are the linchpin of the entire ceremony. They should be the most beautiful and moving words spoken at your wedding.' "

I look up expectantly at Luke, but he's gazing out of the window again.

"It says in this book, we must think about what sort of couple we are," I press on. "Are we Young Lovers or Autumn Companions?"

Luke isn't even listening. Perhaps I should find a few specific examples. My eye falls on a page marked Summertime Wedding, which would be quite appropriate.

"'*As the roses bloom in summertime, so did my love bloom for you. As the white clouds soar above, so does my love soar,*'" I read aloud.

I pull a face. Maybe not. I flick through a few more pages, glancing down as I go.

You helped me through the pain of rehab . . .
Though you are incarcerated for murder, our love will shine like a beacon . . .

"Ooh, look," I say suddenly. "This is for high school sweethearts. *'Our eyes met in a math class. How were we to know that trigonometry would lead to matrimony?'* "

"Our eyes met across a crowded press conference," says Luke. "How were we to know love would blossom as I announced an exciting new range of unit trusts investing in European growth companies with tracking facility, fixed-rate costs, and discounted premiums throughout the first accounting period?"

"Luke—"

Well, OK. Maybe this isn't the time for vows. I shut the book and look anxiously at Luke. "Are you all right?"

"I'm fine."

"Are you worried about Michael?" I reach for his hand. "Because honestly, I'm sure he's going to be fine. You heard what he said. It was just a wake-up call."

There's silence for a while—then Luke turns his head.

"While you were going to the rest room," he says slowly, "I met the parents of the guy in the room next to Michael's. He had a heart attack last week. Do you know how old he is?"

"How old?" I say apprehensively.

"Thirty-three."

"God, really? That's awful!"

Luke's only a year older than that.

"He's a bond trader, apparently. Very successful." He exhales slowly. "It makes you think, doesn't it? Think about what you're doing with your life. And wonder."

"Er . . . yes," I say, feeling as though I'm walking across eggshells. "Yes, it does."

Luke's never spoken like this before. Usually if I start conversations about life and what it all means—which, OK, I don't do very often—he either brushes me off or turns it into a joke. He certainly never confesses to doubting what he's doing with his life. I really want to encourage him—but I'm worried I might say the wrong thing and put him off.

Now he's staring silently out of the window again.

"What exactly were you thinking?" I prompt gently.

"I don't know," says Luke after a pause. "I suppose it just makes you see things differently for a moment."

He looks at me—and just for an instant I think I can see deep inside him, to a part of him I rarely have access to. Softer and quieter and full of doubts like everyone else.

Then he blinks—and it's as though he's closed the camera shutter. Back into normal mode. Businesslike. Sure of himself.

"Anyway. I'm glad Michael and I were able to make up," he says, taking a sip from the water bottle he's carrying.

"Me too."

"He saw my point of view in the end. The publicity that we'll get through the foundation will benefit the company enormously. The fact that it's my mother's charity is largely irrelevant."

"Yes," I say reluctantly. "I suppose so."

I really don't want to get into a conversation about Luke's mother right now, so I open the vows book again.

"Hey, here's one in rhyme . . ."

As we arrive back at Penn Station, it's crowded with people. Luke heads off to a rest room, and I head to a kiosk to buy a candy bar. I walk straight past a stand of newspapers—then stop. Hang on a minute. What was that?

I retrace my steps and stare at the *New York Post.* Right at the top, flagging an inside feature, is a little picture of Elinor.

I grab the paper and turn quickly to the inside page.

There's a headline, "How to Fight Charity Fatigue." Then there's a picture of Elinor with a frosty smile, standing on the steps of some big building and handing over a check to some man in a suit. My eyes run puzzledly over the caption. *Elinor Sherman has battled against apathy to raise money for a cause she believes in.*

Wasn't the photo opportunity supposed to be for Luke?

I scan the piece quickly, searching for any mention of Brandon Communications. For any mention of Luke. But I get to the end of the page—and his name hasn't appeared once. It's as though he doesn't figure at all.

I stare down at the page in disbelief.

After everything he's done for her. *How* can she treat him like this?

"What's that?"

I give a startled jump at Luke's voice. For an instant I consider hiding the paper under my coat. But then, there's no point, is there? He'll see it sooner or later.

"Luke . . ." I hesitate—then swivel the page so he can see it.

"Is that my mother?" Luke looks astounded. "She never told me anything was set up. Let me have a look."

"Luke . . ." I take a deep breath. "It doesn't mention you anywhere. Or the company."

I wince as I see him scanning the page; as I watch the sheer disbelief growing on his face. It's been a hard enough day already, without discovering that his mother has completely screwed him.

"Didn't she even tell you she was doing the interview?"

Luke doesn't reply. He takes out his mobile, jabs in a number, and waits for a few moments. Then he makes a noise of frustration. "I forgot. She's gone back to Switzerland."

I'd forgotten that too. She's gone to "visit her friends" again, in time for the wedding. This time she's staying for two whole months, which means she's having the full works. She must have done the interview just before she left.

I try to take Luke's hand, but he doesn't respond. God knows what he's thinking.

"Luke . . . maybe there's some explanation—"

"Let's forget it."

"But—"

"Just forget it." There's an edge to his voice that makes me flinch. "It's been a long, difficult day. Let's just get home."

THE LAST WILL AND TESTAMENT OF Rebecca Bloomwood

I, REBECCA JANE BLOOMWOOD, do make, publish, and declare this to be my Last Will and Testament.

FIRST: I hereby revoke all former Wills and Codicils by me made.

SECOND: (a) I give and bequeath to SUSAN CLEATH-STUART my collection of shoes, all my jeans, my tan leather coat, all my makeup except the Chanel lipstick, my leather floor cube, my red Kate Spade handbag,[1] my silver ring with the moonstone, and my painting of two elephants.

(b) I give and bequeath to my mother JANE BLOOMWOOD all my remaining handbags, my Chanel lipstick, all my jewelry, my Barneys white cotton duvet set, my waffle-weave dressing gown, my suede cushions, my Venetian glass vase, my collection of jam spoons, and my Tiffany watch.[2]

(c) I give and bequeath to my father GRAHAM BLOOMWOOD my chess set, my CDs of classical music that he gave me for Christmas, my Bill Amberg weekend bag, my titanium desk lamp, and the incomplete manuscript of my self-help book *Manage Money the Bloomwood Way,* all rights of which are hereby passed to him.

(d) I give and bequeath to my friend DANNY KOVITZ all my old copies of *British Vogue,*[3] my lava lamp, my customized denim jacket, and my juicer.

(e) I give and bequeath to my friend ERIN GAYLER my Tse cashmere jumper, my Donna Karan evening dress, all my Betsey Johnson dresses, and my Louis Vuitton hair bobbles.

THIRD: I bequeath all the rest, residue, and remainder of my property of whatsoever kind or character and wheresoever situated, apart from any clothes found in carrier bags at the bottom of the wardrobe,[4] to LUKE JAMES BRANDON.

1. Unless she would prefer the new DKNY bag with the long straps.
2. Also my Tiffany keyring, which I have lost, but must be in the apartment somewhere.
3. Plus any other magazines I subsequently buy.
4. Which are to be disposed of discreetly, in secret.

Eleven

THIS IS NOT a good time.

In fact, it's horrendous. Ever since he saw that piece in the paper, Luke has been really withdrawn and silent. He won't talk about it, and the atmosphere in the apartment is getting really tense, and I just don't know how to make things better. A few days ago I tried buying some soothing scented candles, but they didn't really smell of anything except candle wax. So then yesterday I tried rearranging the furniture to make it more feng shui and harmonious. But Luke came into the living room just as I'd jammed a sofa leg into the DVD player, and I don't think he was very impressed.

I wish he'd open up to me, like they do on *Dawson's Creek*. But whenever I say, "Do you want to talk?" and pat the sofa invitingly, instead of saying, "Yes, Becky, I have some issues I'd like to share," he either ignores me or tells me we've run out of coffee.

I know he's tried calling his mother, but the patients at her stupid Swiss clinic aren't allowed mobile phones, so he hasn't been able to speak to her. I also know that he's been on the phone to Michael several times. And that the assistant who had been assigned to work for the Elinor Sherman Foundation is now back working for Brandon Communications. When I asked him about it, though, he just shut off and wouldn't say anything. It's as though he can't bring himself to admit any of it has happened.

The only thing that is going at all well at the moment is the wedding preparations. Robyn and I have had several meetings with the event designer, whose ideas for the room are absolutely spectacular. Then we had the dessert tasting at the Plaza the other day, and I nearly swooned at all the amazing, out-of-this-world sweets there were to choose from. It was champagne all the way through, and deferential waiters, and I was treated exactly like a princess . . .

But if I'm really honest, even that didn't feel quite as relaxed and wonderful as it should. Even while I was sitting there, being served poached white peaches with pistachio mousse and anise biscotti on a gilded plate, I couldn't help feeling little pricks of guilt through the pleasure, like tiny pinpoints of light through a blanket.

I think I'll feel a lot better when I've broken the news to Mum.

I mean, not that there's any reason to feel bad. Because I couldn't do anything about it while they were in the Lake District, could I? I wasn't exactly going to interrupt their nice relaxing holiday. But they get back tomorrow. So then what I'll do is very calmly phone up Mum, and tell her that I really appreciate everything she's done, and it doesn't mean I'm not grateful, but that I've decided . . .

No. That *Luke* and I have decided . . .

No. That Elinor has very kindly offered . . . That we have decided to accept . . .

Oh God. My insides are churning, just thinking about it.

OK, I won't think about it yet. Anyway, I don't want to come out with some stilted, awkward speech. Much better just to wait until the moment and be spontaneous.

As I arrive at Barneys, Christina is sorting through a rack of evening jackets.

"Hi!" she says as I walk in. "Did you sign those letters for me?"

"What?" I say distractedly. "Oh, sorry. I forgot. I'll do it today."

"Becky?" Christina looks at me more closely. "Are you all right?"

"I'm fine! I'm just . . . I don't know, the wedding . . ."

"I saw India from the bridal atelier last night. She said you'd reserved a Richard Tyler dress?"

"Oh yes, I have."

"But I could have sworn I heard you telling Erin the other day about a dress at Vera Wang."

I look away and fiddle with the zip of my bag. "Well. The thing is, I've kind of reserved more than one dress."

"How many?"

"Four," I say after a pause. I needn't tell her about the one at Kleinfeld.

Christina throws back her head in a laugh. "Becky, you can't wear more than one dress! You're going to have to fix on one in the end, you know."

"I know," I say weakly, and disappear into my fitting room before she can say anything else.

My first client is Laurel, who is here because she's been invited on a corporate weekend, dress "casual," and her idea of casual is a pair of track pants and a Hanes T-shirt.

"You look like shit," she says as soon she walks in. "What's wrong?"

"Nothing!" I smile brightly. "I'm just a bit preoccupied at the moment."

"Are you fighting with your mother?"

My head jerks up.

"No," I say cautiously. "Why do you ask that?"

"It's par for the course," says Laurel, taking off her coat. "All brides fight with their mothers. If it's not over the ceremony, it's over the floral arrangements. I threw a tea strainer at mine because she cut three of my friends off the guest list without asking."

"Really? But then you made up."

"We didn't speak for five years afterward."

"Five years?" I stare at her, aghast. "Just over a wedding?"

"Becky, there's no such thing as *just* a wedding," says Laurel. She picks up a cashmere sweater. "This is nice."

"Mmm," I say distractedly. Oh God, now I'm really worried.

What if I fall out with Mum? What if she gets really offended and says she never wants to see me again? And then Luke and I have children and they never get to know their grandparents. And every Christmas they buy presents for Granny and Grandpa Bloomwood, just in case, but every year they sit under the tree unopened, and we quietly put them away, and one year our little girl says, "Mummy, why does Granny Bloomwood hate us?" and I have to choke back my tears and say, "Darling, she doesn't hate us. She just—"

"Becky? Are you all right?"

I snap into the present, to see Laurel peering at me concernedly. "You know, you really don't look yourself. Maybe you need a break."

"I'm fine! Honestly." I summon up a professional smile. "So . . . here are the skirts I was thinking of. If you try this beige one, with the off-white shirt . . ."

As Laurel tries on different pieces, I sit on a stool, nodding and making the odd absent comment, while my mind still frets on the subject of Mum. I feel like I've got so far into this mess, I've lost all sense of proportion. Will she flip out when I tell her about the Plaza? Won't she? I just can't tell.

I mean, take what happened at Christmas. I thought Mum was going to be devastated when I told her Luke and I weren't coming home, and it took me ages to pluck up the courage to tell her. But to my astonishment, she was really nice about it and told me that she and Dad would have a lovely day with Janice and Martin, and I mustn't worry. So maybe this will be the same. When I explain the whole story to her, she'll say, "Oh darling, don't be silly, of course you must get married wherever you want to."

Or else she'll burst into tears, say how could I deceive her like this, and she'll come to the Plaza over her dead body.

"So I was going into Central Park for my marathon training, and who should I see, standing right there like a Barbie doll?"

Laurel's voice filters into my mind and I look up.

"Not the blond intern?"

"Right! So my heart starts thumping, I'm walking toward her and I'm wondering what I'm going to say. Do I yell at her? Do I hit her? Do I completely ignore her? You know, which will give me most satisfaction? And of course half of me wants to run away and hide . . ."

"So what happened?" I say eagerly.

"When I got up close, it wasn't even her. It was some other girl!" Laurel puts a hand to her head. "It's like, now she's messing with my mind. Not content with taking my husband, wrecking my life, stealing my jewelry . . ."

"She's stolen your jewelry?" I say in surprise. "What do you mean?"

"I must have told you this. No? Things started going missing around the time Bill was taking her back to our apartment. An emerald pendant my grandmother gave me. A couple of bracelets. Of course, I had no idea what was going on, so I thought I was being careless. But then it all came out, and I realized. It had to be her."

"Couldn't you do anything?" I say, appalled.

"Oh, I did. I called the police." Laurel's chin tightens as she buttons up her dress. "They went and asked her some questions, but they didn't get anywhere. Of course they didn't." She gives me a strange little smile. "Then Bill found out. He went crazy. He went to the police and told them . . . well, I don't know exactly what he told them. But that same afternoon the police called me back and said they were dropping the case. It was obvious they thought I was just some vindictive, spurned wife. Which of course I was."

She stares at herself in the mirror and slowly the animation seeps out of her face. "You know, I always thought he would come to his senses," she says quietly. "I thought he'd last a month. Maybe two. Then he'd crawl back, I'd send him away, he'd crawl back again, we'd fight, but eventually . . ." She exhales slowly. "But he's not. He's not coming back."

She meets my eye in the mirror and I feel a sudden pang of outrage. Laurel's the nicest person in the world. Why would her stupid husband leave her?

"I like this dress," she adds, sounding more cheerful. "But maybe in the black."

"I'll go and get one for you," I say. "We have it on this floor."

I walk out of the personal shopping department and head toward the rack of Dries van Noten dresses. It's still early for regular shoppers and the floor is nearly empty. But as I'm searching for another dress in Laurel's size, I'm suddenly aware of a familiar figure in the corner of my vision. I turn, puzzled, but the figure has gone.

Weird. Eventually I find the dress, and pick out a matching fringed stole. I turn around—and there he is again. It's Danny. What on earth is he doing in Barneys? As I get nearer, I stare at him. His eyes are bloodshot, his hair is awry, and he's got a wild, fidgety look.

"Danny!" I say—and he visibly jumps. "What are you doing here?"

"Oh!" he says. "Nothing! Just . . . browsing."

"Are you OK?"

"I'm fine! Everything's fine." He glances at his watch. "So—I guess you're in the middle of something?"

"I am, actually," I say regretfully. "I have a client waiting. Otherwise we could go and have a coffee."

"No. That's fine," he says. "You go. I'll see you later."

"OK," I say, and walk back to my fitting room, rather puzzled.

Laurel decides to take three of the outfits I chose for her, and when she leaves she gives me a big hug. "Don't let the wedding get you down," she says. "You shouldn't listen to me. I have a somewhat jaded view. I know you and Luke will be happy."

"Laurel." I squeeze her tightly back. "You're the best."

God, if I ever meet that stupid husband of hers I'm going to let him have it.

When she's gone, I consult my schedule for the rest of the day. I've got an hour before my next client, so I decide to wander up to the bridal department and look at my dress again. It's definitely between this one and the Vera Wang. Or maybe the Tracy Connop.

Definitely one of those three, anyway.

As I walk out onto the sales floor again, I stop in surprise. There's Danny, standing by a rack of tops, fingering one casually. What on earth is he still doing here? I'm about to call out to him, and say does he want to come and see my dress and then go for a quick cappuccino? But then, to my astonishment, he glances around, surreptitiously bends down, and reaches for something in his canvas bag. It's a T-shirt with glittery sleeves, on a hanger. He shoves it onto the rack, looks around again, and reaches for another one.

I stare at him in utter stupefaction. What does he think he's doing?

He looks around again—then reaches into his bag and pulls out a small laminated sign, which he props up at the end of the display.

What the hell is he up to?

"Danny!" I say, heading toward him.

"What?" He gives a startled jump, then turns and sees me. "Sssh! Jesus, Becky!"

"What are you doing with those T-shirts?" I hiss.

"I'm stocking myself."

"What do you mean, stocking yourself?"

He jerks his head toward the laminated sign and I read it in disbelief.

THE DANNY KOVITZ COLLECTION
AN EXCITING NEW TALENT AT BARNEYS

"They're not all on Barneys hangers," says Danny, thrusting another two T-shirts on the rack. "But I figure that won't matter."

"Danny . . . you can't do this! You can't just . . . put your stuff on the racks!"

"I'm doing it."

"But—"

"I have no choice, OK?" says Danny, turning his head. "Randall's on his way here right now, expecting to see a Danny Kovitz line at Barneys."

I stare at him in horror.

"I thought you said he would never check!"

"He wouldn't have!" Danny shoves another hanger onto the rack. "But his stupid girlfriend has to poke her nose in. She never showed any interest in me before, but as soon as she hears the word Barneys, it's like Oh, Randall, you should support your brother! Go to Barneys tomorrow and buy one of his pieces! So I'm saying, you *really* don't have to do that—but now Randall's got the idea in his head, he's like, well, maybe I will pop in and take a look! So I'm up sewing all fucking night . . ."

"You made all of these last night?" I say incredulously, and reach for one of the T-shirts. A piece of leather braid falls off, onto the floor.

"So maybe the finish isn't quite up to my usual standards," says Danny defensively. "Just don't manhandle them, OK?" He starts to count the hangers. "Two . . . four . . . six . . . eight . . . ten. That should be enough."

"Danny . . ." I glance around the sales floor to see Carla, one of the assistants, giving us an odd look. "Hi!" I call brightly. "Just . . . helping one of my clients . . . for his girlfriend . . ." Carla gives us another suspicious look, then moves away. "This isn't going to work!" I mutter as soon as she's out of earshot. "You're going to have to take these down. You wouldn't even be stocked on this floor!"

"I need two minutes," he says. "That's all. Two minutes for him to come in, see the sign, then go. Come on, Becky. No one's even going to . . ." He freezes. "Here he is."

I follow his gaze and see Danny's brother Randall walking across the floor toward us.

For the millionth time I wonder how on earth Randall and Danny can have come from the same parents. While Danny is wiry and constantly on the move, Randall fills his double-breasted suit comfortably, and always wears the same disapproving frown.

"Hello, Daniel," he says, and nods to me. "Becky."

"Hi, Randall," I say, and give what I hope is a natural smile. "How are you?"

"So here they are!" says Danny triumphantly, moving away from the rack and gesturing to the T-shirts. "My collection. In Barneys. Just like I said."

"So I see," says Randall, and carefully scrutinizes the rack of clothes. I feel sure he's about to look up and say, "What on earth are you playing at?" But he says nothing—and with a slight dart of shock I realize that he's been completely taken in.

There again, why is that such a surprise? Danny's clothes don't look so out of place, up there on the rack.

"Well, congratulations," says Randall at last. "This is quite an achievement." He pats Danny awkwardly on the shoulder, then turns to me. "Are they selling well?"

"Er . . . yes!" I say. "Very popular, I believe."

"So, for how much do they retail?" He reaches for a T-shirt, and both Danny and I involuntarily draw breath. We watch, frozen, while he searches for the label, then looks up with a deep frown. "These have no price tags."

"That's because . . . they're only just out," I hear myself saying hurriedly. "But I think they're priced at . . . erm . . . eighty-nine dollars."

"I see." Randall shakes his head. "Well, I never was one for high fashion—"

"Telling me," Danny whispers in my ear.

"But if they're selling, they must have something. Daniel, I take my hat off to you." He reaches for another one, with rivets round the neck, and looks at it with a fastidious dismay. "Now, which one shall I buy?"

"Don't buy one!" says Danny at once. "I'll . . . make you one. As a gift."

"I insist," says Randall. "If I can't support my own brother—"

"Randall, please." Danny's voice crackles with sincerity. "Allow me to make a gift to you. It's the least I can do after all your kindness to me over the years. Really."

"Well, if you're sure," says Randall at last, with a shrug. He looks at his watch. "I must go. Good to see you, Becky."

"I'll walk to the elevator with you," says Danny, and darts me a jubilant look.

As they walk away, I feel a giggle of relief rising in me. I can't quite believe we got away with it so easily.

"Hey!" comes a voice behind me suddenly. "Look at these! They're new, aren't they?" A manicured hand appears over my shoulder and plucks one of Danny's T-shirts off the rail before I can stop it. My head whips round and I feel a plunge of dismay. It's Lisa Farley, a sweet but completely dippy client of Erin's. She's about twenty-two, doesn't seem to have a job, and always says whatever pops into her head, never mind whether someone might be offended. (She once asked Erin in all innocence, "Doesn't it bother you, having such a weird-shaped mouth?")

Now she's holding the T-shirt up against her, looking down at it appraisingly.

Damn it. I should have whipped them down off the rack straight away.

"Hi, Becky!" she says cheerily. "Hey, this is cute! I haven't seen these before."

"Actually," I say quickly, "these aren't for sale yet. In fact, I need to . . . um . . . take them back to the stock room." I try to grab for the T-shirt, but she moves away.

"I'll just take a look in the mirror. Hey, Tracy! What do you think?"

Another girl, wearing the new Dior print jacket, is coming toward us.

"Of what?"

"These new T-shirts. They're cool, aren't they?" She reaches for another one and hands it to Tracy.

"If you could just give them back to me—" I say helplessly.

"This one's nice!"

Now they're both searching through the hangers with brisk

fingers, and the poor T-shirts just can't take the strain. Hems are unraveling, bits of glitter and strings of diamante are coming loose, and sequins are shedding all over the floor.

"Oops, this seam just came apart." Lisa looks up in dismay. "Becky, it just fell apart. I didn't pull it."

"That's OK," I say weakly.

"Is everything supposed to fall off like this? Hey, Christina!" Lisa suddenly calls out. "This new line is so fun!"

Christina?

I wheel round and feel a lurch of horror. Christina is standing at the entrance to the personal shopping department, in conversation with the head of personnel.

"What new line?" she says, looking up. "Oh, hi, Becky."

Shit. I have to stop this right now.

"Lisa—" I say desperately. "Come and see the new Marc Jacobs coats we've got in!"

Lisa ignores me.

"This new . . . what's it called . . ." She squints at the label. "Danny Kovitz! I can't believe Erin didn't tell me these were coming in! Naughty naughty!" She wags a finger in mock reproach.

I watch in dismay as Christina looks up, alert. There's nothing to galvanize her like someone suggesting her department is less than perfect.

"Excuse me a minute," she says to the head of personnel, and comes across the floor toward us, her dark hair gleaming under the lights.

"What didn't Erin tell you about?" she says pleasantly.

"This new designer!" says Lisa. "I never even heard of him before."

"Ow!" says Tracy suddenly, and draws her hand away from the T-shirt. "That was a pin!"

"A pin?" echoes Christina. "Give me that!"

She takes the ragged T-shirt and stares at it bewilderedly. Then she catches sight of Danny's laminated sign.

Oh, I'm so *stupid.* Why didn't I take that down, at least?

As she reads it, her expression changes. She looks up and meets my eye, and I feel my whole body prickle with fear. I've never been in trouble with Christina before. But I've heard her telling people off over the phone, and I know she can be pretty fierce.

"Do you know anything about this, Becky?" she asks pleasantly.

"I . . ." I clear my throat. "The thing is . . ."

"I see. Lisa, I'm afraid there's been a little confusion." She gives Lisa a professional smile. "These items are not for sale. Becky—I think I'd better see you in my office."

"Christina, I'm . . . sorry," I say, feeling my face flush beetroot. "I really am . . ."

"What happened?" says Tracy. "Why aren't they for sale?"

"Is Becky in trouble?" says Lisa in dismay. "Will she get fired? Don't fire Becky! We like her better than Erin . . . Oh." She claps her hand over her mouth. "Sorry, Erin. I didn't see you there."

"That's all right," says Erin, giving a rather pinched smile.

"Christina, all I can do is apologize," I say humbly. "I never meant to cause any trouble. I never meant to mislead the customers . . ."

"In my office," says Christina, lifting a hand to stop me. "If you have anything to say, Becky, then you can say it—"

"Stop!" comes a melodramatic voice behind us, and we all whip round, to see Danny heading toward us, his eyes even wilder than usual. "Just stop right there! Don't blame Becky for this!" he says, placing himself in front of me. "She had nothing to do with it. If you're going to fire anyone—fire me!"

"Danny, she can't fire you," I mutter. "You're not employed by Barneys."

"And you would be?" inquires Christina.

"Danny Kovitz."

"Danny Kovitz. Ah." Light dawns on Christina's face. "So it was you who . . . assembled these garments. And planted them on our racks."

"What? He's not a real designer?" says Tracy in horror. "I knew it! *I* wasn't fooled." She thrusts the hanger she's holding back onto the rack as though she's been contaminated.

"Isn't that breaking the law?" says Lisa, wide-eyed.

"It may well be," says Danny defensively. "But shall I tell you why I'm reduced to criminal measures? Do you know the impossibility of getting a break in this so-called business of fashion?" He glances around to make sure his audience is listening. "I put every ounce of my life-force into my work. I weep, I cry out in pain, I squeeze myself dry of creative blood. But the fashion establishment isn't interested in new talent! They aren't interested in nurturing the newcomer who dares to be a little different!" His voice rises impassionedly. "If I have to take desperate measures, can you blame me? If you cut me, do I not bleed?"

"Wow," breathes Lisa. "I had no idea it was so tough out there."

"You did cut me," puts in Tracy, who looks far less impressed by Danny's speech. "With your stupid pin."

"Christina, you have to give him a chance!" exclaims Lisa. "Look! He's so dedicated!"

"I just want to bring my ideas to people who will love them," begins Danny again. "My only desire is that someone, someday, will wear one of my garments and feel themselves transformed. But as I crawl toward them on my hands and knees, the doors keep being slammed in my face—"

"Enough already!" says Christina, half exasperated, half amused. "You want your big break? Let me have a look at these clothes."

There's a sudden intrigued quiet. I glance quickly at Danny. Perhaps this is going to be it! Christina will spot his genius and Barneys will buy his entire collection and he'll be made! Then Gwyneth Paltrow will wear one of his T-shirts on Leno, and there'll be a rush for them, and suddenly he'll be famous and have his own boutique!

Christina reaches for a T-shirt with spattered dye and rhinestones on the front, and as she runs her eye up and down it, I hold my breath. Lisa and Tracy raise their eyebrows at each other, and although Danny is motionless, I can see his face tightening with hope. There's dead silence as she puts it down—and as she reaches for a second T-shirt we all give an intake of breath, as though the Russian judge's hand has hovered over the perfect six scorecard. With a critical frown, she stretches it out to look at it properly . . . and as she does so, one of the sleeves comes off in her hand, leaving a ragged seam behind.

Everyone stares at it speechlessly.

"That's the look," says Danny, a little too late. "It's a . . . a deconstructive approach to design . . ."

Christina is shaking her head and putting the T-shirt back. "Young man. You certainly have flair. You may even have talent. Unfortunately these are not enough. Until you can finish off your work properly, you're not going to get very far."

"My designs are usually immaculately finished!" says Danny at once. "Perhaps this particular collection was a little hurried . . ."

"I suggest you go back to the beginning, make a few pieces, very carefully . . ."

"Are you saying I'm careless?"

"I'm saying you need to learn how to follow a project through to the end." Christina smiles kindly at him. "Then we'll see."

"I can follow a project through!" says Danny indignantly. "It's one of my strengths! It's one of my— Would I be making Becky's wedding dress otherwise?" He grabs me, as though we're about to sing a duet. "The most important outfit of her whole life? She believes in me, even if nobody else does. When Becky Bloomwood walks down the aisle at the Plaza Hotel in a Danny Kovitz creation, you won't be calling me careless then. And when the phones start ringing off their hooks—"

"What?" I say stupidly. "Danny—"

"You're making Becky's wedding dress?" Christina turns to me. "I thought you were wearing Richard Tyler."

"Richard Tyler?" echoes Danny blankly.

"I thought you were wearing Vera Wang," says Erin, who wandered over to the little scene two minutes ago and has been staring agog ever since.

"I heard you were wearing your mother's dress," chips in Lisa.

"*I'm* making your dress!" says Danny, his eyes wide with shock. "Aren't I? You promised me, Becky! We had an agreement!"

"The Vera Wang sounds perfect," says Erin. "You have to have that."

"I'd go for Richard Tyler," says Tracy.

"What about the dress your mother was married in, though?" says Lisa. "Wouldn't that be so romantic?"

"The Vera Wang would be divine," says Erin determinedly.

"But how can you pass up your own mother's wedding dress?" demands Lisa. "How can you set aside a whole family tradition like that? Becky, don't you agree?"

"The point is to look good!" says Erin.

"The point is to be romantic!" retorts Lisa.

"But what about my dress?" comes Danny's plaintive voice. "What about loyalty to your best friend? What about that, Becky?"

Their voices seem to be drilling into my head, and they're all staring at me avidly, waiting for an answer . . . and with no warning I feel myself snap.

"I don't know, OK?" I cry desperately. "I just . . . don't know what I'm going to do!"

Suddenly I feel almost tearful—which is completely ridiculous. I mean, it's not like I won't *have* a dress.

"Becky, I think we need to have a little chat," says Christina, giving me a shrewd look. "Erin, clear all this up, please, and apologize to Carla, would you? Becky, come with me."

We go into Christina's smart beige suede office and she closes the door. She turns round—and for an awful moment I think she's going to yell at me. But instead she gestures for me to sit down and gives me a long, penetrating look through her tortoiseshell glasses.

"How are you, Becky?"

"I'm fine!"

"You're fine. I see." Christina gives a skeptical nod. "What's going on in your life at the moment?"

"Nothing much," I say brightly. "You know! Same old same old . . ."

"Wedding plans going all right?"

"Yes!" I say at once. "Yes! Absolutely no problems there."

"I see." Christina is silent for a moment, tapping her teeth with a pen. "You visited a friend in the hospital recently. Who was that?"

"Oh, yes. That was . . . a friend of Luke's, actually. Michael. He had a heart attack."

"That must have been a shock for you."

For a moment I'm silent.

"Well . . . yes, I suppose it was," I say at last, running a finger along the arm of my chair. "Especially for Luke. The two of them have always been really close, but they'd had a falling out, and Luke was already feeling really guilty. Then we got the call about Michael—I mean, if he'd died, Luke never would have been able to . . ." I break off and rub my face, feeling emotion rising. "And then of course, there's all this tension between Luke and his mother at the moment, which doesn't help. She completely used him. In fact, she more than used him, she abused him. He feels utterly betrayed by her. But he won't talk to me about it." My voice starts to tremble. "He won't talk to me about anything at the moment. Not the wedding, not the honeymoon . . . Not even where we're going to live! We're being chucked out of our apartment, and we haven't found anywhere else to go yet, and I don't know when we're even going to start looking . . ."

To my astonishment a tear starts trickling down the side of my nose. Where did that come from?

"But you're fine, apart from that," says Christina.

"Oh, yes!" I brush at my face. "Apart from that, everything's great!"

"Becky!" Christina shakes her head. "This is no good. I want you to take some vacation days. You're due some, anyway."

"I don't need a vacation!"

"I'd noticed you've been tense recently, but I had no idea it was this bad. It was only when Laurel talked to me this morning—"

"Laurel?" I say, taken aback.

"She's worried too. She told me she thought you'd lost your sparkle. Even Erin has noticed it. She says she told you about a Kate Spade sample sale yesterday, and you barely looked up. This is not the Becky I hired."

"Are you firing me?" I say dolefully.

"I'm not firing you! I'm *worried* about you. Becky, that's some combination of events you just told me about. Your friend . . . and Luke . . . and your apartment . . ."

She reaches for a bottle of mineral water, pours out two glasses, and hands one to me. "And that's not all. Is it, Becky?"

"What do you mean?" I say apprehensively.

"I think there's another complication you're not telling me about. To do with the wedding." She meets my eyes. "Am I right?"

Oh my God.

How did she find out? I've been so careful, I've been so—

"Am I right?" repeats Christina gently.

For a few more moments I'm completely motionless. Then, very slowly I nod.

It's almost a relief to think that the secret's out.

"How did you find out?" I say, sinking back into my chair.

"Laurel told me."

"*Laurel?*" A fresh shock runs through me. "But I never—"

"She said it was obvious. Plus you let a few little things slip out . . . You know, keeping a secret is never as easy as you might think."

"I just . . . can't believe you know. I haven't dared tell anybody!" I push my hair back off my hot face. "God knows what you think of me now."

"Nobody thinks any the worse of you," says Christina. "Really."

"I never meant things to get this far."

"Of course you didn't! Don't blame yourself."

"But it's all my fault!"

"No it's not. It's perfectly normal."

"*Normal?*"

"Yes! All brides argue with their mothers over the wedding. You're not the only one, Becky!"

I stare at her confusedly. What did she just say?

"I can understand the strain it's been putting you under." Christina looks at me sympathetically. "Especially if you and your mother have always been close in the past?"

Christina thinks . . .

Suddenly I realize she's waiting for an answer.

"Er . . . yes!" I gulp. "It has been . . . rather difficult."

Christina nods, as though I've confirmed every suspicion she had. "Becky, I don't often give you advice, do I?"

"Well . . . no."

"But I want you to listen to me on this. I want you to remember, this is your wedding. Not your mother's. It's yours and Luke's, and you only get one shot. So do it the way *you* want to. Believe me, if you don't, you'll regret it."

"Mmm. The thing is . . ." I swallow. "It's not *quite* that simple—"

"It is that simple. It's exactly that simple. Becky, it's your wedding. *It's your wedding.*"

Her voice is clear and emphatic and I stare at her, glass halfway to my lips, feeling as though a shaft of light is cutting through the cloud.

It's my wedding. I've never thought of it like that before.

It's not Mum's wedding. It's not Elinor's wedding. It's mine.

"It's easy to fall into the trap of wanting to please your mother too much," Christina is saying. "It's a natural, generous instinct. But sometimes you have to put yourself first. When I got married—"

"You were married?" I say in surprise. "I didn't know that."

"A long time ago. It didn't work out. Maybe it didn't work out because I hated every moment of the wedding. From the processional music to the vows that my mother insisted on writing." Her hand tenses around a plastic water stirrer. "From the lurid blue cocktails to that tacky, *tacky* dress . . ."

"Really? That's awful!"

"It's water under the bridge now." The water stirrer snaps and she gives me a slightly brittle smile. "But just bear my words in mind. It's your day. Yours and Luke's. Do it the way you want, and don't feel guilty about it. And Becky?"

"Yes?"

"Remember, you and your mother are both adults now. So have an adult conversation." She raises her eyebrows. "You might be surprised at how it turns out."

Christina is so right.

As I make my way home, I can suddenly see everything clearly. My whole approach to the wedding has changed. I feel full of a fresh, clean determination. This is *my* wedding. It's *my* day. And if I want to get married in New York, then that's where I'll get married. If I want to wear a Vera Wang dress, then that's what I'll wear. It's ridiculous to feel guilty about it.

I've been putting off talking to Mum for far too long. I mean, what am I expecting her to do, burst into tears? We're both adults. We'll have a sensible, mature conversation and I'll put forward my point of view calmly, and the whole thing will be sorted out, once and for all. God, I feel liberated. I'm going to call her straight away.

I march into the bedroom, dump my bag on the bed, and dial the number.

"Hi, Dad," I say as he answers. "Is Mum there? There's something I need to talk to her about. It's rather important."

As I glance at my face in the mirror, I feel like a newsreader on NBC, all crisp and cool and in charge.

"Becky?" says Dad puzzledly. "Are you all right?"

"I'm very well," I say. "I just have to discuss a . . . a couple of issues with Mum."

As Dad disappears off the line I take a deep breath and push my hair back, feeling suddenly very grown-up. Here I am, about to have an adult-to-adult, straight-down-the-line conversation with my mother, for probably the first time in my life.

You know, maybe this is the beginning of a whole new relationship with my parents. A new mutual respect. A shared understanding of life.

"Hello, darling?"

"Hi, Mum." I take a deep breath. Here goes. Calm and mature. "Mum—"

"Oh, Becky, I was going to give you a ring. You'll never guess who we saw up in the Lake District!"

"Who?"

"Auntie Zannie! You used to dress up in all her old necklaces, do you remember? And her shoes. We were laughing about it, the sight you made, tottering around . . ."

"Mum. There's something important I need to discuss with you."

"And they've still got the same grocer in the village. The one who used to sell you strawberry ice-cream cones. Do you remember the time you ate too many and weren't very well? We laughed about that too!"

"Mum—"

"And the Tivertons still live in the same house . . . but . . ."

"What?"

"I'm afraid, love . . . Carrot the donkey has . . ." Mum lowers her voice. "Gone to donkey heaven. But he was very old, darling, and he'll be very happy up there . . ."

This is impossible. I don't feel like a grown-up. I feel about six years old.

"They all send you their love," Mum says, eventually coming to the end of her reminiscences, "and of course they'll all be at the wedding! So, Dad said you wanted to talk about something?"

"I . . ." I clear my throat, suddenly aware of the echoey silence on the line; of the distance between us. "Well, I wanted to . . . um . . ."

Oh God. My mouth is trembling and my newsreader voice has turned into a nervous squeak.

"What is it, Becky?" Mum's voice rises in concern. "Is something wrong?"

"No! It's just that . . . that . . ."

It's no good.

I know what Christina said is right. I know there's no need to feel guilty. It's my wedding, and I'm a grown-up, and I should have it wherever I like. I'm not asking Mum and Dad to pay. I'm not asking them to make any effort.

But even so.

I can't tell Mum I want to get married in the Plaza over the phone. I just can't do it.

"I thought I'd come home and see you," I hear myself saying in a rush. "That's all I wanted to say. I'm coming home."

Finerman Wallstein
Attorneys at Law
Finerman House
1398 Avenue of the Americas
New York, NY 10105

Miss Rebecca Bloomwood
251 W. 11th Street, Apt. B
New York, NY 10014

April 18, 2002

Dear Miss Bloomwood:

Thank you for your letter of April 16 regarding your will. I confirm that under the fourth clause, section (e) I have added the line "And also my new denim high-heeled boots," as requested.

With kind regards,

Jane Cardozo

Twelve

As soon as I see Mum, I feel nervous. She's standing next to Dad at Terminal 4, scanning the arrivals gate, and as she sees me her whole face lights up with a mixture of delight and anxiety. She was quite taken aback when I told her I was coming home without Luke—in fact, I had to reassure her several times that everything was still OK between us.

Then I had to reassure her that I hadn't been sacked.

And then promise I wasn't being chased by international loan sharks.

You know, when I think back over the last few years, I sometimes feel a teeny bit bad about everything I've put my parents through.

"Becky! Graham, she's here!" She runs forward, elbowing a family in turbans out of the way. "Becky, love! How are you? How's Luke? Is everything all right?"

"Hi, Mum," I say, and give her a huge hug. "I'm well. Luke sends his love. Everything's fine."

Except one tiny matter—I've been planning a big wedding in New York behind your back.

Stop it, I instruct my brain firmly, as Dad gives me a kiss and takes my luggage. There's no point mentioning it yet. There's no point even thinking about it yet. I'll bring the subject up later, when we're all at home, when there's a natural opening in the conversation.

Which there's bound to be.

"So, Becky, did you think any more about getting married in America?"

"Well, Mum. It's funny you should ask that . . ."

Exactly. I'll wait for some opportunity like that.

But although I act as relaxed as I can, I can't think about anything else. All the while that Mum and Dad are finding the car, disagreeing on which way the exit is, and arguing over whether £3.60 for an hour's parking is a reasonable amount, I've got an anxious knot in my stomach that tightens every time the words *wedding, Luke, New York,* or *America* are mentioned, even in passing.

This is just like the time when I told my parents I was doing the Further Maths GCSE. Tom next door was doing Further Maths and Janice was really smug about it, so I told Mum and Dad I was too. then the exams came, and I had to pretend I was sitting an extra paper (I spent three hours in Top Shop instead). And then the results came out and they kept saying, "But what did you get in Further Maths?"

So then I made up this story that it took the examiners longer to mark Further Maths than the other subjects because it was harder. And I honestly think they would have believed me, except then Janice came running in, saying, "Tom got an A in Further Maths, what did Becky get?"

Bloody Tom.

"You haven't asked about the wedding yet," says Mum as we zoom along the A3 toward Oxshott.

"Oh! No, I haven't, have I?" I force a bright note into my voice. "So—er . . . how are preparations going?"

"To be honest, we haven't done very much," says Dad as we approach the turning for Oxshott.

"It's early days yet," says Mum easily.

"It's only a wedding," adds Dad. "People get far too het up about these things in my opinion. You can put it all together at the last minute."

"Absolutely!" I say in slight relief. "I couldn't agree more!"

Well, thank goodness for that. I sink back in my seat and feel the anxiety drain out of me. This is going to make everything a lot easier. If they haven't arranged very much yet, it'll take no time to call it all off. In fact, it sounds like they're really not bothered about it. This is going to be fine. I've been worrying about nothing!

"Suzie phoned, by the way," says Mum as we start to get near home. "She said, would you like to meet up later on today? I said I was sure you would . . . Oh, and I should warn you." Mum turns in her seat. "Tom and Lucy."

"Hmm?" I resign myself to hearing the details of the latest kitchen they've had put in, or which promotion Lucy has won at work.

"They've split up." Mum lowers her voice, even though it's just the three of us in the car.

"Split up?" I stare at her, taken aback. "Are you serious? But they've only been married for . . ."

"Not even two years. Janice is devastated, as you can imagine."

"What happened?" I say blankly, and Mum purses her lips.

"That Lucy ran off with a drummer."

"A drummer?"

"In a band. Apparently he's got a pierced . . ." She pauses disapprovingly, and my mind ranges wildly over all the possibilities, some of which I'm sure Mum's never heard of. (To be honest, I hadn't either, till I moved to the West Village.) "Nipple," she says at last, to my slight relief.

"Let me get this straight. Lucy's run off . . . with a drummer . . . with a pierced nipple."

"He lives in a trailer," puts in Dad, signaling left.

"After all the work Tom did on that lovely conservatory," says Mum, shaking her head. "Some girls have no gratitude."

I can't get my head round this. Lucy works for Wetherby's Investment Bank. She and Tom live in Reigate. Their curtains match their sofa. How on earth did she meet a drummer with a pierced nipple?

Suddenly I remember that conversation I overheard in the garden when I was here last. Lucy didn't exactly sound happy. But then she didn't exactly sound like she was about to run off, either.

"So how's Tom?"

"He's coping," says Dad. "He's at home with Janice and Martin at the moment, poor lad."

"If you ask me, he's well out of it," says Mum crisply. "It's Janice

I feel sorry for. After that lovely wedding she put on. They were all fooled by that girl."

We pull up outside the house, and to my surprise there are two white vans parked in the drive.

"What's going on?" I say.

"Nothing," says Mum.

"Plumbing," says Dad.

But they've both got slightly strange expressions. Mum's eyes are bright, and she glances at Dad a couple of times as we walk up to the front door.

"So, are you ready?" says Dad casually. He puts his key into the lock and swings open the door.

"Surprise!" cry Mum and Dad simultaneously, and my jaw drops to the ground.

The old hall wallpaper has gone. The old hall carpet has gone. The whole place has been done in light, fresh colors, with pale carpet and new lighting everywhere. As my eye runs disbelievingly upward I see an unobtrusive man in overalls repainting the banisters; on the landing are two more, standing on a stepladder and putting up a candelabra. Everywhere is the smell of paint and newness. And money being spent.

"You're having the house done up," I say feebly.

"For the wedding!" says Mum, beaming at me.

"You said—" I swallow. "You said you hadn't done much."

"We wanted to surprise you!"

"What do you think, Becky?" says Dad, gesturing around. "Do you like it? Does it meet with your approval?"

His voice is jokey. But I can tell it really matters to him whether I like it. To both of them. They're doing all this for me.

"It's . . . fantastic," I say huskily. "Really lovely."

"Now, come and look at the garden!" says Mum, and I follow her dumbly through to the French windows, where I see a team of uniformed gardeners working away in the flower beds.

"They're going to plant 'Luke and Becky' in pansies!" says Mum. "Just in time for June." And we're having a new water feature put in, right by where the entrance to the marquee will be. I saw it in *Modern Garden.*"

"It sounds . . . great."

"And it lights up at night, so when we have the fireworks—"

"What fireworks?" I say, and Mum looks at me in surprise.

"I sent you a fax about the fireworks, Becky! Don't say you've forgotten."

"No! Of course not!"

My mind flicks back to the pile of faxes Mum's been sending me, and which I've been guiltily thrusting under the bed, some skimmed over, some completely unread.

What have I been doing? Why haven't I paid attention to what's been going on?

"Becky, love, you don't look at all well," says Mum. "You must be tired after the flight. Come and have a nice cup of coffee."

We walk into the kitchen, and I feel my insides gripped with new horror.

"Have you installed a new kitchen too?"

"Oh, no!" says Mum gaily. "We just had the units repainted. They look pretty, don't they? Now. Have a nice croissant. They come from the new bakery."

She hands me a basket—but I can't eat. I feel sick.

"Becky?" Mum peers at me. "Is something wrong?"

"No!" I say quickly. "Nothing's wrong. It's all . . . perfect."

What am I going to do?

"You know . . . I think I'll just go and unpack," I say, and manage a weak smile. "Sort myself out a bit."

As I close my bedroom door behind me, the weak smile is still pasted to my face, but inside my heart is thumping wildly.

This is not going as planned.

This is not going remotely as planned. New wallpaper? Water features? Fireworks displays? How come I didn't know about any of this? I should have been more attentive. This is all my own fault. Oh God, oh God . . .

How can I tell Mum and Dad this has all got to be called off? How can I do it?

I can't.

But I have to.

But I can't, I just can't.

It's *my* wedding, I remind myself firmly, trying to regain my New York kick-ass confidence. I can have it where I like.

But the words ring false in my brain, making me wince. Maybe that was true at the beginning. Before anything had been done, before any effort had been made. But now . . . this isn't just my wedding anymore. This is Mum's and Dad's gift to me. It's the biggest present they've ever given me in my life, and they've invested it with all the love and care they can muster.

And I'm proposing to reject it. To say thanks, but no thanks.

What have I been thinking?

Heart thumping, I reach into my pocket for the notes I scribbled on the plane, trying to remember all my justifications.

Reasons why our wedding should be at the Plaza:

1. Wouldn't you love a trip to New York, all expenses paid?
2. The Plaza is a fantastic hotel.
3. You won't have to make any effort.
4. A marquee would only mess up the garden.
5. You won't have to invite Auntie Sylvia.
6. You get free Tiffany frames.

They seemed so convincing when I was writing them. Now they seem like jokes. Mum and Dad don't know anything about the Plaza. Why would they want to fly off to some snooty hotel they've never clapped eyes on? Why would they want to give up hosting the wedding they've always dreamed of? I'm their only daughter. Their one and only child.

So . . . what am I going to do?

I sit staring at the page, breathing hard, letting my thoughts fight it out. I'm scrabbling desperately for a solution, a loophole to wriggle through, unwilling to give up until I've tried every last possibility. Round and round, over the same old ground.

"Becky?"

Mum comes in and I give a guilty start, crumpling the list in my hand.

"Hi!" I say brightly. "Ooh. Coffee. Lovely."

"It's decaffeinated," says Mum, handing me a mug reading *You Don't Have to Be Mad to Organize a Wedding But Your Mother Does*. "I thought maybe you were drinking decaffeinated these days."

"No," I say in surprise. "But it doesn't matter."

"And how are you feeling?" Mum sits down next to me and I

surreptitiously transfer my screwed-up piece of paper from one hand to the other. "A little bit tired? Sick, too, probably."

"Not too bad." I give a slightly heavier sigh than I meant to. "The airline food was pretty grim, though."

"You must keep your strength up!" Mum squeezes my arm. "Now, I've got something for you, darling!" She hands me a piece of paper. "What do you think?"

I unfold the paper and stare at it in bewilderment. It's house details. A four-bedroom house in Oxshott, to be precise.

"It's nice, isn't it?" Mum's face is glowing. "Look at all the features!"

"You're not going to move, are you?"

"Not for us, silly! You'd be just round the corner from us! Look, it's got a built-in barbecue, two en-suite bathrooms . . ."

"Mum, we live in New York."

"You do at the moment. But you won't want to stay in New York forever, will you? Not in the long term."

There's a sudden thread of concern in her voice; and although she's smiling, I can see the tension in her eyes. I open my mouth to answer—then realize, to my own surprise, that Luke and I haven't ever talked properly about the long term.

I suppose I've always assumed that we'll come back to Britain one day. But when?

"You're not planning to stay there for good, surely?" she adds, and gives a little laugh.

"I don't know," I say confusedly. "I don't know what we want to do."

"You couldn't bring up a family in that poky flat! You'll want to come home! You'll want a nice house with a garden! Especially now."

"Now what?"

"Now . . ." She makes a euphemistic circling gesture.

"What?"

"Oh, Becky." Mum sighs. "I can understand if you're a little . . . shy about telling people. But it's all right, darling! These days, it's perfectly acceptable. There's no stigma!"

"*Stigma?* What are you—"

"The only thing we'll need to know"—she pauses delicately—"is how much to let the dress out by? For the day?"

Let out the dress? What on . . .

Hang on.

"Mum! You haven't got the idea that I'm . . . I'm . . ." I make the same euphemistic gesture that she made.

"You're not?" Mum's face falls in disappointment.

"No! Of course I'm not! Why on earth would you think that?"

"You said you had something important to discuss with us!" says Mum, defensively taking a sip of coffee. "It wasn't Luke, it wasn't your job, and it wasn't your bank manager. And Suzie's having a baby, and you two girls always do things together, so we assumed . . ."

"Well, I'm not, OK? And I'm not on drugs either, before you ask."

"So, then, what *did* you want to tell us?" She puts her coffee down and looks at me anxiously. "What was so important that you had to come home?"

There's silence in the bedroom. My fingers tighten around my mug.

This is it. This is my lead-in moment. This is my opportunity to confess everything. If I'm going to do it, I have to do it right now. Before they go any further. Before they spend any more money.

"Well, it's . . ." I clear my throat. "It's just that . . ."

I stop, and take a sip of coffee. My throat is tight and I feel slightly sick. How can I possibly do this?

I close my eyes and allow the glitter of the Plaza to flash before my eyes, trying to summon up all the excitement and glamour again. The gilded rooms, the plushiness everywhere. Images of myself sweeping around that huge shiny dance floor before an admiring crowd.

But somehow . . . it doesn't seem quite as overpowering as it did before. Somehow it doesn't seem as convincing.

Oh God. What do I want? What do I really want?

"I knew it!"

I look up to see Mum gazing at me in dismay. "I knew it! You and Luke *have* fallen out, haven't you?"

"Mum—"

"I just knew it! I said to your father several times, 'I can feel it in my bones, Becky's coming home to call off the wedding.' He said nonsense, but I could just *feel* it, here." Mum clasps her chest. "A mother knows these things. And I was right, wasn't I? You do want to cancel the wedding, don't you?"

I stare at her dumbly. She knows I came home to cancel the wedding. How does she know that?

"Becky? Are you all right?" Mum puts an arm round my shoulders. "Darling, listen. We won't mind. All Dad and I want is the best for you. And if that means calling off the wedding, then that's what we'll do. Love, you mustn't go ahead with it unless you're 100 percent sure—110 percent!"

"But . . . but you've made so much effort . . ." I mumble. "You've spent all this money . . ."

"That doesn't matter! Money doesn't matter!" She squeezes me tight. "Becky, if you have any doubts at all, we'll cancel straight away. We just want you to be happy. That's all we want."

Mum sounds so sympathetic and understanding, for a few instants I can't speak. Here she is, offering me the very thing I came home to ask for. Without any questions, without any recriminations. Without anything but love and support.

As I look at her kind, cozy, familiar face, I know, beyond any doubt, that it's impossible.

"It's all right," I manage at last. "Mum, Luke and I haven't fallen out. The . . . the wedding's still on." I rub my face. "You know, I think I'll just go outside and . . . and get some air."

As I step out into the garden, a couple of of the hired gardeners look up and say hello, and I smile weakly back. I feel completely paranoid, as though my secret is so huge, I must somehow be giving it away. As though people must be able to see it, bulging out of me, or floating above my head in bubble captions.

I have another wedding planned.

For the same day as this one.

My parents have no idea.

Yes, I know I'm in trouble.

Yes, I know I've been stupid.

Oh, just piss off and leave me alone, can't you see how completely stressed out I am?

"Hello, Becky."

I give a start of surprise and turn round. Standing at the garden fence in the next-door garden, looking mournfully at me, is Tom.

"Tom! Hi!" I say, trying not to give away my shock at his appearance.

But . . . blimey. He looks awful, all pale and miserable and wearing absolutely terrible clothes. Not that Tom's ever been a style king—but while he was with Lucy, he did acquire a veneer of OK-ness. In fact, his hair went through quite a groovy stage. But now it's back to greasy hair and the maroon jumper Janice gave him five Christmases ago.

"Sorry to hear about . . ." I pause awkwardly.

"That's all right."

He hunches his shoulders miserably and looks around at all the gardeners digging and clipping away behind me. "So, how are the wedding preparations going?"

"Oh . . . fine," I say brightly. "You know, it's all lists at this stage. Things to do, things to check, little details to . . . to . . . finalize . . ."

Like which continent to get married in. Oh God. Oh God.

"So . . . er, how are your parents?"

"I remember the preparations for our wedding." Tom shakes his head. "Seems a million years ago now. Different people."

"Oh, Tom." I bite my lip. "I'm sorry. Let's change the—"

"You know the worst thing?" says Tom, ignoring me.

"Er . . ." Your hair, I nearly say.

"The worst thing is, I thought I understood Lucy. We understood each other. But all the time . . ." He breaks off, reaches in his pocket for a handkerchief, and blows his nose. "I mean, now I look back, of course I can see there were signs."

"Really?"

"Oh, yes," says Tom. "I just didn't pick up on them."

"Such as . . ." I prompt gently, trying not to give away how curious I am.

"Well." He thinks for a moment. "Like the way she kept saying if she had to live in Reigate for one more minute she'd shoot herself."

"Right," I say, slightly taken aback.

"Then there was the screaming fit she had in Furniture Village . . ."

"Screaming fit?"

"She began yelling, 'I'm twenty-seven! I'm twenty-seven! What am I doing here?' Security had to come in the end, and calm her down."

"But I don't understand. I thought she loved Reigate! You two seemed so . . ."

Smug is the word I'm searching for.

"So . . . happy!"

"She was happy until all the wedding presents were unwrapped," says Tom thoughtfully. "Then . . . it was like she suddenly looked around and realized . . . this was her life now. And she didn't like what she saw. Including me, I expect."

"Oh, Tom."

"She started saying she was sick of the suburbs, and she wanted to have a bit of life while she was young. But I thought, we've just repainted the house, we're halfway through the new conservatory, this isn't a good time to move—" He looks up, his eyes full of misery. "I should have listened, shouldn't I? Maybe I should even have got the tattoo."

"She wanted you to get a *tattoo*?"

"To match hers."

Lucy Webster with a tattoo! I almost want to laugh. But then, as I look at Tom's miserable face, I feel a surge of anger. OK, Tom and I haven't always seen eye to eye over the years. But he doesn't deserve this. He is what he is. And if Lucy wasn't happy with that, then why did she get married to him in the first place?

"Tom, you can't blame yourself," I say firmly. "It sounds like Lucy was having her own problems."

"Do you think?"

"Of course. She was very lucky to have you. More fool her, not appreciating it." Impulsively I lean across the fence and give him a hug. As I draw away again, he stares at me with huge eyes, like a dog.

"You've always understood me, Becky."

"Well, we've known each other a long time."

"No one else knows me like you do."

His hands are still round my shoulders, and he doesn't seem about to let go, so I step backward under the pretext of gesturing at the house, where a man in overalls is painting a window frame.

"Have you seen all the work Mum and Dad are having done? It's incredible."

"Oh, yes. They're really pushing the boat out. I heard about the fireworks display. You must be very excited."

"I'm really looking forward to it," I say automatically. It's what I've said at once, every time anyone's mentioned the wedding to me. But now, as I watch our old, familiar house being smartened up, like a lady putting on makeup, I start to feel a strange sensation. A strange tugging at my heart.

With a sudden pang, I realize I *am* looking forward to it.

I'm looking forward to seeing our garden all bedecked with balloons. To seeing Mum all dressed up and happy. Getting ready in my own bedroom, at my own dressing table. Saying good-bye to my old life properly. Not in some impersonal suite in a hotel . . . but here. At home, where I grew up.

While I was in New York, I couldn't begin to envisage this wedding. It seemed so tiny and humdrum in comparison to the glamour of the Plaza. But now that I'm here, it's the Plaza that's starting to seem unreal. It's the Plaza that's slipping away, like an exotic, far-off holiday, which I'm already starting to forget. It's been a lot of fun playing the part of a New York princess bride, tasting sumptuous dishes and discussing vintage champagne and million-dollar flower arrangements. But that's the point. I've been playing a part.

The truth is, this is where I belong. Right here in this English garden I've known all my life.

So what am I going to do?

Am I really going to . . .

I can barely even think it.

Am I really even contemplating canceling that whole, huge, expensive wedding?

Just the thought of it makes my insides shrivel up.

"Becky?" Mum's voice penetrates my thoughts and I look up dazedly, to see her standing at the patio doors, holding a tablecloth. "Becky! There's a phone call for you inside."

"Oh. OK. Who is it?"

"Someone called Robin," says Mum. "Hello, Tom, love!"

"Robin?" I frown puzzledly as I walk back toward the house. "Robin who?"

I'm not sure I know any Robins. Apart from Robin Anderson

who used to work for *Investment Monthly,* but I hardly knew him, really—

"I didn't catch the surname, I'm afraid," says Mum. "But she seems very nice. She said she was calling from New York . . ."

Robyn?

I can't move. I'm pinioned with horror to the patio steps.

Robyn is on the phone . . . here?

This is all wrong. Robyn doesn't belong in this world, she belongs in New York. This is like when people go back in time and mess up World War II.

"Is she a friend?" Mum's saying innocently. "We've just had a nice little chat about the wedding . . ."

The ground wobbles beneath me.

"What . . . what did she say?" I manage.

"Nothing in particular!" Mum stares at me in surprise. "She asked me what color I was going to wear . . . and she kept saying something odd about violinists. You don't want violinists at the wedding, do you, love?"

"Of course not!" My voice rises shrilly. "What would I want violinists for?"

"Becky, darling, are you all right?" Mum peers at me. "I'll tell her you'll call back, shall I?"

"No! Don't talk to her again! I mean . . . it's fine. I'll take it."

I hurry into the house, heart thumping. What am I going to say? Should I tell her I've changed my mind?

As I pick up the phone, I see that Mum's followed me inside. Oh God. How am I going to manage this?

"Robyn, hi!" I attempt a natural tone. "How are you?"

OK. I'll just get her off the phone, as quickly as possible.

"Hi! Becky! I'm so glad I got a chance to speak with your mother!" says Robyn. "She seems a lovely lady. I'm so looking forward to meeting her!"

"Me too," I say as heartily as I can. "I can't wait for you to . . . get together."

"Although I was surprised she didn't know about the string orchestra. Tut tut! You really should keep your mom up-to-date, Becky!"

"I know," I say after a pause. "I've just been quite busy . . ."

"I can understand that," says Robyn sympathetically. "Why

don't I send her an information package? It would be so easy to FedEx it over. Then she'll see the whole thing in front of her eyes! If you give me the address—"

"No!" I cry before I can stop myself. "I mean . . . don't worry. I'll pass everything on. Really. Don't . . . send anything. Nothing at all."

"Not even a few menu cards? I'm sure she'd love to see those!"

"No! Nothing!"

My hand is tight around the receiver and my face is sweating. I don't even dare look at Mum.

"Well, OK!" says Robyn at last. "You're the boss! Now, I've spoken to Sheldon Lloyd about the table arrangements . . ."

As she babbles on, I dart a glance at Mum, who is about three feet away from me. Surely she can hear the phone from there? Surely she just heard the word *Plaza*? Surely she just caught *wedding* and *ballroom*?

"Right," I say, without taking in anything that Robyn's saying, "That all sounds fine." I twist the cord around my fingers. "But . . . but listen, Robyn. The thing is, I've come home to get away from it all. So could you possibly not phone me here anymore?"

"You don't want to be updated?" says Robyn in surprise.

"No. That's fine. You just . . . do your thing, and I'll catch up when I get back next week."

"No problem. I understand. You need time out! Becky, I promise, unless it's an emergency, I'll leave you alone. You have a lovely break now!"

"Thanks. I will. Bye, Robyn."

I put the phone down, shaky with relief. Thank God she's gone.

But I don't feel safe. Robyn's got the number here now. She could phone at any time. I mean, what counts as an emergency in wedding planning? Probably anything. Probably a misplaced rose petal. She only has to say one wrong word to Mum, and both of them will realize what's been going on. Mum will immediately realize why I came back here, what I was trying to say.

She'd be so hurt. I can't allow that to happen.

OK, I have two options. Number one: get Mum and Dad to move house immediately. Number two . . .

"Listen, Mum," I say, turning round. "That woman Robyn. She's . . ."

"Yes?"

"She's . . . deranged."

"Deranged?" Mum stares at me. "What do you mean, love?"

"She . . . she's in love with Luke!"

"Oh my goodness!"

"Yes, and she's got this weird delusion that she's going to marry him."

"*Marry* him?" Mum gapes at me.

"Yes! At the Plaza Hotel! Apparently she even tried to . . . um . . . book it. Under my name!"

My fingers are twisting into complicated knots. I must be crazy. Mum'll never fall for this. Never. Not in a million—

"You know, that doesn't surprise me!" says Mum. "I could tell there was something a bit odd about her straight away. All this nonsense about violins! And she seemed obsessed by what color I was going to wear—"

"Oh, she's completely obsessed. So . . . if she ever rings again, just make an excuse and put the phone down. And whatever she says, even if it sounds quite plausible . . . don't believe a word of it. Promise?"

"All right, love," says Mum, nodding. "Whatever you say."

As she goes into the kitchen, I hear her saying "Poor woman. You have to feel sorry for them, really. Graham, did you hear that? That lady from America who phoned for Becky. She's in love with Luke!"

I can't cope with this anymore.

I need to see Suze.

Thirteen

I'VE AGREED TO meet Suze at Sloane Square for a cup of tea. There's a crowd of tourists milling around when I arrive, and for a moment I can't see her. Then the throng disperses—and there she is, sitting by the fountain, her long blond hair haloed by the sun, and the hugest stomach I've ever seen.

As I see her, I'm all set to rush up to her, exclaim, "Oh God, Suze, it's all a nightmare!" and tell her everything.

But then I stop. She looks like an angel, sitting there. A pregnant angel.

Or the Virgin Mary, perhaps. All serene and lovely and perfect.

And suddenly I feel all messed up in comparison. I'd been planning to unburden the entire situation on Suze, like I always do, and wait for her to think of an answer. But now . . . I just can't. She looks so calm and happy. It would be like dumping toxic waste in some beautiful clear sea.

"Bex! Hi!" As she sees me she stands up, and I feel a fresh shock at how . . . well, how big she looks.

"Suze!" I hurry toward her and give her a huge hug. "You look amazing!"

"I'm feeling great!" says Suze. "How are you? How's the wedding?"

"Oh . . . I'm fine!" I say after a pause. "It's all fine. Come on. Let's go and have some tea."

I'm not going to tell her. This is it. For once in my life, I'm going to sort out my problems on my own.

We go to Oriel and get a table by the window. When the waiter comes, I order hot chocolate, but Suze produces a tea bag and hands it to the waiter.

"Raspberry leaf tea," she explains. "It strengthens the uterus. For labor."

"Right." I nod. "Labor. Of course!"

I feel a little shiver at the base of my spine and smile quickly to cover it.

Secretly, I'm really not at all convinced about this whole giving birth thing. I mean, look at the size of Suze's bump. Look at the size of a full-grown baby. And then tell me *that's* going to fit through . . .

I mean, I know the theory. It's just . . . to be honest, I can't see it working.

"When are you due again?" I say, staring at Suze's stomach.

"Four weeks today!"

"So . . . it's going to grow even bigger?"

"Oh yes!" Suze pats her bump fondly. "Quite a bit, I should think."

"Good," I say weakly, as a waiter puts a cup of hot chocolate in front of me. "Excellent. So . . . how's Tarquin?"

"He's fine!" says Suze. "He's up on Craie at the moment. You know, his Scottish island? They're lambing at the moment, so he thought he'd go and help out. Before the baby comes."

"Oh right. And you didn't go with him?"

"Well, it would have been a bit risky." Suze stirs her raspberry tea thoughtfully. "And the thing is, I'm not *quite* as interested in sheep as he is. I mean, they are really interesting," she adds loyally. "But you know, after you've seen a thousand of them . . ."

"But he'll be back in time, will he?"

"Oh yes. He's really excited! He's been to all the classes and everything!"

God, I can't believe in a few weeks' time Suze will have a baby. I won't even be here.

"Can I touch?" I put my hand gingerly on Suze's stomach. "I can't feel anything."

"That's all right," says Suze. "I expect it's asleep."

"Do you know if it's a boy or a girl?"

"I haven't found out." Suze leans forward earnestly. "But I kind of think it's a girl, because I keep being drawn to all these sweet little dresses in the shops. Like a kind of a craving? And they say in all the books, your body will tell you what it needs. So, you know, maybe that's a sign."

"So, what are you going to call her?"

"We can't decide. It's so hard! You know, you buy these books, and all the names are crap . . ." She takes a sip of tea. "What would you call a baby?"

"Ooh! I don't know! Maybe Lauren, after Ralph Lauren." I think for a few moments. "Or Dolce."

"Dolce Cleath-Stuart," says Suze thoughtfully. "I quite like that! We could call her Dolly for short."

"Or Vera. After Vera Wang."

"*Vera*?" Suze stares at me. "I'm not calling my baby Vera!"

"We're not talking about your baby!" I retort. "We're talking about mine. Vera Lauren Comme des Brandon. I think that's got a really good ring to it."

"Vera Brandon sounds like a character off *Coronation Street*! But I like Dolce. What about if it was a boy?"

"Harvey. Or Barney," I say after a little thought. "Depending on whether it was born in London or New York."

I take another sip of hot chocolate—then look up, to see Suze gazing at me seriously.

"You wouldn't really have a baby in America, would you, Bex?"

"I . . . I don't know. Who can tell? We probably won't have children for years yet!"

"You know, we all really miss you."

"Oh, not you, too, Suze." I give a half-laugh. "I had Mum on at me today to move back to Oxshott."

"Well, it's true! Tarkie was saying the other day, London just isn't the same without you."

"Really?" I gaze at her, feeling ridiculously touched.

"And your mum keeps asking me if I think you'll stay in New York forever . . . you won't, will you?"

"I honestly don't know," I say helplessly. "It all depends on Luke . . . and his business . . ."

"He's not the boss!" says Suze. "You have a say, too. Do you want to stay out there?"

"I don't know." I screw up my face, trying to explain. "Sometimes I think I do. When I'm in New York, it seems like the most important place in the world. My job is fantastic, and the people are fantastic, and it's all wonderful. But when I come home, suddenly I think, Hang on, this is my home. This is where I belong." I pick up a sugar packet and begin to shred it. "I just don't know whether I'm ready to come home yet."

"Oh, come back to England and have a baby!" says Suze wheedlingly. "Then we can be mummies together!"

"Honestly, Suze!" I take a sip of chocolate, rolling my eyes. "Like I'm really ready to have a baby!" I get up to go to the ladies' room before she can say anything else.

On the other hand . . . she has got a point. Why shouldn't I have a baby? Other people do—so why not me? I mean, if I could somehow bypass the actual *having* it bit. Maybe I could have one of those operations where you go to sleep and don't feel anything. And then when I woke up I'd have a baby!

I have a sudden pleasant vision of Suze and me walking up the road together, pushing prams. That might be quite fun, actually. I mean, you can buy loads of gorgeous baby things these days. Like cute little hats, and tiny denim jackets . . . And—yes—doesn't Gucci do a really cool baby sling?

We could have cappuccinos together, and walk round the shops, and . . . I mean, that's basically all mothers do, isn't it? Now that I think about it, I'd be perfect at it!

I must definitely have a chat with Luke.

It's not until we're leaving Oriel that Suze says, "So, Bex, you haven't told me anything about the wedding!"

My stomach gives a little swoop, and I turn my head away, under the pretense of putting on my coat.

I'd kind of managed to forget about the whole wedding issue.

"Yes," I say at last. "Well, it's all . . . um . . . fine!"

I'm not going to bother Suze with my problems. I'm not.

"Was Luke all right about you getting married in England?" She looks anxiously at me. "I mean, it didn't cause a rift between you or anything?"

"No," I say after a pause. "I can honestly say that it didn't."

I hold the door open for her and we walk out into Sloane Square. A column of schoolchildren in corduroy knickerbockers is crowding the pavement, and we stand aside, waiting for them to pass.

"You know, you made the right decision." Suze squeezes my arm. "I was so worried you were going to choose New York. What made you finally decide?"

"Er . . . this and that. You know. So, erm . . . did you read about these new proposals to privatize the water system?"

But Suze ignores me. Honestly, isn't she interested in current affairs?

"So what did Elinor say when you called off the Plaza?"

"She said . . . erm . . . well, she wasn't pleased, of course. She said she was very cross, and . . . er . . ."

"Very cross?" Suze raises her eyebrows. "Is that all? I thought she'd be furious!"

"She *was* furious!" I amend hurriedly. "She was so furious, she . . . burst a blood vessel!"

"She burst a blood vessel?" Suze stares at me. "Where?"

"On her . . . chin."

There's silence. Suze is standing still in the street, her expression slowly changing. "Bex—"

"Let's go and look at baby clothes!" I say hurriedly. "There's that really sweet shop on the King's Road . . ."

"Bex, what's going on?"

"Nothing!"

"There is! I can tell. You're hiding something."

"No, I'm not!"

"You did call the American wedding off, didn't you?"

"I . . ."

"Bex?" Her voice is as stern as I've ever heard it. "Tell me the truth."

Oh God. I can't lie any more.

"I . . . I'm going to," I say weakly.

"You're going to?" Suze's voice rises in dismay. "You're *going to*?"

"Suze—"

"I should have known! I should have guessed! But I just assumed you must have called it off, because your mother kept on organizing her wedding, and no one said anything about New York, and I thought, oh, Bex must have decided to get married at home after all . . ."

"Suze, please. Don't worry about it," I say quickly. "Just stay calm . . . breathe deeply . . ."

"How can I not worry about it!" cries Suze. "How can I not worry? Bex, you promised me you were going to sort this out weeks ago! You promised!"

"I know! And I'm going to. It's just . . . it's been so difficult. Deciding between them. They both seemed so perfect, in completely different ways—"

"Bex, a wedding isn't a handbag!" says Suze incredulously. "You can't decide you'll treat yourself to two!"

"I know! I know! Look, I'm going to sort it out—"

"Why didn't you tell me before?"

"Because you're all lovely and serene and happy!" I wail. "And I didn't want to spoil it with my stupid problems."

"Oh, Bex." Suze gazes at me silently—then puts an arm round me. "So . . . what are you going to do?"

I take a deep breath.

"I'm going to tell Elinor the New York wedding is all off. And I'm going to get married here in England."

"Really? You're completely sure about that?"

"Yes. I'm sure. After seeing Mum and Dad . . . and Mum was so sweet . . . and she has no idea what I've been planning behind her back . . ." I swallow hard. "I mean, this wedding is everything to her. Oh God, Suze, I feel so stupid. I don't know what I was thinking. I don't want to get married at the Plaza. I don't want to get married anywhere else except at home."

"You won't change your mind again?"

"No. Not this time. Honestly, Suze, this is it."

"What about Luke?"

"He doesn't care. He's said all along, it's up to me."

Suze is silent for a moment. Then she reaches in her bag for her mobile phone and thrusts it at me.

"OK. If you're going to do it, do it now. Dial the number."

"I can't. Elinor's in a Swiss clinic. I was planning to write her a letter—"

"No." Suze shakes her head firmly. "Do it now. There must be someone you can call. Call that wedding planner, Robyn, and tell her it's off. Bex, you can't afford to leave it any longer."

"OK," I say, ignoring the leap of apprehension inside me. "OK, I'll do it. I'll . . . I'll call her."

I lift up the phone—then put it down again. Making the decision in my head was one thing. Actually making the call is another.

What's Robyn going to say? What's everybody going to say? I wouldn't mind a little time, just to think through exactly what I'm going to tell them . . .

"Go on!" says Suze. "Do it!"

"All right!"

With trembling hands I lift the phone and dial 001 for America—but the display remains blank.

"Oh . . . dear!" I exclaim, trying to sound upset. "I can't get a signal! Oh well, I'll just have to phone later—"

"No you won't! We'll keep walking till you get one. Come on!" Suze starts marching toward the King's Road and I scuttle nervously along behind her.

"Try again," she says as we reach the first pedestrian crossing.

"Nothing," I quaver. God, Suze looks incredible, like the prow of a ship. Her blond hair is streaming out behind her, and her face is flushed with determination. How come she's got so much energy, anyway? I thought pregnant women were supposed to take it easy.

"Try again!" she repeats after every three hundred feet. "Try again! I'm not stopping till you've made that call!"

"There's nothing!"

"Are you sure?"

"Yes!" Frantically I punch at the buttons, trying to trigger a signal. "Look!"

"Well, keep trying! Come on!"

"I am! I am!"

"Oh my God!" Suze gives a sudden shriek and I jump in terror.

"I'm trying! Honestly, Suze, I'm trying as hard as I—"

"No! Look!"

I stop still, and turn round. She's stopped still on the pavement, ten yards behind me, and there's a puddle of water at her feet.

"Suze . . . don't worry," I say awkwardly. "I won't tell anybody."

"No! You don't understand! It's not . . ." She stares at me wildly. "I think my waters have broken!"

"Your what?" I feel a thud of pure fright. "Does that mean . . . Are you going to—"

This can't be happening.

"I don't know." I can see panic rising on Suze's face. "I mean, it's possible . . . But it's four weeks early! It's too soon! Tarkie isn't here, nothing's ready . . . Oh God . . ."

I've never seen Suze look so scared before. A choking dismay creeps over me, and I fight the temptation to burst into tears. What have I done now? As well as everything else, I've sent my best friend into premature labor.

"Suze, I'm so sorry," I gulp.

"It's not your fault! Don't be stupid!"

"It is! You were so happy and serene, and then you saw me. I should just stay away from pregnant people—"

"I'll have to go to the hospital." Suze's face is pale. "They said to come in if this happened."

"Well, let's go! Come on!"

"But I haven't got my bag, or anything. There's loads of stuff I need to take . . ." She bites her lip worriedly. "Shall I go home first?"

"You haven't got time for that!" I say in a panic. "What do you need?"

"Baby clothes . . . nappies . . . stuff like that . . ."

"Well, where do you . . ." I look around helplessly, then, with a sudden surge of relief, spot the sign for Peter Jones.

"OK," I say, and grab her arm. "Come on."

As soon as we get into Peter Jones, I look around for an assistant. And thank goodness, here comes one, a nice middle-aged lady with red lipstick and gold spectacles on a chain.

"My friend needs an ambulance," I gasp.

"A taxi will be fine, honestly," says Suze. "It's just that my waters have broken. So I should probably get to the hospital."

"Goodness!" says the lady. "Come and sit down, dear, and I'll call a taxi for you . . ."

We sit Suze down on a chair by a checkout desk, and a junior assistant brings her a glass of water.

"Right," I say. "Tell me what you need."

"I can't remember exactly." Suze looks anxious. "We were given a list . . . Maybe they'll know in the baby department."

"Will you be OK if I leave you?"

"I'll be fine! Contractions haven't even started."

"You're sure?" I glance nervously at her stomach.

"Bex, just go!"

Honestly. Why on earth do they put baby departments so far away from the main entrances of shops? I mean, what's the point of all these stupid floors of clothes and makeup and bags, which no one's interested in? After sprinting up and down about six escalators, at last I find it, and come to a standstill, panting slightly.

For a moment I look around, dazed by all the names of things I've never heard of.

Reception blanket?

Anticolic teats?

Oh, sod it. I'll just buy everything. I quickly head for the nearest display and start grabbing things indiscriminately. Sleeping suits, tiny socks, a hat . . . a teddy, a cot blanket . . . what else? A Moses basket . . . nappies . . . little glove puppets in case the baby gets bored . . . a really cute little Christian Dior jacket . . . gosh, I wonder if they do that in grown-up sizes too . . .

I shove the lot onto the checkout desk and whip out my Visa card.

"It's for my friend," I explain breathlessly. "She's just gone into labor. Is this everything she needs?"

"I wouldn't know, I'm afraid, dear," says the assistant, scanning a baby bath thermometer.

"I've got a list here," says a nearby woman in maternity dungarees and Birkenstocks. "This is what the National Childbirth Trust recommends you take in."

"Oh, thanks!"

She hands a piece of paper to me and I scan the endless typed list with growing dismay. I thought I'd done so well—but I haven't got half the stuff they say here. And if I miss anything, it'll turn out to be completely vital, and Suze's whole birth experience will be ruined and I'll never forgive myself.

Loose T-shirt . . . Scented candles . . . Plant sprayer . . .

Is this the right list?

"Plant sprayer?" I say bewilderedly.

"To spray the laboring woman's face," explains the woman in dungarees. "Hospital rooms get very hot."

"You'll want the home department for that," puts in the assistant.

"Oh, right. Thanks."

Tape recorder . . . soothing tapes . . . inflatable ball . . .

"Inflatable ball? Won't the baby be a bit young to play with a ball?"

"It's for the mother to lean on," says the woman kindly. "To alleviate the waves of pain. Alternatively she could use a large bean bag."

Waves of pain? Oh God. The thought of Suze in pain makes me feel all wobbly inside.

"I'll get a ball *and* a bean bag," I say hurriedly. "And maybe some aspirin. Extra-strong."

At last I stagger back to the ground floor, red in the face and panting. I just hope I've got all this right. I couldn't find an inflatable ball in the whole of the stupid shop—so in the end I grabbed an inflatable canoe instead, and made the man pump it up for me. I've got it wedged under one arm now, with a Teletubbies bean bag and a Moses basket stuffed under the other, and about six full carrier bags dangling from my wrists.

I glance at my watch—and to my utter horror I see that I've already been twenty-five minutes. I'm half expecting to see Suze sitting on the chair holding a baby in her arms.

But there she is, still on the chair, wincing slightly.

"Bex. There you are! I think my contractions have started."

"Sorry I took so long," I gasp. "I just wanted to get everything you might need." A box of Scrabble falls out of one of the bags onto the ground, and I bend to pick it up. "That's for when you have an epidural," I explain.

"The taxi's here," interrupts the lady with gold spectacles. "Do you need some help with all that?"

As we make our way out to the chugging taxi, Suze is staring at my load in utter bewilderment.

"Bex . . . why did you buy an inflatable canoe?"

"It's for you to lie on. Or something."

"And a watering can?"

"I couldn't find a plant sprayer." Breathlessly I start shoving bags into the taxi.

"But why do I need a plant sprayer?"

"Look, it wasn't my idea, OK?" I say defensively. "Come on, let's go!"

Somehow we cram everything into the taxi. A canoe paddle falls out as we close the door, but I don't bother trying to get it. I mean, it's not like Suze is having a water birth.

"Tarkie's business manager is trying to reach him," says Suze as we zoom along the King's Road. "But even if he gets on a plane straight away, he's going to miss it."

"He might not!" I say encouragingly. "You never know!"

"He will." To my dismay I can hear her voice starting to wobble. "He'll miss the birth of his first child. After waiting all this time. And doing the classes, and everything. He was really good at panting. The teacher made him do it in front of everyone else, he was so good."

"Oh, Suze." I feel like crying. "Maybe you'll take hours and hours, and he'll still make it."

"You'll stay with me, won't you?" She suddenly turns in her seat. "You won't leave me there?"

"Of course not!" I say, appalled. "I'll stay with you all the time, Suze." I hold both her hands tight. "We'll do it together."

"Do you know anything at all about giving birth?"

"Erm . . . yes," I lie. "Loads!"

"Like what?"

"Like . . . um . . . you need hot towels . . . and . . ." Suddenly I spot a baby milk carton poking out of one of the bags. ". . . and many babies require a vitamin K injection after the birth."

Suze stares at me, impressed. "Wow. How did you know that?"

"I just know stuff," I say, pushing the carton out of sight with my foot. "You see? It'll be fine!"

OK, I can do this. I can help Suze. I just have to stay cool and calm and not panic.

I mean, millions of people give birth every day, don't they? It's probably one of those things that *sounds* really scary but is quite easy when it comes to it. Like a driving test.

"Oh God." Suze's face suddenly contorts. "Here it comes again."

"OK! Hang on!" In a flurry of alarm I scrabble inside one of the plastic bags. "Here you are!"

Suze opens her eyes dazedly as I produce a smart cellophaned box. "Bex—why are you giving me perfume?"

"They said get jasmine oil to help ease the pain," I say breathlessly. "But I couldn't find any, so I got Romance by Ralph Lauren instead. It's got jasmine overtones." I rip off the packaging and squirt it at her hopefully. "Does that help?"

"Not really," says Suze. "But it's a nice smell."

"It is, isn't it?" I say, pleased. "And because I spent over thirty quid, I got a free beauty bag with exfoliating body mitt and—"

"St. Christopher's Hospital," says the driver suddenly, drawing up in front of a large redbrick building. We both stiffen in alarm and look at each other.

"OK," I say. "Keep calm, Suze. Don't panic. Just . . . wait there."

I open the taxi door, sprint through an entrance marked "Maternity," and find myself in a reception area with blue upholstered chairs. A couple of women in dressing gowns look up from the magazines they're reading, but other than that, there are no signs of life.

For God's sake. Where is everybody?

"My friend's having a baby!" I yell. "Quick, everyone! Get a stretcher! Get a midwife!"

"Are you all right?" says a woman in white uniform, appearing out of nowhere. "I'm a midwife. What's the problem?"

"My friend's in labor! She needs help immediately!"

"Where is she?"

"I'm here," says Suze, struggling in through the door with three bags under one arm.

"Suze!" I say in horror. "Don't move. You should be lying down! She needs drugs," I say to the nurse. "She needs an epidural and general anesthetic and some laughing gas stuff, and . . . basically, whatever you've got . . ."

"I'm fine," says Suze. "Really."

"OK," says the midwife. "Let's just get you settled into a room. Then we can examine you and take a few details . . ."

"I'll get the rest of the stuff," I say, and start heading back toward the doors. "Suze, don't worry, I'll be back. Go with the midwife and I'll come and find you . . ."

"Wait," says Suze urgently, suddenly turning round. "Wait, Bex!"

"What?"

"You never made that call. You never canceled the New York wedding."

"I'll make it later," I say. "Go on. Go with the midwife."

"Make it now."

"Now?" I stare at her.

"If you don't make it now, you'll never make it! I know you, Bex."

"Suze, don't be stupid! You're about to have a baby! Let's get our priorities right, shall we?"

"I'll have the baby when you've made the call!" says Suze obstinately. "Oh!" Her face suddenly twists. "It's starting again."

"OK," says the midwife calmly. "Now, breathe . . . try to relax . . ."

"I can't relax! Not until she cancels the wedding! Otherwise she'll just put it off again! I know her!"

"I won't!"

"You will, Bex! You've already dithered for months!"

"Is he a bad sort, then?" says the midwife. "You should listen to your friend," she adds to me. "She sounds like she knows what she's talking about."

"Friends can always tell the wrong 'uns," agrees the woman in the pink dressing gown.

"He's not a wrong 'un!" I retort indignantly. "Suze, please! Calm down! Go with the nurse! Get some drugs!"

"Make the call," she replies, her face contorted. "Then I'll go." She looks up. "Go on! Make the call!"

"If you want this baby born safely," says the midwife to me, "I'd make the call."

"Make the call, love!" chimes in the woman in the pink dressing gown.

"OK! OK!" I scrabble for the mobile phone and punch in the number. "I'm calling. Now go, Suze!"

"Not until I've heard you say the words!"

"Breathe *through* the pain . . ."

"Hello!" chirps Robyn in my ear. "Is that wedding bells I hear?"

"There's no one there," I say, looking up.

"Then leave a message," says Suze through gritted teeth.

"Another deep breath now . . ."

"Your call is *so* important to me . . ."

"Go on, Bex!"

"All right! Here goes." I take a deep breath as the bleep sounds. "Robyn, this is Becky Bloomwood here . . . and I'm canceling the wedding. Repeat, I'm canceling the wedding. I'm very sorry for all the inconvenience this is going to cause. I know what a lot you've put into it and I can only guess at how angry Elinor will be . . ." I swallow. "But I've made my final decision—and it's that I want to get married at home in England. If you want to talk to me about this, leave a message at my home and I'll call you back. Otherwise, I guess this is good-bye. And . . . thanks. It was fun while it lasted."

I click off the phone and stare at it, silent in my hand.

I've done it.

"Well done," says the midwife to Suze. "That was a tough one!"

"Well done, Bex," says Suze, pink in the face. She squeezes my hand and gives me a tiny smile. "You've done the right thing." She looks at the midwife. "OK. Let's go."

"I'll just go and . . . get the rest of the stuff," I say, and walk slowly toward the double doors leading out of the hospital.

As I step out into the fresh air I can't help giving a little shiver. So that's it. No more Plaza wedding. No more enchanted forest. No more magical cake. No more fantasy.

I can't quite believe it's all gone.

But then . . . if I'm really honest, it only ever was a fantasy, wasn't it? It never quite felt like real life.

This is real life, right here.

For a few moments I'm silent, letting my thoughts drift, until the sound of an ambulance siren brings me back to the present. Hastily I unload the taxi, pay the driver, then stare at the mound of stuff, wondering how on earth I'm going to get it all inside. And whether I really did need to buy a collapsible playpen.

"Are you Becky Bloomwood?" A voice interrupts my thoughts and I look up, to see a young midwife standing at the door.

"Yes!" I feel a tremor of alarm. "Is Suze all right?"

"She's fine, but her contractions are intensifying now, and we're still waiting for the anesthetist to arrive . . . and she's saying she'd like to try using"—she looks at me puzzledly—"is it . . . a canoe?"

Oh my God.

Oh my God.

I can't even begin to . . . to . . .

It's seven o'clock in the evening, and I'm completely shattered. I have never seen anything like that in my life. I had no idea it would be so—

That Suze would be so—

It took six hours altogether, which is apparently really quick. Well, all I can say is, I wouldn't like to be one of the slow ones.

I can't believe it. Suze has got a baby boy. A tiny, pink, snuffly baby boy. One hour old.

He's been weighed and measured, and apparently he's a really healthy size, considering he came early. A nurse has dressed him in the most gorgeous white and blue baby suit and a little white blanket, and now he's lying in Suze's arms, all curled up and scrumpled, with tufts of dark hair sticking out over his ears. The baby that Suze and Tarquin made. I almost want to cry . . . except I'm so elated. It's the weirdest feeling.

I meet Suze's eyes, and she beams euphorically. She's been beaming ever since he was born, and I'm secretly wondering if they gave her a bit too much laughing gas.

"Isn't he just perfect?"

"He's perfect." I touch his tiny fingernail. To think that's been growing inside Suze, all this time.

"Would you like a cup of tea?" says a nurse, coming into the warm, bright room. "You must be exhausted."

"Thanks very much," I say gratefully, stretching out a hand.

"I meant Mum," says the nurse, giving me an odd look.

"Oh," I say flusteredly. "Yes, of course. Sorry."

"It's all right," says Suze. "Give it to Bex. She deserves it." She gives me an abashed smile. "Sorry I got angry with you."

"That's all right." I bite my lip. "Sorry I kept saying, 'Does it really hurt?' "

"No, you were great. Seriously, Bex. I couldn't have done it without you."

"Some flowers have arrived," says a midwife, coming in. "And we've had a message from your husband. He's stuck on the island for the moment because of bad weather, but he'll be here as soon as he can."

"Thanks," says Suze, managing a smile. "That's great."

But when the midwife goes out again, her lips begin to tremble. "Bex, what am I going to do if Tarkie can't get back? Mummy's in Ulan Bator, and Daddy doesn't know one end of a baby from the other . . . I'm going to be all on my own . . ."

"No, you aren't!" I quickly put an arm round her. "I'll look after you!"

"But don't you have to go back to America?"

"I don't have to go anywhere. I'll change my flight and take more vacation days." I give her a tight hug. "I'm staying here with you for as long as you need me, Suze, and that's the end of it."

"What about the wedding?"

"I don't need to worry about the wedding any more. Suze, I'm staying with you, and that's that."

"Really?" Suze's chin quivers. "Thanks, Bex." She shifts the baby cautiously in her arms, and he gives a little snuffle. "Do you . . . know anything about babies?"

"You don't have to know anything!" I say confidently. "You just have to feed them and dress them up in nice clothes and wheel them around the shops."

"I'm not sure—"

"And anyway, just look at little Armani." I reach into the white bundle of blanket and touch the baby's cheek fondly.

"We're *not* naming him Armani!"

"Well, whatever. He's an angel! He must be what they call an 'easy' baby."

"He is good, isn't he?" says Suze, pleased. "He hasn't even cried once!"

"Honestly, Suze, don't worry." I take a sip of tea and smile at her. "It'll be a blast!"

Finerman Wallstein

Attorneys at Law

Finerman House
1398 Avenue of the Americas
New York, NY 10105

Miss Rebecca Bloomwood
251 W. 11th Street, Apt. B
New York, NY 10014

May 6, 2002

Dear Miss Bloomwood:

Thank you for your message of April 30, and I confirm that under the fourth clause I have added the section "(f) I give and bequeath to my gorgeous godson Ernest, the sum of $1,000."

May I draw your attention to the fact that this is the seventh amendment you have made to your will since drawing it up a month ago?

With kind regards,

Jane Cardozo

Fourteen

I STUMBLE UP THE steps of our building. Swaying slightly, I reach for my key—and, after three goes, manage to get it in the lock.

Home again.

Quiet again.

"Becky? Is that you?" I hear Danny's voice from above and the sound of his footsteps on the stairs.

I stare dazedly up, unable to focus. I feel like I've run a marathon. No, make that six marathons. The last two weeks has been a blurry jumble of nights and days all run into one. Just me and Suze, and baby Ernest. And the crying.

Don't get me wrong, I adore little Ernie. I mean, I'm going to be his godmother, and everything.

But . . . God. That *scream* of his . . .

I just had no idea having a baby was like that. I thought it would be *fun*.

I didn't realize Suze would have to feed him every single hour. I didn't realize he would refuse to go to sleep. Or that he would hate his crib. I mean, it came from the Conran Shop! All lovely beech, with gorgeous white blankets. You'd think he would have loved it! But when we put him in it, all he did was thrash about, going "Waaah!"

Then I tried to take him shopping—and when we started out, it was fine. People were smiling at the pram, and smiling at me, and I was starting to feel quite proud of myself. But then we went into Karen Millen, and I was halfway into a pair of leather trousers when he started to yell. Not a cute little whimper. Not a plaintive little wail. A full-throated, piercing "This Woman Has Kidnapped Me, Call the Cops" scream.

I didn't have any bottles or nappies or anything, and I had to run down the Fulham Road, and by the time I got home, I was red in the face and panting and Suze was crying and Ernest was looking at me like I was a mass murderer or something.

And then, even after he'd been fed, he screamed and screamed all evening . . .

"Jesus!" says Danny, arriving downstairs in the hall. "What happened to you?"

I glance in the mirror and feel a dart of shock. I look pale with exhaustion, my hair is lank and my eyes are drained. Tarquin got home three days ago, and he did do his fair share—but that didn't mean I got any sleep. And it didn't help that when I finally got on the plane to fly home, I was seated next to a woman with six-month-old twins.

"My friend Suze had a baby," I say blearily. "And her husband was stuck on an island, so I helped out for a bit . . ."

"Luke said you were on vacation," says Danny, staring at me in horror. "He said you were taking a rest!"

"Luke . . . has no idea."

Every time Luke phoned, I was either changing a nappy, comforting a wailing Ernie, comforting an exhausted Suze—or flat-out asleep. We did have one brief, disjointed conversation, but in the end Luke suggested I go and lie down, as I wasn't making much sense.

Other than that, I haven't spoken to anyone. Mum called to let me know that Robyn had left a message at the house that I should call her urgently. And I did mean to call back. But every time I had a spare five minutes to myself . . . somehow I just couldn't face it. I've no idea what's been going on; what kind of arguments and fall-out there's been. I know Elinor must be furious. I know there's probably the mother of all rows waiting for me.

But . . . I just don't care. All I care about right now is getting into bed.

"Hey, a bunch of boxes arrived from QVC." Danny looks at me curiously. "Did you order a set of Marie Osmond dolls?"

"I don't know," I say blankly. "I expect so. I ordered pretty much everything they had."

I have a dim memory of myself at three in the morning, rocking Ernest on my lap so Suze could have a sleep, staring groggily at the screen.

"Do you know how terrible the telly is in Britain at three in the morning?" I rub my dry cheeks. "And there's no point watching a film, because the minute it gets to a good bit, the baby cries and you have to leap up and start joggling him around, singing 'Old Macdonald Had a Farm, Ee-I Ee-I Oh . . .' and he still doesn't stop crying. So you have to go into 'Oh what a beautiful mooorr-rning . . .' but that doesn't work either . . ."

"Right," says Danny, backing away. "I'll . . . take your word for it. Becky, I think you need a nap."

"Yes. So do I. See you later."

I stumble into the apartment, shove all the post on the sofa, and head for the bedroom, as single-minded as a junkie craving a hit.

Sleep. I need sleep . . .

A light is blinking on our message machine and as I lie down, I automatically reach out and press the button.

"Hi, Becky! Robyn here. Just to say the meeting with Sheldon Lloyd to discuss table centerpieces has been changed to next Tuesday the twenty-first, at two-thirty. Byee!"

I have just enough time to think "That's odd," before my head hits the pillow and I pass out into a deep, dreamless sleep.

Eight hours later I wake up and sit bolt upright.

What was that?

I reach out to the machine and press the "Repeat" button. Robyn's voice chirps exactly the same message again, and the computer display informs me it was left yesterday.

But . . . that doesn't make any sense. The New York wedding's off.

I look disorientedly around the dim apartment. My body clock's so screwed up, it could be any time at all. I pad into the kitchen for a glass of water and look blearily out of the window at the mural of dancers on the building opposite.

I canceled the wedding. There were witnesses. Why is Robyn still organizing table centerpieces? I mean, it wasn't as though I was vague about it.

What's happened?

I drink my water, pour another glass, and go into the living room. It's 4 P.M. according to the VCR clock, so there's still time to call her. Find out what's going on.

"Hello! Wedding Events Ltd.!" says a girl I don't recognize. "How may I help you?"

"Hi! Excuse me, this is Becky Bloomwood. You're . . . you were organizing a wedding for me?"

"Oh, hi, Becky! I'm Kirsten, Robyn's assistant. Can I just say that I thought your *Sleeping Beauty* concept was totally inspired? I told all my friends about it, and they were all, like, 'I love *Sleeping Beauty*! That's what I'm going to do when *I* get married.' "

"Oh. Er . . . thanks. Listen, Kirsten, this might seem like a strange question . . ."

How am I going to put this? I can't say, Is my wedding still on?

"Is my . . . wedding still on?"

"I certainly hope so!" says Kirsten with a laugh. "Unless you've had a row with Luke!" Her tone suddenly changes. "*Have* you had a row with Luke? Because we have a procedure if that happens . . ."

"No! I haven't! It's just . . . didn't you get my message?"

"Which message was that?" says Kirsten brightly.

"The message I left about two weeks ago!"

"Oh, I'm sorry. What with the flood . . ."

"Flood?" I stare at the phone in dismay. "You had a *flood*?"

"I was sure Robyn had called you in England to let you know! It's OK, nobody was drowned. We just had to evacuate the office for a few days, and some of the telecoms were affected . . . plus unfortunately an antique ring cushion belonging to one of our clients was ruined . . ."

"So you *didn't* get the message?"

"Was it the one about the hors d'oeuvres?" says Kirsten thoughtfully.

I swallow several times, feeling almost light-headed.

"Becky, Robyn's just stepped in," Kirsten's saying, "if you'd like to speak to her . . ."

No way. I'm not trusting the phone anymore.

"Can you tell her," I say, trying to keep calm, "that I'm coming into the office. Tell her to wait. I'll be there as soon as I can."

"Is it urgent?"

"Yes. It's pretty urgent."

Robyn's offices are in a plushy building, right up on Ninety-sixth Street. As I knock on the door, I can hear her gurgling laugh, and as I cautiously open the door, I see her sitting at her desk, champagne glass in one hand, telephone in the other, and an open box of chocolates on the desk.

"Becky!" she says. "Come in! I won't be a second! Jennifer, I think we should go with the devore satin. Yes? OK. See you soon." She puts down the phone and beams at me. "Becky, sweetheart. How are you? How was England?"

"Fine, thanks. Robyn—"

"I have just been to a delightful thank-you lunch given to me by Mrs. Herman Winkler at the Carlton. Now, that was a fabulous wedding. The groom gave the bride a schnauzer puppy at the altar! So adorable . . ." Her brow wrinkles. "Where was I going with this? Oh yes! You know what? Her daughter and new son-in-law just left for England on their honeymoon! I said to her, perhaps they'll bump into Becky Bloomwood!"

"Robyn, I need to talk to you."

"Absolutely. If it's about the dessert flatware, I've spoken to the Plaza—"

"It's not about the flatware!" I cry. "Robyn, listen! While I was England, I canceled the wedding. I left a message! But you didn't get it."

There's silence in the plushy room. Then Robyn's face creases up into laughter.

"Ha-ha-ha! Becky, you're priceless! Isn't she priceless, Kirsten?"

"Robyn, I'm serious. I want to call the whole thing off. I want to get married in England. My mum's organizing a wedding, it's all arranged—"

"Can you imagine if you did that?" says Robyn with a gurgle. "Well, of course you couldn't, because of the prenup. If you canceled now, you'd be in for a lot of money!" She laughs gaily. "Would you like some champagne?"

I stare at her, momentarily halted. "What do you mean, the prenup?"

"The contract you signed, sweetheart." She hands me a glass of champagne, and my fingers automatically close round it.

"But . . . but Luke didn't sign it. He said it wasn't valid if he didn't sign—"

"Not between you and Luke! Between you and me! Or, rather, Wedding Events Ltd."

"What?" I swallow. "Robyn, what are you talking about? I never signed anything."

"Of course you did! All my brides do! I gave it to Elinor to pass along to you, and she returned it to me . . . I have a copy of it somewhere!" She takes a sip of champagne, swivels on her chair, and reaches into an elegant wooden filing cabinet.

"Here we are!" She hands me a photocopy of a document. "Of course, the original is with my lawyer . . ."

I stare at the page, my heart pounding. It's a typed sheet, headed "Terms of Agreement." I look straight down to the dotted line at the bottom—and there's my signature.

My mind zooms back to that dark, rainy night. Sitting in Elinor's apartment. Indignantly signing every single sheet in front of me. Not bothering to read the words above.

Oh God. What have I done?

Feverishly I start to scan the contract, only half taking in the legal phrases.

"The Organizer shall prepare full plans . . . time frame to be mutually agreed . . . the Client shall be consulted on all matters . . . liaise with service providers . . . budget shall be agreed . . . final decisions shall rest with the Client . . . any breach or cancellation for any reason whatsoever . . . reimbursement . . . 30 days . . . full and final payment . . . Furthermore . . ."

As I read the next words, slugs are crawling up and down my back.

"Furthermore, in the case of cancellation, should the Client marry within one year of the date of cancellation, the Client will be liable to a penalty of $100,000, payable to Wedding Events Ltd."

A hundred-thousand-dollar penalty.

And I've signed it.

"A hundred thousand dollars?" I say at last. "That . . . that seems a lot."

"That's only for the silly girls who pretend to cancel and then get married anyway," says Robyn cheerily.

"But why—"

"Becky, if I plan a wedding, then I want that wedding to happen. We've had girls pull out before." Her voice suddenly hardens. "Girls who decided to go their own way. Girls who decided to use my ideas, my contacts. Girls who thought they could exploit my expertise and get away with it." She leans forward with glittering eyes, and I shrink back fearfully.

"Becky, you don't want to be those girls."

She's crazy. The wedding planner's crazy.

"G-good idea," I say quickly. "You have to protect yourself!"

"Of course, Elinor could have signed it herself—but we agreed, this way, she's protecting her investment too!" Robyn beams at me. "It's a neat arrangement."

"Very clever!" I give a shrill laugh and take a slug of champagne.

What am I going to do? There must be some way out of this. There *must* be. People can't force other people to get married. It's not ethical.

"Cheer up, Becky!" Robyn snaps back into cheery-chirrupy mood. "Everything's under control. We've been taking care of everything while you were in Britain. The invitations are being written as we speak."

"Invitations?" I feel a fresh shock. "But they can't be. We haven't done a guest list yet."

"Yes you have, silly girl! What's this?"

She presses a couple of buttons on her computer and a list pops up, and I stare at it, my mouth open. Familiar names and addresses are scrolling past on the screen, one after another. Names of my cousins. Names of my old school friends. With a sudden lurch I spot "Janice and Martin Webster, The Oaks, 41 Elton Road, Oxshott."

How does Robyn know about Janice and Martin? I feel as though I've stumbled into some arch-villainess's lair. Any minute a panel will slide back and I'll see Mum and Dad tied to a chair with gags in their mouths.

"Where . . . where did you get those names?" I ask, trying to make it sound like a lighthearted inquiry.

"Luke gave us a list! I was pressuring him about it, so he had a look around your apartment. He said he found it hidden under the bed, or someplace odd. I said, that's probably the safest place to put it!"

She produces a piece of paper, and my eyes focus on it in disbelief.

Mum's handwriting.

The guest list she faxed over to us, weeks ago. The names and addresses of all the family friends and relations who are being invited to the wedding. The wedding at home.

Robyn's inviting all the same people as Mum.

"Have the invitations . . . gone out yet?" I say in a voice I don't quite recognize.

"Well, no." Robyn wags her finger at me. "Elinor's all went out last week. But we got your guest list so late, I'm afraid yours are still with the calligrapher! She's going to mail them off just as soon as she's finished . . ."

"Stop her," I say desperately. "You have to stop her!"

"What?" Robyn looks at me in surprise, and I'm aware of Kirsten lifting her head in interest. "Why, sweetheart?"

"I . . . I have to post the invitations myself," I say. "It's a . . . a family tradition. The bride always, er . . . posts her own invitations."

I rub my hot face, trying to keep cool. Across the room, I can see Kirsten staring curiously at me. They probably think I'm a complete control freak now. But I don't care. I have to stop those invitations from going out.

"How unusual!" says Robyn. "I never heard that custom before!"

"Are you saying I'm making it up?"

"No! Of course not! I'll let Judith know," says Robyn, picking up the phone and flicking her Rolodex, and I subside, breathing hard.

My head is spinning. Too much is happening. While I've been closeted with Suze and Ernie, everything has been steaming ahead without me realizing it, and now I've completely lost control of the situation. It's like this wedding is some big white horse that was trotting along quite nicely but has suddenly reared up and galloped off into the distance without me.

Robyn wouldn't *really* sue me. Would she?

"Hi, Judith? Yes, it's Robyn. Have you . . . you have? Well, that was quick work!" Robyn looks up. "You won't believe this, but she's already finished them!"

"What?" I look up in horror.

"She's at the mailbox already! Isn't that a—"

"Well, stop her!" I shriek. "Stop her!"

"Judith," says Robyn urgently. "Judith, stop. The bride is very particular. She wants to mail the invitations herself. Some family tradition," she says in a lower tone. "British. Yes. No, I don't know either."

She looks up with a careful smile, as though I'm a tricky three-year-old.

"Becky, I'm afraid a few already went into the mailbox. But you'll get to mail all the rest!"

"A few?" I say agitatedly. "How many?"

"How many, Judith?" says Robyn, then turns to me. "She thinks three."

"Three? Well . . . can she reach in and get them back?"

"I don't think so."

"Couldn't she find a . . . a stick or something . . ."

Robyn stares at me silently for a second, then turns to the phone.

"Judith, let me get the location of that mailbox." She scribbles on a piece of paper, then looks up. "You know what, Becky, I think the best thing is if you go down there, and just . . . do whatever you have to do . . ."

"OK. I will. Thanks."

As I put my coat on, I can see Robyn and Kirsten exchanging glances.

"You know, Becky, you might want to chill out a little," says Robyn. "Everything's under control. There's nothing for you to worry about!" She leans forward cozily. "As I often say to my brides, when they get a little agitated . . . it's just a wedding!"

I can't even bring myself to reply.

The mailbox is off the corner of Ninety-third and Lexington. As I turn into the street I can see a woman who must be Judith, dressed in a dark raincoat, leaning against the side of a building. As I hurry toward her, I see her look at her watch, give an impatient shrug, and head toward the mailbox, a stack of envelopes in her hand.

"Stop!" I yell, increasing my pace to a sprint. "Don't post those!"

I arrive by her side, panting so hard I can barely speak.

"Give me those invitations," I manage to gasp. "I'm the bride. Becky Bloomwood."

"Here you are!" says Judith. "A few already went in. But you know, no one said anything to me about not mailing them," she adds defensively.

"I know. I'm sorry."

"If Robyn hadn't called when she did . . . they would've been gone. All of them!"

"I . . . I appreciate that."

I flip through the thick taupe envelopes, feeling slightly shaky as I see all the names on Mum's list, beautifully written out in Gothic script.

"So are you going to mail them?"

"Of course I am." Suddenly I realize Judith's waiting for me to do it. "But I don't want to be watched," I add quickly. "It's a very private matter. I have to . . . say a poem and kiss each one . . ."

"Fine," says Judith, rolling her eyes. "Whatever."

She walks off toward the corner, and I stand as still as a rock until she's vanished from sight. Then, clutching the pile of invitations to my chest, I hurry to the corner, raise my hand, and hail a cab to take me home.

Luke is still out when I arrive, and the apartment is as dim and silent as it was when I left it. My suitcase is open on the floor—and as I walk in I can see inside it the pile of invitations to the Oxshott wedding that Mum gave me to pass on to Elinor.

I pick up the second pile of invitations and look from one to the other. One pile of white envelopes. One pile of taupe envelopes. Two weddings. On the same day. In less than six weeks.

If I do one, Mum will never speak to me again.

If I do the other, I get sued for $100,000.

OK, just . . . keep calm. Think logically. There has to be a way out of this. There *has* to be. As long as I keep my head and don't get into a—

Suddenly I hear the sound of the front door opening. "Becky?" comes Luke's voice. "Is that you?"

Fuck.

In a complete panic, I open the cocktail cabinet, shove both lots of invitations inside, slam the door, and whip round breathlessly just as Luke comes in.

"Sweetheart!" His whole face lights up and he throws his briefcase down. "You're back! I missed you." He gives me a huge hug—then draws back and looks anxiously at me. "Becky? Is everything all right?"

"I'm fine!" I say brightly. "Honestly, everything's great! I'm just tired."

"You look wiped out. I'll make some tea, and you can tell me all about Suze."

He goes out of the room and I collapse weakly on the sofa.

What the hell am I going to do now?

THE PINES
43 Elton Road
Oxshott
Surrey

FAX MESSAGE

TO BECKY BLOOMWOOD

FROM MUM

20 May 2002

Becky, love, I don't want to worry you. But it looks like that deranged woman you were telling us about has gone one step further and actually printed invitations! Auntie Irene phoned up today and told us she'd got some peculiar invitation through the post, for the Plaza Hotel, just like you said. Apparently it was all bronze and beige, very odd and not like a proper wedding invitation at all!

The best thing is to ignore these people, so I told her to put it straight in the bin and not worry about it. And you must do the same, darling. But I just thought I should let you know.

Much love and talk soon,

Mum xxxxxxxxx

Finerman Wallstein

Attorneys at Law

Finerman House
1398 Avenue of the Americas
New York, NY 10105

Miss Rebecca Bloomwood
251 W. 11th Street, Apt. B
New York, NY 10014

May 21, 2002

INVOICE no. 10956

April 3rd	Receiving instructions to redraft your will	$150
April 6th	Receiving further instructions to redraft your will	$150
April 11th	Receiving instructions for further amendments to your will	$150
April 17th	Receiving further instructions to redraft your will	$150
April 19th	Receiving instructions for further amendments to your will	$150
April 24th	Receiving further instructions to redraft your will	$150
April 30th	Receiving instructions for further amendments to your will	$150
Total:		**$1,050**

With thanks

Fifteen

OK. THE REALLY vital thing is to keep a sense of proportion. I mean, let's face it, every wedding has the odd glitch. You can't expect the whole process to go smoothly. I've just bought a new book, called *The Realistic Bride,* which I'm finding very comforting at the moment. It has a huge chapter all about wedding hitches, and it says: "No matter how insurmountable the problem seems, there will always be a solution! So don't worry!"

So the example they give is of a bride who loses her satin shoe on the way to the reception. Not one who has arranged two different weddings on the same day on different continents, is hiding half the invitations in a cocktail cabinet, and has discovered her wedding planner is a litigious nutcase.

But you know, I'm sure the principle's broadly the same.

I've been back in New York for a week now, and during that time I've been to see about seventeen different lawyers about Robyn's contract. All of them have looked at it carefully, told me they're afraid it's watertight, and advised me in the future to read all documentation before signing it.

Actually, that's not quite true. One lawyer just said, "Sorry, miss, there's nothing we can do," as soon as I mentioned that the contract was with Robyn de Bendern. Another said, "Girl, you're in trouble," and put the phone down.

I can't believe there isn't a way out, though. As a last resort, I've sent it off to Garson Low, the most expensive lawyer in Manhattan. I read about him in *People* magazine, and it said he has the sharpest mind in the legal world. It said he can find a loophole in a piece of concrete. So I'm kind of pinning all my hopes on him—and meanwhile, trying very hard to act normally and not crumple into a gibbering wreck.

"I'm having lunch with Michael today," says Luke, coming into the kitchen with a couple of boxes in his arms. "He seems to have settled into his new place well."

Michael's taken the plunge and moved to New York, which is fantastic for us. He's working part time as a consultant at Brandon Communications, and the rest of the time, as he put it, he's "reclaiming his life." He's taken up painting, and has joined a group that power-walks in Central Park, and last time we saw him he was talking about taking a course in Italian cookery.

"That's great!" I say.

"He said we must come over soon . . ." He peers at me. "Becky, are you all right?"

Abruptly I realize I'm drumming a pencil so hard it's making indentations in the kitchen table.

"I'm absolutely fine," I say with an overbright smile. "Why wouldn't I be?"

I haven't said a word about anything to Luke. In *The Realistic Bride* it says the way to stop your fiancé from getting bored with wedding details is to feed them to him on a need-to-know basis.

I don't feel Luke needs to know anything just yet.

"A couple more wedding presents," he says. He dumps the boxes on the counter and grins at me. "It's getting closer, isn't it?"

"Yes! Yes it is!" I attempt a laugh, not very successfully.

"Another toaster . . . this time from Bloomingdale's." He frowns. "Becky, exactly how many wedding lists have we got?"

"I don't know. A few."

"I thought the whole point of a wedding list was that we *didn't* end up with seven toasters."

"We haven't got seven toasters!" I point to the box. "This is a *brioche grill.*"

"And we also have . . . a Gucci handbag." He raises his eyebrows quizzically at me. "A Gucci handbag for a wedding present?"

"It's his-and-hers luggage!" I say defensively. "I put down a briefcase for you . . ."

"Which no one's bought for me."

"That's not my fault! I don't tell them what to buy!"

Luke shakes his head incredulously. "Did you put down his-and-hers Jimmy Choos too?"

"Did someone get the Jimmy Choos?" I say joyfully—then stop as I see his face. "I'm . . . joking." I clear my throat. "Here. Look at Suze's baby."

I've just had three rolls of film developed, mostly of Suze and Ernie.

"That's Ernie in the bath . . ." I point out, handing him photographs. "And that's Ernie asleep . . . and Suze asleep . . . and Suze . . . hang on a minute . . ." Hastily I pass over the ones of Suze breast-feeding with nothing on except a pair of knickers. She had actually bought a special breast-feeding top from a catalogue, which promised "discretion and ease at home and in public." But she got so pissed off with the stupid concealed zip, she threw it away after one day. "And look! That's the first day we brought him home!"

Luke sits down at the table, and as he leafs through the pictures, a strange expression comes over his face.

"She looks . . . blissful," he says.

"She is," I agree. "She adores him. Even when he screams."

"They seem bonded already." He stares at a photo of Suze laughing as Ernie grabs her hair.

"Oh, they are. Even by the time I left, he yelled if I tried to take him away from her."

I look at Luke, feeling touched. He's completely transfixed by these photographs. Which actually quite surprises me. I never thought he'd be particularly into babies. I mean, most men, if you handed them a load of baby pictures—

"I don't have any pictures of myself as a tiny baby," he says, turning to a picture of Ernie peacefully asleep on Suze.

"Don't you? Oh well . . ."

"My mother took them all with her."

His face is unreadable, and tiny alarm bells start to ring inside my head.

"Really?" I say casually. "Well, anyway—"

"Maybe she wanted to keep them nearby."

"Yes," I say doubtfully. "Maybe she did."

Oh God. I should have realized these pictures would set Luke off brooding about his mother again.

I'm not quite sure what happened between them while I was away. All I know is that eventually Luke managed to get through to her at the clinic. And apparently she came up with some lame explanation for why that newspaper article didn't mention Luke. Something about the journalist wasn't interested.

I don't know whether Luke believed her. I don't know whether he's forgiven her or not. To be honest, I don't think *he* knows. Every so often he goes all blank and withdrawn, and I can tell he's thinking about it.

Part of me wants to say, "Look, Luke, just forget it! She's a complete cow and she doesn't love you and you're better off without her."

Then I remember something his stepmother, Annabel, said—when we had that chat, all those months ago. As we were saying good-bye, she said, "As hard as it may be to believe, Luke needs Elinor."

"No, he doesn't!" I replied indignantly. "He's got you, he's got his dad, he's got me . . ."

But Annabel shook her head. "You don't understand. He's had this longing for Elinor ever since he was a child. It's driven him to work so hard; it's sent him to America; it's part of who he is now. Like a vine twisted round an apple tree." And she gave me this rather penetrating look and said, "Be careful, Becky. Don't try to chop her out of his life. Because you'll damage him too."

How did she read my mind? How did she know that I was exactly picturing myself, and Elinor, and an ax . . .

I look at Luke, and he's staring, mesmerized, at a picture of Suze kissing Ernie on the tummy.

"Anyway!" I say brightly, gathering up the photos and shoving them back into the envelopes. "You know, the bond is just as strong between Tarquin and Ernie. You should have seen them together. Tarquin's making a wonderful dad. He changes nappies and everything! In fact, I often think a mother's love is overrated . . ."

Oh, it's no good. Luke isn't even listening.

The phone rings, and he doesn't move, so I go into the sitting room to answer it.

"Hello?"

"Hello. Is that Rebecca Bloomwood?" says a strange man's voice.

"Yes it is," I say, noticing a new catalogue from Pottery Barn on the table. Perhaps I should register there too. "Who's this?"

"This is Garson Low, from Low and Associates."

My whole body freezes. Garson Low himself? Calling me at home?

"I apologize for calling so early," he's saying.

"No! Not at all!" I say, coming to life and quickly kicking the door shut so Luke can't hear. "Thanks for calling!"

Thank God. He must think I have a case. He must want to help me take on Robyn. We'll probably make groundbreaking legal history or something, and stand outside the courtroom while cameras flash and it'll be like *Erin Brockovich*!

"I received your letter yesterday," says Garson Low. "And I was intrigued by your dilemma. That's quite a bind you've got yourself in."

"I know it is," I say. "That's why I came to you."

"Is your fiancé aware of the situation?"

"Not yet." I lower my voice. "I'm hoping I'll be able to find a solution first—and then tell him. You understand, Mr. Low."

"I certainly do."

This is great. We've got rapport and everything.

"In that case," says Garson Low, "let's get down to business."

"Absolutely!" I feel a swell of relief. You see, this is what you get when you consult the most expensive lawyer in Manhattan. You get quick results.

"First of all, the contract has been very cleverly drawn up," says Garson Low.

"Right." I nod.

"There are several extremely ingenious clauses, covering all eventualities."

"I see."

"I've examined it thoroughly. And as far as I can see, there is no way you can get married in Britain without incurring the penalty."

"Right." I nod expectantly.

There's a short silence.

"So . . . what's the loophole?" I ask eventually.

"There is no loophole. Those are the facts."

"What?" I stare confusedly at the phone. "But . . . that's why you rang, isn't it? To tell me you'd found a loophole. To tell me we could win!"

"No, Miss Bloomwood. I called to tell you that if I were you, I would start making arrangements to cancel your British wedding."

I feel a stab of shock. "But . . . but I can't. That's the whole point. My mum's had the house done up, and everything. It would kill her."

"Then I'm afraid you will have to pay Wedding Events Ltd. the full penalty."

"But . . ." My throat is tight. "I can't do that either. I haven't got a hundred thousand dollars! There must be another way!"

"I'm afraid—"

"There must be some brilliant solution!" I push back my hair, trying not to panic. "Come on! You're supposed to be the cleverest person in America or something! You must be able to think of some way out!"

"Miss Bloomwood, let me assure you. I have looked at this from all angles and there is no brilliant solution. There is no way out." Garson Low sighs. "May I give you three small pieces of advice?"

"What are they?" I say with a flicker of hope.

"The first is, never sign any document before reading it first."

"I know that!" I cry before I can stop myself. "What's the good of everyone telling me that now?"

"The second is—and I strongly recommend this—tell your fiancé."

"And what's the third?"

"Hope for the best."

Is that all a million-pound lawyer can come up with? Tell your fiancé and hope for the best? Bloody stupid . . . expensive . . . complete rip-off . . .

OK, keep calm. I'm cleverer than him. I can think of something. I know I can. I just *know* I—

Hang on.

I saunter casually into the kitchen, where Luke has stopped gazing at the pictures of Suze and is staring broodingly into space instead.

"Hi," I say, running a hand along the back of his chair. "Hey, Luke. You've got loads of money, haven't you?"

"No."

"What do you mean, no?" I say, slightly affronted. "Of course you have!"

"I've got assets," says Luke. "I've got a company. That's not necessarily the same as money."

"Whatever." I wave my hand impatiently. "And we're getting married. You know, 'All thy worldly goods' and everything. So in a way . . ." I pause carefully, "it's mine, too."

"Yeee-s. Is this going anywhere?"

"So . . . if I asked you for some money, would you give it to me?"

"I expect so. How much?"

"Er . . . a hundred thousand dollars," I say, trying to sound nonchalant.

Luke raises his head. "A hundred thousand dollars?"

"Yes! I mean, it's not that much really—"

Luke sighs. "OK, Becky. What have you seen? Because if it's another customized leather coat—"

"It's not a coat! It's a . . . a surprise."

"A hundred-thousand-dollar surprise."

"Yes," I say after a pause. But even I don't sound that convinced.

Maybe this isn't a brilliant solution after all.

"Becky, a hundred thousand dollars *is* that much. It's a lot of money!"

"I know," I say. "I know. Look . . . OK . . . it doesn't matter." And I hurry out before he can question me further.

OK, forget the lawyers. Forget the money. There has to be another solution to this. I just need to think laterally.

I mean, we could always elope. Get married on a beach and change our names and never see our families again.

No, this is it. I go to the Oxshott wedding. And Luke goes to the New York wedding. And we each say we've been jilted . . . and then we secretly meet up . . .

No! I have it! We hire stand-ins! Genius!

I'm riding up the escalator to work as this idea comes to me—and I'm so gripped, I almost forget to step off. This is it. We hire look-alikes, and they stand in for us at the Plaza wedding, and no one ever realizes. I mean, all the guests there are going to be Elinor's friends. People Luke and I barely know. We could get the bride look-alike to wear a really thick veil . . . and the Luke look-alike could say he'd cut his face shaving, and wear a huge bandage . . . and meanwhile we'd have flown back to England . . .

"Watch out, Becky!" says Christina with a smile, and I look up, startled. I was about to walk right into a mannequin.

"Busy thinking about the wedding?" she adds as I go into the personal shopping department.

"That's right," I say brightly.

"You know, you look so much more relaxed these days," says Christina approvingly. "Your break obviously did you the world of good. Seeing your mom . . . catching up with home . . ."

"Yes, it was . . . great!"

"I think it's admirable the way you're so laid-back." Christina takes a sip of coffee. "You've barely mentioned the wedding to any of us since you've been back! In fact, you've almost seemed to be avoiding the subject!"

"I'm not avoiding it!" I say, my smile fixed. "Why would I do that?"

"Some brides seem to make so *much* of a wedding. Almost let it take over their life. But you seem to have it all under control—"

"Absolutely!" I say, even more brightly. "If you'll excuse me, I'll just get ready for my first client—"

"Oh, I had to switch your appointments around," says Christina as I open the door of my room. "You have a first-timer at ten. Amy Forrester."

"I don't like yellow or orange." Amy Forrester's voice is still droning on. "And when I say dressy, I mean not *too* dressy. Just kind of formal . . . but sexy. You know what I mean?" She snaps her gum and looks at me expectantly.

"Er . . . yes!" I say, not having a clue what she's talking about. I can't even remember what she wants. Come on, Becky. Concentrate.

"So, just to recap, you're after . . . an evening dress?" I risk, scribbling on my notebook.

"Or a pantsuit. Whatever. I can pretty much wear any shape." Amy Forrester gazes complacently at herself in the mirror, and I give her a surreptitious Manhattan Onceover, taking in her tight lilac top and turquoise stirrup leggings. She looks like a model in an ad for some dodgy piece of home exercise equipment. Same tacky blond haircut and everything.

"You have a wonderful figure!" I say, realizing a bit late that she's waiting for a compliment.

"Thank you! I do my best."

With the help of Rollaflab! Just roll away that flab . . .

"I already bought my vacation wardrobe." She snaps her gum again. "But then my boyfriend said, why not buy a few more little things? He loves to treat me. He's a wonderful man. So—do you have any ideas?"

"Yes," I say, finally forcing myself to concentrate. "Yes, I do. I'll just go and fetch some pieces that I think might suit you."

I go out onto the floor and start gathering up dresses. Gradually, as I wander from rail to rail, I begin to relax. It's a relief to focus on something else; to think about something other than weddings . . .

"Hi, Becky!" says Erin, passing by with Mrs. Zaleskie, one of her regular clients. "Hey, I was just saying to Christina, we have to plan your shower!"

Oh God.

"You know, my daughter works at the Plaza," puts in Mrs. Zaleskie. "She says *everyone's* talking about your wedding."

"Are they?" I say after a pause. "Well, it's really no big deal—"

"No big deal? Are you kidding? The staff is fighting over who's going to serve! They all want to see the enchanted woodland!" She peers at me through her spectacles. "Is it true you're having a string orchestra, a DJ, *and* a ten-piece band?"

"Er . . . yes."

"My friends are *so* jealous I'm going," says Erin, her face all lit up. "They're like, you have to show us the pictures afterward! We are allowed to take pictures, right?"

"I . . . don't know. I guess so."

"You must be excited," says Mrs. Zaleskie. "You're a lucky girl."

"I . . . I know."

I can't bear this.

"I have to go," I mutter, and hurry back to the personal shopping department.

I can't win. Whatever I do. Either way, I'm going to let down a whole load of people.

As Amy wriggles into the first dress, I stand, staring blankly at the floor, my heart thumping hard. I've been in trouble before. I've been stupid before. But never on this level. Never so large, so expensive, so important . . .

"I like this," says Amy, staring at herself critically. "But is there enough cleavage?"

"Er . . ." I look at her. It's a black chiffon dress, slashed practically to the navel. "I *think* so. But we could always have it altered . . ."

"Oh, I don't have time for that!" says Amy. "I'm only in New York for one more day. We go on vacation tomorrow and then we're moving to Atlanta. That's why I came out shopping. They're packing up the apartment and it's driving me nuts."

"I see," I say absently.

"My boyfriend adores my body," she says smugly as she clambers out of it. "But then, his wife never bothered with her appearance at all. Ex-wife, I should say. They're getting a divorce."

"Right," I say politely, handing her a white and silver sheath dress.

"I can't believe he put up with her for so long. She's this completely jealous harridan. I'm having to take legal action!" Amy steps into the sheath dress. "You know, she mailed me this really offensive letter. It was like a list of completely insulting stuff about me! Our lawyer says we have an excellent case."

That sounds familiar. I look up, my brain starting to tweak. "You're sure it was her who sent it?"

"Oh yes! I mean, she signed it and everything. Plus it was definitely her writing. William recognized it."

I stare at her, my skin prickling. "What . . . what did you say your boyfriend's name was?"

"William." Her lip curls scornfully. "*She* called him Bill."

Oh my God.

It is. It's the blond intern. Right here in front of me.

OK. Just . . . keep smiling. Don't let her know you suspect anything.

Inside I'm hot with outrage. *This* is the woman Laurel was cast aside for? This stupid, tacky airhead?

"That's why we're moving to Atlanta," Amy says, examining her reflection complacently. "We want to start a new life together, so William asked the firm for a transfer. You know, discreetly. We don't want the old witch following us." She frowns. "Now, I like this one better."

She bends down farther and I freeze. Hang on. She's wearing a pendant. A pendant with a . . . is that green stone an *emerald*?

"Amy, I just have to make a call," I say casually. "Keep trying on the dresses!" And I slide out of the room.

When I eventually get through to Laurel's office, her assistant, Gina, tells me she's in a meeting with American Airlines and can't be disturbed.

"Please," I say. "Get her out. It's important."

"So is American Airlines," says Gina. "You'll have to wait."

"But you don't understand! It really is crucial!"

"Becky, a new skirt length from Prada is not crucial," says Gina a little wearily. "Not in the world of airplane leasing."

"It's not clothes!" I say indignantly—then hesitate for a second, wondering how much Laurel confides in Gina. "It's Amy Forrester," I say at last in a lowered voice. "You know who I mean?"

"Yes, I know," says Gina in a voice that makes me thinks she knows even more than I do. "What about her?"

"I have her."

"You *have* her? What do you—"

"She's in my fitting room right now!" I glance behind me to make sure no one can hear. "Gina, she's wearing this pendant with an emerald in it! I'm sure it's Laurel's grandmother's! The one the police couldn't find."

There's a long pause.

"OK," says Gina at last. "I'll get Laurel out of the meeting. She'll probably come right over. Just don't let . . . *her* leave."

"I won't. Thanks, Gina."

I put down the phone and stand still for a moment, thinking. Then I head back to my fitting room, trying to look as natural as possible.

"So!" I say breezily as I go in. "Let's get back to trying on dresses! And remember, Amy, just take your time over each one. As long as you like. We can take all day, if we need to—"

"I don't need to try on any more," says Amy, turning round in a tight red sequined dress. "I'll take this one."

"What?" I say blankly.

"It's great! Look, it fits me perfectly." She does a little twirl, admiring herself in the mirror.

"But we haven't even started yet!"

"So what? I've made my decision. I want this one." She looks at her watch. "Besides, I'm in a bit of a hurry. Can you unzip me, please?"

"Amy . . ." I force a smile. "I really think you should try on some others before you make a decision."

"I don't need to try any others! You have a very good eye."

"No, I don't! It looks terrible!" I say without thinking, and she gives me a strange look. "I mean . . . there was a wonderful pink dress I wanted to see on you . . ." I grab for the hanger. "Just imagine that on you! Or . . . or this halter neck . . ."

Amy Forrester gives me an impatient look. "I'm taking this one. Please, will you help me out of it?"

What can I do? I can't *force* her to stay.

I glance surreptitiously at my watch. Laurel's office is only a block or two away. She should be here any minute.

"Please, will you help me out of it?" she repeats, her voice hardening.

"Yes!" I say flusteredly. "All right!"

I reach for the zip of the sequined red dress and start to pull it down. Then I have a sudden thought.

"Actually," I say. "Actually, it'll be easier to get it off if I pull it over your head—"

"OK," says Amy Forrester impatiently. "Whatever."

I undo the zip a tiny bit more, then tug the tight-fitting dress up over her hips and right over her head.

Ha! She's trapped! The stiff red fabric covers her face completely, but the rest of her is clad only in underwear and high heels. She looks like a Barbie doll crossed with a Christmas cracker.

"Hey. It's gotten stuck." She waves one of her arms fruitlessly, but it's pinned to her head by the dress.

"Really?" I exclaim innocently. "Oh dear. They do that sometimes."

"Well, get me out!" She takes a couple of steps, and I back away nervously in case she grabs my arm. I feel like I'm six years old and playing blindman's bluff at a birthday party.

"Where are you?" comes a furious muffled voice. "Get me out!"

"I'm just . . . trying to . . ." Gingerly I give a little tug at the dress. "It's really stuck," I say apologetically. "Maybe if you bent over and wriggled . . ."

Come *on*, Laurel. Where are you? I open my fitting room and have a quick glance out, but nothing.

"OK! I'm getting somewhere!"

I look up and feel a plunge of dismay. Amy's hand has appeared out of nowhere and somehow she's managed to grasp the zip with two manicured nails. "Can you help me pull the zipper down?"

"Erm . . . I can try . . ."

I take hold of the zip and start pulling it in the opposite direction from the way she's tugging.

"It's stuck!" she says in frustration.

"I know! I'm trying to get it undone . . ."

"Wait a minute." Her voice is suddenly suspicious. "Which way are you pulling?"

"Er . . . the same way as you . . ."

"Hi, Laurel," I suddenly hear Christina saying in surprise. "Are you all right? Did you have an appointment?"

"No. But I think Becky has something for me—"

"Here!" I say, hurrying to the door and looking out. And there's Laurel, cheeks flushed with animation, wearing her new Michael Kors skirt with a navy blue blazer, which looks completely wrong.

How many times have I told her? Honestly, I should do more

spot-checks on my clients. Who knows what they're all wearing out there?

"Here she is," I say, nodding toward the Barbie-doll-Christmas-cracker hybrid, who is still trying to unzip the dress.

"It's OK," says Laurel, coming into the fitting room. "You can leave her to me."

"What? Who's that?" Amy's head jerks up disorientedly. "Oh Jesus. No. Is that—"

"Yes," says Laurel, closing the door. "It's me."

I stand in front of the door, trying to ignore the raised voices coming from my room. After a few minutes, Christina comes out of her room and looks at me.

"Becky, what's going on?"

"Um . . . Laurel bumped into an acquaintance. I thought I'd give them some privacy." A thumping sound comes from the room and I cough loudly. "I think they're . . . chatting."

"Chatting." Christina gives me a hard look.

"Yes! Chatting!"

The door suddenly opens, and Laurel emerges, a bunch of keys in her hand.

"Becky, I'm going to need to pay a little visit to Amy's apartment, and she'd like to stay here until I come back. Isn't that right, Amy?"

I glance past Laurel into the fitting room. Amy is sitting in the corner in her underwear, minus the emerald pendant, looking completely shell-shocked. She nods silently.

As Laurel strides off, Christina gives me an incredulous look. "Becky—"

"So!" I say quickly to Amy, in my best Barneys employee manner. "While we're waiting, would you care to try some more dresses?"

Forty minutes later, Laurel arrives back, her face alive with animation.

"Did you get the rest of it?" I say eagerly.

"I got it all."

Christina, on the other side of the department, looks up, then looks away again. She's said that the only way she can't fire me for what just happened is not to know about it.

So we're basically agreed, she doesn't know about it.

"Here you are." Laurel tosses the keys to Amy. "You can go now. Give my regards to Bill. He deserves you."

As Amy totters, almost running, toward the escalator, Laurel puts an arm round me.

"Becky, you're an angel," she says warmly. "I can't even begin to repay you. But whatever you want, it's yours."

"Don't be silly!" I say at once. "I just wanted to help."

"I'm serious!"

"Laurel—"

"I insist. Name it, and it'll be there in time for your wedding."

My wedding.

It's as though someone's opened a window and the cold air is rushing in.

In all the excitement and urgency, I'd managed briefly to forget about it. But now it all comes piling back into my head.

My two weddings. My two fiascos.

Like two trains traveling toward me. Quicker and quicker, getting nearer even when I'm not looking at them. Gathering momentum with every minute. If I manage to dodge one, I'll only get hit by the other.

I stare at Laurel's warm, open face, and all I want to do is bury my head in her shoulder and wail, "Sort out my life for me!"

"Whatever you want," says Laurel again, and squeezes my shoulders.

As I walk slowly back to my fitting room, the adrenaline has gone. I can feel a familiar, wearying anxiety creeping over me. Another day has gone by, and I'm no nearer to a brilliant solution. I have no idea what I'm going to do. And I'm running out of time.

Maybe the truth is, I can't solve this on my own, I think, sinking heavily down in my chair. Maybe I need help. Fire rescue trucks and SWAT teams.

Or maybe just Luke.

Sixteen

As I arrive home, I'm surprisingly calm. In fact, I almost feel a sense of relief. I've tried everything—and now I'm at the end of the line. There's nothing else I can do but confess everything to Luke. He'll be shocked. Angry too. But at least he'll know.

I stopped in a café on the way, had a coffee, and thought very carefully about how I was going to tell him. Because everyone knows, it's all in the presentation. When the president's going to raise taxes, he doesn't say, "I'm going to raise taxes." He says, "Every American citizen knows the value of education." So I've written out a speech, a bit like the State of the Union address, and I've memorized it word for word, with gaps for interjections from Luke. (Or applause. Though that's a bit unlikely.) As long as I stick to my text, and no one brings up the question of Ugandan policy, then we should be all right.

My legs are trembling slightly as I climb the stairs to our apartment, even though Luke won't be back yet; I still have time to prepare. But as I open the door, to my shock, there he is, sitting at the table with a pile of papers and his back to me.

OK, Becky, come on. Ladies and gentlemen of Congress. Four score and thingummy. I let the door swing shut behind me, get out my notes, and take a deep breath.

"Luke," I begin in a grave, grown-up voice. "I have something to tell you about the wedding. It's quite a serious problem, with no easy solution. If there is a solution, it will be one that I can only achieve with your help. Which is why I'm telling you this now—and asking that you listen with an open mind."

So far so good. I'm quite proud of that bit, actually. The "listen with an open mind" bit was especially inspired, because it means he can't shout at me.

"In order to explain my current predicament," I continue, "I must take you back in time. Back to the beginning. By which I mean not the creation of Earth. Nor even the big bang. But tea at Claridges."

I pause—but Luke is still silent, listening. Maybe this is going to be OK.

"It was there, at Claridges, that my problem began. I was presented with an impossible task. I was, if you will, that Greek god having to choose between the three apples. Except there were only two—and they weren't apples." I pause significantly. "They were weddings."

At last, Luke turns round in his chair. His eyes are bloodshot, and there's a strange expression on his face. As he gazes at me, I feel a tremor of apprehension.

"Becky," he says, as though with a huge effort.

"Yes?" I gulp.

"Do you think my mother loves me?"

"What?" I say, thrown.

"Tell me honestly. Do you think my mother loves me?"

Hang on. Has he been listening to a single word I've been saying?

"Er . . . of course I do!" I say. "And speaking of mothers, that is, in a sense, where my problem originally lay—"

"I've been a fool." Luke picks up his glass and takes a swig of what looks like whiskey. "She's just been using me, hasn't she?"

I stare at him, discomfited—then notice the half-empty bottle on the table. How long has he been sitting here? I look at his face again, taut and vulnerable, and bite back some of the things I could say about Elinor.

"Of course she loves you!" I put down my speech and go over to him. "I'm sure she does. I mean, you can see it, in the way she . . . um . . ." I tail off feebly.

What am I supposed to say? In the way she uses your staff with no recompense or thanks? In the way she stabs you in the back, then disappears to Switzerland?

"What . . . why are you . . ." I say hesitantly. "Has something happened?"

"It's so stupid." He shakes his head. "I came across something earlier on." He takes a deep breath. "I was at her apartment to pick up some papers for the foundation. And I don't know why—maybe it was after seeing those photographs of Suze and Ernie this morning." He looks up. "But I found myself searching in her study for old pictures. Of me as a child. Of us. I don't really know what I was looking for. Anything, I guess."

"Did you find anything?"

Luke gestures to the papers littering the table and I squint puzzledly at one. "What are they?"

"They're letters. From my father. Letters he wrote to my mother after they split up, fifteen, twenty years ago. Pleading with her to see me." His voice is deadpan and I look at him warily.

"What do you mean?"

"I mean that he begged her to let me visit," says Luke evenly. "He offered to pay hotel bills. He offered to accompany me. He asked again and again . . . and I never knew." He reaches for a couple of sheets and hands them to me. "Look, read for yourself."

Trying to hide my shock, I start to scan them, taking in phrases here and there.

Luke is so desperate to see his mother . . . cannot understand your attitude . . .

"These letters explain a lot of things. It turns out her new husband wasn't against her taking me with them, after all. In fact, he sounds like a pretty decent guy. He agreed with my dad, I should come and visit. But she wasn't interested." He shrugs. "Why should she be, I suppose?"

. . . an intelligent loving boy . . . missing out on a wonderful opportunity . . .

"Luke, that's . . . terrible," I say inadequately.

"The worst thing is, I used to take it all out on my parents. When I was a teenager. I used to blame them."

I have a sudden vision of Annabel, and her kind, warm face; of Luke's dad, writing these letters in secret—and feel a pang of outrage toward Elinor. She doesn't deserve Luke. She doesn't deserve any family.

There's silence except for the rain drumming outside. I reach out and squeeze Luke's hand, trying to inject as much love and warmth as I can.

"Luke, I'm sure your parents understood. And . . ." I swallow all the things I really want to say about Elinor. "And I'm sure Elinor wanted you to be there really. I mean, maybe it was difficult for her at the time, or . . . or maybe she was away a lot—"

"There's something I've never told you," interrupts Luke. "Or anybody." He raises his head. "I came to see my mother when I was fourteen."

"What?" I stare at him in astonishment. "But I thought you said you never—"

"There was a school trip to New York. I fought tooth and nail to go on it. Mum and Dad were against it, of course, but in the end they gave in. They told me my mother was away, that, of course, otherwise, she would have loved to see me."

Luke reaches for the whiskey bottle and pours himself another drink. "I couldn't help it, I had to try and see her. Just in case they were wrong." He stares ahead, running his finger round the rim of his glass. "So . . . toward the end of the trip, we had a free day. Everyone else went up the Empire State Building. But I sneaked off. I had her address, and I just came and sat outside her building. It wasn't the building she's in now, it was another one, farther up Park Avenue. I sat on a step, and people kept staring at me as they went by, but I didn't care."

He takes a gulp of his drink and I gaze back at him, rigid. I don't dare make a sound. I hardly dare breathe.

"Then, at about twelve o'clock, a woman came out. She had dark hair, and a beautiful coat. I knew her face from the photograph. It was my mother." He's silent for a few seconds. "I . . . I stood up. She looked up and saw me. She stared at me for less than five seconds. Then she turned away. It was as though she hadn't seen me. She got into a taxi and went off, and that was it." He closes his eyes briefly. "I didn't even have a chance to take a step forward."

"What . . . what did you do?" I say tentatively.

"I left. And I walked around the city. I persuaded myself that she hadn't recognized me. That's what I told myself. That she had no idea what I looked like; that she couldn't possibly have known it was me."

"Well, maybe that's true!" I say eagerly. "How on earth would she have—"

I fall silent as he reaches for a faded blue airmail letter with something paper-clipped to it at the top.

"This is the letter my father wrote her to tell her I was coming," he says. He lifts up the paper and I feel a small jolt. "And this is me."

I'm looking into the eyes of a teenaged boy. A fourteen-year-old Luke. He's wearing a school uniform and he has a terrible haircut; in fact he's barely recognizable. But those are his dark eyes, gazing out at the world with a mixture of determination and hope.

There's nothing I can say. As I stare at his gawky, awkward face, I want to cry.

"You were right all along, Becky. I came to New York to impress my mother. I wanted her to stop dead in the street and turn round and . . . and stare . . . and be proud . . ."

"She is proud of you!"

"She isn't." He gives me a tiny half-smile. "I should just give up."

"No!" I say, a little too late. I reach out and take Luke's arm, feeling completely helpless. Completely sheltered and pampered in comparison. I grew up knowing that Mum and Dad thought I was the best thing in the whole wide world; knowing that they loved me, and always would, whatever I did.

"I'm sorry," says Luke at last. "I've gone on too much about this. Let's forget it. What did you want to talk about?"

"Nothing," I say at once. "It . . . doesn't matter. It can wait."

The wedding seems a million miles away, suddenly. I screw up my notes into a tight ball and throw them in the bin. Then I look around the cluttered room. Letters spread out on the table, wedding presents stacked up in the corner, paraphernalia everywhere. It's impossible to escape your own life when you live in a Manhattan apartment.

"Let's go out and eat," I say, standing up abruptly. "And see a movie or something."

"I'm not hungry," says Luke.

"That's not the point. This is place is just too . . . crowded." I take Luke's hand and tug at it. "Come on, let's get out of here. And just forget about everything. All of it."

We go out and walk, arm in arm, down to the cinema and lose ourselves in a movie about the Mafia. Then when it's over we walk a couple of blocks to a small, warm restaurant we know, and order red wine and risotto.

We don't mention Elinor once. Instead, we talk about Luke's childhood in Devon. He tells me about picnics on the beach, and a tree house his father built for him in the garden, and how his little half-sister Zoe always used to tag along with all her friends and drive him mad. Then he tells me about Annabel. About how fantastic she's always been to him, and how kind she is to everyone; and how he never ever felt she loved him any less than Zoe, who was truly hers.

We talk tentatively about things we've never even touched on. Like having children ourselves. Luke wants to have three. I want . . . well after having watched Suze go through labor, I don't think I want any, but I don't tell him that. I nod when he says "or perhaps even four" and wonder whether maybe I could pretend to be pregnant and secretly adopt them.

By the end of the evening, I think Luke is a lot better. We walk home and fall into bed and both go straight to sleep. During the night I half wake, and I think I see Luke standing by the window, staring out into the night. But I'm asleep again before I'm sure.

I wake up the next morning with a dry mouth and an aching head. Luke's already got up and I can hear clattering from the kitchen, so maybe he's making me a nice breakfast. I could do with some coffee, and maybe some toast. And then . . .

My stomach gives a nervous flip. I've got to bite the bullet. I've got to tell him about the weddings.

Last night was last night. Of course I couldn't do anything about it then. But now it's the morning and I can't wait any longer. I know it's terrible timing, I know it's the last thing he'll want to hear right now. But I just have to tell him.

I can hear him coming along the corridor, and I take a deep breath, trying to steady my nerves.

"Luke, listen," I say as the door swings open. "I know this is a bad time. But I really need to talk to you. We've got a problem."

"What's that?" says Robyn, coming into the room. "Nothing to do with the wedding, I hope!" She's wearing a powder-blue suit and patent leather pumps and carrying a tray of breakfast things. "Here you go, sweetheart. Some coffee to wake you up!"

Am I dreaming? What's Robyn doing in my bedroom?

"I'll just get the muffins," she says brightly, and disappears out of the room. I subside weakly onto my pillow, my head pounding, trying to work out what she might be doing here.

Suddenly last night's Mafia film jumps into my mind and I'm struck with terror. Oh my God. It's obvious.

She's found out about the other wedding—and she's come to murder me.

Robyn appears through the door again, with a basket of muffins, and smiles as she puts it down. I stare back, transfixed with fear.

"Robyn!" I say huskily. "I . . . didn't expect to see you. Isn't it a bit . . . early?"

"When it comes to my clients, there is no such thing as too early," says Robyn, with a twinkle. "I am at your service, day and night." She sits down on the armchair next to the bed and pours me out a cup of coffee.

"But how did you get in?"

"I picked the lock. Only kidding! Luke let me in on his way out!"

I'm alone in the apartment with her. She's got me trapped.

"Luke's gone to work already?"

"I'm not sure he was going to work." Robyn pauses thoughtfully. "It looked more like he was going jogging."

"Jogging?"

Luke doesn't jog.

"Now, drink up your coffee—and then I'll show you what you've been waiting for. What we've all been waiting for." She looks at her watch. "I have to be gone in twenty minutes, remember!"

I stare at her dumbly.

"Becky, are you all right? You do *remember* we have an appointment?"

Dimly a memory starts filtering back into my mind, like a shadow through gauze. Robyn. Breakfast meeting. Oh yes.

Why did I agree to a breakfast meeting?

"Of course I remember!" I say at last. "I'm just a bit . . . you know, hung over."

"You don't have to explain!" says Robyn cheerily. "Fresh orange juice is what you need. And a good breakfast. I say the same thing to all my brides: you must take care of yourself! There's no point starving yourself and then fainting at the altar. Have a muffin." She rummages in her bag. "And look! At last we have it!"

I look blankly at the scrap of shimmering silver material she's holding up.

"What is it?"

"It's the fabric for the cushion pads!" says Robyn. "Flown in especially from China. The one we had all the problems with over customs! You can't have forgotten, surely?"

"Oh! No, of course not," I say hastily. "Yes, it looks . . . lovely. Really beautiful."

"Now, Becky, there was something else," says Robyn. She puts the fabric away and looks up with a serious expression. "The truth is . . . I'm getting a little concerned."

I feel a fresh spasm of nerves and take a sip of coffee to hide it. "Really? What . . . what are you concerned about?"

"We haven't had a single reply from your British guests. Isn't that strange?"

For a moment I'm unable to speak.

"Er . . . yes," I manage at last. "Very."

"Except Luke's parents, who accepted a while ago. Of course they were on Elinor's guest list, so they got their invitation a little earlier, but even so . . ." She reaches for my coffee cup and takes a sip. "Mmm. This is good, if I do say so myself! Now, I don't want to accuse anyone of lacking manners. But we need to start getting some numbers in. So is it OK if I make a few tactful calls to England? I have all the phone numbers in my database . . ."

"No!" I say, suddenly waking up. "Don't call anybody! I mean . . . you'll get the replies, I promise."

"It's just so odd!" Robyn muses. "To have heard nothing . . . They did all receive their invitations, didn't they?"

"Of course they did! I'm sure it's just an oversight." I start pleating the sheet between finger and thumb. "You'll have some replies within a week. I can . . . guarantee it."

"Well, I certainly hope so! Because time is ticking on! We've only got four weeks to go!"

"I know!" I say shrilly, and take another gulp of coffee, wishing desperately it were vodka.

Four weeks.

Oh God.

"Shall I refresh your cup, sweetheart?" Robyn stands up—then bends down again. "What's this?" she says with interest, and picks up a piece of paper lying on the floor. "Is this a menu?"

I look up—and my heart stops. She's got one of Mum's faxes.

The menu for the other wedding.

Everything's right there, under the bed. If she starts looking . . .

"It's nothing!" I say, grabbing it from her. "Just a . . . um . . . a menu for a . . . a party . . ."

"You're holding a party?"

"We're . . . thinking about it."

"Well, if you want any help planning it, just say the word!" Robyn lowers her voice confidentially. "And a tiny tip?" She gestures to Mum's menu. "I think you'll find filo parcels are a little passé."

"Right. Er . . . thanks."

I have to get this woman out of here. At once. Before she finds anything else.

Abruptly I throw back the sheets and leap out of bed.

"Actually, Robyn, I'm still not feeling quite right. Maybe we could . . . could reschedule the rest of this meeting?"

"I understand." She pats my shoulder. "I'll leave you in peace."

"By the way," I say casually as we reach the front door. "I was just wondering . . . You know that financial penalty clause in your contract?"

"Yes!" Robyn beams at me.

"Out of interest." I give a little laugh. "Have you ever actually collected it?"

"Oh, only a few times!" says Robyn. She pauses reminiscently. "One silly girl tried to run off to Poland . . . but we found her in the end . . . See you, Becky!"

"See you!" I say, matching her bright tone, and close the door, my heart thumping hard.

She'll get me. It's only a matter of time.

As soon as I get to work, I call Luke at work and get his assistant, Julia.

"Hi," I say, "can I speak to Luke?"

"Luke called in sick," says Julia, sounding surprised. "Didn't you know?"

I stare at the phone, taken aback. Luke's taken a sickie? Blimey. Maybe his hangover was even worse than mine.

Shit, and I've nearly given the game away.

"Oh, right!" I say quickly. "Yes! Now you mention it . . . of course I knew! He's dreadfully sick, actually. He's got a terrible fever. And his . . . er . . . stomach. I just forgot for a moment, that's all."

"Well, give him all the best from us."

"I will!"

As I put the phone down, I realize I might have overreacted a teeny bit. I mean, it's not like anyone's going to give Luke the sack, is it? After all, it's his company.

In fact, I'm *pleased* he's having a day off.

But still. Luke getting sick. He never gets sick.

And he never jogs. What's going on?

I'm supposed to be going out for a drink after work with Erin, but I make an excuse and hurry home instead. When I let myself in, the apartment's dim, and for a moment I think Luke isn't back. But then I see him, sitting at the table in the gloom, wearing track pants and an old sweatshirt.

At last. We've got the evening to ourselves. OK, this is it. I'm finally going to tell him everything.

"Hi," I say, sliding into a chair next to him. "Are you feeling better? I called your work and they said you were ill."

There's silence.

"I wasn't in the right frame of mind to go to work," says Luke at last.

"What did you do all day? Did you really go jogging?"

"I went for a long walk," says Luke. "And I thought a great deal."

"About . . . your mother?" I say tentatively.

"Yes. About my mother. About a lot of other things too." He turns for the first time and to my surprise I see he hasn't shaved. Mmm. I quite like him unshaven, actually.

"But you're OK?"

"That's the question," he says after a pause. "Am I?"

"You probably just drank a bit too much last night." I take off my coat, marshaling my words. "Luke, listen. There's something really important I need to tell you. I've been putting it off for weeks now—"

"Becky, have you ever thought about the grid of Manhattan?" says Luke, interrupting me. "Really *thought* about it?"

"Er . . . no," I say, momentarily halted. "I can't say I have."

"It's like . . . a metaphor for life. You think you have the freedom to walk anywhere. But in fact . . ." He draws a line with his finger on the table. "You're strictly controlled. Up or down. Left or right. No other options."

"Right," I say after a pause. "Absolutely. The thing is, Luke—"

"Life should be an open space, Becky. You should be able to walk in whichever direction you choose."

"I suppose—"

"I walked from one end of the island to the other today."

"Really?" I stare at him. "Er . . . why?"

"I looked up at one point, and I was surrounded by office blocks. Sunlight was bouncing off the plate-glass windows. Reflected backward and forward."

"That sounds nice," I say inadequately.

"Do you see what I'm saying?" He fixes me with an intense stare, and I suddenly notice the purple shadows beneath his eyes. God, he looks exhausted. "The light enters Manhattan . . . and becomes trapped. Trapped in its own world, bouncing backward and forward with no escape."

"Well . . . yes, I suppose. Except . . . sometimes it rains, doesn't it?"

"And people are the same."

"Are they?"

"This is the world we're living in now. Self-reflecting. Self-obsessed. Ultimately pointless. Look at that guy in the hospital. Thirty-three years old—and he has a heart attack. What if he'd died? Would he have had a fulfilled life?"

"Er—"

"Have *I* had a fulfilled life? Be honest, Becky. Look at me, and tell me."

"Well . . . um . . . of course you have!"

"Bullshit." He picks up a nearby Brandon Communications press release and gazes at it. "This is what my life has been about. Meaningless pieces of information." To my shock, he starts to rip it up. "Meaningless fucking bits of paper."

Suddenly I notice he's tearing up our joint bank statement too.

"Luke! That's our bank statement!"

"So what? What does it matter? It's only a few pointless numbers. Who cares?"

"But . . . but . . ."

Something is wrong here.

"What does any of it matter?" He scatters the shreds of paper on the floor, and I force myself not to bend down and pick any of them up. "Becky, you're so right."

"*I'm* right?" I say in alarm.

Something is very wrong here.

"We're all too driven by materialism. With success. With money. With trying to impress people who'll never be impressed, whatever you . . ." He breaks off, breathing hard. "It's humanity that matters. We *should* know homeless people. We *should* know Bolivian peasants."

"Well . . . yes," I say after a pause. "But still—"

"Something you said a while back has been going round and round in my head all day. And now I can't forget it."

"What was that?" I say nervously.

"You said . . ." He pauses, as though trying to get the words just right. "You said that we're on this planet for too short a time. And at the end of the day, what's more important? Knowing that a few meaningless figures balanced—or knowing that you were the person you wanted to be?"

I gape at him. "But . . . but that was just stuff I made up! I wasn't being *serious*—"

"I'm not the person I want to be, Becky. I don't think I've ever been the person I wanted to be. I've been blinkered. I've been obsessed by all the wrong things—"

"Come on!" I say, squeezing his hand encouragingly. "You're Luke Brandon! You're successful and handsome and rich . . ."

"I'm not the person I should have become. The trouble is, now I don't know who that person is. I don't know who I want to be . . . what I want to do with my life . . . which path I want to take . . ." He slumps forward and buries his head in his hands. "Becky, I need some answers."

I don't believe it. At age thirty-four Luke is having a midlife crisis.

SECOND UNION BANK
53 WALL STREET
NEW YORK, NY 10005

May 23, 2002

Miss Rebecca Bloomwood
Apt. B
251 W. 11th Street
New York, NY 10014

Dear Miss Bloomwood:

Thank you for your letter of May 21. I am glad you are starting to think of me as a good friend, and in answer to your question, my birthday is October 31.

I also appreciate that weddings are expensive affairs. Unfortunately, however, I am unable to extend your credit limit from $5,000 to $105,000 at the current time.

I can instead offer you an increased limit of $6,000, and hope this goes some way to help.

Yours sincerely,

Walt Pitman
Director of Customer Relations

49 Drakeford Road
Potters Bar
Hertfordshire

27 May 2002

Mr. Malcolm Bloomwood thanks Mrs. Elinor Sherman very much for her kind invitation to Becky and Luke's wedding at the Plaza on 22nd June. Unfortunately he must decline, as he has broken his leg.

The Oaks
43 Elton Road
Oxshott, Surrey

27 May 2002

Mr. and Mrs. Martin Webster thank Mrs. Elinor Sherman very much for her kind invitation to Becky and Luke's wedding at the Plaza on 22nd June. Unfortunately they must decline, as they have both contracted glandular fever.

9 Foxtrot Way
Reigate
Surrey

27 May 2002

Mr. and Mrs. Tom Webster thank Mrs. Elinor Sherman very much for her kind invitation to Becky and Luke's wedding at the Plaza on 22nd June. Unfortunately they must decline, as their dog has just died.

Seventeen

THIS IS GETTING beyond a joke. Luke hasn't been to work for over a week. Nor has he shaved. He keeps going out and wandering around God knows where and not coming home until the early hours of the morning. And yesterday I arrived back from work to find he'd given away half his shoes to people on the street.

I feel so helpless. Nothing I do seems to work. I've tried making him bowls of nourishing, homemade soup. (At least, it says they're nourishing and homemade on the can.) I've tried making warm, tender love to him. Which was great as far as it went. (And that was pretty far, as it happens.) He seemed better for a little while—but in the end it didn't change anything. Afterward, he was just the same, all moody and staring into space.

The thing I've tried the most is just sitting down and talking to him. Sometimes I really think I'm getting somewhere. But then he either just reverts back into depression, or says, "What's the use?" and goes out again. The real trouble is, nothing he says seems to be making any sense. One minute he says he wants to quit his company and go into politics, that's where his heart lies and he should never have sold out. (Politics? He's never mentioned politics before.) The next moment he's saying fatherhood is all he's ever wanted, let's have six children and he'll stay at home and be a house-husband.

Meanwhile his assistant keeps phoning every day to see if

Luke's better, and I'm having to invent more and more lurid details. He's practically got the plague by now.

I'm so desperate, I phoned Michael this morning and he's promised to come over and see if he can do anything. If anyone can help, Michael can.

And as for the wedding . . .

I feel ill every time I think about it. It's three weeks away. I still haven't come up with a solution.

Mum calls me every morning and somehow I speak perfectly normally to her. Robyn calls me every afternoon and somehow I also speak perfectly normally to her. I even made a joke recently about not turning up on the day. We laughed, and Robyn quipped, "I'll sue you!" and I managed not to sob hysterically.

I feel like I'm in free fall. Plummeting toward the ground without a parachute.

I don't know how I'm doing it. I've slipped into a whole new zone, beyond normal panic, beyond normal solutions. It's going to take a miracle to save me.

Which is basically what I'm pinning my hopes on now. I've lit fifty candles at St. Thomas's, and fifty more at St. Patrick's, and I've put up a petition on the prayer board at the synagogue on Sixty-fifth, and given flowers to the Hindu god Ganesh. Plus a group of people in Ohio who I found on the Internet are all praying hard for me.

At least, they're praying that I find happiness following my struggle with alcoholism. I couldn't quite bring myself to explain the full two-weddings story to Father Gilbert, especially after I read his sermon on how deceit is as painful to the Lord as is the Devil gouging out the eyes of the righteous. So I went with alcoholism, because they already had a page on that.

There's no respite. I can't even relax at home. The apartment feels like it's closing in on me. There are wedding presents in huge cardboard boxes lining every room. Mum sends about fifty faxes a day, Robyn's taken to popping in whenever she feels like it, and there's a selection of veils and headdresses in the sitting room that Dream Dress sent to me without even asking.

"Becky?" I look up from my breakfast coffee to see Danny wandering into the kitchen. "The door was open. Not at work?"

"I've taken the day off."

"I see." He reaches for a piece of cinnamon toast and takes a bite. "So, how's the patient?"

"Very funny."

"Seriously." For a moment Danny looks genuinely concerned, and I feel myself unbend a little. "Has Luke snapped out of it yet?"

"Not really," I admit, and his eyes brighten.

"So are there any more items of clothing going?"

"No!" I say indignantly. "There aren't. And don't think you can keep those shoes!"

"Brand-new Pradas? You must be kidding! They're mine. Luke gave them to me. If he doesn't want them anymore—"

"He does. He will. He's just . . . a bit stressed at the moment. Everyone gets stressed! It doesn't mean you can take their shoes!"

"Everybody gets stressed. Everybody doesn't give away hundred-dollar bills to total strangers."

"Really?" I look up anxiously. "He did that?"

"I saw him at the subway. There was a guy there with long hair, carrying a guitar . . . Luke just went up to him and handed him a wad of money. The guy wasn't even begging. In fact, he looked pretty offended."

"Oh God—"

"You know my theory? He needs a nice, long, relaxing honeymoon. Where are you going?"

Oh no. Into free fall again. The honeymoon. I haven't even booked one yet. How can I? I don't know which bloody airport we'll be flying out of.

"We're . . . it's a surprise," I say at last. "We'll announce it on the day."

"So what are you cooking?" Danny looks at the stove, where a pot is bubbling away. "Twigs? Mm, tasty."

"They're Chinese herbs. For stress. You boil them up and then drink the liquid."

"You think you'll get Luke to drink this?" Danny prods the mixture.

"They're not for Luke. They're for me!"

"For you? What have you got to be stressed about?" The buzzer sounds and Danny reaches over and presses the entry button without even asking who it is.

"Danny!"

"Expecting anyone?" he says as he replaces the receiver.

"Oh, just that mass murderer who's been stalking me," I say sarcastically.

"Cool." Danny takes another bite of cinnamon toast. "I always wanted to see someone get murdered."

There's a knock at the door, and I get up to answer.

"I'd change into something snappier," says Danny. "The courtroom will see pictures of you in that outfit. You want to look your best."

I open the door, expecting yet another delivery man. But it's Michael, wearing a yellow cashmere jumper and a big smile. My heart lifts in relief just at the sight of him.

"Michael!" I exclaim, and give him a hug. "Thank you so much for coming."

"I would've been here sooner if I'd realized how bad it was," says Michael. He raises his eyebrows. "I was in at the Brandon Communications offices yesterday, and I heard Luke was sick. But I had no idea . . ."

"Yes. Well, I haven't exactly been spreading the news. I thought it would just blow over in a couple of days."

"So is Luke here?" Michael peers into the apartment.

"No, he went out early this morning. I don't know where." I shrug helplessly.

"Give him my love when he comes back," says Danny, heading out of the door. "And remember, I've got dibs on his Ralph Lauren coat."

I make a fresh pot of coffee (decaffeinated—that's all Michael's allowed these days) and stir the herbs dubiously, then we pick our way through the clutter of the sitting room to the sofa.

"So," he says, removing a stack of magazines and sitting down. "Luke's feeling the strain a little." He watches as I pour the milk with a trembling hand. "By the looks of things, you are too."

"I'm OK," I say quickly. "It's Luke. He's completely changed, overnight. One minute he was fine, the next it was all, 'I need some answers' and, 'What's the point of life?' and, 'Where are we all going?' He's depressed, and he isn't going to work . . . I just don't know what to do."

"You know, I've seen this coming for a while," says Michael, taking his coffee from me. "That man of yours pushes himself too hard. Always has. Anyone who works at that pace for that length of time . . ." He gives a rueful shrug and taps his chest. "I should know. Something has to give."

"It's not just work. It's . . . everything." I bite my lip awkwardly. "I think he was affected more than he realized when you had your . . . heart thing."

"Episode."

"Exactly. The two of you had been fighting . . . it was such a jolt. It made him start thinking about . . . I don't know, life and stuff. And then there's this thing with his mother."

"Ah." Michael nods. "I knew Luke was upset over that piece in the *New York Times*. Understandably."

"That's nothing! It's all got a lot worse since then."

I explain all about Luke finding the letters from his father, and Michael winces.

"OK," he says, stirring his coffee thoughtfully. "Now this all makes sense. His mother has been the driving force behind a lot of what he's achieved. I think we all appreciate that."

"It's like . . . suddenly he doesn't know why he's doing what he's doing. So he's given up doing it. He won't go to work, he won't talk about it, Elinor's still in Switzerland, his colleagues keep ringing up to ask how he is, and I don't want to say, 'Actually, Luke can't come to the phone, he's having a midlife crisis right now . . .' "

"Don't worry, I'm going in to the office today. I could spin some story about a sabbatical. Gary Shepherd can take charge for a bit. He's very able."

"Will he be OK, though?" I look at Michael fearfully. "He won't rip Luke off?"

The last time Luke took his eye off his company for more than three minutes, Alicia Bitchface Billington tried to poach all his clients and sabotage the entire enterprise. It was nearly the end of Brandon Communications.

"Gary will be fine," says Michael reassuringly. "And I'm not doing much at the moment. I can keep tabs on things."

"No!" I say in horror. "You mustn't work too hard! You must take it easy."

"Becky, I'm not an invalid!" says Michael with a tinge of annoyance. "You and my daughter are as bad as each other."

The phone rings, and I leave it to click onto the machine.

"So, how are the wedding preparations going?" says Michael, glancing around the room.

"Oh . . . fine!" I smile brightly at him. "Thanks."

"I had a call from your wedding planner about the rehearsal dinner. She told me your parents won't be able to make it."

"No," I say after a pause. "No, they won't."

"That's too bad. What day are they flying over?"

"Erm . . ." I take a sip of coffee, avoiding his eye. "I'm not sure of the *exact* day . . ."

"Becky?" Mum's voice resounds through the room on the machine, and I jump, spilling some coffee on the sofa. "Becky, love, I need to talk to you about the band. They say they can't do 'Dancing Queen' because their bass player can only play four chords. So they've sent me a list of songs they *can* play—"

Oh fuck. I dive across the room and grab the receiver.

"Mum!" I say breathlessly. "Hi. Listen, I'm in the middle of something, can I call you back?"

"But, love, you need to approve the list of songs! I'll send you a fax, shall I?"

"Yes. OK, do that."

I thrust down the receiver and return to the sofa, trying to look composed.

"Your mom's clearly gotten involved in the wedding preparations," says Michael with a smile.

"Oh, er . . . yes. She has."

The phone starts to ring again and I ignore it.

"You know, I always meant to ask. Didn't she mind about you getting married in the States?"

"No!" I say, twisting my fingers into a knot. "Why should she mind?"

"I know what mothers are like about weddings . . ."

"Sorry, love, just a quickie," comes Mum's voice again. "Janice was asking, how do you want the napkins folded? Like bishops' hats or like swans?"

I grab the phone.

"Mum, listen. I've got company!"

"Please. Don't worry about me," says Michael from the sofa. "If it's important—"

"It's not important! I don't give a shit what shape the napkins are in! I mean, they only look like a swan for about two seconds . . ."

"Becky!" exclaims Mum in shock. "How can you talk like that! Janice went on a napkin-arranging course especially for your wedding! It cost her forty-five pounds, and she had to take her own packed lunch—"

Remorse pours over me.

"Look, Mum, I'm sorry. I'm just a bit preoccupied. Let's go for . . . bishops' hats. And tell Janice I'm really grateful for all her help." I put down the receiver just as the doorbell rings.

"Is Janice the wedding planner?" says Michael interestedly.

"Er . . . no. That's Robyn."

"You have mail!" pipes up the computer in the corner of the room.

This is getting to be too much.

"Excuse me, I'll just get the door . . ."

I swing open the front door breathlessly, to see a delivery man holding a huge cardboard box.

"Parcel for Bloomwood," he says. "Very fragile."

"Thanks," I say, awkwardly taking it from him.

"Sign here, please . . ." He hands me a pen, then sniffs. "Is something burning in your kitchen?"

Oh fuck. The Chinese herbs.

I dash into the kitchen and turn off the burner, then return to the man and take the pen. Now I can hear the phone ringing again. Why can't everyone leave me alone?

"And here . . ."

I scribble on the line as best I can, and the delivery man squints suspiciously at it. "What does that say?"

"Bloomwood! It says Bloomwood!"

"Hello," I can hear Michael saying. "No, this is Becky's apartment. I'm Michael Ellis, a friend."

"I need you to sign again, lady. Legibly."

"Yes, I'm Luke's best man. Well, hello! I'm looking forward to meeting you!"

"OK?" I say, after practically stabbing my name into the page. "Satisfied?"

"Lighten up!" says the delivery guy, raising his hands as he saunters away. I close the door with my foot and stagger into the living room just in time to hear Michael saying, "I've heard about the plans for the ceremony. They sound quite spectacular!"

"Who are you talking to?" I mouth.

"*Your mom,*" mouths back Michael with a smile.

I nearly drop the box on the floor.

"I'm sure it'll all run smoothly on the day," Michael's saying reassuringly. "I was just saying to Becky, I really admire your involvement with the wedding. It can't have been easy!"

No. Please, no.

"Well," says Michael, looking surprised. "All I meant was, it must be difficult. What with you based in England . . . and Becky and Luke getting married in—"

"Michael!" I say desperately, and he looks up, startled. "Stop!"

He puts his hand over the receiver. "Stop what?"

"My mum. She . . . she doesn't know."

"Doesn't know what?"

I stare at him, agonized. At last he turns to the phone. "Mrs. Bloomwood, I'm going to have to go. There's a lot going on here. But great to talk to you and . . . I'll see you at the wedding, I'm sure . . . Yes, you too."

He puts down the phone and there's a scary silence.

"Becky, what doesn't your mom know?" he says at last.

"It . . . doesn't matter."

"I get the feeling it does." He looks at me shrewdly. "I get the feeling something's not right."

"I . . . It's nothing. Really . . ."

I stop at the sound of the fax machine whirring in the corner. Mum's fax. I quickly dump the box on the sofa and launch myself at the fax machine.

But Michael's too quick for me. He plucks the page from the machine and starts to read it.

"Playlist for Rebecca and Luke's wedding. Date: 22nd June. Venue: The Pines, 43 Elton Road . . . Oxshott . . ." He looks up, a frown on his face. "Becky, what is this? You and Luke are getting married at the Plaza. Right?"

I can't answer. Blood is pumping through my head, almost deafening me.

"Right?" repeats Michael, his voice becoming sterner.

"I don't know," I say at last in a tiny voice.

"How can you not know where you're getting married?"

He surveys the fax again. I can see comprehension slowly dawning.

"Jesus Christ." He looks up. "Your mom's planning a wedding in England, isn't she?"

I stare at him in mute anguish. This is even worse than Suze finding out. I mean, Suze has known me for so long. She knows how stupid I am and she always forgives me. But Michael. I swallow. Michael's always treated me with respect. He once told me I was sharp and intuitive. He even offered me a job with his company. I can't bear for him to find out what a complete mess I've got into.

"Does your mom know *anything* about the Plaza?"

Very slowly, I shake my head.

"Does Luke's mother know about this?" He hits the fax.

I shake my head again.

"Does anyone know? Does *Luke* know?"

"Nobody knows," I say, finally finding a voice. "And you have to promise not to tell anyone."

"Not *tell* anyone? Are you kidding?" He shakes his head in disbelief. "Becky, how could you have let this happen?"

"I don't know. I don't know. I didn't *mean* for it to happen—"

"You didn't mean to deceive two entire families? Not to mention the expense, the effort . . . You realize you're in big trouble here?"

"It'll work itself out!" I say desperately.

"How is it going to work itself out? Becky, this isn't a double-booked dinner date! This is hundreds of people!"

"Ding-dong, ding-dong!" suddenly chimes my wedding countdown alarm clock from the bookshelf. "Ding-dong, ding-dong! Only twenty-two days to go till the Big Day!"

"Shut up!" I say tensely.

"Ding-dong, ding—"

"Shut *up*!" I cry, and hurl it onto the floor, where the clock face shatters.

"Twenty-two days?" says Michael. "Becky, that's only three weeks!"

"I'll think of something! A lot can happen in three weeks!"

"You'll think of something? That's your only answer?"

"Perhaps a miracle will happen!"

I try a little smile, but Michael's face doesn't react. He still looks just as astounded. Just as angry.

I can't stand Michael being angry with me. My head's pounding and I can feel tears pressing hotly at my eyes. With trembling hands I grab my bag and reach for my jacket.

"What are you going to do?" His voice sharpens. "Becky, where are you going?"

I stare back, my mind feverishly racing. I need to escape. From this apartment, from my life, from this whole hideous mess. I need a place of peace, a place of sanctuary. A place where I'll find solace.

"I'm going to Tiffany," I say with a half-sob, and close the door behind me.

Five seconds after I've crossed the threshold of Tiffany, I'm already calmer. My heart rate begins to subside. My mind begins to turn less frantically. I feel soothed, just looking around at the cases full of glittering jewelry. Audrey Hepburn was right: nothing bad could ever happen in Tiffany.

I walk to the back of the ground floor, dodging the tourists and eyeing up diamond necklaces as I go. There's a girl about my age trying on a knuckle-duster of an engagement ring, and as I see her exhilarated face, I feel a painful pang inside.

It seems like a million years ago that Luke and I got engaged. I feel like a different person. If only I could rewind. God, if I could just have the chance. I'd do it all so differently.

There's no point torturing myself with how it might have been. This is what I've done—and this is how it is.

I get into the elevator and travel up to the third floor—and as I step out, I relax even more. This really is another world. It's different even from the crowded, touristy floor below. It's like heaven.

The whole floor is tranquil and spacious, with silver, china, and glassware displayed on mirror-topped cabinets. It's a world of quiet luxury. A world of glossy, cultured people who don't have to worry about anything. I can see an immaculate girl in navy blue examining a glass candlestick. Another girl, heavily pregnant, is looking at a sterling silver baby's rattle. No one's got any problems here. The only major dilemma facing anyone is whether to have gold or platinum edging their dinner service.

As long as I stay here I'll be safe.

"Becky? Is that you?" My heart gives a little flicker and I turn round, to see Eileen Morgan beaming at me. Eileen is the lady who showed me around the floor when I registered my list here. She's an elderly lady with her hair in a bun, and reminds me of the ballet teacher I used to have when I was little.

"Hi, Eileen," I say. "How are you?"

"I'm well. And I have good news for you!"

"Good news?" I say stupidly.

I can't remember the last time I heard a piece of good news.

"Your list has been going very well."

"Really?" In spite of myself I feel the same twinge of pride I used to when Miss Phipps said my pliés were going well.

"Very well, indeed. In fact, I was planning to call you. I think the time has come . . ." Eileen pauses momentously, ". . . to go for some larger items. A silver bowl. A platter. Some antique hollow-ware."

I stare at her in slight disbelief. In wedding list terms, this is as though she's said I should try for the Royal Ballet.

"You honestly think I'm in that . . . league?"

"Becky, the performance of your list has been very impressive. You're right up there with our top brides."

"I . . . I don't know what to say. I never thought . . ."

"Never underestimate yourself!" says Eileen with a warm smile, and gestures around the floor. "Browse for as long as you like and let me know what you'd like to add. If you need any help, you know where I am." She squeezes my arm. "Well done, Becky."

As she walks away, I feel my eyes pricking with grateful tears. *Someone* doesn't think I'm a disaster. *Someone* doesn't think I've ruined everything. In one area, at least, I'm a success.

I head toward the antiques cabinet and gaze up at a silver tray, filled with emotion. I won't let Eileen down. I'll register the best damn antique hollowware I possibly can. I'll put down a teapot, and a sugar bowl . . .

"Rebecca."

"Yes?" I say, turning round. "I haven't quite decided—"

And then I stop, my words shriveling on my lips. It's not Eileen.

It's Alicia Bitch Longlegs.

Out of the blue, like a bad fairy. She's wearing a pink suit and holding a Tiffany carrier bag and hostility is crackling all around her.

Of all the times.

"So," she says. "So, Becky. I suppose you're feeling pretty pleased with yourself, are you?"

"Er . . . no. Not really."

"Miss Bride of the Year. Miss Enchanted Bloody Forest."

I gaze at her puzzledly. I know Alicia and I aren't exactly best buddies—but isn't this a bit extreme?

"Alicia," I say. "What's wrong?"

"What's wrong?" Her voice rises shrilly. "What could be wrong? Maybe the fact that my wedding planner has dumped me with no warning. Maybe that's irking me a little!"

"What?"

"And why has she dumped me? So she can concentrate on her big, important, Plaza-wedding client. Her extra-special, spare-no-expense client Miss Becky Bloomwood."

I stare at her in horror. "Alicia, I had no idea—"

"My whole wedding's in pieces. I couldn't get another wedding planner. She's bad-mouthed me all over town. Apparently the rumor is I'm 'difficult.' Fucking *'difficult'*! The caterers aren't returning my calls, my dress is too short, the florist is an idiot . . ."

"I'm so sorry," I say helplessly. "I honestly didn't know about this—"

"Oh, I'm sure you didn't. I'm sure you weren't sniggering in Robyn's office while she made the call."

"I wasn't! I wouldn't! Look . . . I'm sure it'll all turn out OK." I take a deep breath. "To be honest, my wedding isn't going that smoothly either . . ."

"Give me a break. I've heard all about your wedding. The whole bloody world has." She turns on her heel and stalks away, and I gaze after her, shaken.

I haven't just ruined my own wedding, I've ruined Alicia's too.

I try to turn my attention back to the antiques cabinet but I feel upset and jittery. OK, come on. Let's pick a few things. That might cheer me up. A nineteenth-century tea strainer. And a sugar bowl with inlaid mother-of-pearl. I mean, that'll always come in handy, won't it?

And look at this silver teapot. Only $5,000. I scribble it down on my list and then look up to see if there's a matching cream jug. A young couple in jeans and T-shirts have wandered over to the same cabinet, and suddenly I notice they're staring up at the same teapot.

"Look at that," says the girl. "A five-thousand-dollar teapot. What would anyone want with that?"

"Don't you like tea?" says her boyfriend with a grin.

"Sure! But I mean, if you had five thousand dollars, would you spend it on a *teapot*?"

"When I have five thousand dollars I'll let you know," says the boyfriend. They both laugh and walk off, hand in hand, light and happy with each other.

Suddenly, standing there in front of the cabinet, I feel ridiculous. Like a child playing with grown-up clothes. What do I want a $5,000 teapot for?

I don't know what I'm doing here. I don't know what I'm doing.

I want Luke.

It hits me like a tidal wave, overwhelming everything else. Brushing all the clutter and rubbish away.

That's all I want. Luke normal and happy again.

The two of us normal and happy. I have a sudden vision of us on a deserted beach somewhere. Watching the sunset. No baggage, no fuss. Just the two of us, being together.

Somehow I've lost sight of what really matters in all this, haven't I? I've been distracted by all the froth. The dress, and the cake, and the presents. When all that really counts is that Luke wants to be with me, and I want to be with him. Oh, I've been such a stupid fool . . .

My mobile phone suddenly bleeps, and I scrabble in my bag for it, filled with sudden hope.

"Luke?"

"Becky! What the hell's going on?" Suze's voice shrieks in my ear so fiercely, I nearly drop the phone in fright. "I just had a call from Michael Ellis! He says you're still getting married in New York! Bex, I can't believe you!"

"Don't shout at me! I'm in Tiffany!"

"What the hell are you doing in Tiffany? You should be sorting this mess out! Bex, you're not going to get married in America. You just can't! It would kill your mum."

"I know! I'm not going to! At least . . ." I push a hand distractedly through my hair. "Oh God, Suze. You just don't know what's been going on. Luke's having a midlife crisis . . . the wedding planner's threatened to sue me . . . I feel like I'm all on my own . . ."

To my horror I feel my eyes welling up with tears. I creep round the back of the cabinet and sink onto the carpeted floor, where no one can see me.

"I've ended up with two weddings and I can't do either of them! Either way, people are going to be furious with me. Either way it's going to be a disaster. It's supposed to be the best day of my life, Suze, and it's going to be the worst! The very worst!"

"Look, Bex, don't get into a state," she says, relenting slightly. "Have you really gone through all the options?"

"I've thought of everything. I've thought of committing bigamy, I've thought of hiring look-alikes . . ."

"That's not a bad idea," says Suze thoughtfully.

"You know what I really want to do?" My throat tightens with emotion. "Just run away from all of this and do it on a beach. Just the two of us and a minister and the seagulls. I mean, that's what really counts, isn't it? The fact that I love Luke and he loves me and we want to be together forever." As I picture Luke kissing me against a Caribbean sunset, I feel tears welling up again. "Who cares about having a posh dress? Who cares about a grand reception and getting lots of presents? None of it is important! I'd just wear a really simple sarong, and we'd be in bare feet, and we'd walk along the sand, and it would be so romantic—"

"Bex!" I jump in fright at Suze's tone. She sounds as angry as I've ever heard her. "Just stop it! Stop right there! God, you're a selfish cow sometimes."

"What do you mean?" I falter. "I just meant all the trappings weren't important . . ."

"They *are* important! People have made a lot of effort over those trappings! You've got two weddings that most people would die to have. OK, you can't do both. But you can do one. If you don't do either of them, then . . . you don't deserve them. You don't deserve any of it. Bex, these weddings aren't just about you! They're about all the people involved. All the people who have made an effort and put time and love and money into creating something really special. You can't just run away from that! You *have* to face this out, even if it means apologizing to four hundred people individually, on bended knee. If you just run away, then . . . then you're selfish and cowardly."

She stops, breathing hard, and I hear Ernie begin to wail plaintively in the background. I feel completely shocked, as though she's slapped me in the face.

"You're right," I say at last.

"I'm sorry," she says, and she sounds quite upset too. "But I am right."

"I know you are." I rub my face. "Look . . . I will face this out: I don't know how. But I will." Ernie's wailing has increased to lusty screaming, and I can barely hear myself over the noise. "You'd better go," I say. "Give my godson my love. Tell him . . . his godmother's sorry she's such a flake. She's going to try and do better."

"He sends all his love back," says Suze. She hesitates. "And he says remember, even though we might get a bit cross with you, we're still ready to help. If we can."

"Thanks, Suze," I say, my throat thick. "Tell him . . . I'll keep you posted."

I put my phone away and sit still, gathering my thoughts. At last I get to my feet, brush myself down, and walk back out onto the shop floor.

Alicia's standing five yards away.

My stomach gives a little flip. How long has she been there for? What did she hear?

"Hi," I say, my voice crackly with nerves.

"Hi," she says. Very slowly she walks toward me, her eyes running over me appraisingly

"So," she says pleasantly. "Does Robyn know you're planning to run off to get married on a beach?"

Fuck.

"I'm . . ." I clear my throat. "I'm not planning to run off to a beach!"

"Sounded to me like you were." Alicia examines a nail. "Isn't there a clause about that in her contract?"

"I was joking! It was . . . you know, just being funny . . ."

"I wonder if Robyn would find it funny." Alicia gives me her most ingratiating smile. "To hear that Becky Bloomwood doesn't care about having a grand reception. To hear that her favorite, goody-two-shoes Little Miss Perfect client . . . is going to fly the coop!"

I have to keep calm. "You wouldn't say anything to Robyn."

"Wouldn't I?"

"You can't! You just . . ." I break off, trying to stay composed.

"Alicia, we've known each other a long time. And I know we haven't always . . . seen eye to eye . . . but come on. We're two British girls in New York. Both getting married. In a way, we're . . . we're practically sisters!"

I force myself to place a hand on her pink bouclé sleeve. "Surely we have to show solidarity? Surely we have to . . . support each other?"

There's a pause as Alicia runs contemptuous eyes over me. Then she jerks her arm away from my hand and starts to stride away.

"See you, Becky," she says over her shoulder.

I have to stop her. Quick.

"Becky!" Eileen's voice is behind me and I turn round in a daze. "Here's the pewterware I wanted to show you . . ."

"Thanks," I say dazedly. "I just have to . . ."

I turn back—but Alicia's disappeared.

Where did she go?

I hurry down the stairs to ground level, not bothering to wait for the lift. As I enter the floor I pause and look around desperately, searching for a flash of pink. But the whole place is crowded with an influx of excited, yabbering tourists. There are bright colors everywhere.

I push my way through them, breathing hard, telling myself Alicia wouldn't really say anything to Robyn; she wouldn't really be so vindictive. And at the same time, knowing that she would.

I can't see her anywhere on the whole floor. At last I manage to squeeze past a group of tourists clustered round a case full of watches and reach the revolving doors. I push my way out and stand on the street, looking from left to right. I can barely see anything. It's a blindingly bright day, with low sunlight glinting off plate-glass windows, turning everything into silhouettes and shadows.

"Rebecca." I feel a hand suddenly pulling sharply at my shoulder. In confusion, I turn round, blinking in the brightness and look up.

As my gaze focuses, I'm gripped by pure, cold terror.

It's Elinor.

Eighteen

I SHOULD NEVER HAVE stepped outside Tiffany.

"Rebecca, I need to talk to you," says Elinor coldly. "At once."

She's wearing a long black coat and oversized black sunglasses and looks exactly like a member of the Gestapo. Oh God, she's found out everything, hasn't she? She's spoken to Robyn. She's spoken to Alicia. She's come to haul me in front of the commandant and condemn me to hard labor.

"How did you know where I was?" I falter.

"Michael Ellis told me," she replies crisply.

Michael told her? Doesn't he think I'm suffering enough?

"Well, I'm er . . . busy," I say, trying to duck back inside Tiffany. "I haven't got time to chat."

"This is not chat."

"Whatever."

"This is very important."

"OK, look, it might *seem* important," I say desperately. "But let's get things in perspective. It's only a wedding. Compared to things like, you know, foreign treaties . . ."

"I don't wish to discuss the wedding." Elinor frowns. "I wish to discuss Luke."

"Luke?" I stare at her, taken aback. "How come . . . have you spoken to him?"

"I had several disturbing messages from him in Switzerland. And yesterday a letter. I returned home immediately."

"What did the letter say?"

"I'm on my way to see Luke now," says Elinor, ignoring me. "I would be glad if you accompany me."

"Are you? Where is he?"

"Michael Ellis went to search for Luke this morning and found him at my apartment. I'm on my way there now. Apparently Luke wishes to speak to me." She pauses. "But I wanted to talk to you first, Rebecca."

"Me? Why?"

Before she can answer, a group of tourists comes out of Tiffany and for a moment we're submerged by them. I could make my getaway under their cover. I could escape.

But now I'm curious. Why does Elinor want to talk to me?

The crowd melts away and we stare at each other.

"Please." She nods toward the curb. "My car is waiting."

"OK," I say, and give a tiny shrug. "I'll come."

Once inside Elinor's plushy limousine, my terror recedes. As I gaze at her pale, impenetrable face, I feel a slow hatred growing inside me instead.

This is the woman who screwed up Luke. This is the woman who ignored her own fourteen-year-old son. Sitting calmly in her limousine. Still behaving as though she owns the world; as though she's done nothing wrong.

"So what did Luke write in his letter?" I say.

"It was . . . confused," she says. "Rambling and nonsensical. He seems to be having some sort of . . ." She gestures regally.

"Breakdown? Yes, he is."

"Why?"

"Why do you think?" I retort, unable to keep a sarcastic edge out of my voice.

"He works very hard," says Elinor. "Perhaps too hard sometimes."

"It's not the work!" I say, unable to stop myself. "It's you!"

"Me." She frowns.

"Yes, you! It's the way you've treated him!"

There's a long pause. Then Elinor says, "What do you mean?"

She sounds genuinely taken aback. Is she really that insensitive?

"OK . . . where shall I start? With your charity! The charity that he has spent all his bloody waking hours working for. The charity that you promised him would benefit the profile of his company. But funnily enough didn't . . . because you took all the credit yourself!"

God, that felt good. Why have I never spoken my mind to Elinor before?

Her nostrils flare slightly and I can tell she's angry, but all she says is, "That version of events is skewed."

"It's not skewed! You used Luke!"

"He never complained about the amount of work he was doing."

"He wouldn't complain! But you *must* have seen how much time he was giving you for nothing! You used one of his staff, for God's sake! I mean, that alone was bound to get him into trouble—"

"I agree," says Elinor.

"What?" I'm momentarily halted.

"To use staff from Brandon Communcations was not my idea. Indeed, I was against it. It was Luke who insisted. And as I have explained to Luke, the newspaper article was not my fault. I was given the option of a last-minute interview. Luke was unavailable. I told the journalist at great length about Luke's involvement and gave him Brandon Communications promotional literature. The journalist promised to read it but then used none of it. I assure you, Rebecca, it was out of my control."

"Rubbish!" I say at once. "A decent journalist wouldn't completely ignore something like . . ."

Hmm. Actually . . . maybe they would. Now that I think about it, when I was a journalist I always ignored half the stuff the interviewees told me. I certainly never read any of the stupid heavy literature they gave me.

"Well . . . OK," I say after a pause. "Maybe that wasn't entirely your fault. But that's not the main issue. That's not why Luke's so upset. A few days ago, he went looking for family photos in your apartment. But he didn't find any. Instead, he found some letters from his dad. All about how you didn't want him when he was a child. How you weren't interested in meeting him, even for ten minutes."

Elinor's face flinches slightly but she says nothing.

"And that brought back a lot of other really painful stuff. Like when he came to see you in New York and sat outside your building and you refused to acknowledge him? Remember that, Elinor?"

I know I'm being harsh. But I don't care.

"That was him," she says at last.

"Of course it was him! Don't pretend you didn't know it was him. Elinor, why do you think he pushes himself so hard? Why do you think he came to New York in the first place? To impress you, of course! He's been obsessed for years! No wonder he's gone over the edge now. To be honest, given the childhood he had, I'm amazed he's lasted this long without cracking!"

As I break off for breath, it occurs to me that maybe Luke wouldn't want me discussing all his secret neuroses with his mother.

Oh well, too late now. Anyway, someone's got to let Elinor have it.

"He had a happy childhood," she says, staring rigidly out of the window. We've stopped at a crossing and I can see the reflection of people walking past the car in her sunglasses.

"But he loved you. He wanted *you*. His mother. But you just didn't want to see him—"

"He's angry with me."

"Of course he's angry! You leave him behind and go off to America, not even caring about him, as happy as a clam."

"Happy." Elinor turns her head. "Do you think I'm happy, Rebecca?"

I'm halted. With a very slight twinge of shame I realize it's never occurred to me to think about whether Elinor is happy or not. I've only ever thought about what a cow she is.

"I . . . don't know," I say at last.

"I made my decision. I stuck to it. That doesn't mean that I don't regret it."

She takes off her sunglasses and I try not to give away my shock at the way she looks. Her skin is stretched even more tightly than ever and there's slight bruising around her eyes. Although she's just had a face-lift, to my eye she looks older than she did before. And kind of more vulnerable.

"I did recognize Luke that day," she says in a quiet voice.

"So why didn't you go over to him?"

There's silence in the car—and then, her lips barely moving, she says, "I was apprehensive."

"Apprehensive?" I echo disbelievingly.

"Giving up a child is a tremendous step. Taking a child back into one's life is . . . equally momentous. Particularly after such a long time. I wasn't prepared for such a step. I wasn't prepared for seeing him."

"Didn't you want to talk to him, though? Didn't you want to . . . to get to know him?"

"Maybe. Maybe I did."

I can see a slight quivering, just below her left eye. Is that an expression of emotion?

"Some people find it easy to embrace new experiences. Others shrink away. It may be difficult for you to understand that, Rebecca. I know you are an impulsive, warm person. It's one of the things I admire about you."

"Yeah, right," I say sarcastically.

"What do you mean?"

"Come on, Elinor," I say, rolling my eyes. "Let's not play games. You don't like me. You never have."

"What makes you think I don't like you?"

She cannot be serious.

"Your doorpeople don't let me into my own party . . . you try to make me sign a prenup . . . you're never *ever* nice to me . . ."

"I regret the incident at the party. That was an error on the part of the party planners." She frowns slightly. "But I have never understood your objection to a prenuptial contract. No one should get married without one." She looks out of the window. "We're here."

The car stops and the driver comes round to open the passenger door. Elinor looks at me.

"I do like you, Rebecca. Very much." She gets out of the car and her eye rests on my foot. "Your shoe is scuffed. It looks shoddy."

"You see?" I say in exasperation. "You see what I mean?"

"What?" She gives me a blank stare.

Oh, I give up.

Elinor's apartment is bright with shafts of morning sun, and completely silent. At first I think she must be wrong and Luke isn't here—but as we enter the living room, I see him. He's standing at the picture window, staring out with a deep frown.

"Luke, are you OK?" I say cautiously, and he wheels round in shock.

"Becky. What are you doing here?"

"I just . . . ran into your mother at Tiffany. Where have you been all morning?"

"Around and about," says Luke. "Thinking."

I glance at Elinor. She's staring at Luke, her face unreadable.

"Anyway, I'll leave, shall I?" I say awkwardly. "If you two are going to talk . . ."

"No," says Luke. "Stay. This won't take long."

I sit down awkwardly on the arm of a chair, wishing I could shrink into it. I've never liked the atmosphere in this apartment—but right now it's like the temperature's dropped ten degrees.

"I received your messages," says Elinor. "And your letter, which made very little sense." She takes off her gloves with jerky movements and places them on a side table. "I have no idea what you're trying to accuse me of."

"I'm not here to accuse you of anything," says Luke, making a visible attempt to stay calm. "I just wanted to let you know that I've had a few realizations. One of which has been that I've been somewhat . . . deluded over the years. You never really wanted me to live with you, did you? Yet you've allowed me to believe that you did."

"Don't be ridiculous, Luke," says Elinor after a pause. "The situation was far more complicated than you might imagine."

"You've played on my . . . my weakness. You've used me. And my company. You've treated me like a . . ." He breaks off, breathing heavily, and takes a couple of moments to calm himself. "What's a little sad is that one of the reasons I came to New York was to spend time with you. Perhaps get to know you as well as Becky knows her mother."

He gestures toward me and I look up in alarm. Don't bring me into this!

"What a waste of time." His voice harshens. "I'm not sure you're even capable of that kind of relationship."

"That's enough!" says Elinor. "Luke, I can't talk to you when you're in this state."

As he and Elinor face each other, I see that they're more alike than I've ever realized. They both get that blank, scary expression when things are going badly. They both set themselves impossibly high standards. And they're both more vulnerable than they want the outside world to know.

"You don't have to talk to me," says Luke. "I'm leaving now. You won't see me or Becky again."

My head jerks up in shock. Is he serious?

"You're talking nonsense," says Elinor.

"I've sent a letter of resignation to the trustees of the Elinor Sherman Foundation. There should be no other reason for our paths to cross."

"You have forgotten the wedding," says Elinor crisply.

"No, we haven't. I haven't forgotten it at all." Luke takes a deep breath and glances at me. "As of now, Becky and I will be making alternative arrangements for our marriage. Naturally, I'll pay whatever expenses you've incurred."

Wh—

What did he say? I stare at Luke, gobsmacked.

Did he really just say what I—

Did he really just . . .

Am I hallucinating?

"Luke," I say, trying to keep calm, trying to keep steady. "Let me just get this . . . Are you saying you want to pull out of the Plaza wedding?"

"Becky, I know I haven't discussed this with you yet." Luke comes over and takes my hands. "I know you've been planning this wedding for months. It's a lot to ask you to pull out. But under the circumstances, I just don't feel I can go through it."

"You want to pull out of the wedding." I swallow. "You do know there's a financial penalty?"

"I don't care."

"You . . . you don't care?"

He doesn't care.

I don't know whether to laugh or cry.

"That's not what I meant!" says Luke, seeing my expression. "I do care! Of course I care about us. But to stand up in public, and pretend to be a loving son to . . ." He glances at Elinor. "It would be farcical. It would debase the whole thing. Can you understand that?"

"Luke . . . of course I understand," I say, trying to keep the exhilaration out of my voice. "If you want to pull out, then I'm happy to go along."

I can't believe it. I'm saved. I'm saved!

"You're serious, aren't you?" He stares at me incredulously.

"Of course I'm serious! If you want to cancel the wedding, then I'm not going to put up a fight. In fact . . . let's call it off straight away!"

"You are a girl in a million, Becky Bloomwood." Luke's voice is suddenly thick. "To agree without even hesitating . . ."

"It's what you want, Luke," I say simply. "That's all that matters to me."

It's a miracle!

There's no other explanation.

For once in my life, God was actually listening. Either him or Ganesh.

"You cannot do this." For the first time there's a tremor of emotion in Elinor's voice. "You cannot simply abandon the wedding I have organized for you. Funded for you."

"I can."

"It's a highly significant event! We have four hundred people coming! Important people. Friends of mine, of the charity—"

"Well, you'll just have to make my excuses."

Elinor takes a few steps toward him, and I see to my astonishment that she's shaking with rage. "If you do this, Luke, I can promise you. We will never speak again."

"That's fine by me. Come on, Becky." He tugs at my hand and I follow him, stumbling slightly on the rug.

I can see Elinor's face twitching again, and to my extreme astonishment, I feel a bit sorry for her. But then, as we turn and stride together out of the apartment, I squash it. Elinor's been mean enough to me and my parents. She deserves all she gets.

We walk downstairs in silence. I think we're both completely shell-shocked. Luke lifts his hand for a cab, gives our address to the driver, and we both get in.

After about three blocks we look at each other. Luke is pale and shaking slightly.

"I don't know what to say," he says. "I can't believe I just did that."

"You were brilliant," I say firmly. "She had it coming."

He swivels in his seat and looks at me earnestly. "Becky, I'm so sorry about the wedding. I know how much you've been looking forward to it. I'll make it up to you. I promise. Just tell me how."

I stare at him, my mind working fast. OK. I have to play this one very carefully. If I make the wrong move, everything could still fall about my ears.

"So . . . you do still want to get married? You know, in principle."

"Of course I do!" Luke looks shocked. "Becky, I love you. Even more than I did before. In fact, I've never loved you as much as I did in that room. When you made that incredible sacrifice for me, without even a moment's hesitation."

"What? Oh, the wedding! Yes." I compose my features hastily. "Yes, well. It was quite a lot to ask of me. And um . . . speaking of . . . weddings . . ."

I almost can't bring myself to say it. I feel as though I'm trying to balance the last card on top of the pyramid. I have to get it exactly right.

"How would you feel about getting married in . . . Oxshott?"

"Oxshott. Perfect." Luke closes his eyes and leans back on his seat, looking exhausted.

I'm numb with disbelief. It's all fallen into place. The miracle is complete.

As we drive down Fifth Avenue I look out of the window of the cab, suddenly taking in the world outside. Noticing for the first time that it's summer. That it's a beautiful sunshiny day. That Saks has a new window display of swimwear. Little things I haven't been able to see, let alone appreciate, because I've been so preoccupied, so stressed.

I feel as though I've been walking around with a heavy weight on my back for such a long time, I've forgotten what it's like to walk upright. But at last the burden is lifted, and I can cautiously stand up and stretch, and start to enjoy myself. The months of nightmaresville are over. Finally, I can sleep easy.

Nineteen

EXCEPT I DON'T.

In fact, I don't sleep at all.

Long after Luke's crashed out, I'm staring at the ceiling, feeling uncomfortable. There's something wrong here. I'm just not quite sure what.

On the surface, everything's perfect. Elinor is out of Luke's life for good. We can get married at home. I don't have to worry about Robyn. I don't have to worry about anything. It's like a great big bowling ball has arrived in my life and knocked down all the bad ninepins in one fell swoop, leaving only good ones behind.

We had a lovely celebration supper, and cracked open a bottle of champagne, and toasted the rest of Luke's life, and the wedding, and each other. Then we started talking about where we should go on our honeymoon, and I made a strong case for Bali and Luke said Moscow and we had one of those laughing, almost hysterical arguments you have when you're high on exhilaration and relief. It was a wonderful, happy evening. I should be completely content.

But now that I'm in bed and my mind's settled down, things keep niggling at me. The way Luke looked tonight. Almost too exhilarated. Too bright-eyed. The way we both kept laughing, as though we didn't dare stop.

And other things. The way Elinor looked when we left. The conversation I had with Annabel, all those months ago.

I should feel triumphant. I should feel vindicated. But . . . somehow this doesn't feel right.

At last, at about three in the morning, I slide out of bed, go into the living room, and dial Suze's number.

"Hi, Bex!" she says in surprise. "What time is it there?" I can hear the tinny sound of British breakfast television on in the background, and little gurgles from Ernie. "God, I'm sorry I gave you a hard time yesterday. I've been feeling really bad ever since—"

"It's OK. Honestly, I've forgotten all about it." I huddle on the floorboards, pulling my dressing gown tightly around me. "Listen, Suze. Luke had a huge bust-up with his mum today. He's pulled out of the Plaza wedding. We can get married in Oxshott after all."

"*What?*" Suze's voice explodes down the line. "That's incredible! That's fantastic! Bex, I've been so worried! I honestly didn't know what you were going to do. You must be dancing on the ceiling! You must be—"

"I am. Kind of."

Suze comes to a breathless halt. "What do you mean, kind of?"

"I know everything's worked out. I know it's all fantastic." I wind my dressing gown cord tightly round my finger. "But somehow . . . it doesn't feel fantastic."

"What do you mean?" I can hear Suze turning the volume down. "Bex, what's wrong?"

"I feel bad," I say in a rush. "I feel like . . . I've won but I don't want to have won. I mean, OK, I've got everything I wanted. Luke's had it out with Elinor, he's going to pay off the wedding planner, we can have the wedding at home . . . On the one hand it's great. But on the other hand—"

"What other hand?" says Suze. "There isn't another hand!"

"There is. At least . . . I think there is." I start to nibble my thumbnail distractedly. "Suze, I'm worried about Luke. He really attacked his mother. And now he says he's never going to talk to her again . . ."

"So what? Isn't that a good thing?"

"I don't know. Is it?" I stare at the floor for a few moments. "He's all euphoric at the moment. But what if he starts feeling guilty? What if this screws him up just as badly in the future? You know, Annabel, his stepmum, once said if I tried to chop Elinor out of Luke's life it would damage him."

"But you didn't chop her out of his life," points out Suze. "He did."

"Well, maybe he's damaged himself. Maybe it's like . . . he's chopped his own arm off or something."

"Err, gross!"

"And now there's this huge wound, which nobody can see, and it'll fester away, and one day it'll erupt again . . ."

"Bex! Stop it! I'm eating my breakfast."

"OK, sorry. I'm just worried about him. He's not right. And the other thing is . . ." I close my eyes, almost unable to believe I'm about to say this. "I've kind of . . . changed my mind about Elinor."

"You *what*?" screeches Suze. "Bex, please don't say things like that! I nearly dropped Ernie on the floor!"

"I don't *like* her or anything," I say hastily. "But we had this talk. And I do think maybe she loves Luke. In her own weird, icebox Vulcan way."

"But she abandoned him!"

"I know. But she regrets it."

"Well, so what! She bloody well ought to regret it!"

"Suze, I just think . . . maybe she deserves another chance." I gaze at my fingertip, which is slowly turning blue. "I mean . . . look at me. I've done millions of stupid, thoughtless things. I've let people down. But they've always given me another chance."

"Bex, you're nothing like bloody Elinor! You'd never leave your child!"

"I'm not saying I'm *like* her! I'm just saying . . ." I tail away feebly, letting the dressing gown cord unravel.

I don't really know what I'm saying. And I don't think Suze will ever quite understand where I'm coming from. She's never made any mistakes in her life. She's always cruised through easily, never upsetting anyone, never getting herself in trouble. But I haven't. I know what it feels like to do something stupid—or worse than stupid—and then wish, above anything else, that I hadn't.

"So what does all this mean? Why are you—" Suze's voice sharpens in alarm. "Hang on. Bex, this isn't your way of saying you're going to get married in New York after all, is it?"

"It's not as simple as that," I say after a pause.

"Bex . . . I'll kill you. I really will. If you tell me now that you want to get married in New York—"

"Suze, I don't *want* to get married in New York. Of course I don't! But if we abandon the wedding now . . . then that'll be it. Elinor'll never speak to either of us again. Ever."

"I don't believe it. I just don't believe it! You're going to fuck everything up again, aren't you?"

"Suze—"

"Just as everything is all right! Just as for once in your life, you *aren't* in a complete mess and I can start to relax . . ."

"Suze—"

"Becky?"

I look up, startled. Luke is standing there in his boxers and T-shirt, staring in bleary puzzlement at me.

"Are you OK?" he says.

"I'm fine," I say, putting a hand over the receiver. "Just talking to Suze. You go back to bed. I won't be long."

I wait until he's gone and then shuffle closer to the radiator, which is still giving out a feeble heat.

"OK, Suze, listen," I say. "Just . . . just hear me out. I'm not going to fuck anything up. I've been thinking really hard, and I've had this genius idea . . ."

By nine the next morning I'm at Elinor's apartment. I've dressed very carefully and am wearing my smartest linen U.N. diplomatic envoy-style suit, together with a pair of nonconfrontational rounded-toe shoes. Although I'm not sure Elinor quite appreciates the effort I've made. As she answers the door she looks even paler than usual and her eyes are like daggers.

"Rebecca," she says stonily.

"Elinor," I reply, equally stonily. Then I remember I've come here in order to be conciliatory. "Elinor," I repeat, trying to inject the word with some warmth. "I've come to talk."

"To apologize," she says, heading down the corridor.

God, she is a cow. And anyway, what did I do? Nothing! For a moment I consider turning round and leaving. But I've decided to do this, so I will.

"Not really," I say. "Just to talk. About you. And Luke."

"He has regretted his rash actions."

"No."

"He wishes to apologize."

"No! He doesn't! He's hurt and angry and he has no desire to go near you again!"

"So why are you here?"

"Because . . . I think it would be a good thing if the two of you tried to make up. Or at least talk to each other again."

"I have nothing to say to Luke," replies Elinor. "I have nothing to say to you. As Luke indicated yesterday, the relationship is terminated."

God, they are *so* like each other.

"So . . . have you told Robyn yet about the wedding being off?" This is my secret fear, and I hold my breath for an answer.

"No. I thought I would give Luke a chance to reconsider. Clearly this was a mistake."

I take a deep breath. "I'll get Luke to go through with the wedding. If you apologize to him." My voice is a little shaky. I can't quite believe I'm doing this.

"What did you say?" Elinor turns and stares at me.

"You apologize to Luke and tell him . . . well, basically, that you love him. And I'll persuade him to get married at the Plaza. You'll have your big smart wedding for all your friends. That's the deal."

"You're . . . *bargaining* with me?"

"Er . . . yes." I turn to face her square-on and clench my fists tightly by my sides. "Basically, Elinor, I'm here for completely selfish reasons. Luke has been screwed up about you all his life. Now he's decided he never wants to see you again. Which is all fine and good—but I'm worried that's not the end. I'm worried in two years' time he'll suddenly decide he's got to come back to New York and find you and see if you really are as bad as he thinks you are. And it'll all start again."

"This is preposterous. How dare you—"

"Elinor, you want this wedding. I know you do. You just have to be nice to your son and you can have it. I mean, it's not that much to ask!"

There's silence. Gradually Elinor's eyes narrow, as closely as they can since her last bout of plastic surgery.

"You want this wedding too, Rebecca. Please don't pretend this is a purely altruistic offer. You were as dismayed as I was when he pulled out. Admit it. You're here because you want to get married at the Plaza."

"You think that's why I'm here?" I gape at her. "Because I'm upset that the Plaza wedding was canceled?"

I almost feel like laughing hysterically. I almost want to tell her the whole truth, right from the beginning.

"Believe me, Elinor," I say at last. "That's not why I'm here. I can live without the Plaza wedding. Yes, I was looking forward to it and it was exciting. But if Luke doesn't want it . . . that's it. I can drop it just like that. It's not my friends. It's not my home city. I really don't care."

There's another sharp silence. Elinor moves away to a polished side table and, to my utter astonishment, takes out a cigarette and lights it. She's kept that habit very quiet!

"I can persuade Luke," I say, watching her put the box away. "And you can't."

"You are . . . beyond belief," she says. "Using your own wedding as a bargaining tool."

"I know I am. Is that a yes?"

I've won. I can see it in her face. She's already decided.

"Here's what you have to say." I get out a piece of paper from my bag. "It's all the stuff Luke needs to hear. You have to tell him you love him, you have to say how much you missed him when he was a child, how you thought he'd be better off in Britain, how the only reason you didn't want to see him was you were afraid of disappointing him . . ." I hand the paper to Elinor. "I know none of it is going to sound remotely natural. So you'd better start off by saying 'These words don't come naturally to me.' "

Elinor stares blankly at the sheet. She's breathing heavily and for a moment I think she's going to throw it at me. Then, carefully, she folds up the piece of paper and puts it on the side table. Is that another twitch of emotion beneath her eye? Is she upset? Livid? Or just disdainful?

I just can't get my head round Elinor. One minute I think she's carrying round a huge untapped love deep inside her—and the next I think she's a coldhearted cow. One minute I think she completely hates me. Then I think, maybe she just has no idea how she comes across. Maybe, all this time, she's genuinely believed she was being friendly.

I mean, if no one's ever *told* her what an awful manner she has . . . how's she to know?

"What did you mean by saying that Luke might decide to come back to New York?" she says frostily. "Are you planning to leave?"

"We haven't talked about it yet," I say after a pause. "But yes. I think we might. New York's been great, but I don't think it's a good place for us to be anymore. Luke's burned out. He needs a change of scene."

He needs to be away from you, I add silently.

"I see." Elinor draws on her cigarette. "You appreciate I had arranged an interview with the co-op board of this building? At considerable effort."

"I know. Luke told me. But to be honest, Elinor, we would never have lived here."

Her face flickers again, and I can tell she's suppressing some kind of feeling. But what? Is it fury with me for being so ungrateful? Is it distress that Luke's not going to live in her building after all? Part of me is desperately curious, wants to pick away at her facade, nose in, and find out all about her.

And another, more sensible part of me says, just leave it, Becky. Just leave it.

As I reach the door, though, I can't resist turning round. "Elinor, you know how they say inside every fat person there's a thin person struggling to get out? Well . . . the more I think about you, the more I think there might—possibly—be a nice person inside you. But as long as you keep being mean to people and telling them their shoes are shoddy, no one's ever going to know."

There. She'll probably kill me now. I'd better get out. Trying not to look as though I'm running, I head down the corridor and out of the apartment. I close the door behind me and lean against it, my heart thudding.

OK. So far so good. Now for Luke.

"I have absolutely no idea why you want to go to the Rainbow Room." Luke leans back in his taxi seat and scowls out of the window.

"Because I never have, OK? I want to see the view!"

"But why now? Why today?"

"Why not today?" I glance at my watch and then survey Luke anxiously.

He's pretending he's happy. He's pretending he's liberated. But he's not. He's brooding.

Superficially, things have started to get slightly better. At least he hasn't given away any more items of clothing, and this morning he actually shaved. But he's still far from his old self. He didn't go into work today but sat all day watching a triple bill of old black-and-white films starring Bette Davis.

Funnily enough, I'd never seen the resemblance between Bette Davis and Elinor before.

The truth is, Annabel was right, I think as I watch him. Well, of course she was. She knows her stepson as though he were her own child. And she knows that Elinor is right inside Luke, part of his very being. He can't just cut her out and move on. He needs at least the chance of some kind of resolution. Even if it is painful.

I shut my eyes and send a silent plea to all gods. Please let this work. Please. And then maybe we'll be able to draw a line under all of it and get on with our lives.

"Rockefeller Center," says the taxi driver, pulling up, and I smile at Luke, trying to hide my nerves.

I tried to think of the least likely place that Elinor would ever be found—and came up with the Rainbow Room at Rockefeller Center, where tourists go to drink cocktails and gawk at the view over Manhattan. As we head up to the sixty-fifth floor in the lift, we're both silent, and I pray desperately that she'll be there, that it'll all work out, that Luke won't get too pissed off with me—

We walk out of the lift . . . and I can already see her. Sitting at a window table in a dark jacket, her face silhouetted against the view.

As he spots her, Luke gives a start.

"Becky. What the fuck—" He turns on his heel and I grab his arm.

"Luke, please. She wants to talk to you. Just . . . give her a chance."

"You set this up?" His face is white with anger. "You brought me here deliberately?"

"I had to! You wouldn't have come otherwise. Just five minutes. Listen to what she says."

"Why on earth should I—"

"I really think the two of you need to talk. Luke, you can't leave it like you did. It's eating you up inside! And it's not going to get any better unless you talk to her . . . Come on, Luke." I loosen my grip on his arm and look at him pleadingly. "Just five minutes. That's all I'm asking."

He has to agree. If he stalks out now, I'm dead.

A group of German tourists have come up behind us and I watch them milling around at the window, gasping admiringly at the view.

"Five minutes," says Luke at last. "That's all." Slowly he walks across the room and sits down opposite Elinor. She glances over at me and nods, and I turn away, my heart beating fast. Please don't let her fuck this one up. Please.

I walk out of the bar and make my way into an empty function room, where I stand at the floor-length window, gazing out over the city. After a while I glance at my watch. It's been five minutes and he hasn't stormed out yet.

She's delivered on her side of the deal. Now I have to deliver on mine.

I get out my mobile phone, feeling sick with dread. This is going to be hard. This is going to be really hard. I don't know how Mum's going to react. I don't know what she's going to say.

But the point is, whatever she says, however furious she gets, I know Mum and I will last. Mum and I are there for the duration.

Whereas this could be Luke's only chance to reconcile with Elinor.

As I listen to the ringing tone, I stare out over the endless silvery blocks and towers of Manhattan. The sun's glinting off one building, only to be reflected off another, just like Luke said. Backward and forward, never leaving. The yellow taxis are so far down they look like Tonka toys and the people scurrying about are like tiny insects. And there in the middle is the green rectangular form of Central Park, like a picnic rug laid down for the children to play on.

I gaze out, mesmerized by the sight. Did I really mean what I said to Elinor yesterday? Do I really want for Luke and me to leave this amazing city?

"Hello?" Mum's voice breaks my thoughts, and my head jolts upward. For a moment I'm paralyzed with nerves. I can't do this.

But I have to.

I have no choice.

"Hi, Mum," I say at last, digging my nails into the palm of my hand. "It's . . . it's Becky. Listen, I've got something to tell you. And I'm afraid you're not going to like it—"

MRS. JAMES BRANDON
RIDGE HOUSE
RIDGEWAY
NORTH FULLERTON
DEVON

2 June 2002

Dear Becky,

We were a little bewildered by your phone call. Despite your assurances that all will be clear when you have explained it to us, and that we must trust you, we do not really understand what is going on.

However, James and I have talked long and hard and have at last decided to do as you ask. We have canceled our flights to New York and alerted the rest of the family.

Becky dear, I do hope this all works out.

With very best wishes, and with all our love to Luke—

Annabel

SECOND UNION BANK
53 WALL STREET
NEW YORK, NY 10005

June 10, 2002

Miss Rebecca Bloomwood
Apt. B
251 W. 11th Street
New York, NY 10014

Dear Miss Bloomwood:

Thank you very much for your wedding invitation addressed to Walt Pitman.

After some discussion we have decided to take you into our confidence. Walt Pitman does not in fact exist. It is a generic name, used to represent all our customer care operatives.

The name "Walt Pitman" was chosen after extensive focus group research to suggest an approachable yet competent figure. Customer feedback has shown that the continual presence of Walt in our customers' lives has increased confidence and loyalty by over 50 percent.

We would be grateful if you would keep this fact to yourself. If you would still like a representative from Second Union Bank at your wedding, I would be glad to attend. My birthday is March 5th and my favorite color is blue.

Yours sincerely,

Bernard Lieberman
Senior Vice-President

Twenty

OK. DON'T PANIC. This is going to work. If I just keep my head and remain calm, it'll work.

"It'll never work," says Suze's voice in my ear.

"Shut up!" I say crossly.

"It'll never work in a million years. I'm just warning you."

"You're not supposed to be warning me! You're supposed to be encouraging me!" I lower my voice. "And as long as everyone does what they're supposed to, it will work. It has to."

I'm standing at the window of a twelfth-floor suite at the Plaza, staring at Plaza Square below. Outside, it's a hot sunny day. People are milling around in T-shirts and shorts, doing normal things like hiring horse carriages to go round the park and tossing coins into the fountain.

And here am I, dressed in a towel, with my hair teased beyond recognition into a *Sleeping Beauty* style, and makeup an inch thick, walking around in the highest white satin shoes I've ever come across in my life. (Christian Louboutin, from Barneys. I get a discount.)

"What are you doing now?" comes Suze's voice again.

"I'm looking out the window."

"What are you doing that for?"

"I don't know." I watch a woman with denim shorts sit down on a bench and snap open a can of Coke, completely unaware she's being watched. "To try to get a grip on normality, I suppose."

"Normality?" I hear Suze splutter down the phone. "Bex, it's a bit late for normality!"

"That's not fair!"

"If normality is planet earth, do you know where you are right now?"

"Er . . . the moon?" I hazard.

"You're fifty million light-years away. You're . . . in another galaxy. A long long time ago."

"I do feel a bit like I'm in a different world," I admit, and turn to survey the palatial suite behind me.

The atmosphere is hushed and heavy with scent and hairspray and expectation. Everywhere I look there are lavish flower arrangements, baskets of fruit and chocolates, and bottles of champagne on ice. Over by the dressing table the hairdresser and makeup girl are chatting to one another while they work on Erin. Meanwhile the reportage photographer is changing his film, his assistant is watching Madonna on MTV, and a room-service waiter is clearing away yet another round of cups and glasses.

It's all so glamorous, so expensive. But at the same time, what I'm reminded of most of all is getting ready for the summer school play. The windows would be covered in black material, and we'd all crowd round a mirror getting all overexcited, and out the front we'd hear the parents filing in, but we wouldn't be allowed to peek out and see them . . .

"What are you doing now?" comes Suze's voice again.

"Still looking out the window."

"Well, stop looking out the window! You've got less than an hour to go!"

"Suze, relax."

"How can I relax?"

"It's all fine. It's under control."

"And you haven't told anyone," she says for the millionth time. "You haven't told Danny."

"Of course not! I'm not that stupid!" I edge casually into a corner where no one can hear me. "Only Michael knows. And Laurel. That's it."

"And no one suspects anything?"

"Not a thing," I say, just as Robyn comes into the room. "Hi, Robyn! Suze, I'll talk to you later, OK—"

I put the phone down and smile at Robyn, who's wearing a bright pink suit and a headset and carrying a walkie-talkie.

"OK, Becky," she says in a serious, businesslike way. "Stage one is complete. Stage two is under way. But we have a problem."

"Really?" I swallow. "What's that?"

"None of Luke's family have arrived yet. His father, his stepmother, some cousins who are on the list . . . You told me they'd spoken to you?"

"Yes, they did." I clear my throat. "Actually . . . they just called again. I'm afraid there's a problem with their plane. They said to seat other people in their places."

"Really?" Robyn's face falls. "This is too bad! I've never known a wedding to have so many last-minute alterations! A new maid of honor . . . a new best man . . . a new officiant . . . it seems like everything's changed!"

"I know," I say apologetically. "I'm really sorry, and I know it's meant a lot of work." I cross my fingers behind my back. "It just suddenly seemed so obvious that Michael should marry us, rather than some stranger. I mean, since he's such an old friend and he's qualified to do it and everything. So then Luke had to have a new best man . . ."

"But to change your minds three weeks before the wedding! And you know, Father Simon was quite upset to be rejected. He wondered if it was something to do with his hair."

"No! Of course not! It's nothing to do with him, honestly—"

"And then your parents both catching the measles. I mean, what kind of odds is that?"

"I know!" I pull a rueful face. "Sheer bad luck."

There's a crackle from the walkie-talkie and Robyn turns away.

"Yes," she says. "What's that? No! I said radiant *yellow* light! Not blue! OK, I'm coming . . ." As she reaches the door she looks back.

"Becky, I have to go. I just needed to say, it's been so hectic, what with all the changes, there are a couple of tiny additional details we didn't have time to discuss. So I just went ahead with them. OK?"

"Whatever," I say. "I trust your judgment. Thanks, Robyn."

As Robyn leaves, there's a tapping on the door and in comes Christina, looking absolutely amazing in pale gold Issey Miyake and holding a champagne glass.

"How's the bride?" she says with a smile. "Feeling nervous?"

"Not really!" I say.

Which is kind of true.

In fact, it's completely true. I'm beyond nervous. Either everything goes to plan and this all works out. Or it doesn't and it's a complete disaster. There's not much I can do about it.

"I just spoke to Laurel," she says, taking a sip of champagne. "I didn't know she was so involved with the wedding."

"Oh, she's not really," I say. "There's just this tiny little favor she's doing for me—"

"So I understand." Christina eyes me over her glass, and I suddenly wonder how much Laurel has said to her.

"Did she tell you . . . what the favor was?" I say casually.

"She gave me the gist. Becky, if you pull this off . . ." says Christina. She shakes her head. "If you pull this off, you deserve the Nobel Prize for chutzpah." She raises her glass. "Here's to you. And good luck."

"Thanks."

"Hey, Christina!" We both look round to see Erin coming toward us. She's already in her long violet maid-of-honor dress, her hair up in a medieval knot, eyes lit up with excitement. "Isn't this *Sleeping Beauty* theme cool? Have you seen Becky's wedding dress yet? I can't believe I'm the maid of honor! I was never a maid of honor before!"

I think Erin's a tad excited about her promotion. When I told her my best friend, Suze, couldn't make it, and would she like to be maid of honor, she actually burst into tears.

"I haven't seen Becky's wedding dress yet," says Christina. "I hardly dare to."

"It's really nice!" I protest. "Come and look."

I lead her into the sumptuous dressing area, where Danny's dress is hanging up.

"It's all in one piece," observes Christina laconically. "That's a good start."

"Christina," I say. "This isn't like the T-shirts. This is in a different league. Take a look!"

I just can't believe what a fantastic job Danny has done. Although I'd never admit it to Christina, I wasn't exactly counting on wearing his dress. In fact, to be perfectly honest, I was having secret Vera Wang fittings right up until a week ago.

But then one night Danny knocked on the door, his whole face lit up with excitement. He dragged me upstairs to his apartment, pulled me down the corridor, and flung open the door to his room. And I was speechless.

From a distance it looks like a traditional white wedding dress, with a tight bodice, full, romantic skirt, and long train. But the closer you get, you more you start spotting the fantastic customized details everywhere. The white denim ruffles at the back. The trademark Danny little pleats and gatherings at the waistline. The white sequins and diamante and glitter scattered all over the train, like someone's emptied a candy box over it.

I've never seen a wedding dress like it. It's a work of art.

"Well," says Christina. "I'll be honest. When you told me you were wearing a creation by young Mr. Kovitz, I was a little worried. But this . . ." She touches a tiny bead. "I'm impressed. Assuming the train doesn't fall off as you walk down the aisle."

"It won't," I assure her. "I walked around our apartment in it for half an hour. Not even one sequin fell off!"

"You're going to look amazing," says Erin dreamily. "Just like a princess. And in that room . . ."

"The room is spectacular," says Christina. "I think a lot of jaws are going to be dropping."

"I haven't seen it yet," I say. "Robyn didn't want me going in."

"Oh, you should take a look," says Erin. "Just have a peek. Before it gets filled up with people."

"I can't! What if someone sees me?"

"Go on," says Erin. "Put on a scarf. No one'll know it's you."

I creep downstairs in a borrowed hooded jacket, averting my face when I pass anyone, feeling ridiculously naughty. I've seen the designer's plans, and as I push open the double doors to the Terrace Room, I think I know roughly what I'm expecting to see. Something spectacular. Something theatrical.

Nothing could have prepared me for walking into that room.

It's like walking into another land.

A silvery, sparkling, magical forest. Branches are arching high above me as I look up. Flowers seem to be growing out of clumps of earth. There are vines and fruits and an apple tree covered with silver apples, and a spider's web covered with dewdrops . . . and are those *real* birds flying around up there?

Colored lights are dappling the branches and falling on the rows of chairs. A pair of women are methodically brushing lint off every upholstered seat. A man in jeans is taping a cable to the carpet. A man on a lighting rig is adjusting a silvery branch. A violinist is playing little runs and trills, and there's the dull thud of timpani being tuned up.

This is like being backstage at a Broadway show.

I stand at the side, staring around, trying to take in every detail. I have never seen anything like this in my life before, and I don't think I ever will again.

Suddenly I see Robyn entering the room at the far end, talking into her headpiece. Her eyes scan the room, and I shrink into my hooded jacket. Before she can spot me, I back out of the Terrace Room and get into the lift to go up to the Grand Ballroom.

As the doors are about to close, a couple of elderly women in dark skirts and white shirts get in.

"Did you see the cake?" says one of them. "Three thousand dollars minimum."

"Who's the family?"

"Sherman," says the first woman. "Elinor Sherman."

"Oh, *this* is the Elinor Sherman wedding."

The doors open and they walk out.

"Bloomwood," I say, too late. "I think the bride's name is Becky . . ."

They weren't listening, anyway.

I cautiously follow them into the Grand Ballroom. The enormous white and gold room where Luke and I will lead the dancing.

Oh my God. It's even huger than I remember. It's even more gilded and grandiose. Spotlights are circling the room, lighting up the balconies and chandeliers. They suddenly switch to strobe effects, then flashing disco lights, playing on the faces of waiters putting finishing touches to the tables. Every circular table has an ornate centerpiece of cascading white flowers. The ceiling has been tented with muslin, festooned with fairy lights like strings of pearls. The dance floor is vast and polished. Up on the stage, a ten-piece band is doing a sound check. I look round dazedly and see two assistants from Antoine's cake studio balancing on chairs, sticking the last few sugar tulips into the eight-foot cake. Everywhere is the smell of flowers and candle wax and anticipation.

"Excuse me." I jump aside as a waiter wheels a cart past.

"Can I help you?" says a woman with a Plaza badge on her lapel.

"I was just, er . . . looking around . . ." I say.

"Looking around?" Her eyes narrow suspiciously.

"Yes! In case I ever . . . er . . . want to get married." I back away before she can ask any more. I've seen enough, anyway.

I'm not sure how to get back to the suite from here, and this place is so huge I'm bound to get lost, so I head back down to the ground floor and walk as inconspicuously as I can past the Palm Court to the elevators.

As I pass an alcove containing a sofa, I stop. There's a familiar dark head. A familiar hand, holding what looks like a gin and tonic.

"Luke?" He turns round and peers at me blankly—and I suddenly realize my face is half hidden. "It's me!" I hiss.

"Becky?" he says incredulously. "What are you doing here?"

"I wanted to see it all. Isn't it amazing?" I look around to see if I'm being observed, then slide into the chair opposite him. "You look great."

He looks more than great. He's looking completely gorgeous, in an immaculate dinner jacket and crisp white dress shirt. His dark hair is glossy under the lights, and I can just smell the familiar scent of his aftershave. As he meets my eyes, I feel something release inside me, like a coil unwinding. Whatever happens today—whether I pull this off or not—the two of us are together. The two of us will be all right.

"We shouldn't be talking to each other, you know," he says with a little smile. "It's bad luck."

"I know," I say, and take a sip of his gin and tonic. "But to be honest, I think we're beyond superstition by now."

"What do you mean?"

"Oh . . . nothing." I count to five, psyching myself up, then say, "Did you hear about your parents being delayed?"

"Yes, I was told." Luke frowns. "Did you speak to them? Do you know when they'll get here?"

"Oh, soon, I expect," I say vaguely. "Don't worry, they said they would definitely be there to see you walk down the aisle."

Which is true. In its way.

Luke doesn't know anything of my plans. He's had enough to deal with as it is. For once, I'm the one in charge.

I feel like I've seen a completely different Luke over the last few weeks. A younger, more vulnerable Luke, whom the rest of the world doesn't know anything about. After he had that meeting with Elinor, he was very quiet for a while. There was no huge emotional outburst, no dramatic scene. In some ways, he simply went back to normal. But he was still fragile, still exhausted. Still nowhere near being able to go to work. For about two weeks, he just slept and slept, fourteen or fifteen hours a day. It was as though ten years of driving himself too hard were finally catching up with him.

Now he's gradually becoming his usual self. He's getting back that veneer of confidence. That blank expression when he doesn't want people to know what he's feeling. That abrupt, businesslike manner. He's been into the office during the past week, and it's been like old times.

Although not quite. Because although the veneer's back, the point is, I've seen underneath it. I've seen the way Luke works. The way he thinks and what he's scared of and what he really wants out of life. Before all this happened, we'd been together for over two years. We'd lived together, we were a successful couple. But now I feel I know him in a way I never did before.

"I keep thinking back to that conversation I had with my mother," he says, frowning into his drink. "Up in the Rainbow Room."

"Really?" I say warily. "What exactly—"

"I still find it confusing."

"Confusing?" I say after a pause. "Why's that?"

"I've never heard her speak that way before. It didn't seem real." He looks up. "I don't know whether I should believe her."

I lean forward and take his hand. "Luke, just because she's never said those things to you before, it doesn't mean they aren't true."

This is what I've said to him nearly every day since he had the meeting with Elinor. I want to stop him picking away at it. I want him to accept what she said, and be happy. But he's too intelligent for that. He's silent for a few moments, and I know he's replaying the conversation in his mind.

"Some of the things she said seemed so true, and others, so false."

"Which bits sounded false?" I say lightly. "Out of interest?"

"When she told me that she was proud of everything I'd done, from the founding of my company to choosing you as a wife. It just didn't quite . . . I don't know . . ." He shakes his head.

"I thought that was rather good!" I retort before I can stop myself. "I mean . . . you know . . . quite a likely thing for her to say—"

"But then she said something else. She said there wasn't a single day since I was born that she hadn't thought about me." He hesitates. "And the way she said it . . . I really believed her."

"She said that?" I say, taken aback.

There was nothing about that on the piece of paper I gave Elinor. I reach for Luke's gin and tonic and take a sip, thinking hard.

"I really do think she meant what she said," I say at last. "In fact . . . I know it. The point is, she wanted to tell you she loved you. Even if everything she said didn't sound completely natural, that's what she wanted you to know."

"I suppose so." He meets my eyes. "But still. I can't feel the same way about her. I can't go back to where I was."

"No," I say after a short silence. "Well . . . I think that's probably a good thing."

The spell's been lifted. Luke has finally woken up.

I lean over and kiss him, then take another sip of his drink. "I should go and put my frock on."

"You're not wearing that fetching anorak?" says Luke with a grin.

"Well, I was *going* to. But now you've seen it, I'll just have to find something else, I suppose . . ." I get up to go—then hesitate. "Listen, Luke. If things seem a bit strange today, just . . . go with it, OK?"

"OK," says Luke in surprise.

"You promise?"

"I promise." He gives me a sideways look. "Becky, is there anything I should know?"

"Er . . . no," I say innocently. "No, I don't think so. See you in there."

Twenty-one

I CAN'T BELIEVE I'VE made it to this moment. I honestly can't believe it's really happening.

I'm wearing a wedding dress and a sparkly tiara in my hair.

I'm a bride.

As I'm led by Robyn down the empty, silent Plaza corridors, I feel a bit like the president in a Hollywood movie. "The Beauty is on the move," she's muttering into her headset as we walk along the plushy red carpet. "The Beauty is approaching."

We turn a corner and I catch a glimpse of myself in a huge antique mirror, and feel a dart of shock. Of course I know what I look like. I've just spent half an hour staring at myself in the suite upstairs, for goodness' sake. But still, catching myself unawares, I can't quite believe that girl in the veil is me. It's *me*.

I'm about to walk up the aisle at the Plaza. Four hundred people watching every move. Oh God.

Oh God. What am I thinking?

As I see the doors of the Terrace Room, I start to panic, and my fingers tighten around my bouquet. This is never going to work. I must be mad. I can't do it. I want to run away.

But there's nowhere to run. There's nothing else to do but go forward.

Erin and the other bridesmaids are waiting, and as we draw

near, they all begin to coo over my dress. I've no idea what their names are. They're daughters of Elinor's friends. After today I'll probably never see them again.

"String orchestra. Stand by for Beauty," Robyn is saying into her headset.

"Becky!" I look up, and thank God, it's Danny, wearing a brocade frock coat over leather trousers, and carrying a taupe and bronze Ceremony Program. "You look amazing."

"Really? Do I look OK?"

"Spectacular," says Danny firmly. He adjusts the train, stands back for a look, then takes out a pair of scissors and snips at a piece of ribbon.

"Ready?" says Robyn.

"I guess," I say, feeling slightly sick.

The double doors swing open, and I hear the rustle of four hundred people turning in their seats. The string orchestra starts to play the theme from *Sleeping Beauty,* and the bridesmaids begin to walk up the aisle.

And suddenly I'm walking forward. I'm walking into the enchanted forest, carried on the swell of the music. Little lights are twinkling overhead. Pine needles are giving off their scent under my feet. There's the smell of fresh earth and the sound of birds chirruping, and the trickle of a tiny waterfall. Flowers are magically blooming as I take each step, and leaves are unfurling, and people are gasping as they look up. And there's Luke up ahead, my handsome prince, waiting for me.

Finally, I start to relax. To savor it.

As I take each step, I feel as though I'm a prima ballerina doing the perfect arabesque at Covent Garden. Or a movie star arriving at the Oscars. Music playing, everyone looking at me, jewels in my hair and the most beautiful dress I've ever worn. I know I will never experience anything like this again in my life. Never. As I reach the top of the aisle, I slow my pace right down, breathing in the atmosphere, taking in the trees and the flowers and the wonderful scent. Trying to impress every detail on my mind. Relishing every magical second.

I reach Luke's side and hand my bouquet to Erin. I smile warmly at Gary, Luke's new best man—then take Luke's hand. He gives a little squeeze, and I squeeze it back.

And here's Michael stepping forward, wearing a dark, vaguely clerical-looking suit.

He gives me a tiny, conspiratorial smile, then takes a deep breath and addresses the congregation.

"Dearly beloved. We are gathered here together to witness the love between two people. We are here to watch them pledging their love for each other. And to join with them in celebrating the joy of their sharing of that love. God blesses all who love, and God will certainly bless Luke and Becky today as they exchange their vows."

He turns to me, and I can hear the rustling behind me as people try to get a good view.

"Do you, Rebecca, love Luke?" he says. "Do you pledge yourself to him for better for worse, for richer for poorer, in sickness and in health? Do you put your trust in him now and forever?"

"I do," I say, unable to stop a tiny tremor in my voice.

"Do you, Luke, love Rebecca? Do you pledge yourself to her for better for worse, for richer for poorer, in sickness and in health? Do you put your trust in her now and forever?"

"Yes," says Luke firmly. "I do."

"May God bless Luke and Becky and may they have happiness always." Michael pauses and looks around the room, as though daring anyone to argue with him, and my fingers tighten around Luke's. "May they know the joy of a shared understanding, the delight of a growing love, and the warmth of an everlasting friendship. Now let us applaud the happy couple." He smiles at Luke. "You may kiss the bride."

As Luke bends to kiss me, Michael determinedly begins to clap. There's a slightly uncertain pause . . . then a smattering of people join in, and soon the whole room is applauding.

Gary is murmuring something in Luke's ear, and he turns to me, looking puzzled.

"What about the ring?"

"Don't mention the ring," I say through a fixed smile.

My heart is beating so hard, I can barely breathe. I keep waiting for someone to stand up. For someone to say, "Hang on a minute . . ."

But no one does. No one says anything.

It's worked.

I meet Michael's eye for an instant—then look away before anyone notices. I can't relax yet. Not quite yet.

The photographer comes forward and I take Luke's arm firmly in mine, and Erin gives me my bouquet, wiping away her tears as she does so.

"That was such a beautiful ceremony!" she says. "The bit about the warmth of an everlasting friendship really got to me. You know, because that's all I want." She clasps my bouquet to her chest. "That's all I've ever wanted."

"Well, you know, I'm sure you'll find it," I say, and give her a hug. "I know you will."

"Excuse me, miss?" says the photographer. "If I could just get the bride and groom . . ."

Erin gives me my flowers and ducks out of the way, and I adopt my most radiant, newlywed expression.

"But, Becky," Luke says. "Gary says—"

"Take the ring from Gary," I say without moving my head. "Say you're really embarrassed that it got left out, and we'll do it later."

Some guests have come forward to take photographs, and I rest my head on Luke's shoulder and smile happily at them.

"Something else is wrong," Luke is saying. "Michael didn't proclaim us husband and wife. And don't we have to sign something?"

"Sssshh!" There's a bright flash, and we both blink.

"Becky, what's going on?" He pulls me round to face him. "Are we married?"

"That's a good shot!" says the photographer. "Stay like that."

"Are we married?" Luke's eyes scan my face intently.

"Well . . . OK," I say reluctantly. "As it happens, we're not."

There's another blinding flash. When my eyes focus again, Luke's gazing at me incredulously. "We're not married?"

"Look, just trust me, OK?"

"*Trust* you?"

"Yes! Like you just promised to do five seconds ago! Remember?"

"I promised to do that when I thought we were getting married!"

Suddenly the string orchestra launches into the "Bridal March," and a team of minders usher away the guests with their cameras.

"Go," says a crackling, disembodied voice. "Start walking."

Where on earth is it coming from? Are my flowers talking to me?

Suddenly my eyes zoom in on a tiny speaker, attached to a rosebud. Robyn's planted a speaker in my bouquet?

"Bride and groom! Walk!"

"OK!" I say to the flowers. "We're going!"

I grab Luke's arm tight and begin to walk down the aisle, back through the enchanted forest.

"We're not married," Luke is saying disbelievingly. "A whole bloody forest, four hundred people, a big white dress, and we're not married."

"Sssh!" I say crossly. "Don't tell everybody! Look, you promised if things were a bit strange you'd go with it. Well, go with it!"

As we walk along arm in arm, rays of sunlight are piercing the branches of the forest, dappling the floor. Suddenly there's a whirring noise, and to my astonishment the branches creakily begin to retreat, to reveal rainbows playing on the ceiling. A heavenly chorus breaks into song, and a fluffy cloud descends from the sky, on which a pair of fat pink doves are reposing.

Oh God. I've got the giggles. This is too much. Are these the tiny additional details Robyn was talking about?

I look up at Luke, and his mouth is twitching suspiciously too.

"What do you think of the forest?" I say brightly. "It's cool, isn't it? They flew the birch trees over from Switzerland especially."

"Really?" says Luke. "Where did they fly the doves over from?" He peers up at them. "Those are too big to be doves. They must be turkeys."

"They're not turkeys!"

"Love turkeys."

"Luke, shut up," I mutter, trying desperately not to giggle. "They're doves."

We're passing row after row of smartly dressed guests, all smiling warmly at us except the girls, who are giving me the Manhattan Onceover.

"Who the hell are all these people?" says Luke, surveying the rows of smiling strangers.

"I have no idea." I shrug. "I thought you might know some of them."

We reach the back of the room for a final session of photographs, and Luke looks at me quizzically. "Becky, my parents aren't here. And neither are yours."

"Er . . . no. They're not."

"No family. No ring. And we're not married." He pauses. "Call me crazy—but this isn't quite how I expected our wedding to be."

"This isn't our wedding," I say, and kiss him for the cameras.

I can't quite believe we're getting away with it. No one's said anything. No one's questioned a thing. A couple of people have asked to see the ring, and I've just flashed them the band of my engagement ring, turned round.

We've eaten sushi and caviar. We've had an amazing four-course dinner. We've drunk toasts. It's all gone according to plan. We cut the cake with a huge silver sword and everybody cheered, and then the band started to play "The Way You Look Tonight" and Luke led me onto the dance floor and we started dancing. That was one of those moments I'll keep in my scrapbook forever. A whirl of white and gold and glitter and music, and Luke's arms around me, and my head giddy from champagne, and the knowledge that this was it, this was the high, and soon it would be over.

And now the party's in full swing. The band's playing a jazzy number I don't recognize, and the dance floor's full. Amid the throng of well-dressed strangers, I can pick out a few familiar faces. Christina's dancing with her date, and Erin is chatting to one of the groomsmen. And there's Laurel, dancing very energetically with . . . Michael!

Well now. That's a thought.

"So. Guess how many people have asked for my card?" says a voice in my ear. I turn round, to see Danny looking triumphant, a glass of champagne in each hand and a cigarette in his mouth. "Twenty! At least! One wanted me to take her measurements, right then and there. They all think the dress is to die for. And when I told them I'd worked with John Galliano . . ."

"Danny, you've never worked with John Galliano!"

"I passed him a cup of coffee once," he says defensively. "And he thanked me. That was, in its way, an artistic communication . . ."

"If you say so." I grin at him happily. "I'm so pleased for you."

"So are you enjoying yourself?"

"Of course!"

"Your mother-in-law is in her element."

We both turn to survey Elinor, who is sitting at a nearby table, surrounded by smart ladies. There's a slight glow to her cheek and she looks about as animated as I've ever seen her. She's wearing a long sweeping pale green dress and huge quantities of diamonds, and looks like the belle of the ball. Which, in a way, she is. These are her friends. This is really her party, not Luke's or mine. It's a wonderful spectacle. It's a wonderful occasion to be a guest at.

And that's kind of what I feel I am.

A group of women go by, chattering loudly, and I hear snatches of conversation.

"Spectacular . . ."

"So imaginative . . ."

They smile at me and Danny, and I smile back. But my mouth is feeling a bit stiff. I'm tired of smiling at people I don't know.

"It's a great wedding," says Danny, looking around the glittering room. "Really spectacular. Although it's less *you* than I would have thought."

"Really? What makes you say that?"

"I'm not saying it's not fantastic. It's very slick, very lavish. It's just . . . not like I imagined you'd have your wedding. But I was wrong," he adds hastily as he sees my expression. "Obviously."

I look at his wiry, comical, unsuspecting face. Oh God. I have to tell him. I *can't* not tell Danny.

"Danny, there's something you should know," I say in an undertone.

"What?"

"About this wedding—"

"Hi, kids!"

I break off guiltily and turn around—but it's only Laurel, all flushed and happy from dancing.

"Great party, Becky," she says. "Great band. Christ, I'd forgotten how much I love to dance."

I survey her appearance in slight dismay.

"Laurel," I say. "You don't roll up the sleeves of a thousand-dollar Yves St. Laurent dress."

"I was hot," she says with a cheerful shrug. "Now, Becky, I hate to tell you." She lowers her voice. "But you're going to have to get going pretty soon."

"Already?" I look instinctively at my wrist, but I'm not wearing a watch.

"The car's waiting outside," says Laurel. "The driver has all the details. He'll take you to Teterboro Airport and show you where to go. It's a different procedure for private planes, but it should be straightforward. Any problems, you call me." She lowers her voice to a whisper, and I glance at Danny, who's pretending not to be listening. "You should be in England in plenty of time. I really hope it all works out."

I reach out and hug her tightly. "Laurel . . . you're a star," I mutter. "I don't know what to say."

"Becky, believe me. This is nothing. After what you did for me, you could have had ten planes." She hugs me back, then looks at her watch. "You'd better find Luke. I'll see you in a bit."

After she's gone there's a short, interested silence.

"Becky, did I just catch the words *private plane*?" says Danny.

"Er . . . yes. Yes, you did."

"You're flying on a private plane?"

"Yes." I try to sound nonchalant. "We are. It's Laurel's wedding present to us."

"She snapped up the private jet?" Danny shakes his head. "Damn. You know, I was planning to get you that myself. It was between that and the eggbeater . . ."

"Idiot! She's president of a plane company."

"Jesus. A private plane. So . . . where are you heading? Or is it still a big secret?" I watch as he takes a drag from his cigarette, and feel a sudden huge wave of affection for him.

I don't just want to tell Danny what's going on.

I want him to be part of this.

"Danny," I say. "How do you feel about going on a little trip?"

It takes me a while to find Luke. He's been trapped in a corner by two corporate financiers, and leaps up gratefully as soon as I appear. We go around the huge crowded room, saying good-bye and thank you for coming to all the guests we know. To be honest, it doesn't take that long.

Last of all, we approach the top table and interrupt Elinor as discreetly as we can.

"Mother, we're going now," says Luke.

"Now?" Elinor frowns. "It's too early."

"Well . . . we're going."

"Thank you for a wonderful wedding," I say sincerely. "It was really amazing. Everyone's been saying how wonderful it is." I bend to kiss her. "Good-bye."

"Good-bye, Becky," she says in that formal way of hers. "Good-bye, Luke."

"Good-bye, Mother."

They gaze at each other—and for a moment I think Elinor's going to say something else. But instead she leans forward rather stiffly and kisses Luke on the cheek.

"Becky!" I feel someone poking me on the shoulder. "Becky, you're not going yet!" I turn round to see Robyn looking perturbed.

"Er . . . yes. We're off. Thank you so much for everything you've—"

"You can't go yet!"

"No one'll notice," I say, glancing around the party.

"They have to notice! We have an exit planned, remember? The rose petals? The music?"

"Well . . . maybe we could forget the exit—"

"Forget the exit?" Robyn stares at me. "Are you joking? Orchestra!" she says urgently into her headpiece. "Segue to 'Some Day.' Do you copy? Segue to 'Some Day.' " She lifts the walkie-talkie. "Lighting crew, stand by with rose petals."

"Robyn," I say helplessly. "Honestly, we just wanted to slip away quietly . . ."

"My brides do not slip away quietly! Cue fanfare," she mutters into her headpiece. "Lighting crew, prepare exit spotlight."

There's a sudden loud fanfare of trumpets, and the guests on the dance floor all jump. The lighting changes from disco beat to a radiant pink glow, and the band starts to play "Some Day My Prince Will Come."

"Go, Beauty and Prince," says Robyn, giving me a little shove. "Go! *One* two three, *one* two three . . ."

Exchanging looks, Luke and I make it onto the dance floor, where the guests part to let us through. The music is all around us, a spotlight is following our path, and all of a sudden, rose petals start falling gently from the ceiling.

This is rather lovely, actually. Everyone's beaming benevolently, and I can hear some "Aahs" as we go by. The glow of pink light is like being inside a rainbow, and the rose petals smell wonderful as they land on our heads and arms and drift to the floor. Luke and I are smiling at each other, and there's a petal in his hair—

"Stop!"

As I hear the voice, I feel a sudden chill, right to the marrow of my bones.

The double doors have opened, and there she is, standing in the doorway. Wearing a black suit and the highest, pointiest black boots I've ever seen.

Everyone turns to look, and the orchestra peters out uncertainly.

"Oh, look!" I hear someone saying in delight. "That's so cute, they even thought of a witch!"

"Alicia?" says Luke in astonishment. "What are you doing here?"

"Having a good wedding, Luke?" she says sweetly, and takes a few steps into the room.

"Come in," I say quickly. "Come on in and join the party. We would have invited you . . ."

"I know what you're doing, Becky."

"We're getting married!" I say, trying to sound lighthearted. "No prizes for guessing that!"

"I know exactly what you're doing." She meets my eye. "I've got friends in Surrey, and they've been checking things out."

No.

Please, no.

"I think you have a teeny little secret you're not sharing with the rest of your guests." Alicia pulls a mock-concerned face. "That's not very polite, is it?"

I need my fairy godmothers, quick. I need someone to zap her with twinkle dust.

Laurel shoots me a horrified look.

Christina puts down her champagne glass.

"Code red, Code red," I hear Robyn's voice crackling from the bouquet. "Urgent. Code red."

Now Alicia's walking around the dance floor, taking her time, relishing the attention.

"The truth is," she says pleasantly, "this is all a bit of a sham. Isn't it, Becky?"

My eye flickers behind her. Two burly minders in tuxedos are approaching the dance floor. But they're not going to get there in time. It's all going to be ruined.

"It all looks so lovely. It all looks so romantic." Her voice suddenly hardens. "But what people might like to know is that this so-called perfect Plaza wedding is actually a complete and utter . . . *arrrgh*!" Her voice rises to a scream. "Put me down!"

I don't believe it. It's Luke.

He's calmly walked up to her and hoisted her up onto his shoulder. And now he's carrying her out, like a naughty toddler.

"Put me down!" she cries. "Someone bloody well help me!"

But the guests are starting to laugh. She starts kicking Luke with her pointy boots, and he raises his eyebrows but doesn't stop striding.

"It's a fake!" she shrieks as they reach the door. "It's a fake! They're not really—"

The door slams, cutting her off, and there's a silent, shocked moment. No one moves, not even Robyn. Then, slowly, the door opens again, and Luke reappears, brushing his hands.

"I don't like gate-crashers," he says dryly.

"Bravo!" shouts a woman I don't recognize. Luke gives a little bow, and there's a huge, relieved laugh, and soon the whole room is applauding.

My heart is thumping so hard I'm not sure I can keep standing. As Luke rejoins me, I reach for his hand and he squeezes mine hard. I just want to go now. I want to get away.

Now there's an interested babble around the room, and I can hear people murmuring things like "deranged" and "must be jealous." A woman in head-to-toe Prada is even saying brightly, "You know, exactly the same thing happened at *our* wedding—"

Oh God, and now here come Elinor and Robyn, side by side like the two queens in *Alice in Wonderland*.

"I'm so sorry!" says Robyn as soon as she gets near. "Don't let it upset you, sweetheart. She's just a sad girl with a grudge."

"Who *was* that?" says Elinor with a frown. "Did you know her?"

"A disgruntled ex-client," says Robyn. "Some of these girls become very bitter. I've no idea what happens to them! One minute they're sweet young things, the next minute they're throwing lawsuits around! Don't worry, Becky. We'll do the exit again. Attention, orchestra," she says urgently. "Reprise 'Some Day' at the signal. Lighting crew, stand by with emergency rose petals."

"You have emergency rose petals?" I say in disbelief.

"Sweetheart, I have every eventuality covered." She twinkles at me. "This is why you hire a wedding planner!"

"Robyn," I say honestly, "I think you're worth every penny." I put an arm round her and give her a kiss. "Bye. And bye again, Elinor."

The music swells through the air again, we start walking again, and more rose petals start cascading from the ceiling. I really have to hand it to Robyn. People are crowding around and applauding—and is it my imagination, or do they look a bit friendlier, following the Alicia incident? At the end of the line I spot Erin leaning eagerly forward, and I toss my bouquet into her outstretched hands.

And then we're out.

The heavy double doors close behind us and we're in the silent, plushy corridor, empty but for the two bouncers, who stare studiously ahead.

"We did it," I say, half laughing in relief; in exhilaration. "Luke, we did it!"

"So I gather," says Luke, nodding. "Well done, us. Now, do you mind telling me what the fuck is going on?"

Twenty-two

Laurel arranged it all perfectly. After a quick detour to the West Village for Danny's passport, we arrived at Teterboro to find the plane all ready for us. We arrived at Gatwick at about eight in the morning, where another car was waiting for us. And now we're speeding through Surrey toward Oxshott. We'll be there soon! I can't quite believe how seamless it's all been.

"Of course, you know your big mistake," says Danny, stretching luxuriously back in the leather Mercedes seat.

"What's that?" I say, looking up from the phone.

"Sticking to two weddings. I mean, as long as you're going to do it more than once, why not three times? Why not six times? Six parties . . ."

"Six dresses . . ." puts in Luke.

"Six cakes . . ."

"Look, shut up!" I say indignantly. "I didn't do all this intentionally, you know! It just . . . happened."

"Just happened," echoes Danny scoffingly. "Becky, you needn't pretend to us. You wanted to wear two dresses. There's no shame in it."

"Danny, I'm on the phone—" I look out of the window. "OK, Suze, I think we're about ten minutes away."

"I just can't believe you've made it," says Suze down the line. "I can't believe it all worked out! I feel like rushing around, telling everyone!"

"Well, don't!"

"But it's so incredible! To think last night you were at the Plaza, and now—" She stops in sudden alarm. "Hey, you're not still wearing your wedding dress, are you?"

"Of course not!" I giggle. "I'm not a complete moron. We changed on the plane."

"And what was that like?"

"It was *so* cool. Honestly, Suze, I'm only ever traveling by Learjet from now on."

It's a bright sunny day, and as I look out of the window at the passing fields, I feel a swell of happiness. I can't quite believe it's all fallen into place. After all these months of worry and trouble. We're here in England. The sun is shining. And we're going to get married.

"You know, I'm a tad concerned," says Danny, peering out of the window. "Where are all the castles?"

"This is Surrey," I explain. "We don't have castles."

"And where are the soldiers with bearskins on their heads?" He narrows his eyes. "Becky, you're sure this is England? You're sure that pilot knew where he was going?"

"Pretty sure," I say, getting out my lipstick.

"I don't know," he says doubtfully. "This looks a lot more like France to me."

We pull up at a traffic light and he winds down the window.

"Bonjour," he says to a startled woman. *"Comment allez-vous?"*

"I . . . I wouldn't know," says the woman, and hurries across the road.

"I knew it," says Danny. "Becky, I hate to break it to you . . . but this is France."

"It's Oxshott, you idiot," I retort. "And . . . here's our road."

I feel a huge spasm of nerves as I see the familiar sign. We're nearly there.

"OK," says the driver. "Elton Road. Which number?"

"Number 43. The house over there," I say. "The one with the balloons and the bunting . . . and the silver streamers in the trees . . ."

Blimey. The whole place looks like a fairground. There's a man up in the horse chestnut tree at the front, threading lightbulbs through the branches, and a white van parked in the drive, and women in green and white stripy uniforms bustling in and out of the house.

"Looks like they're expecting you, anyway," says Danny. "You OK?"

"Fine," I say—and it's ridiculous, but my voice is shaking.

The car comes to a halt, and so does the other car behind, which is carrying all our luggage.

"What I don't understand," says Luke, staring out at all the activity, "is how you managed to shift an entire wedding forward by a day. At three weeks' notice. I mean, you're talking the caterers, you're talking the band, you're talking a million different very busy professionals . . ."

"Luke, this isn't Manhattan," I say, opening the car door. "You'll see."

As we get out, the front door swings open, and there's Mum, wearing tartan trousers and a sweatshirt reading "Mother of the Bride."

"Becky!" she cries, and runs over to give me a hug.

"Mum." I hug her back. "Is everything OK?"

"Everything's under control, I think!" she says a little flusteredly. "We had a problem with the table posies, but fingers crossed, they should be on their way . . . Luke! How are you? How was the financial conference?"

"It went er . . . very well," he says. "Very well indeed, thank you. I'm just sorry it's caused so much trouble with the wedding arrangements—"

"Oh, that's all right!" says Mum. "I'll admit, I was a bit taken aback when Becky phoned. But in the end, it didn't take much doing! Most of the guests were staying over for Sunday brunch, anyway. And Peter at the church was most understanding, and said he didn't usually conduct weddings on a Sunday, but in this case he'd make an exception—"

"But what about . . . the catering, for instance? Wasn't that all booked for yesterday?"

"Oh, Lulu didn't mind! Did you, Lulu?" she says to one of the women in green and white stripes.

"No!" says Lulu brightly. "Of course not. Hello, Becky! How are you?"

Oh my God! It's Lulu who used to take me for Brownies.

"Hi!" I say, "I didn't know you did catering!"

"Oh well." She makes a self-deprecating little gesture. "It's just to keep me busy, really. Now that the children are older . . ."

"You know, Lulu's son Aaron is in the band!" says Mum proudly. "He plays the keyboards! And you know, they're very good! They've been practicing 'Unchained Melody' especially—"

"Now, just taste this!" says Lulu, reaching into a foil-covered tray and producing a canapé. "It's our new Thai filo parcels. We're rather pleased with them. You know, filo pastry is very in now."

"Really?"

"Oh yes." Lulu nods knowledgeably. "*No one* has shortcake tartlets anymore. And as for vol-au-vents . . ." She pulls a little face. "Over."

"You are so right," says Danny, his eyes bright. "The vol-au-vent is dead. The vol-au-vent is toast, if you will. May I ask where you stand on the asparagus roll?"

"Mum, this is Danny," I put in quickly. "My neighbor, remember?"

"Mrs. B., it's an honor to meet you," says Danny, kissing Mum's hand. "You don't mind my tagging along with Becky?"

"Of course not!" says Mum. "The more the merrier! Now, come and see the marquee!"

As we walk round to the garden, my jaw drops. A huge silver and white striped marquee is billowing on the lawn. All the flower beds read "Becky and Luke" in pansies. There are fairy lights strung up in every available bush and shrub. A uniformed gardener is polishing a new granite water feature, someone else is sweeping the patio, and inside the marquee I can see lots of middle-aged women sitting in a semicircle, holding notebooks.

"Janice is just giving the girls the team briefing," says Mum in an undertone. "She's really got into this wedding organizing lark now. She wants to start doing it professionally!"

"Now," I hear Janice saying as we approach. "The emergency rose petals will be in a silver basket by Pillar A. Could you all please mark that on your floorplans—"

"You know, I think she'll be a success," I say thoughtfully.

"Betty and Margot, if you could be in charge of buttonholes. Annabel, if you could please take care of—"

"Mum?" says Luke, peering into the marquee incredulously.

Oh my God. It's Annabel! It's Luke's stepmum, sitting there along with everyone else.

"Luke!" Annabel looks round and her entire face lights up. "Janice, excuse me for a moment—"

She hurries toward us and envelops Luke in a tight hug.

"You're here. I'm so glad to see you." She peers anxiously into his face. "Are you all right, darling?"

"I'm fine," says Luke, "I think. A lot's been going on . . ."

"So I understand," says Annabel, and gives me a sharp look. "Becky." She reaches out with one arm and hugs me, too. "I'm going to have a long chat with you later," she says into my ear.

"So . . . you're helping with the wedding?" says Luke to his stepmother.

"Oh, it's all hands to the deck around here," says Mum gaily. "Annabel's one of us now!"

"And where's Dad?" says Luke, looking around.

"He's gone to get some extra glasses with Graham," says Mum. "Those two have really hit it off. Now, who's for a cup of coffee?"

"You're getting on well with Luke's parents!" I say, following Mum toward the kitchen.

"Oh, they're super!" she says happily. "Really charming. They've already invited us down to stay in Devon. Nice, normal, down-to-earth people. Not like . . . that woman."

"No. They're quite different from Elinor."

"She didn't seem at all interested in the wedding," says Mum, her voice prickling slightly. "You know, she never even replied to her invitation!"

"Didn't she?"

Damn. I thought I'd done a reply from Elinor.

"Have you seen much of her recently?" says Mum.

"Er . . . no," I say. "Not much."

We carry a tray of coffee upstairs to Mum's bedroom, and open the door to find Suze and Danny sitting on the bed, with Ernie lying between them, kicking his little pink feet. And hanging on the wardrobe door opposite, Mum's wedding dress, as white and frilly as ever.

"Suze!" I exclaim, giving her a hug. "And gorgeous Ernie! He's got so *big*—" I bend down to kiss his cheek, and he gives me an enormous gummy smile.

"You made it." Suze grins at me. "Well done, Bex."

"Suze has just been showing me your family heirloom wedding dress, Mrs. B.," says Danny, raising his eyebrows at me. "It's . . . quite unique."

"This dress is a real survivor!" says Mum delightedly. "We thought it was ruined, but all the coffee came out!"

"What a miracle!" says Danny.

"And even just this morning, little Ernie tried to throw apple puree over it—"

"Oh, really?" I say, glancing at Suze, who flushes slightly.

"But luckily I'd covered it in protective plastic!" says Mum. She reaches for the dress and shakes out the frills, slightly pink about the eyes. "This is a moment I've been dreaming about for so long. Becky wearing my wedding dress. I am a silly, aren't I?"

"It's not silly," I say, and give her a hug. "It's what weddings are all about."

"Mrs. Bloomwood, Becky described the dress to me," says Danny. "And I can honestly say she didn't do it justice. But you won't mind if I make a couple of teeny tiny alterations?"

"Not at all!" says Mum, and glances at her watch. "Well, I must get on. I've still got to chase these posies!"

As the door closes behind her, Danny and Suze exchange glances.

"OK," says Danny. "What are we going to do with this?"

"You could cut the sleeves off, for a start," says Suze. "And all those frills on the bodice."

"I mean, how much of it do we actually need to keep?" Danny looks up. "Becky, what do you think?"

I don't reply. I'm staring out of the window into the garden. I can see Luke and Annabel walking round the garden, their heads close together, talking. And there's Mum talking to Janice, and gesturing to the flowering cherry tree.

"Becky?" says Danny again.

"Don't touch it," I say, turning round.

"What?"

"Don't do anything to it." I smile at Danny's appalled face. "Just leave it as it is."

By ten to three I'm ready. I'm wearing the sausage roll dress. My face has been made up by Janice as Radiant Spring Bride, only slightly toned down with a tissue and water. I've got a garland of bright pink carnations and gypsophila in my hair, which Mum ordered along with my bouquet. The only remotely stylish thing about me is my Christian Louboutin shoes, which you can't even see.

And I don't care. I look exactly how I want to look.

We've had our photos taken by the flowering cherry tree, and Mum has wept all down her "Summer Elegance" makeup and had to be retouched. And now everyone has gone off to the church. It's me and Dad, waiting to go.

"Ready?" he says, as a white Rolls-Royce purrs into the drive.

"I think so," I say, a slight wobble to my voice.

I'm getting married. I'm really getting married.

"Do you think I'm doing the right thing?" I say, only half joking.

"Oh, I think so." Dad looks into the hall stand mirror and adjusts his silk tie. "I remember saying to your mother, the very first day I met Luke, 'This one will keep up with Becky.' " He meets my eye in the mirror. "Was I right, love? Does he keep up with you?"

"Not quite." I grin at him. "But . . . he's getting there."

"Good." Dad smiles back. "That's probably all he can hope for."

The driver is ringing the doorbell, and as I open the door, I peer at the face under the peaked cap. I don't believe it. It's my old driving instructor, Clive.

"Clive! Hi! how are you?"

"Becky Bloomwood!" he exclaims. "Well, I never! Becky Bloomwood, getting married! Did you ever pass your test, then?"

"Er . . . yes. Eventually."

"Who would have thought it?" He shakes his head, marvelingly. "I used to go home to the wife and say, 'If that girl passes her test, I'm a fried egg.' And then of course, when it came to it—"

"Yes, well, anyway—"

"That examiner said he'd never known anything like it. Has your husband-to-be seen you drive?"

"Yes."

"And he still wants to marry you?"

"Yes!" I say crossly.

Honestly. This is my wedding day. I shouldn't have to be reminded about stupid driving tests that happened years ago.

"Shall we get in?" says Dad tactfully. "Hello, Clive. Nice to see you again."

We walk out into the drive, and as we reach the car I look back at the house. When I see it again I'll be a married woman. I take a deep breath and step into the car.

"Stooooop!" comes a voice. "Becky! Stop!"

I freeze in terror, one foot inside the car. What's happened? Who's found out? What do they know?

"I can't let you go through with this!"

What? This doesn't make any sense. Tom Webster from next door is pelting toward us in his morning suit. What does he think he's doing? He's supposed to be ushering at the church.

"Becky, I can't stand by and watch," he says breathlessly, planting a hand on the Rolls-Royce. "This could be the biggest mistake of your life. You haven't thought it through."

Oh, for God's sake.

"Yes, I have," I say, and try to elbow him out of the way.

But he grabs my shoulder. "It hit me last night. We belong together. You and me. Think about it, Becky. We've known each other all our lives. We've grown up together. Maybe it's taken us a while to discover our true feelings for each other . . . but don't we deserve to give them a chance?"

"Tom, I haven't got any feelings for you," I say. "And I'm getting married in two minutes. So can you get out of my way?"

"You don't know what you're letting yourself in for! You have no idea of the reality of marriage! Becky, tell me honestly. Do you really envisage yourself spending the rest of your days with Luke? Day after day, night after night? Hour after endless hour?"

"Yes!" I say, losing my temper. "I do! I love Luke very much and I do want to spend the rest of my days with him! Tom, it has taken a lot of time and effort and trouble for me to get to this moment. More than you can possibly imagine. And if you don't get out of my way right now and let me get to my wedding, I'll . . . I'll . . ."

"Tom," puts in Dad. "I think the answer's no."

"Oh." Tom is silent for a moment. "Well . . . OK." He gives an abashed shrug. "Sorry."

"You never did have any sense of timing, Tom Webster," says Clive scornfully. "I remember the first time you ever pulled out into a roundabout. Nearly killed us both, you did!"

"It's OK. No harm done. Can we go now?" I step into the car, arranging my dress around me, and Dad gets in beside me.

"I'll see you there, then, shall I?" says Tom mournfully, and I raise my eyes heavenward.

"Tom, do you want a lift to the church?"

"Oh, thanks. That'd be great. Hi, Graham," he says awkwardly to my father as he clambers in. "Sorry about that."

"That's quite all right, Tom," says my father, patting him on the back. "We all have our little moments." He pulls a face at me over Tom's head and I quell a giggle.

"So. Are we all set?" says Clive, turning in his seat. "Any sudden changes of heart? Any more last-minute protestations of love? Any three-point turns?"

"No!" I say. "There's nothing else. Let's go already!"

As we arrive at the church, the bells are ringing, the sun is shining, and a couple of last-minute guests are hurrying in. Tom opens the car door and dashes down the path without a backward glance, while I fluff out my train to the admiring glances of passersby.

God, it is fun being a bride. I'm going to miss it.

"All set?" says Dad, handing me my bouquet.

"I think so." I grin at him and take his outstretched arm.

"Good luck," says Clive, then nods ahead. "You've got a couple of late ones here."

A black taxi is pulling up in front of the church, and both passenger doors are flung open. I stare ahead incredulously, wondering if I'm dreaming, as Michael gets out, still in his evening dress from the Plaza. He extends a hand back into the taxi, and the next moment Laurel appears, still in her Yves St. Laurent with the sleeves rolled up.

"Don't let us put you off!" she says. "We'll just sneak in somewhere—"

"But . . . but what the hell are you *doing* here?"

"Language," says Clive reprovingly.

"What's the point of being in control of a hundred private jets if you can't fly wherever you want?" says Laurel as she comes over to hug me. "We decided we wanted to see you get married."

"For real," says Michael into my ear. "Hats off to you, Becky."

Dad and I wait until they've disappeared into the church, then make our way down the path to the porch where Suze is excitedly waiting. She's wearing a silvery blue dress and carrying Ernie, who's wearing a matching romper suit. As I peep inside the church, I can see the gathered faces of all my family, all my old friends, all Luke's friends and relations. Sitting side by side, happy and expectant.

The organ stops playing, and I feel a stab of nerves.

It's finally happening. I'm finally getting married. For real.

Then the "Bridal March" starts and Dad gives my arm a squeeze, and we start to walk up the aisle.

Twenty-three

WE'RE MARRIED.

We're really married.

I look down at the shiny wedding band that Luke slid onto my finger in the church. Then I look around at the scene before me. The marquee is glowing in the summer dusk, and the band is playing a ropy version of "Smoke Gets in Your Eyes," and people are dancing. Maybe the music isn't as smooth as it was at the Plaza. And maybe the guests aren't all as well dressed. But they're ours. They're all ours.

We had a lovely dinner of watercress soup, rack of lamb, and summer pudding, and we drank lots of champagne and the wine that Mum and Dad got in France. And then Dad rattled his fork in a glass and made a speech about me and Luke. He said that he and Mum had often talked about the kind of man I would marry, and they'd always disagreed on everything except one thing—"he'll have to be on his toes." Then he looked at Luke, who obligingly got up and turned a pirouette, and everyone roared with laughter. Dad said he'd become very fond of Luke and his parents and that this was more than just a marriage, it was a joining of families. And then he said he knew I would be a very loyal and supportive wife, and told the story of how when I was eight I wrote to Downing Street and proposed my father as prime minister—and then a week later wrote again to ask why they hadn't replied—and everyone laughed again.

Then Luke made a speech about how we met in London when I was a financial journalist, and how he noticed me at my very first press conference, when I asked the PR director of Barclays Bank why they didn't make fashion checkbook covers like they have for mobile phones. And then he confessed that he'd started sending me invitations to PR events even when they weren't relevant to my magazine, just because I always livened up proceedings.

(He's never told me that before. But now it all makes sense! That's why I kept being invited to all those weird conferences on commodity brokering and the state of the steel industry.)

Last of all, Michael stood up, and introduced himself in his warm, gravelly voice, and spoke about Luke. About how fantastically successful he is but how he needs someone by his side, someone who really loves him for the person he is and will stop him from taking life too seriously. Then he said it was an honor to meet my parents, and they'd been so friendly and welcoming to a pair of complete strangers, he could see where I got what he called the "Bloomwood bloom" of good-hearted happiness. And he said that I'd really grown up recently. That he'd watched me cope with some very tricky situations, and he wouldn't go into details, but I'd had quite a few challenges to deal with and somehow I'd managed to solve them all.

Without using a Visa card, he added, and there was the hugest roar of laughter, all around the marquee.

And then he said he'd attended many weddings in his time, but he'd never felt the contentment he was feeling right now. He knew Luke and I were meant to be with each other, and he was extremely fond of us both, and we didn't know how lucky we were. And if we were blessed with children, they wouldn't know how lucky they were, either.

Michael's speech nearly made me cry, actually.

Now I'm sitting with Luke on the grass. Just the two of us, away from everyone else for a moment. My Christian Louboutins are all smeared with grass stains, and Ernie's strawberry-covered fingers have left their mark on my bodice. I should think I look a complete mess. But I'm happy.

I think I'm the happiest I've ever been in my life.

"So," says Luke. He leans back on his elbows and stares up at the darkening blue sky. "We made it."

"We made it." My garland of flowers is starting to fall down over one eye, so I carefully unpin it and place it on the grass. "And no casualties."

"You know . . . I feel as though the past few weeks have been a weird dream," says Luke. "I've been in my own, preoccupied world, with no idea what was happening in real life." He shakes his head. "I think I nearly went off the rails back then."

"Nearly?"

"OK, then. I did go off the rails." He turns to look at me, his dark eyes glowing in the light from the marquee. "I owe a lot to you, Becky."

"You don't owe me anything," I say in surprise. "We're married now. It's like . . . everything's a joint account."

There's a rumbling sound from the side of the house, and I look up to see Dad loading our suitcases into the car. All ready for us to go.

"So," says Luke, following my gaze. "Our famous honeymoon. Am I allowed to know where we're going yet? Or is it still a secret?"

I feel a spasm of nerves. Here it comes. The last bit of my plan. The very last cherry on top of the cake.

"OK," I say, and take a deep breath. "Here goes. I've been thinking a lot about us recently, Luke. About being married, about where we should live. Whether we should stay in New York or not. What we should do . . ." I pause, carefully marshaling my words. "And what I've realized is . . . I'm not ready to settle down. Tom and Lucy tried to settle down too early, and look what happened to them. And I adore little Ernie, but seeing what it was like for Suze . . . It made me realize I'm not ready for a baby either. Not yet." I look up apprehensively. "Luke, there are so many things I've never done. I've never really traveled. I've never seen the world. Neither have you."

"You've lived in New York," points out Luke.

"New York is a great city and I do love it. But there are other great cities, all over the world. I want to see those too. Sydney. Hong Kong . . . and not just cities!" I spread my arms. "Rivers . . . mountains . . . all the sights of the world . . ."

"Right," says Luke amusedly. "So, narrowing this all down to one honeymoon . . ."

"OK." I swallow hard. "Here's what I've done. I've . . . I've cashed in all the wedding presents we got in New York. Stupid silver candlesticks and teapots and stuff. And I've . . . I've bought us two first-class tickets round the world."

"Round the world?" Luke looks genuinely taken aback. "Are you serious?"

"Yes! Round the world!" I plait my fingers together tightly. "We can take as long as we like. As little as three weeks, or as long as . . ." I look at him, tense with hope. "A year."

"A year?" Luke stares back at me. "You're joking."

"I'm not joking. I've told Christina I may or may not come back to work at Barneys. She's fine about it. Danny will clear out our apartment for us and put it all in storage—"

"Becky!" says Luke, shaking his head. "It's a nice idea. But I can't possibly just up sticks and—"

"You can. You can! It's all set up. Michael will keep an eye on the New York office. The London office is running itself anyway. Luke, you can do it. Everyone thinks you should."

"Everyone?"

I count off on my fingers. "Your parents . . . my parents . . . Michael . . . Laurel . . . Clive, my old driving instructor . . ."

Luke stares at me.

"Clive, your old driving instructor?"

"OK," I say hastily, "don't bother about him. But everyone whose opinion you respect. They all think you need a break. You've been working so hard, for so long . . ." I lean forward earnestly. "Luke, this is the time to do it. While we're still young. Before we have children. Just picture it. The two of us, wandering through the world. Seeing amazing sights. Learning from other cultures."

There's silence. Luke gazes at the ground, frowning.

"You spoke to Michael," he says at last. "And he'd really be willing to—"

"He'd be more than willing. He's bored living in New York with nothing to do except go power walking! Luke, he said even if you don't go away, you need a long breathing space. You need a proper holiday."

"A year," says Luke, rubbing his forehead. "That's more than a holiday."

"It could be shorter. Or longer! The point is, we can decide as we go along. We can be free spirits, for once in our lives. No ties, no commitments, nothing weighing us down—"

"Becky, love," calls Dad from the car. "Are you sure they'll let you take six suitcases?"

"It's OK, we'll just pay the excess baggage—" I turn back to Luke. "Come on. How about it?"

Luke says nothing for a few moments—and my heart sinks. I have a horrible feeling he's going to revert back to old Luke. Old, workaholic, single-minded, corporate Luke.

Then he looks up—and there's a wry little smile on his face. "Do I have a choice?"

"No." I grab his hand in relief. "You don't."

We're going round the world! We're going to be travelers!

"These last two are very light!" shouts Dad, and waves the cases in the air. "Is there anything in them?"

"No, they're empty!" I turn to Luke, glowing with delight. "Oh, Luke, it'll be so great! This is our one chance to have a year of escape. A year of . . . simplicity. Just us. Nothing else!"

There's a pause. Luke looks at me, his mouth twitching.

"And we're taking two great big empty suitcases with us because . . ."

"Well, you never know," I explain. "We might pick a few things up along the way. Travelers should always support the local economies—" I break off as Luke starts to laugh.

"What?" I say indignantly. "It's true!"

"I know." Luke wipes his eyes. "I know it is. Becky Bloomwood, I love you."

"I'm Becky Brandon now, remember!" I retort, glancing down at my lovely new ring. "Mrs. Rebecca Brandon."

But Luke shakes his head. "There's only one Becky Bloomwood. Never stop being her." He takes both hands in mine and gazes at me with a strange intensity. "Whatever you do, never stop being Becky Bloomwood."

"Well . . . OK," I say, taken aback. "I won't."

"Becky! Luke!" Mum's voice comes across the lawn. "It's time to cut the cake! Graham, put on the fairy lights!"

"Right-o!" calls Dad.

"Coming!" I shout back. "Just let me put my garland back on!"

"Let me." Luke reaches for the garland of pink flowers and puts it on my head with a little smile.

"Do I look stupid?" I say, pulling a face.

"Yes. Very." He gives me a kiss, then stands up and helps me to my feet. "Come on, Becky B. Your audience is waiting."

As fairy lights begin to twinkle all around us, we walk back over the dusky grass to the wedding, Luke's hand clasped firmly around mine.

PRENUPTIAL AGREEMENT
Between Rebecca Bloomwood and Luke Brandon

22 June 2002

5. JOINT BANK ACCOUNT

5.1 The joint account shall be used for necessary expenditure on household expenses.

"Household expenses" shall be defined to include Miù Miù skirts, pairs of shoes, and other items of apparel deemed essential by the Bride.

5.2 The Bride's decision regarding such expenses shall be final in all cases.

5.3 Questions regarding the joint account shall not be sprung on the Bride by the Groom with no warning, but submitted in writing, with a 24-hour period for reply.

6. SIGNIFICANT DATES

6.1 The Groom shall remember all birthdays and anniversaries, and shall mark said dates with surprise gifts.*

6.2 The Bride shall demonstrate surprise and delight at the Groom's choices.

7. MARITAL HOME

The Bride shall make the best attempt within her powers to maintain order and tidiness in the marital home. HOWEVER, failure to abide by this clause shall not be regarded as a breaking of the contract.

8. TRANSPORT

The Groom shall not comment on the Bride's driving ability.

9. SOCIAL LIFE

9.1 The Bride shall not require the Groom to remember the names and past romantic history of all her friends including those he has never met.

9.2 The Groom shall make every effort to set aside a significant portion of each week for leisure and relaxing activities.

9.3 Shopping shall be defined as a relaxing activity.

*The surprise gifts shall comprise those items marked discreetly by the Bride in catalogues and magazines, to be left around the marital home in the weeks leading up to said dates.

Acknowledgments

Writing this book was tremendous fun; researching it even more so. I am exceedingly grateful to all, both in Britain and in the States, who gave me so much inspiration, and allowed me to come and ask them lots of stupid questions.

My thanks to Lawrence Harvey at the Plaza, who could not have been more helpful, and to the ever wonderful Sharyn Soleimani at Barneys. Also to Ron Ben-Israel, Elizabeth and Susan Allen, Fran Bernard, Preston Bailey, Clare Mosley, Joe Dance at Crate and Barrel, Julia Kleyner and Lillian Sabatelli at Tiffany, Charlotte Curry at *Brides*, Robin Michaelson, Theresa Ward, Guy Lancaster and Kate Mailer, David Stefanou and Jason Antony, and lovely Lola Bubbosh.

A million thanks, as always, to my wonderful agent Araminta Whitley and to Celia Hayley, Kim Witherspoon, and David Forrer. And of course deep gratitude to the endlessly fantastic team at The Dial Press, with particular thanks to Susan Kamil, Zoë Rice, and Nita Taublib.

And lastly to the people who've been there all the way through: Henry, Freddy, and Hugo, and the purple posse. You know who you are.

Coming in 2004

an all-new

Sophie Kinsella
adventure

introducing her latest hilarious heroine

EMMA CORRIGAN

who has a few secrets . . .

Of course I have secrets.

Everyone has a few secrets. I'm not talking about big, earth-shattering secrets. Not the-president-is-planning-to-bomb-Japan-and-only-Will-Smith-can-save-the-world type secrets.

Just normal, everyday little ones. Like, for example, here are a few random secrets of mine, off the top of my head:

1. My Kate Spade bag is a fake.
2. I love sweet sherry, the least cool drink in the universe.
3. I have no idea what NATO stands for. Or even what it is.

EMMA CORRIGAN HAS SECRETS FROM HER BOYFRIEND . . .

4. I weigh one hundred and twenty-eight pounds. Not one eighteen, like Connor thinks.
5. I've always thought Connor looks a bit like Ken. As in Barbie and Ken.
6. Sometimes, when we're right in the middle of passionate sex, I suddenly want to laugh.

EMMA CORRIGAN HAS SECRETS FROM HER COLLEAGUES . . .

7. When Artemis really annoys me, I feed her plant orange juice. (Which is pretty much every day.)
8. It was me who jammed the copier that time. In fact, all the times.
9. Just sometimes, when I'm reading *Marketing Week* at my desk, I really have *Entertainment Weekly* inside.

EMMA CORRIGAN HAS SECRETS FROM HER PARENTS . . .

10. I lost my virginity in the spare bedroom with Danny Nussbaum, while Mum and Dad were downstairs watching *Ben-Hur.*
11. I've already drunk the wine that Dad told me to lay down for twenty years.
12. The goldfish in the kitchen isn't the same one Mum and Dad gave me to look after when they went to Egypt.

EMMA CORRIGAN HAS SECRETS SHE WOULD NEVER SHARE WITH ANYBODY . . .

13. My G-string is hurting me.
14. I've always had this deep-down conviction that I'm not like everybody else, and there's an amazingly exciting new life waiting for me just around the corner.
15. I often have no idea what people are talking about. None whatsoever . . .

UNTIL SHE SPILLS THEM ALL TO A STRANGER ON A PLANE . . .

The plane suddenly drops down again, and I give an involuntary shriek. "We're going to die!" I stare into his face. This could be the last person I ever see alive. I take in the lines etched around his dark eyes, his strong jaw, shaded with stubble.

"I don't think we're going to die," he says. But he's gripping hard onto his seat arms, too. "They said it was just turbulence—"

"Of course they did!" I can hear the hysteria in my voice. "They wouldn't exactly say, 'OK, folks, that's it, you're all goners!'" The plane gives another terrifying swoop and I find myself clutching the man's hand in panic. "We're not going to make it. I know we're not. This is it. I'm twenty-five years old, for God's sake, I'm not ready to die. I haven't achieved anything. I've never had children, I've never saved a life . . ." My eyes fall randomly on the "30 Things to Do Before You're 30" magazine article in front of me. "I haven't ever climbed a mountain; I haven't got a tattoo; I don't even *know* if I've got a G spot . . ."

"I'm sorry?" says the man, sounding taken aback, but I barely hear him.

"I'm not a top businesswoman!" I gesture half tearfully to my suit. "I'm just a crappy assistant and I just had my first-ever big meeting and it was a total disaster. I don't know what *logistical* means, and I've never read a Dickens novel, and my underwear's too small, and I owe my dad four thousand quid, and I've never really been in love . . ."

AT LEAST, SHE THOUGHT HE WAS A STRANGER . . .

So this is the new big boss. The guy in the baseball cap turns, and as I see his face I feel an almighty thud, as though a bowling ball's landed hard in my chest. Oh my God. It's him. The same dark eyes. The same lines etched around them. The stubble's gone, but it's definitely him. It's the man from the plane—the man I told all my secrets to. What's he doing here at the office? And . . . and why has he got everyone's attention? He's speaking now, and everyone is lapping up every word he says. He turns again, and I instinctively duck back out of sight, trying to keep calm. What's he doing here? He can't— That can't be— That can't possibly be. If this is the new mega-boss, I'm in big, big trouble . . .

CAN YOU KEEP A SECRET?

THE NEW NOVEL COMING FROM

Sophie Kinsella

The trouble with telling secrets is . . . you can't get them back

And don't miss the novel that introduced the fabulous Becky Bloomwood!

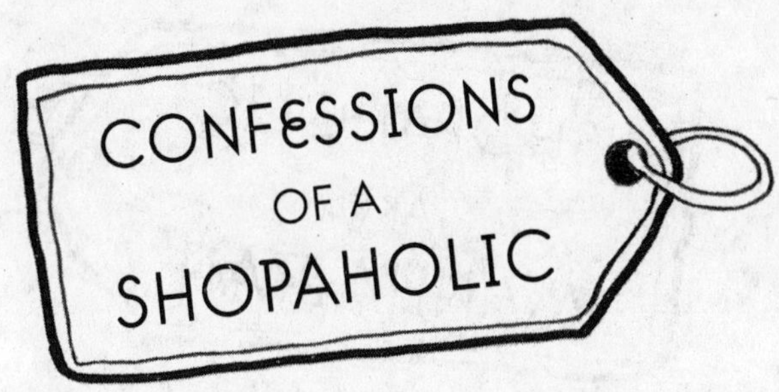

Becky Bloomwood has everything: a fabulous flat in London's trendiest neighborhood, a troupe of glamorous socialite friends, and a closet brimming with the season's must-haves. The only problem is that she can't actually afford it—not any of it. Her job as a financial journalist not only bores her to tears, it doesn't pay much at all. And lately, Becky's been chased by dismal letters from Visa and the Endwich Bank—letters with large red sums she can't bear to read—and they're getting ever harder to ignore. She tries cutting back; she even tries making more money. But none of her efforts succeeds. Becky's only consolation is to buy herself something . . . just a little something . . .

Finally a story arises that Becky actually *cares* about, and her front-page article catalyzes a chain of events that will transform her life—and the lives of those around her—forever.

Sophie Kinsella brilliantly taps into our collective consumer conscience to deliver a novel of our times—and a heroine who grows stronger every time she weakens. Becky Bloomwood's hysterical schemes to pay back her debts are as endearing as they are desperate. Her "confessions" are the perfect pick-me-up when life is hanging in the (bank) balance.

"Packing Light" takes on a whole new meaning

"This expensive, glossy world is where I've been headed all along. Limos and flowers; waxed eyebrows and designer clothes from Barneys. These are my people; this is where I'm meant to be."

—Becky Bloomwood.

With her shopping excesses (somewhat) in check and her career as a TV financial guru thriving, Becky's biggest problem seems to be tearing her entrepreneur boyfriend, Luke, away from work for a romantic country weekend. And worse, figuring out how to "pack light." But packing takes on a whole new meaning when Luke announces he's moving to New York for business—and asks Becky to go with him! Before you can say "Prada sample sale," Becky has landed in the Big Apple, home of Park Avenue penthouses and luxury department stores. Surely it's only a matter of time until she becomes an American TV celebrity, and she and Luke are the toast of Gotham society. Nothing can stand in their way, especially with Becky's bills miles away in London. But then an unexpected disaster threatens her career prospects, her relationship with Luke, and her available credit line! *Shopaholic Takes Manhattan*—but will she have to return it?

Shopping anywhere is great—
but the advantages of doing it abroad are:

1. You can buy things you can't get in Britain.
2. You can name-drop when you get back home.
3. Foreign money doesn't count, so you can spend as much as you like.

Okay, I know that last one isn't entirely true. Somewhere in my head I know that dollars are proper money, with a real value. But I mean, *look* at them. I've got a whole wodge of them in my purse, and I feel as though I'm carrying around the bank from Monopoly. Yesterday I went and bought some magazines from a newsstand, and as I handed over a twenty-dollar bill, it was just like playing shop. It's like some weird form of jet lag—you move into another currency and suddenly feel as though you're spending nothing.

So as I walk around the handbag department, trying out gorgeous bag after gorgeous bag, I'm not taking too much notice of the prices. Because this is America, and everyone knows that prices in America are really low. It's common knowledge. So basically, I'm working on the principle that everything's a bargain.

Eventually I choose a beautiful Kate Spade bag in tan leather. It costs five hundred dollars, which sounds quite a lot—but then "a million lira" sounds a lot too, doesn't it? And it's only about fifty pence.

Also by Sophie Kinsella

CONFESSIONS OF A SHOPAHOLIC

SOPHIE KINSELLA

SHOPAHOLIC

takes

MANHATTAN

A DELTA TRADE PAPERBACK

A Delta Book
Published by
Dell Publishing
a division of
Random House, Inc.
1540 Broadway
New York, New York 10036

This novel is a work of fiction. Names, characters, places, and incidents either are the product of the author's imagination or are used fictitiously. Any resemblance to actual persons, living or dead, events, or locales is entirely coincidental.

Cover design by Belina Huey
Cover art © 2002 by Diane Bigda

ISBN: 0-385-33588-1

LIBRARY OF CONGRESS CATALOGING-IN-PUBLICATION INFORMATION
Kinsella, Sophie.
Shopaholic takes Manhattan / Sophie Kinsella.
p. cm.
"Delta trade paperbacks."
"A Delta book"—T.p. verso.
ISBN 0-385-33588-1 (pbk.)
1. British—New York (State)—New York—Fiction.
2. Manhattan (New York, N.Y.)—Fiction.
3. Young women—Fiction.
4. Shopping—Fiction.
I. Title.
PR6061.I54 S56 2001
823'.92—dc21 2001047364

MANUFACTURED IN THE UNITED STATES OF AMERICA
First published in 2001 by Transworld, United Kingdom, as *Shopaholic Abroad*

Published simultaneously in Canada

February 2002

20 19 18 17
BVG

For Gemma, who has always known the importance to a girl of a Denny and George scarf

SHOPAHOLIC

takes

MANHATTAN

· ENDWICH BANK ·

FULHAM BRANCH

3 Fulham Road

London SW6 9JH

Ms. Rebecca Bloomwood
Flat 2
4 Burney Rd.
London SW6 8FD

18 July 2000

Dear Ms. Bloomwood:

Thank you for your letter of 15 July.

It is true that we have known each other a long time, and I am pleased that you consider me "more than just a bank manager." I agree that friendship is important and was glad to hear that you would always lend me money should I need it.

However, I cannot reciprocate, as you suggest, by wiping £1,000 off your overdraft "accidentally on purpose." I can assure you, the money *would* be missed.

Instead, I am prepared to extend your overdraft limit by another £500, taking it up to £4,000, and suggest that we meet before too long to discuss your ongoing financial needs.

Yours sincerely,

Derek Smeath
Manager

• ENDWICH—BECAUSE WE CARE •

· ENDWICH BANK ·

FULHAM BRANCH

3 Fulham Road

London SW6 9JH

Ms. Rebecca Bloomwood
Flat 2
4 Burney Rd.
London SW6 8FD

23 July 2000

Dear Ms. Bloomwood:

I am glad that my letter of 18 July proved helpful.

I should, however, be grateful if you refrained from referring to me personally on your television show as "Sweetie Smeathie" and "the best bank manager in the world."

Although naturally I am pleased you feel this way, my superiors are a little anxious at the image of Endwich Bank which is being presented, and have asked that I write to you on the matter.

With all best wishes,

Derek Smeath
Manager

• ENDWICH—BECAUSE WE CARE •

· ENDWICH BANK ·

FULHAM BRANCH

3 Fulham Road

London SW6 9JH

Ms. Rebecca Bloomwood
Flat 2
4 Burney Rd.
London SW6 8FD

20 August 2000

Dear Ms. Bloomwood:

Thank you for your letter of 18 August.

I was sorry to hear that keeping within your new overdraft limit is proving so difficult. I understand that the Pied a Terre summer sale is a unique opportunity to save money in the long run, and I can certainly increase your limit by £63.50 if, as you say, this would "make all the difference."

However, I would also recommend that you come into the branch for a more comprehensive review of your financial situation. My assistant, Erica Parnell, will be pleased to set up an appointment.

Yours sincerely,

Derek Smeath
Manager

• ENDWICH—BECAUSE WE CARE •

One

OK, DON'T PANIC. Don't *panic*. It's simply a question of being organized and staying calm and deciding what exactly I need to take. And then fitting it all neatly into my suitcase. I mean, just how hard can that be?

I step back from my cluttered bed and close my eyes, half-hoping that if I wish hard enough, my clothes might magically organize themselves into a series of neatly folded piles. Like in those magazine articles on packing, which tell you how to go on holiday with one cheap sarong and cleverly turn it into six different outfits. (Which I always think is a complete con, because, OK, the sarong costs ten quid, but then they add loads of accessories which cost hundreds, and we're not supposed to notice.)

But when I open my eyes again, the clutter is all still there. In fact, there seems to be even more of it, as if while my eyes were shut, my clothes have been secretly jumping out of the drawers and running around on my bed. Everywhere I look, there are huge great tangled piles of . . . well . . . *stuff*. Shoes, boots, T-shirts, magazines . . . a Body Shop gift basket that was on sale . . . a Linguaphone Italian course which I'm *definitely* going to start soon . . . a facial sauna thingy . . . And, sitting proudly on my dressing table, a fencing mask and sword which I bought yesterday. Only forty quid from a charity shop!

I pick up the sword and experimentally give a little lunge toward my reflection in the mirror. It was a real coincidence, because I've been meaning to take up fencing for ages, ever since I read this article about it in *The Daily World*. Did you know that fencers have better legs than any other athletes? Plus, if you're an expert you can become a stunt double in a film and earn loads of money! So what I'm planning to do is find some fencing lessons nearby, and get really good, which I should think I'll do quite quickly.

And then—this is my secret little plan—when I've got my gold badge, or whatever it is, I'll write to Catherine Zeta-Jones. Because she must need a stunt double, mustn't she? And why shouldn't it be me? In fact she'd probably *prefer* someone British. Maybe she'll phone back and say she always watches my television appearances on cable, and she's always wanted to meet me! We'll probably really hit it off, and turn out to have the same sense of humor and everything. And then I'll fly out to her luxury home, and get to meet Michael Douglas and play with the baby. We'll be all relaxed together like old friends, and some magazine will do a feature on celebrity best friends and have us in it, and maybe they'll even ask me to be . . .

"Hi, Bex!" With a jolt, the happy pictures of me laughing with Michael and Catherine vanish, and my brain snaps into focus. Suze, my flatmate, is wandering into my room, wearing a pair of ancient paisley pajamas, with her blond hair in plaits. "What are you doing?" she asks curiously.

"Nothing!" I say, hastily putting the fencing sword back. "Just . . . you know. Keep fit."

"Oh right," she says vaguely. "So—how's the packing going?" She wanders over to my mantelpiece, picks up a lipstick, and begins to apply it. Suze always does this in my room—just wanders about picking things up and looking at them and putting them down again. She says she loves the way you never know what you might find, like in a junk shop. Which I'm fairly sure she means in a nice way.

"It's going really well," I say. "I'm just deciding which suitcase to take."

"Ooh," says Suze, turning round, her mouth half bright pink. "What about that little cream one? Or your red holdall?"

"I thought maybe this one," I say, hauling my new acid-green shell case out from under the bed. I bought it last weekend, and it's absolutely gorgeous.

"Wow!" says Suze, her eyes widening. "Bex! That's fab! Where did you get it?"

"Fenwicks," I say, grinning broadly. "Isn't it amazing?"

"It's the coolest case I've ever seen!" says Suze, running her fingers admiringly over it. "So . . . how many suitcases have you got now?" She glances up at my wardrobe, on which are teetering a brown leather case, a lacquered trunk, and three vanity cases.

"Oh, you know," I say, shrugging a little defensively. "The normal amount."

I suppose I have been buying quite a bit of luggage recently. But the thing is, for ages I didn't have any, just one battered old canvas bag. Then, a few months ago I had an incredible revelation in the middle of Harrods, a bit like Saint Paul on the road to Mandalay. *Luggage.* And since then, I've been making up for all the lean years.

Besides which, everyone knows good luggage is an investment.

"I'm just making a cup of tea," says Suze. "D'you want one?"

"Ooh, yes please!" I say. "And a KitKat?" Suze grins.

"Definitely a KitKat."

Recently, we had this friend of Suze's to stay on our sofa—and when he left he gave us this huge box full of a hundred KitKats. Which is such a great thank-you present, but it means all we eat, all day long, is KitKats. Still, as Suze pointed out last night, the quicker we eat them, the quicker they'll be gone—so in a way, it's healthier just to stuff in as many as possible right away.

Suze ambles out of the room and I turn to my case. Right. Concentrate. Packing. This really shouldn't take long. All I need is a very basic, pared-down capsule wardrobe for a romantic minibreak in Somerset. I've even written out a list, which should make things nice and simple.

Jeans: two pairs. Easy. Scruffy and not quite so scruffy.

T-shirts:

Actually, make that three pairs of jeans. I've *got* to take my new Diesel ones, they're just so cool, even if they are a bit tight. I'll just wear them for a few hours in the evening or something.

T-shirts:

Oh, and my embroidered cutoffs from Oasis, because I haven't worn them yet. But they don't really count because they're practically shorts. And anyway, jeans hardly take up any room, do they?

OK, that's probably enough jeans. I can always add some more if I need to.

T-shirts: selection. So let's see. Plain white, obviously. Gray, ditto. Black cropped, black vest (Calvin Klein), other black vest (Warehouse, but actually looks nicer), pink sleeveless, pink sparkly, pink—

I stop, halfway through transferring folded-up T-shirts into my case. This is stupid. How am I supposed to predict which T-shirts I'm going to want to wear? The whole point about T-shirts is you choose them in the morning according to your mood, like crystals, or aromatherapy oils. Imagine if I woke up in the mood for my "Elvis Is Groovy" T-shirt and I didn't have it with me?

You know, I think I'll just take them all. I mean, a few T-shirts aren't going to take up much room. I'll hardly even notice them.

I tip them all into my case and add a couple of cropped bra-tops for luck.

Excellent. This capsule approach is working really well. OK, what's next?

Ten minutes later, Suze wanders back into the room, holding two mugs of tea and three KitKats to share. (We've come to agree that four sticks, frankly, doesn't do it.)

"Here you are," she says—then gives me a closer look. "Bex, are you OK?"

"I'm fine," I say, rather pink in the face. "I'm just trying to fold up this insulated vest a bit smaller."

I've already packed a denim jacket and a leather jacket, but you just can't count on September weather, can you? I mean, at the moment it's hot and sunny, but it might well start snowing tomorrow. And what happens if Luke and I go for a really rustic country walk? Besides which, I've had this gorgeous Patagonia vest for ages, and I've only worn it once. I try to fold it again, but it slithers out of my hands and onto the floor. God, this reminds me of camping trips with the Brownies, trying to get my sleeping bag back into its tube.

"How long are you going for, again?" asks Suze.

"Three days." I give up trying to squash the vest into the size of a matchbox, and it springs jauntily back to shape. Discomfited, I sink onto the bed and take a sip of tea. What I don't understand is, how do other people manage to pack so lightly? You see businesspeople all the time, striding onto planes with only a tiny shoe-box suitcase on wheels. How do they do it? Do they have magic shrinking clothes?

"Why don't you take your holdall as well?" suggests Suze.

"D'you think?" I look uncertainly at my overflowing suitcase. Come to think of it, maybe I don't need three pairs of boots. Or a fur stole.

Then suddenly it occurs to me that Suze goes away nearly every weekend, and she only takes a tiny squashy bag. "Suze, how do *you* pack? Do you have a system?"

"I dunno," she says vaguely. "I suppose I still do what they taught us at Miss Burton's. You work out an outfit for each occasion—and stick to that." She begins to tick off on her fingers. "Like . . . driving outfit, dinner, sitting by the pool, game of tennis . . ." She looks up. "Oh yes, and each garment should be used at least three times."

God, Suze is a genius. She knows all this kind of stuff. Her parents sent her to Miss Burton's Academy when she was eighteen, which is some posh place in London where they teach you things like how to talk to a bishop and get out of a sports car in a miniskirt. She knows how to make a rabbit out of chicken wire, too.

Quickly I start to jot some broad headings on a piece of paper. This is much more like it. Much better than randomly stuffing things into a case. This way, I won't have any superfluous clothes, just the bare minimum.

Outfit 1: Sitting by pool (sunny).
Outfit 2: Sitting by pool (cloudy).
Outfit 3: Sitting by pool (bottom looks huge in morning).
Outfit 4: Sitting by pool (someone else has same swimsuit).
Outfit 5:

The phone rings in the hall, but I barely look up. I can hear Suze talking excitedly—then a moment later, she appears in the doorway, her face all pink and pleased.

"Guess what?" she says. "Guess what?"

"What?"

"Box Beautiful has sold out of my frames! They just phoned up to order some more!"

"Oh, Suze! That's fantastic!" I shriek.

"I know!" She comes running over, and we have a big hug, and sort of dance about, before she realizes she's holding a cigarette and is about to burn my hair.

The amazing thing is, Suze only started making photograph frames a few months ago—but already she's supplying four shops in London, and they're doing really well! She's been in loads of magazines, and everything. Which isn't surprising, because her frames are *so* cool. Her latest range is in purple tweed, and they come in these gorgeous gray sparkly boxes, all wrapped in bright turquoise tissue paper. (I helped choose the exact color, by the way.) She's so successful, she doesn't even make them all herself anymore, but sends off her designs to a little workshop in Kent, and they come back, all made up.

"So, have you finished working your wardrobe out?" she says, taking a drag on her cigarette.

"Yes," I say, brandishing my sheet of paper at her. "I've got it all sorted out. Down to every last pair of socks."

"Well done!"

"And the *only* thing I need to buy," I add casually, "is a pair of lilac sandals."

"Lilac sandals?"

"Mmm?" I look up innocently. "Yes. I need some. You know, just a nice cheap little pair to pull a couple of outfits together . . ."

"Oh right," says Suze, and pauses, frowning slightly. "Bex . . . weren't you talking about a pair of lilac sandals last week? Really expensive, from LK Bennett?"

"Was I?" I feel myself flush a little. "I . . . I don't remember. Maybe. Anyway—"

"Bex." Suze gives me a suddenly suspicious look. "Now tell me the truth. Do you really *need* a pair of lilac sandals? Or do you just want them?"

"No!" I say defensively. "I really need them! Look!"

I take out my clothes plan, unfold it, and show it to Suze. I have to say, I'm quite proud of it. It's quite a complicated flow chart, all boxes and arrows and red asterisks.

"Wow!" says Suze. "Where did you learn how to do that?"

"At university," I say modestly. I got my degree in Business and Accounting—and it's amazing how often it comes in handy.

"What's this box?" she asks, pointing at the page.

"That's . . ." I squint at it, trying to remember. "I think that's if we go out to some really smart restaurant and I've already worn my Whistles dress the night before."

"And this one?"

"That's if we go rock-climbing. And this"—I point to an empty box—"is where I need a pair of lilac sandals. If I don't have them, then this outfit won't work, and neither will this one . . . and the whole thing will disintegrate. I might as well not bother going."

Suze is silent for a while, perusing my clothes plan while I bite my lip anxiously and cross my fingers behind my back.

I know this may seem a little unusual. I know most people don't run every single purchase past their flatmate. But the fact is, a while ago I kind of made Suze a little promise, which was that I'd let her keep tabs on my shopping. You know. Just keep an eye on things.

Don't get the wrong idea here. It's not like I have a problem or anything. It's just that a few months ago, I did get into a . . . Well. A very slight money scrape. It was really just a tiny blip—nothing to worry about. But Suze got really freaked out when she found out how much I owed, and said that for my own good, she'd vet all my spending from now on.

And she's been as good as her word. She's very strict, actually. Sometimes I'm really quite scared she might say no.

"I see what you mean," she says at last. "You haven't really got a choice, have you?"

"Exactly," I say in relief. I take the plan from her, fold it up, and put it into my bag.

"Hey, Bex, is that new?" says Suze suddenly. She pulls my wardrobe door open and I feel a twinge of nerves. She's frowning at my lovely new honey-colored coat, which I smuggled into the flat the other day when she was in the bath.

I mean, obviously I was planning to tell her about it. I just never got round to it.

Please don't look at the price tag, I think feverishly. Please don't look at the price tag.

"Erm . . . yes," I say. "Yes, it is new. But the thing is . . . I need a good coat, in case I get asked to do an outside broadcast for *Morning Coffee.*"

"Is that likely?" asks Suze, puzzledly. "I mean, I thought your job was just sitting in the studio, giving financial advice."

"Well . . . you never know. It's always best to be prepared."

"I suppose so . . ." says Suze doubtfully. "And what about this top?" She pulls at a hanger. "That's new, too!"

"That's to wear on the show," I reply promptly.

"And this skirt?"

"For the show."

"And these new trousers?"

"For the—"

"Bex." Suze looks at me with narrowed eyes. "How many outfits have you got to wear on the show?"

"Well—you know," I say defensively. "I need a few backups. I mean, Suze, this is my career we're talking about. My *career.*"

"Yes," says Suze eventually. "Yes, I suppose it is." She reaches for my new red silk jacket. "This is nice."

"I know," I beam. "I bought it to wear on my January special!"

"Have you got a January special?" says Suze. "Ooh, what's it about?"

"It's going to be called *Becky's Fundamental Financial Principles,*" I say, reaching for my lip gloss. "It should be really good. Five ten-minute slots, just me!"

"So—what *are* your fundamental financial principles?" asks Suze interestedly.

"Erm . . . well, I haven't really got any yet," I say, carefully painting my lips. "But you know. I'll work them out a bit nearer the time." I snap my lip gloss shut and reach for my jacket. "See you later."

"OK," says Suze. "And remember. Just one pair of shoes!"

"All right! I promise!"

It's really sweet of Suze to be so concerned about me. But she doesn't need to be. To be honest, she doesn't really understand what a changed person I am. OK, I did have a very slight financial crisis earlier this year. In fact, at one point, I was in debt by . . . Well. Really quite a lot.

But then I landed my job on *Morning Coffee*, and everything changed. I turned my life around completely, worked really hard, and paid off all my debts. Yes, I paid them all off! I wrote out check after check—and cleared every single outstanding credit card, every store card, every scribbled IOU to Suze. (She couldn't believe it when I presented her with a check for several hundred pounds. At first she didn't want to take it, but then she changed her mind and went out and bought this most amazing sheepskin coat.)

Honestly, paying off those debts was the most wonderful, exhilarating feeling in the world. It was a few months ago now—

but I still feel high as I think about it. There's really nothing to beat being completely and utterly financially solvent, is there?

And just look at me now. I'm a completely different person from the old Becky. I'm a reformed character. I haven't even got an overdraft!

Two

WELL, OK. I have got a bit of an overdraft. But the only reason is, I've been taking the long view recently, and investing quite heavily in my career. Luke, my boyfriend, is an entrepreneur. He's got his own financial PR company and everything. And he said something a few weeks ago which really made sense to me: "People who want to make a million borrow a million first."

Honestly, I must have a naturally entrepreneurial mind or something, because as soon as he said it, I felt this amazing chord of recognition. I even found myself murmuring it aloud. He's so right. How can you expect to make any money if you don't spend it first?

So I've invested in quite a few outfits to wear on television—plus a few good haircuts, and quite a few manicures and facials. And a couple of massages. Because everyone knows you can't perform well if you're all stressed.

I've also invested in a new computer, which cost £2,000—but is an essential item because guess what? I'm writing a self-help book! Just after I'd become a regular on *Morning Coffee,* I met these really nice publishers, who took me out to lunch and said I was an inspiration to financially challenged people everywhere. Wasn't that nice? They paid me £1,000 before I'd even written a word—and I get a lot more when it's actually published. The book's going to be called *Becky Bloomwood's Guide to Money.* Or possibly *Manage Money the Becky Bloomwood Way.*

I haven't quite had time to start writing it yet, but I really think the most important thing is to get the title right, and then the rest will just fall into place. And I've already jotted down *loads* of ideas about what to wear in the author photograph.

So basically, it's no surprise that I'm a little overdrawn at the moment. But the point is, all that money is out there, working for me. And luckily my bank manager, Derek Smeath, is very sympathetic to my needs. He's a real sweetie, actually. For a long time we didn't get on at all—which I think was more a communications problem than anything else. But then we met up and had a nice long chat (plus I gave him some advice on what to buy his wife for Christmas) and now I really think he understands where I'm coming from. And the truth is, of course, I'm a lot more sensible than I used to be.

For example, I have a completely different attitude toward shopping. My new motto is "Buy Only What You Need." I know, it sounds almost *too* simple—but it really does work. Before each purchase, I ask myself one question: "Do I *need* this?" And only if the answer is yes do I make the purchase. It's all just a matter of self-discipline.

So, for example, when I get to LK Bennett, I'm incredibly focused and direct. As I walk in, a pair of high-heeled red boots catches my eye—but I quickly look away and head straight for the display of sandals. This is how I shop these days: no pausing, no browsing, no eyeing up other items. Not even that gorgeous new range of sequined pumps over there. I simply go straight to the sandals I want, take them from the rack, and say to the assistant, "I'd like to have these in a six, please."

Direct and to the point. Just buy what you need and nothing else. This is the key to controlled shopping. I'm not even going to *glance* at those cool pink stilettos, even though they'd match my new pink denim skirt perfectly.

Nor those slingbacks with the glittery heels.

They are nice though, aren't they? I wonder what they look like on?

Oh God. This is really hard.

What *is* it about shoes? I mean, I like most kinds of clothes, but a good pair of shoes can just reduce me to jelly. Sometimes, when Suze isn't at home, I open my wardrobe and just *stare* at all my pairs of shoes, like some mad collector. And once I lined them all up on my bed and took a photograph of them. Which might seem a bit weird—but I thought, I've got loads of photos of people I don't really like, so why not take one of something I really love?

"Here you are!"

Thank goodness, the assistant is back, with my lilac sandals in a box—and as I see them, my heart leaps. Oh, these are gorgeous. *Gorgeous.* All delicate and strappy, with a tiny little blackberry by the toe. I fell in love with them as soon as I saw them. They're a bit expensive—but then, everyone knows you should never skimp on shoes, because you'll hurt your feet.

I slip my feet into them with a frisson of delight—and they're just fantastic. My feet suddenly look elegant, and my legs look longer . . . and OK, it's a tiny bit difficult to walk in them, but that's probably because the shop floor is all slippery.

"I'll take them, please," I say, and beam happily at the assistant.

You see, this is the reward for taking such a controlled approach to shopping. When you buy something, you really feel as though you've *earned* it.

We both head toward the checkout, and I keep my eyes carefully away from the rack of accessories. In fact, I barely even notice that purple bag with the jet beading. And I'm just reaching for my wallet, congratulating myself on being so single-minded, when the assistant says conversationally, "You know, we've got these sandals in clementine, as well."

Clementine?

"Oh . . . right," I say after a pause.

I'm not interested. I've got what I came in to buy—and that's the end of the story. Lilac sandals. Not clementine.

"They've just come in," she adds, rooting around on the floor. "I think they're going to be even more popular than the lilac."

"Really?" I say, trying to sound as indifferent as I can. "Well, I'll just take these, I think . . ."

"Here it is!" she exclaims. "I knew there was one around here somewhere . . ."

And I freeze, as she puts the most exquisite sandal I've ever seen onto the counter. It's a pale, creamy orange color, with the same strappy shape as the lilac one—but instead of the blackberry, there's a tiny clementine by the toe.

It's instant love. I can't move my eyes away.

"Would you like to try it?" says the girl, and I feel a lurch of desire, right to the pit of my stomach.

Just look at it. It's delicious. It's the most darling shoe I've ever seen. Oh God.

But I don't need a pair of clementine shoes. I don't need them.

Come on, Becky. Just. Say. No.

"Actually . . ." I swallow hard, trying to get control of my voice. "Actually . . ." I can hardly say it. "I'll just take the lilac ones today," I manage eventually. "Thank you."

"OK . . ." The girl punches a code into the till. "That'll be £89, then. How would you like to pay?"

"Er . . . VISA, please," I say. I sign the slip, take my bag, and leave the shop, feeling slightly numb.

I did it! I did it! I completely controlled my desires! I only needed one pair of shoes—and I only bought one. In and out of the shop, completely according to plan. You see, this is what I can do when I really want to. This is the new Becky Bloomwood.

Having been so good, I deserve a little reward, so I go to a coffee shop and sit down outside in the sun with a cappuccino.

I want those clementine shoes, pops into my head as I take the first sip.

Stop. Stop it. Think about . . . something else. Luke. The holiday. Our first ever holiday together. God, I can't wait.

I've been wanting to suggest a holiday ever since Luke and I started going out, but he works so hard, it would be like asking the prime minister to give up running the country for a bit. (Except come to think of it, he does that every summer, doesn't he? So why can't Luke?)

Luke's so busy, he hasn't even met my parents yet, which I'm a bit upset about. They asked him over for Sunday lunch a few weeks ago, and Mum spent ages cooking—or at least, she bought apricot-stuffed loin of pork from Sainsbury's and a really posh chocolate meringue pudding. But at the last minute he had to cancel because there was a crisis with one of his clients in the Sunday papers. So I had to go on my own—and it was all rather miserable, to be honest. You could tell Mum was really disappointed, but she kept saying brightly, "Oh well, it was only a casual arrangement," which it wasn't. He sent her a huge bouquet of flowers the next day to apologize (or at least, Mel, his assistant, did), but it's not the same, is it?

The worst bit was that our next-door neighbors, Janice and Martin, popped in for a glass of sherry "to meet the famous Luke," as they put it, and when they found out he wasn't there, they kept giving me all these pitying looks tinged with smugness, because their son Tom is getting married to his girlfriend Lucy next week. And I have a horrible suspicion that they think I have a crush on him. (Which I don't—in fact, quite the reverse. I actually turned *him* down when we were teenagers. But once people believe something like that, it's completely impossible to convince them otherwise. Hideous.)

When I got upset with Luke, he pointed out that I've never met his parents, either. But I have once—although very briefly. And anyway it's not the same thing, because his family lives miles away, and it's all much more complicated.

To be honest, I find Luke's family setup just a tad weird. He's got a dad and a stepmum in Britain who brought him up with his two half-sisters, and whom he calls Mum and Dad. And then he's got his real mum, Elinor, who left his dad when he was little, married some rich American, and left Luke behind. Then she left the rich American and married another, even richer

American and then . . . was there another one? Anyway, the point is, she lives in New York. So of course I haven't met her. And the rest of his family is in Devon, not exactly handy for a quick Sunday lunch.

I said all this to Luke and I think he got my point. And at least he's making the effort to come on this little holiday. It was Mel, actually, who suggested the weekend idea. She told me Luke hadn't had a proper holiday for three years—and maybe he had to warm up to the idea. So I stopped talking about holidays and started talking about weekends away—and that did the trick! All of a sudden Luke told me to set aside this weekend. He booked the hotel himself and everything. I'm *so* looking forward to it. We'll just do nothing but relax and take it easy—and actually spend some time with each other for a change. Lovely.

I want those clementine shoes.

Stop it.

I take another sip of coffee, lean back, and force myself to survey the bustling street. People are striding along, holding bags and chatting, and there's a girl crossing the road with nice trousers on, which I think come from Nicole Farhi and . . . Oh God.

A middle-aged man in a dark suit is coming along the road toward me, and I recognize him. It's Derek Smeath, my bank manager.

Oh, and I think he's seen me.

OK, don't panic, I instruct myself firmly. There's no need to panic. Maybe once upon a time I would have been thrown by seeing him. I might have tried to hide behind a menu, or perhaps even run away. But that's all in the past. These days, Sweetie Smeathie and I have a very honest and amicable relationship.

Still, I find myself shifting my chair slightly farther away from my LK Bennett bag, as though it hasn't got anything to do with me.

"Hello, Mr. Smeath!" I say brightly as he approaches. "How are you?"

"Very well," says Derek Smeath, smiling. "And you?"

"Oh, I'm fine, thanks. Would you . . . would you like a coffee?" I add politely, gesturing to the empty chair opposite me. And I'm not really expecting him to say yes—but to my astonishment he sits down and picks up a menu.

How civilized is this? I'm having coffee with my bank manager at a pavement cafe! You know, maybe I'll find a way to work this into my *Morning Coffee* slot. "I myself prefer the informal approach to personal finance," I'll say, smiling warmly into the camera. "My own bank manager and I often share a friendly cappuccino as we discuss my current financial strategies . . ."

"As it happens, Rebecca, I've just written a letter to you," says Derek Smeath, as a waitress puts an espresso down in front of him. Suddenly his voice is more serious, and I feel a small lurch of alarm. Oh God, what have I done now? "You and all my customers," he adds. "To tell you that I'm leaving."

"What?" I put my coffee cup down with a little crash. "What do you mean, leaving?"

"I'm leaving Endwich Bank. I've decided to take early retirement."

"But . . ."

I stare at him, appalled. Derek Smeath can't leave Endwich Bank. He can't just leave me in the lurch, just as everything was going so well. I mean, I know we haven't always exactly seen eye to eye—but recently we've developed a really good rapport. He understands me. He understands my overdraft. What am I going to do without him?

"Aren't you too young to retire?" I say, aware of the dismay in my voice. "Won't you get bored?"

He leans back in his chair and takes a sip of espresso. "I'm not planning to give up work altogether. But I think there's a little more to life than looking after people's bank accounts, don't you? Fascinating though some of them have been."

"Well . . . yes. Yes, of course. And I'm glad for you, honestly." I shrug, a little embarrassed. "But I'll . . . miss you."

"Believe it or not," he says, smiling slightly, "I think I'll miss you too, Rebecca. Yours has certainly been one of the most . . . interesting accounts I've dealt with."

He gives me a penetrating look and I feel myself flush

slightly. Why does he have to remind me of the past? The point is, that's all over. I'm a different person now. Surely one should be allowed to turn over a new leaf and start again in life.

"Your new career in television seems to be going well," he says, taking a sip of espresso.

"I know! It's so great, isn't it? And it pays really well," I add, a little pointedly.

"Your income has certainly gone up in recent months." He puts down his coffee cup and my heart sinks slightly. "However . . ."

I knew it. *Why* does there always have to be a *however*?

"However," repeats Derek Smeath. "Your outgoings have also risen. Substantially. In fact, your overdraft is now higher than it was at the height of your . . . shall we say, your excesses."

Excesses? That is so mean.

"You really must make more effort to keep within your overdraft limit," he's saying now. "Or, even better, pay it off."

"I know," I say vaguely. "I'm planning to."

I've just spotted a girl on the other side of the road, with an LK Bennett bag. She's holding a great big bag—with *two* shoe boxes in it.

If she's allowed to buy two pairs of shoes, then why aren't I? What's the rule that says you can only buy one pair of shoes at a time? I mean, it's so arbitrary.

"What about your other finances?" Derek Smeath is asking. "Do you have any store card bills, for example?"

"No," I say with a tinge of smugness. "I paid them all off months ago."

"And you haven't spent anything since?"

"Only bits and pieces. Hardly anything."

And what's ninety quid, really? In the greater scheme of things?

"The reason I'm asking these questions," says Derek Smeath, "is that I feel I should warn you. The bank is restructuring somewhat, and my successor, John Gavin, may not have quite the same relaxed approach which I have taken toward your account.

I'm not sure you're aware quite how lenient I have been with you."

"Really?" I say, not really listening.

I mean, suppose I took up smoking. I'd easily spend ninety quid on cigarettes without even thinking about it, wouldn't I?

In fact, think of all the money I've saved by *not* smoking. Easily enough to afford one little pair of shoes.

"He's a very capable man," Derek Smeath is saying. "But also very . . . rigorous. Not particularly known for his flexibility."

"Right," I say, nodding absently.

"I would certainly recommend that you address your overdraft without delay." He takes a sip of coffee. "And tell me, have you done anything about taking out a pension?"

"Erm . . . I went to visit that independent adviser you recommended."

"And did you fill in any of the forms?"

Unwillingly, I drag my attention back to him.

"Well, I'm just considering my options," I say, and put on my wise, financial-expert look. "There's nothing worse than rushing into the wrong investment, you know. Particularly when it comes to something as important as a pension."

"Very true," says Derek Smeath. "But don't spend too long considering, will you? Your money won't save itself."

"I know!" I say and take a sip of cappuccino.

Now I feel a bit uncomfortable. Maybe he's right. Maybe I should put £90 into a pension fund instead of buying another pair of shoes.

But on the other hand—what good is a pension fund of £90? I mean, that's not exactly going to keep me in my old age, is it? Ninety measly quid. And by the time I'm old, the world will probably have blown up, or something.

Whereas a pair of shoes is tangible, it's there in your hand . . .

Oh, sod it. I'm going to get them.

"Mr. Smeath, I have to go," I say abruptly, putting down my cup. "There's something I have to . . . do."

I *have* to get back there as quickly as possible. I pick up my carrier bag and drop a fiver on the table. "Lovely to see you. And good luck in your retirement."

"Best of luck to you too, Rebecca," says Derek Smeath, smiling kindly at me. "But do remember what I've said. John Gavin won't indulge you in the way that I have. So please be careful with your spending."

"I will!" I say brightly.

And without quite running, I'm off down the street, as quick as I can, back to LK Bennett.

Perhaps strictly speaking I didn't exactly need to buy a pair of clementine shoes. But what occurred to me while I was trying them on was, I haven't actually broken my new rule. Because the point is, I *will* need them.

After all, I will need new shoes *at some point,* won't I? Everyone needs shoes. And surely it's far more prudent to stock up now in a style I really like, than to wait until my last pair wears out and then find nothing nice in the shops. It's only sensible. It's like . . . hedging my future position in the shoe market.

As I come out of LK Bennett, gleefully grasping my two shiny new bags, there's a warm, happy glow all around me, and I'm not in the mood to go home. So I decide to pop across the street to Gifts and Goodies. This is one of the shops that carries Suze's frames, and I have a little habit of going in whenever I pass, just to see if anyone's buying one.

I push the door open with a little ping, and smile at the assistant, who looks up. This is such a lovely shop. It's all warm and scented, and full of gorgeous things like chrome wine racks and etched glass coasters. I sidle past a shelf of pale mauve leather notebooks, and look up—and there they are! Three purple tweed photo frames, made by Suze! I still get a thrill, every time I see them.

And oh my God! I feel a sudden zing of excitement. There's a customer standing there, and she's holding one. She's actually holding one!

To be perfectly honest, I've never actually seen anyone buying one of Suze's frames. I mean, I know people must buy them, because they keep selling out—but I've never actually seen it happen. This is so exciting!

I walk quietly forward just as the customer turns the frame over. She frowns at the price, and my heart gives a little flurry.

"That's a really beautiful photo frame," I say casually. "Really unusual."

"Yes," she says, and puts it back down on the shelf.

No! I think in dismay. Pick it up again!

"It's so difficult to find a nice frame these days," I say conversationally. "Don't you think? When you find one, you should just . . . buy it! Before someone else gets it."

"I suppose so," says the customer, giving me an odd look.

Now she's walking away. What can I do?

"Well, I think I'll get one," I say distinctly, and pick it up. "It'll make a perfect present. For a man, or a woman . . . I mean, everyone needs photograph frames, don't they?"

The customer doesn't seem to be taking any notice. But never mind, when she sees *me* buying it, maybe she'll rethink.

I hurry to the checkout, and the woman behind the till smiles at me. I think she's the shop owner, because I've seen her interviewing staff and talking to suppliers. (Not that I come in here very often, it's just coincidence or something.)

"Hello again," she says. "You really like those frames, don't you?"

"Yes," I say loudly. "And such *fantastic* value!" But the customer's looking at a glass decanter, and not even listening.

"How many of them have you bought, now? It must be about . . . twenty?"

What? My attention snaps back to the shop owner. What's she saying?

"Or even thirty?"

I stare at her in shock. Has she been monitoring me, every time I've been in here? Isn't that against the law?

"Quite a collection!" she adds pleasantly, as she wraps it up in tissue paper.

I've got to say something, or she'll get the idea that it's me buying all Suze's frames instead of the general public. Which is ridiculous. I ask you, thirty! I've only bought about . . . four. Five, maybe.

"I haven't got that many!" I say hurriedly. "I should think you've been mixing me up with . . . other people. And I didn't just come in to buy a frame!" I laugh gaily to show what a ludicrous idea that is. "I actually wanted some of . . . these, too." I grab randomly at some big carved wooden letters in a nearby basket, and hand them to her. She smiles, and starts laying them out on tissue paper one by one.

"P . . . T . . . R . . . R."

She stops, and looks at the letters puzzledly. "Were you trying to make *Peter*?"

Oh for God's sake. Does there always have to be a *reason* to buy things?

"Erm . . . yes," I say. "For my . . . my godson. He's three."

"Lovely! Here we are then. Two E's, and take away one R . . ."

She's looking at me kindly, as if I'm a complete halfwit. Which I suppose is fair enough, since I can't spell *Peter* and it's the name of my own godson.

"That'll be . . . £48," she says, as I reach for my purse. "You know, if you spend £50, you get a free scented candle."

"Really?" I look up with interest. I could do with a nice scented candle. And for the sake of £2 . . .

"I'm sure I could find something . . ." I say, looking vaguely round the shop.

"Spell out the rest of your godson's name in wooden letters!" suggests the shop owner helpfully. "What's his surname?"

"Um, Wilson," I say without thinking.

"Wilson!" And to my horror, she begins to root around in the basket. "W . . . L . . . here's an O . . ."

"Actually," I say quickly, "actually, better not. Because . . . because . . . actually, his parents are divorcing and he might be changing his surname."

"Really?" says the shop owner, and pulls a sympathetic face

as she drops the letters back in. "How awful. Is it an acrimonious split, then?"

"Yes," I say, looking around the shop for something else to buy. "Very. His . . . his mother ran off with the gardener."

"Are you serious?" The shop owner's staring at me, and I suddenly notice a couple nearby listening as well. "She ran off with the *gardener*?"

"He was . . . very hunky," I improvise, picking up a jewelry box and seeing that it costs £75. "She couldn't keep her hands off him. The husband found them together in the toolshed. Anyway—"

"Goodness me!" says the shop owner. "That sounds incredible!"

"It's completely true," chimes in a voice from across the shop.

What?

My head whips round—and the woman who was looking at Suze's frames is walking toward me. "I assume you're talking about Jane and Tim?" she says. "Such a terrible scandal, wasn't it? But I thought the little boy was called Toby."

I stare at her, unable to speak.

"Maybe Peter is his baptismal name," suggests the shop owner, and gestures to me. "This is his godmother."

"Oh, you're the godmother!" exclaims the woman. "Yes, I've heard all about you."

This isn't happening.

"Now, perhaps *you* can tell me." The woman comes forward and lowers her voice confidentially. "Did Tim accept Maud's offer?"

I look around the silent shop. Everyone is waiting for my answer.

"Erm . . . yes, he did! Actually, I think I'll pay by cash." I fumble in my purse, and plonk £50 on the counter. "Keep the change."

"What about your scented candle?" says the shop owner. "You can choose from vanilla, sandalwood—"

"Never mind," I say, hurrying toward the door.

"Wait!" calls the woman urgently. "What happened to Ivan?"

"He . . . he emigrated to Australia," I say, and slam the door behind me.

God, that was a bit close. I think I'd better go home.

As I reach the corner of our road, I pause and do a little rearranging of my bags. Which is to say, I put them all in one LK Bennett carrier, and push them down until you can't see them. But it's not that I'm hiding them or anything.

I'm kind of hoping I'll be able to scuttle into my room without Suze seeing me, but as I open the front door, she's sitting on the floor of the hall, parceling something up.

"Hi!" she says. "Did you get the shoes?"

"Yes," I say brightly. "Absolutely. Right size, and everything."

"Let's have a look then!"

"I'll just . . . unpack them," I say casually, and head toward my room, trying to keep relaxed. But I know I look guilty. I'm even *walking* guiltily.

"Bex," she says suddenly. "What else is in that bag? That's not just one pair of shoes."

"Bag?" I turn as though in surprise. "Oh, *this* bag. Erm . . . just a few . . . bits and pieces. You know . . . odds and ends . . ."

I tail away guiltily as Suze folds her arms, looking as stern as she can.

"Show me."

"OK, listen," I say in a rush. "I know I said only one pair. But before you get angry, just look." I reach into my second LK Bennett bag, slip open the box, and slowly pull out one of the clementine sandals. "Just . . . look at that."

"Oh my God," breathes Suze, staring at it. "That's absolutely . . . stunning." She takes it from me and strokes the soft leather gently—then suddenly her stern expression returns. "But did you *need* them?"

"Yes!" I say defensively. "Or at least . . . I was just stocking up for the future. You know, like a kind of . . . investment."

"An investment?"

"Yes. And in a way, it's *saving* money—because now I've got these, I won't need to spend any money on shoes next year. None!"

"Really?" says Suze suspiciously. "None at all?"

"Absolutely! Honestly, Suze, I'm going to live in these shoes. I won't need to buy any more for at least a year. Probably two!"

Suze is silent and I bite my lip, waiting for her to tell me to take them back to the shop. But she's looking down at the sandal again, and touching the little clementine.

"Put them on," she says suddenly. "Let me see!"

With a small thrill I pull out the other sandal and slip them on—and they're just perfect. My perfect clementine slippers, just like Cinderella.

"Oh, Bex," says Suze—and she doesn't have to say anything else. It's all there in her eyes.

Honestly, sometimes I wish I could marry Suze.

After I've paraded back and forth a few times, Suze gives a contented sigh, then reaches inside the big carrier for the Gifts and Goodies bag. "So—what did you get from here?" she says interestedly. The wooden letters spill out, and she begins to arrange them on the carpet.

"P-E-T-E-R. You got a present for Peter!"

"Erm . . . yes," I say vaguely, grabbing for the Gifts and Goodies bag before she can spot her own frame in there. (She once caught me buying one in Fancy Free and got all cross, and said she would always make me one if I wanted it.) "Who's Peter?"

"My machinist!" says Suze. "But you've never met him!"

"Well . . . you know. He sounds nice on the phone . . . anyway, I'd better go and get ready for tomorrow."

"Ooh, that reminds me," says Suze, reaching for a piece of paper. "Luke rang for you!"

"Really?" I say, trying to hide my delight. I always get a little thrill when Luke rings, because, to be honest, he doesn't do it that much. I mean, he phones to arrange times of meeting and that kind of stuff—but he doesn't often phone for a chat. Sometimes he sends me e-mails, but they're not what you'd call chatty, more . . . Well, I don't exactly want to give away our intimate secrets—but put it like this, the first time I got one, I was quite shocked! (But I sort of look forward to them now.)

"He said he'll pick you up from the studio tomorrow at twelve. And the Mercedes has had to go into the garage, so you'll be going down in the MGF."

"Really?" I say. "That's so cool!"

"I know," says Suze, beaming back at me. "Isn't it great? Oh, and he also said can you pack light, because the boot isn't very big."

I stare at her, my smile fading.

"What did you say?"

"Pack light," repeats Suze. "You know: not much luggage, maybe one small bag or holdall . . ."

"I know what 'pack light' means!" I say, my voice shrill with alarm. "But . . . I can't!"

"Of course you can!"

"Suze, have you *seen* how much stuff I've got?" I say, going to my bedroom door and flinging it open. "I mean, just look at that."

Suze follows my gaze uncertainly, and we both stare at my bed. My big acid-green suitcase is full. Another pile of clothes is sitting beside it. And I haven't even *got* to makeup and stuff yet.

"I can't do it, Suze," I wail. "What am I going to do?"

"Phone Luke and tell him?" suggests Suze, "and say he'll have to hire a car with a bigger boot?"

For a moment I'm silent. I try to imagine Luke's face if I tell him he has to hire a bigger car to hold my clothes.

"The thing is," I say at last, "I'm not sure he'd *completely* understand . . ."

The doorbell rings and Suze gets up.

"That'll be Special Express for my parcel," she says. "Listen, Bex, it'll be fine! Just . . . prune away a few things." She goes to answer the door and I'm left staring at my jumbled bed.

Prune away? But prune away what, exactly? I mean, it's not

as though I've packed a load of stuff I don't need. If I just start removing things at random my whole system will collapse.

Come on. Think laterally. There *must* be a solution.

Maybe I could . . . secretly fix a trailer onto the car when Luke isn't looking?

Or maybe I could *wear* all my clothes, on top of each other, and say I'm feeling a bit chilly . . .

Oh, this is hopeless. What am I going to do?

Distractedly, I wander out of my room and into the hall, where Suze is handing a padded envelope to a man in uniform.

"That's great," he says. "If you could just sign there . . . Hello!" he adds cheerfully to me, and I nod back, staring blankly at his badge, which reads: *Anything, anywhere, by tomorrow morning.*

"Here's your receipt," says the man to Suze, and turns to leave. And he's halfway out of the door, when the words suddenly start jumping about in my mind.

Anything.

Anywhere.

By tomorrow—

"Hey, wait!" I call, just as the door's about to slam. "Could you just hold on one sec—"

PARADIGM BOOKS LTD

695 Soho Square

London W1 5As

Ms. Rebecca Bloomwood
Flat 2
4 Burney Rd.
London SW6 8FD

4 September 2000

Dear Becky:

You may remember, when we spoke two weeks ago you assured me the first draft of your book would be with me within days. I'm sure it's on its way—or has it possibly gotten lost in the post? Maybe you could send me another copy?

As far as the author photograph goes, just wear whatever you feel comfortable with. An Agnes B top sounds fine, as do the earrings you described. And thanks for sending me a Polaroid of your orange sandals—I'm sure they will look great.

I look forward to seeing the manuscript—and again, let me say how thrilled and delighted we are that you're writing for us.

With all best wishes,

Pippa Brady
Editor

PARADIGM BOOKS LTD

Helping you to help yourself

COMING SOON! *Jungle Survival* by Brig. Roger Flintwood

Three

At five to twelve the next day I'm sitting under the bright lights of the *Morning Coffee* set, wondering how much longer we'll be. Normally my financial advice slot is over by eleven forty, but they got so engrossed with the psychic who reckons she's the reincarnated spirit of Mary Queen of Scots that everything's overrun since then. And Luke will be here any minute, and I've still got to change out of this stuffy suit . . .

"Becky?" says Emma, who's one of the presenters of *Morning Coffee* and is sitting opposite me on a blue sofa. "This sounds like quite a problem."

"Absolutely," I say, dragging my mind back to the present. I glance down at the sheet in front of me, then smile sympathetically at the camera. "So, to recap, Judy, you and your husband Bill have inherited some money. You'd like to invest some of it in the stock market—but he's refusing."

"It's like talking to a brick wall!" comes Judy's indignant voice. "He says I'll lose it all, and it's his money too, and if all I want to do is gamble it away, then I can go to . . ."

"Yes," interrupts Emma smoothly. "Well. This does sound quite a problem, Becky. Two partners disagreeing about what to do with their money."

"I just don't understand him!" exclaims Judy. "This is our

one chance to make a serious investment! It's a fantastic opportunity! Why can't he *see* that?"

She breaks off—and there's an expectant silence around the studio. Everyone's waiting for my answer.

"Judy . . ." I pause thoughtfully. "May I ask a question? What outfit is Bill wearing today?"

"A suit," says Judy, sounding taken aback. "A gray suit for work."

"What kind of tie? Plain or patterned?"

"Plain," says Judy at once. "All his ties are plain."

"Would he ever wear, say . . . a polka-dot tie?"

"Never!"

"I see." I raise my eyebrows. "Judy, would it be fair to say Bill is generally quite an unadventurous person? That he doesn't like taking risks?"

"Well . . . yes," says Judy. "Now that you say it, I suppose he is."

"Ah!" says Rory suddenly, on the other side of the sofa. Rory is the other presenter of *Morning Coffee*. He's very chiseled-looking and is great at flirting with film stars, but he's not exactly the Brain of Britain. "I think I see where you're going here, Becky."

"Yes, thanks Rory," says Emma, rolling her eyes at me. "I think we all do. So Becky, if Bill doesn't like risk—are you saying he's right to avoid the stock market?"

"No," I reply. "Actually, I'm not saying that at all. Because maybe what Bill isn't quite seeing is that there's more than one kind of risk. If you invest in the stock market, yes, you risk losing some money in the short term. But if you simply tuck it away in the bank for years and years, an even greater risk is that this inheritance will be eroded over time by inflation."

"Aha," puts in Rory wisely. "Inflation."

"In twenty years' time, it could well be worth very little—compared to what it would probably have achieved on the market. So if Bill is only in his thirties and wants to make a long-term investment—although it seems risky, it's in many ways *safer* to choose a balanced stock market portfolio."

"I see!" says Emma, and gives me an admiring look. "I would never have looked at it like that."

"Successful investment is often simply a question of thinking laterally," I say, smiling modestly.

I *love* it when I get the answer right and everyone looks impressed.

"Does that help you, Judy?" says Emma.

"Yes," says Judy. "Yes, it does! I've videotaped this call, so I'll show it to Bill tonight."

"Oh right!" I say. "Well, check what kind of tie he's wearing first."

Everyone laughs, and I join in after a pause—though I wasn't actually joking.

"Time for one more quick call," says Emma. "And we have Enid from Northampton, who wants to know if she's got enough money to retire on. Enid, is that right?"

"Yes, that's right," comes Enid's voice down the line. "My husband Tony's recently retired, and I was on holiday last week—just at home with him, cooking and so forth. And he . . . we got to thinking . . . how about I retire early, too? But I wasn't sure I had enough saved up, so I thought I'd call in."

"What kind of financial provision have you made for retirement, Enid?" I ask.

"I've a pension which I've contributed to all my life," says Enid hesitantly, "and I've a couple of savings plans . . . and I've a recent inheritance which should see off the mortgage . . ."

"Well!" says Emma brightly. "Even *I* can see that you're pretty well set up, Enid. I'd say, happy retirement!"

"Right," says Enid. "I see. So—there's no reason for me not to retire. It's just as Tony said." There's silence apart from her breathing unsteadily down the line, and Emma gives me a quick glance. I know the producer, Barry, must be yelling into her earpiece to fill the space.

"So good luck, Enid!" she says brightly. "Becky, on the subject of retirement planning—"

"Just . . . hold on a moment," I say, frowning slightly. "Enid, there's no obvious financial reason for you not to retire. But . . ."

what about the most important reason of all? Do you actually *want* to retire?"

"Well." Enid's voice falters slightly. "I'm in my fifties now. I mean, you have to move on, don't you? And as Tony said, it'll give us a chance to spend more time together."

"Do you enjoy your job?"

There's another silence.

"I do. Yes. It's a good crowd, at work. I'm older than most of them, but somehow that doesn't seem to matter when we're having a laugh . . ."

"Well, I'm afraid that's all we've got time for," cuts in Emma, who has been listening intently to her earpiece. She smiles at the camera. "Good luck in your retirement, Enid . . ."

"Wait!" I say quickly. "Enid, please stay on the line if you'd like to talk about this a bit more. OK?"

"Yes," says Enid after a pause. "Yes, I'd like that."

"We're going to go to weather now," says Rory, who always perks up as the finance slot comes to an end. "But a final word, Becky?"

"Same as always," I say, smiling at the camera. "Look after your money . . ."

". . . and your money will look after you!" chime in Rory and Emma. After a frozen pause, everyone relaxes and Zelda, the assistant producer, strides onto the set.

"Well done!" she says. "Great stuff. Now, Becky, we've still got Enid on line four. But we can get rid of her if you like . . ."

"No!" I say. "I really want to talk to her. You know, I reckon she doesn't want to retire at all!"

"Whatever," says Zelda, ticking something on her clipboard. "Oh, and Luke's waiting for you at reception."

"Already?" I look at my watch. "Oh God . . . OK—can you tell him I won't be long?"

I honestly don't intend to spend that long on the phone. But once I get talking to Enid, it all comes out—about how she's dreading retirement, and how her husband just wants her at home to cook for him. How she really loves her job and she was thinking about taking a computer course but her husband says it's a waste of money . . . By the end I'm completely outraged. I've said exactly what I think, several times over, and am in the middle of asking Enid if she considers herself a feminist, when Zelda taps me on the shoulder and suddenly I remember where I am.

It takes me about another five minutes to apologize to Enid and say I've got to go, then for her to apologize to *me*—and for us both to say good-bye and thank you and don't mention it, about twenty times. Then, as quickly as possible, I head to my dressing room and change out of my *Morning Coffee* outfit into my driving outfit.

I'm quite pleased with my appearance as I look at myself in the mirror. I'm wearing: a Pucci-esque multicolored top, frayed denim cutoffs, my new sandals, Gucci shades (Harvey Nichols sale—half price!), and my treasured pale blue Denny and George scarf.

Luke's got a real thing about my Denny and George scarf. When people ask us how we met, he always says, "Our eyes met across a Denny and George scarf," which is actually kind of true. He lent me some of the money I needed to buy it, and he still maintains I never paid him back so it's partly his. (Which is *so* not true. I paid him back straight away.)

Anyway, I tend to wear it quite a lot when we go out together. Also when we stay in together. In fact, I'll tell you a small secret—sometimes we even . . .

Actually, no. You don't need to know that. Forget I mentioned it.

As I eventually hurry into reception I glance at my watch—and oh God, I'm forty minutes late. And there's Luke sitting on a squashy chair, wearing the gorgeous polo shirt I bought him in the Ralph Lauren sale. He's talking intently on his mobile phone and sipping a cup of coffee and frowning at something in the paper. But then he looks up and his dark eyes meet mine, and his whole face breaks into a smile. A true, affectionate smile, which makes him seem like a different person.

When I first knew Luke, I only ever saw him businesslike and polite, or scarily angry, or—very occasionally—amused. Even after we started seeing each other, it was a long time before he really let his guard down. In fact, the first time he really, really laughed, I was so surprised, I snorted lemonade through my nose.

Even now, whenever I see his face creasing into a real smile, I feel a bit of a lift inside. Because I know he's not like that with everyone. He's smiling like that because it's me. For me.

"I'm really sorry I took so long," I say. "I was just . . ."

"I know," says Luke, closing his paper and standing up. "You were talking to Enid." He gives me a kiss and squeezes my arm. "I saw the last couple of calls. Good for you."

"You just won't believe what her husband's like!" I say as we go through the swing doors and out into the car park. "No wonder she wants to keep working!"

"I can imagine."

"He just thinks she's there to give him an easy life." I shake my head fiercely. "You know, I'm never going to just . . . stay at home and cook your supper. Never in a million years."

There's a short silence, and I look up to see Luke's amused expression.

"Or . . . you know," I add hastily. "Anyone's supper."

"I'm glad to hear it," says Luke mildly. "I'm especially glad if you're never going to cook me Moroccan couscous surprise."

"You know what I mean," I say, flushing slightly. "And you promised you weren't going to talk about that anymore."

My famous Moroccan evening was quite soon after we started going out. I really wanted to show Luke that I could cook—and I'd seen this program about Moroccan cooking which made it look really easy and impressive. Plus there was some gorgeous Moroccan tableware on sale in Debenhams, so it should have all been perfect.

But that soggy couscous. It was the most revolting stuff I've ever seen in my life. Even after I tried Suze's suggestion of stir-frying it with mango chutney. And there was so *much* of it, all swelling up in bowls everywhere . . .

Anyway. Never mind. We had quite a nice pizza in the end.

We're approaching Luke's convertible in the corner of the car park, and he bleeps it open.

"You got my message, did you?" he says. "About luggage?"

"Yes, I did. Here it is."

I hand him the dinkiest little suitcase in the world, which I got from a children's gift shop in Guildford. It's white canvas with red hearts stenciled round it, and I use it as a vanity case.

"Is that it?" says Luke, looking astonished, and I stifle a giggle. Ha! This'll show him who can pack light.

All I've got in this case is my makeup and shampoo—but Luke doesn't need to know that, does he?

"Yes, that's it," I say, raising my eyebrows slightly. "You did say, 'pack light.' "

"So I did," says Luke. "But this—" He gestures at the case. "I'm impressed."

As he opens the boot, I get into the driving seat and adjust the seat forward so I can reach the pedals. I've always wanted to drive a convertible!

The boot slams behind me, and Luke comes round, a quizzical look on his face.

"You're driving, are you?"

"Part of the way, I thought," I say carelessly. "Just to take the pressure off you. You know, it's very dangerous to drive for too long."

"You can drive, can you, in those shoes?" He's looking down at my clementine sandals—and I have to admit, the heel is a bit high for pedaling. But I'm not going to let him know that. "They're new, aren't they?" he adds, looking more closely at them.

And I'm about to say yes, when I remember that the last time I saw him, I had new shoes on—and the time before that, too. Which is really weird and must be one of those random cluster things.

"No!" I reply instead. "Actually, I've had them for ages. Actually . . ." I clear my throat. "They're my driving shoes."

"Your driving shoes," echoes Luke skeptically.

"Yes!" I say, and start the engine before he can say any more. God, this car is amazing! It makes a fantastic roaring sound, and a kind of screech as I move it into gear.

"Becky—"

"I'm fine!" I say, and slowly move off across the car park into the street. Oh, this is such a fantastic moment. I wonder if anybody's watching me. I wonder if Emma and Rory are looking out the window. And that sound guy who thinks he's so cool with his motorbike. He hasn't got a convertible, has he? Accidentally on purpose, I lean on the horn, and as the sound echoes round the car park I see at least three people turning to look. Ha! Look at me! Ha-ha-ha . . .

"My petal," says Luke beside me. "You're causing a traffic jam."

I glance into my rear mirror—and there are three cars creeping along behind me. Which is ridiculous, because I'm not going *that* slowly.

"Try moving it up a notch," suggests Luke. "Ten miles an hour, say?"

"I *am*," I say crossly. "You can't expect me just to whiz off at a million miles an hour! There is a speed limit, you know."

I reach the exit, smile nonchalantly at the porter at the gate, who gives me a surprised look, and pull out into the road. I signal left and take a last glance back to check if anyone I know has just come out and is watching me admiringly. Then, as a car behind me starts to beep, I carefully pull in at the pavement.

"There we are," I say. "Your turn."

"My turn?" Luke stares at me. "Already?"

"I have to do my nails now," I explain. "And anyway, I know you think I can't drive. I don't want to have you pulling faces at me all the way down to Somerset."

"I do not think you can't drive," protests Luke, half-laughing. "When have I ever said that?"

"You don't need to say it. I can see it coming out of your head in a thought bubble: 'Becky Bloomwood cannot drive.' "

"Well, that's where you're wrong," retorts Luke. "The bubble actually reads: 'Becky Bloomwood cannot drive in her new orange shoes because the heels are too high and pointy.' "

He raises his eyebrows, and I feel myself flush slightly.

"They're my driving shoes," I mutter, shifting over to the passenger seat. "And I've had them for years."

As I reach into my bag for my nail file, Luke gets into the driver's seat, leans over, and gives me a kiss.

"Thank you for doing that stint, anyway," he says. "I'm sure it'll lessen my risk of fatigue on the motorway."

"Well, good!" I say, starting on my nails. "You need to conserve your energy for all those long country walks we're going to go on tomorrow."

There's silence, and after a while I look up.

"Yes," says Luke—and he isn't smiling anymore. "Becky . . . I was going to talk to you about tomorrow." He pauses and I stare at him, feeling my own smile fade slightly.

"What is it?" I say, trying not to sound anxious.

Luke exhales sharply. "Here's the thing. A business opportunity has arisen which I really would like to . . . to take advantage of. And there are some people over from the States who I need to talk to. Urgently."

"Oh," I say, a little uncertainly. "Well—that's OK. If you've got your phone with you . . ."

"Not by phone." He looks straight at me. "I've scheduled a meeting for tomorrow."

"Tomorrow?" I echo, and give a little laugh. "But you can't have a meeting. We'll be at the hotel."

"So will the people I need to talk to," says Luke. "I've invited them down."

I stare at him in shock.

"You've invited businesspeople down on our holiday?"

"Purely for the meeting," says Luke. "The rest of the time it'll just be the two of us."

"And how long will the meeting go on?" I exclaim. "Don't tell me! All day!"

I just can't believe it. After waiting all this time, after getting all excited, after all my packing . . .

"Becky, it won't be as bad as that . . ."

"You *promised* me you'd take time off! You said we'd have a lovely romantic time."

"We will have a lovely romantic time."

"With all your business friends. With all your horrible contacts, networking away like . . . like maggots!"

"They won't be networking with us," says Luke with a grin. "Becky—" He reaches for my hand, but I pull it away.

"To be honest, I don't see any point in my coming if it's just you doing business!" I say miserably. "I might as well just stay at home. In fact—" I open the car door. "In fact, I think I'll go home right now. I'll call a taxi from the studio."

I slam the car door and begin to stride off along the street, my clementine sandals making a click-clack sound against the hot pavement. And I've almost got to the studio gate before I hear his voice, raised so loud that several people turn to look.

"Becky! Wait there!"

I stop and slowly turn on the spot—to see him standing up in the car, dialing a number on his mobile phone.

"What are you doing?" I call suspiciously.

"I'm phoning my horrible business contact," says Luke. "To put him off. To cancel."

I fold my arms and stare at him with narrowed eyes.

"Hello?" he says. "Room 301, please. Michael Ellis. Thanks. I guess I'll just have to fly out and see him in Washington," he adds to me in deadpan tones. "Or wait until the next time he and his associates are all together in Britain. Which could be a while, bearing in mind their completely crazy schedules. Still, it's only business, after all. Only a deal. It's only the deal I've been wanting to make for . . ."

"Oh . . . stop it!" I say furiously. "Stop it. Have your stupid meeting."

"Are you sure?" says Luke, putting a hand over the receiver. "Absolutely sure?"

"Quite sure," I say, giving a morose shrug. "If it's *that* important . . ."

"It's pretty important," says Luke, and meets my eyes, suddenly serious. "Believe me, I wouldn't be doing it otherwise."

I walk slowly back to the car as Luke puts away his mobile phone.

"Thanks, Becky," he says as I get in. "I mean it." He touches my cheek gently, then reaches for the keys and starts up the engine.

As we drive off toward a set of traffic lights, I glance at him, and then at his mobile phone, still sticking out of his pocket.

"Were you *really* phoning your business contact?" I say.

"Were you really going home?" he replies, without moving his head.

This is what's so annoying about going out with Luke. You can't get away with anything.

We drive for about an hour into the countryside, stop for lunch in a little village pub, then drive for another hour and a half down to Somerset. By the time we reach Blakeley Hall, I feel like a different person. It's so good to get out of London—and I'm already incredibly energized and refreshed by all this wonderful country air. As I step out of the car I do a few stretches—and honestly, I already feel fitter and more toned. I reckon if I came to the country every week, I'd lose half a stone, if not more.

"Do you want any more of these?" says Luke, reaching down and picking up the nearly empty packet of Maltesers which I've been snacking on. (I have to eat in the car, otherwise I get carsick.) "And what about these magazines?" He picks up the stack of glossies which have been at my feet, then makes a grab as they all start slithering out of his hands.

"I'm not going to read magazines here!" I say in surprise. "This is the country!"

Honestly. Doesn't Luke know anything about rural life?

As he's getting the bags out of the boot I wander over to a fence and gaze peacefully at a field full of browny-yellow stuff. You know, I reckon I have a real natural affinity for the countryside. It's like I've got this whole nurturing, earth-mother side, which has been gradually creeping up on me. For example, the other day I found myself buying a Fair Isle jersey from French Connection. And I've recently started gardening! Or at least, I've bought some sweet little ceramic flowerpots from The Pier, marked "Basil" and "Coriander"—and I'm definitely going to get some of those little plants from the supermarket and have a whole row of them on the windowsill. (I mean, they're only about 50 pence, so if they die you can just buy another one.)

"Ready?" says Luke.

"Absolutely!" I say, and teeter back toward him, cursing the mud.

We crunch over the gravel to the hotel—and I have to say, I'm impressed. It's a great big old-fashioned country house, with beautiful gardens, and modern sculptures in the gardens and its own cinema, according to the brochure! Luke's been here quite a few times before, and he says it's his favorite hotel. And lots of celebrities come here, too! Like Madonna. (Or was it Sporty Spice? Someone, anyway.) But apparently they're always very discreet and usually stay in some separate coach-housey bit, and the staff never lets on.

Still, as we go into the reception hall I have a good look around, just in case. There are lots of cool-looking people in trendy spectacles and denim, and there's a blonde girl who sort of looks famous-ish, and standing over there . . .

I freeze in excitement. It's him, isn't it? It's Elton John! Elton John himself is standing right there, only a few—

Then he turns round—and it's just a dumpy guy in an anorak and spectacles. Damn. Still, it was *nearly* Elton John.

We've reached the reception desk by now, and a concierge in a trendy Nehru jacket smiles at us. "Good afternoon, Mr. Brandon," he says. "And Miss Bloomwood. Welcome to Blakeley Hall."

He knew our names! We didn't even have to tell him! No wonder celebrities come here.

"I've put you in room 9," he says, as Luke starts to fill in a form. "Overlooking the rose garden."

"Great," says Luke. "Becky, which paper would you like in the morning?"

"The *Financial Times,*" I say smoothly.

"Of course," says Luke, writing. "So that's one *FT*—and a *Daily World* for me."

I give him a suspicious look, but his face is completely blank.

"Would you like tea in the morning?" says the concierge, tapping at his computer. "Or coffee?"

"Coffee, please," says Luke. "For both of us, I think." He looks at me questioningly, and I nod.

"You'll find a complimentary bottle of champagne in your room," says the concierge, "and room service is available twenty-four hours."

I have to say I'm very impressed. This really is a top-class place. They know your face immediately, they give you champagne—and they haven't even mentioned my Special Express parcel yet. Obviously they realize it's a matter of discretion. They realize that a girl doesn't necessarily want her boyfriend knowing about every single package that is delivered to her—and are going to wait until Luke is out of earshot until they tell me about it. *This* is why it's worth coming to a good hotel.

"If there's anything else you require, Miss Bloomwood," says the concierge, looking at me meaningfully, "please don't hesitate to let me know."

You see? Coded messages and everything.

"I will, don't worry," I say, and give him a knowing smile. "In just a moment." I flick my eyes meaningfully toward Luke, and the concierge gives me a blank stare, exactly as though he's got no idea what I'm talking about. God, these people are good!

Eventually, Luke finishes the forms and hands them back. The concierge hands him a big, old-fashioned room key, and summons a porter.

"I don't think we need any help," says Luke, with a smile, and lifts up my dinky suitcase. "I'm not exactly overburdened."

"You go on up," I say. "I just want to . . . check something. For tomorrow." I smile at Luke and after a moment, to my relief, he heads off toward the staircase.

As soon as he's out of earshot, I swivel back to the desk.

"I'll take it now," I murmur to the concierge, who has turned away and is looking in a drawer. He raises his head and looks at me in surprise.

"I'm sorry, Miss Bloomwood?"

"It's OK," I say more meaningfully. "You can give it to me now. While Luke's gone."

A flicker of apprehension passes over the concierge's face.

"What exactly—"

"You can give me my package." I lower my voice. "And thanks for not letting on."

"Your . . . package?"

"My Special Express."

"What Special Express?"

I stare at him, feeling a few misgivings.

"The parcel with all my clothes in it! The one you weren't mentioning! The one . . ."

I tail away at the sight of his face. He doesn't have a clue what I'm talking about, does he? OK. Don't panic. Someone else will know where it is.

"I should have a parcel waiting for me," I explain. "About this big . . . It should have arrived this morning . . ."

The concierge is shaking his head.

"I'm sorry, Miss Bloomwood. There aren't any packages for you."

Suddenly I feel a little hollow.

"But . . . there has to be a package. I sent it by Special Express, yesterday. To Blakeley Hall."

The concierge frowns.

"Charlotte?" he says, calling into a back room. "Has a parcel arrived for Rebecca Bloomwood?"

"No," says Charlotte, coming out. "When was it supposed to arrive?"

"This morning!" I say, trying to hide my agitation. " 'Anything, anywhere, by tomorrow morning'! I mean, this is anywhere, isn't it?"

"I'm sorry," says Charlotte, "but nothing's come. Was it very important?"

"Rebecca?" comes a voice from the stairs, and I turn to see Luke peering down at me. "Is something wrong?"

"No!" I say brightly. "Of course not! What on earth could be wrong?" Quickly I swivel away from the desk and, before Charlotte or the concierge can say anything, hurry toward the stairs.

"Everything all right?" he says as I reach him, and smiles at me.

"Absolutely!" I say, my voice two notches higher than usual. "Everything's absolutely fine!"

I have no clothes. This cannot be happening.

I'm on holiday with Luke, in a smart hotel—and I have no clothes. What am I going to do?

I can't tell him the truth. I just *can't* admit that my dinky suitcase was only the tip of the clothes-berg. Not after having been so smug about it. I'll just have to . . . improvise, I think wildly, as we turn a corner and start walking down another plushy corridor. Wear *his* clothes, like Annie Hall or . . . or rip down the curtains and find some sewing stuff . . . and quickly learn how to sew . . .

Calm down, I tell myself firmly. Just . . . calm down. The parcel is bound to arrive tomorrow morning, so I've only got to last one night. And at least I've got my makeup with me . . .

"Here we are," says Luke, stopping at a door and opening it. "What do you think?"

Oh wow. For a moment all my worries are swept away as I gaze around the enormous airy room. Now I can see why Luke likes this hotel so much. It's gorgeous—exactly like his flat, all huge white bed with an enormous waffle duvet, and a state-of-the-art music system and two suede sofas.

"Take a look at the bathroom," says Luke, and I follow him

through—and it's stunning. A great sunken mosaic Jacuzzi, with the hugest shower I've ever seen above, and a whole rack of gorgeous-looking aromatherapy oils.

Maybe I could just spend the whole weekend in the bath.

"So," he says, turning back into the room. "I don't know what you'd like to do . . ." He walks over to his suitcase and clicks it open—and I can see serried rows of shirts, all ironed by his housekeeper. "I suppose we should unpack first . . ."

"Unpack! Absolutely!" I say brightly. I walk over to my own little suitcase and finger the clasp, without opening it. "Or else . . ." I say, as though the idea's just occurring to me, "why don't we go and have a drink—and unpack later!"

Genius. We'll go downstairs and get really pissed, and then tomorrow morning I'll just pretend to be really sleepy and stay in bed until my package comes. Thank God. For a moment there I was starting to—

"Excellent idea," says Luke. "I'll just get changed." And he reaches into his case and pulls out a pair of trousers and a crisp blue shirt.

"Changed?" I say after a pause. "Is there . . . a strict dress code?"

"Oh no, not strict," says Luke. "You just wouldn't go down in . . . say, in what you're wearing at the moment." He gestures to my denim cutoffs with a grin.

"Of course not!" I say, laughing as though the idea's ridiculous. "Right. Well. I'll just . . . choose an outfit, then."

I turn to my case again, snap it open, lift the lid, and look at my makeup bag.

What am I going to do? Luke's unbuttoning his shirt. He's calmly reaching for the blue one. In a minute he's going to look up and say, "Are you ready?"

I need a radical plan of action here.

"Luke—I've changed my mind," I say, and close the lid of my case. "Let's not go down to the bar." Luke looks up in surprise, and I give him the most seductive smile I can muster. "Let's stay up here, and order room service, and . . ." I take a few steps toward him, loosening my wrap top, ". . . and see where the night leads us."

Luke stares at me, his hands still halfway up the buttons of his blue shirt.

"Take that off," I say huskily. "What's the point of dressing up when all we want to do is undress each other?"

A slow smile spreads across Luke's face, and his eyes begin to gleam.

"You're so right," he says, and walks toward me, unbuttoning his shirt and letting it fall to the floor. "I don't know what I was thinking of."

Thank God! I think in relief, as he reaches for my wrap top and gently starts to untie it. This is perfect. This is exactly what I—

Ooh. Mmm.

Actually, this *is* pretty bloody perfect.

Four

BY EIGHT THIRTY the next morning, I still haven't got up. I don't want to move an inch. I want to stay in this lovely comfortable bed, wrapped up in this gorgeous white waffle duvet.

"Are you staying there all day?" says Luke, smiling at me. "Not that I don't want to join you." He kisses me on the forehead and I snuggle down in the pillows without replying. I just don't want to get up. I'm so cozy and warm and happy here.

Plus—just a very small point—I still don't have any clothes.

I've already secretly rung down to reception three times about my Special Express. (Once while Luke was in the shower, once while I was in the shower—from the posh bathroom phone—and once very quickly when I sent Luke into the corridor because I said I heard a cat meowing.)

And it hasn't arrived. I have nil clothes. Nada.

Which hasn't mattered up until now, because I've just been lounging around in bed. But I can't possibly eat any more croissants or drink any more coffee, nor can I have another shower, and Luke's half-dressed already.

I'm just going to have to put on yesterday's clothes again. Which is really hideous, but what else can I do? I'll just pretend

I'm sentimental about them, or maybe hope I can slip them on and Luke won't even realize. I mean, do men really *notice* what you . . .

Hang on.

Hang on a minute. Where *are* yesterday's clothes? I'm sure I dropped them just there on the floor . . .

"Luke?" I say, as casually as possible. "Have you seen the clothes I was wearing yesterday?"

"Oh yes," he says, glancing up from his suitcase. "I sent them to the laundry this morning, along with my stuff."

I stare at him, unable to breathe.

My only clothes in the whole world have *gone to the laundry*?

"When . . . when will they be back?" I say at last.

"Tomorrow morning." Luke turns to look at me. "Sorry, I should have said. But it's not a problem, is it? I mean, I don't think you have to worry. They do an excellent job."

"Oh no!" I say in a high, brittle voice. "No, I'm not worried!"

"Good," he says, and smiles.

"Good," I say, and smile back.

What am I going to do?

"Oh, and there's plenty of room in the wardrobe," says Luke, "if you want me to hang anything up." He reaches toward my little case and in a panic, I hear myself crying "Nooo!" before I can stop myself. "It's all right," I add, as he looks at me in surprise. "My clothes are mostly . . . knitwear."

Oh God. Oh God. Now he's putting on his shoes. *What am I going to do?*

OK, come on, Becky, I think frantically. Clothes. Something to wear. Doesn't matter what.

One of Luke's suits?

No. He'll just think it's too weird, and anyway, his suits all cost about £1,000 so I won't be able to roll the sleeves up.

My hotel robe? Pretend robes and waffle slippers are the latest fashion? Oh, but I can't walk around in a dressing gown as if I think I'm in a spa. Everyone will laugh at me.

Come on, there *must* be clothes in a hotel. What about . . .

the chambermaids' uniforms! Yes, that's more like it! They must keep a rack of them somewhere, mustn't they? Neat little dresses with matching hats. I could tell Luke they're the latest thing from Prada—and just hope no one asks me to clear out their room . . .

"By the way," says Luke, reaching into his case, "you left this behind at my flat."

And as I look up, startled, he chucks something across the room at me. It's soft, it's fabric . . . as I catch it, I want to weep with relief. It's clothes! A single oversized Calvin Klein T-shirt, to be precise. I have never been so glad to see a plain washed-out gray T-shirt in my life.

"Thanks!" I say. And I force myself to count to ten before I add casually, "Actually, maybe I'll wear this today."

"That?" says Luke, giving me a strange look. "I thought it was a nightshirt."

"It is! It's a nightshirt-slash-dress," I say, popping it over my head—and thank God, it comes to halfway down my thighs. It could easily be a dress. And ha! I've got a stretchy black headband in my makeup bag, which just about fits me as a belt.

"Very nice," says Luke quizzically, watching me wriggle into it. "A *little* on the short side . . ."

"It's a minidress," I say firmly, and turn to look at my reflection. And . . . oh God, it is a bit short. But it's too late to do anything about that now. I step into my clementine sandals and shake back my hair, not allowing myself to think about all the great outfits I had planned for this morning.

"Here," says Luke. He reaches for my Denny and George scarf and winds it slowly round my neck. "Denny and George scarf, no knickers. Just the way I like it."

"I'm going to wear knickers!" I say indignantly.

Which is true. I'll wait till Luke's gone, then pinch a pair of his boxer shorts.

"So—what's your deal about?" I ask hurriedly, to change the subject. "Something exciting?"

"It's . . . pretty big," says Luke after a pause. He holds up a pair of silk ties. "Which one will bring me luck?"

"The red one," I say after a little consideration. "It matches your eyes."

"It matches my eyes?" Luke starts to laugh. "Do I look that rough?"

"It *goes* with your eyes. You know what I mean."

"No, you were right first time," says Luke, peering into the mirror. "It matches my eyes perfectly." He glances at me. "You'd almost think I'd had no sleep last night."

"No sleep?" I raise my eyebrows. "Before an important meeting? Surely that's not the way Luke Brandon behaves."

"Very irresponsible," agrees Luke, putting the tie round his neck. "Must be thinking of someone else."

I watch as he knots the tie with brisk, efficient movements. "So come on—tell me about this deal. Is it a big new client?"

But Luke smiles and shakes his head.

"Is it Nat West? I know, Lloyds Bank!"

"Let's just say . . . it's something I want very much," Luke says eventually. "Something I've always wanted. But this is all very boring," he adds in a different tone.

"No, it's not!"

"Very dull indeed. Now—what are you going to do today? Will you be all right?" And now he sounds like *he's* changing the subject.

Actually, I think Luke's a bit sensitive about boring me with his work. Don't get me wrong, I think his business is really fascinating. But there was this one occasion when it was really late at night, and he was telling me about a new range of technical products he was going to represent and I kind of . . . fell asleep.

I think he took it to heart, because recently he's hardly talked about work at all.

"Have you heard the pool is closed this morning?" he says.

"I know," I say, reaching for my blusher. "But that doesn't matter. I'll easily amuse myself."

There's silence and I look up to see Luke surveying me doubtfully.

"Would you like me to order you a taxi to take you to the shops? Bath is quite near here—"

"No," I say indignantly. "I don't want to go shopping!"

Which is true. When Suze found out how much those clementine sandals were, she got all worried that she hadn't been strict enough with me, so I promised not to do any shopping this weekend. She made me cross my heart and swear on—well, on my clementine sandals, actually. And I'm going to make a real effort to keep to it.

I mean, I should be able to last forty-eight hours.

"I'm going to do all lovely rural things," I say, snapping my blusher closed.

"Like . . ."

"Like look at the scenery . . . and maybe go to a farm and watch them milking the cows, or something . . ."

"I see."

"What?" I say suspiciously. "What's that supposed to mean?"

"You're just going to pitch up at a farm, are you, and ask if you can milk the cows?"

"I didn't say *I* was going to milk the cows," I say with dignity. "I said I was going to *watch* the cows. And anyway, I might not go to a farm, I might go and look at some local attractions." I reach for a pile of leaflets on the dressing table. "Like . . . this tractor exhibition. Or . . . St. Winifred's Convent with its famous Bevington Triptych."

"A convent," echoes Luke after a pause.

"Yes, a convent!" I give him an indignant look. "Why shouldn't I visit a convent? I'm actually a very spiritual person."

"I'm sure you are, my darling," says Luke, giving me a quizzical look. "You *might* want to put on more than a T-shirt before you go . . ."

"It's a dress!" I say indignantly, pulling the T-shirt down over my bum. "And anyway, spirituality has nothing to do with clothes. 'Consider the lilies of the field.' " I shoot him a satisfied glance.

"Fair enough." Luke grins. "Well, enjoy yourself." He gives me a kiss. "And Becky, I really am sorry about all this. This wasn't the way I wanted our first weekend away to be."

"Yeah, well," I say, and give him a little poke in the chest. "You just make sure this mysterious deal is worth it."

And I'm expecting Luke to laugh, or at least smile—but he just gives me a tiny nod, picks up his briefcase, and heads for the door.

I don't actually mind having this morning to myself, because I've always secretly wanted to see what it's like inside a convent. I mean, I know I don't exactly make it to church every week, but I do have a very spiritual side to me. It seems obvious to me that there's a greater force out there at work than us mere mortals—which is why I always read my horoscope in *The Daily World.* Plus I love that plainchant they play in yoga classes, and all the lovely candles and incense. And Audrey Hepburn in *The Nun's Story.*

In fact, to tell you the truth, a part of me has always been attracted to the simplicity of a nun's life. No worries, no decisions, no having to work. Just lovely singing and walking around all day. I mean, wouldn't that be great?

So when I've done my makeup and watched a bit of telly, I go down to reception—and after asking fruitlessly again about my package (honestly, I'm going to sue), I order a taxi to St. Winifred's. As we trundle along the country lanes, I look out at all the lovely scenery, and find myself wondering what Luke's deal can be about. What on earth is this mysterious "something he's always wanted"? I mean, I would have thought he's already got everything he wants. He's the most successful publicist in the financial field, he's got a thriving company, he's won loads of prizes . . . So what could it be? Big new client? New offices? Expanding the company, maybe?

I screw up my face, trying to remember if I've overheard anything recently—then, with a jolt, I remember hearing him on the phone a few weeks ago. He was talking about an advertising agency, and even at the time, I wondered why.

Yes. It's obvious, now that I think about it. He's always secretly wanted to be an ad director. That's what this deal is all about. He's going to branch out from PR and start making adverts.

And I could be in them! Yes!

I'm so excited at this thought, I almost swallow my chewing gum. I can be in an ad! Oh, this is going to be *so* cool. Maybe I'll be in one of those Bacardi ads where they're all on a boat, laughing and water-skiing and having a great time. I mean, I know it's usually fashion models, but I could easily be somewhere in the background. Or I could be the one driving the boat. It'll be so fantastic. We'll fly out to Barbados or somewhere, and it'll be all hot and sunny and glamorous, with loads of free Bacardi, and we'll stay in a really amazing hotel . . . I'll have to buy a new bikini, of course . . . or maybe two . . . and some new flip-flops . . .

"St. Winifred's," says the taxi driver—and with a start I come to. I'm not in Barbados, am I? I'm in the middle of bloody nowhere, in Somerset.

We've stopped outside an old honey-colored building, and I peer through the window curiously. So this is a convent. It doesn't look that special, actually—just like a school, or a big country house. And I'm wondering whether I should even bother getting out, when I see a nun. Walking past, in black robes, and a wimple, and everything! A real live nun, in her real habitat. And she's completely natural. She hasn't even *looked* at the taxi. This is like being on safari!

I get out and pay the driver—and as I walk toward the heavy front door, I feel prickles of intrigue. There's an elderly woman going in at the same time who seems to know the way, so I follow her along a corridor toward the chapel. And as we walk in, I feel this amazing, holy, almost euphoric sensation coming over me. Maybe it's the lovely smell in the air or the organ music, but I'm definitely getting something.

"Thank you, Sister," says the elderly woman to the nun. And she starts walking off to the front of the chapel—but I stand still, slightly transfixed.

Sister. Wow.

Sister Rebecca.

And one of those lovely flowing black habits, and a fantastic clear nun complexion all the time.

Sister Rebecca of the Holy . . .

"You look a little lost, my dear," a nun says behind me, and I jump. "Were you interested in seeing the Bevington Triptych?"

"Oh," I say. "Erm . . . yes. Absolutely."

"Up there," she points, and I walk tentatively toward the front of the chapel, hoping it will become obvious what the Bevington Triptych is. A statue, maybe? Or a . . . a piece of tapestry?

But as I reach the elderly lady, I see that she's staring up at a whole wall of stained-glass windows. And I have to admit, they're pretty amazing. I mean, look at that huge blue one in the middle. It's fantastic!

"The Bevington Triptych," says the elderly woman. "It simply has no parallel, does it?"

"Wow," I breathe reverentially, staring up with her. "It's beautiful."

And it really is stunning. It just shows, there's no mistaking a real work of art, is there? Real genius just leaps out at you. And I'm not even an expert.

"Wonderful colors," I murmur.

"The detail," says the woman, clasping her hands, "is absolutely incomparable."

"Incomparable," I echo.

And I'm just about to point out the rainbow, which I think is a really nice touch—when I suddenly notice that the elderly woman and I aren't looking at the same window. She's looking at a much smaller, dingier one which I hadn't even noticed.

As inconspicuously as possible, I shift my gaze to the right one—and feel a pang of disappointment. Is *this* the Bevington Triptych? But it isn't even pretty!

"Whereas this Victorian rubbish," the woman suddenly adds savagely, "is absolutely criminal! That rainbow! Doesn't it make you feel sick?" She gestures to my big blue window, and I gulp.

"I know," I say. "It's shocking, isn't it? Absolutely . . . You know, I think I'll just go for a little wander . . ."

Hastily I back away, before she can say any more. And I'm sidling back down the side of the pews, wondering vaguely what to do next, when suddenly I notice a little side chapel in the corner.

Spiritual retreat, reads a notice outside. *A place to sit quietly, pray, and discover more about the Catholic faith.*

Cautiously I poke my head inside the side chapel—and there's an old nun, sitting on a chair, doing embroidery. She smiles at me, and nervously I smile back and walk inside.

I sit down on a dark wooden pew, trying not to make any creaking sounds, and for a while I'm too awestruck to say anything. This is just amazing. The atmosphere is fantastic, all quiet and still—and I feel incredibly cleansed and holy just from being here. I smile again at the nun, shyly, and she puts down her embroidery and looks at me as though waiting for me to speak.

"I really like your candles," I say in a quiet, reverent voice. "Are they from Habitat?"

"No," says the nun, looking a bit startled. "I don't believe so."

"Oh right."

I give a tiny yawn—because I'm still sleepy from all this country air—and as I do so, I notice that one of my nails has chipped. So very quietly, I unzip my bag, get out my nail file, and start to buff it. The nun looks up, and I give her a rueful smile, and point to my nail (silently, because I don't want to ruin the spiritual atmosphere). Then, when I've finished, the edge is looking a bit ragged, so I take out my Maybelline express dry polish and very quickly touch it up.

All the while, the nun is watching me with a perplexed expression, and as I'm finishing, she says, "My dear, are you a Catholic?"

"No, I'm not, actually," I say.

"Was there anything you wanted to talk about?"

"Um . . . not really." I run my hand fondly over the pew I'm sitting on, and give her a friendly smile. "This carving is really nice, isn't it. Is all your furniture as nice as this?"

"This is the chapel," says the nun, giving me a strange look.

"Oh, I know! But you know, loads of people have pews in their houses, too, these days. I saw this article in *Harpers*—"

"My child . . ." The nun lifts a hand to interrupt me. "My child, this is a place of spiritual retreat. Of quietness."

"I know!" I say in surprise. "That's why I came in. For quietness."

"Good," says the nun, and we lapse into silence again.

In the distance, a bell starts tolling, and I notice the nun begins murmuring very quietly under her breath. I wonder what she's saying? My granny used to knit things, and mutter the pattern to herself. Maybe she's lost track of her embroidery.

"Your sewing's going really well," I say encouragingly. "What's it going to be?" She gives a tiny start, and puts down her embroidery.

"My dear," she says, and exhales sharply. Then she gives me a warm smile. "My dear, we have some quite famous lavender fields. Would you like to go and see them?"

"No, it's all right." I beam at her. "I'm just happy, sitting here with you."

The nun's smile wavers slightly. "What about the crypt?" she says. "Would you be interested in that?"

"Not particularly. But honestly, I'm not bored! It's just so lovely here. So . . . tranquil. Just like *The Sound of Music.*"

She stares at me as though I'm speaking gibberish, and I realize she's probably been in the convent so long, she doesn't know what *The Sound of Music* is.

"There was this film . . ." I start to explain. Then it occurs to me, maybe she doesn't know what a film is, even. "It's like, moving pictures," I say carefully. "You watch it on a screen. And there was this nun called Maria . . ."

"We have a shop," interrupts the nun urgently. "A shop. What about that?"

A shop! For a moment I feel all excited, and want to ask what they sell. But then I remember the promise I made to Suze.

"I can't," I say regretfully. "I told my flatmate I wouldn't go shopping today."

"Your flatmate?" says the nun. "What does she have to do with it?"

"She just gets really worried about me spending money—"

"Does your flatmate run your life?"

"Well, it's just I made her this quite serious promise a while ago. You know, a bit like a vow, I suppose . . ."

"She'll never know!" says the nun. "Not if you don't tell her."

I stare at her, a bit taken aback.

"But I'd feel really bad, breaking my promise! No, I'll just stay here with you for a bit longer, if that's OK." I pick up a little statue of Mary which has caught my eye. "This is nice. Where did you get it?"

The nun stares at me, her eyes narrowing.

"Don't think of it as shopping," she says at last. "Think of it as making a donation." She leans forward. "You donate the money—and we give you a little something in return. You couldn't really count it as shopping at all. More . . . an act of charity."

I'm silent for a few moments, letting this idea sink in. The truth is, I do always mean to do more for charity, and maybe this is my chance.

"So, it'll be like doing a good deed?" I say, just to be sure.

"Exactly the same. And Jesus and all his angels will bless you for it." She takes hold of my arm. "Now, you go along and have a browse. Come on, I'll show you the way . . ."

As we leave the side chapel, the nun shuts the door and takes down the Spiritual Retreat notice.

"Aren't you coming back?" I say in surprise.

"Not today, no," she says, and gives me an odd look. "I think I'll leave it for today."

You know, it's just like they say—virtue is its own reward. As I arrive back at the hotel later that afternoon, I'm glowing with happiness at all the good I've done. I must have donated at least £50 in that shop, if not more! In fact, not to show off or anything, but I'm obviously naturally very altruistic. Because once I started donating, I couldn't stop! Each time I parted with a bit more money, I felt a real high. And although it's a completely incidental point, I ended up with some really nice stuff in return. Lots of lavender honey, and lavender essential oil, and some lavender tea, which I'm sure will be delicious, and a lavender pillow to help me sleep.

The amazing thing is, I'd never really given lavender much thought before. I just thought of it as a plant in people's gardens. But that young nun behind the table was quite right—it has such vital, life-enhancing properties that it should be part of everyone's life. Plus St. Winifred's lavender is completely organic, she explained, so it's vastly superior to other varieties, but the prices are much lower than many competing mail-order catalogues. She was the one who persuaded me to buy the lavender pillow, actually, and to put my name on the mailing list. She was really quite persistent, for a nun.

When I get back to Blakeley Hall, the minicab driver offers to help me lug it all in, because the box of lavender honey is quite heavy. And I'm standing at the reception desk, giving him a nice hefty tip and thinking I might go and have a nice bath with my new lavender bath essence . . . when the front door into reception swings open. Into the hotel strides a girl with blond hair, a Louis Vuitton bag, and long tanned legs.

I stare at her in disbelief. It's Alicia Billington. Or, as I call her, Alicia Bitch Longlegs. What's *she* doing here?

Alicia is one of the account executives in Brandon Communications—which is Luke's PR company—and we've never exactly got along. In fact, between you and me, she's a bit of a cow and, secretly, I wish Luke would fire her. A few months ago, actually, she nearly did get fired—and it was kind of to do with me. (I was a financial journalist then, and I wrote this piece . . . oh, it's a bit of a long story.) But in the end she just got a stiff warning, and since then, she's really pulled her socks up.

I know all this because I have little chats every now and then with Luke's assistant, Mel, who's a real sweetie and keeps me up on all the gossip. She was telling me only the other day that she reckons Alicia's really changed. She isn't any *nicer,* but she certainly works harder. She badgers journalists until they put her clients into their stories, and often stays really late at the office, tapping at her computer. And only the other day she told Mel she wanted a full list of all the company's clients, with contact names, so she could familiarize herself with them. Plus she wrote some company strategy report which Luke was really impressed by. Mel added gloomily that she reckons Alicia wants a promotion—and I think she could be right.

The trouble with Luke is, he only looks at how hard a person works and what results they get—and not at what a completely horrible cow they are. In fact, just the other day I heard him telling someone how reliable Alicia was in stressful situations and how he's really starting to depend on her. So the chances are, she probably will get a promotion—and become even more unbearable.

As I watch her come in, I'm slightly transfixed. Half of me wants to run away and half of me wants to know what she's doing here. But before I can decide, she spots me, and raises her eyebrows slightly. And oh God, suddenly I realize what I must look like—in a grotty old gray T-shirt that, to be honest, looks nothing like a dress, and my hair a mess, and my face all red from lugging carrier bags full of lavender honey. And she's in an immaculate white suit.

"Rebecca!" she says, and puts her hand over her mouth in mock dismay. "You're not supposed to know I'm here! Just pretend you haven't seen me."

"What . . . what do you mean?" I say, trying not to sound as disconcerted as I feel. "What *are* you doing here?"

"I've just popped in for a quick introductory meeting with the new associates," says Alicia. "You know my parents only live five miles away? So it made sense."

"Oh right," I say. "No, I didn't."

"But Luke's given us all *strict* instructions," says Alicia, "we're not allowed to bother you. After all, this is your holiday!"

And there's something about the way she says it that makes me feel like a child.

"Oh, I don't mind," I say robustly. "When something as . . .

as important as this is going on. In fact, Luke and I were talking about it earlier on actually. Over breakfast."

OK, so I only mentioned breakfast to remind her that Luke and I are going out together. Which I *know* is really pathetic. But somehow, whenever I'm talking to Alicia, I feel we're in some secret little competition, and if I don't fight back, she'll think she's won.

"Really?" says Alicia. "How sweet." Her eyes narrow slightly. "So—what do you think of this whole enterprise? You must have an opinion."

"I think it's great," I say after a pause. "Really great."

"You don't mind?" Her eyes are probing my face.

"Well . . . not really." I shrug. "I mean, it was supposed to be a holiday, but if it's that important—"

"I don't mean the meetings!" says Alicia, laughing a little. "I mean—this whole deal. The whole New York thing."

I open my mouth to reply—then feebly close it again. What New York thing?

And like a buzzard sensing weakness, she leans forward, a tiny, malicious smile at her lips. "You do *know,* don't you, Rebecca, that Luke's going to move to New York?"

I can't move for shock. That's what he's so excited about. Luke's moving to New York. But . . . but why hasn't he told me?

My face feels rather hot and there's a horrible thickening in my chest. He's going to New York and he hasn't even told me.

"Rebecca?"

My head jerks up, and I quickly force a smile onto my face. I can't let Alicia realize this is all news to me. I just *can't.*

"Of course I know about it," I say huskily, and clear my throat. "I know all about it. But I . . . I never discuss business in public. Much better to be discreet, don't you think?"

"Oh, absolutely," she answers—and the way she looks at me makes me think she isn't convinced for a minute. "So . . . will you be going out there too?"

I stare back, my lips trembling, unable to think of an answer, my face growing pinker and pinker—when suddenly, thank God, a voice behind me says, "Rebecca Bloomwood. Parcel for a Miss Rebecca Bloomwood."

My head jerks round in astonishment, and, I don't believe it. A man in uniform is approaching the desk, holding my huge, battered Special Express parcel, which I'd honestly given up for lost. All my things, at last. All my carefully chosen outfits. I can wear anything I like tonight!

But somehow . . . I don't really care anymore. I just want to go off somewhere and be on my own and think for a bit.

"That's me," I say, managing a smile. "I'm Rebecca Bloomwood."

"Oh right!" says the man. "That's nice and easy then. If you could just sign here . . ."

"Well, I mustn't keep you!" exclaims Alicia, eyeing my parcel amusedly. "Enjoy the rest of your stay, won't you?"

"Thanks," I reply. "I will." And, feeling slightly numb, I walk away, clutching my clothes tightly to me.

I go up to our room, dump the parcel on the bed, and sit down next to it, trying to keep perspective on this. OK, let's just go over the facts. Luke's making plans to move to New York. And he hasn't told me.

Yet. He hasn't told me *yet.*

As I think this through, my numbness starts to melt away. Of course. He's probably planning to tell me everything this evening. Waiting for the right moment. That's probably why he brought me here in the first place. He couldn't know that Alicia would stick her oar in, could he?

Feeling better already, I reach for a complimentary packet of biscuits, tear it open, and begin to munch one. It's like they say, don't run before you can walk. Don't cross bridges before you come to them. Don't do . . . that other thing you shouldn't do.

I've just finished my third biscuit and have switched on the television to watch *Ready Steady Cook,* when the door opens and

Luke comes in. His eyes are sparkling and he seems full of a suppressed energy. I stare at him, feeling a little weird.

I'm sure he's going to tell me. He wouldn't just move to America without saying anything.

"Did your meetings go well?" I say, my voice feeling false.

"Very well, thanks," says Luke, taking off his tie and throwing it on the bed. "But let's not talk about that." He smiles at me. "Did you have a good day?"

"Fine, thanks!"

"You want to go for a walk? Come on. I haven't seen you all day." He reaches for my hand, pulls me up off the bed, and puts his arms round my waist. "I've missed you," he says against my hair, and his arms tighten around my body.

"Have you?" I give a little laugh. "Well, you know . . . perhaps I should come to your meetings, and hear what they're all about!"

"You wouldn't enjoy them," says Luke, returning my laugh. "Come on, let's go out."

We head down the stairs and out of the heavy front door and start walking over the grass toward a group of trees. The sun is still warm, and some people are playing croquet and drinking Pimms. After a while I take off my sandals and walk along barefoot, feeling myself relax.

"Are you hungry?" says Luke casually as we get near a large oak tree. And I'm about to reply, "No, I've just had three biscuits," when I see it, waiting for us in the long grass.

A red-and-white checked picnic blanket. A little wicker hamper. And . . . is that a bottle of champagne? I turn toward Luke in disbelief.

"Is this . . . did you . . ."

"This," says Luke, touching my cheek, "is in some small way to make up. You've been so incredibly understanding, Becky."

"That's all right," I say awkwardly. "If it was for something as important as . . ." I hesitate. "As . . . well, whatever amazing opportunity this might be . . ."

I look at Luke expectantly. This is the perfect moment for him to tell me.

"Even so," says Luke. He moves away and reaches for the champagne bottle and I sit down, trying not to give away my disappointment.

I'm not going to ask him. If he wants to tell me he can. If he doesn't want to . . . then he must have his reasons.

But there's no harm in prompting him, is there?

"I love the countryside!" I exclaim as Luke hands me my champagne. "And I love cities, too." I gesture vaguely in the air. "London . . . Paris . . ."

"Cheers," says Luke, raising his glass.

"Cheers." I take a sip of champagne and think quickly. "So . . . um . . . you've never really told me much about your family."

Luke looks up, a bit surprised.

"Haven't I? Well, there's me and my sister . . . and Mum and Dad . . ."

"And your real mother, of course." Casual, Becky. Casual. "I've always thought she sounds really interesting."

"She's a truly inspiring person," says Luke, his face lighting up. "So elegant . . . you've seen the picture of her?"

"She looks beautiful," I nod encouragingly. "And where is it she lives again?" I wrinkle my brow as though I can't quite remember.

"New York," says Luke, and takes a swig of his drink.

There's a taut silence. Luke stares ahead, frowning slightly, and I watch him, my heart thumping. Then he turns to me, and I feel a spasm of fright. What's he going to say? Is he going to tell me he's moving thousands of miles away?

"Becky?"

"Yes?" I say, my voice half-strangled by nerves.

"I really think you and my mother would love each other. Next time she's in London, I'll be sure to introduce you."

"Oh . . . right," I say. "That would be really great." And morosely, I drain my glass.

· ENDWICH BANK ·

FULHAM BRANCH
3 Fulham Road
London SW6 9JH

Ms. Rebecca Bloomwood
Flat 2
4 Burney Rd.
London SW6 8FD

8 September 2000

Dear Ms. Bloomwood:

Thank you for your letter of 4 September, addressed to Sweetie Smeathie, in which you ask him to rush through an extension of your overdraft "before the new guy arrives."

I am the new guy.

I am currently reviewing all customer files and will be in touch regarding your request.

Yours sincerely,

John Gavin
Overdraft Facilities Director

• ENDWICH—BECAUSE WE CARE •

Five

We arrive back in London the next day—and Luke still hasn't mentioned his deal or New York, or anything. And I know I should just ask him outright. I should casually say, "So what's this I hear about New York, Luke?" and wait and see what he says. But somehow I can't bring myself to do it.

I mean, for a start, he's made it plain enough that he doesn't want to talk about it. If I confront him, he might think I've been trying to find out stuff behind his back. And for another start, Alicia might have got it wrong—or even be making it up. (She's quite capable of it, believe me. When I was a financial journalist she once sent me to the completely wrong room for a press conference—and I'm sure it was deliberate.) So until I'm absolutely certain of my facts, there's no point saying anything.

At least, this is what I tell myself. But I suppose if I'm really honest, the reason is that I just can't bear the idea of Luke turning to me and giving me a kind look and saying, "Rebecca, we've had a lot of fun, but . . ."

So I end up saying nothing and smiling a lot—even though inside, I feel more and more miserable. As we arrive back outside my flat, I want to turn to him and wail, "Are you going to New York? Are you?"

But instead, I give him a kiss, and say lightly, "You will be OK for Saturday, won't you?"

It turns out Luke's got to fly off to Zurich tomorrow and have lots of meetings with finance people. Which of course is very important and I completely understand that. But Saturday is Tom and Lucy's wedding at home, and that's even more important. He just *has* to be there.

"I'll make it," he says. "I promise." He squeezes my hand and I get out of the car and he says he has to shoot off. And then he's gone.

Disconsolately, I open the door to our flat, and a moment later Suze comes out of the door of her room, dragging a full black bin liner along the ground.

"Hi!" she says. "You're back!"

"Yes!" I reply, trying to sound cheerful. "I'm back!"

Suze disappears out of our door, and I hear her lugging her black bag down the stairs and out of the main front door—then bounding up to our flat again.

"So, how was it?" she says breathlessly, closing the door behind her.

"It was fine," I say, walking into my bedroom. "It was . . . nice."

"Nice?" Suze's eyes narrow and she follows me in. "Only nice?"

"It was . . . good."

"*Good?* Bex, what's wrong? Didn't you have a lovely time?"

I wasn't really planning to say anything to Suze, because after all, I don't know the facts yet. Plus I read in a magazine recently that couples should try to sort their problems out alone, without recourse to others. But as I look at her warm, friendly face, I just can't help it, I hear myself blurting out, "Luke's moving to New York."

"Really?" says Suze, missing the point. "Fantastic! God, I love New York. I went there three years ago, and—"

"Suze, he's moving to New York—but he hasn't told me."

"Oh," says Suze, looking taken aback. "Oh, right."

"And I don't want to bring it up, because I'm not supposed

to know, but I keep thinking, why hasn't he told me? Is he just going to . . . *go*?" My voice is rising in distress. "Will I just get a postcard from the Empire State Building saying, 'Hi, I live in New York now, love Luke'?"

"No!" says Suze at once. "Of course not! He wouldn't do that!"

"Wouldn't he?"

"No. Definitely not." Suze folds her arms and thinks for a few moments—then looks up. "Are you absolutely sure he hasn't told you? Like, maybe when you were half asleep or daydreaming or something?"

She looks at me expectantly and for a few moments I think hard, wondering if she could be right. Maybe he told me in the car and I just wasn't listening. Or last night, while I was eyeing up that girl's Lulu Guinness handbag in the bar . . . But then I shake my head.

"No. I'm sure I'd remember if he'd mentioned New York." I sink down miserably onto the bed. "He's just not telling me because he's going to chuck me."

"No, he's not!" retorts Suze. "Honestly, Bex, men never mention things. That's just what they're like." She picks her way over a pile of CDs and sits cross-legged on the bed beside me. "My brother never mentioned when he got done for drugs. We had to find it out from the paper! And my father once bought a whole island without telling my mother."

"Really?"

"Oh yes! And then he forgot about it, too. And he only remembered when he got this letter out of the blue inviting him to roll the pig in the barrel."

"To do *what*?"

"Oh, this ancient ceremony thing," says Suze vaguely. "My dad gets to roll the first pig, because he owns the island." Her eyes suddenly brighten. "In fact, he's always looking for people to do it instead of him. I don't suppose you fancy doing it this year, do you? You get to wear this funny hat, and you have to learn a poem in Gaelic, but it's quite easy . . ."

"Suze—"

"Maybe not," says Suze hurriedly. "Sorry." She leans back on my pillow and chews a fingernail thoughtfully. Then suddenly she looks up. "Hang on a minute. Who told you about New York? If it wasn't Luke?"

"Alicia," I say gloomily. "She knew all about it."

"Alicia?" Suze stares at me. "Alicia Bitch Longlegs? Oh, for goodness' sake. She's probably making it up. Honestly, Bex, I'm surprised you even listened!"

And she sounds so sure that I feel my heart giving a joyful leap. Of course. That must be the answer. Didn't I suspect it myself? Didn't I tell you what Alicia was like?

The only thing—tiny niggle—is I'm not sure Suze is completely 100 percent unbiased here. There's a bit of history between Suze and Alicia, which is that they both started working at Brandon Communications at the same time—but Suze got the sack after three weeks and Alicia went on to have a high-flying career. Not that Suze really wanted to be a PR girl, but still.

"I don't know," I say doubtfully. "Would Alicia really do that?"

"Of course she would!" says Suze. "She's just trying to wind you up. Come on, Bex, who do you trust more? Alicia or Luke?"

"Luke," I say after a pause. "Luke, of course."

"Well, then!"

"You're right," I say, suddenly feeling more cheerful. "You're right! I should just trust him, shouldn't I? I shouldn't listen to gossip and rumors!"

"Exactly. Here are your letters. And your messages."

"Ooh, thanks!" I say, and take the bundle with a little pang of excited hope. Because you never know, do you, what might have happened while you're away? Maybe one of these envelopes is a letter from a long-lost friend, or an exciting job offer, or news that I've won a holiday!

But of course, they aren't. It's just one boring old bill after another, which I leaf through dismissively before dropping the whole lot to the floor without even opening them.

You know, this always happens. Whenever I go away, I always think I'll come back to mountains of exciting post, with parcels and telegrams and letters full of scintillating news—and I'm always disappointed. In fact, I really think someone should set up a company called holidaypost.com which you would pay to write you loads of exciting letters, just so you had *something* to look forward to when you got home.

I turn to my phone messages—and Suze has written them down really conscientiously:

Your mum—what are you wearing to Tom and Lucy's wedding?
Your mum—don't wear violet as it will clash with her hat.
Your mum—Luke does know it's morning dress?
Your mum—Luke *is* definitely coming, isn't he?
David Barrow—please could you ring him.
Your mum—

Hang on. David Barrow. Who's that?

"Hey, Suze!" I yell. "Did David Barrow say who he was?"

"No," says Suze, appearing in the hall. "He just said could you ring him."

"Oh right." I look at the message, feeling faintly intrigued. "What did he sound like?" Suze screws up her nose.

"Oh, you know. Quite posh. Quite . . . smooth."

I'm a little excited as I dial the number. David Barrow. It sounds almost familiar. Maybe he's a film producer or something!

"David Barrow," comes his voice—and Suze is right, he is quite posh.

"Hello!" I say. "This is Rebecca Bloomwood. I had a message to call you."

"Ah, Miss Bloomwood! I'm the special customer manager of La Rosa."

"Oh." I screw up my face puzzledly. La Rosa? What on earth's—

Oh yes. That trendy boutique in Hampstead. But I've only been in there about once, and that was ages ago. So why is he calling me?

"May I say, first, what an honor it is to have a television personality of your caliber as one of our customers."

"Oh! Well—thank you!" I say, beaming at the phone. "It's a pleasure, actually."

This is great. I know exactly why he's calling. They're going to give me some free clothes, aren't they? Or maybe . . . yes! They want me to design a new line for them! God, yes. I'll be a designer. They'll call it the Becky Bloomwood collection. Simple, stylish, wearable garments, with maybe one or two evening dresses . . .

"This is simply a courtesy call," says David Barrow, interrupting my thoughts. "I just want to ensure that you are completely happy with our service and ask if you have any other needs we can help you with."

"Well—thanks!" I say. "I'm very happy, thanks! I mean, I'm not exactly a regular customer but—"

"Also to mention the small matter of your outstanding La Rosa Card account," adds David Barrow as though I haven't spoken. "And to inform you that if payment is not received within seven days, further action will have to be taken."

I stare at the phone, feeling my smile fade. This isn't a courtesy call at all, is it? He doesn't want me to design a collection of clothes. He's phoning about money!

I feel slightly outraged. Surely people aren't just allowed to telephone you in your own home and demand money with no warning? I mean, *obviously* I'm going to pay them. Just because I don't send a check off the moment the bill comes through the letter box . . .

"It has been three months now since your first bill," David Barrow is saying. "And I must inform you that our policy after the three-month period is to hand over all outstanding accounts to—"

"Yes, well," I interrupt coolly. "My . . . accountants are dealing with all my bills at the moment. I'll speak to them."

"I'm so glad to hear it. And of course, we look forward to seeing you again in La Rosa very soon!"

"Yeah, well," I say grumpily. "Maybe."

I put the phone down as Suze comes past the door again, dragging another black bin bag. "Suze, what *are* you doing?" I say, staring at her.

"I'm decluttering!" she says. "It's brilliant. So cleansing! You should try it! So—who was David Barrow?"

"Just some stupid bill I hadn't paid," I say. "Honestly! Phoning me at home!"

"Ooh, that reminds me. Hang on . . ."

She disappears for a moment, then appears again, holding a bundle of envelopes.

"I found these under my bed when I was tidying up, and this other lot were on my dressing table . . . I think you must have left them in my room." She pulls a face. "I think they're all bills, too."

"Oh, thanks," I say, and throw them onto the bed.

"Maybe . . ." says Suze hesitantly, "maybe you should pay some of them off? You know. Just one or two."

"But I have paid them off!" I say in surprise. "I paid them all off in June. Don't you remember?"

"Oh yes!" says Suze. "Yes, of course I do." She bites her lip. "But the thing is, Bex . . ."

"What?"

"Well . . . that was a while ago, wasn't it? And maybe you've built up a few debts since then."

"Since *June*?" I give a little laugh. "But that was only about five minutes ago! Honestly, Suze, you don't need to worry. I mean . . . take this one." I reach randomly for an envelope. "I mean, what have I bought in M&S recently? Nothing!"

"Oh right," says Suze, looking relieved. "So this bill will just be for . . . zero, will it."

"Absolutely," I say ripping it open. "Zero! Or, you know, ten quid. You know, for the odd pair of knickers—"

I pull out the account and look at it. For a moment I can't speak.

"How much is it?" says Suze in alarm.

"It's . . . it's wrong," I say, trying to stuff it back in the envelope. "It has to be wrong. I'll write them a letter . . ."

"Let me see." Suze grabs the bill and her eyes widen. "Three hundred sixty-five pounds? Bex—"

"It has to be wrong," I say—but my voice is holding less conviction. I'm suddenly remembering those leather trousers I bought in the Marble Arch sale. And that dressing gown. And that phase I went through of eating M&S sushi every day.

Suze stares at me for a few minutes, her face creased anxiously.

"Bex—d'you think all of these other bills are as high as that?"

Silently I reach for the envelope from Selfridges, and tear it open. Even as I do so, I'm remembering that chrome juicer, the one I saw and *had* to have . . . I've never even used it. And that fur-trimmed dress. Where did that go?

"How much is it?"

"It's . . . it's enough," I reply, pushing it quickly back inside, before she can see that it's well over £400.

I turn away, trying to keep calm. But I feel alarmed and slightly angry. This is all wrong. The whole point is, I paid off my cards. I *paid them off*. I mean, what's the point of paying off all your credit cards if they all just go and sprout huge new debts again? What is the point?

"Look, Bex, don't worry," says Suze. "You'll be OK! I just won't cash your rent check this month."

"No!" I exclaim. "Don't be silly. You've been good enough to me already! I don't want to owe you anything. I'd rather owe M&S." I look round and see her anxious face. "Suze, don't *worry*! I can easily put this lot off for a bit." I hit the letter. "And meanwhile, I'll get a bigger overdraft or something. In fact, I've just asked the bank for an extension—so I can easily ask for a bit more. In fact, I'll phone them right now!"

"What, this minute?"

"Why not?"

I pick up the phone again, reach for an old bank statement, and dial the Endwich number.

"You see, there really isn't a problem," I say reassuringly. "One little phone call is all it'll take."

"Your call is being transferred to the Central Endwich Call Center," comes a tinny voice down the line. "Kindly memorize the following number for future use: 0800 . . ."

"What's going on?" says Suze.

"I'm being transferred to some central system," I say, as Vivaldi's *Four Seasons* starts to play. "They'll probably be really quick and efficient. This is great, isn't it? Doing it all over the phone."

"Welcome to Endwich Bank!" says a new woman's voice in my ear. "Please key in your account number."

What's my account number? Shit! I've got no idea—

Oh yes. On my bank statement.

"Thank you!" says a voice as I finish pressing the numbers. "Now please key in your personal identification number."

What?

Personal identification number? I didn't know I had a personal identification number. Honestly! They never told me—

Actually . . . maybe that does ring a slight bell.

Oh God. What was it again? Seventy-three-something? Thirty-seven-something?

"Please key in your personal identification number," repeats the voice pleasantly.

"But I don't *know* my bloody personal identification number!" I say. "Quick, Suze, if you were me, what would you choose as a personal identification number?"

"Ooh!" says Suze. "Um . . . I'd choose . . . um . . . 1234?"

"Please key in your personal identification number," says the voice, with a definite edge to it this time.

God, this is really stressful.

"Try my number for my bicycle lock," suggests Suze. "It's 435."

"Suze—I need *my* number. Not yours."

"You might have chosen the same! You never know!"

"Please key in—"

"All right!" I yell, and punch in 435.

"I'm sorry," intones the voice. "This password is invalid."

"I knew it wouldn't work!"

"It might have done!" says Suze defensively.

"It should be four digits, anyway," I say, having a sudden flash of memory. "I had to phone up and register it . . . and I was standing in the kitchen . . . and . . . yes! Yes! I'd just got my new Karen Millen shoes, and I was looking at the price tag . . . and that was the number I used!"

"How much were they?" says Suze in excitement.

"They were . . . £120 reduced to . . . to £84.99!"

"Punch it in! 8499!"

Excitedly I punch in 8499—and to my disbelief, the voice says, "Thank you! You are through to the Endwich Banking Corporation. Endwich—because we care. For debt control, press one. For mortgage arrears, press two. For overdrafts and bank charges, press three. For . . ."

"Right! I'm through." I exhale sharply, feeling a bit like James Bond breaking the code to save the world. "Am I debt control? Or overdrafts and bank charges?"

"Overdrafts and bank charges," says Suze knowledgeably.

"OK." I press three and a moment later a cheerful singsong voice greets me.

"Hello! Welcome to the Endwich Central Call Center. I'm Dawna, how can I help you, Miss Bloomwood?"

"Oh, hi!" I say, taken aback. "Are you real?"

"Yes!" says Dawna, and laughs. "I'm real. Can I help you?"

"Erm . . . yes. I'm phoning because I need an extension to my overdraft. A few hundred pounds if that's all right. Or, you know, more, if you've got it . . ."

"I see," says Dawna pleasantly. "Was there a specific reason? Or just a general need?"

She sounds so nice and friendly, I feel myself start to relax.

"Well, the thing is, I've had to invest quite a bit in my career recently, and a few bills have come in, and kind of . . . taken me by surprise."

"Oh right," says Dawna sympathetically.

"I mean, it's not as if I'm in *trouble.* It's just a temporary thing."

"A temporary thing," she echoes, and I hear her typing in the background.

"I suppose I have been letting things mount up a bit. But the thing was, I paid everything off! I thought I'd be able to relax for a bit!"

"Oh right."

"So you understand?" I give a relieved beam to Suze, who offers me thumbs-up in return. This is more like it. Just one quick and easy call, like in the adverts. No nasty letters, no tricky questions . . .

"I completely understand," Dawna's saying. "It happens to us all, doesn't it?"

"So—can I have the overdraft?" I say joyfully.

"Oh, I'm not authorized to extend your overdraft by more than £50," says Dawna in surprise. "You'll have to get in touch with your branch overdraft facilities director. Who is a . . . let me see . . . Fulham . . . a Mr. John Gavin."

I stare at the phone in dismay.

"But I've already written to him!"

"Well, that's all right, then, isn't it? Now, is there anything else I can help you with?"

"No," I say. "No, I don't think so. Thanks anyway."

I put down the phone disconsolately.

"Stupid bank. Stupid call center."

"So are they going to give you the money?" asks Suze.

"I don't know. It all depends on this John Gavin bloke." I look up and see Suze's anxious face. "But I'm sure he'll say yes," I add hastily. "He's just got to review my file. It'll be fine!"

"I suppose if you just don't spend anything for a while, you'll easily get back on track, won't you?" she says hopefully. "I mean, you're making loads of money from the telly, aren't you?"

"Yes," I say after a pause, not liking to tell her that after rent, taxi fares, meals out, and outfits for the show, it doesn't actually amount to that much.

"And there's your book, too . . ."

"My book?"

For a moment I stare at her blankly. Then suddenly, with a lift of the heart, I remember. Of course! My self-help book! I've been meaning to do something about that.

Well, thank God. This is the answer. All I have to do is write my book really quickly and get a nice big check—and then I'll pay all these cards off and everything will be happy again. Ha. I don't need any stupid overdraft. I'll start straight away. This evening!

And the truth is, I'm rather looking forward to getting down to my book. I have so many important themes I want to address in it, like poverty and wealth, comparative religion, philosophy maybe. I mean, I know the publishers have just asked for a simple self-help book, but there's no reason why I can't encompass broader questions too, is there?

In fact, if it does really well, I might give lectures. God, that would be great, wouldn't it? I could become a kind of lifestyle guru and tour the world, and people would flock to see me, and ask my advice on all sorts of issues—

"How's it going?" says Suze, appearing at my door in a towel, and I jump guiltily. I've been sitting at my computer for quite a while now but I haven't actually turned it on.

"I'm just thinking," I say, hastily reaching to the back of the computer and flipping the switch. "You know, focusing my thoughts and . . . and letting the creative juices meld into a coherent pattern."

"Wow," says Suze, and looks at me in slight awe. "That's amazing. Is it hard?"

"Not really," I say, after a bit of thought. "It's quite easy, actually."

The computer suddenly bursts into a riot of sound and color, and we both stare at it, mesmerized.

"Wow!" says Suze again. "Did you do that?"

"Erm . . . yes," I say. Which is true. I mean, I did switch it on.

"God, you're so clever, Bex," breathes Suze. "When do you think you'll finish it?"

"Oh, quite soon, I expect," I say breezily. "You know. Once I get going."

"Well, I'll leave you to get on with it, then," says Suze. "I just wanted to borrow a dress for tonight."

"Oh right," I say, with interest. "Where are you going?"

"Venetia's party," says Suze. "D'you want to come too? Oh, go on, come! Everyone's going!"

For a moment I'm tempted. I've met Venetia a few times, and I know she gives amazing parties at her parents' house in Kensington.

"No," I say at last. "I'd better not. I've got work to do."

"Oh well." Suze's face droops briefly. "But I can borrow a dress, can I?"

"Of course!" I screw up my face for a moment, thinking hard. "Why don't you wear my new Tocca dress with your red shoes and my English Eccentrics wrap?"

"Excellent!" says Suze, going to my wardrobe. "Thanks, Bex. And . . . could I borrow some knickers?" she adds casually. "And some tights and makeup?"

I turn in my chair and give her a close look.

"Suze—when you decluttered your room, did you keep *anything*?"

"Of course I did!" she says, a little defensively. "You know. A few things." She meets my gaze. "OK, perhaps I went a bit too far."

"Do you have *any* underwear left?"

"Well . . . no. But you know, I feel so good, and kind of positive about life—it doesn't matter! It's feng shui. You should try it!"

I watch as Suze gathers up the dress and underwear and rifles through my makeup bag. Then she leaves the room and I stretch my arms out in front of me, flexing my fingers. Right. To work.

I open a file, type "Chapter One," and stare at it proudly.

Chapter One! This is so cool! Now all I have to do is come up with a really memorable, striking opening sentence.

I sit quite still for a while, concentrating on the empty screen in front of me, then type briskly,

Finance is the

I stop, and take a sip of Diet Coke. Obviously the right sentence takes a bit of honing. You can't just expect it to land straight in your head.

Finance is the most

God, I wish I were writing a book about clothes. Or makeup. *Becky Bloomwood's Guide to Lipstick.*

Anyway, I'm not. So concentrate.

Finance is something which

You know, my chair's quite uncomfortable. I'm sure it can't be healthy, sitting on a squashy chair like this for hours on end. I'll get repetitive strain injury, or something. Really, if I'm going to be a writer, I should invest in one of those ergonomic ones which swivel round and go up and down.

Finance is very

Maybe they sell chairs like that on the Internet. Maybe I should just have a quick little look. Since the computer's on, and everything.

In fact—surely it would be irresponsible of me if I didn't. I mean, you have to look after yourself, don't you? *Mens sana in healthy sana,* or whatever it is.

I reach for my mouse, quickly click onto the Internet icon, and search for "office chairs"—and soon I'm coasting happily through the list. And I've already noted down a few good possibilities—when all of a sudden I land on this incredible Web site which I've never seen before, all full of office supplies. Not just boring white envelopes, but really amazing high-tech stuff. Like smart chrome filing cabinets, and cool pen holders, and really nice personalized nameplates to put on your door.

I scroll through all the photographs, utterly mesmerized. I mean, I know I'm not supposed to be spending money at the moment—but this is different. This is investment in my career. After all—this is my office, isn't it? It should be well equipped. It *needs* to be well equipped. In fact, I can't believe how short-sighted I've been. How on earth was I expecting to write a book without the necessary equipment? It would be like climbing Everest without a tent.

I'm so dazzled by the array of stuff you can get that I almost can't decide what to get. But there are a few essentials which I absolutely must buy.

So I click on an ergonomic swivel chair upholstered in purple to match my iMac, plus a Dictaphone which translates stuff straight into your computer. And then I find myself adding a really cool steel claw which holds up notes while you're typing, a set of laminated presentation folders—which are bound to come in useful—and a mini paper shredder. Which is a complete essential because I don't want the whole world seeing my first drafts, do I? And I'm toying with the idea of some modular reception furniture—except I don't really have a reception area in my bedroom—when Suze comes back into the room.

"Hi! How's it going?"

I jump guiltily, quickly click on "send" without even bothering to check what the final amount was, click off the Internet—and look up just as my Chapter One reappears on the screen.

"You're working really hard!" says Suze, shaking her head. "You should take a break. How much have you done?"

"Oh . . . quite a lot," I say.

"Can I read it?" And to my horror she starts coming toward me.

"No!" I exclaim. "I mean—it's a work in progress. It's . . .

sensitive material." Hastily I close the document and stand up. "You look really great, Suze. Fantastic!"

"Thanks!" She beams at me and twirls around in my dress as the doorbell rings. "Ooh! That'll be Fenny."

Fenella is one of Suze's weird posh cousins from Scotland. Except to be fair, she's not actually that weird anymore. She used to be as peculiar as her brother, Tarquin, and spend the whole time riding horses and shooting fish, or whatever they do. But recently she's moved to London and got a job in an art gallery, and now she just goes to parties instead. As Suze opens the front door I can hear her high-pitched voice—and a whole gaggle of girls' voices following her. Fenny can't move three feet without a huge cloud of shrieking people around her. She's like some socialite version of a rain god.

"Hi!" she says, bursting into my room. She's wearing a really nice pink velvet skirt from Whistles, which I've also got—but she's teamed it with a disastrous brown Lurex polo neck. "Hi, Becky! Are you coming tonight?"

"Not tonight," I say. "I've got to work."

"Oh well." Fenella's face droops just like Suze's did—then brightens. "Then can I borrow your Jimmy Choos? We've got the same size feet, haven't we?"

"OK," I say. "They're in the wardrobe." I hesitate, trying to be tactful. "And do you want to borrow a top? It's just I've actually got the top that goes with your skirt. Pink cashmere with little beads. Really nice."

"Have you?" says Fenny. "Ooh, yes! I shoved on this polo neck without really thinking." As she peels it off, a blond girl in a black shift comes in and beams at me.

"Hi, er . . . Milla," I say, remembering her name just in time. "How are you?"

"I'm fine!" she says, and gives me a hopeful look. "Fenny said I could borrow your English Eccentrics wrap."

"I'm lending it to Suze," I say, pulling a regretful face. "But what about . . . a purple shawl with sequins?"

"Yes, please! And Binky says, have you still got that black wraparound skirt?"

"I have," I say thoughtfully. "But actually, I've got another skirt I think would look even better on her . . ."

It's about half an hour before everyone has borrowed what they want. Eventually they all pile out of my room, shrieking to me that they'll return it all in the morning, and Suze comes in, looking completely stunning with her hair piled up on her head and hanging down in blond tendrils.

"Bex, are you sure you don't want to come?" she says. "Tarquin's going to be there, and I know he'd like to see you."

"Oh right," I say, trying not to look too appalled at the idea. "Is he in London, then?"

"Just for a few days." Suze looks at me, a little sorrowfully. "You know, Bex, if it weren't for Luke . . . I reckon Tarkie still likes you."

"I'm sure he doesn't," I say quickly. "That was ages ago now. Ages!"

My one and only date with Tarquin is one of those events I am trying very hard never to remember again, ever.

"Oh well," says Suze, shrugging. "See you later. And don't work too hard!"

"I won't," I reply, and give a world-weary sigh. "Or at least, I'll try not to."

I wait until the front door bangs behind her, and the taxis waiting outside have roared off. Then I take a sip of tea and turn back to my first chapter.

Chapter One

Finance is very

Actually, I'm not really in the mood for this anymore. Suze is right, I should have a break. I mean, if I sit here hour after hour, I'll get all jaded, and lose the creative flow. And the point is, I've made a good start.

I stand up and stretch, then wander into the sitting room, and pick up a copy of *Tatler.* It's *EastEnders* in a minute, and then it might be *Changing Rooms* or something, or that documentary about the vets. I'll just watch that—and then I'll go back to work. I mean, I've got a whole evening ahead, haven't I? I need to pace myself.

Idly, I flick open the magazine and am scanning the contents page for something interesting when suddenly my eye stops in surprise. It's a little picture of Luke, with the caption *Best of Brandon,* page seventy-four! Why on earth didn't he tell me he was going to be in *Tatler*?

The photograph is his new official one, the one I helped him choose an outfit for (blue shirt, dark blue Fendi tie). He's staring at the camera, looking all serious and businesslike—but if you look closely at his eyes, there's a little friendly spark in there. As I stare at his face I feel a tug of affection and realize Suze is right. I should just trust him, shouldn't I? I mean—what does Alicia Bitchy-pants know about anything?

I turn to page seventy-four, and it's an article on "Britain's Top Movers and Shakers." I scan down the page, and I can't help noticing that some of the movers and shakers are pictured with their partners. Maybe there'll be a picture of me with Luke! After all, somebody might have taken a picture of us together at a party or something, mightn't they? Come to think of it, we were once snapped by the *Evening Standard* at a launch for some new magazine, although it never actually got into the paper.

Ooh! Here he is, number thirty-four! And it's just him, in that same official photo, with not a glimpse of me. Still, I feel a twinge of pride as I see his picture (much bigger than some of the others, ha!) and a caption reading: "Brandon's ruthless pursuit of success has knocked lesser competitors off the starting blocks." Then the piece starts: "Luke Brandon, dynamic owner and founder of Brandon Communications, the blah-di blah-di . . ."

I skim over the text, feeling a pleasant anticipation as I reach the section labeled "Vital Statistics." This is the bit where I'll be mentioned! "Currently dating TV personality Rebecca Bloomwood." Or maybe, "Partner of well-known finance expert Rebecca Bloomwood." Or else—

Luke James Brandon
Age: 34
Education: Cambridge
Current status: Single.

Single?

Luke told them he was *single*?

A hurt anger begins to rise through me as I stare at Luke's confident, arrogant gaze. Suddenly I've had enough of all this. I've had enough of being made to feel insecure and paranoid and wondering what's going on. Hands trembling, I pick up the phone and jab in Luke's number.

"Yes," I say, as soon as the message has finished. "Yes, well. If you're single, Luke, then I'm single too. OK? And if you're going to New York, then I'm going to . . . to Outer Mongolia. And if you're . . ."

Suddenly my mind goes blank. Shit, and it was going so well.

". . . if you're too cowardly to tell me these things yourself, then maybe it's better for both of us if we simply . . ."

I'm really struggling here. I should have written it all down before I began.

". . . if we just call it a day. Or perhaps that's what you think you've already done," I finish, breathing hard.

"Becky?" Suddenly Luke's deep voice is in my ear, and I jump with fright.

"Yes?" I say, trying to sound dignified.

"What *is* all this gibberish you're spouting on my machine?" he asks calmly.

"It's not gibberish!" I reply indignantly. "It's the truth!"

" 'If you're single, then I'm single'? What's that supposed to be? Lyrics to a pop song?"

"I was talking about you! And the fact that you've told the whole world you're single."

"I've done what?" says Luke, sounding amused. "When did I do that?"

"It's in *Tatler*!" I say furiously. "This month!" I grab for the magazine and flip it open. "Britain's top movers and shakers. Number thirty-four, Luke Brandon."

"Oh, for God's sake," says Luke. "That thing."

"Yes, that thing!" I exclaim. "That thing! And it says you're single. How do you think it felt for me to see you'd said you were single?"

"It quotes me, does it?"

"Well . . . no," I say after a pause. "It doesn't exactly quote you. But I mean, they must have phoned you up and asked you—"

"They did phone me up and ask me," he says. "And I said no comment."

"Oh." I'm silenced for a moment, trying to think clearly. OK, so maybe he didn't say he was single—but I'm not at all sure I like "no comment." Isn't that what people say when things are going really badly?

"Why did you say no comment?" I say at last. "Why didn't you say you were going out with me?"

"My darling," says Luke, sounding a little weary, "think about it. Do you *want* our private life splashed all over the media?"

"Of course not." I twist my hands into a complicated knot. "Of course not. But you . . ." I stop.

"What?"

"You told the media when you were going out with Sacha," I say in a small voice.

Sacha is Luke's ex-girlfriend.

I can't quite believe I just said that.

Luke sighs.

"Becky, *Sacha* told the media about us. She would have had *People* magazine photographing us in the bath if they'd been interested. That's the kind of girl she was."

"Oh," I say, winding the telephone cord round my finger.

"I'm not interested in that kind of thing. My clients can do what they like, but personally, I can't think of anything worse. Hence the no comment." He pauses. "But you're right. I should have thought. I should have warned you. I'm sorry."

"That's all right," I say awkwardly. "I suppose I shouldn't have jumped to conclusions."

"So are we OK?" says Luke, and there's a warm, teasing note to his voice. "Are we back on course?"

"What about New York?" I say, hating myself. "Is that all a mistake, too?"

There's a long, horrible silence.

"What have you heard about New York?" says Luke at last—and to my horror, he sounds all businesslike and distant.

Oh God. *Why* couldn't I keep my mouth closed?

"Nothing really!" I stammer. "I . . . I don't know. I just . . ."

I tail off feebly, and for what seems like hours, neither of us says anything. My heart is pounding hard, and I'm clutching the receiver so hard, my ear's starting to hurt.

"Becky, I need to talk to you about a few things," says Luke finally. "But now is not the time."

"Right," I say, feeling a pang of fright. "What . . . sort of things?"

"Not now. We'll talk when I get back, OK? Saturday. At the wedding."

"Right," I say again, talking brightly to hide the nerves in my voice. "OK! Well, I'll . . . I'll see you then, then . . ."

But before I can say any more, he's gone.

MANAGING YOUR MONEY

A Comprehensive Guide to Personal Finance

By Rebecca Bloomwood

FIRST EDITION (UK)

(FIRST DRAFT)

PART ONE

Chapter one.

Finance is very

· ENDWICH BANK ·

FULHAM BRANCH

3 Fulham Road

London SW6 9JH

Ms. Rebecca Bloomwood
Flat 2
4 Burney Rd.
London SW6 8FD

12 September 2000

Dear Ms. Bloomwood:

Further to my letter of 8 September, I have conducted a thorough examination of your account. Your current overdraft limit vastly exceeds the bank's approved ratios. I cannot see any need for this excessive level of debt, nor that any genuine attempts have been made to reduce it. The situation is little short of a disgrace.

Whatever special status you have enjoyed in the past will not be continuing in the future. I will certainly not be increasing your overdraft limit as you request, and would ask as a matter of urgency that you make an appointment with me to discuss your position.

Yours sincerely,

John Gavin
Overdraft Facilities Director

• ENDWICH—BECAUSE WE CARE •

Six

I ARRIVE AT MY PARENTS' house at ten o'clock on Saturday, to find the street full of festivity. There are balloons tied to every tree, our drive is full of cars, and a billowing marquee is just visible from next door's garden. I get out of my car, reach for my overnight bag, then just stand still for a few moments, staring at the Websters' house. God, this is strange. Tom Webster getting married. I can hardly believe it. To be honest—and this may sound a bit mean—I can hardly believe that anyone would *want* to marry Tom Webster. He has smartened up his act recently, admittedly. He's got a few new clothes, and a better hairstyle. But his hands are still all huge and clammy—and frankly, he's not Brad Pitt.

Still, that's the point of love, I think, closing my car door with a bang. You love people despite their flaws. Lucy obviously doesn't mind that Tom's got clammy hands—and he obviously doesn't mind that her hair's all flat and boring. It's quite romantic, I suppose.

As I'm standing there, gazing at the house, a girl in jeans with a circlet of flowers in her hair appears at the Websters' front door. She gives me an odd, almost aggressive look, then disappears inside the house again. One of Lucy's bridesmaids, obviously. I expect she's a bit nervous, being seen in her jeans.

Lucy's probably in there too, it occurs to me—and instinctively I turn away. I know she's the bride and everything, but to be honest, I'm not desperately looking forward to seeing Lucy again. I've only met her a couple of times and we've never jelled. Probably because she had the idea I was in love with Tom. Still, at least when Luke arrives I'll finally be able to prove them all wrong.

At the thought of Luke, there's a painful stab in my chest, and I take a deep, slow breath to calm myself. I'm determined I'm not going to put the cart before the horse this time. I'm going to keep an open mind, and see what he says today. And if he does tell me he's moving away to New York then I'll just . . . deal with it. Somehow.

Anyway. Don't think about it now. Briskly I head for the front door and let myself in. I head for the kitchen and find my dad drinking coffee in his waistcoat, while Mum, dressed in a nylon cape with her hair in curlers, is buttering a round of sandwiches.

"I just don't think it's right," she's saying as I walk in. "It's not right. They're supposed to be leading our country, and look at them. They're a mess! Dowdy jackets, dreadful ties . . ."

"You really think the ability to govern is affected by what you wear, do you?"

"Hi, Mum," I say, dumping my bag on the floor. "Hi, Dad."

"It's the principle of the thing!" says Mum. "If they're not prepared to make an effort with their dress, then why should they make any effort with the economy?"

"It's hardly the same thing!"

"It's exactly the same thing. Becky, *you* think the chancellor should dress more smartly, don't you? All this lounge suit nonsense."

"I don't know," I say vaguely. "Maybe."

"You see? Becky agrees with me. Now, let me have a look at you, darling." She puts down her knife and surveys me properly, and I feel myself glowing a little, because I know I look good. I'm wearing a shocking pink dress and jacket, a Philip Treacy feathered hat, and the most beautiful black satin shoes, each decorated with a single gossamer butterfly. "Oh, Becky," says Mum at last. "You look lovely. You'll upstage the bride!" She reaches for my hat and looks at it. "This is very unusual! How much did it cost?"

"Erm . . . I can't remember," I say vaguely. "Maybe . . . fifty quid?"

This is not quite true. It was actually more like . . . Well, anyway, quite a lot. Still, it was worth it.

"So, where's Luke?" says Mum, popping my hat back on my head. "Parking the car?"

"Yes, where's Luke?" says my father, looking up, and gives a jocular laugh. "We've been looking forward to meeting this young man of yours at last."

"Luke's coming separately," I say—and flinch slightly as I see their faces fall.

"Separately?" says Mum at last. "Why's that?"

"He's flying back from Zurich this morning," I explain. "He had to go there for business. But he'll be here, I promise."

"He does know the service starts at twelve?" says Mum anxiously. "And you've told him where the church is?"

"Yes!" I say. "Honestly, he'll be here."

I'm aware that I sound slightly snappy, but I can't help it. To be honest, I'm a bit stressed out myself about where Luke's got to. He was supposed to be ringing me when he landed at the airport—and that was supposed to be half an hour ago. But so far I haven't heard anything.

Still. He said he'd be here.

"Can I do anything to help?" I ask, to change the subject.

"Be a darling, and take these upstairs for me," says Mum, cutting the sandwiches briskly into triangles. "I've got to pack away the patio cushions."

"Who's upstairs?" I say, picking up the plate.

"Maureen's come over to blow-dry Janice's hair," says Mum. "They wanted to keep out of Lucy's way. You know, while she's getting ready."

"Have you seen her yet?" I ask interestedly. "Has she got a nice dress?"

"I haven't seen it," says Mum, and lowers her voice. "But apparently it cost £3,000. And that's not including the veil!"

"Wow," I say, impressed. And for a second I feel ever so slightly envious. A £3,000 dress. And a party . . . and loads of presents . . . I mean, people who get married have it all.

As I go up the stairs, there's the sound of blow-drying coming from Mum and Dad's bedroom—and as I go in, I see Janice sitting on the dressing-room stool, wearing a dressing gown, holding a sherry glass, and dabbing at her eyes with a hanky. Maureen, who's been doing Mum's and Janice's hair for years now, is brandishing a hair dryer at her, and a woman I don't recognize with a mahogany tan, dyed blond curly hair, and a lilac silk suit is sitting on the window seat.

"Hello, Janice," I say, going over and giving her a hug. "How are you feeling?"

"I'm fine, dear," she says, and gives a sniff. "A little wobbly. You know. To think of Tom getting married!"

"I know," I say sympathetically. "It doesn't seem like yesterday that we were kids, riding our bikes together!"

"Have another sherry, Janice," says Maureen comfortably, and sloshes a deep brown liquid into her glass. "It'll help you relax."

"Oh, Becky," says Janice, and squeezes my hand. "This must be a hard day for you, too."

I knew it. She does still think I fancy Tom, doesn't she? *Why* do all mothers think their sons are irresistible?

"Not really!" I say, as brightly as I can. "I mean, I'm just pleased for Tom. And Lucy, of course . . ."

"Becky?" The woman on the window seat turns toward me, eyes narrowed suspiciously. "This is Becky?"

And there's not an ounce of friendliness in her face. Oh God, don't say *she* thinks I'm after Tom, too.

"Erm . . . yes." I smile at her. "I'm Rebecca Bloomwood. And you must be Lucy's mother?"

"Yes," says the woman, still staring at me. "I'm Angela

Harrison. Mother of the bride," she adds, emphasizing "the bride" as though I don't understand English.

"You must be very excited," I say politely. "Your daughter getting married."

"Yes, well, of course, Tom is devoted to Lucy," she says aggressively. "Utterly devoted. Never *looks* in any other direction." She gives me a sharp glance and I smile feebly back.

Honestly, what am I supposed to do? Throw up all over Tom or something? Tell him he's the ugliest man I've ever known? They'd all still just say I was jealous. They'd say I was in denial.

"Is . . . Luke here, Becky?" says Janice, and gives me a hopeful smile. And suddenly—which is rather bizarre—everyone in the room is completely still, waiting for my answer.

"Not yet, I'm afraid," I say. "I think he must have been held up."

There's silence, and I'm aware of glances flying around the room.

"Held up," echoes Angela, and there's a tone to her voice that I don't much like. "Is that right? Well, there's a surprise."

What's that supposed to mean?

"He's coming back from Zurich," I explain. "I should think the flight's been delayed or something." I look at Janice and, to my surprise, she flushes.

"Zurich," she says, nodding a little too emphatically. "I see. Of course. Zurich." And she shoots me an embarrassed, almost sympathetic look.

What's wrong with her?

"This *is* Luke Brandon we're talking about here," says Angela, taking a puff on her cigarette. "The famous entrepreneur."

"Well—yes," I say, a bit surprised. I mean, I don't *know* any other Lukes.

"And he's your boyfriend."

"Yes!"

There's a slightly awkward silence—and even Maureen seems to be gazing at me curiously. Then, suddenly, I see a copy of this month's *Tatler* lying on the floor by Janice's chair. Oh God.

"That article in *Tatler*, by the way," I say hastily, "is all wrong. He didn't say he was single. He said no comment."

"Article?" says Janice unconvincingly. "I don't know what you're talking about, dear."

"I . . . I don't read magazines," says Maureen, who blushes bright red and looks away.

"We just look forward to meeting him," says Angela, and blows out a cloud of smoke. "Don't we, Janice?"

I stare at her in confusion—then turn to Janice, who will barely meet my eye, and Maureen, who's pretending to root about in a beauty case.

Hang on a minute.

They surely don't think—

"Janice," I say, trying to keep my voice steady. "You know Luke's coming. He even wrote you a reply!"

"Of course he did, Becky!" says Janice, staring at the floor. "Well—as Angela says, we're all looking forward to meeting him."

I feel a swoosh of humiliated color fill my cheeks. What does she think? That I've just *made up* that I'm going out with Luke?

"Well, enjoy your sandwiches, won't you?" I say, trying not to sound as flustered as I feel. "I'll just . . . see if Mum needs me."

When I find Mum, she's on the top-floor landing, packing patio cushions into transparent plastic bags, then suctioning all the air out with the nozzle of her vacuum cleaner.

"I've some of these bags on order for you, by the way," she shouts over the noise of the vacuum. "From Country Ways. Plus some turkey foil, a casserole dish, a microwave egg poacher . . ."

"I don't want any turkey foil!" I yell.

"It's not for you!" says Mum, turning off the vacuum. "They had a special offer—introduce a friend and receive a set of earthenware pots. So I nominated you as the friend. It's a very good catalogue, actually. I'll give it to you to have a browse."

"Mum—"

"Lovely duvet covers. I'm sure you could do with a new—"

"Mum, listen!" I say agitatedly. "Listen. You do believe I'm going out with Luke, don't you?"

There's a slightly too long pause.

"Of course I do," she says eventually.

I stare at her in horror.

"You don't, do you? You all think I've just made it up!"

"No!" says Mum firmly. She puts down her hoover and looks me straight in the eye. "Becky, you've told us you're going out with Luke Brandon, and as far as Dad and I are concerned, that's enough."

"But Janice and Martin. Do they think I've made it up?"

Mum gazes at me—then sighs, and reaches for another patio cushion.

"Oh, Becky. The thing is, love, you have to remember, they once believed you had a stalker. And that turned out to be . . . well. Not quite true. Didn't it?"

A cold dismay creeps over me. OK, maybe I did once kind of pretend I had a stalker. Which I shouldn't have done. But I mean, just because you invent one tiny stalker—that doesn't make you a complete nutcase, does it?

"And the trouble is, we've never actually . . . well, *seen* him with you, have we, love?" Mum's continuing, as she stuffs the cushion into its transparent bag. "Not in the flesh. And then there was that piece in the paper saying he was single . . ."

"He didn't say single!" My voice is shrill with frustration. "He said no comment! Mum, have Janice and Martin told you they don't believe me?"

"No!" Mum lifts her chin defiantly. "They wouldn't dare say a thing like that to me."

"But you know that's what they're saying behind our backs."

We stare at each other, and suddenly I see the strain in Mum's face, hidden behind her bright facade. She must have been *so* hoping we'd pull up together in Luke's flash car, I suddenly realize. She must have been so wanting to prove Janice wrong. And instead, here I am, on my own again . . .

"He'll be here," I say, almost to reassure myself. "He'll be here any minute."

"Of course he will!" exclaims Mum brightly. "And as soon as he turns up—well, then everyone will have to eat their words, won't they?"

The doorbell rings and we both stiffen, staring at each other.

"I'll get that, shall I?" I say, trying to sound casual.

"Why don't you?" agrees Mum, and I can see a tiny shine of hope in her eyes.

Trying not to run, I hurry down the stairs and, with a light heart, fling the front door open. And it's . . . not Luke.

It's a man laden with flowers. Baskets of flowers, a bouquet of flowers, and several flat boxes at his feet.

"Wedding flowers," he says. "Where do you want them?"

"Oh," I say, trying to hide my disappointment. "Actually, you've got the wrong house, I'm afraid. They need to go next door. Number 41."

"Really?" The man frowns. "Let me just look at my list . . . Hold that, would you?"

He thrusts the bridal bouquet at me and starts rooting around his pocket.

"Honestly," I say, "they need to go next door. Look, I'll just get my—"

I turn round, holding Lucy's bouquet with both hands, because it's quite heavy. And to my horror, Angela Harrison is just arriving at the foot of the stairs. She stares at me, and for a moment I almost think she's going to kill me.

"What are you doing?" she snaps. "Give me that!" She wrenches the bouquet out of my hands and brings her face so close to mine I can smell the gin on her breath. "Listen, young lady," she hisses. "I'm not fooled by the smiles. I know what you're up to. And you can just forget it, all right? I'm not having my daughter's wedding wrecked by some deranged little psychopath."

"I'm not deranged!" I exclaim furiously. "And I'm not going to wreck anything! I don't fancy Tom! I've got a boyfriend!"

"Oh yes," she says, folding her arms. "The famous boyfriend. Is he here yet?"

"No, he isn't," I say, and flinch at the expression on her face. "But he . . . he just called."

"He just called," echoes Angela with a little sneer. "To say he can't make it?"

Why won't these people believe that Luke's coming?

"Actually . . . he's half an hour away," I hear myself saying defiantly.

"Good!" says Angela Harrison, and gives me a nasty smile. "Well—we'll see him very soon, then, won't we?"

Oh shit.

By twelve o'clock, Luke still hasn't arrived, and I'm beside myself. This is a complete nightmare. Where *is* he? I loiter outside the church until the very last minute, desperately dialing his number, hoping against hope I'm suddenly going to see him running up the road. But the bridesmaids have arrived, and another Rolls-Royce has just pulled up, and he's still not here. As I see the car door open and a glimpse of wedding dress, I hastily retreat into the church before anyone can think I'm waiting outside to disrupt the bridal procession.

As I creep in, trying not to disturb the organ music, Angela Harrison darts me an evil look, and there's a rippling and whispering from Lucy's side of the church. I sit down near the back, trying to keep composed and tranquil—but I'm well aware that all Lucy's friends are shooting surreptitious glances at me. What the hell has she been telling everyone?

For a second I feel like getting up and walking out. I never wanted to come to this stupid wedding anyway. I only said yes because I didn't want to offend Janice and Martin. But it's too late, the bridal march is starting, and Lucy's walking in. And I have to hand it to her, she's wearing the most drop-dead gorgeous dress I've ever seen. I stare wistfully after it, trying not to imagine what I would look like in a dress like that.

The music stops and the vicar starts talking. I'm aware that people on Lucy's side of the church are still darting me little looks—but I adjust my hat and lift my chin and ignore them.

". . . to join together this man and this woman in holy matrimony," intones the vicar, "which is an honorable estate . . ."

The bridesmaids have got really nice shoes, I notice. I wonder where they're from?

Shame about the dresses, though.

". . . reverently, discreetly, advisedly, soberly, and in the fear of God . . ."

He pauses to look around the congregation, just as I hear a little trilling sound coming from my bag.

Shit. It's my phone.

I pull at the zip—but it's stuck. I don't believe this. You buy an expensive bag, and the bloody zip sticks.

There's another, louder trill. At the front of the church, Angela Harrison turns round in her pew and gives me the evil eye.

"Sorry," I mouth. "I'm just trying to get it . . ."

As it trills for a third time, the vicar stops talking. And oh God, now Tom and Lucy are turning round, too.

"I'm sorry," I gulp, giving another frantic tug at the zip. "I'll just . . . try to . . ."

Face burning, I stand up, squeeze my way past the row of people, and hurry out of the church. As the door clangs shut behind me I wrench so hard at the zip that I pull the stitching undone. I scrabble inside for the phone, and jab at the green button.

"Hello?" I say breathlessly into the mouthpiece. "Luke?"

"Good morning!" says a cheery voice. "Would you be interested in adding a hundred minutes to your monthly plan?"

After carefully turning off my phone I creep back into the church, where the rest of the service goes by in a blur. When it's all over, Lucy and Tom process out, studiously ignoring me as they do so—and everyone gathers around them in the graveyard to throw confetti and take photos. I slip away without anyone noticing, and hurry feverishly up the road to the Websters' house. Because Luke must be there by now. He *must.* He must have arrived late, and decided not to come to the church, but go straight to the reception. It's obvious, when you think about it. It's what any sensible person would do.

I hurry through the Websters' house, which is full of caterers and waitresses—and head straight for the marquee. There's already a joyful smile on my face at the thought of seeing him, and telling him about that awful moment in the church, and seeing his face crease up in laughter—

But the marquee's empty. Completely empty.

I stand there, bewildered, for a few moments—then quickly head out again and hurry toward my parents' house. Because maybe Luke went there, instead, it suddenly occurs to me. Maybe he got the time wrong, or maybe he had to get changed into his wedding outfit. Or maybe—

But he's not there either. Not in the kitchen, not upstairs. And when I dial his mobile number, it clicks straight onto messages.

Slowly, I walk into my bedroom and sink down onto the bed, trying not to let myself think all the bad thoughts which are creeping into my mind.

He's coming, I tell myself again and again. He's just . . . on his way.

Through the window I can see Tom and Lucy and all the guests starting to arrive in next door's garden. There are lots of hats and morning suits, and waitresses handing round champagne. In fact, it all looks rather jolly. And I know I should be down there with them, but I just can't face it. Not without Luke, not all on my own.

But after sitting there for a while, it occurs to me that by staying up here, I'll just be fueling the intrigue. They'll all think I can't face the happy couple and that I'm off slitting my wrists somewhere. It'll confirm all their suspicions forever. I *have* to go and show my face, even if just for half an hour.

I force myself to stand up, take a deep breath, and put some fresh lipstick on. Then I walk out of the house and round to the Websters'. I slip inconspicuously into the marquee through a side flap and stand watching for a moment. There are people milling about everywhere, and the hubbub is huge, and no one even notices me. Near the entrance, there's a formal lineup with Tom and Lucy and their parents, but no way am I going near that. So instead I sidle off to an empty table and sit down, and after a bit a waitress comes and gives me a glass of champagne.

For a while I just sit there, sipping my drink and watching people and feeling myself start to relax. But then there's a rustling sound in front of me. I look up—and my heart sinks. Lucy is standing right in front of me in her beautiful wedding dress, flanked by a large bridesmaid in a really unflattering shade of green. (Which I think says quite a lot about Lucy.)

"Hello, Rebecca," says Lucy pleasantly—and I can just tell, she's congratulating herself on being so polite to the loony girl who nearly wrecked her wedding.

"Hi," I say. "Listen, I'm really sorry about the service. I honestly didn't mean to . . ."

"That doesn't matter," says Lucy, and gives me a tight smile. "After all, Tom and I are married. That's the main thing." And she gives her wedding-ringed hand a satisfied glance.

"Absolutely!" I say. "Congratulations. Are you going on—"

"We were just wondering," interrupts Lucy pleasantly. "Is Luke here yet?"

My heart sinks.

"Oh," I say, playing for time. "Well . . ."

"It's only that Mummy said you told her he was half an hour away. But no sign of him! Which seems a bit strange, don't you think?" She raises her eyebrows innocently, and her bridesmaid gives a half-snort of laughter. I glance over Lucy's shoulder and see Angela Harrison standing with Tom, a few yards away, watching with gimlet, triumphant eyes. God, they're enjoying this, aren't they?

"After all, that was, oh, a good two hours ago now," Lucy's saying. "At least! So if he *isn't* here, it does seem a teeny bit peculiar." She gives me a mock-concerned look. "Or maybe he's had an accident? Maybe he's got held up in . . . Zurich, was it?"

I stare at her smug, mocking face, and something violent rushes to my head.

"He's here," I say before I can stop myself.

There's a stunned silence. Lucy and her bridesmaid glance at each other, while I take a deep gulp of champagne.

"He's *here*?" says Lucy at last. "You mean, here at the wedding?"

"Absolutely!" I say. "He's . . . he's been here a while, actually."

"But where? Where is he?"

"Well . . . he was here just a few moments ago . . ." I gesture to the chair next to me. "Didn't you see him?"

"No!" says Lucy, with wide eyes. "Where is he now?" And she starts to look around the marquee.

"Just there," I say, pointing vaguely through the crowd. "He's wearing a morning coat . . ."

"And? What else?"

"And he's . . . he's holding a glass of champagne . . ."

Thank *God* all men look alike at weddings.

"Which one!" says Lucy impatiently.

"The dark one," I say, and take another gulp of champagne. "Look, he's waving at me." I lift my hand and give a little wave. "Hi, Luke!"

"*Where?*" exclaims Lucy, peering into the crowd. "Kate, can you see him?"

"No!" says the bridesmaid hopelessly. "What does he look like?"

"He's . . . actually, he's just disappeared," I say. "He must be getting me a drink or something."

Lucy turns to me again.

"So—how come he wasn't at the service?"

"He didn't want to interrupt," I say after a pause, and force myself to smile naturally. "Well—I won't keep you. You must want to mingle with your guests!"

"Yes," says Lucy after a pause. "Yes, I will."

Giving me another suspicious look, she rustles off toward her mother, and they all start hobnobbing in a little group, shooting glances at me every so often. Then one of the bridesmaids rushes off to another group of guests, and they all start giving me glances, too. And then one runs off to *another* group. It's like seeing a bushfire begin.

A few moments later, Janice comes up, all flushed and teary looking, with a flowery hat perched lopsidedly on her head.

"Becky!" she says. "Becky, we've just heard that Luke's here!"

And my heart plummets. Putting down the bride from hell was one thing. But I can't bring myself to lie to Janice. I just can't do it. So I quickly take a gulp of champagne, and wave my glass at her in a vague manner that could mean anything.

"Oh, Becky . . ." Janice clasps her hands. "Becky, I feel absolutely . . . Have your parents met him yet? I know your mother will be over the moon!"

Oh fuck.

Suddenly I feel a bit sick. My parents. I didn't think of that.

"Janice, I've just got to go and . . . and powder my nose," I say, and get hastily to my feet. "See you later."

"And Luke!" she says.

"And Luke, of course!" I say, and give a shrill little laugh.

I hurry to the portaloos without meeting anyone's eye, lock myself in a cubicle, and sit, swigging the last warm dregs of my champagne. OK, let's not panic about this. Let's just . . . think clearly, and go over my options.

Option One: Tell everybody that Luke isn't really here, I made a mistake.

Not unless I want to be stoned to death with champagne glasses and never show my face in Oxshott again.

Option Two: Tell Mum and Dad in private that Luke isn't really here.

But they'll be so disappointed. They'll be mortified, and they won't enjoy the day and it'll be all my fault.

Option Three: Bluff it out—and tell Mum and Dad the truth at the end of the day.

Yes. That could work. It has to work. I can easily convince everyone Luke's here for about an hour or so—and then I'll say he's got a migraine, and has gone off to lie down quietly.

Right, this is what I'm going to do. OK—let's go.

And you know, it's easier than I thought. Before long, everyone seems to be taking it for granted that Luke is around somewhere. Tom's granny even tells me she's already spotted him, and isn't he handsome and will it be my turn next? I've told countless people that he was here just a minute ago, have collected two plates of food from the buffet—one for me, one for Luke (tipped one into the flower bed), and have even borrowed some stranger's morning coat and put it on the chair next to me, as though it's his. The great thing is, no one can prove he's not here! There are so many people milling about, it's impossible to keep track of who's here and who isn't. I should have done this ages ago.

"Group photograph in a minute," says Lucy, bustling up to me. "We all have to line up. Where's Luke?"

"Talking to some guy about property prices," I reply without hesitation. "They were over by the drinks table."

"Well, make sure you introduce me," says Lucy. "I still haven't met him!"

"OK!" I say, and give her a bright smile. "As soon as I track him down!" I take a swig of champagne, look up—and there's Mum in her lime-green wedding outfit, heading toward me.

So far, I've managed to avoid her and Dad completely, basically by running away whenever they've come close. I know it's really bad of me—but I just won't be able to lie to Mum. Quickly I slip out of the marquee into the garden, and head for the shrubbery, dodging the photographer's assistant, who's rounding up all the children. I sit down behind a tree and finish my glass of champagne, staring up blankly at the blue afternoon sky.

I stay there for what seems like hours, until my legs are starting to ache and the breeze is making me shiver. Then at last, I slowly wander back, and slip inconspicuously into the tent. I won't hang around much longer. Just long enough to have a piece of wedding cake, maybe, and some more champagne . . .

"There she is!" comes a voice behind me.

I freeze for an instant—then slowly turn round. To my utter

horror, all the guests are standing in neat rows in the center of the marquee, while a photographer adjusts a tripod.

"Becky, where's Luke?" says Lucy sharply. "We're trying to get everybody in."

Shit. *Shit.*

"Erm . . ." I swallow, trying to stay nonchalant. "Maybe he's in the house?"

"No, he's not," says Kate the bridesmaid. "I've just been looking in there."

"Well, he must be . . . in the garden, then."

"But you were in the garden!" says Lucy, narrowing her eyes. "Didn't you see him?"

"Erm . . . I'm not sure." I look round the marquee hurriedly, wondering if I could pretend to spot him in the distance. But it's different when there are no milling crowds. Why did they have to stop milling?

"He must be somewhere!" says a cheerful woman. "Who saw him last?"

There's a deathly silence. Two hundred people are staring at me. I catch Mum's anxious eye, and quickly look away again.

"Actually . . ." I clear my throat. "Now I remember, he was saying he had a bit of a headache! So maybe he went to—"

"Who's seen him *at all*?" cuts in Lucy, ignoring me. She looks around the assembled guests. "Who here can say they've actually seen Luke Brandon in the flesh? Anyone?"

"I've seen him!" comes a wavering voice from the back. "Such a good-looking young man . . ."

"Apart from Tom's gran," says Lucy, rolling her eyes. "Anyone?"

And there's another awful silence.

"I've seen his morning coat," ventures Janice timidly. "But not his actual . . . body," she whispers.

"I knew it. I knew it!" Lucy's voice is loud and triumphant. "He never was here, was he?"

"Of course he was!" I say, trying to sound confident. "I expect he's just in the—"

"You're not going out with Luke Brandon at all, are you?"

Her voice lashes across the marquee. "You just made the whole thing up! You're just living in your own sad little fantasy land!"

"I'm not!" To my horror, my voice is thickening, and I can feel tears pricking at my eyes. "I'm not! Luke and I are a couple!"

But as I look at all the faces gazing at me—some hostile, some astonished, some amused—I don't even feel so sure of that anymore. I mean, if we were a couple, he'd be here, wouldn't he? He'd be here with me.

"I'll just . . ." I say in a trembling voice. "I'll just check if he's . . ."

And without looking anyone in the eye, I back out of the marquee.

"She's a bloody fruit loop!" I hear Lucy saying. "Honestly, Tom, she could be dangerous!"

"*You're* dangerous, young lady!" I hear Mum retorting, her voice shaking a little. "Janice, I don't know how you could let your daughter-in-law be so rude! Becky's been a good friend to you, over the years. And to you, Tom, standing there, pretending this has nothing to do with you. And this is the way you treat her. Come on, Graham. We're going."

And a moment later, I see Mum stalking out of the marquee, Dad in tow, her lime-green hat quivering on her head. They head toward the front drive, and I know they're going back to our house for a nice, calming cup of tea.

But I don't follow them. I can't bring myself to see them—or anyone.

I walk quickly, stumbling slightly, toward the other end of the garden. Then, when I'm far enough away, I sink down onto the grass. I bury my head in my hands—and, for the first time today, feel tears oozing out of my eyes.

This should have been such a good day. It should have been such a wonderful, happy occasion. Seeing Tom get married, introducing Luke to my parents and all our friends, dancing together into the night . . . And instead, it's been spoiled for everyone. Mum, Dad, Janice, Martin . . . I even feel sorry for

Lucy and Tom. I mean, they didn't want all this disruption at their wedding, did they?

For what seems like ages I sit without moving, staring down at the ground. From the marquee I can hear the sounds of a band starting up, and Lucy's voice bossing somebody about. Some children are playing with a bean bag in the garden and occasionally it lands near me. But I don't flicker. I wish I could just sit here forever, without having to see any of them ever again.

And then I hear my name, low across the grass.

At first I think Lucy's right, and I'm hearing imaginary voices. But as I look up, my heart gives an almighty flip and I feel something hard blocking my throat. I don't believe it.

It's him.

It's Luke, walking across the grass, toward me, like a dream. He's wearing morning dress and holding two glasses of champagne, and I've never seen him looking more handsome.

"I'm sorry," he says as he reaches me. "I'm beyond sorry. Four hours late is . . . well, it's unforgivable." He shakes his head.

I stare up at him dazedly. I'd almost started to believe that Lucy was right, and he only existed in my own imagination.

"Were you . . . held up?" I say at last.

"A guy had a heart attack. The plane was diverted . . ." He frowns. "But I left a message on your phone as soon as I could. Didn't you get it?"

I grab for my phone, realizing with a sickening thud that I haven't checked it for a good while. I've been too busy dealing with imaginary Luke to think about the real one. And sure enough, the little message icon is blinking merrily.

"No, I didn't get it," I say, staring at it blankly. "I didn't. I thought . . ."

I break off and shake my head. I don't know what I thought anymore.

"Are you all right?" says Luke, sitting down beside me and handing me a glass of champagne. He runs a finger gently down my face and I flinch.

"No," I say, rubbing my cheek. "Since you ask, I'm not all right. You promised you'd be here. You *promised,* Luke."

"I *am* here."

"You know what I mean." I hunch my arms miserably round my knees. "I wanted you to be there at the service, not arrive when it's all nearly over. I wanted everyone to meet you, and see us together . . ." My voice starts to wobble. "It's just been . . . awful! They all thought I was after the bridegroom—"

"The bridegroom?" says Luke incredulously. "You mean the pale-faced nonentity called Tom?"

"Yes, him." I look up and give a reluctant half-giggle as I see Luke's expression. "Did you meet him, then?"

"I met him just now. And his very unlovely wife. Quite a pair." He takes a sip of champagne and leans back on his elbows. "By the way—she looked rather taken aback to meet me. Almost . . . gobsmacked, one might say. As did most of the guests." He gives me a quizzical look. "Anything I should know?"

"Erm . . ." I clear my throat. "Erm . . . not really. Nothing important."

"I thought as much," says Luke. "So the bridesmaid who cried out, 'Oh my God, he exists!' when I walked in. She's presumably . . ."

"Mad," I say without moving my head.

"Right." He nods. "Just checking."

He reaches out for my hand, and I let him take it. For a while we sit in silence. A bird is wheeling round and round overhead, and in the distance I can hear the band playing "Lady in Red."

"Becky, I'm sorry I was late." His voice is suddenly grave. "There was really nothing I could do. I gave a lot of people a lot of grief, believe me."

"I'm sure you did." I exhale sharply. "You couldn't help it. Just one of those things."

For a while longer we're both silent.

"Good champagne," says Luke eventually, and takes a sip.

"Yes," I say. "It's . . . very nice. Nice and . . . dry . . ." I break off and rub my face, trying to hide how nervous I am.

There's part of me that wants to sit here, making small talk for as long as we can. But another part is thinking, what's the point in putting it off any longer? There's only one thing I want to know. I feel a spasm of nerves in my stomach, but somehow force myself to take a deep breath and turn to him.

"So. How did your meetings in Zurich go? How's the . . . the new deal coming along?"

I'm trying to stay calm and collected—but I can feel my lips starting to tremble, and my hands are twisting themselves into knots.

"Becky . . ." says Luke. He stares into his glass for a moment, then puts it down. "There's something I need to tell you. I'm moving to New York."

I feel cold and heavy. So this is the end to a completely disastrous day. Luke's leaving me. It's the end. It's all over.

"Right," I manage, and give a careless shrug. "I see. Well—OK."

There's silence—and I force myself to look up. The love in Luke's dark eyes hits me like a thunderbolt.

"And I'm really, *really* hoping . . ." He takes both my hands and squeezes them tight. ". . . that you'll come with me."

HEAD OFFICE • PRESTON HOUSE • 354 KINGSWAY • LONDON WC2 4TH

Ms. Rebecca Bloomwood
Flat 2
4 Burney Rd.
London SW6 8FD

17 September 2000

Dear Rebecca Bloomwood:

Thank you for your letter of 15 September.

I am glad that you are looking forward to flying with us and have already recommended us highly to all your friends. I agree that word-of-mouth business is invaluable for a company such as ours and may well send our revenues "rocketing."

Unfortunately this does not, as you suggest, qualify you for "a special little thank-you" regarding luggage. Regal Airlines is unable to increase your luggage allowance beyond the standard 20 kg. Any excess weight will be subject to a charge; I enclose an explanatory leaflet.

Please enjoy your flight.

Mary Stevens
Customer Care Manager

PGNI FIRST BANK VISA

7 CAMEL SQUARE

LIVERPOOL L1 5NP

Ms. Rebecca Bloomwood
Flat 2
4 Burney Rd.
London SW6 8FD

19 September 2000

GOOD NEWS!
YOUR NEW CREDIT LIMIT IS £10,000

Dear Ms. Bloomwood:

We are delighted to announce that you have been given an increase to your credit limit. Your new credit limit of £10,000 is available for you to spend immediately and will be shown on your next statement.

You can use your new credit limit to do many things. Pay for a holiday, a car, even transfer balances from other cards!

However, we realize that some customers do not wish to take advantage of increased credit limits. If you would prefer your credit limit to remain at its original level, please call one of our Customer Satisfaction Representatives, or return the form below.

Yours sincerely,

Michael Hunt
Customer Satisfaction Manager

- -

Name: REBECCA BLOOMWOOD   Account Number: 0003 4572 0990 2765

I **would / would not** like to take up the offer of my new £10,000 credit limit.

Please delete as appropriate.

Seven

NEW YORK! I'm going to New York! *New York!*

Everything is transformed. *This* is why Luke has been so secretive. We had a lovely long chat at the wedding, and Luke explained everything to me, and suddenly it all made sense. It turns out he's opening up a new office of Brandon Communications in New York, in partnership with some advertising supremo called Michael Ellis who is based in Washington. And Luke's going to go over there and head it up. He said he's been wanting to ask me all along to come with him—but he knew I wouldn't want to give up my career just to trail along with him. So—this is the best bit—he's been speaking to some contacts in television, and he reckons I'll be able to get a job as a financial expert on an American TV show! In fact, he says I'll get "snapped up" because Americans love British accents. Apparently one producer has already practically offered me a job just from seeing a tape Luke sent him. Isn't that great?

The reason he didn't say anything before was he didn't want to raise my hopes before things started looking definite. But now, apparently, all the investors are on board, and everyone's really positive, and they're hoping to finalize the deal as soon as possible. Michael Ellis's agency advertises for most of the big financial players—and he's already been talking to them all about the new company. So there are loads of potential clients out there for Luke, and that's before he's even started.

And guess what? We're going over there in three days' time! Hooray! Luke's going to have meetings with some of his backers—and I'm going to have some interviews with TV people and explore the city. God, it's exciting. In just seventy-two hours, I'll be there. In the Big Apple. The city that never sleeps. The—

"Becky?"

Oh shit. I snap to attention and hastily smile brightly. I'm sitting on the set of *Morning Coffee,* doing my usual phone-in, and Jane from Lincoln has been explaining over the line that she wants to buy a property but doesn't know which kind of mortgage to take out.

Oh, for goodness' sake. How many times have I explained the difference between repayment plans and endowment policies? You know, sometimes this job can be so interesting, hearing about people and their problems and trying to help them. But other times—to be honest—it's just as boring as *Successful Saving* ever was. I mean, mortgages *again*? I feel like yelling, "Didn't you watch last week's show?"

"Well, Jane!" I say, stifling a yawn. "You're right to be concerned about redemption penalties."

As I speak, my mind begins to drift again toward New York. Just think. We'll have an apartment in Manhattan. In some amazing Upper East Side condo—or maybe somewhere really cool in Greenwich Village. Yes! It's just going to be perfect.

To be honest, I hadn't thought of Luke and me living together for . . . well, for ages. I reckon if we'd stayed in London, perhaps we wouldn't have. I mean, it's quite a big step, isn't it? But as Luke said, this is the chance of a lifetime for both of us. It's a whole new beginning. It's yellow taxicabs and skyscrapers, and Woody Allen and *Breakfast at Tiffany's.*

The weird thing is that although I've never actually been to New York, I already feel an affinity toward it. Like for example, I adore sushi—and that was invented in New York, wasn't it? And I always watch *Friends,* unless I'm going out that night. And

Cheers. (Except now I come to think of it, that's Boston. Still, it's the same thing, really.)

"So really, Jane, whatever you're buying," I say dreamily, "be it a . . . a Fifth Avenue duplex . . . or an East Village walk-up . . . you must maximize the potential of your dollar. Which means . . ."

I stop as I see both Emma and Rory staring at me strangely.

"Becky, Jane is planning to buy a semidetached house in Skegness," says Emma.

"And surely it's pounds?" says Rory, looking around, as though for support. "Isn't it?"

"Yes, well," I say hurriedly. "Obviously, I was just using those as examples. The principles apply wherever you're buying. London, New York, Skegness . . ."

"And on that international note, I'm afraid we'll have to finish," says Emma. "Hope that helped you, Jane, and thanks once again to Becky Bloomwood, our financial expert . . . do you have time for a last word, Becky?"

"The same message as ever," I say, smiling warmly into the camera. "Look after your money . . ."

"And your money will look after you," everyone choruses dutifully.

"And that brings us to the end of the show," says Emma. "Join us tomorrow, when we'll be making over a trio of teachers from Teddington . . ."

". . . talking to the man who became a circus performer at sixty-five . . ." says Rory.

". . . and giving away £5,000 in 'Go On—Have a Guess!' Good-bye!"

There's a frozen pause—then everyone relaxes as the signature music starts blaring out of the loudspeakers.

"So—Becky—are you going to New York or something?" says Rory.

"Yes," I say, beaming back at him. "For two weeks!"

"How nice!" says Emma. "What brought this on?"

"Oh, I don't know . . ." I shrug vaguely. "Just a sudden whim."

I'm not telling anyone at *Morning Coffee* yet about moving to New York. It was Luke's advice, actually. Just in case.

"Becky, I wanted a quick word," says Zelda, one of the assistant producers, bustling onto the set with some papers in her hand. "Your new contract is ready to be signed, but I'll need to go through it with you. There's a new clause about representing the image of the station." She lowers her voice. "After all that business with Professor Jamie."

"Oh right," I say, and pull a sympathetic face. Professor Jamie is the education expert on *Morning Coffee.* Or at least he was, until *The Daily World* ran an exposé on him last month in their series "Are They What They Seem?" revealing that he isn't a real professor at all. In fact, he hasn't even got a degree, except the fake one he bought from the "University of Oxbridge." All the tabloids picked up the story, and kept showing photographs of him in the dunce's hat he wore for last year's telethon. I felt really sorry for him, actually, because he used to give good advice.

And I was a bit surprised at *The Daily World* being so vicious. I've actually written for *The Daily World* myself, once or twice, and I'd always thought they were quite reasonable, for a tabloid.

"It won't take five minutes," says Zelda. "We could go into my office—"

"Well . . ." I say, and hesitate. Because I don't really want to sign anything at the moment. Not if I'm planning to switch jobs. "I'm in a bit of a hurry, actually." Which is true, because I've got to get to Luke's office by twelve, and then start getting my stuff ready for New York. (Ha! Ha-ha!) "Can it wait till I come back?"

"OK," says Zelda. "No problem." She puts the contract back in its brown envelope and grins at me. "Have a great time. Hey, you know, you must do some shopping while you're there."

"Shopping?" I say, as though it hadn't occurred to me. "Yes, I suppose I could."

"Ooh yes!" says Emma. "You can't go to New York without shopping! Although I suppose Becky would tell us we should put our money into a savings plan instead."

She laughs merrily and Zelda joins in. And I smile back, feeling a bit uncomfortable. Somehow, all the people at *Morning Coffee* have got the idea I'm incredibly organized with my money—and, without quite meaning to, I've gone along with it. Still, I don't suppose it really matters.

"A savings plan is a good idea, of course . . ." I hear myself saying. "But as I always say, there's no harm going shopping once in a while as long as you stick to a budget."

"Is that what you're going to do, then?" asks Emma interestedly. "Give yourself a budget?"

"Oh, absolutely," I say wisely. "It's the only way."

Which is completely true. I mean, obviously I'm planning to give myself a New York shopping budget. I'll set realistic limits and I'll stick to them. It's really very simple.

Although what I'll do is make the limits fairly broad and flexible. Because it's always a good idea to allow some extra leeway for emergencies or one-offs.

"You're so virtuous!" says Emma, shaking her head. "Still—that's why you're the financial expert and I'm not . . ." Emma looks up as the sandwich man approaches us with a tray of sandwiches. "Ooh lovely, I'm starving! I'll have . . . bacon and avocado."

"And I'll have tuna and sweet corn," says Zelda. "What do you want, Becky?"

"Pastrami on rye," I say casually. "Hold the mayo."

"I don't think they do that," says Zelda, wrinkling her brow. "They've got ham salad . . ."

"Then a bagel. Cream cheese and lox. And a soda."

"Soda water, do you mean?" says Zelda.

"What's lox?" says Emma puzzledly—and I pretend I haven't heard. I'm not actually sure what lox is—but everyone eats it in New York, so it's got to be delicious.

"Whatever it is," says the sandwich man, "I 'aven't got it. You can 'ave cheese and tomato and a nice packet of Hula Hoops."

"OK," I say reluctantly, and reach for my purse. As I do so, a pile of post that I picked up this morning falls out of my bag, onto the floor. Shit. Hastily, I gather all the letters up, and shove them into my Conran Shop carrier bag, hoping no one spotted them. But bloody Rory was looking straight at me.

"Hey, Becky," he says, giving a guffawing laugh. "Was that a red bill I saw there?"

"No!" I say at once. "Of course not! It's a . . . a birthday card. A joke birthday card. For my accountant. Anyway, I must run. Ciao!"

OK, so that wasn't quite true. It was a red bill. To be honest, there have been quite a few red bills arriving for me over the last few days, which I'm completely intending to get round to paying off when I've got the cash. But I mean, I've got more important things happening in my life than a few crappy final demands. In a few months' time, I'm going to be living on the other side of the Atlantic. I'm going to be an American television star!

Luke says I'll probably earn twice in the States what I do here. If not more! So a few crummy bills won't exactly matter then, will they? A few outstanding pounds won't exactly ruin my sleep when I'm a household name and living in a Park Avenue penthouse.

God, and that'll completely suss that horrible John Gavin. Just imagine his face when I march in and tell him I'm going to be the new anchorwoman on CNN, on a salary six times what he earns. That'll teach him to be so nasty. I finally got round to opening his latest letter this morning, and it actually quite upset me. What does he mean, "excessive level of debt"? What does he mean, "special status"? You know, Derek Smeath would never have been so rude to me, not in a million years.

Luke's in a meeting when I arrive, but that's OK, because I don't mind hanging around. I love visiting the Brandon Communications offices—in fact, I pop in there quite a lot, just for the atmosphere. It's such a cool place—all blond-wood floors and spotlights and trendy sofas, and people rushing around being really busy and dynamic. Everyone stays really late every night, even though they don't have to—and at about seven o'clock someone always opens a bottle of wine and passes it around.

I've got a present to give his assistant Mel for her birthday, which was yesterday. I'm quite pleased with it actually—it's a gorgeous pair of cushions from the Conran Shop—and as I hand over the carrier bag, I actually hear her gasp, "Oh, Becky! You shouldn't have!"

"I wanted to!" I beam, and perch companionably on her desk as she admires them. "So—what's the latest?"

Ooh, you can't beat a good gossip. Mel puts down the carrier bag and gets out a box of toffees, and we have a lovely old natter. I hear all about her terrible date with an awful guy her mother's been trying to set her up with, and she hears all about Tom's wedding. And then she lowers her voice and starts filling me in on all the office gossip.

She tells me all about the two receptionists who haven't been speaking ever since they came to work in the same Next jacket and both refused to take it off—and the girl in accounts who has just come back from maternity leave and is throwing up every morning but won't admit anything.

"And here's a really juicy one!" she says, handing me the box of toffees. "I reckon Alicia's having an affair in the office."

"No!" I stare at her in amazement. "Really? With who?"

"With Ben Bridges."

I screw up my face, trying to place the name.

"That new guy who used to be at Coupland Foster Bright."

"Him?" I stare at Mel. "Really?"

I have to say I'm surprised. He's very sweet, but quite short and pushy. Not what I would have said was Alicia's type.

"I keep seeing them together, kind of whispering. And the other day Alicia said she was going to the dentist—but I went into Ratchetts and there they were, having a secret lunch—"

She breaks off as Luke appears at the door of his office, ushering out a man in a purple shirt.

"Mel, order a taxi for Mr. Mallory, would you please?"

"Of course, Luke," says Mel, switching into her efficient secretary voice. She picks up the phone and we grin at each other—then I walk into Luke's office.

His office is so smart. I always forget how grand he is. He's got a sweeping maple desk that was designed by some award-winning Danish designer, and on the shelves in the alcove behind it are all his shiny PR awards.

"Here you are," he says, handing me a sheaf of papers. The top one is a letter from someone called "Howski and Forlano, U.S. Immigration Lawyers," and as I see the words "your proposed relocation to the United States," I feel a tingle of excitement which reaches right to my fingertips.

"This is really happening, isn't it?" I say, walking over to his floor-length window and gazing down at the busy street below. "We're really going to New York."

"The flights are booked," he says, grinning at me.

"You know what I mean."

"I do know just what you mean," he echoes, and wraps me in his arms. "And it's very exciting."

For a while we just stand there, the two of us, looking down at the busy London street below. I can hardly believe I'm planning to leave all this to live in a foreign country. It's exciting and wonderful—but just a little scary, at the same time.

"Do you really think I'll get a job out there?" I say, as I have every time I've seen him in the past week. "Do you honestly think I will?"

"Of course you will." He sounds so assured and confident, I feel myself relax into his arms. "They'll love you. You're talented, and you're charming, and you come with a record of success . . . no question at all." He kisses me and holds me tight for a moment. Then he moves away to his desk, frowns absently, and opens a huge file labeled "New York." No wonder it's so huge. He told me the other day that he's been working toward a New York deal for three years. Three years!

"I can't believe you've been planning this for so long and

never told me," I say, watching him scribble something on a Post-it.

"Mmm," says Luke. I clench the papers in my hands slightly harder and take a deep breath. There's something I've been wanting to say for a while—and now is as good a moment as any.

"Luke, what would you have done if I hadn't wanted to go to New York?"

There's silence apart from the hum of the computer.

"I knew you'd want to go," says Luke at last. "It's the next obvious step for you."

"But . . . what if I hadn't?" I bite my lip. "Would you still have gone?" Luke sighs.

"Becky—you do want to go to New York, don't you?"

"Yes! You know I do!"

"So—what's the point in asking what-if questions? The point is, you want to go, I want to go . . . it's all perfect." He smiles at me and puts down his pen. "How are your parents doing?"

"They're . . . OK," I say hesitantly. "They're kind of getting used to the idea."

Which is sort of true. They were fairly shocked when I told them, I have to admit. In hindsight, perhaps I should have introduced Luke to them *before* making the announcement. Because how it happened was, I hurried into the house—where they were still sitting in their wedding gear, drinking tea in front of *Countdown*—and I switched off the telly and said joyfully, "Mum, Dad, I'm moving to New York with Luke!"

Whereupon Mum just looked at Dad and said, "Oh, Graham. She's gone."

She said afterward she didn't mean it like that—but I'm not so sure.

Then they actually met Luke, and he told them about his plans, and explained about all the opportunities in American TV for me—and I could see Mum's smile fading. Her face seemed to get smaller and smaller, and sort of closed in on itself. She went off to make some tea in the kitchen, and I followed her—and I could see she was upset. But she refused to show it. She just made the tea, with slightly shaking hands, and put out some biscuits—and then she turned to me and smiled brightly, and said, "I've always thought you would suit New York, Becky. It's the perfect place for you."

I stared at her, suddenly realizing what I was talking about. Going and living thousands of miles away from home, and my parents, and . . . my whole life, apart from Luke.

"You'll . . . you'll come and visit lots," I said, my voice trembling slightly.

"Of course we will, darling! All the time!"

She squeezed my hand and looked away—and then we went out into the sitting room, and didn't say much more about it.

But the next morning, when we came down for breakfast, she and Dad were poring over an ad in the *Sunday Times* for holiday properties in Florida, which they claimed they had been thinking about anyway. As we left that afternoon, they were arguing vigorously over whether the Disneyland in Florida was better than the one in California—even though I happen to know neither of them has ever set foot near Disneyland in their lives.

"Becky, I have to get on," says Luke, interrupting my thoughts. "Scottish Prime's new fund launch is tomorrow, and I've got a lot to do." He picks up the phone and dials a number. "I'll see you this evening, OK?"

"OK," I say, still loitering by the window. Then, suddenly remembering, I turn round. "Hey, have you heard about Alicia?"

"What about her?" Luke frowns at the receiver and puts it down.

"Mel reckons she's having an affair! With Ben Bridges! Can you believe it?"

"No, frankly," says Luke, tapping at his keyboard. "I can't."

"So what do you think's going on?" I perch on his desk and look excitedly at him.

"My sweet—" says Luke patiently. "I really do have to get on."

"Aren't you *interested*?"

"No. As long as they're doing their jobs."

"People are more than just their jobs," I say reprovingly. But Luke isn't even listening. He's got that faraway, cutoff look which comes over him when he's concentrating on business.

"Oh well," I say, and roll my eyes. "See you later."

As I come out, Mel is not at her desk—but Alicia is standing there in a smart black suit, staring at some papers. Her face seems more flushed than usual, and I wonder with an inward giggle if she's just been canoodling with Ben.

"Hi, Alicia," I say politely. "How are you?"

Alicia jumps, and she quickly gathers up whatever it is she's reading—then looks at me with a strange expression, as though horns have sprouted from my head.

"Becky," she says slowly. "Well, I never. The financial expert herself. The money guru!"

What *is* it about Alicia? Why does everything she say sound like she's playing some stupid game?

"Yes," I say. "It's me. Where's Mel gone?"

As I approach Mel's desk, I feel sure I left something on it. But I can't quite think what. Did I have an umbrella?

"She's gone to lunch," says Alicia. "She showed me the present you bought her. Very stylish."

"Thanks," I say shortly.

"So." She gives a faint smile. "I gather you're tagging along with Luke to New York. Must be nice to have a rich boyfriend."

God, she's a cow! She'd never say that in front of Luke.

"I'm not 'tagging along,' actually," I retort pleasantly. "I've got lots of meetings with television executives. It's a completely independent trip."

"But . . ." Alicia frowns thoughtfully. "Your flight's on the company, is it?"

"No! I paid for it myself!"

"Just wondering!" Alicia lifts her hands apologetically. "Well, have a great time, won't you?" She gathers up some folders and pops them into her briefcase, then snaps it shut. "I must run. Ciao."

"See you later," I say, and watch as she walks briskly off to the lifts.

I stand there by Mel's desk for a few seconds longer, still wondering what on earth it was that I put down. Oh, I don't suppose it can be important.

I get home to find Suze in the hall, talking on the phone. Her face is all red and shiny and her voice is trembling, and at once I'm seized by the terror that something awful has happened. Fearfully, I raise my eyebrows at her—and she nods frantically back, in between saying "Yes," and "I see," and "When would that be?"

I sink onto a chair, feeling weak with worry. What's she talking about? A funeral? A brain operation? As soon as I decide to go away—this happens.

"Guess what's happened?" she says shakily as she puts down the phone, and I leap up.

"Suze, I won't go to New York," I say, and impulsively take her hands. "I'll stay here and help you get through whatever it is. Has someone . . . died?"

"No," says Suze dazedly, and I swallow hard.

"Are you ill?"

"No, no, Bex, this is *good* news! I just . . . don't quite believe it."

"Well—what, then? Suze, what is it?"

"I've been offered my own line of home accessories in Hadleys. You know, the department store?" She shakes her head disbelievingly. "They want me to design a whole line! Frames, vases, stationery . . . whatever I want."

"Oh my God!" I clap a hand over my mouth. "That's *fantastic*!"

"This guy just rang up, out of the blue, and said his scouts have been monitoring sales of my frames. Apparently they've never seen anything like it!"

"Oh, Suze!"

"I had no idea things were going so well." Suze still looks shell-shocked. "This guy said it was a phenomenon! Everyone in the industry is talking about it. Apparently the only shop that hasn't done so well is that one which is miles away. Finchley or somewhere."

"Oh, right," I say vaguely. "I don't think I've ever even been to that one."

"But he said that had to be a blip—because all the other ones, in Fulham and Notting Hill and Chelsea, have all soared." She gives an embarrassed smile. "Apparently in Gifts and Goodies, around the corner, I'm the number-one best-seller!"

"Well, I'm not surprised!" I exclaim. "Your frames are easily the best thing in that shop. *Easily* the best." I throw my arms around her. "I'm so proud of you, Suze. I always knew you were going to be a star."

"Well, I never would have done it if it weren't for you! I mean, it was you who got me started making frames in the first place . . ." Suddenly Suze looks almost tearful. "Oh, Bex—I'm really going to miss you."

"I know," I say, biting my lip. "Me too."

For a while, we're both silent, and I honestly think I might start crying any second. But instead, I take a deep breath and look up. "Well, you'll just have to launch a New York branch."

"Yes!" says Suze, brightening. "Yes, I could do that, couldn't I?"

"Of course you could. You'll be all over the world soon." I give her a hug. "Hey, let's go out tonight and celebrate."

"Oh, Bex, I'd love to," says Suze, "but I can't. I'm going up to Scotland. In fact—" She looks at her watch, and pulls a face. "Oh, I didn't realize how late it was. Tarquin'll be here any moment."

"Tarquin's coming here?" I say in shock. "Now?"

Tarquin is Suze's cousin and is one of the richest people in Britain. (He's also one of the worst-dressed.) He's very sweet, and I never used to take much notice of him—until, a few months ago, we spent a truly toe-curling evening together. Even the memory of it makes me feel uncomfortable. Basically, the date was going fine (at least, fine given that I didn't find him attractive or have anything in common with him)—until Tarquin caught me flicking through his checkbook. Or at least, I think he did. I'm still not quite sure what he saw—and to be honest, I'm not keen to find out.

"I'm driving him up to my aunt's house for this dreary family party thing," says Suze. "We're going to be the only ones there under ninety."

As she hurries off to her room, the doorbell rings and she calls over her shoulder, "Could you get that, Bex? It's probably him."

Oh God. Oh God. I *really* don't feel prepared for this.

Trying to assume an air of confident detachment I swing open the front door and say brightly, "Tarquin!"

"Becky," he says, staring at me as though I'm the lost treasure of Tutankhamen.

And he's looking as bony and strange as ever, with an odd green hand-knitted jersey stuffed under a tweed waistcoat, and a huge old fob watch dangling from his pocket. I'm sorry, but surely the fifteenth richest man in England, or whatever he is, should be able to buy a nice new Timex?

"Well—come on in," I say overheartily, throwing my hand out like an Italian restaurant owner.

"Great," says Tarquin, and follows me into the sitting room. There's an awkward pause while I wait for him to sit down; in fact, I start to feel quite impatient as he hovers uncertainly in the middle of the room. Then suddenly I realize he's waiting for *me* to sit down, and hastily sink down onto the sofa.

"Would you like a titchy?" I ask politely.

"Bit early," says Tarquin, with a nervous laugh.

("Titchy" is Tarquin-speak for drink, by the way. And trousers are "tregs" and . . . you get the picture.)

We lapse into another dreadful silence. I just can't stop remembering awful details from our date—like when he tried to kiss me and I pretended to be absorbed in a nearby picture. Oh God. Forget. Forget.

"I . . . I heard you were moving to New York," Tarquin says suddenly, staring at the floor. "Is that true?"

"Yes," I say, unable to stop myself smiling. "Yes, that's the plan."

"I went to New York once myself," Tarquin says. "Didn't really get on with it."

"No," I say consideringly. "No, I can believe that. It's a bit different from Scotland, isn't it? Much more . . . frantic."

"Absolutely!" he exclaims, as if I've said something very insightful. "That was just it. Too frantic. And the people are absolutely extraordinary. Quite mad, in my opinion."

Compared to what? I want to retort. At least they don't call water "Ho" and sing Wagner in public.

But that wouldn't be kind. So I say nothing, and he says nothing—and when the door opens, we both look up gratefully.

"Hi!" says Suze, appearing at the door. "Tarkie, you're here! Listen, I've just got to get the car, because I had to park a few streets away the other night. I'll beep when I get back, and we can whiz off. OK?"

"OK," says Tarquin, nodding. "I'll just wait here with Becky."

"Lovely!" I say, trying to smile brightly.

Suze disappears, I shift awkwardly in my seat, and Tarquin stretches his feet out and stares at them. Oh, this is excruciating. The very sight of him is niggling at me more and more—and suddenly I realize I *have* to say something now, otherwise I'll disappear off to New York and the chance will be lost.

"Tarquin," I say, and exhale sharply. "There's something I . . . I really want to say to you. I've been wanting to say it for a while, actually."

"Yes?" he says, his head jerking up. "What . . . what is it?" He meets my eyes anxiously, and I feel a slight pang of nerves. But now I've started, I've got to carry on. I've got to tell him the truth. I push my hair back, and take a deep breath.

"That jumper," I say. "It *really* doesn't go with that waistcoat."

"Oh," says Tarquin, looking taken aback. "Really?"

"Yes!" I say, feeling a huge relief at having got it off my chest. "In fact . . . it's frightful."

"Should I take it off?"

"Yes. In fact, take the waistcoat off, too."

Obediently he peels off the jumper and the waistcoat—and it's amazing how much better he looks when he's just in a plain blue shirt. Almost . . . normal! Then I have a sudden inspiration.

"Wait here!"

I hurry to my room and seize one of the carrier bags sitting on my chair. There's a jumper inside which I bought a few days ago for Luke's birthday, but I've discovered he's already got exactly the same one, so I was planning to take it back.

"Here!" I say, arriving back in the sitting room. "Put this on. It's Paul Smith."

Tarquin slips the plain black jumper over his head and pulls it down—and what a difference! He's actually starting to look quite distinguished.

"Your hair," I say, staring critically at him. "We need to do something with that."

Ten minutes later I've wetted it, blow-dried it, and smoothed it back with a bit of mousse. And . . . I can't tell you. It's a transformation.

"Tarquin, you look wonderful!" I say—and I really mean it. He's still got that thin, bony look, but suddenly he doesn't look geeky anymore, he looks kind of . . . interesting.

"Really?" says Tarquin, staring down at himself. He looks a little shell-shocked, but the point is, he'll thank me in the long run.

A car horn sounds from outside, and we both jump.

"Well—have a good time," I say, suddenly feeling like his mother. "Tomorrow morning, just wet your hair again and push your fingers through it, and it should look OK."

"Right," says Tarquin, looking as though I've just given him a long mathematical formula to memorize. "I'll try to remember. And the jersey? Shall I return it by post?"

"Don't return it!" I say in horror. "It's yours to keep, and *wear.* A gift."

"Thank you," says Tarquin. "I'm . . . very grateful, Becky." He comes forward and pecks me on the cheek, and I pat him awkwardly on the hand. And as he disappears out of the door, I find myself hoping that he'll get lucky at this party, and find someone. He really does deserve it.

As I hear Suze's car drive away, I wander into the kitchen and make a cup of tea, wondering what to do for the rest of the afternoon. I was half-planning to do some more work on my self-help book. But my other alternative is to watch *Manhattan,* which Suze taped last night, and would be really useful research for my trip. Because after all, I need to be well prepared.

I can always work on the book when I get back from New York. Exactly.

I'm just happily putting the video into the machine when the phone rings.

"Oh, hello," says a girl's voice. "Sorry to disturb you. Is that Becky Bloomwood, by any chance?"

"Yes," I say, reaching for the remote control.

"This is Sally," says the girl. "I'm the new secretary at *Morning Coffee.* We met the other day."

"Oh. Erm . . . yes!" I wrinkle my brow, trying to remember.

"We just wanted to check on which hotel you're staying at in New York, in case we need to contact you urgently."

"I'll be at the Four Seasons."

"Four . . . Seasons," says Sally carefully. "Excellent."

"Do you think they might want me to do a report from New York or something?" I ask excitedly. That would be so cool! A special report from New York!

"Maybe," says Sally. "And that's with a Mr. . . . Luke Brandon?"

"That's right."

"For how many nights?"

"Erm . . . thirteen? Fourteen? I'm not sure." I'm squinting at the telly, wondering if I've gone too far back. Surely they don't show that Walker's crisps ad anymore?

"And are you staying in a room or a suite?"

"I think it's a suite. I could find out . . ."

"No, don't worry," says Sally pleasantly. "Well, I won't trouble you anymore. Enjoy your trip."

"Thanks!" I say, just as I find the start of the film. "I'm sure we will!"

The phone goes dead, and I walk over to the sofa, frowning slightly. Why did Sally need to know whether I was in a suite? Unless—maybe she was just curious.

But then I forget all about it, as Gershwin's *Rhapsody in Blue* suddenly crashes through the air, and the screen is filled with pictures of Manhattan. I stare at the television, utterly gripped. This is where we're going! In three days' time we'll be there! I just cannot, cannot wait!

"Little Ridings"
34 Copse Road
Eastbourne
Sussex

21 September 2000

Dear Rebecca:

Thank you for your letter and good wishes. I am thoroughly enjoying my retirement, thank you.

I am sorry to hear that you are having such difficulties dealing with John Gavin. May I assure you that he is not a heartless android programmed to make your life miserable. If you ever were cast out on the street with nothing but a pair of shoes, I'm sure he would be concerned, rather than "laugh evilly and walk away."

If you persevere with your good intentions, I'm certain your relationship with him will improve. You have every ability to keep your accounts in check, as long as your resolve remains steady.

I look forward to hearing how you get along.

With very best wishes,
Derek Smeath

HEAD OFFICE • PRESTON HOUSE • 354 KINGSWAY • LONDON WC2 4TH

Ms. Rebecca Bloomwood
Flat 2
4 Burney Rd.
London SW6 8FD

23 September 2000

Dear Rebecca Bloomwood:

Thank you for your letter of 18 September, and I was sorry to hear that our luggage policy has been giving you anxiety attacks and frown lines.

I accept that you may well weigh considerably less than, as you put it, "a fat businessman from Antwerp, stuffing his face full of doughnuts." Unfortunately Regal Airlines is still unable to increase your luggage allowance beyond the standard 20 kg.

You are welcome to start a petition and to write to Cherie Blair. However, our policy will remain the same.

Please enjoy your flight.

Mary Stevens
Customer Care Manager

Eight

I WAS *made* to live in America.

We've only been here one night, but already I'm completely in love with the place. For a start, our hotel is fantastic—all limestone and marble and amazing high ceilings. We're staying in an enormous suite overlooking Central Park, with a paneled dressing room and the most incredible bath that fills up in about five seconds. Everything is so grand, and luxurious, and kind of . . . *more.* Like last night, after we arrived, Luke suggested a quick nightcap downstairs—and honestly, the martini they brought me was the hugest drink I've ever seen. In fact, I nearly couldn't finish it. (But I managed it in the end. And then I had another one, just because it would have been churlish to refuse.)

Plus, everyone is so nice all the time. The hotel staff smile whenever they see you—and when you say "thank you," they reply, "you're welcome," which they would *never* do in Britain, just kind of grunt. To my amazement, I've already been sent a lovely bouquet of flowers and an invitation to lunch from Luke's mother, Elinor, and another bouquet from the TV people I'm meeting on Wednesday, and a basket of fruit from someone I've never heard of but who is apparently "desperate" to meet me!

I mean, when did Zelda from *Morning Coffee* last send me a basket of fruit?

I take a sip of coffee, and smile blissfully at Luke. We're sitting in the restaurant finishing breakfast before he whizzes off for a meeting, and I'm just deciding what to do with my time. I haven't got any interviews for a couple of days—so it's completely up to me whether I take in a few museums, or stroll in Central Park . . . or . . . pop into a shop or two . . .

"Would you like a refill?" comes a voice at my ear, and I look up to see a smiling waiter offering me a coffeepot. You see what I mean? They've been offering us endless coffee since we sat down, and when I asked for an orange juice they brought me a huge glass, all garnished with frosted orange peel. And as for those scrummy pancakes I've just polished off . . . I mean, pancakes for breakfast. It's pure genius, isn't it?

"So—I guess you'll be going to the gym?" says Luke, as he folds up his copy of the *Daily Telegraph.* He reads all the papers every day, American and British. Which is quite good, because it means I can still read my *Daily World* horoscope.

"The gym?" I say puzzledly.

"I thought that was going to be your routine," he says, reaching for the *FT.* "A workout every morning."

And I'm about to say, "Don't be ridiculous!"—when it occurs to me that I might have rashly announced something along those lines last night. After that second martini.

Still—that's OK. I can go to the gym. In fact, it would be *good* to go to the gym. And then I could . . . well, I could always take in a few sights, I suppose. Maybe look at a few famous buildings.

You know, I'm sure I read somewhere that Bloomingdale's is quite an admired piece of architecture.

"And then what will you do?"

"I don't know," I say vaguely, watching as a waiter puts a plate of French toast down on the table next to ours. God, that looks delicious. Why don't we have stuff like this in Europe? "Go and explore New York, I guess."

"I was asking at reception—and there's a guided walking tour which leaves from the hotel at eleven. The concierge highly recommended it."

"Oh right," I say, taking a sip of coffee. "Well, I suppose I could do that . . ."

"Unless you wanted to get any shopping out of the way?" Luke adds, reaching for the *Times,* and I stare at him slightly incredulously. You don't "get shopping out of the way." You get *other things* out of the way.

Which, in fact, makes me think. Maybe I should do this tour—and then I've got sightseeing ticked off.

"The guided tour sounds good," I say. "In fact, it'll be a great way to get to know my new home city. The Statue of Liberty, Central Park . . ."

"Don't go to Central Park," puts in Luke.

"Why not? Is it dangerous?"

"It can be, but that's not why." Luke looks up with that serious, affectionate expression of his. "The truth is, I'd love to introduce it to you myself. It's one of my favorite places in the world."

"OK." I smile at him, feeling touched. "I won't go to Central Park."

As he shakes open the *Times* I look at him more carefully. His jaw is set and he doesn't quite have his usual confident demeanor. In fact he looks . . . nervous, I realize in surprise.

"Feeling all right?" I say encouragingly. "All set for your meeting? Who's it with, anyway?"

"Mason Forbes Stockbrokers," says Luke. "One of the companies I'm very much hoping to sign up as a client."

"Excellent! Well, I'm sure it'll go brilliantly."

"I hope so." He's silent for a moment. "It's all been talk up to now. Talk and plans and promises. But now I need to start getting a few results. A few signatures on the line."

"You'll get your signatures!" Confidently, I pick up *The Daily World.* "Just listen to your horoscope: 'A day for doing deals and winning hearts. If you have faith in yourself, others will too. You are beginning a streak of success.' " I look up. "You see? It's in your stars!"

"Let me see that," says Luke, and plucks the paper from my hand before I can stop him.

Damn.

"You do *slightly* have to read between the lines . . ." I add quickly.

"I see," he says, gazing down at the horoscope page with a smile. "Yes, that would explain it. So, do you want to hear yours?"

"I've already—"

" 'Spend today exploring new surroundings,' " says Luke, as though reading. " 'Remember to hold your bag tightly to you and that over here it's called a purse. Have a nice day—but don't feel obliged to tell complete strangers to have one.' "

He smiles at me and I laugh. As he puts away the paper I take a sip of coffee and glance around the dining room at all the smart businessmen and groomed women sitting on luxurious striped chairs. Piano music is tinkling discreetly and I feel like I'm at the hub of some cosmopolitan, civilized world. At a nearby table a woman in black is talking about the First Lady's wardrobe, and I listen eagerly until she gives me a look.

The First Lady. I mean, it sounds so much more impressive than "prime minister's wife."

"God, just think, Luke," I say dreamily. "In a few weeks' time, this will be our home city. We'll be real New Yorkers!"

I'll have to buy a few more black things before then, I find myself thinking. Everyone here seems to wear black . . .

"Becky—" says Luke. He puts down his paper—and suddenly he looks rather grave. "There's something I've been meaning to say to you. Everything's been such a rush, I haven't had a chance—but it's something I really think you need to hear."

"OK," I say apprehensively. "What is it?"

"It's a big step, moving to a new city, especially a city as extreme as New York. It's not the same as London . . ."

"I know," I nod. "You have to have your nails done."

Luke gives a puzzled frown before carrying on: "I've been here many times—and even I find it overwhelming at times. The sheer pressure and pace of life here is, frankly, on another level from London."

"Right. So—what are you saying?"

"I'm saying I think you should take it slow. Don't expect to fit in straight away. You may well find it a bit of a shock to begin with."

I stare at him, discomfited.

"Don't you think I'll be able to stand the pace?"

"I'm not saying that," says Luke. "I'm just saying—get to know the city gradually. Get the feel of it; see if you can really see yourself living here. You may hate it! You may decide you can't possibly move here. Of course, I very much hope you don't—but it's worth keeping an open mind."

"Right," I say slowly. "I see."

"So just see how today goes—and we'll talk some more this evening. OK?"

"OK," I say, and drain my coffee thoughtfully.

I'll show Luke I can fit into this city. I'll show him I can be a true New Yorker. I'll go to the gym, and then I'll eat a bagel, and then I'll . . . shoot someone, maybe?

Or maybe just the gym will be enough.

I'm actually quite looking forward to doing a workout, because I bought this fab DKNY exercise outfit in the sales last year, and this is the first time I've had the chance to wear it! I did mean to join a gym, in fact I even went and got a registration pack from Holmes Place in Fulham. But then I read this really interesting article which said you could lose loads of weight just by fidgeting. Just by twitching your fingers and stuff! So I thought I'd go for that method instead, and spend the money I saved on a new dress.

But it's not that I don't like exercise or anything. And if I'm going to live in New York, I'll have to go to the gym every day. I mean, it's the law or something. So this is a good way to acclimatize.

As I reach the entrance to the fitness center I glance at my reflection—and I'm secretly quite impressed. They say people in New York are all pencil thin and fit, don't they? But I reckon I look much fitter than some of these characters. I mean, look at that balding guy over there in the gray T-shirt. He looks like he's never been near a gym in his life!

"Hi there," says a voice. I look up and see a muscular guy in trendy black Lycra coming toward me. "I'm Tony. How are you today?"

"I'm fine, thanks," I say, and casually do a little hamstring stretch. (At least, I think it's my hamstring. The one in your leg.) "Just here for a workout."

Nonchalantly I swap legs, clasp my hands, and stretch my arms out in front of me. I can see my reflection on the other side of the room—and though I say it myself, I look pretty bloody cool.

"Do you exercise regularly?" asks Tony.

"Not in a gym," I say, reaching down to touch my toes—then changing my mind halfway down and resting my hands on my knees. "But I walk a lot."

"Great!" says Tony. "On a treadmill? Or cross-country?"

"Round the shops, mostly."

"OK . . ." he says doubtfully.

"But I'm often holding quite heavy things," I explain. "You know, carrier bags and stuff."

"Right . . ." says Tony, not looking that convinced. "Well . . . would you like me to show you how the machines work?"

"It's all right," I say confidently. "I'll be fine."

Honestly, I can't be bothered listening to him explain every single machine and how many settings it has. I mean, I'm not a moron, am I? I take a towel from the pile, drape it around my neck, and head off toward a running machine, which should be fairly simple. I step up onto the treadmill and survey the buttons in front of me. A panel is flashing the word "time" and after some thought I enter "40 minutes," which sounds about right. I mean, that's how long you'd go on a walk for, isn't it? It flashes "program" and after scrolling down the choices I select "Everest," which sounds much more interesting than "hill walk." Then it flashes "level." Hmm. Level. I look around for some advice—but Tony is nowhere to be seen.

The balding guy is getting onto the treadmill next to mine, and I lean over.

"Excuse me," I say politely. "Which level do you think I should choose?"

"That depends," says the guy. "How fit are you?"

"Well," I say, smiling modestly. "You know . . ."

"I'm going for level 5, if it's any help," says the guy, briskly punching at his machine.

"OK," I say. "Thanks!"

Well, if he's level 5, I must be at least level 7. I mean, frankly, look at him—and look at me.

I reach up to the machine and punch in "7"—then press "start." The treadmill starts moving, and I start walking. And this is really pleasant! I really should go to the gym more often. Or, in fact, join a gym.

But it just shows, even if you don't work out, you can still have a level of natural baseline fitness. Because this is causing me absolutely no problems at all. In fact, it's far too easy. I should have chosen level—

Hang on. The machine's tilting upward. And it's speeding up. I'm running to catch up with it.

Which is OK. I mean, this is the point, isn't it? Having a nice healthy jog. Running along, panting a little, but that just means my heart is working. Which is perfect. Just as long as it doesn't get any—

It's tilting again. And it's getting faster. And faster.

I can't do this. My face is red. My chest is hurting. I'm panting frenziedly, and clutching the sides of the machine. I can't run this fast. I have to slow down a bit.

Feverishly I jab at the panel—but the treadmill keeps whirring round—and suddenly cranks up even higher. Oh no. Please, no.

"Time left: 38.00" flashes brightly on a panel in front of me. *Thirty-eight more minutes?*

I glance to my right—and the balding guy is sprinting easily along as though he's running through a field of daisies. I want to ask him for help, but I can't open my mouth. I can't do anything except keep my legs moving as best I can.

But all of a sudden he glances in my direction—and his expression changes.

"Miss? Are you all right?"

He hastily punches at his machine, which grinds to a halt, then leaps down and jabs at mine.

The treadmill slows down, then comes to a rather abrupt standstill—and I collapse against one of the side bars, gasping for breath.

"Have some water," says the man, handing me a cup.

"Th-thanks," I say, and stagger down off the treadmill, still gasping. My lungs feel as if they're about to burst, and when I glimpse my reflection opposite, my face is beet red.

"Maybe you should leave it for today," says the man, gazing at me anxiously.

"Yes," I say. "Yes, maybe I will." I take a swig of water, trying to get my breath back. "I think actually the trouble is, I'm not used to American machines."

"Could be," says the man, nodding. "They can be tricky. Of course, this one," he adds, slapping it cheerfully, "was made in Germany."

"Right," I say after a pause. "Yes. Well, anyway. Thanks for your help."

"Any time," says the man—and as he gets back onto his treadmill I can see him smiling.

Oh God, that was really embarrassing. As I make my way, showered and changed, to the foyer of the hotel for the walking tour, I feel a little deflated. Maybe Luke's right. Maybe I won't cope with the pace of New York. Maybe it's a stupid idea, my moving here with him. I mean, if I can't keep up with a treadmill, how am I going to keep up with a whole city?

A group of sightseers has already assembled—mostly much older than me and attired in a variety of sensible windbreakers and sneakers. They're all listening to a young, enthusiastic man who's saying something about the Statue of Liberty.

"Hi there!" he says, breaking off as I approach. "Are you here for the tour?"

"Yes, please," I say.

"And your name?"

"Rebecca Bloomwood," I say, flushing a little as all the others turn to look at me. "I paid at the desk, earlier."

"Well, hi, Rebecca!" says the man, ticking something off on his list. "I'm Christoph. Welcome to our group. Got your walking shoes on?" He looks down at my boots (bright purple, kitten heel, last year's Bertie sale) and his cheery smile falters. "You realize this is a three-hour tour? All on foot?"

"Absolutely," I say in surprise. "That's why I put these boots on."

"Right," says Christoph after a pause. "Well—OK." He looks around. "I think that's it, so let's start our tour!"

He leads the way out of the hotel, onto Fifty-seventh Street. It's a wide and busy street, with canopied entrances and trees planted at intervals and limousines pulling up in front of expensive-looking shops. As everyone else follows Christoph briskly along the pavement, I find myself walking slowly, staring upward. It's an amazingly clear, fresh day—with almost blinding sunlight bouncing off the pavements and buildings—and as I look around I'm completely filled with awe. God, this city is an incredible place. I mean, obviously I knew that New York would be full of tall skyscrapers. But it's only when you're actually standing in the street, staring up at them, that you realize how . . . well, how *huge* they are. I gaze up at the tops of the buildings against the sky, until my neck is aching and I'm starting to feel dizzy. Then slowly my eyes wander down, floor by floor to shop-window level. And I find myself staring at two words. *Prada* and *Shoes.*

Ooh.

Prada Shoes. Right in front of me.

I'll just have a really quick look.

As the others all march on, I hurry up to the window and stare at a pair of deep brown pumps with cream stitching. God, those are divine. I wonder how much they are? You know, Prada is probably really cheap over here. Maybe I should just pop in and—

"Rebecca?"

With a start I come to and look round to see the tour group twenty yards down the street, all staring at me.

"Sorry," I say, and reluctantly pull myself away from the window. "I'm coming."

"There'll be time for shopping later," says Christoph cheerfully.

"I know," I say, and give a relaxed laugh. "Sorry about that."

"Don't worry about it!"

Of course, he's quite right. There'll be plenty of time to go shopping. Plenty of time.

Right. I'm really going to concentrate on the tour.

"So, Rebecca," says Christoph brightly, as I rejoin the group. "I was just telling the others that we're heading down East Fifty-seventh Street to Fifth Avenue, the most famous avenue of New York City."

"Great!" I say. "That sounds really good!"

"Fifth Avenue serves as a dividing line between the 'East Side' and the 'West Side,' " continues Christoph. "Anyone interested in history will like to know that . . ."

I'm nodding intelligently as he speaks, and trying to look interested. But as we walk down the street, my head keeps swiveling from left to right, like someone watching a tennis game. Christian Dior, Hermès, Chanel . . . This street is just incredible. If only we could just slow down a bit, and have a proper look—but Christoph is marching on ahead like a hike leader, and everybody else in the group is following him happily, not even glancing at the amazing sights around them. Do they not have eyes in their heads?

". . . where we're going to take in two well-known landmarks: Rockefeller Center, which many of you will associate with ice-skating . . ."

We swing round a corner—and my heart gives a swoop of excitement. Tiffany's. It's Tiffany's, right in front of me! I *must* just have a quick peek. I mean, this is what New York is all about. Little blue boxes, and white ribbon, and those gorgeous silver beans . . . I sidle up to the window and stare longingly at the beautiful display inside. Wow. That necklace is absolutely stunning. Oh God, and look at that watch, with all those little diamonds round the edge. I wonder how much something like that would—

"Hey, everybody, wait up!" rings out Christoph's voice. I look up—and they're all bloody miles ahead again. How come they walk so fast, anyway? "Are you OK there, Rebecca?" he calls, with a slightly forced cheeriness. "You're going to have to try to keep up! We have a lot of ground to cover!"

"Sorry," I say, and scuttle toward the group. "Just having a quick little look at Tiffany's." I grin at a woman next to me, expecting her to smile back. But she looks at me blankly and pulls the hood of her baggy gray sweatshirt more tightly over her head.

"As I was saying," Christoph says as we stride off again, "above Fourteenth Street, Manhattan was designed as a grid, so that . . ."

And for a while I really try to concentrate. But it's no good. I can't listen. I mean, come on. This is Fifth Avenue! There are women striding along in immaculate coats and sunglasses, yellow taxicabs honking at each other, two men are standing on a street corner, arguing in Italian . . . And everywhere I look, there are fabulous shops. There's Gucci—and that's the hugest Gap I've ever seen in my life . . . and oh God, look at that window display over there! And we're just walking straight past Armani Exchange and no one's even pausing . . .

What is *wrong* with these people? Are they complete philistines?

We walk on a bit farther, and I'm trying my best to catch a glimpse inside a window full of amazing-looking hats when . . . oh my God. Just . . . just look there. It's Saks Fifth Avenue. Right there, across the street. One of the most famous department stores in the world. Floors and floors of clothes and shoes and bags . . . And thank God, at *last,* Christoph is coming to his senses and stopping.

"This is one of New York's most famous landmarks," he's saying, with a gesture. "Many New Yorkers regularly visit this magnificent place of worship—once a week or even more often. Some even make it here daily! We don't have time to do more than have a quick look inside—but those that are interested can always make a return trip."

"Is it very old?" asks a man with a Scandinavian accent.

"The building dates from 1879," says Christoph, "and was designed by James Renwick."

Come on, I think impatiently, as someone else asks a question about the architecture. Who cares who designed it? Who cares about the stonework? It's what's inside that matters.

"Shall we go in?" says Christoph at last.

"Absolutely!" I say joyfully, and hurry across the street toward the entrance.

It's only as my hand is actually on the door that I realize no one else is with me. Where've they all gone? Puzzled, I look back—and the rest of the group is processing into a big stone church, outside which there's a board reading "St. Patrick's Cathedral."

Oh.

Oh, I see. When he said "magnificent place of worship" he meant . . .

Right. Of course.

I hesitate, hand on the door, feeling torn. I should go into the cathedral. I should take in some culture and come back to Saks later.

But then—how is that going to help me get to know whether I want to live in New York or not? Looking around some old cathedral?

Put it like this—how many millions of cathedrals do we have in England? And how many branches of Saks Fifth Avenue?

"Are you going in?" says an impatient voice behind me.

"Yes!" I say, coming to a decision. "Absolutely. I'm going in."

I push my way through the heavy wooden doors and into the store, feeling almost sick with anticipation. I haven't felt this excited since Octagon relaunched their designer floor and I was invited to the cardholders' champagne reception.

I mean, visiting any shop for the first time is exciting. There's always that electric buzz as you push open the door; that hope, that *belief,* that this is going to be the shop of all shops, which will bring you everything you ever wanted, at magically low prices. But this is a thousand times better. A million times. Because this isn't just any old shop, is it? This is a world-famous shop. I'm actually here. I'm in Saks on Fifth Avenue in New York. As I walk slowly into the store—forcing myself not to rush—I feel as though I'm setting off for a date with a Hollywood movie star.

I wander through the perfumery, gazing around at the elegant Art Deco paneling; the high, airy ceilings; the foliage everywhere. God, this has to be one of the most beautiful shops I've ever been in. At the back are old-fashioned lifts which make you feel you're in a film with Cary Grant, and on a little table is a pile of store directories. I pick one up, just to get my bearings . . . and I don't quite believe it. There are ten floors to this store.

Ten.

I stare at the list, transfixed. I feel like a child trying to choose a sweetie in a chocolate factory. Where am I going to start? How should I do this? Start at the top? Start at the bottom? All these names, jumping out at me, calling to me. Anna Sui. Calvin Klein. Kate Spade. Kiehl's. I am going to hyperventilate.

"Excuse me?" A voice interrupts my thoughts and I turn to see a girl with a Saks name badge smiling at me. "Can I help you?"

"Um . . . yes," I say, still staring at the directory. "I'm just trying to work out where to start, really."

"Were you interested in clothes? Or accessories? Or shoes?"

"Yes," I say dazedly. "Both. All. Everything. Erm . . . a bag," I say randomly. "I need a new bag!"

Which is true. I mean, I've brought bags with me—but you can always do with a new bag. Plus, I've been noticing that all the women in Manhattan seem to have very smart designer bags—so this is a very good way of acclimatizing myself to the city.

The girl gives me a friendly smile.

"Bags and accessories are through there," she says, pointing. "You might want to start there and work your way up."

"Yes," I say. "That's what I'll do. Thanks!"

God, I adore shopping abroad. I mean, shopping anywhere is always great—but the advantages of doing it abroad are:

1. You can buy things you can't get in Britain.
2. You can name-drop when you get back home. ("Actually, I picked this up in New York.")
3. Foreign money doesn't count, so you can spend as much as you like.

OK, I know that last one isn't entirely true. Somewhere in my head I know that dollars are proper money, with a real value. But I mean, *look* at them. I just can't take them seriously. I've got a whole wodge of them in my purse, and I feel as though I'm carrying around the bank from a Monopoly set. Yesterday I went and bought some magazines from a newsstand, and as I handed over a twenty-dollar bill, it was just like playing shop. It's like some weird form of jet lag—you move into another currency and suddenly feel as though you're spending nothing.

So as I walk around the bag department, trying out gorgeous bag after gorgeous bag, I'm not taking too much notice of the prices. Occasionally I lift a price tag and make a feeble attempt to work out how much that is in real money—but I have to confess, I can't remember the exact exchange rate.

But the point is, it doesn't matter. Because this is America, and everyone knows that prices in America are really low. It's common knowledge. So basically, I'm working on the principle that everything's a bargain. I mean, look at all these gorgeous designer handbags. They're probably half what they'd cost in England, if not less!

As I'm hovering over the DKNY display, an elderly woman wearing a gold-colored suit and carrying a Gucci tote comes up to me.

"Which one matches?" she says. "This . . . " She holds out a tan satin bag. ". . . or this . . . " She holds out a paler one. "It's for evening," she adds.

"Erm . . ." I look at her suit and at the bags again—and wonder how to tell her they don't match at all. "The thing is, they're both a kind of brownish color . . . and your suit's more of a golden, yellowish . . ."

"Not the suit!" she exclaims. "The dog!"

I look at her perplexedly—then spot a tiny face poking out of the Gucci tote. Oh my God! Is that a real live *dog*?

"Don't hide, Muffy!" says the woman, reaching into the bag and hauling it out. And honestly, it's more like a rat than a dog—except a rat with a Gucci collar and a diamante name tag.

"You want your bag to match your . . . dog?" I say, just to be sure.

"If I can't find anything, I'll just have to have her hair tinted again." The woman sighs. "But it's so time-consuming . . ."

"No, don't do that!" I say hastily. "I think the paler bag goes perfectly."

"I think you're right." She gives it a critical look, then nods. "Thank you for your help. Do you have a dog?"

"Erm . . . not on me."

The woman stares at me suspiciously—then stuffs the dog back in the Gucci tote. She walks off, and I resume my search, wondering if I need to buy a dog in order to be a real New Yorker. Except I only like big ones. And you couldn't exactly lug a Labrador around in a Fendi clutch, could you?

Eventually I choose a beautiful Kate Spade bag in tan leather, and take it up to the counter. It costs five hundred dollars, which sounds quite a lot—but then, "a million lira" sounds like a lot too, doesn't it? And that's only about fifty pence. So this is *sure* to be a bargain.

As the assistant hands me my receipt, she even says something about it being "a gift"—and I beam in agreement.

"A complete gift! I mean, in London, it would probably cost—"

"Gina, are you going upstairs?" interrupts the woman, turning to a colleague. "Gina will show you to the seventh floor," she says, and smiles at me.

"Right," I say, in slight confusion. "Well . . . OK."

Gina beckons me briskly and, after a moment's hesitation, I follow her, wondering what's on the seventh floor. Maybe some complimentary lounge for Kate Spade customers, with free champagne or something!

It's only as we're approaching a department entitled "Gift Wrapping" that I suddenly realize what's going on. When I said *gift,* she must have thought I meant it was an actual—

"Here we are," says Gina brightly. "The Saks signature box is complimentary—or choose from a range of quality wrap."

"Right!" I say. "Well . . . thanks very much! Although actually, I wasn't really planning to—"

But Gina has already gone—and the two ladies behind the gift wrap counter are smiling encouragingly at me.

This is a bit embarrassing.

"Have you decided which paper you'd like?" says the elder of the two ladies, beaming at me. "We also have a choice of ribbons and adornments."

Oh, sod it. I'll get it wrapped. I mean, it only costs $7.50—and it'll be nice to have something to open when I get back to the hotel room.

"Yes!" I say, and beam back. "I'd like that silver paper, please, and some purple ribbon . . . and one of those clusters of silver berries."

The lady reaches for the paper and deftly begins to wrap up my bag—more neatly than I've ever wrapped anything in my life. And you know, this is quite fun! Maybe I should always get my shopping gift wrapped.

"Who's it to?" says the lady, opening a card and taking out a silver pen.

"Um . . . to Becky," I say vaguely. Three girls, all wearing jeans and high-heeled boots, have come into the gift wrap room—and I'm slightly intrigued by their conversation.

". . . below wholesale . . ."

". . . sample sale . . ."

". . . Earl jeans . . ."

"And who is it from?" says the gift wrap lady pleasantly.

"Um . . . from Becky," I say without thinking. The gift wrap lady gives me a rather strange look and I suddenly realize what I've said. "A . . . a different Becky," I add awkwardly.

". . . sample sale . . ."

". . . Alexander McQueen, pale blue, 80 percent off . . ."

". . . sample sale . . ."

". . . sample sale . . ."

I cannot bear this any longer.

"Excuse me," I say, turning round. "I didn't mean to eavesdrop on your conversation—but I just have to know one thing. What is a sample sale?"

The whole gift wrap area goes quiet. Everyone is staring at me, even the lady with the silver pen.

"You don't know what a sample sale is?" says a girl in a leather jacket eventually, as though I've said I don't know my alphabet.

"Erm . . . no," I say, feeling myself flush red. "No, I . . . I don't." The girl raises her eyebrows, reaches in her bag, rummages around, and eventually pulls out a card. "Honey, *this* is a sample sale."

I take the card from her—and as I read, my skin starts to prickle with excitement.

SAMPLE SALE

Designer clothes, 50–70% off.

Ralph Lauren, Comme des Garçons, Gucci.

Bags, shoes, hosiery, 40–60% off.

Prada, Fendi, Lagerfeld.

"Is this for real?" I breathe at last, looking up. "I mean, could . . . could *I* go to it?"

"Oh yeah," says the girl. "It's for real. But it'll only last a day."

"A day?" My heart starts to thump in panic. "Just one day?"

"One day," affirms the girl solemnly. I glance at the other girls—and they're nodding in agreement.

"Sample sales come without much warning," explains one.

"They can be anywhere. They just appear overnight."

"Then they're gone. Vanished."

"And you just have to wait for the next one."

I look from face to face, utterly mesmerized. I feel like an explorer learning about some mysterious nomadic tribe.

"So you wanna catch this one today," says the girl in blue, tapping the card and bringing me back to life, "you'd better hurry."

I have never moved as fast as I do out of that shop. Clutching my Saks Fifth Avenue carrier, I hail a taxi, breathlessly read out the address on the card, and sink back into my seat.

I have no idea where we're heading or what famous landmarks we're passing—but I don't care. As long as there are designer clothes on sale, then that's all I need to know.

We come to a stop, and I pay the driver, making sure I tip him about 50 percent so he doesn't think I'm some stingy English tourist—and, heart thumping, I get out. And I have to admit, on first impression, things are not promising. I'm in a street full of rather uninspiring-looking shop fronts and office blocks. On the card it said the sample sale was at 405, but when I follow the numbers along the road, 405 turns out to be just another office building. Am I in the wrong place altogether? I walk along the pavement for a little bit, peering up at the buildings—but there are no clues. I don't even know which district I'm in.

Suddenly I feel deflated and rather stupid. I was supposed to be going on a nice organized walking tour today—and what have I done instead? I've gone rushing off to some strange part of the city, where I'll probably get mugged any minute. In fact, the whole thing was probably a scam, I think morosely. I mean, honestly. Designer clothes at 70 percent discount? I should have realized it was far too good to be—

Hang on. Just . . . hang on a minute.

Another taxi is pulling up, and a girl in a Miu Miu dress is getting out. She consults a piece of paper, walks briskly along the pavement, and disappears inside the door of 405. A moment later, two more girls appear along the street—and as I watch, they go inside, too.

Maybe this *is* the right place.

I push open the glass doors, walk into a shabby foyer, and nod nervously at the concierge sitting at the desk.

"Erm . . . excuse me," I say politely. "I was looking for the—"

"Twelfth floor," he says in a bored voice. "Elevators are in the rear."

I hurry toward the back of the foyer, summon one of the rather elderly lifts, and press twelve. Slowly and creakily the lift rises—and I begin to hear a kind of faint hubbub, rising in volume as I get nearer. The lift suddenly pings and the doors open and . . . Oh my God. Is this the *queue*?

A line of girls is snaking back from a door at the end of the corridor. Girls in cashmere coats, girls in black suits, girls tossing their springy ponytails around, and chattering excitedly into their mobile phones. There's not a single one who isn't wearing full makeup and smart shoes and carrying some sort of designer bag, even if it's the teeniest little Louis Vuitton coin purse—and the babble of conversation is peppered with names of fashion houses. They're all pressing forward, firmly moving their stilettos inch by inch along the floor, and all have the same urgent look in their eyes. Every so often somebody pushes their way out of the door, holding an enormous, nameless carrier bag—and about three girls push their way in. Then, just as I join the end of the line, there's a rattling sound, and a woman opens up a door, a few yards behind me.

"Another entrance this way," she calls. "Come this way!"

In front of me, a whole line of heads whips round. There's a collective intake of breath—and then it's like a tidal wave of girls, all heading toward me. I find myself running toward the door, just to avoid being knocked down—and suddenly I'm in the middle of the room, slightly shaken, as everybody else peels off and heads for the racks.

I look around, trying to get my bearings. There are racks and racks of clothes, tables covered in bags and shoes and scarves. I can already spot Ralph Lauren knitwear . . . a rack full of fabulous coats . . . there's a stack of Prada bags . . . I mean, this is like a dream come true! Everywhere I look, girls are feverishly sorting through garments, looking for labels, trying out bags. Their manicured nails are descending on the stuff like the claws of birds of prey and I can't believe quite how fast they're working. As I see the girl who was standing in front of me in the line, I feel a surge of panic. She's got a whole armful of stuff, and I haven't even started. If I don't get in there, everything will be gone. I have to grab something now!

I fight my way through to one of the racks and start leafing through chiffon pleated dresses. Three hundred dollars, reduced to seventy dollars! I mean, even if you only wore it once . . . And oh God, here are some fantastic print trousers, some label I've never heard of, but they're reduced by 90 percent! And a leather coat . . . and those Prada bags. I *have* to get one of the Prada bags!

As I breathlessly reach for one, my hand collides with another girl's.

"Hey!" she says at once, and snatches the bag up. "I was there first!"

"Oh," I say. "Erm . . . sorry!" I quickly grab another one which, to be honest, looks exactly the same. As the girl starts examining the interior of her bag, I can't help staring at her nails. They're filed into square shapes and carefully decorated in two different shades of pink. How long did that take to do? As she looks up, I see her hair is two-tone as well—brown with aubergine tips—while her mouth is carefully lined with purple and filled in with pale mauve.

"Got a problem?" she says, suddenly looking at me, and I jump.

"No! I was just wondering—where's the changing room?"

"Changing room?" She chuckles. "Are you kidding? No such thing."

"Oh." I look around again, and notice a spectacular black girl, about nine feet tall, stripping off to her bra and knickers. "I see. So we . . . change right here? Great!" I swallow. "No problem at all."

Hesitantly I start unbuttoning my coat, telling myself that I've got no alternative—and no one's watching anyway. But Two-Tone Girl's expression is changing as she gazes at me.

"Are you British?"

"Yes! Did you recognize my accent?"

"I love the British!" Her eyes light up. "That film, *Notting Hill*? I loved that!"

"Oh right! So did I, actually."

"That Welsh guy. He was hilarious!" She suddenly frowns as I step out of my shoes. "Hey, but wait. You shouldn't have to get changed out here."

"Why not?"

"Because you're British! Everyone knows the Brits are reserved. It's like . . . your national disease or something."

"Honestly, it's fine . . ."

"Don't worry about it. I'll take care of it." To my horror the girl strides over and pokes the woman in black standing by the door. "Excuse me? This girl is British. She needs privacy to try on her things. OK?"

The woman turns to stare at me as though I'm a Martian and I smile nervously back.

"Really, don't worry. I don't mind . . ."

"She needs privacy!" insists the girl. "They're different than us. It's a whole other culture. Can she go behind those racks there?"

"Please. I don't want to—"

"Whatever," says the woman, rolling her eyes. "Just don't mess up the displays."

"Thanks," I say to the girl, a little awkwardly. "I'm Becky, by the way."

"Jodie." She gives me a wide grin. "Love your boots!"

I disappear behind the rack and begin trying on all the

clothes I've gathered. With each one I feel a little frisson of delight—and when I get to the Prada bag, it's a surge of pure joy. Prada at 50 percent off! I mean, this would make the whole trip worthwhile, just on its own.

When I've eventually finished, I come out from behind the rack to see Jodie wriggling into a stretchy white dress.

"This sample sale is so great!" she exclaims. "I'm just like . . . where do I stop?"

"I know what you mean." I give her a blissful smile. "That dress looks great, by the way."

"Are you going to buy all that?" she says, giving my armload an impressed look.

"Not all of it." I reach into the pile. "Not . . . these trousers. But everything else."

"Cool! Go, girl."

As I happily head toward the paying table, the room is reverberating with high-pitched female voices and I can hear snippets of conversation floating around.

"I have to have it," a girl is saying, holding up a coat against herself. "I just *have* to have it."

"OK, what I'm going to do is, I'm just going to put the $450 I spent today onto my mortgage," another girl is saying to her friend as they walk out, laden with bags. "I mean, what's $450 over thirty years?"

"One hundred percent cashmere!" someone else is exclaiming. "Did you see this? It's only fifty dollars! I'm going to take three."

I dump my stuff on the table and look around the bright, buzzing room at the girls milling about, grabbing at merchandise, trying on scarves, piling their arms full of glossy new gorgeous things. And I feel a sudden warmth, an overwhelming realization. These are my people. I've found my homeland.

Several hours later, I arrive back at the Four Seasons, still on a complete high. After the sample sale, I ended up going out for a "welcome to New York" coffee with Jodie. We sat at a marble table, sipping our decaf Frappuccinos and nibbling at nonfat cranberry muffins, and both worked out exactly how much money we'd saved on our bargains ($1,230 in my case!). We agreed to meet up again during my visit—and then Jodie told me all about this amazing Web site that sends you information on these kind of events every day. Every day! I mean, the possibilities are limitless. You could spend your *whole life* going to sample sales!

You know. In theory.

I go up to our room—and as I open the door I see Luke sitting at the desk, reading through some papers.

"Hi!" I say breathlessly, dumping my bags on the enormous bed. "Listen, I need to use the laptop."

"Oh right," says Luke. "Sure." He picks up the laptop from the desk and hands it to me, and I go and sit on the bed. I open the laptop, consult the piece of paper Jodie gave me, and type in the address.

"So, how was your day?" asks Luke.

"It was great!" I say, tapping the keys impatiently. "I made a new friend, and I saw lots of the city . . . Ooh, and look in that blue bag! I got you some really nice shirts!"

"Did you start to get a feel for the place?"

"Oh, I think so. I mean, obviously it's early . . ." I frown at the screen. "Come *on,* already."

"But you weren't too overwhelmed?"

"Mmm . . . not really," I say absently. Aha! Suddenly the screen is filling up with images. A row of little sweeties at the top—and logos saying, *It's fun. It's fashion. In New York City.* The Daily Candy home page!

I click on "Subscribe" and briskly start to type in my e-mail details, as Luke gets up and comes toward me, a concerned look on his face.

"So tell me, Becky," he says. "I know it must all seem very strange and daunting to you. I know you couldn't possibly find your feet in just one day. But on first impressions—do you think you could get used to New York? Do you think you could ever see yourself living here?"

I type the last letter with a flourish, press "Send," and look at him thoughtfully.

"You know what? I think I probably could."

HOWSKI AND FORLANO
U.S. IMMIGRATION LAWYERS
568 E. 56TH STREET
NEW YORK, N.Y. 10016

Ms. Rebecca Bloomwood
Flat 2
4 Burney Rd.
London SW6 8FD
UNITED KINGDOM

September 28, 2000

Dear Ms. Bloomwood:

Thank you for your completed U.S. immigration forms. As you know, the authorities will wish to evaluate the assets and unique talents which you can bring to this country.

Under section B69 referring to special abilities, you write, "I'm really good at chemistry, ask anyone at Oxford." We did in fact contact the vice-chancellor of Oxford University, who failed to display any familiarity with your work.

As did the British Olympic long-jump coach.

We enclose fresh forms and request that you fill them out again.

With kind regards,

Edgar Forlano

Nine

Two days later, I'm feeling quite dazzled by all the sights and sounds of New York. I've walked so many blocks my feet ache, and I've really seen some awe-inspiring things. Like, in Bloomingdale's, they have a chocolate factory! And there's a whole district full of nothing but shoe shops!

I keep trying to get Luke along to look at all these amazing sights—but he just has meeting after meeting. He's seeing about twenty people a day—wooing potential clients and networking with media people, and even looking round office spaces in the financial district. As he said yesterday at breakfast, he needs to hit the ground running when he arrives. I was about to make a little joke about "Break a leg!" . . . but then I decided against it. Luke's taking everything a bit seriously at the moment.

As well as setting up the new company, he's had briefings from Alicia in London every morning—and she keeps sending through faxes for him to approve, and needlessly long e-mails. I just know she's only doing it all to show off to Luke—and the really annoying thing is, it's working. Like, a couple of clients rang up to complain about things, but when he called Alicia she had already leapt into action and sorted it out. So then I had to hear for fifteen minutes about how marvelous she is, and what a great job she's doing—and keep nodding my head as though I completely agreed. But I still can't stand her. She rang up the other morning when Luke was out, and when I picked up, she said "*So* sorry to disturb your beauty sleep!" in this really patronizing way, and rang off before I could think of a good reply.

Still, never mind. On the positive side, Luke and I did manage to get our walk in Central Park—even if it was only for five minutes. And one afternoon, Luke took me on the Staten Island Ferry, which was fantastic—except for the moment when I lost my new baseball cap overboard.

Obviously, I didn't *mean* to shriek so loudly. Nor did I mean for that old woman to mishear and think I'd lost my "cat"—and I certainly didn't want her to insist the boat should be stopped. It caused a bit of a kerfuffle, actually, which was rather embarrassing. Still, never mind—as Luke said, at least all those tourists with their video cameras had something to film.

But now it's Wednesday morning. The holiday is over—and I've got a slight dentisty feeling of dread. It's my first appointment today with a pair of important TV people from HLBC. I'm actually quite scared.

Luke's left early for a breakfast meeting with Michael and some top PR headhunter who's going to supply him with staff, so I'm left alone in bed, sipping coffee and nibbling at a croissant, and telling myself not to get nervous. The key is not to panic, but to stay calm and cool. As Luke kept reassuring me, this meeting is not an interview as such, it's simply a first-stage introduction. A "getting-to-know-you" lunch, he called it.

But in a way, lunch is even more scary than an interview. What if I knock something over? What if I don't tip all the right people? What if I can't think of anything to say and we sit there in an embarrassing silence?

I spend all morning in our room, trying to read the *Wall Street Journal* and watching CNN—but that only freaks me out even more. I mean, these American television presenters are so slick and immaculate. They never fluff their words, and they never make jokes, and they know everything. Like who's the trade secretary of Iraq, and the implications of global warming for Peru. And here I am, thinking I can do what they do.

My other problem is, I haven't done a proper interview for years. *Morning Coffee* never bothered to interview me, I just kind of fell into it. And for my old job on *Successful Saving*, I just had a cozy chat with Philip, the editor, who already knew me from press conferences. So the idea of having to impress a pair of complete strangers from scratch is completely terrifying.

"Just be yourself," Luke kept saying. But frankly, that's a ridiculous idea. Everyone knows, the point of an interview is not to demonstrate who you are, but to pretend to be whatever sort of person they want for the job. That's why they call it "interview technique."

My interview outfit consists of a beautiful black suit I got at Whistles, with quite a short skirt and discreet red stitching. I've teamed it with high-heeled court shoes and some very sheer, very expensive tights. (Or "hose" as I must now start calling them. But honestly. It sounds like Shakespeare or something.) As I arrive at the restaurant where we're meeting, I see my reflection in a glass door—and I'm quite impressed. But at the same time, half of me wants to run away, give up on the idea, and buy myself a nice pair of shoes to commiserate.

I can't, though. I have to go through with this. The reason my stomach feels so hollow and my hands feel so damp is that this really matters to me. I can't tell myself I don't care and it's not important, like I do about most things. Because this really does matter. If I don't manage to get a job in New York, then I won't be able to live here. If I screw this interview up, and word gets around that I'm hopeless—then it's all over. Oh God. Oh God . . .

OK, calm down, I tell myself firmly. I can do this. I can do it. And afterward, I'm going to reward myself with a little treat. The Daily Candy Web site e-mailed me this morning, and apparently this huge makeup emporium in SoHo called Sephora is running a special promotion today, until four. Every customer gets a goody bag—and if you spend fifty dollars, you get a free special engraved beauty box! I mean, how cool would that be?

About two seconds after the e-mail arrived, I got one from Jodie, the girl I met at the sample sale. I'd been telling her I was a bit nervous about meeting Luke's mother—and she said I should get a makeover for the occasion and Sephora was definitely the place, did I want to meet up? So that will be fun, at least . . .

There, you see, I feel better already, just thinking about it. OK, go girl. Go get 'em.

I force myself to push open the door, and suddenly I'm in a very smart restaurant, all black lacquer and white linen and colored fish swimming in tanks.

"Good afternoon," says a maître d' dressed entirely in black.

"Hello," I say. "I'm here to meet—"

Shit, I've completely forgotten the names of the people I'm meeting.

Oh, great start, Becky. This is really professional.

"Could you just . . . hang on?" I say, and turn away, flushing red. I scrabble in my bag for the piece of paper—and here we are. Judd Westbrook and Kent Garland.

Kent? Is that really a name?

"It's Rebecca Bloomwood," I say to the maître d', hastily shoving the paper back in my bag, "meeting Judd Westbrook and Kent Garland of HLBC."

He scans the list, then gives a frosty smile. "Ah yes. They're already here."

Taking a deep breath, I follow him to the table—and there they are. A blond woman in a beige trouser suit and a chiseled-looking man in an equally immaculate black suit and sage-green tie. I fight the urge to run away, and advance with a confident smile, holding out my hand. They both look up at me, and for a moment neither says anything—and I feel a horrible conviction that I've already broken some vital rule of etiquette. I mean, you do shake hands in America, don't you? Are you supposed to kiss? Or bow?

But thankfully the blond woman is getting up and clasping my hand warmly.

"Becky!" she says. "*So* thrilled to meet you. I'm Kent Garland."

"Judd Westbrook," says the man, gazing at me with deep-set eyes. "We're very excited to meet you."

"Me too!" I say. "And thank you so much for your lovely flowers!"

"Not at all," says Judd, and ushers me into a chair. "It's a delight."

"An enormous pleasure," says Kent.

There's an expectant silence.

"Well, it's a . . . a fantastic pleasure for me, too," I say hastily. "Absolutely . . . phenomenal."

So far so good. If we just keep telling each other what a pleasure this is, I should do OK. Carefully I place my bag on the floor, along with my copies of the *FT* and the *Wall Street Journal.* I thought about the *South China Morning Post,* too, but decided that might be a bit much.

"Would you like a drink?" says a waiter, appearing at my side.

"Oh yes!" I say, and glance nervously around at the table to see what everyone else is having. Kent and Judd have both got tumblers full of what looks like G&T, so I'd better follow suit. "A gin and tonic, please."

To be honest, I think I need it, just to relax. As I open my menu, both Judd and Kent are gazing at me with an alert interest, as though they think I might suddenly burst into blossom or something.

"We've seen your tapes," says Kent, leaning forward. "And we're very impressed."

"Really?" I say—and then realize I shouldn't sound quite so astonished. "Really," I repeat, trying to sound nonchalant. "Yes, well, I'm proud of the show, obviously . . ."

"As you know, Rebecca, we produce a show called *Consumer Today,*" says Kent. "We don't have a personal finance segment at present, but we'd love to bring in the kind of advisory slot you're doing in Britain." She glances at Judd, who nods in agreement.

"It's obvious you have a passion for personal finance," he says.

"Oh," I say, taken aback. "Well—"

"It shines through your work," he asserts firmly. "As does the pincerlike grip you have on your subject."

Pincerlike grip?

"You know, you're pretty unique, Rebecca," Kent is saying.

"A young, approachable, charming girl, with such a high level of expertise and conviction in what you're saying . . ."

"You're an inspiration for the financially challenged everywhere," agrees Judd.

"What we admire the most is the patience you show these people."

"The empathy you have with them . . ."

". . . that faux-simplistic style of yours!" says Kent, and looks at me intently. "How do you keep that up?"

"Erm . . . you know! It just . . . comes, I suppose . . ." The waiter puts a drink in front of me and I grab it thankfully. "Well, cheers, everyone!" I say, lifting my glass.

"Cheers!" says Kent. "Are you ready to order, Rebecca?"

"Absolutely!" I reply, quickly scanning the menu. "The ahm . . . sea bass, please, and a green salad." I look at the others. "And shall we share some garlic bread?"

"I'm wheat-free," says Judd politely.

"Oh, right," I say. "Well . . . Kent?"

"I don't eat carbohydrates," she says pleasantly. "But you go ahead. I'm sure it's delicious!"

"No, it's OK," I say hastily. "I'll just have the sea bass."

God, how could I be so stupid? Of course Manhattanites don't eat garlic bread.

"And to drink?" says the waiter.

"Erm . . ." I look around the table. "I don't know. A sauvignon blanc, maybe? What does everyone else want?"

"Sounds good," says Kent with a friendly smile, and I breathe a sigh of relief. "Just some more Pellegrino for me," she adds, and gestures to her tumbler.

"And me," says Judd.

Pellegrino? They're on *Pellegrino*?

"I'll just have water too!" I say quickly. "I don't need wine! It was just an idea. You know—"

"No!" says Kent. "You must have whatever you like!" She smiles at the waiter. "A bottle of the sauvignon blanc, please, for our guest."

"Honestly—" I say, flushing red.

"Rebecca," says Kent, lifting a hand with a smile. "Whatever makes you comfortable."

Oh great. Now she thinks I'm a complete alcoholic. She thinks I can't survive one getting-to-know-you lunch without hitting the booze.

Well, never mind. It's done now. And it'll be OK. I'll just drink one glass. One glass, and that's it.

And that is honestly what I mean to do. Drink one glass and leave it at that.

But the trouble is, every time I finish my glass, a waiter comes along and fills it up again, and somehow I find myself drinking it. Besides which, it would look rather ungrateful to order a whole bottle of wine and leave it undrunk.

So the upshot is, by the time we've finished our food, I'm feeling quite . . . Well. I suppose one word might be *drunk.* Another might be *pissed.* But it's not a problem, because we're having a really good time, and I'm actually being really witty. Probably because I've relaxed a little. I've told them lots of funny stories about behind the scenes at *Morning Coffee,* and they've listened carefully and said it all sounds "quite fascinating."

"Of course, you British are very different from us," says Kent thoughtfully, as I finish telling her about the time Dave the cameraman arrived so pissed he keeled over in the middle of a shot, and got Emma picking her nose. God, that was funny. In fact, I can't stop giggling, just remembering it.

"We just love your British sense of humor," says Judd, and stares intently at me as though expecting a joke.

OK, quick. Think of something funny. British sense of humor. Erm . . . *Fawlty Towers? Ab Fab?*

"Don't mention the war!" I hear myself exclaiming. "Sweetie darling." I give a snort of laughter, and Judd and Kent exchange puzzled looks.

Just then, the coffee arrives. At least, I'm having coffee, Kent's having English breakfast tea, and Judd's having some weird herbal thing which he gave to the waiter to make.

"I adore tea," says Kent, giving me a smile. "So calming. Now, Rebecca. In England, the custom is that you turn the pot three times clockwise to keep away the devil. Is that right? Or is it counterclockwise?"

Turn the pot? I've never heard of turning the bloody pot.

"Erm . . . let me remember."

I screw my face up thoughtfully, trying to remember the last time I drank tea from a teapot. But the only image that comes to me is of Suze dunking a teabag in a mug while she tears a KitKat open with her teeth.

"I think it's counterclockwise," I say at last. "Because of the old saying, 'The devil he creeps around the clock . . . but never backward he will go.' "

What the hell am I talking about? Why have I suddenly put on a Scottish accent?

"Fascinating!" says Kent, taking a sip of tea. "I adore all these quaint old British customs. Do you know any others?"

"Absolutely!" I say brightly. "I know loads!"

Stop it, Becky. Just stop now.

"Like, we have a very old custom of . . . of . . . 'turning the tea cake.' "

"Really?" says Kent. "I've never heard of that one."

"Oh yes," I say confidently. "What happens is, you take your tea cake . . ." I grab a bread roll from a passing waiter. "And you . . . rotate it above your head like so . . . and you . . . you say a little rhyme . . ."

Crumbs are starting to fall on my head, and I can't think of anything to rhyme with *tea cake,* so I put my bread roll down and take a sip of coffee. "They do it in Cornwall," I add.

"Really?" says Judd with interest. "My grandmother comes from Cornwall. I'll have to ask her about it!"

"Only in some bits of Cornwall," I explain. "Just in the pointy bits."

Judd and Kent give each other puzzled looks—then both burst into laughter.

"Your British sense of humor!" says Kent. "It's so refreshing."

For a moment I'm not quite sure how to react—then I start

laughing too. God, this is great. We're getting on like a house on fire! Then Kent's face lights up.

"Now, Rebecca, I was meaning to say. I have rather an exciting opportunity for you. I don't know what your plans were for this afternoon. But I have a rather unique ticket . . . to . . ."

She pauses for effect, smiling widely, and I stare at her in sudden excitement. A Gucci invitation sample sale! It has to be!

". . . the Association of Financiers Annual Conference!" she finishes proudly.

For a few moments I can't speak.

"Really?" I say at last, my voice slightly more high-pitched than usual. "You're . . . you're joking!"

How on earth am I going to get out of this one?

"I know!" says Kent delightedly. "I thought you'd be pleased. So if you're not doing anything else this afternoon . . ."

I *am* doing something! I want to wail. I'm going to Sephora to get made over!

"There are some very high-profile speakers," puts in Judd. "Bert Frankel, for one."

"Really?" I say. "Bert Frankel!"

I've never heard of bloody Bert Frankel.

"So . . . I have the pass right here . . ." says Kent, reaching for her bag.

Quick. I have to say something or I'll find myself spending a precious afternoon in New York sitting in some dreary conference hall.

"What a shame!" I hear myself exclaiming. "Because actually . . ."

I *can't* tell them I have to go and try on lipstick.

"Actually . . . I was planning to visit the Guggenheim this afternoon."

Phew. No one can argue with culture.

"Really?" says Kent, looking disappointed. "Couldn't it wait until another day?"

"I'm afraid not," I say. "There's a particular exhibit I've been absolutely longing to see since . . . since I was a child of six."

"Really?" says Kent, eyes wide.

"Yes." I lean forward earnestly. "Ever since I saw a photograph of it in my granny's art book, it's been my ambition since childhood to come to New York City and see this piece of art. And now that I'm here . . . I just can't wait any longer. I hope you understand . . ."

"Of course!" says Kent. "Of course we do! What an inspiring story!" She exchanges impressed looks with Judd, and I smile modestly back. "So—which piece of art is it?"

I stare at her, still smiling. OK, quick, think. The Guggenheim. Modern paintings? Sculpture?

I'm fifty-fifty on modern paintings. If only I could phone a friend.

"Actually . . . I'd rather not say," I say at last. "I consider artistic preference a very . . . private matter."

"Oh," says Kent, looking a little taken aback. "Well, of course, I didn't mean to intrude in any way—"

"Kent," says Judd, glancing at his watch again. "We really have to—"

"You're right," says Kent. She takes another sip of tea, and stands up. "I'm sorry, Rebecca, we have a meeting at two thirty. But it's been such a pleasure."

"Of course!" I say. "No problem!"

I struggle to my feet and follow them out of the restaurant. As I pass the wine bucket I realize with a slight lurch that I've more or less drunk the whole bottle. How embarrassing. But I don't think anybody noticed.

We arrive outside the restaurant, and Judd has already hailed a taxi for me.

"Great to meet you, Rebecca," he says. "We'll report back to our vice-president of production, and we'll . . . be in touch! Enjoy the Guggenheim."

"Absolutely!" I say, shaking hands with each of them. "I will. And thank you so much!"

I get into the taxi and slam the door behind me.

"Hi," I say to the taxi driver, watching as Judd and Kent walk away. "I'd like to go to—"

"The Guggenheim," chips in the driver. "I heard."

"No, actually, I'd like to go to SoHo. Sephora on Broadway."

The driver swivels in his seat to look at me. He's huge and swarthy, and his face is creased in a frown.

"What about the Guggenheim?"

"Erm . . . I'll go later on."

"Later on?" says the driver. "You can't rush the Guggenheim. The Guggenheim is a very fine museum. Picasso. Kandinsky. You don't want to miss it."

"I won't miss it! Honestly, I promise. If we could just go to Sephora now? Please?"

There's a disapproving silence from the front.

"All right," he says at last, and starts the engine.

As we drive off, I sink happily into my seat. I think lunch went really well, actually. Except maybe when I told them the anecdote about Rory and the guide dog. And when I tripped over on my way to the loos. But then, that could happen to anybody. The truth is, I really am settling into New York. It's only been three days, but I'm getting the language and everything. Like, yesterday, I said "Go figure" without even thinking. And I called a skirt *cute*!

We pull up at a pedestrian crossing and I'm peering interestedly out, wondering which street we're at—when suddenly I freeze in horror.

There are Judd and Kent. Right there, in front of us. They're crossing the road, and Kent is saying something animatedly, and Judd is nodding. Oh God. I can't let them see me heading in the wrong direction. Quick, hide.

My heart thumping, I sink down off my seat and kind of crouch on the floor, trying to hide behind my *Wall Street Journal*. God, why isn't there more *space* in these taxis?

"You OK back there?" says the taxi driver.

"Fine," I gulp. I raise my head cautiously—and thank goodness Judd and Kent have disappeared. As I scramble back up onto the seat, I bump my head on the window.

"Hey there!" says a disembodied voice, making me jump with fright. "You be careful! Safety counts, OK? So buckle up!"

"OK," I say humbly. "Sorry about that. I'm really sorry. I won't do it again."

I fasten my seat belt with clumsy fingers, and catch the eye of the driver in the mirror.

"It's a recorded announcement," he says scornfully. "You're talking to a tape machine."

I knew that.

We arrive at Sephora on Broadway, and I thrust wodges of dollars at the driver. As I get out of the cab, he looks closely at me.

"Have you been drinking, lady?"

"No," I say indignantly. "I mean . . . yes. But it was just a bit of wine at lunch . . ."

The taxi driver shakes his head and drives off, and I head unsteadily into Sephora. To be honest, I am feeling a little giddy. I push open the door and . . . wow. Spotlights are dancing about the bright interior, landing on shiny black counters; on the deep-red carpet underfoot; on the glass packaging of a thousand nail polishes. There's music pounding, and girls milling everywhere, and trendy guys in black polo necks and headsets handing out goody bags. As I turn dazedly around, I've never seen so much makeup in my life. Rows and rows of lipsticks. Rows and rows of eye shadows. In all the colors of the rainbow. And oh look, there are little chairs where you can sit and try it all on, with personal mirrors. This place is . . . I mean, it's heaven.

"Hi, Becky, you made it!" I look up to see Jodie waving across a display of hairbrushes. She's wearing a stripy red-and-white jersey dress today, and as she gets nearer I see that her nails have been revarnished stripy red-and-white to match. "Ready for your makeover?"

She ushers me to one of the little chairs and I get into it, feeling a pleasant anticipation. A girl in black comes over with a friendly smile and introduces herself as Mona, my makeup specialist for today.

"Had you thought what look you were after?" she says as she switches on a spotlight and guides it toward my face.

"Well, it's for lunch with my boyfriend's mother," I explain. "I want to look kind of . . . groomed."

"Polished but subtle?"

"Exactly!"

"I have you," says Mona, nodding. "Taupes and beiges. The hardest look to pull off."

"Taupe?" says Jodie, wrinkling her brow. "Did anyone ever look good in taupe?"

"And maybe a soft color on the lips," says Mona, ignoring Jodie. "Let me start with a light base . . ."

She reaches for a cosmetic sponge and smooths color gently over my face. As she starts shading my eyes I see Jodie standing back, a critical look on her face.

"For this elegant look, less is more," says Mona.

"Right," I say, nodding knowledgeably. "Absolutely."

"I'll just fetch a mascara . . ."

She disappears toward the front of the shop and I close my eyes. If I'm honest, my head's still spinning from all that wine, and I'm finding it quite hard to balance on this tiny chair.

Suddenly I feel a coldness on my cheek, and look up. Jodie is standing in front of me, dipping her fingers into a small pot.

"What are you doing?" I say feebly.

"Jazzing you up a bit!" she says, and dabs my other cheek. "All this neutral crap! Like that's what you wanted from a makeover."

"Well—"

"I know you're too polite to complain. You Brits really need to get some attitude." She stands back and gives a satisfied nod. "Now, did you ever wear false eyelashes? Because they have a great range here."

"Jodie, I'm not sure . . ."

"Hey!" We both look up to see Mona approaching, an affronted expression on her face. "What the hell is going on? What's happened to her face?"

"She looked boring," says Jodie defiantly.

"She looked classic!" Mona sticks her hands on her hips. "Well, you've ruined it now."

"What have I got on my face?" I demand, and pull the mirror toward me. My own face stares back. Smooth and beige, with softly shadowed eyes, discreetly colored lips . . . and silver sparkles on my cheeks.

"Looks great, doesn't it?" says Jodie unapologetically. "Much better with the glitter."

I glance at Mona's annoyed face and suddenly feel a bit guilty.

"Actually, Mona," I say quickly, "I'd really like to buy some of the products you used. In fact . . . all of them. Would that be possible?"

"Oh," says Mona, unbending a little. "Well—yes, of course. They are from a rather expensive line . . ."

"That doesn't matter!" I turn hastily to Jodie. "And . . . I'll buy the glitter too. I'll buy it all!"

Ten minutes later I find myself outside Sephora, clutching two carrier bags full of makeup, a whole set of new cosmetic brushes, a silver shower cap, and something called "buffing paste," which I threw in at the last moment. I'm not sure quite what it is—but the jar is absolutely gorgeous!

"OK," I say, looking dazedly around the busy street in front of me. "Where next?"

"Babe, I have to go," says Jodie, looking up from her pager. "I've already had a five-hour lunch break. But if you want the true SoHo experience, there's Dean and Deluca right in front of you . . ." She swivels me by the shoulders until I'm facing across the street. ". . . and just along is Scoop, which is *the* place to pick up the most expensive T-shirt in the universe . . ."

"What about that?" I say, pointing to a gorgeous, glowing shop window that has caught my eye.

"Kate's Paperie. To die for."

"What does it sell?" I say puzzledly. "Just paper?"

"Just paper!" She gives a raucous chuckle. "You go take a look. And listen, you want to get together again sometime?"

"I'd love to!" I say in delight. "I'll be here for at least another week. Thanks, Jodie."

"No problem."

I watch as Jodie hurries off toward the subway and suddenly notice that the spiky heels of her shoes are painted in red-and-white stripes, too. That's so cool! Where did she get them?

"Jodie!" I cry, but she can't hear me. Never mind, I'll ask her next time.

As she disappears down into the subway station I walk slowly toward Kate's Paperie. I'm not really interested in paper, to be honest. In fact, I probably won't bother going in. But it can't hurt to have a little—

I stop in my tracks as I reach the window, and stare at the display, astounded. When Jodie said *paper,* I imagined piles of photocopying sheets. I had no idea she meant . . . I mean, just look at that display of marbled wrapping paper. And that decoupage box. And that amazing beaded ribbon! I've never seen anything like it!

I push the door open and walk around, marveling at the arrangements of beautiful wrapping paper adorned with dried flowers, raffia, and bows, the photograph albums, the boxes of exquisite writing paper . . . And oh God, just look at the greeting cards!

You see, this is it. This is why New York is so great. They don't just have boring old cards saying Happy Birthday. They have handmade creations with twinkly flowers and witty collages, saying things like "Congratulations on adopting twins!" and "So sad to hear you broke up!"

I walk up and down, utterly dazzled by the array. I just *have* to have some of these cards. Like this fantastic pop-up castle, with the flag reading "I love your remodeled home!" I mean, I don't actually know anyone who's remodeling their home, but I can always keep it until Mum decides to repaper the hall. And this one covered in fake grass, saying "To a smashing tennis coach with thanks." Because I'm planning to have some tennis lessons next summer, and I'll want to thank my coach, won't I?

I scoop up a few more, and then move on to the invitation rack. And they're even better! Instead of just saying "Party" they say things like "We're Meeting at the Club for Brunch!" and "Come Join Us for an Informal Pizza!"

You know, I think I should buy some of those. It would be shortsighted not to. Suze and I might easily hold a pizza party, mightn't we? And we'll never find invitations like this in Britain. And they're so sweet, with glittery little pizza slices all the way down the sides! I carefully put five boxes of invitations in my basket, along with all my lovely cards, and a few sheets of candy-striped wrapping paper, which I just can't resist, then head to the checkout. As the assistant scans everything through, I look around the shop again, wondering if I've missed anything—and it's only when she announces the total that I look up in slight shock. That much? Just for a few cards?

For a moment I wonder whether I really do need them all. Like the card saying "Happy Hanukkah, Boss!"

But then—they're bound to come in useful one day, aren't they? And if I'm going to live in New York, I'm going to have to get used to sending expensive cards all the time, so really, this is a form of acclimatization.

As I head toward the door, I'm dimly aware of a ringing, burbling sort of sound—and all of a sudden I realize it's my own mobile phone.

"Hi!" I say, clutching it to my ear. "Who's this?"

"Hi. It's me," says Luke. "I heard your lunch went well."

"Really?" I say, feeling a jolt of surprise. "Where did you hear that?"

"I've just been speaking to some people at HLBC. Apparently you were quite a hit. Very entertaining, they said."

"Wow! Really? Are you sure?"

"Quite sure. They were saying how charming you were, and how cultured . . . I even hear they put you in a taxi to the Guggenheim afterward."

"That's right," I say, reaching to look at a paper knife. "They did."

"Yes, I was quite intrigued to hear all about your burning childhood dream," says Luke. "Kent was very impressed."

"Really?" I say vaguely. "Well, that's good."

"Absolutely." Luke pauses. "Slightly strange that you didn't mention the Guggenheim this morning, though, isn't it? Or indeed . . . ever. Bearing in mind you've been longing to go there since you were a child of six."

Suddenly I hear the amusement in his voice, and snap to attention. He's bloody well rung up to tease me, hasn't he?

"Have I never mentioned the Guggenheim?" I say innocently, and put the paper knife back. "How very odd."

"Isn't it?" says Luke. "Most peculiar. So, are you there now?"

Bugger.

For a moment, I'm silenced. I simply can't admit to Luke that I've gone shopping again. Not after all that teasing he gave me about my so-called guided tour. I mean OK, I know ten minutes out of a three-hour city tour isn't that much—but I got as far as Saks, didn't I?

"Yes," I say defiantly. "Yes, I am, actually."

Which is kind of almost true. I mean, I can easily go there after I've finished here.

"Great!" says Luke. "What particular exhibit are you looking at?"

Oh, shut up.

"What's that?" I say, suddenly raising my voice. "Sorry, I didn't realize! Luke, I have to turn my mobile off. The . . . um . . . curator is complaining. But I'll see you later."

"Six at the Royalton Bar," he says. "You can meet my new associate, Michael. And I'll look forward to hearing all about your afternoon."

Now I feel a bit guilty. I shouldn't have told Luke I was at the Guggenheim. I should have told the truth.

But it doesn't matter . . . because what I'll do is I'll go there right now. Right this minute! After all, I can always come back to SoHo another day, can't I?

I walk slowly along the crowded street, telling myself that what I'll do is hail a cab and go straight up there. Without delay. Straight to the Guggenheim and immerse myself in some wonderful culture. Excellent. I can't wait, actually.

I arrive at a street corner and come to a standstill. A lit-up taxi crawls past—but for some strange reason my arm doesn't rise. Across the street is a stall selling fake designer sunglasses, and I feel a sudden pang of longing to go and rifle through them. And look there, that shop's doing a discount on Calvin Klein jeans. And I do actually *need* some new jeans . . . And I haven't even been into Dean and Deluca . . .

Oh, why couldn't the Guggenheim be in SoHo?

Hang on a minute.

People are pushing past me but I don't move. My eye is riveted by something fixed to the facade above an entrance. I don't quite believe what I'm seeing.

The word GUGGENHEIM stares back at me, as large as life. It's like God heard my prayers.

But what's going on? Has the Guggenheim suddenly *moved*? Are there two Guggenheims?

As I hurry toward the doors, I realize this place looks quite small for a museum—so maybe it's not the main Guggenheim. Maybe it's some trendy SoHo offshoot! Yes! I mean, if London can have the Tate Gallery and Tate Modern, why can't New York have the Guggenheim and Guggenheim SoHo? That sounds so cool!

I cautiously push the door open—and sure enough, it's all white and spacious, with modern art on pedestals and people wandering around quietly, whispering to one another.

You know, this is what all museums should be like. Nice and small, for a start, so you don't feel exhausted as soon as you walk in. I mean, you could probably do this lot in about half an hour. Plus, all the things look really interesting. Like, look at those amazing red cubes in that glass cabinet! And this fantastic abstract print, hanging on the wall.

As I'm gazing admiringly at the print, a couple come over and look at it too, and start murmuring to each other about how nice it is. Then the girl says casually, "How much is it?"

And I'm about to turn to her with a friendly smile and say, "That's what I always want to know, too!"—when to my astonishment the man reaches for it and turns it over. And there's a price label fixed onto the back!

A price label in a museum! I don't believe it! This place is perfect! *Finally,* some forward-thinking person has agreed with me—that people don't want to just look at art, they want to know how much it is. I'm going to write to the people at the Victoria and Albert about this.

And you know, now that I look around properly, *all* the exhibits seem to have a price on them. Those red cubes in the cabinet have got a price label, and so has that chair, and so has that . . . that box of pencils.

How weird, having a box of pencils in a museum. Still, maybe it's installation art. I walk over to have a closer look—and there's something printed on each pencil. Probably some really meaningful message about art, or life . . . I lean close, interested, and find myself reading the words "Guggenheim Museum Store."

What?

Is this a—

I lift my head and look around bewilderedly.

Am I in a *shop*?

Suddenly I start noticing things I hadn't seen before. Like a pair of cash registers on the other side of the room. And there's somebody walking out with a couple of carrier bags.

How could I have not recognized a *shop*? But . . . this makes less and less sense. Is it just a shop on its own?

"Excuse me," I say, to a fair-haired boy wearing a name badge. "Can I just check—this *is* a shop?"

"Yes, ma'am," says the boy politely. "This is the Guggenheim Museum Store."

"And where's the actual Guggenheim Museum? With all the Picassos and things?"

"To see the Picassos you have to go to the main museum, on Fifth Avenue at Eighty-ninth Street," says the boy.

"Right." I look at him confusedly. "So let me just get this straight. You can come here and buy loads of stuff—and no one minds whether you've been to the museum or not? I mean, you don't have to show your ticket or anything?"

"No, ma'am."

"So you . . . you can just shop?" My voice rises in delight. "It's perfect!" Suddenly I see the boy's shocked expression and quickly add, "I mean, obviously I *do* want to look at the art. Very much so. I was just . . . you know. Checking."

"If you're interested in visiting the museum," says the boy, "I can give you a location map. Did you want to pay a visit?"

"Erm . . ."

Now, let's not make any hasty decisions.

"Erm . . . I'm not sure," I say carefully. "Could you just give me a minute?"

"Sure," says the boy, giving me a slightly odd look, and I sit down on a white seat, thinking hard.

OK, here's the thing. I mean, obviously I could get in a cab, and whiz up to wherever it is, and spend all afternoon looking at the Picassos.

Or else . . . I could just buy a book *about* the Picassos. Because the thing is, do you actually need to see a piece of art in the flesh to appreciate it? Of course you don't. And in a way, flicking through a book would be *better* than trekking round lots of galleries—because I'm bound to cover more ground more quickly and actually learn far more.

Besides, what they have in this shop is art, isn't it? I mean, I've already taken in some pretty good culture. Exactly.

Several hours later, I arrive at the Royalton with a huge, exhilarated grin on my face. I haven't had such a successful afternoon shopping since . . . well, since yesterday.

I check all my carrier bags in at the cloakroom, then head for the small circular bar where Luke has told me to meet him and his new associate, Michael Ellis.

I've heard quite a lot about this Michael Ellis during the last few days. Apparently he owns a huge advertising agency in Washington and is best friends with the president. Or is it the vice-president? Something like that, anyway. Basically, he's a big shot, and crucial to Luke's new deal. So I'd better make sure I impress him.

God, this place is trendy, I think as I walk in. All leather and chrome and people in severe black outfits with haircuts to match. I walk into the dim circular bar, and there's Luke, sitting at a table. To my surprise, he's on his own.

"Hi!" I say, and kiss him. "So—where's your friend?"

"Making a call," says Luke. He gestures to a waiter. "Another gimlet here, please." He gives me a quizzical look as I sit down. "So, my darling. How was the Guggenheim?"

"It was good," I say with a triumphant beam. Ha, ha-di-ha. I've been doing my homework in the cab. "I particularly enjoyed a fascinating series of acrylic forms based on simple Euclidean shapes."

"Really?" says Luke, looking a bit surprised.

"Absolutely. The way they absorb and reflect pure light . . . Riveting. Oh and by the way, I bought you a present." I plonk a book on his lap entitled *Abstract Art and Artists,* and take a sip of the drink that has been placed in front of me, trying not to look too smug.

"You really went to the Guggenheim!" says Luke, leafing through the book incredulously.

"Erm . . . yes," I say. "Of course I did!"

OK, I know you shouldn't lie to your boyfriend. But it's kind of true, isn't it? I *did* go to the Guggenheim. In the broadest sense of the word.

"This is really interesting," Luke's saying. "Did you see that famous sculpture by Brancusi?"

"Erm . . . well . . ." I squint over his shoulder, trying to see what he's talking about. "Well, I was more concentrating on the . . . um . . ."

"What's that on your cheek?" says Luke, suddenly staring at me. I put a hand up in surprise and feel a trace of silver glitter. I'd forgotten all about that.

"It was . . . a piece of installation art," I hear myself saying. "Entitled *Constellations.* They had all this, um . . . glitter, and they smeared it on you . . ."

"Here comes Michael now," interrupts Luke. He closes the book and I quickly put it back in its carrier bag. Thank God for that. I look up interestedly to see what this famous Michael looks like—and nearly choke on my drink.

I don't believe it. It's him. Michael Ellis is the balding guy from the gym. Last time he saw me, I was dying at his feet.

"Hi!" says Luke, standing up. "Becky, meet Michael Ellis, my new associate."

"Hi again," I say, trying to smile composedly. "How are you?"

Oh, this shouldn't be allowed. There should be a rule which says that people you've met in the gym should *never* meet you in real life.

"We've already had the pleasure of meeting," says Michael Ellis, shaking my hand with a twinkle and sitting down opposite. "Becky and I worked out together at the hotel gym. Didn't catch you there this morning, though."

"This morning?" says Luke, giving me a puzzled look as he sits down again. "I thought you said the gym was closed, Becky."

Shit.

"Oh. Um, well . . ." I take a deep gulp of my drink and clear my throat. "When I said it was *closed,* what I really meant was . . . was . . ." I tail away feebly into silence.

And I so wanted to make a good impression.

"What am I thinking of?" exclaims Michael suddenly. "I must be going crazy! It wasn't this morning. The gym *was* closed this morning. Due to vital repair work, I believe." He grins broadly and I feel myself blushing.

"So, anyway," I say, hurriedly changing the subject. "You're . . . you're doing a deal with Luke. That's great! How's it all going?"

I only really ask to be polite, and steer attention away from my gym activities. I'm expecting them both to start explaining it to me at great length, and I can nod my head at intervals and enjoy my drink. But to my surprise, there's an awkward pause.

"Good question," says Luke at last, and looks at Michael. "What did Clark say?"

"We had a long conversation," says Michael. "Not entirely satisfactory."

I look from face to face, feeling disconcerted.

"Is something going wrong?"

"That all depends," says Michael.

He starts to tell Luke about his phone call with whoever Clark is, and I try to listen intelligently to their conversation. But the trouble is, I'm starting to feel quite giddy. How much have I drunk today? I don't even want to think about it, to be honest. I loll against the leather backrest, my eyes closed, listening to their voices chatting what seems far above my head.

". . . some sort of paranoia . . ."

". . . think they can change the goalposts . . ."

". . . overheads . . . cost reduction . . . with Alicia Billington heading up the London office . . ."

"Alicia?" I struggle to an upright position. "Alicia's going to run the London office?"

"Almost definitely," says Luke, stopping midsentence. "Why?"

"But—"

"But what?" says Michael, looking at me with interest. "Why shouldn't she run the London office? She's bright, ambitious . . ."

"Oh. Well . . . no reason," I say feebly.

I can't very well say, "Because she's a complete cow."

"You've heard she's just got engaged, by the way?" says Luke. "To Ed Collins at Hill Hanson."

"Really?" I say in surprise. "I thought she was having an affair with . . . whassisname."

"With who?" says Michael.

"Erm . . . thingy." I take a sip of gimlet to clear my head. "She was having secret lunches with him, and everything!"

What's his name again? I really am pissed.

"Becky likes to keep abreast of the office gossip," says Luke with an easy laugh. "Unfortunately one can't always vouch for its accuracy."

I stare at him crossly. What's he trying to say? That I'm some kind of rumormonger?

"Nothing wrong with a bit of office gossip," says Michael with a warm smile. "Keeps the wheels turning."

"Absolutely!" I say emphatically. "I couldn't agree more. I always say to Luke, you should be *interested* in the people who work for you. It's like when I give financial advice on my TV show. You can't just look at the numbers, you have to *talk* to them. Like . . . like Enid from Northampton!" I look at Michael expectantly, before remembering that he doesn't know who Enid is. "On paper she was ready to retire," I explain. "Pension and everything. But in real life . . ."

"She . . . wasn't ready?" suggests Michael.

"Exactly! She was really enjoying work and it was only her stupid husband who wanted her to give up. She was only fifty-five!" I gesture randomly with my glass. "I mean, don't they say life begins at fifty-five?"

"I'm not sure they do," says Michael, smiling. "But maybe they should." He gives me an interested look. "I'd like to catch your show one day. Is it shown in the States?"

"No, it isn't," I say regretfully. "But I'll be doing the same thing on American TV soon, so you'll be able to watch it then!"

"I look forward to that." Michael looks at his watch and drains his glass. "I have to go, I'm afraid. We'll speak later, Luke. And very nice to meet you, Becky. If I ever need financial advice, I'll know where to come."

As he leaves the bar, I lean back against my squashy seat and turn to look at Luke. His easy demeanor has vanished, and he's staring tensely into space while his fingers methodically tear a matchbook into small pieces.

"Michael seems really nice!" I say. "Really friendly."

"Yes," says Luke distantly. "Yes, he is."

I take a sip of gimlet and look at Luke more carefully. He's got exactly the same expression he had last month, when one of his staff cocked up a press release and some confidential figures were made public by mistake. My mind spools back over the conversation I was half-listening to—and as I watch his face I start to feel a bit worried.

"Luke," I say at last. "What's going on? Is there some kind of hitch with your deal?"

"No," says Luke without moving.

"So what did Michael mean when he said, 'That all depends'? And all that stuff about them changing the goalposts?"

I lean forward and try to take his hand, but Luke doesn't respond. As I gaze at him in anxious silence, I gradually become aware of the background chatter and music all around us in the dim bar. At the next table a woman's opening a little box from Tiffany's and gasping—something which would normally have me throwing my napkin onto the floor and sidling over to see what she's got. But this time I'm too concerned.

"Luke?" I lean forward. "Come on, tell me. Is there a problem?"

"No," says Luke shortly, and tips his glass back into his mouth. "There's no problem. Things are fine. Come on, let's go."

Ten

I WAKE UP the next morning with a pounding headache. We went on from the Royalton to someplace for dinner, and I drank even more there—and I can't even remember getting back to the hotel. Thank God I don't have an interview today. To be honest, I could quite happily spend the whole day in bed with Luke.

Except that Luke is already up, sitting by the window, talking grimly into the phone.

"OK, Michael. I'll talk to Greg today. God knows. I have no idea." He listens for a bit. "That may be the case. But I'm not having a second deal collapse on us." There's a pause. "Yes, but that would put us back—what, six months? OK. I hear what you're saying. Yes, I will. Cheers."

He puts down the receiver and stares tensely out of the window, and I rub my sleepy face, trying to remember if I packed any aspirin.

"Luke, what's wrong?"

"You're awake," says Luke, turning round, and gives me a quick smile. "Did you sleep well?"

"What's wrong?" I repeat, ignoring him. "What's wrong with the deal?"

"Everything's fine," says Luke shortly, and turns back to the window.

"Everything isn't fine!" I retort. "Luke, I'm not blind. I'm not deaf. I can tell something's up."

"A minor blip," says Luke after a pause. "You don't need to worry about it." He reaches for the phone again. "Shall I order you some breakfast? What would you like?"

"Stop it!" I cry frustratedly. "Luke, I'm not some . . . some stranger! We're going to live together, for God's sake! I'm on your side. Just tell me what's really going on. Is your deal in trouble?"

There's silence—and for an awful moment I think Luke's going to tell me to mind my own business. But then he pushes his hands through his hair, exhales sharply, and looks up.

"You're right. The truth is, one of our backers is getting nervous."

"Oh," I say, and pull a face. "Why?"

"Because some *fucking* rumor's going around that we're about to lose Bank of London."

"Really?" I stare at him, feeling a cold dismay creep down my back. Even I know how important Bank of London is to Brandon Communications. They were one of Luke's first clients—and they still bring in about a quarter of the money the company makes every year. "Why would people be saying that?"

"Fuck knows." He pushes his hair back with his hands. "Bank of London denies it completely, of course. But then, they would. And of course it doesn't help that I'm here, not there . . ."

"So are you going to fly back to London?"

"No." He looks up. "That would give out completely the wrong signals. Things are shaky enough here already. If I suddenly disappear . . ." He shakes his head and I stare at him apprehensively.

"So—what happens if your backer pulls out?"

"We find someone else."

"But what if you can't? Will you have to give up on coming to New York?"

Luke turns to look at me—and he's suddenly got that blank,

scary expression that used to make me want to run away from him at press conferences.

"Not an option."

"But I mean, you've got a really successful business in London," I persist. "I mean, you don't *have* to set up one in New York, do you? You could just . . ."

I tail away at the look on his face.

"Right," I say nervously. "Well—I'm sure it'll all be OK. In the end."

For a while we're both silent—then Luke seems to come to, and looks up.

"I'm afraid I'm going to have to hold a few hands today," he says abruptly. "So I won't be able to make this charity lunch with you and my mother."

Oh shit. Luke's mother. Of course, that's today.

"Can't she rearrange?" I suggest. "So we can both go?"

"Unfortunately not," says Luke. He gives a quick smile, but I can see true disappointment on his face, and I feel a flash of indignation toward his mother.

"Surely she could find time—"

"She's got a very busy schedule. And as she pointed out, I didn't give her very much warning." He frowns. "You know, my mother's not just some . . . society lady of leisure. She has a lot of important commitments. She can't just drop everything, much as she would like to."

"Of course not," I say hurriedly. "Anyway, it'll be fine. I'll just go along to this lunch with her on my own, shall I?" I add, trying to sound as though I'm not at all intimidated by this prospect.

"She has to go to the spa first," says Luke, "and she suggested you accompany her."

"Oh right!" I say cautiously. "Well, that could be fun . . ."

"And then there's the charity lunch she's going to take you to. It'll be a chance for you two to get to know one another. I really hope you hit it off."

"Of course we will," I say firmly. "It'll be really nice." I get out of bed and go and put my arms around Luke's neck. His face still looks strained, and I put up my hand to smooth away the creases in his brow. "Don't worry, Luke. People will be queuing up to back you. Round the block."

Luke gives a half-smile and kisses my hand.

"Let's hope so."

As I sit in reception, waiting for Luke's mother to arrive, I feel a combination of nerves and intrigue. I mean, for a start, what are we going to talk about? If I were meeting his stepmum, she could tell me all about Luke when he was a little boy, and bring out all the embarrassing photographs. But Luke's real mum barely saw him when he was a little boy. Apparently she just used to send him huge presents at school, and visit about every three years.

You'd think that would have made him a bit resentful—but he adores her. In fact, he simply can't find one bad thing to say about her. I once asked him whether he minded that she left him—and he got all defensive and said she had no choice. And he's got this enormous glamorous photograph of her in his study at home—much bigger than the one of his dad and stepmum on their wedding day. I do sometimes wonder what they think about that. But it's not something I really feel I can bring up.

"Rebecca?" A voice interrupts my thoughts and I look up, startled. A tall, elegant woman in a pale suit, with very long legs and crocodile shoes, is staring down at me. It's the glamorous photograph in the flesh! And she looks just the same as she does in the picture, with high cheekbones and dark, Jackie Kennedy–style hair—except her skin is kind of tighter, and her eyes are unnaturally wide. In fact, it looks as though she might have some difficulty closing them.

"Hello!" I say, getting awkwardly to my feet and holding out my hand. "How do you do?"

"Elinor Sherman," she says in a strange half-English, half-American drawl. Her hand is cold and bony, and she's wearing two enormous diamond rings that press into my flesh. "So pleased to meet you."

"Luke was very sorry he couldn't make it," I say, and hand her the present he gave me to give. As she undoes the wrapping, I can't help goggling. A Hermès scarf!

"Nice," she says dismissively, and puts it back into the box. "My car is waiting."

"Luke was really hoping we might get to know each other a bit," I say, with a friendly smile.

"I have until two fifteen," says Elinor crisply.

"Oh," I say. "Well, never m—"

"So that should be ample time. Shall we go?"

Blimey. A car with a chauffeur. And a crocodile Kelly bag—and are those earrings *real* emeralds?

As we drive away, I can't help surreptitiously staring at Elinor. Now I'm close up I realize she's older than I first thought, probably in her fifties. And although she looks wonderful, it's a bit as though that glamorous photo has been left out in the sun and lost its color—and then been painted over with makeup. Her lashes are heavy with mascara and her hair is shiny with lacquer and her nails are so heavily varnished, they could be red porcelain. She's so completely . . . done. Groomed in a way I know I could never be, however many people went to work on me.

I mean, I'm looking quite nice today, I think. In fact, I'm looking really sharp. There was a spread in American *Vogue* on how black and white is *the* look at the moment, so I've teamed a black pencil skirt with a white shirt I found in the sample sale the other day, and black shoes with fantastic high heels. And I've shaded my eyes just like Mona showed me. I was really pleased with myself this morning. But now, as Elinor surveys me, I'm suddenly aware that one of my nails is very slightly chipped, and my shoe has got a tiny smear on the side—and oh God, is that a thread hanging down from my skirt? Should I quickly try to pull it off?

Casually, I put my hand down on my lap to cover up the loose thread. Maybe she didn't see. It's not that obvious, is it?

But Elinor is silently reaching into her bag, and a moment

later she hands me a pair of small silver tortoiseshell-handled scissors.

"Oh . . . er, thanks," I say awkwardly. I snip the offending thread, and hand back the scissors, feeling like a schoolchild. "That always happens," I add, and give a nervous little giggle. "I look in the mirror in the morning and I think I look fine, but then the minute I get out of the house . . ."

Great, now I'm gabbling. Slow down, Becky.

"The English are incapable of good grooming," says Elinor. "Unless it's a horse."

The corners of her lips move a couple of millimeters up into a smile—although the rest of her face is static—and I burst into sycophantic laughter.

"That's really good! My flatmate loves horses. But I mean, you're English, aren't you? And you look absolutely . . . immaculate!"

I'm really pleased I've managed to throw in a little compliment, but Elinor's smile abruptly disappears. She gives me a blank stare and suddenly I can see where Luke gets that impassive scary expression from.

"I'm a naturalized American citizen."

"Oh right," I say. "Well, I suppose you've been here for a while. But I mean, in your heart, aren't you still . . . wouldn't you say you're a . . . I mean, Luke's very English . . ."

"I have lived in New York for the majority of my adult life," says Elinor coldly. "Any attachment of mine to Britain has long disappeared. The place is twenty years out of date."

"Right." I nod fervently, trying to look as though I understand completely. God, this is hard work. I feel like I'm being observed under a microscope. Why couldn't Luke have come? Or why couldn't she have rescheduled? I mean, doesn't she *want* to see him?

"Rebecca, who colors your hair?" says Elinor abruptly.

"It's . . . it's my own," I say, nervously touching a strand.

"Meione," she echoes suspiciously. "I don't know the name. At which salon does she work?"

For a moment I'm completely silenced.

"Erm . . . well," I flounder at last. "Actually . . . I . . . I'm not sure you'll have heard of it. It's very . . . tiny."

"Well, I think you should change colorist," says Elinor. "It's a very unsubtle shade."

"Right!" I say hurriedly. "Absolutely."

"Guinevere von Landlenburg swears by Julien on Bond Street. Do you know Guinevere von Landlenburg?"

I hesitate thoughtfully, as though going through a mental address book. As though checking all the many, many Guineveres I know.

"Um . . . no," I say at last. "I don't think I do."

"They have a house in South Hampton." She takes out a compact and checks her reflection. "We spent some time there last year with the de Bonnevilles."

I stiffen. The de Bonnevilles. As in Sacha de Bonneville. As in Luke's old girlfriend.

Luke never told me they were friends of the family.

OK, I'm not going to stress. Just because Elinor is tactless enough to mention Sacha's family. It's not as though she's actually mentioned *her*—

"Sacha is such an accomplished girl," says Elinor, snapping her compact shut. "Have you ever seen her water-ski?"

"No."

"Or play polo?"

"No," I say morosely. "I haven't."

Suddenly Elinor is rapping imperiously on the glass panel behind the driver.

"You took that corner too fast!" she says. "I won't tell you again, I don't wish to be rocked in my seat. So, Rebecca," she says, sitting back in her seat and giving me a dissatisfied glance. "What are your own hobbies?"

"Uhm . . ." I open my mouth and close it again. My mind's gone completely blank. Come on, I must have some hobbies. What do I do at the weekends? What do I do to relax?

"Well, I . . ."

This is completely ridiculous. There *must* be things in my life other than shopping.

"Well, obviously, I enjoy . . . socializing with friends," I begin hesitantly. "And also the . . . the study of fashion through the um . . . medium of magazines . . ."

"Are you a sportswoman?" says Elinor, eyeing me coldly. "Do you hunt?"

"Erm . . . no. But . . . I've recently taken up fencing!" I add in sudden inspiration. I've got the outfit, haven't I? "And I've played the piano since I was six."

Completely true. No need to mention that I gave up when I was nine.

"Indeed," says Elinor, and gives a wintry smile. "Sacha is also very musical. She gave a recital of Beethoven piano sonatas in London last year. Did you go to it?"

Bloody Sacha. With her bloody water-skiing and bloody sonatas.

"No," I say defiantly. "But I . . . I gave one myself, as it happens. Of . . . of Wagner sonatas."

"Wagner sonatas?" echoes Elinor suspiciously.

"Erm . . . yes." I clear my throat, trying to think how to get off the subject of accomplishments. "So! You must be very proud of Luke!"

I'm hoping this comment will trigger a happy speech from her lasting ten minutes. But Elinor simply looks at me silently, as though I'm speaking nonsense.

"With his . . . his company and everything," I press on doggedly. "He's such a success. And he seems very determined to make it in New York. In America." Elinor gives me a patronizing smile.

"No one is anything till they make it in America." She looks out of the window. "We're here."

Thank God for that.

To give Elinor her due, the beauty spa is absolutely amazing. The reception area is exactly like a Greek grotto, with pillars and soft music and a lovely scent of essential oils in the air. We go up to the reception desk, where a smart woman in black linen calls Elinor "Mrs. Sherman" very deferentially. They talk for a while in lowered voices, and the woman occasionally gives me a glance and nods her head, and I try to pretend not to be listening, looking at the price list for bath oils. Then abruptly Elinor turns away and ushers me to a seating area where there's a jug of mint tea and a sign asking patrons to respect the tranquility of the spa and keep their voices down.

We sit in silence for a while—then a girl in a white uniform comes to collect me and takes me to a treatment room, where a robe and slippers are waiting, all wrapped in embossed cellophane. As I get changed, she's busying herself at her counter of goodies, and I wonder pleasurably what I've got in store. Elinor insisted on paying for all my treatments herself, however much I tried to chip in—and apparently she selected the "top-to-toe grooming" treatment, whatever that is. I'm hoping it'll include a nice relaxing aromatherapy massage—but as I sit down on the couch, I see a pot full of wax heating up.

I feel an unpleasant lurch in my tummy. I've never been that great at having my legs waxed. Which is not because I'm afraid of pain, but because—

Well, OK. It's because I'm afraid of pain.

"So—does my treatment include waxing?" I say, trying to sound lighthearted.

"You're booked in for a full waxing program," says the beautician, looking up in surprise. "The 'top-to-toe.' Legs, arms, eyebrows, and Brazilian."

Arms? Eyebrows? I can feel my throat tightening in fear. I haven't been this scared since I had my jabs for Thailand.

"Brazilian?" I say in a scratchy voice. "What . . . what's that?"

"It's a form of bikini wax. A total wax."

I stare at her, my mind working overtime. She can't possibly mean—

"So if you'd like to lie down on the couch—"

"Wait!" I say, trying to keep my voice calm. "When you say 'total,' do you mean . . ."

"Uh-huh." The beautician smiles. "Then, if you wish, I can apply a small crystal tattoo to the . . . area. A love heart is quite popular. Or perhaps the initials of someone special?"

No. This can't be real.

"So, if you could just lie back on the couch and relax—"

Relax? *Relax?*

She turns back to her pot of molten wax—and I feel a surge of pure terror.

"I'm not doing it," I hear myself saying, and slither off the couch. "I'm not having it."

"The tattoo?"

"Any of it."

"*Any* of it?"

The beautician comes toward me, the wax pot in hand—and in panic I dodge behind the couch, clasping my robe defensively around me.

"But Mrs. Sherman has already prepaid for the entire treatment—"

"I don't care what she's paid for," I say, backing away. "You can wax my legs. But not my arms. And definitely not . . . that other one. The crystal love heart one."

The beautician looks worried.

"Mrs. Sherman is one of our most regular customers. She specifically requested the 'top-to-toe wax' for you."

"She'll never know!" I say desperately. "She'll never know! I mean, she's not exactly going to *look,* is she? She's not going to ask her son if his initials are tattooed on his girlfriend's . . ." I can't bring myself to say *area.* "I mean, come on. Is she?"

I break off, and there's a tense silence, broken only by the sound of tootling panpipes.

Then suddenly the beautician gives a snort of laughter. I catch her eye—and find myself starting to laugh, too, albeit slightly hysterically.

"You're right," says the beautician, sitting down and wiping her eyes. "You're right. She'll never know."

"How about a compromise?" I say. "You do my legs and eyebrows and we keep quiet about the rest."

"I could give you a massage instead," says the beautician. "Use up the time."

"There we are, then!" I say in relief. "Perfect!"

Feeling slightly drained, I lie down on the couch, and the beautician covers me up expertly with a towel.

"So, does Mrs. Sherman have a son, then?" she says, smoothing back my hair.

"Yes." I look up, taken aback. "Has she never even mentioned him?"

"Not that I recall. And she's been coming here for years . . ." The beautician shrugs. "I guess I always assumed she didn't have any children."

"Oh right," I say, and lie back down, trying not to give away my surprise.

When I emerge an hour and a half later, I feel fantastic. I've got brand-new eyebrows, smooth legs, and a glow all over from the most wonderful aromatherapy massage.

Elinor is waiting for me in reception, and as I come toward her, she runs her eyes appraisingly up and down my body. For a horrible moment I think she's going to ask me to roll up my sleeves to check the smoothness of my arms—but all she says is, "Your eyebrows look a lot better." Then she turns and walks out, and I hurry after her.

As we get back into the car, I ask, "Where are we having lunch?"

"Nina Heywood is holding a small informal charity lunch for Ugandan famine relief," she replies, examining one of her immaculate nails. "She holds events like this nearly every month. Do you know the Heywoods? Or the van Gelders?"

Of course I don't bloody know them.

"No," I hear myself saying. "But I know the Websters."

"The Websters?" She raises her arched eyebrows. "The Newport Websters?"

"The Oxshott Websters. Janice and Martin." I give her an innocent look. "Do you know them?"

"No," says Elinor, giving me a frosty look. "I don't believe I do."

For the rest of the journey we travel in silence. Then suddenly the car is stopping and we're getting out, and walking into the grandest, most enormous lobby I've ever seen, with a doorman in uniform and mirrors everywhere. We go up what seems like a zillion floors in a gilded lift with a man in a peaked cap, and into an apartment. And I have *never* seen anything like it.

The place is absolutely enormous, with a marble floor and a double staircase and a grand piano on a platform. The pale silk walls are decorated with enormous gold-framed paintings, and on pedestals around the room there are cascading flower arrangements like I've never seen before. Pin-thin women in expensive clothes are talking animatedly to one another, a smaller number of well-dressed men are listening politely, there are waitresses handing out champagne, and a girl in a flowing dress is playing the harp.

And this is a *small* charity lunch?

Our hostess Mrs. Heywood is a tiny woman in pink, who is about to shake hands with me when she's distracted by the arrival of a woman in a bejeweled turban. Elinor introduces me to a Mrs. Parker, a Mr. Wunsch, and a Miss Kutomi, then drifts away, and I make conversation as best I can, even though everyone seems to assume I must be a close friend of Prince William.

"Tell me," says Mrs. Parker urgently. "How is that poor young man bearing up after his . . . great loss?" she whispers.

"That boy has a natural nobility," says Mr. Wunsch fiercely. "Young people today could learn a lot from him. Tell me, is it the army he's headed for?"

"He . . . he hasn't mentioned it," I say helplessly. "Would you excuse me."

I escape to the bathroom—and that's just as huge and sumptuous as the rest of the apartment, with racks of luxury soaps and bottles of free perfume, and a comfy chair to sit in. I kind of wish I could stay there all day, actually. But I don't dare linger too long in case Elinor comes looking for me. So with a final squirt of Eternity, I force myself to get up and go back into the throng, where waiters are moving quietly around, murmuring, "Lunch will be served now."

As everyone moves toward a set of grand double doors I look around for Elinor but I can't see her. There's an old lady in black lace sitting on a chair near to me, and she begins to stand up with the aid of a walking stick.

"Let me help," I say, hurrying forward as her grip falters. "Shall I hold your champagne glass?"

"Thank you, my dear!" The lady smiles at me as I take her arm, and we walk slowly together into the palatial dining room. People are pulling out chairs and sitting down at circular tables, and waiters are hurrying round with bread rolls.

"Margaret," says Mrs. Heywood, coming forward and holding out her hands to the old lady. "There you are. Now let me find your seat . . ."

"This young lady was assisting me," says the old lady as she lowers herself onto a chair, and I smile modestly at Mrs. Heywood.

"Thank you, dear," she says absently. "Now, could you take my glass too, please . . . and bring some water to our table?"

"Of course!" I say with a friendly smile. "No problem."

"And I'll have a gin and tonic," adds an elderly man nearby, swiveling in his chair.

"Coming right up!"

It just shows, what Mum says is right. The way to make a friend is to give a helping hand. I feel quite special, helping out the hostess. It's almost like I'm throwing the party with her!

I'm not sure where the kitchen is, but the waiters are all heading toward one end of the room. I follow them through a set of double doors, and find myself in the kind of kitchen Mum would absolutely die for. Granite and marble everywhere, and a fridge which looks like a space rocket, and a pizza oven set into the wall! There are waiters in white shirts hurrying in and out with trays, and two chefs standing at a central island hob, holding sizzling pans, and someone's yelling, "Where the *fuck* are the napkins?"

I find a bottle of water and a glass, and put them on a tray, then start looking around to see where the gin might be. As I bend down to open a cupboard door, a man with cropped bleached hair taps me on the shoulder.

"Hey. What are you doing?"

"Oh hi!" I say, standing up. "I'm just looking for the gin, actually. Somebody wanted a gin and tonic."

"We haven't got time for that!" he barks. "Do you realize how short-staffed we are? We need food on tables!"

Short-staffed? I stare at him blankly for a moment. Then, as my eye falls on my black skirt and the realization hits me, I give a shocked laugh.

"No! I'm not a . . . I mean, I'm actually one of the . . ."

How do I say this without offending him? I'm sure being a waiter is actually very fulfilling. Anyway, he's probably an actor in his spare time.

But while I'm dithering, he dumps a silver platter full of smoked fish in my arms.

"Get! Now!"

"But I'm not—"

"Now! *Food on tables!*"

With a pang of fright I quickly hurry away. OK. What I'll do is I'll just get away from him, and put this platter down somewhere, and find my place.

Cautiously I walk back into the dining room, and wander about between the tables, looking for a handy surface to leave the platter. But there don't seem to be any side tables or even spare chairs. I can't really leave it on the floor, and it would be a bit too awkward to reach between the guests and dump it on a table.

This is really annoying, actually. The platter's quite heavy, and my arms are starting to ache. I pass by Mr. Wunsch's chair and give him a little smile, but he doesn't even notice me. It's as though I'm suddenly invisible.

This is ridiculous. There *must* be somewhere I can put it down.

"Will-you-serve-the-food!" hisses a furious voice behind me, and I feel myself jump.

"OK!" I retort, feeling slightly rattled. "OK, I will!"

Oh, for goodness' sake. It's probably easier just to serve it. Then at least it'll be gone, and I can sit down. Hesitantly I approach the nearest table.

"Erm . . . would anyone like some smoked fish? I think this is salmon . . . and this is trout . . ."

"Rebecca?"

The elegantly coiffured head in front of me swivels round and I give a startled leap. Elinor is staring up at me, her eyes like daggers.

"Hi," I say nervously. "Would you like some fish?"

"*What* do you think you're doing?" she says in a low, furious voice.

"Oh!" I swallow. "Well, I was just, you know, helping out . . ."

"I'll have some smoked salmon, thanks," says a woman in a gold jacket. "Do you have any nonfat French dressing?"

"Erm . . . well, the thing is, I'm not actually . . ."

"Rebecca!" Elinor's voice comes shooting out of her barely opened mouth. "Put it down. Just . . . sit down."

"Right. Of course." I glance uncertainly at the platter. "Or should I serve it, since I'm here anyway . . ."

"Put it down. Now!"

"Right." I look helplessly about for a moment, then see a waiter coming toward me with an empty tray. Before he can protest I deposit the smoked fish platter on his tray, then hurry round with trembling legs to my empty chair, smoothing down my hair.

As I sit down, and spread my thick napkin over my knees, there's silence around the table. I try a friendly little smile, but nobody responds. Then an old lady wearing about six rows of huge pearls and a hearing aid leans toward Elinor and whispers, so audibly we can all hear, "Your son is dating . . . a *waitress*?"

BECKY BLOOMWOOD'S NEW YORK BUDGET

DAILY BUDGET (PROPOSED)

Food	$50
Shopping	~~$50~~ $100
Expenses	~~$50~~ ~~$60~~ $100
TOTAL	$250

DAILY BUDGET (REVISED)

DAY THREE

Food	$50
Shopping	$100
Expenses	$365
Other expenses	$229
Unique sample sale opportunity	$567
Further unique sample sale opportunity	$128
Unavoidable contingency expense	$49
Essential business-linked expense (shoes)	

Eleven

"She did?" There's a long pause. Luke frowns and glances at me. "Well, I'm sure she didn't . . ." He breaks off into silence and I feel a flutter of apprehension.

It's a couple of days later, and on the other end of the phone, speaking to Luke, is Elinor. God only knows what she's saying about me. I wish we had a speaker phone.

On second thought, no, I don't.

"Really?" Luke looks surprised. "I see. Interesting." He clears his throat. "And on that matter—what about the two of us trying to meet up?"

Thank goodness. They've stopped talking about me.

"Oh, I see." The deflation in Luke's voice is unmistakable. "No, of course I understand. Yes, I will. Bye, then." He puts down the phone and gazes down at it for a few seconds.

"So!" I say, trying to sound relaxed. "What did your mother think of me?"

"Oh! Well . . ." Luke screws up his face puzzledly. "She said you were . . . overzealous. What did she mean by that?"

"I've no idea!" I give a shrill laugh. "Probably just . . . you know . . . hardworking! So, erm . . . did she mention your gift?" I add, changing the subject.

"No," says Luke after a pause. "As a matter of fact, she didn't."

"Oh," I say, feeling a pang of indignation toward Elinor. "Well, you know, she did absolutely love it."

"Do you think?"

"Absolutely!" I say emphatically. "She . . . she almost cried, she was so pleased. And she said you were the best son in the whole world."

"Really?" Luke's face glows with pleasure. "She said that?"

I smile vaguely and reach down for my shoes. Maybe that wasn't quite true. But I mean, I can't tell him she just shoved it back into the box as though it were a pair of socks from Woolworth's, can I?

"See you later." Luke picks up his briefcase and gives me a kiss. "And good luck this morning."

"Thanks!" I beam back, and feel a small trickle of excitement.

All of a sudden, things have started to happen over here. I keep getting phone calls from people who want to meet me, which Luke says is the "snowball effect" and he expected it all along. Yesterday I had three meetings with different sets of TV executives—today I've got a breakfast meeting with a Greg Walters from Blue River Productions. He's the one who sent me the basket of fruit and was "desperate" to see me. I've never had anyone desperate to see me before in my entire life!

An hour later, I'm sitting in the Four Seasons restaurant, feeling like a movie star. Greg Walters is tall and tanned and has already dropped the name of every TV network I've ever heard of.

"You're hot," he now keeps saying, in between bites of croissant. "You realize that?"

"Erm . . . well . . ."

"No." He lifts a hand. "Don't be coy. You're all over town. Folks are fighting over you." He takes a sip of coffee and looks me in the eye. "I'll be frank—I want to give you your own show."

I stare at him, almost unable to breathe for excitement.

"Really? My own show? Doing what?"

"Whatever. We'll find you a winning format." He takes a gulp of coffee. "You're a political commentator, right?"

"Um . . . not really," I say awkwardly. "I do personal finance. You know, mortgages and stuff?"

"Right." Greg nods. "Finance. So I'm thinking . . . off the top of my head . . . Wall Street. Wall Street meets *Ab Fab* meets Oprah. You could do that, right?"

"Erm . . . absolutely!"

I beam confidently at him and take a bite of croissant.

"I have to go," he says as he finishes his coffee. "But I'm going to call you tomorrow and set up a meeting with our head of development. Is that OK?"

"Fine!" I say, trying to look as nonchalant as possible. "That would be good."

As he walks off, a huge grin of delight spreads across my face. My own show! Things are just going better and better. Everyone I speak to seems to want to offer me a job, and they all keep buying me nice meals, and yesterday, someone said I could have a career in Hollywood, no question. Hollywood!

I mean, just imagine if I get my own show in Hollywood! I'll be able to live in some amazing house in Beverly Hills, and go to parties with all the film stars. Maybe Luke will start a Los Angeles branch of his company. I mean, people out there need PR—and he could easily switch from finance to movies. And . . . yes! We could set up a film production company together!

"What a pleasant surprise," says a cheerful voice, and I look up dazedly to see Michael Ellis pulling out a chair at another table.

"Oh," I say, wrenching my mind away from the Oscars. "Oh, hello. Do join me!" And I gesture politely to the chair opposite.

"I'm not disturbing you?" he says, sitting down.

"No. I was having a meeting but it's over." I look around vaguely. "Is Luke with you?"

Michael shakes his head.

"He's talking to some people at JD Slade this morning. The big guns."

A waiter comes and clears away Greg's plate, and Michael orders a cappuccino.

"So—how are things going?" I ask, lowering my voice slightly. "Luke told me about one of the backers getting nervous."

"Right." Michael nods gravely. "I don't know what the hell's going on there."

"But why do you *need* backers?" I ask. "I mean, Luke's got loads of money . . ."

"Never invest your own money," says Michael. "First rule of business. Besides which, Luke has very grand plans, and grand plans tend to need a lot of capital." He looks up. "You know, he's very driven, that man of yours. *Very* determined to succeed over here."

"I know," I say, rolling my eyes. "All he ever does is work."

"Work is good," says Michael, frowning into his coffee. "Obsession is . . . not so good." He's silent for a moment, then looks up with a smile. "But I gather things are going well for you?"

"They are, actually," I say, unable to maintain my calm. "In fact, they're going brilliantly! I've had all these fantastic meetings, and everybody says they want to give me a job! I just had a meeting with Greg Walters from Blue River Productions—and he said he was going to give me my own show. And yesterday, someone was talking about Hollywood!"

"That's great," says Michael. "Really great." He takes a sip of coffee and looks at me thoughtfully. "If I could just say a word?"

"What?"

"These TV people. You don't necessarily want to believe every single word they say."

I look at him, a little discomfited.

"What do you mean?"

"These guys like talking big," says Michael, slowly stirring his coffee. "It makes them feel good. And they believe everything they say at the time when they're saying it. But when it comes to the cold hard dollar . . ." He stops, and looks up at me. "I just don't want you to be disappointed."

"I won't be disappointed!" I retort indignantly. "Greg Walters said the whole town was fighting over me!"

"I'm sure he did," says Michael. "And I very much hope they are. All I'm saying is—"

He stops as a uniformed concierge stops by our table.

"Miss Bloomwood," he says. "I have a message for you."

"Thanks!" I say in surprise.

I open the envelope he gives me, and pull out the sheets of paper—and it's a message from Kent Garland at HLBC.

"Well!" I say, unable to stop a smile of triumph. "It looks like HLBC wasn't just talking big. It looks like they mean business." I give the piece of paper to Michael Ellis, wanting to add, "So there!"

" 'Please call Kent's assistant to arrange a screen test,' " reads Michael aloud. "Well, looks like I'm wrong," he says, smiling. "And I'm very glad about it." He lifts his coffee cup toward me. "So here's to a successful screen test."

OK. What am I going to wear tomorrow? *What am I going to wear?* I mean, this is the most important moment of my life, a screen test for American television. My outfit has to be sharp, flattering, photogenic, immaculate . . . I mean, I've got nothing. Nothing.

I leaf through all my clothes for the millionth time, and flop back down on the bed, exhausted. I can't believe I've come all this way without one single screen-test outfit.

Well, there's nothing for it. I've got no choice.

I pick up my bag and check that I've got my wallet—and I'm just reaching for my coat when the phone rings.

"Hello?" I say into the receiver, hoping it might be Luke.

"Bex!" comes Suze's voice, all tinny and distant.

"Suze!" I say in delight. "Hi!"

"How's it going?"

"It's going really well!" I say. "I've had loads of meetings, and everyone's being really positive! It's just brilliant!"

"Bex! That's great."

"How about you?" I frown slightly at her voice. "Is everything OK?"

"Oh yes!" says Suze. "Everything's fine. Except . . ." She hesitates. "I just thought you should know, a man phoned up this morning about some money you owe a shop. La Rosa, in Hampstead."

"Really?" I pull a face. "Them again?"

"Yes. He asked me when you were going to be out of the artificial limb unit."

"Oh," I say after a pause. "Right. So—what did you say?"

"Bex, why did he think you were in the artificial limb unit?"

"I don't know," I say evasively. "Maybe he heard something. Or . . . or I may possibly have written him the odd little letter . . ."

"Bex," interrupts Suze, and her voice is quivering slightly. "You told me you'd taken care of all those bills. You promised!"

"I have taken care of them!" I reach for my hairbrush and begin to brush my hair.

"By telling them your *parachute* didn't open in time?" cries Suze. "I mean, honestly, Bex—"

"Look, don't stress. I'll sort it all out as soon as I come home."

"He said he was going to have to take extreme action! He said he was very sorry, but enough allowances had been made, and—"

"They always say that," I say soothingly. "Suze, you really don't have to worry. I'm going to earn loads over here. I'll be loaded! And I'll be able to pay everything off, and everything will be fine."

There's silence, and I imagine Suze sitting on the floor of the sitting room, winding her hair tightly round her fingers.

"Really?" she says at last. "Is it all going well, then?"

"Yes! I've got a screen test tomorrow, and this guy wants to give me my own show, and they're even talking about Hollywood!"

"Hollywood?" breathes Suze. "That's amazing."

"I know!" I beam at my own reflection. "Isn't it great? I'm hot! That's what the guy from Blue River Productions said."

"So—what are you going to wear for your screen test?"

"I'm just off to Barneys," I say happily. "Choose a new outfit!"

"*Barneys?*" exclaims Suze in horror. "Bex, you *promised* me you weren't going to go overboard! You completely promised me you were going to stick to a budget."

"I have! I've completely stuck to it! It's all written out and everything! And anyway, this is a business expense. I'm investing in my career."

"But—"

"Suze, you can't make money unless you spend it first. Everyone knows that! I mean, you have to spend money on your materials, don't you?"

There's a pause.

"I suppose so," says Suze doubtfully.

"And anyway, what are credit cards for?"

"Oh Bex . . ." Suze sighs. "Actually, that's funny—that's just what the council tax girl said yesterday."

"What council tax girl?" I frown at my reflection and reach for an eyeliner.

"The girl who came round this morning," says Suze vaguely. "She had a clipboard. And she asked loads of questions about me, and the flat, and how much rent you paid me . . . we had a really nice chat. And I was telling her all about you being in America, and Luke . . . and your TV job . . ."

"Great," I say, not really listening. "That sounds really good. Listen, Suze, I've got to run. But honestly, don't worry. If anyone else phones for me, just don't take the call. OK?"

"Well . . . OK," says Suze. "And good luck tomorrow!"

"Thanks!" I say, and put down the phone. Ha-ha-ha! Off to Barneys!

Barneys. I've kind of been saving it for last, like an extra-special chocolate. Now, as I push through the distinctive black revolving doors and walk slowly across the pale mosaic floor, looking at all the beautiful people peering into cabinets full of contemporary jewelry . . . I feel like Goldilocks picking the right chair. The music is buzzy and the atmosphere is great, and everyone looks like they're having a great time . . .

For a while I linger at a cabinet with a stunning aquamarine crystal necklace in it. I'd look just like a mermaid in that. I wonder how much it is? I'm just peering to see the price tag when an assistant approaches—and I come to with a jolt. I'm not here to buy a necklace. I'm going to buy what I *need.*

Feeling virtuous, I force myself to move away from the cabinet. Down to business. I study the store guide, then I take the escalator up to the top floor of the store, glimpsing tanks of fish, cages of brightly colored birds . . . and everywhere I look, gorgeous clothes.

Oh God, the *clothes.* They are just the most beautiful things I've ever seen! Everywhere I look, I see shapes and colors and designs I just want to grab and touch and stroke. But I can't just spend all day marveling at candy-colored knitwear and beaded mules. I have to be focused. An outfit for tomorrow, nothing else.

Right. So what exactly do I want? Maybe a jacket, so I look authoritative—but it has to be the right jacket. Not too boxy, not too stiff . . . just nice clean lines. And maybe a skirt. Or just look at those trousers. They would look fantastic, if I had the right shoes . . .

I wander slowly round each floor, making mental notes. Then at last, when I'm sure I haven't left anything out, I start collecting all my possibilities. A Calvin Klein jacket . . . and a skirt . . .

"Excuse me?"

A voice interrupts me just as I'm reaching for a sleeveless top, and I turn in surprise. A woman in a black trouser suit is smiling at me.

"Would you like any help with your shopping today?"

"Erm . . . oh, thanks!" I say. "If you could hold these . . ." I hand her the garments I've already picked out and her smile flickers slightly.

"When I said help . . . we're running a unique promotion of

our personal shopping department today. We'd like to introduce the concept to a wider audience. So if you'd like to take up the offer of an introductory session, there are some slots still available."

"Oh right," I say interestedly. "What exactly would that—"

"Our trained, experienced personal shoppers can help you find exactly what you're searching for," says the woman pleasantly. "They can help you find your own style, focus on designs that suit you, and guide you through the daunting fashion maze." She gives a tight little laugh, and I get the feeling she's said this little spiel quite a few times today.

"I see," I say thoughtfully. "The thing is . . . I'm not sure I really need guiding. So thanks very much, but—"

"The service is complimentary," says the woman. "Today we're also offering tea, coffee, or a glass of champagne."

Champagne? Free champagne?

"Ooh!" I say. "Well, actually—that sounds really good. Yes, please!"

And actually, I think as I follow her to the third floor, these trained shoppers must really know their stuff—and they'll probably have a completely different eye. They'll probably show me a whole side of myself that I've never even seen before!

We arrive at a suite of large dressing rooms, and the woman shows me in with a smile.

"Your personal shopper today will be Erin," she says. "Erin has only recently joined us, so she will be receiving some occasional guidance from a senior Barneys shopper. Will that be all right?"

"Absolutely!" I say, taking off my coat.

"Would you prefer tea, coffee, or champagne?"

"Champagne," I say quickly. "Thanks."

"Very well," she says with a smile. "Ah, and here's Erin."

I look up with interest, to see a tall thin girl coming into the dressing room. She's got straight blond hair and a small, kind of squashed-looking mouth. In fact her whole face looks as though she were once squeezed between a pair of lift doors and never quite recovered.

"Hello," she says, and I watch her mouth in fascination as she smiles. "I'm Erin—and I'll be helping you find the outfit to best suit your needs."

"Great!" I say. "Can't wait!"

I wonder how this Erin got her job. Not by her taste in shoes, certainly.

"So . . ." Erin looks at me thoughtfully. "What were you looking for today?"

"I have a screen test tomorrow," I explain. "I want to look kind of . . . smart and sassy, but approachable, too. Maybe with a little witty twist somewhere."

"A witty twist," echoes Erin, scribbling on her pad. "Right. And were you thinking . . . a suit? A jacket?"

"Well," I say, and launch into an exact explanation of what I'm looking for. Erin listens carefully, and I notice a dark-haired woman in tortoiseshell glasses occasionally coming to the door of our dressing room and listening too.

"Right," says Erin, when I've finished. "Well, you certainly have some ideas there . . ." She taps her teeth for a moment. "I'm thinking . . . we have a very nice fitted jacket by Moschino, with roses on the collar . . ."

"Oh, I know the one!" I say in delight. "I was thinking of that, too!"

"Along with . . . there's a new skirt in the Barneys collection . . ."

"The black one?" I say. "With the buttons just here? Yes, I thought of that, but it's a bit short. I was thinking of the knee-length one. You know, with the ribbon round the hem . . ."

"We'll see," says Erin, with a pleasant smile. "Let me line up some pieces for you, and we can have a look."

As she goes off to gather up clothes, I sit down and sip my champagne. This isn't bad, actually. I mean, it's much less effort than trawling round the shop myself. I can half-hear a murmured conversation going on in the dressing room next door—and suddenly a woman's voice rises in distress, saying, "I just want to show that bastard. I just want to *show* him!"

"And we will show him, Marcia," replies a calm, soothing

voice, which I think belongs to the woman in tortoiseshell glasses. "We will. But not in a cherry-red pantsuit."

"Okaaay!" Erin is back in the dressing room, wheeling in a rack of clothes. I run my eye quickly over them, and notice quite a few of the things I'd already picked out for myself. But what about the knee-length skirt? And what about that amazing aubergine trouser suit with the leather collar?

"So, here's the jacket for you to try . . . and the skirt . . ."

I take the clothes from her, and look doubtfully at the skirt. I just know it's going to be too short. But then, she's the expert, I suppose . . . Quickly I change into the skirt and jacket—then come and stand in front of the mirror, next to Erin.

"The jacket's fabulous!" I say. "And it fits me perfectly. I *love* the cut."

I don't really want to say anything about the skirt. I mean, I don't want to hurt her feelings—but it looks all wrong.

"Now, let's see," says Erin. She stands with her head on one side and squints at my reflection. "I'm thinking a skirt to the knee might look better, after all."

"Like the one I told you about!" I say in relief. "It's on the seventh floor, right next to the—"

"Possibly," she says, and smiles. "But I have a few other skirts in mind . . ."

"Or the Dolce & Gabbana one on the third floor," I add. "I was looking at it earlier. Or the DKNY."

"DKNY?" says Erin, wrinkling her brow. "I don't believe . . ."

"The assistant there told me they're new in. *So* nice. You should have a look at them!" I turn round and look carefully at her outfit. "You know what? The mauve DKNY would look really good with that turtleneck you're wearing. And you could team it with a pair of those new Stephane Kelian boots with the spiky heels. You know the ones?"

"I know the ones," says Erin tightly. "The crocodile and suede ones." I look at her in surprise.

"No, not those ones. The *new* range. With the stitching up the back. They're so gorgeous! In fact they'd go well with the knee-length skirt . . ."

"Thank you!" interrupts Erin sharply. "I'll bear that in mind."

Honestly. I'm only giving her a few hints. You'd think she'd be pleased I was so interested in her shop!

Although, I have to say, she doesn't seem to know it very well.

"Hello there!" comes a voice from the door—and the woman in tortoiseshell glasses is leaning against the door frame, looking at me interestedly. "Everything all right?"

"Great, thanks!" I say, beaming at her.

"So," says the woman, looking at Erin. "You're going to try the knee-length skirt for our customer. Is that right?"

"Yes," says Erin, and gives a rather forced smile. "I'll just go get it."

As she disappears, I can't resist sidling over to the rack of clothes, just to see what else she brought. The woman in glasses watches me for a moment, then comes in and holds out her hand.

"Christina Rowan," she said. "I head up the personal shopping department."

"Well, hello!" I say, looking at a pale blue Jill Stuart shirt. "I'm Becky Bloomwood."

"And you're from England, I guess, by your accent?"

"London, but I'm going to move to New York!"

"Are you, indeed." Christina Rowan gives me a friendly smile. "Tell me, what do you do, Becky? Do you work in fashion?"

"Oh no. I'm in finance."

"Finance! Really." She raises her eyebrows.

"I give financial advice on the telly. You know, pensions and stuff . . ." I reach for a pair of soft cashmere trousers. "Aren't these beautiful? Much better than the Ralph Lauren ones. *And* they're cheaper."

"They're great, aren't they?" She gives me a quizzical look. "Well, it's nice to have such an enthusiastic customer." She reaches into the pocket of her jacket and pulls out a business card. "Do come back and visit us when you're here again."

"I will!" I beam at her. "And thanks very much!"

It's four o'clock by the time I finally leave Barneys. I hail a cab and travel back to the Four Seasons. As I push open the door to our room and look at my reflection in the silent dressing table mirror, I'm still on a kind of glittery high, almost a hysterical excitement at what I've just done. What I've just bought.

I know I went out just planning to buy a single outfit for my screen test. But I ended up . . . Well, I suppose I just got a bit . . . a bit carried away. So my final list of purchases goes like this:

1. Moschino jacket
2. Knee-length Barneys skirt
3. Calvin Klein underwear
4. Pair of new tights

   and . . .

5. Vera Wang cocktail dress.

Just . . . before you say anything, I *know* I wasn't supposed to be buying a cocktail dress. I *know* that when Erin said, "Are you interested in evening wear?" I should simply have said no.

But oh God. Oh *God.* That Vera Wang dress. Inky purple, with a low back and glittering straps. It just looked so completely movie-star perfect. Everyone crowded round to see me in it—and when I drew back the curtain, they all gasped.

And I just stared at myself, mesmerized. Entranced by what I could look like, by the person I could be. There was no question. I had to have it. I *had* to. As I signed the credit card slip . . . I wasn't me anymore. I was Grace Kelly. I was Gwyneth Paltrow. I was a glittering somebody else, who can casually sign a credit card slip for thousands of dollars while smiling and laughing at the assistant, as though this were a nothing-purchase.

Thousands of dollars.

Although, for a designer like Vera Wang, that price is actually quite . . .

Well, it's really very . . .

I feel slightly sick. I don't even want to think about how much it cost. The point is, I'll be able to wear it for years. Yes!

Years and years. And I *need* designer clothes if I'm going to be a famous television star. I mean, I'll have important events to go to—and I can't just turn up in M&S, can I? Exactly.

And I've got a £10,000 credit card limit. That's the real point. I mean, they wouldn't give it to me if they didn't think I could afford it.

Suddenly I hear a sound at the door, and quickly rise to my feet. Heart thumping, I go to the wardrobe I've been stashing all my shopping in, open the door, and quickly shove my Barneys bags inside—then close the door and turn round with a smile, just as Luke enters the room, talking on his mobile.

"Of course I'm in fucking control," he's spitting furiously into the phone. "What the fuck do they think they're—" He breaks off and is silent for a few moments. "I don't need to fly back to London! Alicia has it all in hand. She says there's absolutely no problem with Provident Assurance, she spoke to them today and they're very happy. Someone's just shit-stirring, God knows who. Yes, I know," he says in a calmer voice. "Yes. OK, will do. I'll see you tomorrow, Michael. Thanks."

He switches off his mobile, puts it away, and looks at me as though he's almost forgotten who I am. But then his brow softens and he smiles.

"Hi!" he says, and drops his briefcase onto a chair.

"Hi!" I say brightly, moving away from the wardrobe door. "Stranger."

"I know," says Luke, rubbing his face wearily. "I'm sorry. Things have been . . . a bit of a nightmare, to be frank. I heard about your screen test, though. Fantastic news."

He goes to the minibar, pours himself a scotch, and downs it. Then he pours himself another one and takes a slug while I watch anxiously. His face is pale and tense, I notice, and there are shadows under his eyes.

"Is it all . . . going OK?" I ask gingerly.

"It's going," he replies. "That's about as much as I can say." He walks over to the window and stares out over the glittering Manhattan skyline, and I bite my lip nervously.

"Luke—couldn't someone else go to all these meetings?

Couldn't someone else fly out and take some of the load? Like . . . Alicia?"

It nearly kills me even to mention her name—but I honestly am getting a bit worried. Slightly to my relief, though, Luke shakes his head.

"I can't bring in somebody new at this stage. I've been managing it all until now; I'll just have to see it through. I just had no idea they'd be so pedantic. I had no idea they'd be so . . ." He sits down in an armchair and takes a slug of his drink. "I mean, Jesus, they ask a lot of questions. I know Americans are thorough but—" He shakes his head disbelievingly. "They have to know *everything*. About every single client, every single potential client, everybody who's ever worked for the company, every single bloody memo I've ever sent . . . Is there any possibility of litigation here? Who was your receptionist in 1993? What car do you drive? What fucking . . . toothpaste do you use? And now, with these rumors . . . they're picking everything apart all over again."

He breaks off and drains his glass, and I stare at him in dismay.

"They sound awful!" I say, and the flicker of a smile passes across Luke's face.

"They're not awful. They're just very conservative, old-school investors—and something's rattling them. I don't know what." He exhales sharply. "I just need to keep them steady."

His voice is trembling slightly—and as I glance at his hand I see that it's clenched tightly around his glass. I've never seen Luke like this, to be honest. He usually looks so utterly in control, so completely smooth . . .

"Luke, I think you should have an evening off. You haven't got a meeting tonight, have you?"

"No," says Luke, looking up. "But I need to go through some of these forecasts again. Big meeting tomorrow, with all the investors. I need to be prepared."

"You are prepared!" I reply. "What you need is to be *relaxed*. If you work all night, you'll just be tired and tense and ratty." I go over to him, take his glass out of his hand, and start to massage his shoulders. "Come on, Luke. You really need a night off. I bet Michael would agree. Wouldn't he?"

"He's been telling me to lighten up," admits Luke after a long pause.

"Well, then, lighten up! Come on, a few hours of fun never did anybody any harm. Let's both dress up and go somewhere really nice, and dance, and drink cocktails . . ." I kiss him gently on the back of his neck. "I mean, why on earth come to New York and not enjoy it?"

There's silence—and for an awful moment I think Luke's going to say he hasn't got time. But then suddenly he turns round—and thank God, I can see the faint glimmer of a smile.

"You're right," he says. "Come on. Let's do it."

It turns into the most magical, glamorous, glossy evening of my life. I put on my Vera Wang dress and Luke puts on his smartest suit, and we go to a fabulous restaurant all done like an Art Deco cruise ship, where beautiful people are eating lobster and there's an old-fashioned jazz band, just like in the movies. Luke orders Bellinis, and we toast each other, and as he relaxes, he tells me more about his deal. In fact, he confides in me more than he ever has before.

"This city," he says, shaking his head. "It's a demanding place. Like . . . skiing down the edge of a precipice. If you make one mistake—that's it. You fall."

"But if you don't make any mistakes?"

"You win," says Luke. "You win it all."

"You're going to win," I say confidently. "You're going to wow them all tomorrow."

"And you're going to wow them at your screen test," says Luke, as a waiter appears at our table with our first course—the most amazing sculptures made out of seafood, presented on hexagonal plates. He pours our wine, and Luke lifts his glass in a toast.

"To you, Becky. You're going to be a huge success."

"No, *you're* going to be a huge success," I reply, feeling a glow of pleasure all around me. "We're both going to be huge successes!"

Maybe it's the Bellini, going to my head—but suddenly I feel again exactly as I did in Barneys. I'm not the old Becky—I'm someone new and sparkling. Surreptitiously I glance at myself in a nearby mirror, and feel a twinge of delight. I mean, just look at me! All poised and groomed, in a New York restaurant, wearing a thousands-of-dollars dress, with my wonderful, successful boyfriend—and a screen test tomorrow for American television!

I feel completely intoxicated with happiness. This expensive, glossy world is where I've been heading all along. Limos and flowers; waxed eyebrows and designer clothes from Barneys; a purse stuffed with business cards of TV executives. These are my people; this is where I'm meant to be. My old life seems a million, zillion miles away, like a tiny dot on the horizon. Mum and Dad and Suze . . . my untidy room in Fulham . . . *EastEnders* with a pizza . . . I mean, let's face it. That was never really me, was it?

We end up staying out for hours. We dance to the jazz band, eat passion fruit sorbet, and talk about everything in the world but work. Luke asks the band to play "These Foolish Things," which is a song I completely love—and then sings along as we dance (very out of tune, but I don't say anything). When we get back to the hotel we're both laughing, and tripping slightly as we walk, and Luke's hand is making its way deftly inside my dress.

"Miss Bloomwood?" says the concierge as we pass the desk. "There's a message for you to call a Susan Cleath-Stuart, in London. Whatever time you get in. Apparently it's urgent."

"Oh God," I say, rolling my eyes. "She'll just be calling to lecture me about how much I spent on my new dress. 'How much? Oh Bex, you *shouldn't* have . . .' "

"It's a fantastic dress," says Luke, running his hands appreciatively up and down it. "Although there's far too much of it. You could lose this bit here . . . and this bit . . ."

"Would you like the number?" says the concierge, holding out a piece of paper.

"No, thanks," I say, waving my hand. "I'll call her tomorrow."

"And please," adds Luke, "hold all calls to our room, until further notice."

"Very well," says the concierge with a twinkle. "Good night, sir. Good night, ma'am."

We travel up in the lift, grinning stupidly at each other in the mirrors—and as we arrive at our room, I realize that I'm really feeling quite drunk. My only consolation is, Luke looks completely plastered, too.

"That," I say, as the door closes behind us, "was the best night of my life. The very best."

"It isn't over yet," says Luke, coming toward me with a meaningful gleam in his eye. "I feel I need to reward you for your most insightful comments, Miss Bloomwood. You *were* right. All work and no play . . ." He starts to pull my Vera Wang straps gently down off my shoulders. "Makes Jack . . ." he murmurs against my skin. "A very . . ."

And suddenly we're tumbling down onto the bed together, and his mouth is on mine, and my mind is wheeling with alcohol and delight. As he's pulling off his shirt, I catch a glimpse of myself in the mirror. I stare at my intoxicated, happy self for an instant, and hear a voice inside saying: remember this moment forever. Remember this moment, Becky, because right now, life is perfect.

The rest is a haze of drunken, blurry pleasure, drifting into oblivion. The last thing I remember is Luke kissing me on the eyelids and telling me to sleep well and that he loves me. That's the last thing.

And then, like a car crash, it happens.

Are They What They Seem?

FINANCE GURU IS MONEY MESS!

She sits on the *Morning Coffee* sofa, advising millions of viewers on financial issues. But *The Daily World* can exclusively reveal that hypocritical Becky Bloomwood is herself on the brink of financial disaster. Becky, whose catchphrase is "Look after your money–and it will look after you," is being pursued for debts totaling thousands, and her own bank manager has labeled her a "disgrace."

Summons

La Rosa clothes boutique has issued a summons against bankrupt Becky, while flatmate Susan Cleath-Stuart (right) admits Becky is often behind in her rent. Meanwhile feckless Becky is unashamedly jet-setting in New York with entrepreneur boyfriend Luke Brandon (below, right). "Becky quite blatantly uses Luke for his money," said one inside source at Brandon Communications. Miss Cleath-Stuart meanwhile admits she would like to see Becky gone. "I could do with more space for my work," she says. "Maybe I'll have to hire an office."

Spendaholic

Staying in the swanky Four Seasons Hotel, the wayward 26-year-old revealed she had no idea how much her accommodation cost. Our reporter watched as she splurged over £100 on greeting cards alone, then went on a further spree, buying luxury clothes and gifts totaling £1,000, in just a few hours.

Shocked

Viewers of *Morning Coffee* were outraged to discover the truth about the self-styled money expert. "I'm quite appalled," commented Irene Watson of Sevenoaks. "I phoned Becky a few weeks ago to ask advice on my banking arrangements. Now I wish I'd never listened to a word, and will certainly be taking further advice." Mother-of-two Irene added, "I'm shocked and disgusted that the producers of *Morning Coffee* **turn to page 4**

Twelve

AT FIRST, I don't realize anything is wrong. I wake up feeling extremely bleary—to see Luke handing me a cup of tea.

"Why don't you check the messages?" he says, giving me a kiss, and heads toward the shower. After a few sips of tea, I lift the telephone receiver and press the star button.

"You have twenty-three messages," says the telephone voice—and I gape at it in astonishment. Twenty-three?

Perhaps they're all job offers! is my first thought. Perhaps it's people calling from Hollywood! In great excitement I press the button to hear the first one. But it's not a job offer—it's Suze—and she's sounding really hassled.

"Bex, please ring me. As soon as you get this. It's . . . it's really urgent. Bye."

The voice asks me if I'd like to hear my remaining messages—and for a moment I hesitate. But Suze did sound pretty desperate—and I remember with a twinge of guilt that she called last night, too. I dial the number—and to my surprise, it clicks onto her answer machine.

"Hi! It's me!" I say as soon as Suze's voice has finished speaking. "Well, you're not in, so I hope whatever it is has sorted itself—"

"Bex!" Suze's voice practically bursts my eardrum. "Oh my God, Bex, where have you been?"

"Out," I say puzzledly. "And then asleep. Suze, is everything—"

"Bex, I never said those things!" she interrupts, sounding distressed. "You have to believe me. I'd never say *anything* like that. They just . . . twisted everything round. I told your mum, I didn't have any idea—"

"My mum?" I say in puzzlement. "Suze, slow down. What are you talking about?"

There's silence.

"Oh God," says Suze. "Bex, haven't you seen it?"

"Seen what?" I say.

"The Daily World," says Suze. "I . . . I thought you got all the British papers."

"We do," I say, rubbing my dry face. "But they'll still be outside the door. Is there . . . is there something about me?"

"No," says Suze a little too quickly. "No. I mean . . . there is this one very tiny thing. But it's not worth looking at. I really wouldn't bother. In fact—throw *The Daily World* away, I would. Just . . . put it in the bin, without even opening it."

"There's something nasty, isn't there?" I say apprehensively. "Do my legs look really fat?"

"It's really nothing!" says Suze. "Nothing! So anyway . . . have you been to Rockefeller Center yet? It's supposed to be great! Or FAO Schwarz? Or . . ."

"Suze, stop," I interrupt. "I'm going to go and get it. I'll call you back."

"OK, look, Bex, just remember," says Suze in a rush. "Hardly *anyone* reads *The Daily World.* You know, like about three people. And it's tomorrow's fish-and-chips. And everyone knows the newspapers make up complete lies . . ."

"Right," I say, trying to sound relaxed. "I'll remember that. And don't worry, Suze! These stupid little things don't faze me!"

But as I put the phone down, my hand is trembling slightly. What on earth can they have said about me? I hurry to the door, grab the pile of papers, and cart them all back to the bed. I seize hold of *The Daily World* and feverishly start to leaf through it. Page after page . . . but there's nothing there. I go back to the beginning and leaf through more carefully, looking at all the tiny box items—and there really is no mention of me at all. I lean back on my pillows, bemused. What on earth is Suze going on about? Why on earth is she so—

And then I spot the center double-page spread. A single folded sheet, lying on the bed, which must have fallen out as I grabbed hold of the paper. Very slowly I reach for it. I open it. And it's as though someone's punched me in the stomach.

There's a picture of me. It's a photo I don't recognize—not very flattering. I'm walking along, in some street . . . A New York street, I realize with a lurch. And I'm holding lots of shopping bags. And there's a picture of Luke, in a circle. And a little picture of Suze. And the headline reads . . .

I can't even tell you what it says. I can't even say it. It's . . . it's too awful.

It's a huge article, spanning the whole center spread. As I read it, my heart is thudding; my head feels hot and cold. It's so nasty. It's so . . . personal. Halfway through I can't stand it anymore. I close the paper, and stare ahead, breathing hard, feeling as though I might throw up.

Then almost immediately, with trembling hands, I open it again. I have to see exactly what they've said. I have to read every horrible, humiliating line.

When I've finally finished, I sit, breathing hard, trying to keep control. I can't quite believe this is really happening. This paper has already been printed millions of times. It's too late to stop it. In Britain, I suddenly realize, this has been out for hours. My parents will have seen it. Everyone I know will have seen it. I'm powerless.

As I'm sitting there, the telephone gives a shrill ring, and I jump with fright. After a moment it rings again, and I stare at it in terror. I can't answer. I can't talk to anybody, not even Suze.

The phone rings for the fourth time, and Luke strides out of the bathroom, a towel round his waist and his hair slicked back.

"Aren't you going to get that?" he says shortly, and grabs for the receiver. "Hello? Yes, Luke Brandon here."

I feel a swoop of fear, and wrap the duvet more tightly around me.

"Right," Luke is saying. "Fine. I'll see you then." He puts the phone down and scribbles something on a pad of paper.

"Who was that?" I say, trying to keep my voice steady.

"A secretary from JD Slade," he says, putting his pen down. "Change of venue."

He starts to get dressed, and I say nothing. My hand tightens around the *Daily World* page. I want to show him . . . but I don't want to show him. I don't want him to read those horrible things about me. But I can't let him see it from someone else.

I can't sit here forever, saying nothing. I close my eyes—then take a deep breath and say, "Luke, there's a thing about me in the paper."

"Good," says Luke absently, doing up his tie. "I thought you might get a bit of publicity. Which paper?"

"It's . . . it's not good," I say, and lick my dry lips. "It's really awful."

Luke looks at me properly and sees my expression.

"Oh, Becky," he says, "it can't be that bad. Come on, show me. What does it say?" He holds out his hand, but I don't move.

"It's just . . . really horrible. And there's a great big picture—"

"Did you have a bad hair day?" says Luke teasingly, and reaches for his jacket. "Becky, no piece of publicity is ever 100 percent perfect. You're always going to find *something* to fret about, whether it's your hair, or something you said . . ."

"Luke!" I say despairingly. "It's nothing like that. Just . . . have a look."

Slowly I unfold the paper and give it to Luke. He takes it cheerfully—but as he gazes at it, his smile slowly disappears.

"What the fuck— Is that *me*?" He glances at me briefly, and I swallow, not daring to say anything. Then he scans the page while I watch nervously.

"Is this true?" he says at last. "Any of it?"

"N-no!" I stammer. "At least . . . not . . . not all of it. Some of it is . . ."

"Are you in debt?"

I meet his gaze, feeling my face turn crimson.

"A . . . a little bit. But I mean, not like they say . . . I mean, I don't know anything about a summons . . ."

"Tuesday afternoon!" He hits the paper. "For Christ's sake. You were at the Guggenheim. Find your ticket, we'll prove you were there, get a retraction—"

"I . . . Actually . . . Luke . . ." He looks up and I feel a lurch of pure fear. "I didn't go to the Guggenheim. I . . . I went . . . shopping."

"You went . . ." He stares at me—then silently starts to read again.

When he's finished he stares ahead expressionlessly.

"I don't believe this," he says, so quietly I can barely hear him.

He looks as grim as I feel—and for the first time this morning I feel tears pricking at my eyes.

"I know," I say shakily. "It's awful. They must have been following me. They must have been there all along, watching me, *spying* on me . . ." I look at him for a response, but he's just staring straight ahead. "Luke, don't you have anything to say? Do you realize—"

"Becky, do *you* realize?" he interrupts. He turns toward me—and at his expression I feel the blood draining from my face. "Do you realize quite how bad this is for *me*?"

"I'm really sorry," I gulp. "I know you hate being in the paper . . ."

"It's not a bloody question of—" He stops himself, and says more calmly, "Becky, do you realize how this is going to make me look? Today of all fucking days?"

"I . . . I didn't . . ." I whisper.

"I have to go into a meeting in an hour's time and convince a stuffy, conservative New York investment bank that I'm fully in control of every aspect of my business and personal life. They'll all have seen this. I'll be a joke!"

"But of course you're in control!" I say in alarm. "Luke, surely they'll realize . . . surely they won't—"

"Listen," says Luke, turning round. "Do you know what the perception of me is in this city? The general perception here—for some inexplicable reason—is that I'm losing my touch."

"Losing your touch?" I echo in horror.

"That's what I've heard." Luke takes a deep, controlled breath. "What I've been doing over the last few days is working my fucking *arse* off to convince these people that their perception is wrong. That I'm on top of it. That I have the media taped. And now . . ." He hits the paper sharply and I wince.

"Maybe . . . maybe they won't have seen it."

"Becky, they see everything," says Luke. "That's their job. That's—"

He breaks off as the phone rings. After a pause, he picks it up.

"Hi, Michael. Ah. You've seen it. Yes, I know. Unfortunate timing. All right. See you in a sec." He puts down the phone and reaches for his briefcase, without looking at me.

I feel cold and shivery. What have I done? I've wrecked everything. Phrases from the article keep popping into my mind, making me feel sick. *Feckless Becky* . . . *hypocritical Becky* . . . And they're right. They're all right.

When I look up, Luke's closing his briefcase with a snap.

"I have to go," he says. "I'll see you later." At the door he hesitates, and turns round, looking suddenly confused. "But I don't understand. If you weren't at the Guggenheim—where did you get the book you gave me?"

"At the museum shop," I whisper. "On Broadway."

"But the sparkle stuff on your face. You said it was—"

"I . . . I had a makeover. Luke, I'm so sorry . . . I . . ."

I tail away into a hideous silence. I can feel my heart thumping, the blood pulsing in my ears. I don't know what to say, how to redeem myself.

Luke stares at me blankly, then gives a brief nod, turns, and reaches for the door handle.

When the door has closed behind him, I sit quite still for a while, staring straight ahead. I can't quite believe all this is really happening. Just a few hours ago we were toasting each other with Bellinis. I was wearing my Vera Wang dress and we were dancing to Cole Porter and I was giddy with happiness. And now . . .

The phone starts to ring, but I don't move. Only on the eighth ring do I stir myself and pick it up.

"Hello?"

"Hello!" says a bright voice. "Is that Becky Bloomwood?"

"Yes," I say cautiously.

"Becky, it's Fiona Taggart from the *Daily Herald.* I'm so glad I've tracked you down! Becky, we'd be really interested in running a two-part feature on you and your . . . little problem, shall we call it?"

"I don't want to talk about it," I mutter.

"Do you deny it, then?"

"No comment," I say, and thrust the phone down with a trembling hand. Immediately it rings again, and I pick it up.

"No comment, all right?" I exclaim. "No comment! No—"

"Becky? Darling?"

"Mum!" At the sound of her voice I feel myself dissolving into tears. "Oh, Mum, I'm so sorry," I gulp. "It's so awful. I've messed everything up. I just didn't know . . . I didn't realize . . ."

"Becky!" comes her voice down the line, familiar and reassuring. "Love! You don't have to be sorry! It's those scumbag reporters who should be sorry. Making up all those stories. Putting words in people's mouths. Poor Suzie phoned us up, very upset. You know, she gave that girl three bourbon biscuits and a KitKat, and this is the thanks she gets. A load of outlandish lies! I mean, pretending to be from the council tax. They should be prosecuted!"

"Mum . . ." I close my eyes, almost unable to say it. "It's not all lies. They . . . they didn't make everything up." There's a short silence, and I can hear Mum breathing anxiously down the line. "I am kind of in a . . . a bit of debt."

"Well," says Mum after a pause—and I can hear her gearing herself up to be positive. "Well. So what? Even if you are, is it any of their business?" She pauses, and I hear a voice in the background. "Exactly! Dad says, 'if the American economy can be in debt by billions and still survive, then so can you.' "

God, I love my parents. If I told them I'd committed murder they'd soon find some reason why the victim had it coming to him.

"I suppose so," I gulp. "But it's Luke's big meeting today, and all his investors will have seen it . . ."

"So what? There's no such thing as bad publicity. Now you keep your chin up, Becky! Best foot forward. Suzie told us you've got a screen test today. Is that right?"

"Yes. I just don't know what time. The producer's supposed to call me."

"Well, then. You put a nice brave face on. Run yourself a bath and have a nice cup of tea and put three sugars in it. And a brandy, Dad says. And if any reporters ring up, just tell them to get lost."

"Have you had any reporters bothering you?" I say in alarm.

"A chap came round asking questions this morning," says Mum breezily. "But Dad went for him with the hedge trimmer."

In spite of myself I giggle.

"I'd better go, Mum. But I'll call you later. And . . . thanks."

As I put down the phone, I feel a million times better. Mum's right. I've just got to be positive and go to my screen test and do as well as I possibly can. And Luke probably did overreact a little bit. He'll probably come back in a much better mood.

I ring up the hotel reception and tell them to hold all calls except from HLBC. Then I run my bath, empty a whole bottle of Uplift bath oil from Sephora into it, and wallow for half an hour in rose geranium. As I dry myself I put on MTV and dance around the room to Janet Jackson—and by the time I'm dressed in my knock-'em-dead outfit from Barneys I'm feeling pretty positive, if a little wobbly around the knees. I can do this. I *can.*

They haven't called yet, so I pick up the phone and ring down to reception.

"Hi," I say. "Just checking if HLBC have called for me this morning."

"I don't believe so," says the girl pleasantly.

"Are you sure? They didn't leave a message?"

"No, ma'am."

"OK. Thanks."

I put the phone down and think for a few moments. Well—that's all right, I'll just call them. I mean, I need to know what time the test is, don't I? And Kent told me to call her anytime, whatever I needed. She said, don't even hesitate.

I take her business card out of my bag and carefully punch in the number.

"Hello!" says a bright voice. "Kent Garland's office, this is her assistant, Megan. How can I help you?"

"Hello!" I say. "It's Rebecca Bloomwood here. Could I speak to Kent, please?"

"Kent's in a meeting right now," says Megan pleasantly. "Could I take a message?"

"Well, I'm just phoning to see what time my screen test is today," I say. And just saying it gives me a surge of confidence. Who cares about the crappy *Daily World,* anyway? I'm going to be on American television. I'm going to be a huge celebrity.

"I see," says Megan. "Rebecca, if you could just hold on a moment . . ."

She puts me on hold, and I find myself listening to a tinny version of "Heard It through the Grapevine." It comes to an end, and a voice tells me how important my call is to the HLBC Corporation . . . and then it starts again . . . when suddenly Megan is back.

"Hi, Rebecca? I'm afraid Kent's going to have to postpone the screen test. She'll give you a call if she wants to rearrange."

"What?" I say, staring blankly at my made-up face in the mirror. "Postpone? But . . . why? Do you know when it'll be rescheduled?"

"I'm not sure," says Megan pleasantly. "Kent's very busy right now with the new series of *Consumer Today.*"

"But . . . but that's what the screen test is for! The new series of *Consumer Today*!" I take a deep breath, trying not to sound too anxious. "Do you know when she'll rearrange it for?"

"I really couldn't say. Her diary's very full at the moment . . . and then she has a two-week vacation . . ."

"Listen," I say, trying to stay calm. "I'd really like to talk to Kent, please. It's quite important. Couldn't you get her for me? Just for a second."

There's a pause—then Megan sighs.

"I'll see if I can fetch her."

The tinny song begins again—then suddenly Kent is on the line.

"Hi, Becky. How are you?"

"Hi!" I say, trying to sound relaxed. "I'm fine. I just thought I'd see what was happening today. About the screen test?"

"Right," says Kent thoughtfully. "Tell the truth, Becky, a couple of issues have come up, which we need to think about. OK? So we'll be passing on the screen test until we're a little more decided about things."

Suddenly I feel paralyzed by fear. Oh, please, no.

She's seen *The Daily World,* hasn't she? That's what she's talking about. I clutch the receiver tightly, my heart thudding, desperately wanting to explain it all; wanting to tell her that it all sounds far worse than it really is. That half of it isn't even true; that it doesn't mean I'm not good at what I do . . .

But I just can't bring myself to. I can't bring myself even to mention it.

"So we'll be in touch," Kent says. "Apologies for putting you out today—I was going to have Megan call you later . . ."

"That's all right!" I say, trying to sound bright and easy. "So . . . when do you think we might reschedule?"

"I'm really not sure . . . Sorry, Becky. I'm going to have to run. There's a problem on the set. But thanks for calling. And enjoy the rest of your trip!"

The phone goes silent and I slowly put it down.

I'm not having my screen test. They don't want me, after all.

And I bought a new outfit and everything.

I can feel my breath coming quicker and quicker—and for an awful moment I think I might cry.

But then I think of Mum—and force myself to lift my chin.

I'm not going to let myself collapse. I'm going to be strong and positive. HLBC aren't the only fish in the sea. There are plenty of other people who want to snap me up. Plenty! I mean, look at . . . look at Greg Walters. He said he wanted me to meet his head of development, didn't he? Well, maybe we can fix something up for today. Yes! Perhaps by the end of today, I'll have my own show!

Quickly I find the number and dial it with trembling hands—and to my joy, I get straight through. This is more like it. Straight to the top.

"Hi, Greg? It's Becky Bloomwood here."

"Becky! Great to hear from you!" says Greg, sounding a little distracted. "How're you doing?"

"Erm . . . fine! It was really nice to meet you yesterday," I say, aware that my voice is shrill with nerves. "And I was very interested in all your ideas."

"Well, that's great! So—are you enjoying your trip?"

"Yes! Yes, I am." I take a deep breath. "Greg, you were saying yesterday that I should meet up with your head of development—"

"Absolutely!" says Greg. "I know Dave would adore to meet you. We both think you have huge potential. Huge."

Relief floods over me. Thank God. Thank—

"So next time you're in town," Greg is saying, "you give me a call, and we'll set something up."

I stare at the phone, prickly with shock. Next time I'm in town? But that could be months. It could be never. Doesn't he want to—

"Promise you'll do that?"

"Erm . . . OK," I say, trying to keep the thickening dismay out of my voice. "That would be great!"

"And maybe we'll meet up when I next come over to London."

"OK!" I say brightly. "I hope so. Well . . . see you soon. And good to meet you!"

"Great to meet you too, Becky!"

I'm still smiling my bright fake smile as the phone goes

dead. And this time I just can't stop the tears from gathering in my eyes and dripping slowly down my face, taking my makeup with them.

I sit alone in the hotel room for hours. Lunchtime comes and goes, but I can't face any food. The only positive thing I do is listen to the messages on the phone and delete them all except one from Mum, which I listen to over and over again. It's the one she must have left as soon as she got *The Daily World.*

"Now," she's saying. "There's a bit of fuss here over a silly article in the paper. Don't take any notice of it, Becky. Just remember, that picture will be going in a million dog baskets tomorrow."

For some reason that makes me laugh each time I hear it. So I sit there, half-crying, half-laughing, letting a pool of wet tears gather on my skirt and not even bothering to wipe it away.

I want to go home. For what seems like an eternity I sit on the floor, rocking backward and forward, letting my thoughts circle round and round. Going over the same ground over and over again. How could I have been so stupid? What am I going to do now? How can I face anyone, ever again?

I feel as though I've been on a crazy roller coaster ever since I got to New York. Like some sort of magical Disney ride—except instead of whizzing through space, I've been whizzing through shops and hotels and interviews and lunches, surrounded by light and glitter and voices telling me I'm the next big thing.

And I believed every moment of it. I had no idea it wasn't real.

When, at long last, I hear the door opening, I feel almost sick with relief. I have a desperate urge to go and throw myself into Luke's arms, burst into tears, and listen to him tell me it's all right. But as he comes in, I feel my whole body contract in fear. His expression is taut and set; he looks as though his face is carved out of stone.

"Hi," I say at last. "I . . . I wondered where you were."

"I had lunch with Michael," says Luke shortly. "After the meeting." He takes off his coat and puts it carefully onto a hanger while I watch fearfully.

"So . . ." I hardly dare ask the question. "Did it go well?"

"Not particularly well, no."

My stomach gives a nervous flip. What does that mean? Surely . . . surely it can't be . . .

"Is it . . . off?" I manage at last.

"Good question," says Luke. "The people from JD Slade say they need more time."

"Why do they need time?" I say, licking my dry lips.

"They have a few reservations," says Luke evenly. "They didn't specify exactly what those reservations were."

He pulls off his tie roughly and starts to unbutton his shirt. He's not even looking at me. It's as though he can't bring himself to see my face.

"Do you . . ." I swallow. "Do you think they'd seen the piece?"

"Oh, I think so," says Luke. There's an edge to his voice which makes me flinch. "Yes, I'm pretty sure they'd seen it."

He's fumbling over the last shirt button. Suddenly, in irritation, he rips it off.

"Luke," I say helplessly. "I'm . . . I'm so sorry. I . . . I don't know what I can do." I take a deep breath. "I'll do anything I can."

"There's nothing," says Luke flatly.

He heads into the bathroom and after a few moments I hear the sound of the shower. I don't move. I can't even think. I feel paralyzed, as though I'm crouching on a ledge, trying not to slip.

Eventually Luke comes out and, without even acknowledging me, pulls on a pair of black jeans and a black turtleneck. He pours himself a drink and there's silence. Outside the window I can see right across Manhattan. The air is turning dusky and lights are coming on in windows everywhere, right into the distance. But I feel as though the world has shrunk to this room, these four walls. I haven't been out all day, I abruptly realize.

"I didn't have my screen test, either," I say at last.

"Really." Luke's voice is flat and uninterested, and in spite of myself, I feel a faint spark of resentment.

"Don't you even want to know why?" I say, tugging at the fringe of a cushion.

There's a pause—then Luke says, as though with tremendous effort, "Why?"

"Because no one's interested in me anymore." I push my hair back off my head. "You're not the only one who's had a bad day, Luke. I've wrecked all my chances. No one wants to know me anymore."

Humiliation creeps over me as I remember all the telephone messages I had to listen to this morning, politely canceling meetings and calling off lunches.

"And I know it's all my own fault," I continue. "I *know* that. But even so . . ." My voice starts to wobble treacherously, and I take a deep breath. "Things really aren't great for me either." I look up—but Luke hasn't moved an inch. "You could . . . you could show a little sympathy."

"Show a little sympathy," echoes Luke evenly.

"I know I brought it on myself . . ."

"That's right! You did!" Luke's voice explodes in pent-up frustration, and at last he turns to face me. "Becky, no one forced you to go and spend that money! I mean, I know you like shopping. But for Christ's sake. To spend like this . . . It's bloody irresponsible. Couldn't you have stopped yourself?"

"I don't know!" I retort shakily. "Probably. But I didn't know it was going to become such a . . . a bloody life-and-death issue, did I? I didn't *know* I was being followed, Luke. I didn't do this on purpose." To my horror, I feel a tear making its way down my cheek. "You know, I didn't hurt anybody. I didn't kill anybody. Maybe I was a bit naive . . ."

"A bit naive. That's the understatement of the year."

"OK, so I was naive! But I didn't commit any crime—"

"You don't think throwing away opportunity is a crime?" says Luke furiously. "Because as far as I'm concerned . . ." He shakes his head. "Jesus, Becky! We both had it all. We *had* New York." His hand clenches into a fist. "And now, look at us both. All because you're so bloody *obsessed* by shopping—"

"Obsessed?" I cry. Suddenly I can't stand his accusing gaze anymore. "*I'm* obsessed? What about you?"

"What do you mean?" he says dismissively.

"You're obsessed by work! By making it in New York! The first thing you thought of when you saw that piece wasn't me or . . . or how I was feeling, was it? It was how it affected you and your deal." My voice rises tremulously. "All you care about is your own success, and I always come second. I mean, you didn't even bother to *tell* me about New York until it was all decided! You just expected me to . . . to fall in line and do exactly what you wanted. No wonder Alicia said I was tagging along!"

"You're not tagging along," he says impatiently.

"Yes, I am! That's the way you see me, isn't it? As some little nobody, who has to be . . . to be slotted into your grand magnificent plan. And I was so stupid, I just went along with it . . ."

"I haven't got time for this," says Luke, standing up.

"You've never got time!" I say tearfully. "Suze has got more time for me than you have! You didn't have time to come to Tom's wedding; our holiday turned into a meeting; you didn't have time to visit my parents . . ."

"So I don't have a lot of time!" yells Luke suddenly, shocking me into silence. "So I can't sit around making mindless tittle-tattle with you and Suze." He shakes his head in frustration. "Do you realize how fucking *hard* I work? Do you have any idea how important this deal is?"

"*Why* is it important?" I hear myself shrieking. "Why is it so bloody important to make it in America? So you can impress your complete cow of a mother? Because if you're trying to impress her, Luke, then I'd give up now! She'll never be impressed. Never! I mean, she hasn't even bothered to *see* you! God, you buy her an Hermès scarf—and she can't even rearrange her schedule to find five minutes for you!"

I break off, panting, into complete silence.

Oh fuck. I shouldn't have said that.

I dart a look at Luke, and he's staring at me, his face ashen with anger.

"What did you call my mother?" he says slowly.

"Look, I . . . I didn't mean it." I swallow, trying to keep control of my voice. "I just think . . . there's got to be a sense of proportion in all this. All I did was a bit of shopping . . ."

"A bit of shopping," echoes Luke scathingly. "A *bit* of shopping." He gives me a long look—then, to my horror, heads to the huge cedar-wood wardrobe where I've been stashing all my stuff. He opens it silently and we both stare at the bags crammed to the ceiling.

And as I see it all, I feel a slight nausea overcoming me. All those things which seemed so vital when I bought them, all those things which I got so excited about . . . now just look like a great big pile of rubbish bags. I could barely even tell you what's in any of the packages. It's just . . . stuff. Piles and piles of stuff.

Without saying anything, Luke closes the door again, and I feel shame drenching over me like hot water.

"I know," I say, in a voice barely above a whisper. "I know. But I'm paying for it. I really am."

I turn away, unable to meet his eye, and suddenly I just have to get out of this room. I have to get away from Luke, from myself in the mirror, from the whole horrendous day.

"I'll . . . I'll see you later," I mutter and without looking back, head for the door.

The bar downstairs is dimly lit, soothing, and anonymous. I sink into a sumptuous leather chair, feeling weak and achy, as though I've got the flu. When a waiter comes up, I order an orange juice, then, as he's walking away, change my order to a brandy. It arrives in a huge glass, warm and reviving, and I take a few sips—then look up as a shadow appears on the table in front of me. It's Michael Ellis. I feel my heart sink. I really don't feel up to talking.

"Hello," he says. "May I?" He gestures to the chair opposite and I nod weakly. He sits down and gives me a kind look as I drain my glass. For a while, we're both silent.

"I could be polite, and not mention it," he says at last. "Or I could tell you the truth—which is that I was very sorry for you this morning. Your British papers are vicious. No one deserves that kind of treatment."

"Thank you," I mumble.

A waiter appears, and Michael orders two more brandies without even asking.

"All I can tell you is, people aren't dumb," he says as the waiter walks off. "No one's going to hold it against you."

"They already have," I say, staring at the table. "My screen test for HLBC was called off."

"Ah," says Michael after a pause. "I'm sorry to hear that."

"No one wants to know me anymore. They're all saying they've 'decided to go another way' or they 'feel I don't really suit the American market' and . . . you know. Basically just, 'Go away.' "

As I talk, I can feel my eyes filling up with hot tears. I so wanted to tell all this to Luke. I wanted to pour out all my woes—and for him to give me a huge, uncritical hug. Tell me it was their loss, not mine, like my parents would, or Suze would. But instead, he made me feel even worse about myself. He's right—I've thrown everything away, haven't I? I had opportunities people would kill for, and I wasted them.

Michael is nodding gravely.

"That happens," he says. "I'm afraid these idiots are like a pack of sheep. One gets spooked, they all get spooked."

"I just feel like I've wrecked everything," I say, feeling my throat tightening. "I was going to get this amazing job, and Luke was going to be this huge success. It was all going to be perfect. And I've just chucked it all in the bin. It's all my fault."

To my horror, tears are spilling out of my eyes. I can't stop them. And suddenly I give a huge sob. Oh, this is so embarrassing.

"I'm sorry," I whisper. "I'm just a complete disaster."

I bury my hot face in my hands and hope that Michael Ellis will tactfully slip away and leave me alone. Instead, I feel a hand on mine, and a handkerchief being slipped into my fingers. I wipe my face gratefully with the cool cotton and eventually raise my head.

"Thanks," I gulp. "Sorry about that."

"That's quite all right," says Michael calmly. "I'd be the same."

"Yeah, right," I mutter.

"You should see me when I lose a contract. I bawl my eyes out. My secretary has to run out for Kleenex every half hour." He sounds so completely deadpan, I can't help giving a little smile. "Now, drink your brandy," he says, "and let's get a few things straight. Did you invite *The Daily World* to take pictures of you with a long-range lens?"

"No."

"Did you call them, offering an exclusive on your personal habits and suggesting a choice of offensive headlines?"

"No." I can't help giving a half-giggle.

"So." He gives me a quizzical look. "This would be all your fault because . . ."

"I was naive. I should have realized. I should have . . . seen it coming. I was stupid."

"You were unlucky." He shrugs. "Maybe a little foolish. But you can't heap all the blame on yourself."

An electronic burble sounds from his pocket, and he reaches for his mobile.

"Excuse me a moment," he says, and turns away. "Hi there."

As he talks quietly into the phone I fold a paper coaster over and over. I want to ask him something—but I'm not sure I want to hear the answer.

"Sorry about that," says Michael. As he puts his phone away he gives me a rueful smile and shakes his head. "Never do business with friends."

"Really? Was that a friend?"

Michael nods. "An old friend of the family. I did a campaign for him on credit as a favor. He promised when business picked up, he'd write a check. Well, as far as I'm concerned, business has picked up."

"And he hasn't paid you?" I take a sip of my drink, grateful to have something to distract me.

"He's bought himself a nice new Mercedes."

"That's terrible!" I exclaim.

"That's what friends are for. To exploit the shit out of you. I should have learned that by now." He rolls his eyes humorously, but I'm still frowning.

"Do you know his family?"

"Sure. We used to spend Thanksgiving together."

"Right." I think for a moment. "So—have you mentioned this to his wife?"

"His wife?" Michael looks surprised, and I raise my eyebrows knowingly at him.

"I bet you if you told his wife, you'd get the money back."

Michael stares at me for a second—then bursts into laughter.

"You know, I think you have something there. I'll try it!" He drains his glass, then glances down at the mangled coaster in my fingers. "So. Are you feeling better?"

"Yes. Thanks. But there's something I wanted to—" I take a deep breath. "Michael, was it my fault that Luke's deal fell through? I mean, did the *Daily World* thing come into it?"

He gives me a sharp look. "We're being frank here, right?"

"Yes," I say, feeling a shaft of apprehension. "We're being frank."

"Then, to be honest, I can't say it helped proceedings," says Michael. "There were various . . . remarks made this morning. Some oh-so-funny jokes. I have to hand it to Luke, he took it all pretty well."

I stare at him, feeling cold.

"Luke didn't tell me that."

Michael shrugs. "I wouldn't have thought he particularly wanted to repeat any of the comments."

"So it *was* my fault."

"Uh-uh." Michael shakes his head. "That's not what I said."

He leans back in his chair. "Becky, if this deal had been really strong, it would have survived a bit of adverse publicity. My guess is JD Slade used your little . . . embarrassment as an excuse. There's some bigger reason, which they're keeping to themselves . . ."

"What?"

"Who knows? The rumor about Bank of London? A difference in business ethos? For some reason, they seem to have suffered a general loss of confidence in the whole idea."

I stare at him, remembering what Luke said.

"Do people really think Luke's losing his touch?"

"Luke is a very talented individual," says Michael carefully. "But something's gotten into him over this deal. He's almost *too* driven. I told him this morning, he needs to prioritize. There's obviously a situation with Bank of London. He should be talking to them. Reassuring them. Frankly, if he loses them, he's in big trouble. And it's not just them. Some problem or other seems to have cropped up with Provident Assurance—another huge client." He leans forward. "If you ask me, he should be on a plane back to London this afternoon."

"And what does he want to do?"

"He's already setting up meetings with every New York investment bank I've ever heard of." He shakes his head. "That boy seems fixated by making it in America."

"I think he wants to prove something," I mutter. *To his mother,* I nearly add.

"So Becky . . ." Michael gives me a kind look. "What are you going to do? Try to set up some more meetings?"

"No," I say after a pause. "To be honest, I don't think there's any point."

"So will you stay out here with Luke?"

An image of Luke's frozen face flashes through my mind, and I feel a stab of pain.

"I don't think there's much point doing that, either." I take a deep swig of wine and try to smile. "You know what? I think I'm just going to go home."

Thirteen

I GET OUT OF THE TAXI, hoist my suitcase onto the pavement, and look miserably up at the gray English sky. It's really all over.

Until the very last minute, I had a secret, desperate hope that someone might change their mind and offer me a job. Or that Luke might beg me to stay. Every time the phone rang I felt jittery, hoping that somehow a miracle was about to happen. But nothing happened. Of course it didn't.

When I said good-bye to Luke it was as though I were acting a part. I wanted to throw myself on him in tears, slap his face, *something*. But I just couldn't. I had to salvage some kind of dignity, somewhere. So it was almost businesslike, the way I phoned the airline, packed up my stuff, and ordered a cab. I couldn't bring myself to kiss him on the mouth when I left, so I gave him two brisk pecks on each cheek and then turned away before either of us could say anything.

Now, twelve hours later, I feel completely exhausted. I sat awake all through the overnight flight, stiff with misery and disappointment. Only a few days ago I was flying out, thinking I was about to start a fantastic new life in America, and instead, I'm back here with less than I even started with. And everyone, but *everyone*, knows it. A couple of girls at the airport obviously recognized me, and started whispering and giggling as I was waiting for my bags.

And oh God, I know I'd have been just the same if I'd been them. But right then, I felt so raw with humiliation, I nearly burst into tears.

I lug my bags dejectedly up the steps and let myself into the flat. And for a few moments I just stand there, looking around at the coats and old letters and keys in the bowl. Same old hall. Same old life. Back to square one. I catch sight of my haggard reflection in the mirror and quickly look away.

"Hi!" I call. "Anyone in? I'm back."

There's a pause—then Suze appears at her door in a dressing gown. "Bex?" she exclaims. "I didn't expect you back so early! Are you all right?" She comes nearer, pulling her dressing gown around her, and peers worriedly at my face. "Oh, Bex." She bites her lip. "I don't know what to say."

"It's fine," I say. "I'm fine. Honestly."

"Bex—"

"Really. I'm fine." I turn away before the sight of Suze's anxious face reduces me to tears, and scrabble in my bag. "So anyway . . . I got you that Clinique stuff you asked for . . . and the special face stuff for your mum . . ." I hand the bottles to her and begin to root roughly around again. "There's some more stuff for you in here somewhere . . ."

"Bex—don't worry about it. Just come and sit down, or something." Suze clutches the Clinique bottles to her and peers at me uncertainly. "Would you like a drink or something?"

"No!" I make myself smile. "I'm all right, Suze! I've decided the best thing is just to get on, and not think about what's happened. In fact—I'd rather we didn't talk about it at all."

"Really?" says Suze. "Well . . . OK. If you're sure that's what you want."

"That's what I want." I take a deep breath. "Really. I'm fine. So, how are *you*?"

"I'm OK," says Suze, and gives me another anxious look. "Bex, you look really pale. Have you eaten anything?"

"Airplane food. You know." I take off my coat with trembling fingers and hang it on a peg.

"Was the . . . the flight OK?" says Suze.

"It was great!" I say with a forced brightness. "They were showing the new Billy Crystal film."

"Billy Crystal!" says Suze. She gives me a hesitant glance, as though I'm some psychotic patient who has to be handled carefully. "Was it a . . . a good film? I love Billy Crystal."

"Yes, it was. It was a good film. I was really enjoying it, actually." I swallow hard. "Until my earphones stopped working in the middle."

"Oh dear!" says Suze.

"It was a really crucial bit. Everyone else on the plane was laughing away—and I couldn't hear anything." My voice starts to wobble treacherously. "So I . . . I asked this stewardess if I could have some new earphones. But she didn't understand what I meant, and she got really ratty with me because she was trying to serve drinks . . . And then I didn't want to ask her again. So I don't quite know how the film finished. But apart from that, it was really good . . ." Suddenly I give a huge sob. "And you know, I can always rent it on video or something . . ."

"Bex!" Suze's face crumples in dismay and she drops the Clinique bottles on the floor. "Oh God, Bex. Come here." She envelops me in a hug, and I bury my head in her shoulder.

"Oh, it's all awful," I weep. "It was just so humiliating, Suze. Luke was so cross . . . and they canceled my screen test . . . and suddenly it was like . . . like I had some infectious disease or something. And now nobody wants to know me, and I'm not going to move to New York after all . . ."

I look up, wiping my eyes—and Suze's face is all pink and distressed.

"Bex, I feel so bad," she exclaims.

"*You* feel bad? Why should you feel bad?"

"It's all my fault. I was such a moron! I let that girl from the paper in here, and she probably poked about when I was making her cup of stupid coffee. I mean, why did I have to offer her coffee? It's all my stupid fault."

"Of course it's not!"

"Will you ever forgive me?"

"Will I ever forgive *you*?" I stare at her, my face quivering. "Suze . . . I should be asking you to forgive *me*! You tried to keep tabs on me. You tried to warn me, but I didn't even bother to call you back . . . I was just so . . . stupid, so *thoughtless* . . ."

"No, you weren't!"

"I was." I give another huge sob. "I just don't know what happened to me in New York. I went mad. Just . . . the shops . . . all these meetings . . . I was going to be this huge star and earn loads of money . . . And then it all just disappeared."

"Oh, Bex!" Suze is practically crying herself. "I feel so terrible!"

"It's not your fault!" I reach for a tissue and blow my nose. "If it's anyone's fault, it's *The Daily World*'s."

"I *hate* them!" says Suze savagely. "They should be strung up and flogged. That's what Tarkie said."

"Oh right," I say after a pause. "So . . . he . . . he saw it, did he?"

"To be honest, Bex—I think most people saw it," says Suze reluctantly.

I feel a painful lurch as I think about Janice and Martin reading it. About Tom and Lucy reading it. All my old school friends and teachers reading it. All the people I've ever known, reading my most humiliating secrets.

"Look, come on," says Suze. "Leave all your stuff. Let's have a nice cup of tea."

"OK," I say after a pause. "That would be really nice." I follow her into the kitchen and sit down, leaning against the warm radiator for comfort.

"So—how are things going with Luke now?" says Suze cautiously as she puts on the kettle.

"Not great." I fold my arms tightly round myself. "In fact . . . it's not going at all."

"Really?" Suze gazes at me in dismay. "God, Bex, what happened?"

"Well, we had this big row . . ."

"About the article?"

"Kind of." I reach for a tissue and blow my nose. "He said it messed up his deal, and I was obsessed by shopping. And I said he was obsessed with work . . . and I . . . I said his mother was a . . . a complete cow . . ."

"You called his mother a *cow*?" Suze looks so taken aback, I give a shaky giggle.

"Well, she is! She's awful. And she doesn't even love Luke. But he can't see it . . . all he wants is to land the biggest deal in the world and impress her. He can't think about anything else but that."

"So what happened then?" says Suze, handing me a mug of tea.

I bite my lip, remembering that last painful conversation we had, while I was waiting for my taxi to take me to the airport. The polite stilted voices, the way we didn't look each other in the eye.

"Before I left, I said I didn't think he had time for a proper relationship at the moment."

"Really?" Suze's eyes widen. "You called it off?"

"I didn't mean to." My voice is barely above a whisper. "I wanted him to say he *did* have time. But he didn't say anything. It was . . . awful."

"Oh, Bex." Suze stares at me over her mug. "Oh, Bex."

"Still, never mind," I say, trying to sound upbeat. "It's probably all for the best." I take a sip of tea and close my eyes. "Oh God, that's good. That's so good." For a while I'm silent, letting the steam warm my face, feeling myself relax. I take a few more sips, then open my eyes. "They just cannot make tea in America. I went to one place, and they gave me this . . . cup full of hot water, and a tea bag in a packet. And the cup was *see-through*."

"Ooh." Suze pulls a face. "Yuck." She reaches for the tin of biscuits and takes out a couple of Hobnobs. "Who needs America, anyway?" she says robustly. "I mean, everyone knows American TV is rubbish. You're better off here."

"Maybe I am." I stare into my mug for a while, then take a deep breath and look up. "You know, I thought a lot on the plane. I decided I'm going to make this a real turning point in my life. I'm going to concentrate on my career, and finish my book, and be really focused—and just . . ."

"Show them," finishes Suze.

"Exactly. Just show them."

It's amazing what a bit of home comfort does for the spirit. Half an hour and three cups of tea later, I'm feeling a million times better. I'm even quite enjoying telling Suze about New York, and all the things I did. When I tell her about going to the spa, and where exactly they wanted to put a crystal tattoo, she starts laughing so hard she almost chokes.

"Hey," I say, a sudden thought striking me. "Have you finished the KitKats?"

"No, I haven't," says Suze, wiping her eyes. "They seem to go more slowly when you're not around. So, what did Luke's mum say? Did she want to see the results?" And she starts gurgling with laughter again.

"Hang on, I'll just get a couple," I say, and start to head toward Suze's room, where they're kept.

"Actually—" says Suze, and her laughter abruptly stops. "No, don't go in there."

"Why?" I say, stopping in surprise. "What's in your . . ." I tail off as Suze's cheeks slowly turn pink. "Suze!" I say, backing quietly away from the door. "No. Is there someone in there?"

I stare at her, and she pulls her dressing gown around her defensively, without saying anything.

"I don't believe it!" My voice squeaks incredulously. "I go away for five minutes and you start having a torrid affair!"

This is cheering me up more than anything else. There's nothing like hearing a juicy piece of gossip to raise your spirits.

"It's not a torrid affair!" says Suze at last. "It's not an affair at all."

"So, who is it? Do I know him?"

Suze gives me an agonized look.

"OK, just . . . I just have to explain. Before you . . . you jump to the wrong conclusion, or . . ." She closes her eyes. "God, this is hard."

"Suze, what's wrong?"

Suddenly there's the sound of stirring from inside Suze's bedroom, and we stare at each other.

"OK, listen. It was just a one-off," she says quickly. "Just a . . . a really impetuous, stupid . . . I mean . . ."

"What's wrong, Suze?" I pull a face. "Oh God, it's not Nick, is it?"

Nick is Suze's last boyfriend—the one who was constantly depressed and getting drunk and blaming Suze. A complete nightmare, to be honest. But I mean, that was over months ago.

"No, it's not Nick. It's . . . Oh God."

"Suze—"

"OK! But you have to promise to—"

"To what?"

"To not . . . react."

"Why should I react?" I say, laughing a little. "I mean, I'm not a prude! All we're talking about is . . ."

I tail off as Suze's door opens—and it's only Tarquin, looking not at all bad, in chinos and the jumper I gave him.

"Oh," I say in surprise. "I thought you were going to be Suze's new—"

I break off and look at Suze with a grin.

But she doesn't grin back. She's chewing her nails, avoiding my eyes—and her cheeks growing redder and redder.

I glance at Tarquin—and *he* looks away, too.

No. *No.*

She can't mean—

No.

But . . .

No.

My brain can't cope with this. Something's about to short-circuit.

"Erm, Tarquin," says Suze, in a high-pitched voice. "Could you go and buy some croissants?"

"Oh, ahm . . . OK," says Tarquin, a little stiltedly. "Morning, Becky."

"Morning!" I say. "Nice to . . . to see you. Nice . . . jumper."

There's a frozen silence in the kitchen as he walks out, which remains until we hear the front door slam. Then, very slowly, I turn to face Suze.

"Suze . . ."

I don't even know how to begin.

"Suze . . . that was Tarquin."

"Yes, I know," she says, studying the kitchen counter intently.

"Suze . . . are you and Tarquin—"

"No!" she exclaims, as though she's been scalded. "No, of course not! It's just . . . we just . . ." She stops.

"You just . . ." I say encouragingly.

"Once or twice . . ."

There's a long pause.

"With Tarquin," I say, just to make sure.

"Yes," she says.

"Right," I say, nodding my head as though this is a completely reasonable scenario. But my mouth is twitching and I can feel a strange pressure rising inside me—half shock, half hysterical laughter. I mean, Tarquin. *Tarquin!*

A sudden giggle escapes from me and I clamp my hand over my mouth.

"Don't laugh!" wails Suze. "I knew you'd laugh!"

"I'm not laughing!" I protest. "I think it's great!" I give another snort of laughter, and try to pretend I'm coughing. "Sorry! Sorry. So—how did it happen?"

"It was at that party in Scotland!" she wails. "There was no one else there except loads of ancient aunts. Tarquin was the only other person under ninety. And somehow . . . he looked all different! He had on this really nice Paul Smith jersey, and his hair looked kind of cool—and it was like, is that really Tarquin? And I got quite pissed—and you know what that does to me. And there he was . . ." She shakes her head helplessly. "I don't know. He was just . . . transformed. God knows how it happened!"

There's silence. I can feel my cheeks growing redder and redder.

"You know what, Suze," I admit sheepishly at last. "I think it kind of might have been . . . my fault."

"*Your* fault?" She raises her head and stares at me. "How come?"

"I gave him the jumper. And the hairstyle." I flinch at her expression. "But I mean, I had no idea it would lead to . . . to this! All I did was give him a look!"

"Well, you've got a lot to answer for!" cries Suze. "I've been so stressed. I just keep thinking, I must be a complete pervert."

"Why?" I say, my eyes brightening. "What does he get you to do?"

"No, silly! Because we're cousins. Well, distant cousins, but still . . ."

"Ooh." I pull a face—then realize that isn't exactly tactful. "But I mean, it's not against the law or anything, is it?"

"Oh God, Bex!" wails Suze. "That really makes me feel better."

She picks up her mug and mine, takes them over to the sink, and starts to run the tap.

"I just can't believe you're having a relationship with Tarquin!" I say.

"We're not having a relationship!" squeals Suze, as though I've scalded her. "That's the point. Last night was the very last time. We're both completely agreed. It'll never happen again. *Never.* And you mustn't tell anyone."

"I won't."

"No, I'm serious, Bex. You mustn't tell anyone. No one!"

"I won't! I promise! In fact—" I say, having a sudden idea. "I've got something for you."

I hurry into the hall, open one of my suitcases, and scrabble for the Kate's Paperie carrier bag. I pluck a card from the pile, scribble "To Suze, love Bex" inside, and return to the kitchen, sealing the envelope.

"Is this for me?" says Suze in surprise. "What is it?"

"Open it!"

She tears it open, looks at the picture of a zipped-up pair of lips, and reads aloud the printed message:

Roomie—your secret's safe with me.

"Wow!" she says, wide-eyed. "That's so cool! Did you buy it especially? But I mean . . ." She frowns. "How did you know I'd have a secret?"

"Er . . . just a hunch," I say. "You know. Sixth sense."

"You know, Bex, that reminds me," says Suze, flipping the envelope back and forth in her fingers. "You got quite a lot of post while you were away."

"Oh right."

In the astonishment of hearing about Suze and Tarquin, I'd kind of forgotten about everything else. But now the hysteria which has been lifting my spirits starts to evaporate. As Suze brings over a pile of unfriendly-looking envelopes, my stomach gives a nasty flip, and I suddenly wish I'd never come home. At least while I was away, I didn't have to know about any of this.

"Right," I say, trying to sound nonchalant and on top of things. I leaf through the letters without really looking at them—then put them down. "I'll look at them later. When I can give them my full attention."

"Bex . . ." Suze pulls a face. "I think you'd better open this one now." She reaches for the pile and pulls out a brown envelope with the word SUMMONS on the front.

I stare at it, feeling mortified. A summons. It was true. I've been summonsed. I take the envelope from Suze, unable to meet her eye, and rip it open with trembling fingers. I scan the letter without saying anything, feeling a growing coldness at the base of my spine. I can't quite believe people would actually take me to court. I mean, court is for criminals. Like drug dealers and murderers. Not for people who just miss a couple of bills.

I stuff the letter back into its envelope and put it on the counter, breathing hard.

"Bex . . . what are you going to do?" says Suze, biting her lip. "You can't just ignore that one."

"I won't. I'll pay them."

"But can you afford to pay them?"

"I'll have to."

There's silence, apart from the drip-drip of the cold-water tap into the sink. I look up, to see Suze's face contorted with worry.

"Bex—let me give you some money. Or Tarkie will. He can easily afford it."

"No!" I say, more sharply than I'd intended. "No, I don't want any help. I'll just . . ." I rub my face. "I'll go and see the guy at the bank. Today. Right now."

With a sudden surge of determination I scoop up the pile of letters and head to my room. I'm not going to let all this defeat me. I'm going to wash my face, and put on some makeup, and get my life back in order.

"What will you say?" says Suze, following me down the corridor.

"I'll explain the situation to him honestly, and ask him for a bigger overdraft . . . and take it from there. I'm going to be independent and strong, and stand on my own two feet."

"Good for you, Bex!" says Suze. "That's really fantastic. Independent and strong. That's really great!" She watches as I try to open my suitcase with shaking fingers. As I struggle with the clasp for the third time, she comes over and puts a hand on my arm. "Bex—would you like me to come too?"

"Yes, please," I say in a small voice.

Suze won't let me go anywhere until I've sat down and had a couple of brandies for Dutch courage. Then she tells me how she read an article the other day that said your best negotiating weapon is your appearance—so I must choose my outfit for seeing John Gavin very carefully. We go right through my wardrobe and end up with a plain black skirt and gray cardigan which I reckon shouts "frugal, sober, and steady." Then she has to choose her own "sensible, supportive friend" outfit (navy trousers and a white shirt). And we're almost ready to go when Suze decides that if nothing else works, we might have to flirt outrageously with him, so we both change into sexy underwear. Then I look at myself in the mirror and suddenly decide I look too drab. So I quickly change into a pale pink cardigan, which means changing my lipstick.

At last we get out of the house and arrive at the Fulham branch of Endwich Bank. As we go in, Derek Smeath's old assistant, Erica Parnell, is showing out a middle-aged couple. Between you and me, she and I have never exactly got on. I don't think she can be quite human—she's been wearing exactly the same navy blue shoes every time I've seen her.

"Oh, hello," she says, shooting me a look of dislike. "What do you want?"

"I'd like to see John Gavin, please," I say, trying to sound matter-of-fact. "Is he available?"

"I shouldn't think so," she says coldly. "Not without notice."

"Well . . . could you possibly just check?"

Erica Parnell rolls her eyes.

"Wait there," she says and disappears behind a door marked "Private."

"God, they're horrible here!" says Suze, lolling against a glass partition. "When I go to see my bank manager he gives me a glass of sherry and asks me about all the family! You know, Bex, I really think you should move to Coutts."

"Yes, well," I say. "Maybe."

I'm feeling slightly jittery as I leaf through a pile of insurance brochures. I'm remembering what Derek Smeath said about John Gavin being rigorous and inflexible. Oh God, I miss old Smeathie.

Oh God, I miss Luke.

The feeling hits me like a hammer blow. Since I got back from New York I've been trying not to think about him at all. But as I stand here, all I wish is that I could talk to him. I wish I could see him looking at me like he used to before everything went wrong. With that quizzical little smile on his face, and his arms wrapped tightly around me.

I wonder what he's doing now. I wonder how his meetings are going.

"Come this way," comes Erica Parnell's voice, and my head jerks up. Feeling slightly sick, I follow her down a blue-carpeted corridor, into a chilly little room furnished with a table and plastic chairs. As the door closes behind her, Suze and I look at each other.

"Shall we run away?" I say, only half-joking.

"It's going to be fine!" says Suze. "He'll probably turn out to be really nice! You know, my parents once had this gardener, and he seemed really grumpy—but then we found out he had a pet rabbit! And it was like, he was a completely different—"

She breaks off as the door swings open and in strides a guy of about thirty. He's got thinning dark hair, is wearing a rather nasty suit, and is holding a plastic cup of coffee.

He doesn't look as though he's got a friendly bone in his body. Suddenly I wish we hadn't come.

"Right," he says with a frown. "I haven't got all day. Which of you is Rebecca Bloomwood?"

The way he says it, it's like he's asking which one of us threw up on the carpet.

"Erm . . . I am," I say nervously.

"And who's this?"

"Suze is my—"

"People," says Suze confidently. "I'm her people." She looks around the room. "Do you have any sherry?"

"No," says John Gavin, looking at her as though she's subnormal. "I don't have any sherry. Now what's this about?"

"OK, first of all," I say nervously, "I've brought you something." I reach into my bag and hand him another Kate's Paperie envelope.

It was my own idea to bring him a little something to break the ice. After all, it's only good manners. And in Japan, this is how business is done all the time.

"Is this a check?" says John Gavin.

"Erm . . . no," I say, coloring slightly. "It's a . . . a handmade card."

John Gavin gives me a look, then rips the envelope open and pulls out a card printed in silver, with pink feathers glued to the corners.

Now that I look at it, maybe I should have chosen a less girly one.

Or not brought one at all. But it seemed so perfect for the occasion.

Friend—I know I've made mistakes, but can we start over?

John Gavin reads incredulously. He turns it over, as though suspecting a joke. "Did you *buy* this?"

"It's nice, isn't it!" says Suze. "You get them in New York."

"I see. I'll bear that in mind." He puts it up on the table and we all look at it. "Miss Bloomwood, why exactly are you here?"

"Right!" I say. "Well. As my greeting card states, I'm aware that I have . . ." I swallow. "Perhaps not been the perfect . . . ideal customer. However, I'm confident that we can work together as a team, and achieve harmony."

So far so good. I learned that bit off by heart.

"Which means?" says John Gavin.

I clear my throat. "Um . . . due to circumstances beyond my control, I have recently found myself in a slight financial . . . situation. So I was wondering whether you could perhaps temporarily . . ."

"Very kindly . . ." puts in Suze.

"Very kindly . . . perhaps extend my overdraft a little further, on a . . . a short-term . . ."

"Goodwill . . ." interjects Suze.

"Goodwill . . . temporary . . . short-term basis. Obviously to be paid back as soon as is feasibly and humanly possible." I stop, and draw breath.

"Have you finished?" says John Gavin, folding his arms.

"Erm . . . yes." I look to Suze for confirmation. "Yes, we have."

There's silence while John Gavin drums his Biro on the table. Then he looks up and says, "No."

"No?" I look at him puzzledly. "Is that just . . . no?"

"Just no." He pushes back his chair. "So if you'll excuse me—"

"What do you mean, no?" says Suze. "You can't just say no! You have to weigh up the pros and cons!"

"I have weighed up the pros and the cons," says John Gavin. "There are no pros."

"But this is one of your most valued customers!" Suze's voice rises in dismay. "This is Becky Bloomwood of TV fame, who has a huge, glittering career in front of her!"

"This is Becky Bloomwood who has had her overdraft limit extended six times in the last year," says John Gavin in a rather nasty voice. "And who each time has failed to keep within those limits. This is Becky Bloomwood who has consistently lied, who has consistently avoided meetings, who has treated bank staff with little or no respect, and who seems to think we're all here solely to fund her appetite for shoes. I've looked at your file, Miss Bloomwood. I know the picture."

There's a subdued little silence. I can feel my cheeks getting hotter and hotter and I've got a horrible feeling I might cry.

"I don't think you should be so mean!" says Suze in a burst. "Becky's just had a really awful time! Would *you* like to be in the tabloids? Would *you* like to have someone stalking you?"

"Oh, I see!" His voice glints with sarcasm. "You expect me to feel sorry for you!"

"Yes!" I say. "No. Not exactly. But I think you should give me a chance."

"You think I should give you another chance. And what have you done to *merit* another chance?" He shakes his head, and there's silence.

"I just . . . I thought if I explained it all to you . . ." I tail off feebly and shoot Suze a hopeless look to say, "Let's just forget it."

"Hey, is it hot in here?" says Suze in a sudden husky voice. She takes off her jacket, shakes back her hair, and runs one hand down her cheek. "I'm feeling really . . . hot. Are you feeling hot, John?"

John Gavin shoots her an irritated look.

"What precisely did you want to explain to me, Miss Bloomwood?"

"Well. Just that I really want to sort things out," I say, my voice trembling. "You know, I really want to turn things around. I want to stand on my own two feet, and—"

"Stand on your own two feet?" interrupts John Gavin scathingly. "You call taking handouts from a bank 'standing on your own two feet'? If you were really standing on your own two feet, you'd have no overdraft. You'd have a few *assets* by now! You, of all people, shouldn't need telling that."

"I . . . I know," I say, my voice barely above a whisper. "But the fact is, I have got an overdraft. And I just thought—"

"You thought what? That you're special? That you're an exception because you're on the television? That the normal rules don't apply to you? That this bank *owes* you money?"

His voice is like a drill in my head and suddenly I feel myself snap.

"No!" I cry. "I don't think that. I don't think any of that. I know I've been stupid, and I know I've done wrong. But I think that everyone does wrong occasionally." I take a deep breath. "You know, if you look at your files, you'll see I *did* pay off my overdraft. And I *did* pay off my store cards. And OK, I'm in debt again. But I'm trying to sort it out—and all you can do is . . . is sneer. Well, fine. I'll sort myself out without your help. Come on, Suze."

Shaking slightly, I get to my feet. My eyes are hot, but I'm *not* going to cry in front of him. There's a shaft of determination inside me, which strengthens as I turn to face him.

"Endwich—because we care," I say.

There's a long, tense silence. Then, without saying anything else, I open the door and walk out.

As we walk home, I feel almost high with determination. I'll show him. I'll show that John Gavin. And all of them. The whole world.

I'm going to pay off my debts. I don't know how—but I'm going to do it. I'll take an extra job waitressing, maybe. Or I'll get down to it, and finish my self-help book. I'll just make as much money as I can, as quickly as I can. And then I'll go into that bank with a huge check, and plonk it down in front of him, and in a dignified but pointed voice, I'll say—

"Bex?" Suze grabs my arm—and I realize I'm walking straight past our house.

"Are you OK?" says Suze as she lets us in. "Honestly, what a bastard."

"I'm fine," I say, lifting my chin. "I'm going to show him. I'm going to pay off my overdraft. Just wait. I'm going to show them all."

"Excellent!" says Suze. She bends down and picks up a letter from the doormat.

"It's for you," she says. "From *Morning Coffee*!"

"Oh right!" As I'm opening the envelope, I feel a huge leap of hope. Maybe they're offering me a new job! Something with a huge salary, enough to pay off my debts straight away. Maybe they've sacked Emma and I'm going to take her place as the main presenter! Or maybe . . .

Oh my God. Oh my God, no.

East-West Televison
Corner House
London NW8 4DW

Ms. Rebecca Bloomwood
Flat 2
4 Burney Rd.
London SW6 8FD

2 October 2000

Dear Becky:

First of all, bad luck on your recent unfortunate bout of publicity! I really felt for you, and I know I also speak for Rory, Emma, and all the rest of the team.

As you know, the *Morning Coffee* family is a fiercely loyal and supportive one, and it is our policy never to allow adverse publicity to stand in the way of talent. However, completely coincidentally, we have recently been reviewing all our regular contributors. Following some discussion, we have decided to rest you from your slot for a while.

I must emphasize that this is just a temporary measure. However, we would appreciate it if you would return your East-West TV pass in the envelope provided and also sign the enclosed release document.

The work you've done for us has been fabulous (obviously!). We just know that your talents will flourish elsewhere and that this will not prove a setback to someone as dynamic as yourself!

With very best wishes,

Zelda Washington

Assistant Producer

PARADIGM BOOKS LTD

695 SOHO SQUARE
LONDON W1 5AS

Ms. Rebecca Bloomwood
Flat 2
4 Burney Rd.
London SW6 8FD

4 October 2000

Dear Becky:

Thank you very much for your first draft of *Manage Money the Bloomwood Way.* We appreciated the care that had gone into your work. Your writing is well paced and fluent, and you certainly made some interesting points.

Unfortunately, 500 words—however excellent they are—is not quite enough for a self-help book. Your suggestion that we could "pad out the rest with photographs" is unfortunately not really workable.

Sadly, we have therefore decided that this is not a viable project and, as a result, would request that you return our advance forthwith.

With all best wishes,

Pippa Brady
Editor

PARADIGM BOOKS LTD

Helping you to help yourself

OUT NOW! *Jungle Survival* by Brig. Roger Flintwood (deceased) says Clare. "All savers should choose a spread of investments suitable to their individual requirements and tax status."

"Absolutely!" says Emma after a pause. "Right. Well—let's go to the phones, shall we? And it's Mandy from Norwich."

As the first caller is put through, the phone in our sitting room rings.

"Hello?" says Suze, picking it up and zapping the sound on the television, "Ooh, hello, Mrs. Bloomwood. Do you want to speak to Becky?"

She raises her eyebrows at me and I wince back. I've only spoken to Mum and Dad briefly since my return. They know I'm not going to move to New York—but that's all I've said them so far. I just can't face telling them how badly everything else has turned out too.

"Becky, love, I was just watching *Morning Coffee*!" exclaims Mum. "What's that girl doing, giving out financial advice?"

"It's . . . it's OK, Mum, don't worry!" I say, feeling my nails dig into my palm. "They just . . . they got her to cover while I was away."

"Well. They could have chosen someone better! She's got a miserable face on her, hasn't she?" Her voice goes muffled. "What's that, Graham? Dad says, at least she shows how good *you* are! But surely, now that you're back, they can let her go?"

"I don't think it's as simple as that," I say after a pause. "Contracts and . . . things."

"So, when will you be back on? Because I know Janice will be asking."

"I don't know, Mum," I say desperately. "Listen, I've got to go, OK? There's someone at the door. But I'll talk to you soon!"

I put down the phone and bury my head in my hands.

"What am I going to do?" I say hopelessly. "What am I going to do, Suze? I can't tell them I've been fired. I just can't." To my dismay, tears squeeze out of the sides of my eyes. "They're so proud of me. And I just keep letting them down."

"You don't let them down!" retorts Suze hotly. "It wasn't your fault that stupid *Morning Coffee* completely overreacted. And I bet they're regretting it now. I mean, *look* at her!"

She turns up the sound, and Clare's voice drones sternly through the room. "Those who fail to provide for their own retirement are the equivalent of leeches on the rest of us."

"I say," says Rory. "Isn't that a bit harsh?"

"I mean, listen to her!" says Suze. "She's awful!"

"Maybe she is," I say after a pause. "But even if they get rid of her too they'll never ask me back. It would be like saying they made a mistake."

"They *have* made a mistake!"

The phone rings again and she looks at me. "Are you in or out?"

"Out. And you don't know when I'll be back."

"OK . . ." She picks up the phone. "Hello? Sorry, Becky's out at the moment."

"Wendy, you've made every mistake possible," Clare Edwards is saying on the screen. "Have you never heard of a deposit account? And as for remortgaging your house to buy a boat . . ."

"No, I don't know when she'll be back," says Suze. "Would you like me to take a message?" She picks up a pen and starts writing. "OK . . . fine . . . yes. Yes, I'll tell her. Thanks."

"So," I say as she puts the phone down. "Who was that?"

And I know it's stupid—but as I look up at her, I can't help feeling a hot flicker of hope. Maybe it was a producer from another show. Maybe it was someone wanting to offer me my own column. Maybe it was John Gavin, ringing to apologize and offer me free, unlimited overdraft facilities. Maybe it was the one phone call that will make everything all right.

"It was Mel. Luke's assistant."

"Oh." I stare at her in apprehension. "What did she want?"

"Apparently some parcel has arrived at the office, addressed to you. From the States. From Barnes & Noble."

I stare at her blankly—then, with a pang, suddenly remember that trip to Barnes & Noble I made with Luke. I bought a whole pile of coffee-table books, and Luke suggested I send them back on the company courier bill instead of lugging them around. It seems like a million years ago now.

"Oh yes, I know what that is." I hesitate. "Did she . . . mention Luke?"

"No," says Suze apologetically. "She just said pop in anytime you want. And she said she was really sorry about what happened . . . and if you ever want a chat, just call."

"Right." I hunch my shoulders up, hug my knees, and turn up the television volume.

For the next few days, I tell myself I won't bother going. I don't really want those books anymore. And I can't quite cope with the thought of having to go in there—having to face all the curious looks from Luke's staff, and hold my head up and pretend to be OK.

But then, gradually, I start to think I'd like to see Mel. She's the only one I can talk to who really knows Luke, and it would be nice to have a heart-to-heart with her. Plus, she might have heard something of what's going on in the States. I know Luke and I are effectively over, I know it's really nothing to do with me anymore. But I still can't help caring about whether he's got his deal or not.

So four days later, at about six o'clock in the evening, I walk slowly toward the doors of Brandon Communications, my heart thumping. Luckily it's the friendly doorman on duty. He's seen me visit enough times to just wave me in, so I don't have to have any big announcements of my arrival.

I walk out of the lift at the fifth floor, and to my surprise, there's no one on reception. How weird. I wait for a few seconds—then wander past the desk and down the main corridor. Gradually my steps slow down—and a puzzled frown comes to my face. There's something wrong here. Something different.

It's too quiet. The whole place is practically dead. When I look across the open-plan space, most of the chairs are empty. There aren't any phones ringing; there aren't any people striding about; there aren't brainstorming sessions going on.

What's going on? What's happened to the buzzy Brandon C atmosphere? What's *happened* to Luke's company?

As I pass the coffee machine, two guys I half-recognize are standing, talking by it. One's got a disgruntled expression and the other is agreeing—but I can't quite hear what they're talking about. As I come near, they stop abruptly. They shoot me curious looks, then glance at each other and walk off, before starting to talk again, but in lowered voices.

I can't quite believe this is Brandon Communications. There's a completely different feel about the place. This is like some deadbeat company where no one cares about what they're doing. I walk to Mel's desk—and, along with everyone else, she's already left for the night. Mel, who normally stays till at least seven, then takes a glass of wine and gets changed in the loos for whatever great night out she's got planned.

I root around behind her chair until I find the parcel addressed to me, and scribble a note to her on a Post-it. Then I stand up, hugging the heavy package to me, and tell myself that I've got what I came for. Now I should leave. There's nothing to keep me.

But instead of walking away, I stand motionless. Staring at Luke's closed office door.

Luke's office. There are probably faxes from him in there. Messages about how things are going in New York. Maybe even messages about me. As I gaze at the smooth blank wood, I feel almost overwhelmed by an urge to go in and find out what I can.

But then—what exactly would I do? Look through his files? Listen to his voice mail? I mean, what if someone caught me?

I'm standing there, torn—knowing I'm not *really* going to go and rifle through his stuff, yet unable just to walk away—when suddenly I stiffen in shock. The handle of his office door is starting to move.

Oh shit. *Shit.* There's someone in there! They're coming out!

In a moment of pure panic, I find myself ducking down out of sight, behind Mel's chair. As I curl up into a tiny ball I feel a thrill of terror, like a child playing hide-and-seek. I hear some voices murmuring—and then the door swings open and someone comes out. From my vantage point, all I can see is that it's a female, and she's wearing those new Chanel shoes which cost an absolute bomb. She's followed by two pairs of male legs, and the three begin to walk down the corridor. I can't resist peeping out from behind the chair—and of course. It's Alicia Bitch Longlegs, with Ben Bridges and a man who looks familiar but whom I can't quite place.

Well, I suppose that's fair enough. She's in charge while Luke is away. But does she have to take over Luke's office? I mean, why can't she just use a meeting room?

"Sorry we had to meet here," I can just hear her saying. "Obviously, next time, it'll be at 17 King Street."

They continue talking until they reach the lifts, and I pray desperately that they'll all get inside one and disappear. But as the lift doors ping open, only the familiar-looking man gets in—and a moment later, Alicia and Ben are heading back toward Luke's office.

"I'll just get those files," says Alicia, and goes back into Luke's office, leaving the door open. Meanwhile, Ben is lolling against the water dispenser, pressing the buttons on his watch and staring intently at the tiny screen.

This is horrendous! I'm trapped until they leave. My knees are starting to hurt and I've got an awful feeling that if I move an inch, one of them will crack. What if Ben and Alicia stay here all night? What if they come over to Mel's desk? What if they decide to *make love* on Mel's desk?

"OK," says Alicia, suddenly appearing at the door. "I think that's it. Good meeting, I thought."

"I suppose." Ben looks up from his watch. "Do you think Frank's right? Do you think he might sue?"

Frank! Of course. That other man was Frank Harper. The publicity guy from Bank of London. I used to see him at press conferences.

"He won't sue," says Alicia calmly. "He's got too much face to lose."

"He's lost a fair amount already," says Ben, raising his eyebrows. "He'll be the invisible man before too long."

"True," says Alicia, and smirks back at him. She looks at the pile of folders in her arms. "Have I got everything? I think so. Right, I'm off. Ed will be waiting for me. See you tomorrow."

They both disappear down the corridor and this time, thank God, they get into a lift. When I'm quite sure they've gone, I sit back on my heels with a puzzled frown. What's going on? Why were they talking about suing? Suing who? And how come Bank of London was here?

Is Bank of London going to sue Luke? It sounds like everything's a complete mess! I thought Alicia was supposed to have everything under control.

For a while I just sit still, trying to work it all out. But I'm not really getting anywhere—and suddenly it occurs to me that I ought to get out while the going's good. I get up, wincing at the cramp in my foot, and shake out my legs as the circulation returns to them. Then I pick up my parcel, shake back my head, and as nonchalantly as possible, walk down the corridor toward the lifts. Just as I'm pressing the "Summon" button, my mobile phone rings inside my bag, and I give a startled jump. Shit, my phone! Thank *God* that didn't happen while I was hiding behind Mel's desk!

"Hello?" I say, as I get into the lift.

"Bex! It's Suze."

"Suze!" I say, and give a shaky giggle. "You have no idea how you nearly just got me in trouble! If you'd rung like, five minutes ago, you would have completely . . ."

"Bex, listen," says Suze urgently. "You've just had a call."

"Oh right?" I press the ground-floor button. "From who?"

"From Zelda at *Morning Coffee*! She wants to talk to you! She said, do you want to meet for a quick lunch tomorrow?"

That night, I barely get an hour's sleep. Suze and I stay up till late, deciding on what I should wear—and when I've gone to bed, I lie awake, staring at the ceiling, feeling my mind flip around like a fish. Will they offer my old job back after all? Will they offer me a different job? Maybe they'll upgrade me! Maybe they'll give me my own show!

But by the early hours of the morning, all my wild fantasies have faded away, leaving the simple truth. The truth is, all I really want is my old job back. I want to be able to tell Mum to start watching again, and to start paying off my overdraft . . . and to start my life all over again. Another chance. That's all I want.

"You see?" says Suze the next morning as I'm getting ready. "You see? I *knew* they'd want you back. That Clare Edwards is crap! Completely and utterly—"

"Suze," I interrupt. "How do I look?"

"Very good," says Suze, looking me up and down approvingly. I'm wearing my black Banana Republic trousers and a pale fitted jacket over a white shirt, and a dark green scarf round my neck.

I would have worn my Denny and George scarf—in fact, I even picked it up from the dressing table. But then, almost immediately, I put it down again. I don't quite know why.

"Very kick-ass," adds Suze. "Where are you having lunch?"

"Lorenzo's."

"*San Lorenzo?*" Her eyes widen impressively.

"No, I don't think so. Just . . . Lorenzo's. I've never been there before."

"Well, you make sure you order champagne," says Suze. "And tell them you're fighting off loads of other offers, so if they want you to come back, they're going to have to pay big bucks. That's the deal, take it or leave it."

"Right," I say, unscrewing my mascara.

"If their margins suffer, then so be it," says Suze emphatically. "For a quality product you have to pay quality prices. You want to close the deal at *your* price, on *your* terms."

"Suze . . ." I stop, mascara wand on my lashes. "Where are you getting all this stuff?"

"What stuff?"

"All this . . . margins and close the deal stuff."

"Oh, that! From the Hadleys conference. We had a seminar from one of the top salespeople in the U.S.! It was great! You know, a product is only as good as the person selling it."

"If you say so." I pick up my bag and check that I've got everything—then look up and take a deep breath. "Right, I'm going."

"Good luck!" says Suze. "Except you know, there is no luck in business. There's only drive, determination, and more drive."

"OK," I say dubiously. "I'll try to remember that."

The address I've been given for Lorenzo's is a street in Soho—and as I turn into it, I can't see anything that looks obviously like a restaurant. It's mostly just office blocks, with a few little newsagenty-type shops, and a coffee shop, and a . . .

Hang on. I stop still and stare at the sign above the coffee shop. "Lorenzo's coffee shop and sandwich bar."

But surely . . . this can't be where we're meeting?

"Becky!" My head jerks up, and I see Zelda walking along the street toward me, in jeans and a Puffa. "You found it all right!"

"Yes," I say, trying not to look discomfited. "Yes, I found it."

"You don't mind just a quick sandwich, do you?" she says, sweeping me inside. "It's just that this place is quite convenient for me."

"No! I mean . . . a sandwich would be great!"

"Good! I recommend the Italian chicken!" She eyes me up and down. "You look very smart. Off somewhere nice?"

I stare at her, feeling a pang of mortification. I can't admit I dressed up specially to see her.

"Erm . . . yes." I clear my throat. "A . . . a meeting I've got later."

"Oh well, I won't keep you long. Just a little proposition we wanted to put to you." She shoots me a quick smile. "We thought it would be nicer to do it face to face."

This isn't exactly what I imagined for our power lunch. But as I watch the sandwich guy smoothing Italian chicken onto our bread, adding salad, and slicing each sandwich into four quarters, I start to feel more positive. OK, maybe this isn't a grand place with tablecloths and champagne. Maybe they aren't pushing the boat out. But then, that's probably good! It shows they still think of me as part of the team, doesn't it? Someone to have a relaxed sandwich with, and thrash out ideas for the forthcoming season.

Maybe they want to take me on board as a features consultant. Or train me to become a producer!

"We all felt for you dreadfully, Becky," says Zelda as we make our way to a tiny wooden table, balancing our trays of sandwiches and drinks. "How are things going? Have you got a job lined up in New York?"

"Um . . . not exactly," I say, and take a sip of my mineral water. "That's all kind of . . . on hold." I see her eyes watching me appraisingly, and quickly add, "But I've been considering lots of offers. You know—various projects, and . . . and ideas in development . . ."

"Oh good! I'm so glad. We all felt very bad that you had to go. And I want you to know, it wasn't my decision." She puts her hand on mine briefly, then removes it to take a bite of her sandwich. "So now—to business." She takes a sip of tea, and I feel my stomach flutter with nerves. "You remember our producer, Barry?"

"Of course I do!" I say, slightly taken aback. Are they expecting me to have forgotten the name of the producer already?

"Well, he's come up with quite an interesting idea." Zelda beams at me, and I beam back. "He thinks the *Morning Coffee* viewers would be really interested to hear about your . . . little problem."

"Right," I say, feeling my smile freeze on my face. "Well, it's . . . it's not really a—"

"And he thought perhaps you would be ideal to take part in a discussion and/or phone-in on the subject." She takes a sip of tea. "What do you think?"

I stare at her in confusion.

"Are you talking about going back to my regular slot?"

"Oh no! I mean, we could hardly have you giving financial advice, could we?" She gives a little laugh. "No, this would be more of a one-off, topical piece. 'How shopping wrecked my life.' That kind of thing." She takes a bite of sandwich. "And ideally, it would be quite a . . . how can I put this? An *emotional* piece. Maybe you could bare your soul a little. Talk about your parents, how this has ruined their lives too . . . problems in your childhood . . . relationship trouble . . . these are just ideas, obviously!" She looks up. "And you know, if you were able to cry . . ."

"To . . . to cry?" I echo disbelievingly.

"It's not compulsory. By *any* means." Zelda leans earnestly forward. "We want this to be a good experience for you too, Becky. We want to help. So we'd have Clare Edwards in the studio too, to offer you advice . . ."

"Clare Edwards!"

"Yes! You used to work with her, didn't you? That was why we thought of approaching her. And you know, she's quite a hit! She really tells the callers off! So we've decided to rename her Scary Clare and give her a whip to crack!"

She beams at me but I can't smile back. My whole face is prickling with shock and humiliation. I've never felt so belittled in my life.

"So what do you think?" she says, slurping at her smoothie.

I put down my sandwich, unable to take another bite.

"I'm afraid my answer's no."

"Oh! There'd be a fee, of course!" she says. "I should have mentioned that at the beginning."

"Even so. I'm not interested."

"Don't answer yet. Think about it!" Zelda flashes me a cheery smile, then glances at her watch. "I must dash, I'm afraid. But it's lovely to see you, Becky. And I'm *so* glad things are going well for you."

After she's gone I sit still for a while, sipping at my mineral water. I'm outwardly calm—but inside I'm burning with mortified rage. They want me to go on and cry. That's all they want. One article in one crappy tabloid—and suddenly I'm not Becky

Bloomwood, financial expert. I'm Becky Bloomwood, failure and flake. I'm Becky Bloomwood, watch her cry and pass the hankies.

Well, they can just bloody well stuff their bloody hankies. They can just take their stupid, bloody . . . stupid . . . stupid . . . bloody . . .

"Are you all right?" says the man at the next table—and to my horror I realize I'm muttering aloud.

"I'm fine," I say. "Thanks." I put down my glass and walk out of Lorenzo's, my head high and my chin stiff.

I walk down the road and turn a corner without even noticing where I'm going. I don't know the area and I don't have anyplace I need to get to—so I just walk, almost hypnotizing myself with the rhythm of my steps, thinking eventually I'll hit a tube station.

As I walk, my eyes start to smart and I tell myself it's the cold air. It's the wind. I shove my hands in my pockets and tighten my chin and start to walk faster, trying to keep my mind empty. But there's a blank dread inside me; a hollow panic that is getting worse and worse. I haven't got my job back. I haven't even got the prospect of a job. What am I going to say to Suze? What am I going to say to Mum?

What am I going to do with my life?

"Oy! Watch out!" yells someone behind me—and to my horror I realize I've stepped off the pavement in front of a cyclist.

"Sorry," I say in a husky voice as the cyclist swerves off, shooting me the finger. This is ridiculous. I've got to pull myself together. I mean, where am I, for a start? I start to walk more slowly along the pavement, peering up at the glass doors of offices, looking for the name of the road I'm on. And I'm just about to ask a traffic warden—when suddenly I see a sign. King Street.

For a moment I stare at it blankly, wondering why it's chiming a bell inside my head. Then, with a jolt, I remember: 17 King Street. Alicia.

I peer at the number embossed on the glass doors nearest me—and it's 23. Which means . . . I must have just walked past number 17.

Now I'm completely consumed by curiosity. What on earth goes on at 17 King Street? Is it some secret cult, or something? God, it wouldn't surprise me if she was a witch in her spare time.

My whole body is prickling with intrigue as I retrace my steps until I'm standing outside a modest set of double doors marked 17. It's obviously a building with lots of different little companies inside, but as I run my eye down the list, none sounds familiar.

"Hi!" says a bloke in a denim jacket, holding a cup of coffee. He comes up to the doors, presses a code into the keypad, and pushes the door open. "You look lost. Who are you after?"

"Erm . . . I'm not sure actually," I say hesitantly. "I thought I knew somebody who worked here, but I can't remember the name of the company."

"What's her name?"

"It's . . . it's Alicia," I say—then immediately wish I hadn't. What if this guy knows Alicia? What if she's in there somewhere and he goes and fetches her?

But he's frowning puzzledly. "I don't know an Alicia . . . Mind you, there's a few new faces around at the moment . . . What sort of business is she in?"

"PR," I say after a pause.

"PR? We're mostly graphic design, here . . ." Suddenly his face clears. "Hey, but maybe she's with the new company. B and B? BBB? Something like that. They haven't started trading yet, so we haven't met them." He takes a sip of cappuccino and I stare at him. My mind is starting to twitch.

"A new PR company? Based here?"

"As far as I know, yes. They've taken a big space on the second floor."

Thoughts are sparking round my head like fireworks.

B and B. Bridges and Billington. Billington and Bridges.

"Do you . . ." I try to keep calm. "Do you know what sort of PR?"

"Ah! Now, this I *do* know. It's financial. Apparently one of their biggest clients is Bank of London. Or will be. Which must be a nice little earner . . . But as I say, we haven't met them yet, so . . ." He looks at me and his face changes expression. "Hey. Are you OK?"

"I'm fine," I manage. "I think. I just have to . . . I have to make a phone call."

I dial the number of the Four Seasons three times—and each time hang up before I can bring myself to ask for Luke Brandon. At last I take a deep breath, dial the number again, and ask to speak to Michael Ellis.

"Michael, it's Becky Bloomwood here," I say when I'm put through.

"Becky!" he says, sounding genuinely pleased to hear from me. "How are you doing?"

I close my eyes, trying to keep calm. But just the sound of his voice has taken me back to the Four Seasons with a whoosh. Back to that dim, expensive lobby. Back to that New York dream-world.

"I . . ." I take a deep breath. "I'm fine. You know . . . back to normal life . . . busy, busy!"

I'm not going to admit I've lost my job. I'm not going to have everyone feeling sorry for me.

"I'm just on my way to the studio," I say, crossing my fingers. "But I wanted a quick word. I think I know why there's a rumor going around that Luke's going to lose Bank of London."

I tell him exactly what I overheard in the office, how I went to King Street, and what I've discovered.

"I see," says Michael at intervals, sounding grim. "I see. You know, there's a clause in their contracts forbidding employees to do this? If they poach a client, Luke could sue them."

"They talked about that. They seem to think he won't sue because he'd lose too much face."

There's silence—and I can almost hear Michael thinking down the line.

"They have a point," he says at last. "Becky, I have to talk to Luke. You did a great job finding out what you did . . ."

"That's not the only thing." I take a deep breath. "Michael, someone's got to talk to Luke. I went into the Brandon Communications office, and it was completely dead. No one's making any effort, everyone's going home early . . . it's a whole different atmosphere. It's not good." I bite my lip. "He needs to come home."

"Why don't you tell him this yourself?" says Michael gently. "I'm sure he'd like to hear from you."

He sounds so kind and concerned, I feel a sudden prickle in my nose.

"I can't. If I ring him up, he'll just think . . . he'll think I'm trying to prove some point, or it's just some more stupid gossip . . ." I break off, and swallow hard. "To be honest, Michael, I'd rather you just kept me out of it. Pretend someone else spoke to you. But someone's got to tell him."

"I'm seeing him in half an hour," Michael says. "I'll talk to him then. And, Becky . . . well done."

Mrs. Marion Jefferson
Apt. 3
24 E. 88th Street
New York

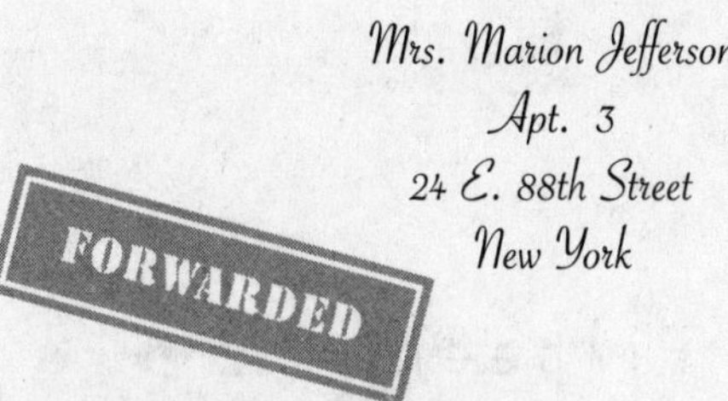

Miss Rebecca Bloomwood
c/o Four Seasons Hotel
57 East 57th Street
New York 10022

October 3, 2000

Dear Miss Bloomwood:

I was delighted to meet you at Nina Heywood's luncheon the other day. It was a great pleasure to meet such a cultured and well-connected young lady as yourself.

I write because I am coming to England in two weeks' time and I was very much hoping that you might be able to introduce me to Prince William and, if possible, the queen? I would be honored to take the three of you to dinner, whenever is convenient.

I look forward to hearing from you.

With kind regards,

Marion Jefferson (Mrs.)

P.S. If not the queen, then maybe Prince Philip?

Fifteen

After a week, I give up on hearing anything from Michael. Whatever he's said to Luke, I'm never going to hear about it. I feel as though that whole part of my life is over. Luke, America, television, everything. Time to start again.

I'm trying to keep positive, and tell myself I've lots of avenues open to me. But what *is* the next career move for an ex–television financial expert? I rang up a television agent, and to my dismay, she sounded exactly like all those TV people in America. She said she was thrilled to hear from me, she'd have absolutely no problem finding me work—if not my own series—and that she'd ring back that day with lots of exciting news. I haven't heard from her since.

So now I'm reduced to looking through the *Media Guardian*, looking for jobs I might just have half a chance of getting. So far, I've ringed a staff writer job on *Investor's Chronicle*, an assistant editorship of *Personal Investment Periodical*, and editor of *Annuities Today*. I don't know much about annuities, but I can always quickly read a book about it.

"How are you doing?" says Suze, coming into the room with a bowl of crunchy nut cornflakes.

"Fine," I say, trying to raise a smile. "I'll get there." Suze takes a mouthful of cereal and eyes me thoughtfully.

"What have you got planned for today?"

"Nothing much," I say morosely. "You know—just trying to get a job. Sort out my mess of a life. That kind of thing."

"Oh right." Suze pulls a sympathetic face. "Have you found anything interesting yet?"

I flick my fingers toward a ringed advertisement.

"I thought I'd go for editor of *Annuities Today.* The right candidate may also be considered for editorship of the annual *Tax Rebate* supplement!"

"Really?" She involuntarily pulls a face—then hastily adds, "I mean . . . that sounds good! Really interesting!"

"Tax rebates? Suze, please."

"Well—you know. Relatively speaking."

I rest my head on my knees and stare at the sitting-room carpet. The sound on the television has been turned down, and there's silence in the room apart from Suze munching. I close my eyes and slump down farther on the floor, until my head's resting on the sofa seat. I feel as though I could stay here for the rest of my life.

"Bex, I'm worried about you," says Suze. "You haven't been out for days. What else are you planning to do today?"

I open my eyes briefly and see her peering anxiously down at me.

"Dunno. Watch *Morning Coffee.*"

"You are *not* watching *Morning Coffee*!" says Suze firmly. "Come on." She closes the *Media Guardian.* "I've had a really good idea."

"What?" I say suspiciously as she drags me to my room. She swings open the door, leads me inside, and spreads her arms around, gesturing to the mess everywhere.

"I think you should spend the morning decluttering."

"What?" I stare at her in horror. "I don't want to declutter."

"Yes, you do! Honestly, you'll feel so great, like I did. It was brilliant! I felt so good afterward."

"Yes, and you had no clothes! You had to borrow knickers from me for three weeks!"

"Well, OK," she concedes. "Maybe I went a bit too far. But the point is, it completely transforms your life."

"No, it doesn't."

"It does! It's feng shui! You have to let things *out* of your life to allow the new good things *in*."

"Yeah, right."

"It's true! The moment I decluttered, I got Hadleys phoning me up with an offer. Come on, Bex . . . Just a little bit of decluttering would do you a world of good."

She throws open my wardrobe and begins to leaf through my clothes.

"I mean, look at this," she says, pulling out a blue fringed suede skirt. "When did you last wear that?"

"Erm . . . quite recently," I say, crossing my fingers behind my back. I bought that skirt off a stall in the Portobello Road without trying it on—and when I got it home it was too small. But you never know, I might lose loads of weight one day.

"And these . . . and these . . ." She gives an incredulous frown. "Blimey, Bex, how many pairs of black trousers have you got?"

"Only one! Two, maybe."

"Four . . . five . . . six . . ." She's leafing through the hangers, sternly plucking out pairs of trousers.

"Those ones are just for when I feel fat," I say defensively as she pulls out my comfy old Benetton boot-cuts. "And those are jeans!" I exclaim as she starts rooting around at the bottom. "Jeans don't count as trousers!"

"Says who?"

"Says everybody! It's common knowledge!"

"Ten . . . eleven . . ."

"Yeah . . . and those are for skiing! They're a completely different thing! They're *sportswear.*" Suze turns to look at me.

"Bex, you've never been skiing."

"I know," I say after a short silence. "But . . . you know. Just in case I ever get asked. And they were on sale."

"And what's this?" She picks up my fencing mask gingerly. "This could go straight in the bin."

"I'm taking up fencing!" I say indignantly. "I'm going to be Catherine Zeta-Jones's stunt double!"

"I don't even understand how you can fit all this stuff in here. Don't you *ever* chuck things out?" She picks up a pair of shoes decorated with shells. "I mean, these. Do you ever wear these anymore?"

"Well . . . no." I see her expression. "But that's not the point. If I did chuck them out, then shells would come back in the next day—and I'd have to buy a new pair. So this is like . . . insurance."

"Shells are *never* going to come back in."

"They might! It's like the weather. You just can't tell."

Suze shakes her head, and picks her way over the piles of stuff on the floor toward the door. "I'm giving you two hours and when I come back I want to see a transformed room. Transformed room—transformed life. Now start!"

She disappears out of the room and I sit on my bed, staring disconsolately around at my room.

Well, OK, maybe she does have a point. Maybe I should have a little tidy-up. But I don't even know where to start. I mean, if I start throwing things out just because I never wear them—where will I stop? I'll end up with nothing.

And it's all so hard. It's all so much *effort*.

I pick up a jumper, look at it for a few seconds, then put it down again. Just the thought of trying to decide whether to keep it or not exhausts me.

"How are you doing?" comes Suze's voice from outside the door.

"Fine!" I call back brightly. "Really good!"

Come on, I've got to do something. OK, maybe I should start in one corner, and work my way round. I pick my way to the corner of my room, where a heap of stuff is teetering on my dressing table, and try to work out what everything is. There's all that office equipment I ordered off the Internet . . . There's that wooden bowl I bought ages ago because it was in *Elle Decoration* (and then saw exactly the same one in Woolworth's) . . . a tie-dye kit . . . some sea salt for doing body rubs . . . What *is* all this stuff, anyway? What's this box which I haven't even opened?

I open up the package and stare at a fifty-meter roll of turkey foil. Turkey foil? Why would I buy that? Was I once planning to cook a turkey? Puzzledly I reach for the letter on top, and see the words, "Welcome to the world of Country Ways. We're so pleased your good friend, Mrs. Jane Bloomwood, recommended our catalogue to you . . ."

Oh God, of course. It's just that stuff Mum ordered to get her free gift. A casserole dish, some turkey foil . . . some of those plastic bags she was stuffing patio cushions into . . . some weird gadget for putting in the . . .

Hang on.

Just hang on a minute. I drop the gadget and slowly reach for the plastic bags again. A woman with a dodgy blond haircut is staring proudly at me over a shrink-wrapped duvet, and a bubble from her mouth reads, "With up to 75 percent reduction, I have so much more room in my closet now!"

Cautiously I open my door, and tiptoe along to the broom cupboard. As I pass the sitting room I look in—and to my astonishment Suze is sitting on the sofa with Tarquin, talking earnestly.

"Tarquin!" I say, and both their heads jerk up guiltily. "I didn't hear you arrive."

"Hello, Becky," he says, not meeting my eye.

"We just had to . . . talk about something," says Suze, giving me an embarrassed look. "Have you finished?"

"Erm . . . nearly," I say. "I just thought I'd hoover my room. To make it look really good!"

I shut my door behind me, and pull the bags out of their packaging. Right. This should be nice and easy. Just stuff them full, and suck out the air. Ten sweaters per bag, it says—but frankly, who's going to count?

I start to stuff clothes into the first bag, until it's as tightly packed as I can get it. Panting with effort, I close the plastic zip—then attach the hoover nozzle to the hole. And I don't believe this. It works. It works! Before my eyes, my clothes are shrinking away into nothing!

Oh, this is fantastic. This is going to revolutionize my life! Why on earth declutter when you can just shrink-wrap?

There are eight bags in all—and when they're all full, I cram them all into my wardrobe and close the door. It's a bit of a tight squash—and I can hear a bit of a hissing sound as I force the door shut—but the point is, they're in. They're contained.

And just look at my room now! It's incredible! OK, it's not exactly immaculate—but it's so much better than it was before. I quickly shove a few stray items under my duvet, arrange some cushions on top, and stand back. As I look around, I feel all warm and proud of myself. I've never seen my room look so good before. And Suze is right—I do feel different, somehow.

You know, maybe feng shui's got something to it after all. Maybe this is the turning point. My life will be transformed from now on.

I take one final admiring look at it, then call out of the door, "I'm done!"

As Suze comes to the door I perch smugly on the bed and beam at her astounded expression.

"Bex, this is fantastic!" she says, peering disbelievingly around the cleared space. "And you're so quick! It took me ages to sort all my stuff out!"

"Well, you know." I shrug nonchalantly. "Once I decide to do something, I do it."

She takes a few steps in, and looks in astonishment at my dressing table.

"I never knew that dressing table had a marble top!"

"I know!" I say proudly. "It's quite nice, isn't it?"

"But where's all the rubbish? Where are the bin bags?"

"They're . . . I've already got rid of them."

"So did you chuck loads out?" she says, wandering over to the almost-empty mantelpiece. "You must have done!"

"A . . . a fair amount," I say evasively. "You know. I was quite ruthless in the end."

"I'm so impressed!" She pauses in front of the wardrobe, and I stare at her, suddenly nervous.

Don't open it, I pray silently. Just *don't* open it.

"Have you got anything left?" she says, with a grin, and pulls open the door of the wardrobe. And we both scream.

It's like a nail-bomb explosion.

Except, instead of nails, it's clothes.

I don't know what happened. I don't know *what* I did wrong. But one of the bags bursts open, showering jumpers everywhere, and pushing all the other bags out. Then another one bursts open, and another one. It's a clothes storm. Suze is completely covered in stretchy tops. A sequinned skirt lands on the light shade. A bra shoots across the room and hits the window. Suze is half-shrieking and half-laughing, and I'm flapping my arms madly and yelling, "Stop! Stop!"

And oh no.

Oh no. Please stop. Please.

But it's too late. Now a cascade of gift-shop carrier bags is tumbling down from their hiding place on the top shelf. One after another, out into the daylight. They're hitting Suze on the head, landing on the floor, and spilling open—and revealing the same contents in each. Gray sparkly boxes with a silver S C-S scrawled on the front.

About forty of them.

"What . . ." Suze pulls a T-shirt off her head and stares at them, open-mouthed. "Where on earth did you . . ." She scrabbles among the clothes littering the floor, picks up one of the boxes, and pulls it open and stares in silence. There, wrapped in turquoise tissue paper, is a photo frame made out of tan leather.

Oh God. Oh God.

Without saying anything, Suze bends down and picks up a Gifts and Goodies carrier bag. As she pulls it open, a receipt flutters to the floor. Silently she takes out the two boxes inside—and opens each to reveal a frame made of purple tweed.

I open my mouth to speak—but nothing comes out. For a moment we just stare at each other.

"Bex . . . how many of these have you got?" says Suze at last, in a slightly strangled voice.

"Um . . . not many!" I say, feeling my face grow hot. "Just . . . you know. A few."

"There must be about . . . fifty here!"

"No!"

"Yes!" She looks around, cheeks growing pink with distress. "Bex, these are really expensive."

"I haven't bought that many!" I give a distracting laugh. "And I didn't buy them all at once . . ."

"You shouldn't have bought *any*! I told you, I'd make you one!"

"I know," I say a little awkwardly. "I know you did. But I wanted to buy one. I just wanted to . . . to support you."

There's silence as Suze reaches for another Gifts and Goodies bag, and looks at the two boxes inside.

"It's you, isn't it?" she says suddenly. "You're the reason I've sold so well."

"It's not! Honestly, Suze—"

"You've spent all your money on buying my frames." Her voice starts to wobble. "All your money. And now you're in debt."

"I haven't!"

"If it weren't for you, I wouldn't have my deal!"

"You would!" I say in dismay. "Of course you would! Suze, you make the best frames in the world! I mean . . . look at this one!" I grab for the nearest box and pull out a frame made out of distressed denim. "I would have bought this even if I hadn't known you. I would have bought all of them!"

"You wouldn't have bought this many," she gulps. "You would have bought maybe . . . three."

"I would have bought them all! They're the best frames in the world! They'd make a perfect present, or a . . . an ornament for the house . . ."

"You're just saying that," she says tearfully.

"No, I'm not!" I say, feeling tears coming to my own eyes. "Suze, everybody loves your frames. I've seen people in shops saying how brilliant they are!"

"No, you haven't."

"I have! There was this woman admiring one in Gifts and Goodies, just the other day, and everyone in the shop was agreeing!"

"Really?" says Suze in a small voice.

"Yes. You're so talented, and successful . . ." I look around my bomb-site room, and feel a sudden wave of despair. "And I'm such a mess. John Gavin's right, I should have assets by now. I should be all sorted out. I'm just . . . worthless." Tears start to trickle down my face.

"You're not!" says Suze in horror. "You're not worthless!"

"I am!" Miserably, I sink to the carpet of clothes on the floor. "Suze, just look at me. I'm unemployed, I haven't got any prospects, I'm being taken to court, I owe thousands and thousands of pounds, and I don't know how I'm even going to start paying it all off . . ."

There's an awkward cough at the door. I look up, and Tarquin is standing at the door, holding three mugs of coffee.

"Refreshments?" he says, picking his way across the floor.

"Thanks, Tarquin," I say, sniffing, and take a mug from him. "Sorry about all this. It's just . . . not a great time."

He sits down on the bed and exchanges looks with Suze.

"Bit short of cash?" he says.

"Yes," I gulp, and wipe my eyes. "Yes, I am." Tarquin gives Suze another glance.

"Becky, I'd be only too happy to—"

"No. No, thanks." I smile at him. "Really."

There's silence as we all sip our coffee. A shaft of winter sunlight is coming through the window, and I close my eyes, feeling the soothing warmth on my face.

"Happens to the best of us," says Tarquin sympathetically. "Mad Uncle Monty was always going bust, wasn't he, Suze?"

"God, that's right! All the time!" says Suze. "But he always bounced back, didn't he?"

"Absolutely!" says Tarquin. "Over and over again."

"What did he do?" I say, looking up with a spark of interest.

"Usually sold off a Rembrandt," says Tarquin. "Or a Stubbs. Something like that."

Great. What is it about these millionaires? I mean, even Suze, who I love. They just don't get it. They *don't know what it's like to have no money.*

"Right," I say, trying to smile. "Well . . . unfortunately, I don't have any spare Rembrandts lying around. All I've got is . . . a zillion pairs of black trousers. And some T-shirts."

"And a fencing outfit," puts in Suze.

Next door, the phone starts ringing, but none of us move.

"And a wooden bowl which I hate." I give a half-giggle, half-sob. "And forty photograph frames."

"And fifty million pots of lavender honey."

"And a Vera Wang cocktail dress." I look around my room, suddenly alert. "And a brand-new Kate Spade bag . . . and . . . and a whole wardrobe full of stuff which I've never even worn . . . Suze . . ." I'm almost too agitated to speak. "Suze . . ."

"What?"

"Just . . . just think about it. I haven't got nothing. I *have* got assets! I mean, they might have depreciated a little bit . . ."

"What do you mean?" says Suze puzzledly—then her face lights up. "Ooh, have you got an ISA that you forgot about?"

"No! Not an ISA!"

"I don't understand!" wails Suze. "Bex, what are you talking about?"

And I'm just opening my mouth to answer, when the answer machine clicks on next door, and a gravelly American voice starts speaking, which makes me stiffen and turn my head.

"Hello, Becky? It's Michael Ellis here. I've just arrived in London for a conference, and I was wondering—could we perhaps meet up for a chat?"

It's so weird to see Michael here in London. In my mind he belongs firmly in New York, in the Four Seasons. Back in that other world. But here he is, large as life, in the River Room at the Savoy, his face creased in a beam. As I sit down at the table he lifts a hand to a waiter.

"A gin and tonic for the lady, please." He raises his eyebrows at me. "Am I right?"

"Yes, please." I smile at him gratefully, and shake out my napkin to cover my awkwardness. Even though we talked so much in New York, I'm feeling a bit shy at seeing him again.

"So," he says, as the waiter brings me my drink. "Quite a lot has been going on since we last spoke." He lifts his glass. "Cheers."

"Cheers." I take a sip. "Like what?"

"Like Alicia Billington and four others have been fired from Brandon Communications."

"*Four* others?" I gape at him. "Were they all planning together?"

"Apparently so. It turns out Alicia has been working on this little project for some time. This wasn't just some tiny little pie-in-the-sky scheme. This was well organized and thought out. Well backed, too. You know Alicia's future husband is very wealthy?"

"I didn't," I say, and remember her Chanel shoes. "But it makes sense."

"He put together the finance. As you suspected, they were planning to poach Bank of London."

I take a sip of gin and tonic, relishing the sharp flavor.

"So what happened?"

"Luke swooped in, took them all by surprise, herded them into a meeting room, and searched their desks. And he found plenty."

"Luke did?" I feel a deep thud in my stomach. "You mean—Luke's in London?"

"Uh-huh."

"How long has he been back?"

"Three days now." Michael gives me a quick glance. "I guess he hasn't called you, then."

"No," I say, trying to hide my disappointment. "No, he hasn't." I reach for my glass and take a deep swig. Somehow while he was still in New York, I could tell myself that Luke and I weren't speaking because of geography as much as anything else. But now he's in London—and he hasn't even called—it feels different. It feels kind of . . . final.

"So . . . what's he doing now?"

"Damage limitation," says Michael wryly. "Upping morale. It turns out as soon as he left for New York, Alicia got busy spreading rumors he was going to close the U.K. branch down completely. That's why the atmosphere plummeted. Clients have been neglected, the staff has all been on the phone to headhunters . . . Meanwhile Alicia was spinning a completely different story to Luke." He shakes his head. "That girl is trouble."

"I know."

"Now, that's something I've been wondering. *How* do you know?" He leans forward interestedly. "You picked up on Alicia in a way neither Luke nor I did. Was that based on anything?"

"Not really," I say honestly. "Just the fact that she's a complete cow."

Michael throws his head back and roars with laughter.

"Feminine intuition. Why should there be any other reason?"

He chuckles for a few moments more—then puts his glass down and gives me a twinkling smile. "Speaking of which—I heard the gist of what you said to Luke about his mom."

"Really?" I look at him in horror. "He told you?"

"He spoke to me about it, asked if you'd said anything to me."

"Oh!" I feel a flush creeping across my face. "Well, I was . . . angry. I didn't *mean* to say she was a . . ." I clear my throat. "I just spoke without thinking."

"He took it to heart, though." Michael raises his eyebrows. "He called his mom up, said he was damned if he was going to go home without seeing her, and arranged a meeting."

"Really?" I stare at him, feeling prickles of intrigue. "And what happened?"

"She never showed up. Sent some message about having to go out of town. Luke was pretty disappointed." Michael shakes his head. "Between you and me—I think you were right about her."

"Oh. Well."

I give an awkward shrug and reach for the menu to hide my embarrassment. I can't *believe* Luke told Michael what I said about his mother. What else did he tell him? My bra size?

For a while I stare at the list of dishes without taking any of them in—then look up, to see Michael gazing seriously at me.

"Becky, I haven't told Luke it was you who tipped me off. The story I've given him is I got an anonymous message and decided to look into it."

"That sounds fair enough," I say, gazing at the tablecloth.

"You're basically responsible for saving his company," says Michael gently. "He should be very grateful to you. Don't you think he should know?"

"No." I hunch my shoulders. "He'd just think . . . he'd think I was . . ." I break off, feeling my eyes grow hot.

I can't believe Luke's been back for three days and hasn't called. I mean—I knew it was over. Of course I did. But secretly, a tiny part of me thought . . .

Anyway. Obviously not.

"What would he think?" probes Michael.

"I dunno," I mutter gruffly. "The point is, it's all over between us. So I'd rather just . . . not be involved."

"Well, I guess I can understand that." Michael gives me a kind look. "Shall we order?"

While we eat, we talk about other things. Michael tells me about his advertising agency in Washington, and makes me laugh with stories of all the politicians he knows and all the trouble they get themselves into. I tell him in turn about my family, and Suze, and the way I got my job on *Morning Coffee.*

"It's all going really well, actually," I say boldly as I dig into a chocolate mousse. "I've got great prospects, and the producers really like me . . . they're thinking of expanding my slot . . ."

"Becky," interrupts Michael gently. "I heard. I know about your job."

I stare at him dumbly, feeling my whole face prickle in shame.

"I felt really bad for you," continues Michael. "That shouldn't have happened."

"Does . . . does Luke know?" I say huskily.

"Yes. I believe he does."

I take a deep swig of my drink. I can't bear the idea of Luke pitying me.

"Well, I've got lots of options open," I say desperately. "I mean, maybe not on television . . . but I'm applying for a number of financial journalism posts . . ."

"On the *FT*?"

"On . . . well . . . on *Personal Investment Periodical* . . . and *Annuities Today* . . ."

"*Annuities Today*," echoes Michael disbelievingly. At his expression I can't help giving a snort of shaky laughter. "Becky, do any of these jobs really excite you?"

I'm about to trot out my stock answer—"Personal finance is more interesting than you'd think, actually!" But suddenly I realize I can't be bothered to pretend anymore. Personal finance *isn't* more interesting than you'd think. It's just as boring as you'd think. Even on *Morning Coffee*, it was only really when callers started talking about their relationships and family lives that I used to enjoy it.

"What do you think?" I say instead, and take another swig of gin and tonic.

Michael sits back in his chair and dabs his mouth with a napkin. "So why are you going for them?"

"I don't know what else to do." I give a hopeless shrug. "Personal finance is the only thing I've ever done. I'm kind of . . . pigeonholed."

"How old are you, Becky? If you don't mind my asking?"

"Twenty-six."

"Pigeonholed at twenty-six." Michael shakes his head. "I don't think so." He takes a sip of coffee and gives me an appraising look.

"If some opportunity came up for you in America," he says, "would you take it?"

"I'd take anything," I say frankly. "But what's going to come up for me in America now?"

There's silence. Thoughtfully, Michael reaches for a chocolate mint, unwraps it, and puts it in his mouth.

"Becky, I have a proposition for you," he says, looking up. "We have an opening at the advertising agency for a head of corporate communications."

I stare at him, glass halfway to my lips. Not daring to hope he's saying what I think he is.

"We want someone with editorial skills, who can coordinate a monthly newsletter. You'd be ideal on those counts. But we also want someone who's good with people. Someone who can pick up on the buzz, make sure people are happy, report to the board on any problems . . ." He shrugs. "Frankly, I can't think of anyone better suited to it."

"You're . . . you're offering me a job," I say disbelievingly, trying to ignore the little leaps of hope inside my chest, the little stabs of excitement. "But . . . but what about *The Daily World*? The . . . shopping?"

"So what?" Michael shrugs. "So you like to shop. I like to eat. Nobody's perfect. As long as you're not on some international 'most wanted' blacklist . . ."

"No. No," I say hurriedly. "In fact, I'm about to sort all that out."

"And immigration?"

"I've got a lawyer." I bite my lip. "I'm not sure he exactly likes me very much . . ."

"I have contacts in immigration," says Michael reassuringly. "I'm sure we can sort something out." He leans back and takes a sip of coffee. "Washington isn't New York. But it's a fun place to be, too. Politics is a fascinating arena. I have a feeling you'd take to it. And the salary . . . Well. It won't be what CNN might have offered you. But as a ballpark . . ." He scribbles a figure on a piece of paper and pushes it across the table.

And I don't believe it. It's about twice what I'd get for any of those crappy journalism jobs.

Washington. An advertising agency. A whole new career.

America. Without Luke. On my own terms.

I can't quite get my head round all of this.

"Why are you offering this to me?" I manage at last.

"I've been very impressed by you, Becky," says Michael seriously. "You're smart. You're intuitive. I took your advice about my friend, by the way," he adds with a twinkle. "He paid up the next day."

"Really?" I say in delight.

"You have a good head on your shoulders—and you're someone who gets things done." I stare at him, feeling an embarrassed color come to my cheeks. "And maybe I figured you deserve a break," he adds kindly. "Now, you don't have to decide at once. I'm over here for a few more days, so if you want to, we can talk again about it. But, Becky—"

"Yes?"

"I'm serious now. Whether you decide to take up my offer or not, don't fall into anything else." He shakes his head. "You're too young to settle. Look into your heart—and go after what you really want."

Sixteen

I DON'T DECIDE straight away. It takes me about two weeks of pacing around the flat, drinking endless cups of coffee, talking to my parents, Suze, Michael, my old boss Philip, this new television agent Cassandra . . . basically everyone I can think of. But in the end I know. I know in my heart what I really want to do.

Luke hasn't called—and to be honest, I shouldn't think I'll ever speak to him again. Michael says he's working about seventeen hours a day—trying simultaneously to salvage Brandon Communications and keep interest open in the States—and is very stressed indeed. Apparently he still hasn't got over the shock of discovering that Alicia was plotting against him—and that Bank of London was still considering moving with her. The shock of discovering he wasn't "immune to shit," as Michael so poetically put it. "That's the trouble with having the whole world love you," he said to me the other day. "One day, you wake up and it's flirting with your best friend instead. And you don't know what to do. You're thrown."

"So—has Luke been thrown by all this?" I asked, twisting my fingers into a knot.

"Thrown?" exclaimed Michael. "He's been hurled across the paddock and trampled on by a herd of wild boar."

Several times I've picked up the phone with a sudden longing to speak to him. But then I've always taken a deep breath and put it down again. That's his life now. I've got to get on with mine. My whole new life.

There's a sound at the door, and I look round. Suze is standing in the doorway, staring into my empty room.

"Oh, Bex," she says miserably. "I don't like it. Put it all back. Make it messy again."

"At least it's all feng shui now," I say, attempting a smile. "It'll probably bring you loads of luck."

She comes in and walks across the empty carpet to the window, then turns round.

"It seems smaller," she says slowly. "It should look bigger without all your clutter, shouldn't it? But somehow . . . it doesn't work like that. It looks like a nasty bare little box."

There's silence for a while as I watch a tiny spider climbing up the windowpane.

"Have you decided what you're going to do with it?" I say at last. "Are you going to get a new flatmate?"

"I don't think so," says Suze. "I mean, there's no rush, is there. Tarkie said why not just have it as my office for a while."

"Did he?" I turn to look at her with raised eyebrows. "That reminds me. Did I hear Tarquin here again last night? And creeping out this morning?"

"No," says Suze, looking flustered. "I mean—yes." She catches my eye and blushes. "But it was completely the last ever time. Ever."

"You make such a lovely couple," I say, grinning at her.

"Don't *say* that!" she exclaims in horror. "We're not a couple."

"OK," I say, relenting. "Whatever." I look at my watch. "You know, we ought to be going."

"Yes. I suppose so. Oh, Bex—"

I look at Suze—and her eyes are suddenly full of tears.

"I know." I squeeze her hand tightly and for a moment neither of us says anything. Then I reach for my coat. "Come on."

We walk along to the King George pub at the end of the road. We make our way through the bar and up a flight of wooden stairs to a large private room furnished with red velvet curtains, a bar, and lots of trestle tables set up on both sides. A makeshift platform has been set up at one end, and there are rows of plastic chairs in the middle.

"Hello!" says Tarquin, spotting us as we enter. "Come and have a drink." He lifts his glass. "The red's not at all bad."

"Is the tab all set up behind the bar?" says Suze.

"Absolutely," says Tarquin. "All organized."

"Bex—that's on us," says Suze, putting her hand on me as I reach for my purse. "A good-bye present."

"Suze, you don't have to—"

"I wanted to," she says firmly. "So did Tarkie."

"Let me get you some drinks," says Tarquin—then adds, lowering his voice, "It's a pretty good turnout, don't you think?"

As he walks off, Suze and I turn to survey the room. There are tables set out round the room, and people are milling around, looking at neatly folded piles of clothes, shoes, CDs, and assorted bits of bric-a-brac. On one table is a pile of typed, photocopied catalogues, and people are marking them as they wander round.

I can hear a girl in leather jeans saying, "Look at this coat! Ooh, and these Hobbs boots! I'm definitely going to bid for those!" On the other side of the room, two girls are trying pairs of trousers up against themselves while their boyfriends patiently hold their drinks.

"Who *are* all these people?" I say disbelievingly. "Did you invite them all?"

"Well, I went down my address book," says Suze. "And Tarquin's address book. And Fenny's . . ."

"Oh well," I say with a laugh. "That explains it."

"Hi, Becky!" says a bright voice behind me—and I swivel round to see Fenella's friend Milla, with a pair of girls I half-recognize. "I'm going to bid for your purple cardigan! And Tory's going to go for that dress with the fur, and Annabel's seen about six thousand things she wants! We were just wondering, is there an accessories section?"

"Over there," says Suze, pointing to the corner of the room.

"Thanks!" says Milla. "See you later!" The three girls trip off into the melee, and I hear one of them saying, "I *really* need a good belt . . ."

"Becky!" says Tarquin, suddenly coming up behind me. "Here's some wine. And let me introduce Caspar, my chum from Christie's."

"Oh hello!" I say, turning round to see a guy with floppy blond hair, a blue shirt, and an enormous gold signet ring. "Thank you so much for doing this! I'm really grateful."

"Not at all, not at all," says Caspar. "Now, I've been through the catalogue and it all seems fairly straightforward. Do you have a list of reserve prices?"

"No," I say without pausing. "No reserves. Everything must go."

"Fine." He smiles at me. "Well, I'll go and get set up."

As he walks off I take a sip of my wine. Suze has gone off to look round some of the tables, so I stand alone for a while, watching as the crowd grows. Fenella arrives at the door, and I give her a wave—but she's immediately swallowed up in a group of shrieking friends.

"Hi, Becky," comes a hesitant voice behind me. I wheel round in shock, and find myself staring up at Tom Webster.

"Tom!" I exclaim in shock. "What are you doing here? How do you know about this?" He takes a sip from his glass and gives a little grin.

"Suze called your mum, and she told me all about it. She and my mum have put in some orders, actually." He pulls a list out of his pocket. "Your mum wants your cappuccino maker. If it's for sale."

"Oh, it's for sale," I say. "I'll tell the auctioneer to make sure you get it."

"And my mum wants that pink hat you wore to our wedding."

"Right. No problem." At the reminder of his wedding, I feel myself growing slightly warm.

"So—how's married life?" I say, examining one of my nails.

"Oh . . . it's all right," he says after a pause.

"Is it as blissful as you expected?" I say, trying to sound lighthearted.

"Well, you know . . ." He stares into his glass, a slightly hunted look in his eye. "It would be unrealistic to expect everything to be perfect straight off. Wouldn't it?"

"I suppose so."

There's an awkward silence between us. In the distance I can hear someone saying, "Kate Spade! Look, brand new!"

"Becky, I'm really sorry," says Tom in a rush. "The way we behaved toward you at the wedding."

"That's all right!" I say, a little too brightly.

"It's not all right." He shakes his head. "Your mum was bang on. You're one of my oldest friends. I've been feeling really bad, ever since."

"Honestly, Tom. It was my fault, too. I mean, I should have just admitted Luke wasn't there!" I smile ruefully. "It would have been a lot simpler."

"But if Lucy was giving you a hard time, I can really understand why you felt you just had to . . . to . . ." He breaks off, and takes a deep swig of his drink. "Anyway. Luke seemed like a nice guy. Is he coming tonight?"

"No," I say after a pause, and force a smile. "No, he isn't."

After half an hour or so, people begin to take their seats on the rows of plastic chairs. At the back of the room are five or six friends of Tarquin's holding mobile phones, and Caspar explains to me that they're on the line to telephone bidders.

"They're people who heard about it but couldn't come, for whatever reason. We've been circulating the catalogues fairly widely, and a lot of people are interested. The Vera Wang dress alone attracted a great deal of attention."

"Yes," I say, feeling a sudden lurch of emotion, "I expect it did." I look around the room, at the bright, expectant faces, at the people still taking a last look at the tables. A girl is leafing through a pile of jeans; someone else is trying out the clasp on my dinky little white case. I can't quite believe that after tonight, none of these things will be mine anymore. They'll be in other people's wardrobes. Other people's rooms.

"Are you all right?" says Caspar, following my gaze.

"Yes!" I say brightly. "Why shouldn't I be all right?"

"I've done a lot of house sales," he says kindly. "I know what it's like. One gets very attached to one's possessions. Whether it's an eighteenth-century chiffonier, or . . ." He glances at the catalogue. "A pink leopard-print coat."

"Actually—I never much liked that coat." I gave him a resolute smile. "And anyway, that's not the point. I want to start again and I think—I *know*—this is the best way." I smile at him. "Come on. Let's get going, shall we?"

"Absolutely." He raps on his lectern and raises his voice. "Ladies and gentlemen! First, on behalf of Becky Bloomwood, I'd like to welcome you all here this evening. We've got quite a lot to get through, so I won't delay you—except to remind you that 25 percent of everything raised tonight is going to a range of charities—plus any remainder of the proceeds after Becky has paid off all her outstanding accounts."

"I hope they're not holding their breath," says a dry voice from the back, and everyone laughs. I peer through the crowd to see who it is—and I don't believe it. It's Derek Smeath, standing there with a pint in one hand, a catalogue in the other. He gives me a little smile, and I give a shy wave back.

"How did he know about this?" I hiss to Suze, who has come to join me on the platform.

"I told him, of course!" she says. "He said he thought it was a marvelous idea. He said when you use your brain, no one comes near you for ingenuity."

"Really?" I glance at Derek Smeath again and flush slightly.

"So," says Caspar. "I present Lot One. A pair of clementine

sandals, very good condition, hardly worn." He lifts them onto the table and Suze squeezes my hand sympathetically. "Do I have any bids?"

"I bid £15,000," says Tarquin, sticking up his hand at once.

"Fifteen thousand pounds," says Caspar, sounding a bit taken aback. "I have a bid of £15,000—"

"No, you don't!" I interrupt. "Tarquin, you can't bid £15,000!"

"Why not?"

"You have to bid *realistic* prices." I give him a stern look. "Otherwise you'll be banned from the bidding."

"OK . . . £1,000."

"No! You can bid . . . £10," I say firmly.

"All right, then. Ten pounds." He puts his hand down meekly.

"Fifteen pounds," comes a voice from the back.

"Twenty!" cries a girl near the front.

"Twenty-five," says Tarquin.

"Thirty!"

"Thirt—" Tarquin catches my eye, blushes, and stops.

"Thirty pounds. Any further bids on 30 . . ." Caspar looks around the room, his eyes suddenly like a hawk's. "Going . . . going . . . gone! To the girl in the green velvet coat." He grins at me, scribbles something on a piece of paper, and hands the shoes to Fenella, who is in charge of distributing sold items.

"Your first £30!" whispers Suze in my ear.

"Lot Two!" says Caspar. "Three embroidered cardigans from Jigsaw, unworn, with price tags still attached. Can I start the bidding at . . ."

"Twenty pounds!" says a girl in pink.

"Twenty-five!" cries another girl.

"I have a telephone bid of 30," says a guy raising his hand at the back.

"Thirty pounds from one of our telephone bidders . . . Any advance on 30? Remember, ladies and gentlemen, this *will* be raising funds for charity . . ."

"Thirty-five!" cries the girl in pink, and turns to her neighbor. "I mean, they'd be more than that each in the shop, wouldn't they? And they've never even been worn!"

God, she's right. I mean, thirty-five quid for three cardigans is nothing. Nothing!

"Forty!" I hear myself crying, before I can stop myself. The whole room turns to look at me, and I feel myself furiously blushing. "I mean . . . does anyone want to bid 40?"

The bidding goes on and on, and I can't believe how much money is being raised. My shoe collection raises at least £1,000, a set of Dinny Hall jewelry goes for £200—and Tom Webster bids £600 for my computer.

"Tom," I say anxiously, as he comes up to the platform to fill in his slip. "Tom, you shouldn't have bid all that money."

"For a brand-new Apple Mac?" says Tom. "It's worth it. Besides, Lucy's been saying she wants her own computer for a while." He gives a half-smile. "I'm kind of looking forward to telling her she's got your castoff."

"Lot Seventy-three," says Caspar beside me. "And one which I know is going to attract a great deal of interest. A Vera Wang cocktail dress." He slowly holds up the inky purple dress, and there's an appreciative gasp from the crowd.

But actually—I don't think I can watch this go. This is too painful, too recent. My beautiful glittering movie-star dress. I can't even look at it without remembering it all, like a slow-motion cine-film. Dancing with Luke in New York; drinking cocktails; that heady, happy excitement. And then waking up and seeing everything crash around me.

"Excuse me," I murmur, and get to my feet. I head quickly out of the room, down the stairs, and into the fresh evening air. I lean against the side of the pub, listening to the laughter and chatter inside, and take a few deep breaths, trying to focus on all the good reasons why I'm doing this.

A few moments later, Suze appears beside me.

"Are you OK?" she says, and hands me a glass of wine. "Here. Have some of this."

"Thanks," I say gratefully, and take a deep gulp. "I'm fine, really. It's just . . . I suppose it's just hitting me. What I'm doing."

"Bex . . ." She pauses and rubs her face awkwardly. "Bex, you could always change your mind. You could always stay. I mean—after tonight, with any luck, all your debts will be paid off! You could get a job, stay in the flat with me . . ."

I look at her for a few silent moments, feeling a temptation so strong, it almost hurts. It would be so easy to agree. Go home with her, have a cup of tea, and fall back into my old life.

But then I shake my head.

"No. I'm not going to fall into anything again. I've found something I really want to do, Suze, and I'm going to do it."

"Rebecca." A voice interrupts us, and we both look up to see Derek Smeath coming out of the door of the pub. He's holding the wooden bowl, one of Suze's photograph frames, and a big hard-backed atlas which I remember buying once when I thought I might give up my Western life and go traveling.

"Hi!" I say, and nod at his haul. "You did well."

"Very well." He holds the bowl up. "This is a very handsome piece."

"It was in *Elle Decoration* once," I tell him. "Very cool."

"Really? I'll tell my daughter." He puts it slightly awkwardly under his arm. "So you're off to America tomorrow."

"Yes. Tomorrow afternoon. After I've paid a small trip to your friend John Gavin."

A wry smile passes over Derek Smeath's face.

"I'm sure he'll be pleased to see you." He extends his hand as best he can to shake mine. "Well, good luck, Becky. Do let me know how you get on."

"I will," I say, smiling warmly. "And thanks for . . . You know. Everything."

He nods, and then walks off into the night.

I stay outside with Suze for quite a time. People are leaving now, carrying their loot, and telling each other how much they got it all for. A guy walks by clutching the mini paper shredder, a girl drags a bin liner full of clothes, someone else has got the invitations with the twinkly pizza slices. Just as I'm starting to get cold, a voice hails us from the stairs.

"Hey," calls Tarquin. "It's the last lot. D'you want to come and see?"

"Come on," says Suze, stubbing out her cigarette. "You've got to see the last thing go. What is it?"

"I don't know," I say as we mount the stairs. "The fencing mask, perhaps?"

But as we walk back into the room, I feel a jolt of shock. Caspar's holding up my Denny and George scarf. My precious Denny and George scarf. Shimmering blue, silky velvet, overprinted in a paler blue, and dotted with iridescent beading.

I stand staring at it, with a growing tightness in my throat, remembering with a painful vividness the day I bought it. How desperately I wanted it. How Luke lent me the twenty quid I needed. The way I told him I was buying it for my aunt.

The way he used to look at me whenever I wore it.

My eyes are going blurry, and I blink hard, trying to keep control of myself.

"Bex . . . don't sell your scarf," says Suze, looking at it in distress. "Keep one thing, at least."

"Lot 126," says Caspar. "A very attractive silk and velvet scarf."

"Bex, tell them you've changed your mind!"

"I haven't changed my mind," I say, staring fixedly ahead. "There's no point hanging on to it now."

"What am I bid for this fine designer accessory by Denny and George?"

"Denny and George!" says the girl in pink, looking up. She's got the hugest pile of clothes around her, and I've no idea how she's going to get them all home. "I collect Denny and George! Thirty pounds!"

"I have a bid at £30," says Caspar. He looks around the room—but it's swiftly emptying. People are queueing up to collect their items, or buy drinks at the bar, and the very few left sitting on the chairs are mostly chatting.

"Any further bids for this Denny and George scarf?"

"Yes!" says a voice at the back, and I see a girl in black raising a hand. "I have a telephone bid of £35."

"Forty pounds," says the girl in pink promptly.

"Fifty," says the girl in black.

"Fifty?" says the pink girl, swiveling on her chair. "Who is it bidding? Is it Miggy Sloane?"

"The bidder wishes to remain anonymous," says the girl in black after a pause. She catches my eye and for an instant my heart stops still.

"I bet it's Miggy," says the girl, turning back. "Well, she's not going to beat me. Sixty pounds."

"Sixty pounds?" says the chap next to her, who's been eyeing her pile of stuff with slight alarm. "For a scarf?"

"A *Denny and George* scarf, stupid!" says the pink girl, and takes a swig of wine. "It would be at least two hundred in a shop. Seventy! Ooh, silly. It's not my turn, is it?"

The girl in black has been murmuring quietly into the phone. Now she looks up at Caspar. "A hundred."

"A hundred?" The pink girl swivels on her chair again. "Really?"

"The bidding stands at one hundred," says Caspar calmly. "I am bid £100 for this Denny and George scarf. Any further bids?"

"A hundred and twenty," says the pink girl. There are a few moments' silence, and the girl in black talks quietly into the phone again. Then she looks up and says, "A hundred and fifty."

There's an interested murmuring around the room, and people who had been chatting at the bar all turn toward the auction floor again.

"One hundred and fifty pounds," says Caspar. "I am bid £150 for Lot 126, a Denny and George scarf."

"That's more than I *paid* for it!" I whisper to Suze.

"Bidding rests with the telephone buyer. At £150. One hundred and fifty pounds, ladies and gentlemen."

There's a tense silence—and suddenly I realize I'm digging my nails into the flesh of my hands.

"Two hundred," says the girl in pink defiantly, and there's a gasp around the room. "And tell your so-called anonymous bidder, Miss Miggy Sloane, that whatever *she* bids, *I* can bid."

Everyone turns to look at the girl in black, who mutters something into the receiver, then nods her head.

"My bidder withdraws," she says, looking up. I feel an inexplicable pang of disappointment, and quickly smile to cover it.

"Two hundred pounds!" I say to Suze. "That's pretty good!"

"Going . . . going . . . gone," says Caspar, and raps his gavel. "To the lady in pink."

There's a round of applause, and Caspar beams happily around. He picks up the scarf, and is about to hand it to Fenella, when I stop him.

"Wait," I say. "I'd like to give it to her. If that's all right."

I take the scarf from Caspar and hold it quite still for a few moments, feeling its familiar gossamer texture. I can still smell my scent on it. I can feel Luke tying it round my neck.

The Girl in the Denny and George Scarf.

Then I take a deep breath and walk down, off the platform, toward the girl in pink. I smile at her and hand it over to her.

"Enjoy it," I say. "It's quite special."

"Oh, I know," she says quietly. "I know it is." And just for a moment, as we look at each other, I think she understands completely. Then she turns and lifts it high into the air in triumph, like a trophy. "Sucks to you, Miggy!"

I turn away and walk back to the platform, where Caspar is sitting down, looking exhausted.

"Well done," I say, sitting down next to him. "And thank you so much again. You did a fantastic job."

"Not at all!" says Caspar. "I enjoyed it, actually. Bit of a change from early German porcelain." He gestures to his notes. "I think we raised a fair bit, too."

"You did brilliantly!" says Suze, coming to sit down too, and handing Caspar a beer. "Honestly, Bex, you'll be completely out of the woods now." She gives an admiring sigh. "You know, it just shows, you were right all along. Shopping *is* an investment.

I mean, like, how much did you make on your Denny and George scarf?"

"Erm . . ." I close my eyes, trying to work it out. "About . . . 60 percent?"

"Sixty percent return! In less than a year! You see? That's better than the crummy old stock market!" She takes out a cigarette and lights it. "You know, I think I might sell all my stuff, too."

"You haven't got any stuff," I point out. "You decluttered it all."

"Oh yeah." Suze's face falls. "God, why did I do that?"

I lean back on my elbow and close my eyes. Suddenly, for no real reason, I feel absolutely exhausted.

"So you're off tomorrow," says Caspar, taking a swig of beer.

"I'm off tomorrow," I echo, staring up at the ceiling. Tomorrow I'm leaving England and flying off to America to live. Leaving everything behind and starting again. Somehow, it just doesn't feel real.

"Not one of these crack-of-dawn flights, I hope?" he says, glancing at his watch.

"No, thank God. I'm not flying until about five."

"That's good," says Caspar, nodding. "Gives you plenty of time."

"Oh yes." I sit up and glance at Suze, who grins back. "Plenty of time for just a couple of little things I've got to do."

"Becky! We're so glad you changed your mind!" cries Zelda as soon as she sees me. I get up from the sofa where I've been sitting in reception, and give her a quick smile. "Everyone's so thrilled you're coming on! What made you decide?"

"Oh, I'm not sure," I say pleasantly. "Just . . . one of those things."

"Well, let me take you straight up to makeup . . . we're completely chaotic, as usual, so we've brought your slot forward slightly . . ."

"No problem," I say. "The sooner the better."

"I have to say, you look very well," says Zelda, surveying me with a slight air of disappointment. "Have you lost weight?"

"A little, I suppose."

"Ah . . . stress," she says wisely. "Stress, the silent killer. We're doing a feature on it next week. Now!" she exclaims, bustling me into the makeup room. "This is Becky . . ."

"Zelda, we know who Becky is," says Chloe, who's been doing my makeup ever since I first appeared on *Morning Coffee*. She pulls a face at me in the mirror and I stifle a giggle.

"Yes, of course you do! Sorry, Becky, I've just got you down in my mind as a guest! Now, Chloe. Don't do too good a job on Becky today. We don't want her looking too glowing and happy, do we?" She lowers her voice. "And use waterproof mascara. In fact, everything waterproof. See you later!"

Zelda sweeps out of the room, and Chloe shoots her a scornful glance.

"OK," she says. "I'm going to make you look as good as you've ever looked in your life. Extra happy and extra glowing."

"Thanks, Chloe," I say, grinning at her, and sit down on a chair.

"Oh, and please don't tell me you're really going to need waterproof mascara," she adds, tying a cape around me.

"No way," I say firmly. "They'll have to shoot me first."

"Then they probably will," says a girl from across the room, and we all start giggling helplessly.

"All I can say is, I hope they're paying you well to do this," says Chloe, as she starts to smooth foundation onto my skin.

"Yes," I say. "They are, as it happens. But that's not why I'm doing it."

Half an hour later, I'm sitting in the Green Room when Clare Edwards comes walking in. She's wearing a dark green suit that really doesn't do much for her—and is it my imagination, or has someone made her up far too pale? She's going to look really pasty under the lights.

"Oh," says Clare, looking discomfited as she sees me. "Hello, Becky."

"Hi, Clare," I say. "Long time no see."

"Yes. Well." She twists her hands into a knot. "I was very sorry to read of your troubles."

"Thanks," I say lightly. "Still—it's an ill wind, eh, Clare?"

Clare immediately blushes bright red and looks away—and I feel a bit ashamed of myself. It's not her fault I got sacked.

"Honestly, I'm really pleased you got the job," I say more kindly. "And I think you're doing it really well."

"Right!" says Zelda, hurrying in. "We're ready for you. Now, Becky." She puts a hand on my arm as we walk out. "I know this is going to be very traumatic for you. We're quite prepared for you to take your time . . . again, if you break down completely, start sobbing, whatever . . . don't worry."

"Thanks, Zelda," I say, and nod seriously. "I'll bear that in mind."

We get to the set, and there are Rory and Emma, sitting on the sofas. I glance at a monitor as I walk past, and see that they've blown up that awful picture of me in New York, tinted it red, and headlined it "Becky's Tragic Secret."

"Hi, Becky," says Emma, as I sit down, and pats me sympathetically on the hand. "Are you all right? Would you like a tissue?"

"Erm . . . no, thanks." I lower my voice. "But, you know. Perhaps later."

"Terrifically brave of you to come and do this," says Rory, and squints at his notes. "Is it true your parents have disowned you?"

"Ready in five," calls Zelda from the floor. "Four . . . three . . ."

"Welcome back," says Emma somberly to camera. "Now, we've got a very special guest with us today. Thousands of you will have followed the story of Becky Bloomwood, our former financial expert. Becky was, of course, revealed by *The Daily World* to be far from financially secure herself."

The picture of me shopping appears on the monitor, followed by a series of tabloid headlines, accompanied by the song "Hey Big Spender."

"So, Becky," says Emma, as the music dies away. "Let me begin by saying how *extremely* sorry and sympathetic we are for you in your plight. In a minute, we'll be asking our new financial expert, Clare Edwards, just what you should have done to prevent this catastrophe. But now—just to put our viewers straight . . . could you tell us exactly how much in debt you are?"

"I'd be glad to, Emma," I say, and take a deep breath. "At the present moment, my debt amounts to . . ." I pause, and I can feel the whole studio bracing itself for a shock. "Nothing."

"Nothing?" Emma looks at Rory as though to check she's heard correctly. *"Nothing?"*

"My overdraft facilities director, John Gavin, will be glad to confirm that this morning, at nine thirty, I paid off my overdraft completely. I've paid off every single debt I had."

I allow myself a tiny smile as I remember John Gavin's face this morning, as I handed over wads and wads of cash. I so wanted him to wriggle and squirm and look pissed off. But to give him his due, after the first couple of thousand he started smiling, and beckoning people round to watch. And at the end, he shook my hand really quite warmly—and said now he understood what Derek Smeath meant about me.

I wonder what old Smeathie can have said?

"So you see, I'm not really in a plight at all," I add. "In fact, I've never been better."

"Right . . ." says Emma. "I see." There's a distracted look in her eye—and I know Barry must be yelling something in her earpiece.

"But even if your money situation is temporarily sorted out, your life must still be in ruins." She leans forward sympathetically again. "You're unemployed . . . shunned by your friends . . ."

"On the contrary, I'm not unemployed. This afternoon I'm flying to the States, where I have a new career waiting for me. It's a bit of a gamble . . . and it'll certainly be a challenge. But I genuinely think I'll be happy there. And my friends . . ." My voice wobbles a little, and I take a deep breath. "It was my friends who helped me out. It was my friends who stood by me."

Oh God, I don't believe it. After all that, I've got bloody tears in my eyes. I blink them back as hard as I can, and smile brightly at Emma.

"So really, my story isn't one of failure. Yes, I got myself into debt; yes, I was fired. But I did something about it." I turn to the camera. "And I'd like to say to anyone out there who's got themselves in a mess like I did . . . you can get out of it, too. Take action. Sell all your clothes. Apply for a new job. You can start again, like I'm going to."

There's silence around the studio. Then suddenly, from behind one of the cameras, there's the sound of clapping. I look over in shock—and it's Dave, the cameraman. He grins at me and mouths "Well done." Suddenly Gareth the floor manager joins in . . . and someone else . . . and now the whole studio is applauding, apart from Emma and Rory, who are looking rather nonplussed—and Zelda, who's talking frantically into her mouthpiece.

"Well!" says Emma, over the sound of the applause. "Um . . . We're taking a short break now—but join us in a few moments to hear more on our lead story today: Becky's . . . Tragic . . . umm . . ." She hesitates, listening to her earpiece. ". . . or rather, Becky's . . . um, *Triumphant* . . . um . . ."

The signature tune blares out of a loudspeaker and she glances at the producer's box in irritation. "I wish he'd make up his bloody mind!"

"See you," I say, and get up. "I'm off now."

"Off?" says Emma. "You can't go yet!"

"Yes, I can." I reach toward my microphone, and Eddie the sound guy rushes forward to unclip it.

"Well said," he mutters as he unthreads it from my jacket. "Don't take their shit." He grins at me. "Barry's going ballistic up there."

"Hey, Becky!" Zelda's head jerks up in horror. "Where are you going?"

"I've said what I came to say. Now I've got a plane to catch."

"You can't leave now! We haven't finished!"

"I've finished," I say, and reach for my bag.

"But the phone lines are all red!" says Zelda, hurrying toward me. "The switchboard's jammed! The callers are all saying . . ." She stares at me as though she's never seen me before. "I mean, we had no idea. Who would ever have thought . . ."

"I've got to go, Zelda."

"Wait! Becky!" says Zelda as I reach the door of the studio. "We . . . Barry and I . . . we were having a quick little chat just now. And we were wondering whether . . ."

"Zelda," I interrupt gently. "It's too late. I'm going."

It's nearly three by the time I arrive at Heathrow Airport. I'm still a little flushed from the farewell lunch I had in the pub with Suze, Tarquin, and my parents. To be honest, there's a small part of me that feels like bursting into tears and running back to them all. But at the same time, I've never felt so confident in my life. I've never been so sure I'm doing the right thing.

There's a promotional stand in the center of the terminus, giving away free newspapers, and as I pass it, I reach for a *Financial Times*. Just for old times' sake. Plus, if I'm carrying the *FT,* I might get upgraded. I'm just folding it up to place it neatly under my arm, when I notice a name which makes me stop dead.

Brandon in bid to save company. Page 27.

With slightly shaky fingers, I unfold the paper, find the page, and read the story.

Financial PR entrepreneur Luke Brandon is fighting to keep his investors on board after severe loss of confidence following the recent defection of several senior employees. Morale is said to be low at the formerly groundbreaking PR agency, with rumors of an uncertain future for the company causing staff to break ranks. In crisis meetings to be held today, Brandon will be seeking to persuade backers to approve his radical restructuring plans, which are said to involve . . .

I read to the end of the piece, and gaze for a few seconds at Luke's picture. He looks as confident as ever—but I remember Michael's remark about him being hurled across the paddock. His world's crashed around him, just like mine did. And chances are, his mum won't be on the phone telling him not to worry.

For a moment I feel a twinge of pity for him. I almost want to call him up and tell him things'll get better. But there's no point. He's busy with his life—and I'm busy with mine. So I fold the paper up again, and resolutely walk forward to the check-in desk.

"Anything to check?" says the check-in girl, smiling at me.

"No," I say. "I'm traveling light. Just me and my bag." I casually lift my *FT* to a more prominent position. "I don't suppose there's any chance of an upgrade?"

"Not today, sorry." She pulls a sympathetic face. "But I can put you by the emergency exit. Plenty of legroom there. If I could just weigh your bag, please?"

"Sure."

And I'm just bending down to put my little case on the belt, when a familiar voice behind me exclaims, "Wait!"

I feel a lurch inside as though I've just dropped twenty feet. I turn disbelievingly—and it's him.

It's Luke, striding across the concourse toward the check-in desk. He's dressed as smartly as ever, but his face is pale and haggard. From the shadows under his eyes he looks as though he's been existing on a diet of late nights and coffee.

"Where the fuck are you going?" he demands as he gets nearer. "Are you moving to Washington?"

"What are you doing here?" I retort shakily. "Aren't you at some crisis meeting with your investors?"

"I was. Until Mel came in to hand round tea, and told me she'd seen you on the television this morning. So I called Suze and got the flight number out of her—"

"You just *left* your meeting?" I stare at him. "What, right in the middle?"

"She told me you're leaving the country." His dark eyes search my face. "Is that right?"

"Yes," I say, and clutch my little suitcase more tightly. "Yes, I am."

"Just like that? Without even telling me?"

"Yes, just like that," I say, plonking my case on the belt. "Just like you came back to Britain without even telling me." There's an edge to my voice, and Luke flinches.

"Becky—"

"Window or aisle seat?" interrupts the check-in girl.

"Window, please."

"Becky—"

His mobile phone gives a shrill ring, and he switches it off irritably. "Becky . . . I want to talk."

"*Now* you want to talk?" I echo disbelievingly. "Great. Perfect timing. Just as I'm checking in." I hit the *FT* with the back of my hand. "And what about this crisis meeting?"

"It can wait."

"The future of your company can *wait*?" I raise my eyebrows. "Isn't that a little . . . irresponsible, Luke?"

"My company wouldn't *have* a fucking future if it weren't for you," he exclaims, almost angrily, and in spite of myself I feel a tingling all over my body. "I've just been on the phone to Michael. He told me what you did. How you cottoned on to Alicia. How you warned him, how you sussed the whole thing." He shakes his head. "I had no idea. Jesus, if it hadn't been for you, Becky . . ."

"He shouldn't have told you," I mutter furiously. "I told him not to. He promised."

"Well, he did tell me! And now . . ." Luke breaks off. "And now I don't know what to say," he says more quietly. " 'Thank you' doesn't even come close."

We stare at each other in silence for a few moments.

"You don't have to say anything," I say at last, looking away. "I only did it because I can't stand Alicia. No other reason."

"So . . . I've put you on row thirty-two," says the check-in girl brightly. "Boarding should be at four thirty . . ." She takes one further look at my passport and her expression changes. "Hey! You're the one off *Morning Coffee,* aren't you?"

"I used to be," I say with a polite smile.

"Oh right," she says puzzledly. As she hands over my passport and boarding card, her eye runs over my *FT,* and stops at Luke's photograph. She looks up at Luke, and down again.

"Hang on. Are you him?" she says, jabbing at the picture.

"I used to be," says Luke after a pause. "Come on, Becky. Let me buy you a drink, at least."

We sit down at a little table with glasses of Pernod. I can see the light on Luke's phone lighting up every five seconds, indicating that someone's trying to call him. But he doesn't even seem to notice.

"I wanted to ring you," he says, staring into his drink. "Every single day, I wanted to ring. But . . . it's been so crazy since I got back. And what you said about me not having time for a real relationship? That really stuck with me. Plus . . ." He breaks off into silence.

"Plus what?" I say at last.

"I wasn't sure," he says, and looks up with frank brown eyes. "The truth is, I didn't know whether we could make it work. It seemed in New York that we suddenly split apart, and started going in different directions. It was as though we didn't understand each other anymore."

I should be able to hear this without reacting. But for some reason the back of my throat feels tight all over again.

"So—what happened?" I say, forcing myself to sound matter-of-fact. "Why are you here? The day when all your investors have flown in to see you."

"Not ideal. I'll give you that." A flicker of amusement passes briefly across his face. "But how was I to know you were planning to skip the country? Michael's been a secretive bastard. And when I heard you were leaving . . ." He meets my eyes. "I suddenly realized."

"Realized . . . what?" I manage.

"That I'd been a fucking . . . stupid . . ."

He pushes his glass around the table abstractly, as though searching for something, and I stare at him apprehensively. "You were right," he says suddenly. "I was obsessed with making it in New York. It was a kind of madness. I couldn't see anything else. Jesus, I've fucked everything up, haven't I? You . . . us . . . the business . . ."

"Come on, Luke," I say awkwardly. "You can't take credit for everything. I fucked up a good few things for you . . ." I stop as Luke shakes his head. He drains his glass and gives me a frank look.

"There's something you need to know. Becky—how do you think *The Daily World* got hold of your financial details?"

I look at him in surprise.

"It . . . it was the council tax girl. The girl who came to the flat and snooped around while Suze was . . ." I tail away as he shakes his head again.

"It was Alicia."

For a moment I'm too taken aback to speak.

"Alicia?" I manage at last. "How do you . . . why would she . . ."

"When we searched her office we found some bank statements of yours in her desk. Some letters, too. Christ alone knows how she got hold of them." He exhales sharply. "This morning, I finally got a guy at *The Daily World* to admit she was the source. They just followed up what she gave them."

I stare at him, feeling rather cold. Remembering that day I visited his office. The Conran bag with all my letters in it. Alicia standing by Mel's desk, looking like a cat with a mouse.

I *knew* I'd left something behind. Oh God, how could I have been so *stupid*?

"You weren't her real target," Luke's saying. "She did it to discredit me and the company—and distract my attention from what she was up to. They won't confirm it, but I'm sure she was also the 'inside source' giving all those quotes about me." He takes a deep breath. "The point is, Becky—I got it all wrong. My deal wasn't ruined because of you." He looks at me matter-of-factly. "Yours was ruined because of me."

I sit still for a few moments, unable to speak. It's as though something heavy is slowly lifting from me. I'm not sure what to think or feel.

"I'm just so sorry," Luke's saying. "For everything you've been through . . ."

"No." I take a deep, shaky breath. "Luke, it wasn't your fault. It wasn't even Alicia's fault. Maybe she fed them the details. But I mean, if I hadn't got myself into debt in the first place, and if I hadn't gone crazy shopping in New York—they wouldn't have had anything to write about, would they?" I rub my dry face. "It was horrible and humiliating. But in a funny way, seeing that article was a good thing for me. It made me realize a few things about myself, at least."

I pick up my glass, see that it's empty, and put it down again.

"Do you want another one?" says Luke.

"No. No, thanks."

There's silence between us. In the distance, a voice is telling passengers on flight BA 2340 for San Francisco to please proceed to Gate 29.

"I know Michael offered you a job," said Luke. He gestures to my case. "I assume this means you accepted it." He pauses, and I stare at him, trembling slightly, saying nothing. "Becky—don't go to Washington. Come and work for me."

"Work for *you*?" I say, startled.

"Come and work for Brandon Communications."

"Are you mad?"

He pushes his hair back off his face—and suddenly he looks young and vulnerable. Like someone who needs a break.

"I'm not mad. My staff's been decimated. I need someone like you at a senior level. You know about finance. You've been a journalist. You're good with people, you already know the company . . ."

"Luke, you'll easily find someone else like me," I chip in.

"You'll find someone better! Someone with PR experience, someone who's worked in—"

"OK, I'm lying," Luke interrupts. "I'm lying." He takes a deep breath. "I don't just need someone like you. I need you."

He meets my eyes candidly—and with a jolt I realize he's not just talking about Brandon Communications.

"I need you, Becky. I rely on you. I didn't realize it until you weren't there anymore. Ever since you left, your words have been going round and round in my head. About my ambitions. About our relationship. About my mother, even."

"Your mother?" I stare at him apprehensively. "I heard you tried to arrange a meeting with her . . ."

"It wasn't her fault." He takes a swig of Pernod. "Something came up, so she couldn't make it. But you're right, I *should* spend more time with her. Really get to know her better, and forge a closer relationship, just like you have with your mother." He looks up and frowns at my dumbfounded expression. "That is what you meant, isn't it?"

I try for a moment to imagine Luke and his mother chatting away in the kitchen like me and Mum—and fail completely.

"Erm . . . yes!" I say hastily. "Yes, that's exactly what I meant. Absolutely."

"That's what I mean. You're the only person who'll tell me the stuff I need to hear, even when I don't want to hear it. I should have confided in you right from the start. I was . . . I don't know. Arrogant. Stupid."

He sounds so bleak and hard on himself, I feel a twinge of dismay.

"Luke—"

"Becky, I know you've got your own career—and I completely respect that. I wouldn't even ask if I didn't think this could be a good step for you too. But . . . please." He reaches across the table and puts a warm hand on mine. "Come back. Let's start again."

I stare helplessly at him, feeling emotion swelling in me like a balloon.

"Luke, I can't work for you." I swallow, trying to keep control of my voice. "I have to go to the States. I have to take this chance."

"I know it seems like a great opportunity. But what I'm offering could be a great opportunity, too."

"It's not the same," I say, clenching my hand tightly round my glass.

"It can be the same. Whatever Michael's offered you, I'll match it." He leans forward. "I'll more than match it. I'll—"

"Luke," I interrupt. "Luke, I didn't take Michael's job."

Luke's face jerks in shock.

"You didn't? Then what—"

He looks at my suitcase and back up to my face—and I stare back in resolute silence.

"I understand," he says at last. "It's none of my business."

He looks so defeated, I feel a sudden stab of pain in my chest. I want to tell him—but I just can't. I can't risk talking about it, listening to my own arguments waver, wondering whether I've made the right choice. I can't risk changing my mind.

"Luke, I've got to go," I say, my throat tight. "And . . . and you've got to get back to your meeting."

"Yes," says Luke after a long pause. "Yes. You're right. I'll go. I'll go now." He stands up and reaches into his pocket. "Just . . . one last thing. You don't want to forget this."

Very slowly, he pulls out a long, pale blue, silk and velvet scarf, scattered with iridescent beads.

My scarf. My Denny and George scarf.

I feel the blood drain from my face.

"How did you—" I swallow. "The bidder on the phone was you? But . . . but you withdrew. The other bidder got the—" I tail off and stare at him in confusion.

"Both the bidders were me."

He ties the scarf gently round my neck, looks at me for a few seconds, then kisses me on the forehead. Then he turns round and walks away, into the airport crowds.

Seventeen

Two Months Later

OK. SO IT'S TWO PRESENTATIONS, one to Saatchis, one to Global Bank. One awards lunch with McKinseys, and dinner with Merrill Lynch."

"That's it. It's a lot. I know."

"It'll be fine," I say reassuringly. "It'll be fine."

I scribble something in my notebook and stare at it thinking hard. This is the moment of my new job I love the most. The initial challenge. Here's the puzzle—find the solution. For a few moments I sit without saying anything, doodling endless small five-pointed stars and letting my mind work it out, while Lalla watches me anxiously.

"OK," I say at last. "I have it. Your Helmut Lang pantsuit for the meetings, your Jil Sander dress for the lunch—and we'll find you something new for the dinner." I squint at her. "Maybe something in a deep green."

"I can't wear green," says Lalla.

"You can wear green," I say firmly. "You look great in green."

"Becky," says Erin, putting her head round my door. "Sorry to bother you, but Mrs. Farlow is on the phone. She loves the jackets you sent over—but is there something lighter she can wear for this evening?"

"OK," I say. "I'll call her back." I look at Lalla. "So, let's find you an evening dress."

"What am I going to wear with my pantsuit?"

"A shirt," I say. "Or a cashmere tee. The gray one."

"The gray one," repeats Lalla carefully, as though I'm speaking in Arabic.

"You bought it three weeks ago? Armani? Remember?"

"Oh yes! Yes. I think."

"Or else your blue shell top."

"Right," says Lalla, nodding earnestly. "Right."

Lalla is high up in some top computer consultancy, with offices all over the world. She has two doctorates and an IQ of about a zillion—and claims she has severe clothes dyslexia. At first I thought she was joking.

"Write it down," she says, thrusting a leather-bound organizer at me. "Write down all the combinations."

"Well, OK . . . but, Lalla, I thought we were going to try to let you start putting a few outfits together yourself."

"I know. I will. One day I will, I promise. Just . . . not this week. I can't deal with that extra pressure."

"Fine," I say, hiding a smile, and begin to write in her organizer, screwing up my face as I try to remember all the clothes she's got. I haven't got much time if I'm going to find her an evening dress for tonight, call Mrs. Farlow back, and locate that knitwear I promised for Janey van Hassalt.

Every day here is completely frenetic; everyone is always in a hurry. But somehow the busier I get, and the more challenges are thrown at me—the more I love it.

"By the way," says Lalla. "My sister—the one you said should wear burnt orange . . ."

"Oh yes! She was nice."

"She said she saw you on the television. In England! Talking about clothes!"

"Oh yes," I say, feeling a faint flush come to my face. "I've been doing a little slot for a daytime lifestyle show. 'Becky from Barneys.' It's a kind of New York, fashiony thing . . ."

"Well done!" says Lalla warmly. "A slot on television! That must be very exciting for you!"

I pause, a beaded jacket in my hand, thinking, a few months ago I was going to have my own show on American network television. And now I have a little slot on a daytime show with half the audience of *Morning Coffee.* But the point is, I'm on the path I want to be.

"Yes, it is," I say, and smile at her. "It's very exciting."

It doesn't take too long to sort Lalla out with an outfit for her dinner. As she leaves, clutching a list of possible shoes, Christina, the head of the department, comes in and smiles at me.

"How're you doing?"

"Fine," I say. "Really good."

Which is the truth. But even if it weren't—even if I were having the worst day in the world—I'd never say anything negative to Christina. I'm so grateful to her for remembering who I was. For giving me a chance.

I still can't quite believe how nice she was to me when I hesitantly phoned her up, out of the blue. I reminded her that we'd met, and asked if there was any chance I could come and work at Barneys—and she said she remembered exactly who I was, and how was the Vera Wang dress? So I ended up telling her the whole story, and how I had to sell the dress, and how my TV career was in tatters, and how I'd so love to come and work for her . . . and she was quiet for a bit—and then she said she thought I'd be quite an asset to Barneys. Quite an asset! It was her idea about the TV slot, too.

"Hidden any clothes today?" she says, with a slight twinkle, and I feel myself flush. I'm *never* going to live this down, am I?

It was during that first phone call that Christina also asked me if I had any retail experience. And like a complete moron, I told her all about the time I went to work in Ally Smith—and got the sack when I hid a pair of zebra-print jeans from a customer because I really wanted them myself. I came to the end of the story, and there was silence on the phone, and I thought I'd completely scuppered my chances. But then came this bellow of laughter, so loud I almost dropped the phone in fright. She told me last week that was the moment she decided to hire me.

She's also told the story to all our regular clients, which is a bit embarrassing.

"So." Christina gives me a long, appraising look. "Are you ready for your ten o'clock?"

"Yes." I flush slightly under her gaze. "Yes, I think so."

"D'you want to brush your hair?"

"Oh." My hand flies to my neck. "Is it untidy?"

"Not really." There's a slight sparkle to her eye, which I don't understand. "But you want to look your best for your customer, don't you?"

She goes out of the room, and I quickly pull out a comb. God, I keep forgetting how tidy you have to be in Manhattan. Like, I have my nails done twice a week at a nail bar round the corner from where I live—but sometimes I think I should increase it to every other day. I mean, it's only nine dollars.

Which in real money, is . . . Well. It's nine dollars.

I'm kind of getting used to thinking in dollars. I'm kind of getting used to a lot of things. Jodie was a real star when I called her, and helped me find a studio apartment. It's tiny and pretty grotty and in a place called Hell's Kitchen (which I haven't told Mum. To her it's "Clinton," which she thinks sounds very nice and respectable.). For the first few nights I couldn't sleep for the traffic noise. But the point is, I'm here. I'm here in New York, standing on my own two feet, doing something I can honestly say I adore.

Michael's job in Washington sounded wonderful. In many ways it would have been much more sensible to take it—and I know Mum and Dad wanted me to. But what Michael said at that lunch—about not falling into anything else, about going after what I truly wanted—made me think. About my career, about my life, about what I really wanted to do for a living.

And to give my mum her due, as soon as I explained what this job at Barneys would involve, she stared at me, and said, "But, love, why on earth didn't you think of this before?"

"Hi, Becky?" I give a small start, and look up to see Erin at my door. I've got to be quite good friends with Erin, ever since she invited me home to look at her collection of lipsticks and we ended up watching James Bond videos all night. "I have your ten o'clock here."

"Who *is* my ten o'clock?" I say, frowning puzzledly as I reach for a Richard Tyler sheath. "I couldn't see anything in the book."

"Well . . . uh . . ." Her face is all shiny and excited, for some reason. "Uh . . . here he is."

"Thank you very much," comes a deep male voice.

A deep male British voice.

Oh my God.

I freeze like a rabbit, still holding the Richard Tyler dress, as Luke walks into the room.

"Hello," he says with a small smile. "Miss Bloomwood. I've heard you're the best shopper in town."

I open my mouth and close it again. Thoughts are whizzing round my mind like fireworks. I'm trying to feel surprised, trying to feel as shocked as I know I should. Two months of absolutely nothing—and now here he is. I should be completely thrown.

But somehow—I don't feel thrown at all.

Subconsciously, I realize, I've been expecting him.

"What are you doing here?" I say, trying to sound as composed as I can.

"As I said, I've heard you're the best shopper in town." He gives me a quizzical look. "I thought perhaps you could help me buy a suit. This one is looking rather tired."

He gestures to his immaculate Jermyn Street suit, which I happen to know he's only had for three months, and I hide a smile.

"You want a suit."

"I want a suit."

"Right."

Playing for time, I put the dress back on a hanger, turn away, and place it carefully on the rail. Luke's here.

He's here. I want to laugh, or dance, or cry, or something. But instead I reach for my notepad and, without rushing, turn round.

"What I normally do before anything else is ask my clients to tell me a little about themselves." My voice is a little jumpy and I take a deep breath. "Perhaps you could . . . do the same?"

"Right. That sounds like a good idea." Luke thinks for a moment. "I'm a British businessman. I'm based in London." He meets my eyes. "But I've recently opened an office in New York. So I'm going to be spending quite a bit of time over here."

"Really?" I feel a jolt of surprise, which I try to conceal. "You've opened in New York? That's . . . that's very interesting. Because I had the impression that certain British businessmen were finding it tough to do deals with New York investors. Just . . . something I heard."

"They were." Luke nods. "They were finding it tough. But then they downscaled their plans. They decided to open on a much smaller scale."

"A smaller scale?" I stare at him. "And they didn't mind that?"

"Perhaps," says Luke after a pause, "they realized that they'd been overambitious the first time round. Perhaps they realized that they'd become obsessed to the point where they'd let everything else suffer. Perhaps they realized they needed to swallow their pride and put away their grand plans—and slow down a little."

"That . . . that makes a lot of sense," I say.

"So they put together a new proposal, found a backer who agreed with them, and this time nothing stood in the way. They're already up and running."

His face is gleaming with a suppressed delight, and I find myself beaming back.

"That's great!" I say. "I mean . . ." I clear my throat. "Right. I see." I scribble some nonsense in my notepad. "So—how much time are you going to be spending in New York, exactly?" I add in a businesslike manner. "For my notes, you understand."

"Absolutely," says Luke, matching my tone. "Well, I'll be wanting to keep a significant presence in Britain. So I'll be here for two weeks a month. At least, that's the idea at the moment. It may be more, it may be less." There's a long pause and his dark eyes meet mine. "It all depends."

"On . . . on what?" I say, scarcely able to breathe.

"On . . . various things."

There's a still silence between us.

"You seem very settled, Becky," says Luke quietly. "Very . . . together."

"I'm enjoying it, yes."

"You look as though you're flourishing." He looks around with a little smile. "This environment suits you. Which I suppose comes as no great surprise . . ."

"Do you think I took this job just because I like shopping?" I say, raising my eyebrows. "Do you think this is just about . . . shoes and nice clothes? Because if that's really what you think, then I'm afraid you're sadly misguided."

"That's not what I—"

"It's far more than that. *Far* more." I spread my arms in an emphatic gesture. "It's about helping people. It's about being creative. It's about—"

A knock at the door interrupts me, and Erin pops her head in.

"Sorry to bother you, Becky. Just to let you know, I've put aside those Donna Karan mules you wanted. In the taupe *and* the black, right?"

"Erm . . . yes," I say hurriedly. "Yes, that's fine."

"Oh, and Accounts called, to say that takes you up to your discount limit for this month."

"Right," I say, avoiding Luke's amused gaze. "Right. Thanks. I'll . . . I'll deal with that later." And I wait for Erin to leave, but she's gazing with frank curiosity at Luke.

"So, how are you doing?" she says to him brightly. "Have you had a chance to look around the store?"

"I don't need to look," says Luke in a deadpan voice. "I know what I want."

My stomach gives a little flip, and I stare straight down at my notebook, pretending to make more notes. Scribbling any old rubbish.

"Oh right!" says Erin. "And what's that?"

There's a long silence, and eventually I can't bear it anymore, I have to look up. As I see Luke's expression, my heart starts to thud.

"I've been reading your literature," he says, reaching into his pocket and pulling out a leaflet entitled *The Personal Shopping Service: For busy people who need some help and can't afford to make mistakes.*

He pauses, and my hand tightens around my pen.

"I've made mistakes," he says, frowning slightly. "I want to right those mistakes and not make them again. I want to listen to someone who knows me."

"Why come to Barneys?" I say in a trembling voice.

"There's only one person whose advice I trust." His gaze meets mine and I feel a small tremor. "If she doesn't want to give it, I don't know what I'm going to do."

"We have Frank Walsh over in menswear," says Erin helpfully. "I'm sure he'd—"

"Shut up, Erin," I say, without moving my head.

"What do you think, Becky?" he says, moving toward me. "Would you be interested?"

For a few moments I don't answer. I'm trying to gather all the thoughts I've had over the last couple of months. To organize my words into exactly what I want to say.

"I think . . ." I say at last, "I think the relationship between a shopper and a client is a very close one."

"That's what I was hoping," says Luke.

"There has to be respect." I swallow. "There can't be canceled appointments. There can't be sudden business meetings that take priority."

"I understand," says Luke. "If you were to take me on, I can assure you that you would always come first."

"The client has to realize that sometimes the shopper knows best. And . . . and never just dismiss her opinion. Even when he thinks it's just gossip, or . . . or mindless tittle-tattle."

I catch a glimpse of Erin's confused face, and suddenly want to giggle.

"The client has already realized that," says Luke. "The client is humbly prepared to listen and be put right. On most matters."

"*All* matters," I retort at once.

"Don't push your luck," says Luke, his eyes flashing with amusement, and I feel an unwilling grin spread across my face. I catch Erin's eye and with a sudden blush of comprehension, she hurries out, leaving us alone.

As the door closes, Luke and I stare at each other. My throat is suddenly tight with emotion.

"Well, Mr. Brandon . . ." I say at last. I clear my throat and doodle consideringly on my notepad. "I suppose 'most' would be acceptable. In the circumstances."

"So." His eyes are warm and tender. "Is that a yes, Becky? Will you be my . . . personal shopper?"

He takes a step forward, and I'm almost touching him. I can smell his familiar scent. Oh God, I've missed him.

"Yes," I say happily. "Yes, I will."

FROM: Gildenstein, Lalla [L. Gildenstein@anagram.com]
TO: Bloomwood, Becky [B.Bloomwood@barneys.com]
DATE: Wednesday, January 28, 2001, 8:22 a.m.
SUBJECT: HELP! URGENT!

Becky:

Help! Help! I lost your list. I have a big formal dinner tonight with some new Japanese clients. My Armani is at the cleaners. What should I wear? Please e-mail back soonest.

Thanks, you are an angel.

Lalla.

P.S.: I heard your news—congratulations!

SECOND UNION BANK
53 WALL STREET
NEW YORK

Ms. Rebecca Bloomwood
Apt. 4D
418 W. 46th Street
New York

January 30, 2001

Dear Ms. Bloomwood:

New Account No.: 4567 2346 7689

Welcome to Second Union Bank! We are sure you will be happy with the wide range of banking services we can provide.

We at Second Union Bank pride ourselves on our highly individual approach to clients. May I invite you now to contact me personally at any time if there is anything I can help you with. No matter is too small for my attention.

Thank you for choosing Second Union Bank, and I am sure this is the beginning of a long and fruitful relationship.

With kind regards.

Yours sincerely,

Walt Pitman
Head of Customer Services

Acknowledgments

HUGEST THANKS to Susan Kamil and Zoë Rice for their help and encouragement, to Nita Taublib and everyone at The Dial Press, who made me so incredibly welcome in New York, and again to Zoë for a wonderful afternoon of research (shopping and eating chocolate). Special thanks as always to Araminta Whitley, Celia Hayley, Mark Lucas, Kim Witherspoon and David Forrer, and all at Transworld. Also to David Stefanou for the gimlets and Sharyn Soleimani at Barneys who was so kind, and to all the people who have given me ideas, advice, and inspiration along the way, in particular Athena Malpas, Lola Bubbosh, Mark Malley, Ana-Maria Mosley, and all my family. And of course, Henry, who has the best ideas.